Everdoor

Sin and Sacrifice Edition

Ëverdöör

Sin & Sacrifice Edition

CHAUNCY FELISZ

WWW.CHAUNCYFELISZ.COM

T·O·T·A

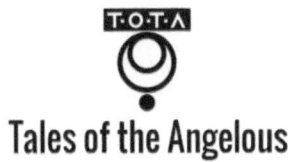

Tales of the Angelous

Other books by Chauncy Felisz:

Traveler's Guide to Eclipse: A Longish Compendium of Things

Message From the Author

ㅂ낌깗ᒪ ㄹ니낌ㅐ ㅏㅎ 凡ㅏ니ㅇㄹ

The Everdoor series has had a tumultuous run, both in error on my part and by publishing issues that have led to multiple reprints and versions of Book 1 and 2. It was because of this that I decided Everdoor would have to undergo a final transformation—and in one last attempt to restore some hope, some sense of stability to my debute series and journey into Eclipse, I thought it best to combine *Everdoor: The Paradise-Purgatory* and *Everdoor: The Owl's Court* into a singular compendium called: *Everdoor Sin & Sacrified Edition.*

It is troubling to move out into such unsure waters with yet another print version of Everdoor; I have taken on so much of the production for my books, and I fear I have made things unnecessarily difficult for myself, but that's part of the learning, I'm afraid. To my friends and family that have watched—perhaps with grimmacing smiles—as I made questionable decisions in getting Everdoor published, I can only say thank you for bearing with me.

There will be no major changes in the *Sin & Sacrifice* version other than to fix some clunky wording and pesky typos that still haunt Everdoor—and the addition of some new art. If you have already read *The Paradise-Purgatory* and *Owl's Court*, I want to make it clear to you that this is merely my last and final edition of those stories—for better or worse—as I continue on with Book 3 and so forth.

Everdoor was originally planned as a 5-Book series, and while I cannot guarantee *how* many more books are needed to complete it *(whether it be one large last installment after this or a few smaller ones)* I will endeavor to conclude it in full—just know that this was never meant to be some long and drawn out affair. After Everdoor, there are other parts of the multiverse I wish to explore, other lives and stories yet to be told, different times and distant voyages that patiently wait for me to wrap up my affairs with this series and pass it along to you, dear reader.

I am saddened that Everdoor had to pass through so many hands up to this point, but nonetheless I want to see this series through to completion. Jerro and Etcher and the whole wonderful motley crew of characters deserve that much. As I package up *Sin & Sacrifice*, know that Book 3 is well underway. Though I have made stumbling errors in getting this series out into the wild world I take heart in knowing there have been a fair few of you that have enjoyed Jerro's and Etcher's journey thus far, and it is also for you that I continue to write.

I don't know what the writing world holds for me after this. I know I must keep telling my stories, one way or another, and though Everdoor has faired rough seas, has been ill treated by some, it has brought me wisdom and experiences that I carry with me as I go forward into that frightful unknown.

It is with a sigh and a sense of relief that I bring you the *Everdoor Sin & Sacrifice Edition*. If you have been here through all of Everdoor's permutations, then you have weathered through just as much as this series and I thank you again for being here still.

May *Sin & Sacrifice* do Everdoor justice, may you enjoy it, and may this series find its way into calmer seas—perhaps find its place of harbor.

But enough lamenting, we go forth now with renewed hope! We push forward despite our hardships and see that there is a tomorrow.

We will see it all through to the end.

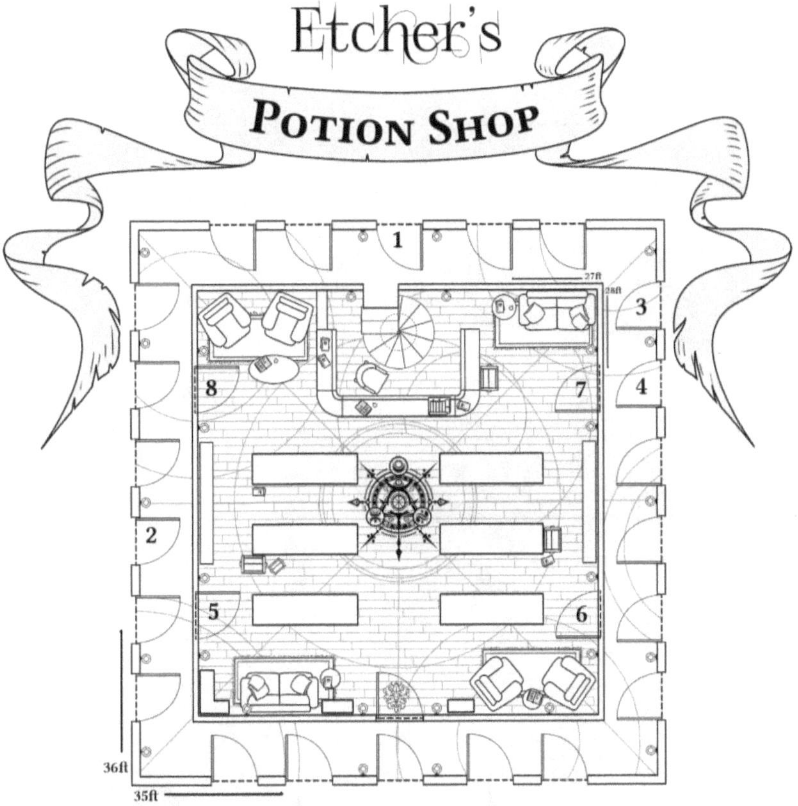

Etcher's
POTION SHOP

Key

The Greenman Door

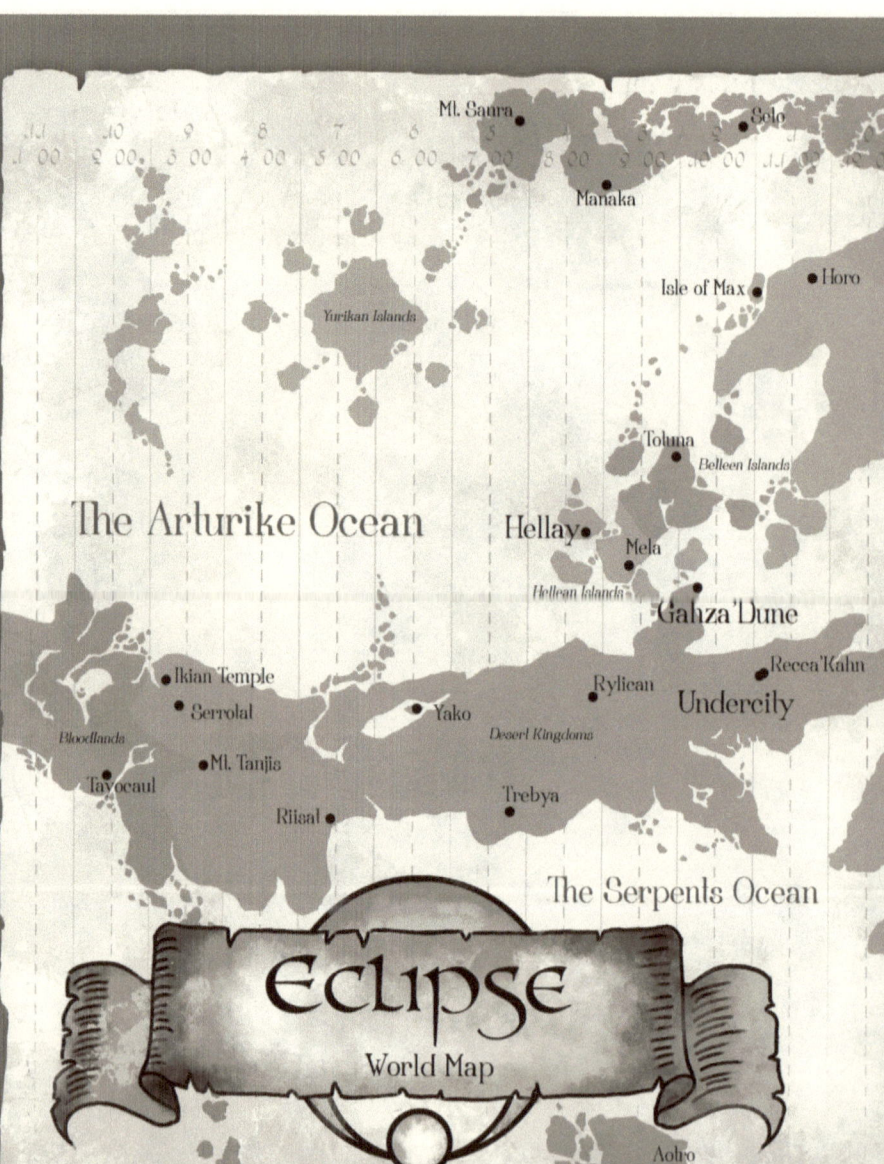

Berro

Arctic Cyzro

Grave of Elheren

3   4   5   6   7   8   9   10   11   12

13:00   14:00   15:00   16:00   17:00   18:00   19:00   20:00   21:00   22:00   23:00   24:00

Crown of Casler

The Guardians

Demi

Sinaku

Kirisha Forests
(Nycan)

Ocean

Yahre

Aru

Aiyun

Si'Ka

"Fire" Treb

Kingdom of Eep

Volyan

Asuralth

Eckla

Leburah

Oxlran

Drem

Darcwood

Bloodlanda

Hourlro

Kingdom of
Tablan

Kyo Temple

Sebrea

Produo

Tembi

Gakara

Cohlosumi

Kingdom of Kalla

The Epli River

Tura

Beheha

Camya Cemetery

Lobii

Pelryo

Petratio Province

The Dark Ocean

Csek

"Ice" Bre

Aurora

Book 1

The Paradise-Purgatory

For Granddad, and all the adventures we shared...

Preface

Young Gods bicker and fight,
But Old Gods, Old Gods play games.

The veranda overlooked the vibrant springtime green of a manicured garden that sprawled out over the gentle rolling slopes of the hillside. Bright-faced pansies and dainty little wild flowers dappled lush flower beds, their perfume rich and decadent, while topiaries stood attentively along the stone walkways as silent sentinels.

The sun-warmed grass brought about a pleasant headiness—an underlying note in an orchestra of earthy fragrance—and shade-chilled dew touched the world with a cooling crispness. But it was the wind that brought life, and in it danced the laden boughs of willow and oak, their leaves playing a symphony of their own, echoing the sea-sighing of lazy waves that lapped against the glittering sands down by an uninhabited coastline. The trees appeared to roll with the undulating wind, rising into a crescendo of sound and gently falling back into place; lifeless once more, awaiting the air to breathe movement back into them for the encore.

In the clear blue sky the kestrels roamed, letting out their long cries as they rounded up flocks of jittery, sparrow-like things. Their efforts made in vain by the occasional looming shadow of greater beasts—the likes of which breathe fire and make even the falcons scatter.

And as all of this went on, it was as calm and as peaceful as it had ever been by the little checkered coffee table on the veranda. An ancient elderly couple, so old their features became androgynous, were contently occupying themselves. Too absorbed in their separate musings to pay much heed to the picturesque scene before them.

One of the elders had a long, elegant pipe, which they puffed at as they read through a newspaper called the *Galactic Times*. The tobacco was fragrant, strangely reminiscent of campfires and toasted almonds. Instead of cloying, the aroma seemed to bathe the veranda in a pocket of comfortable invigoration, beckoning the heart to adventure and tantalizing the mind with images of what *could* be.

The other elder—who had bright blue eyes keen with knowledge—scribbled away with a chewed pencil in a well-worn puzzle book. The presence of the latter elder worked their own kind of magic, much like the tobacco, and around them the world was blanketed in a soothing balm, a type of cheery satisfaction in knowing the day's work had been done.

"D'you know they're *still* finding wreckage from that Nautiloid? The one that plowed into the gate out on the edge of the Angelous Spiral?" said the pipe-smoking elder. Their eyes continued to scan through the paper, never looking up for recognition.

"Artifacts, you mean?" replied the blue-eyed elder. They spared a glance at their opposite and smirked with big pearly dentures.

"Eh?" barked the gruff elder—although it might have also been a cough as a large plume of smoke billowed out from between the elder's lips and nostrils.

"*Artifacts*, Aleph, not wreckage."

"Peh, semantics," harrumphed Aleph before taking a few longer drags from the pipe. The spark in the tobacco had gone out, and the elder diligently worked to rekindle the ember.

Tav—the blue-eyed counterpart—chuckled to themselves and then put down the puzzle book, tapping the end of the chewed pencil against their shallow lips in contemplation. "Shall we get on with it, then?"

Aleph didn't reply right away, seemingly engrossed in their reading. They puffed at the pipe, the ember glowing steadily with each inhale until it burned faithfully on its own. Their eyes slid over to the lush garden, watching as butterflies fluttered between the flower beds and little speckled birds darted out of the bushes. With a long, slow sigh, Aleph relented. "Well, all right, then."

Tav's blue eyes twinkled, and a grin spread across their well-lined face. Together, the two elders cleared away the clutter from the checkered coffee table, leaving only a pair of dainty teacups on gold-leaf saucers and two identical velvet bags sitting across from one another. Tav dipped a knobby-knuckled hand into the closest velvet pouch and withdrew a die with far too many sides and an equal amount of indiscernible symbols. The blue-eyed elder shook the die with an old, arthritic hand, goading Aleph with a mischievous grin.

Aleph's thin lips pursed; the gruff elder took up the other pouch and rummaged through it. With polyhedrons in hand, the elders cast the dice and inspected the results carefully. Aleph peered down the long nose of their solemn-looking face, clutching the pipe stiffly between thin lips and appearing more than a little displeased.

Tav, on the other hand, was smiling. "Looks like I'll be starting this time, Aleph ol' friend."

Aleph—with arms folded and eyes narrowed and glaring—blew out a plume of smoke from the corner of a tight-lipped mouth and said nothing.

It did little to unhinge the cheeky expression plastered all over Tav's face. Picking up their velvet pouch once more—and taking a good long time to rummage through it—the blue-eyed elder carefully withdrew a pawn from the bag. It was no ordinary chess piece however; the little sculpture had been carved into an impish figure—with long ears and a coiling, spade-tipped tail. Tav placed the figure on one of the checkered tiles and leaned back in their chair, looking incredibly smug. "Your move."

Soft padded footsteps slapped hurriedly against the uneven floor of the catacombs, echoing rhythmically along the dark, winding pathways that were the underbelly of the hellish realm. An anguished howl followed. It held all the vigor of a furious gale and shook the walls with its ire, sending an icy chill into the heart of any unfortunate soul within earshot. Then it stopped, and a dreadful quiet took its place.

Drip-drop-drip went the droplets daringly in the dank and musky stillness. Their delicate chorus echoed through the lightless tunnels deep toward the core of Nightmare—where the monsters of Dream slithered and crawled, gnashed and bit, and stared with an uncomfortable number of eyes.

Footsteps once again took up haste, steadily rising out from the depths, splashing puddles, and beating hard against the stony ground. The colorfully clad feet clashed oddly against the earthen tones of the cloak. Slits had been made on either side of the large hood, letting long elven ears poke out freely and bob in time with the petite figure's bounding run. Trailing ever behind the figure like a wisp of smoke was a tail—a long, slender appendage with a spade-shaped tip.

A low guttural growl followed the rhythmic tempo of footsteps, reverberating along the walls and snaking its way up from the depths. Something big and heavy slithered quickly along the slick surfaces of the catacombs and the tunnels became alive with a chorus of clacking, gnashing, whooshing sounds. It was gaining on the cloaked figure, hissing in rage and scraping the stone walls with its many-clawed hands.

The figure pressed on, heading straight for the dim shaft of light just up ahead—their colorfully clad feet beat hard against the ground and shrank the distance as quickly as they could. But as the light grew closer, so did the moist hot breath of the furious pursuer. Flecks of spittle touched the very tip of the cloaked figure's deviltail and urged their feet to move faster still.

The tunnel was coming to an abrupt end, and the light, it seemed, shone down from a long vertical shaft overhead. The figure did not slow down; as they came to the dead end, the figure kicked off from the wall nimbly, jumping back and forth between the sides of the vertical passage and ping-ponging ever higher.

Blinding brightness enveloped the figure as the outside world came within a hairsbreadth. The figure lunged upward with one more mighty leap. They reached out with their hand, their palm aglow with a brilliant, sparkling light. Shimmering into existence in the air just above the gaping mouth of the cave was a vast concentric design written in a glittery malachite. As the figure shot out of the rocky shaft and through the image, the summoning circle rippled like the broken surface tension of a pool. The design then shattered into a shower of green-gold flecks that fizzled out before they hit the ground. On the other side of the collapsed image emerged the figure on the back of a magnificent sapling-green dragon. With a great flap of the beast's wings, the pair lurched toward the sky.

Behind them, however, a thin, pale arm—as long as the dragon itself from nose to tip—shot out from the black gape of the cave. The gangly hand spread wide, talon-like fingers stretched out. It slashed at the winged beast but only managed to pull a single green scale from the dragon's brilliant hide before retreating back into the darkened hollows. A screech of frustration echoed out from the cave as the furious pursuer slithered back down into the bowels of Nightmare.

The dragon yipped in pain and banked hard to the left, careening into a flock of phoenixtail songbirds. A flurry of colorful wings and discordant notes ensued as the birds scrambled to get out of the mighty beast's way. They chittered angrily once the dragon was past, leaving watercolor trails of deep scarlet through the air to illustrate their aggravation.

The dragon soon righted itself and continued onward, sailing gently through the skies. Finally with a moment's peace, the cloaked figure threw back their hood and revealed an elegant tumble of long chestnut hair that trailed freely in the wind. There was a triumphant smirk on the figure's youthful face. Honey-colored eyes, flecked with green, surveyed the endless landscape before them. A timeless ocean blanketed the world, and the bone-white bridge of the Terriss Walk lined the horizon. Floating isles dotted the sky—they were a collective of personal hopes and desires that were scattered throughout the ever-shifting expanse. The youth—with one hand smoothly controlling the reins—rummaged through her tailored cloak and produced a glowing indigo sphere.

Some would call Etcher Everdoor a thief, but that wasn't even the half of it.

Her grin grew wider across her impish face as she inspected the little orb. With her prize clutched protectively in hand and with a flick of her wrist, she conjured a small glowing ball of pinkish light that fluttered on delicate feathered wings. Etcher *ahemed* to clear her throat and then spoke to the bobbing pink creature, "Tell Fairin, *'Deal's done!'*" She then pushed the indigo sphere into the little round body of the pink messenger and dismissed it with a wave. It vanished with a muted *pop*.

Etcher nestled into her saddle and went back to enjoying the magnificent view from atop her dragon. There were other creatures flying among them in the now twilight sky; they were impossible beasts pieced together by pure imagination and whimsy—chimeras of childhood ambitions and the inspired minds of the young at heart. Etcher admired them and calculated absently the going rate of chimera teeth. "We'll get back to the shop and then maybe treat ourselves to a nice restaurant—maybe one with a forest view in the Kirisha Gardens up north. You'd like that, wouldn't you, Hoya?" She patted the side of her powerful dragon, and the beast responded with a deep, resonating purr.

She rested her hands behind her head, confident that Hoya could navigate the rest of the way, and daydreamed about what she would order and where. There was a decent vegetarian place that came to mind with a tasteful selection of imports—particularly a dry-sweet blush that she was partial to. As she pictured it, she began to taste the sweetness of the wine on her tongue and began buttering the freshly baked bread they gave out in little wicker baskets…

But it seemed Fate had a different course for Miss Everdoor. Two messages arrived, pulling Etcher out of her vivid fantasy. One came from an ordinary, white-winged messenger, detailing an intriguing job on a mundane world called *Terra Norse*.

The other came from a golden messenger. There were only two words written on the toothy parchment that unraveled from the body of the golden envoy. The long, looping letters of the scripture were as beautiful as they were distinct, and Etcher recognized the sender immediately. The note read simply:

(Leona Mesa)

CHAUNCY FELISZ

Monday...

An alarm was going off. A loud, buzzing, and utterly obnoxious alarm. Out from beneath a rumpled comforter came a hand that searched fruitlessly for the source of the offensive noise, knocking off knickknacks and loose papers from atop the dresser before finding the edge of the blocky piece of hardware. The hand smacked down on the top of the wailing contraption, frantically smashing buttons until the alarm finally ceased.

And then a groan came from under the bedding, followed by a slow and very reluctant move to rise. Jerro sat up; his pale eyes were dull and zombielike, and his dark hair was a tousled mess. His dry lips smacked together, trying to rid himself of that awful morning taste but doing little more than enhancing it. He scrubbed a hand over his face and blinked furiously, debating with himself why he wasn't still under his cozy covers and sleeping in till well past noon. For a moment he was tempted to flop back down and maybe try again tomorrow—but then he remembered he'd already used most of his sick days and decided it was probably for the best that he got up.

He swung his long legs round to the side of his bed—although *bed* was generous considering it was just a mattress on the floor covered with bed linens and a duvet. He managed one foot on the ground and then two; he was getting very close to *actually* getting up. Then he sat there, poised on the edge and staring off vacantly at a bare wall for as long as he could until the creeping nagging at the back of his mind urged him up. With a reluctant sigh, he pushed off from the mattress and stretched his arms up, extending his full length and nearly grazing the ceiling of his small, boxy room with his fingertips.

He shuffled sluggishly around to the foot of his bed, letting himself fall forward and land right into his daily workout regimen. The sudden rush helped wear away the fogginess of his mind and pull him out of his zombielike stupor—though sleep remained an attractive option. He persevered through his regimen of push-ups and dared a few sets of crunches before calling it good. He sprang back up to his feet, feeling a little livelier than before.

Jerro made ready for a shower, picking through his piles of clothes for a reasonably clean outfit; he found a slightly rumpled button shirt, slacks, and fresh boxers—which he claimed from his dresser and not the questionable floor piles.

"Mornin'," muttered a round-faced youth from the other side of a kitchen island. The young man was wearing a baggy sweater and dark-gray jeans; headphone cables were coiling out from under the hood that was pulled over a tilted baseball cap. There was a splash of color on the front of the otherwise black garment that had to do with some new age club music or trap band— Jerro could never tell. The only thing Jerro knew was that the weird assortment of *thwamping* noises that came out of his flatmate's permanently attached headphones was somehow considered music.

Jerro's tastes were considered tame compared to what Andri Chen—the American of the household—listened to, which was perfectly fine with Jerro. Although every so often there'd be something on the young flatmate's playlist that he actually liked. Whatever band logo Andri was sporting that day, however, was unlikely to be on Jerro's list.

"Morning," Jerro grunted back. He wandered over to the pantry and pulled open the cupboard doors in search of his breakfast. Instead, he found the irritatingly pristine penmanship of *Kristoff.* Kristoff's neatly printed name was written on nearly every bloody thing in the cabinet. Jerro glared at a box of toaster pastries, "Kristoff" printed carefully in black marker along the spine of the box. *To take or not to take? Bugger it,* he thought. The absent flatmate had already left on his routine morning bike ride and wouldn't be back until later. Jerro took a packet of toaster pastries and popped them in the microwave, since the toaster was currently in use.

"He's gonna notice," said Andri; his bored expression never left his phone.

"Yeah, well, Kristoff's an uptight bastard who should learn how to share," said Jerro, meriting a snort of amusement from his flatmate. Jerro plated his "borrowed" breakfast and sat at the kitchen island on one of the barstools.

"It's the first week of Fall," Andri said, tapping away at a little app game.

"And?" Jerro replied through a breathy mouthful of pastry, trying desperately not to burn his tongue and succeeding in looking like a gasping moron and little else.

Andri looked at Jerro incredulously then and exhaled—knowing that he was about to explain something that should be glaringly obvious. "Schedule changes on the third-tier lines start in the Fall."

Jerro stopped chewing. He glanced at the digital clock on the stove as the revelation dawned on him. *"Fuuuuu—"*

The closest third-tier station was about two kilometers away at a direct line; the residential street, however, took a long, leisurely wind through the neighborhood before connecting to the main road—which in turn led to the station entrance. Jerro had opted for a faster route: after scaling a few fences and narrowly missing the jaws of more than one angry guard dog, he found himself navigating his way around a block of council flats atop a squat brick wall that was more or less making a straight line toward his destination.

The morning chill managed to numb the bite out of the rough brick and cold metal railings that his calloused hands were sure to feel later on—but with the adrenaline currently pumping through his veins, he hardly noticed the cuts and scrapes. Another chain-link fence and one daring wall jump through a narrow alleyway and Jerro tumbled out onto the main road, meriting more than a few surprised and disapproving looks from the passing foot traffic.

He booked it across the street and took the station steps two at a time, dodging and weaving between the outpour of transit users. The advantage of being tall was that when a person of average height saw a lean build of six-foot-two hurtling toward them, they tended to get the hell out of the way. The disadvantage being that clothing, bed frames, ceiling fans, and pretty much everything else in existence catered to people about a half foot shorter than Jerro.

The platform was getting closer, and there were a few precious moments left before the train was scheduled to arrive. He skittered across the slick marble floor, quickly ducked around a hairpin turn, jumped the ticket barrier, and arrived, panting and haggard, just in time to see his train barrel through the platform.

Today was going to be swell.

Car horns blared as morning commuters impatiently made their way to work. Most of the vehicles were sleek and otherwise soundless with their quiet, energy-efficient designs. A few outdated clunkers chugged on by spewing out pollutants in an otherwise clean metropolis. After the famine which had started the third World War, cities like Midgard had become the golden standard.

Bullet trains whizzed along magnetized tracks, weaving through the open spaces between skyscrapers. They ran along two main tiers—reflective of the class divisions among the populace. Most of the city commuters traveled along the underground, while the privileged minority dominated the midway tracks, and a handful of executive elites took to the highest level.

Even at ground level, however, Central Midgard oozed opulence. Manicured hedges and pristine shop fronts with big window displays—sporting the latest designer trends—lined the sidewalks of the inner city. There were small faux park areas with cascading water features meant to give the impression of growth and abundance—and worked for that matter.

Central Midgard was a hub of wealth and commerce. Trendy people sat outside cafés, sipping their lattes and looking busy and productive on their overpriced laptops—when in truth most were scrolling through cat funnies and social newsfeeds. There were business-suit types yammering away on their headsets, appearing to be in the midst of important conversations but were, in fact, discussing dinner plans and *"Did you see the new secretary? Yowza!"* Even the casual foot-traffic conducted themselves with a sense of undue purpose.

Nowhere else could you make buying factory-made tartan accessories, overpriced *'rarities'*, gaudy fashion, and supposed handcrafted toiletries seem important. It was all ostentatiously *ritzy*, and so far removed from the Scottish heritage that had once been intrinsic to the land. There was hardly a native accent among the city dwellers these days—as though Midgard had gobbled up what was once Edinburgh and most of Glasgow. Now it was a culturally blurred metropolis like so many others. Simply wander down the street long enough, and you'd feel the itch to buy the latest gadget, start up a diet plan, and dress in something chic and attractive—never mind that more than a few of Midgard's city goers got their threads out of the bargain bins.

But then, of course, there was Jerro—who couldn't care less. It didn't matter to him that his clothes were more than a few years old and his sense of fashion consisted of whether his shirt and trousers were clean enough to be worn together. Jerro just didn't get the same itch that everyone else got. People enjoyed their wealth by spending it; Jerro enjoyed his by having it. And therein lay the quintessential difference that put a wedge between him and everyone else in the city on more than one occasion. As he briskly navigated through the foot traffic, he felt none of the same temptations others did when they passed by the high-end fashion stores and electronic outlets—even if he wasn't about twenty minutes late for work.

It was another five minutes added to the clock before Jerro finally arrived at his destination. His office space was in a magnificent dark-mirrored building that sported smooth, sloping curves. The building loomed over the other skyscrapers of the inner city—a watchful sentinel that boasted its stature with its vertigo-inducing height. There were tall, crisp letters across the front of the colossal tower that spelled out *Kairos Global.* To everyone else the name inspired hushed reverie and gossipy chatter, to Jerro it meant another grueling day at work.

He grunted a *g'morning* to the security guard as he was cleared for entry and headed through the expansive lobby that was all black granite and gold trim—with plush leather seating and elegant little coffee bars where would-be executive sat and sipped, sparing a hungry eye at all the comings and goings, waiting for their chance to pounce on a real elite. Jerro's slightly shabby appearance meant the vultures usually left him be, though he always felt an unwelcome chill whenever their eyes lingered on the employee pass clipped to his belt. He kept his head down and marched straight toward the elevators that were tucked behind the secretary's large oval desk near the back.

The smiley young blonde from behind the desk waved in recognition as Jerro strode by. He gave an awkward half smile back, not yet in the mood for niceties. After fumbling with the clip to free his ID card, Jerro flagged the elevator with it and waited with increasing irritation at each passing second. With a relieving *ding,* the elevator finally arrived. Jerro punched in his floor number and let out a pent-up sigh as he slumped against the inside of the lift.

"Hey, slick! You're going for the record for close calls, I see."

"Tell me Denholm isn't in yet."

"He's not in. Had a meeting this morning with the heads. Won't be in till later this afternoon."

"Oh, thank God."

Jerro's relief was palpable, and his well-dressed colleague took note of it. "Another late one?"

"Huh? No…schedule change—first week of Fall," said Jerro, echoing his flatmate.

The man *tsked.* "I'm telling you, Jerr', you've *got* to invest in a second-tier pass. They always run on time—just like clockwork."

His colleague had the same kind of itch as the rest of Midgard and never missed an opportunity to try and pass it along to Jerro. Despite being vastly different on many standings, Jerro and Daag were somehow friends—or the closest thing to it. While Jerro wore whatever semi-decent ensemble he could dig out of the piles on his floor, Daag was the type of person who wore tailored suits with silk ties and shoes polished to such a shine you could check your teeth in them, which he probably did. There were glaring differences on their views of personal upkeep as well: you had Jerro who was satisfied by simply showering and keeping down his stubble, and then there was Daag—who had his thick eyebrows shaped, his ruffled bedhead look purposefully styled and gelled, and his teeth whitened to an immaculate level. To be fair, it was a rather typical look around the office—or Central Midgard, for that matter—and Jerro had even spied a Daag doppelgänger on one of the lower floors of the office building.

"I'm not spending a few hundred on a ticket when I can get my pass for free." Jerro chuffed at the very notion.

"Suit yourself." Daag shrugged. He drained what was left in his disposable cup and went to pour out more from an exotic-looking cooler. It had that modern high-tech look, with long, sloping curves and a lot of polished glass and metal, making it fit in aptly with the rest of the office decor. With a satisfied, if not slightly overdone, "*Aah!*" Daag continued on to say, "You can really taste the difference when they import from the aquifers, not this *purified-water* business. We only had distilled at the last company I worked for." He grimaced.

Jerro could feel his brow knotting together as it often did when Daag said something so utterly ridiculous he couldn't be sure if it was meant to be a joke. "It's water, Daag. It doesn't taste like anything."

Jerro was about to argue his point further when he saw a perky redhead in a tight skirt and fitted blouse round the corner. *Shit.* Jerro quickly moved to the side so that Daag was blocking the line of sight between Jerro and the redhead.

Daag caught on. Snobbish and showy though he was, he was anything but dim-witted. He took one look at the redhead and one at Jerro's sudden evasive behavior and started smirking. "You *didn't?*"

Jerro rolled his eyes and let out a terse breath. "It was one night. We went out for drinks after work, and she invited me back to her flat. Oh, wipe that smirk off your face. It's not like I *meant* to hook up with her."

"Does *she* know that?" Daag tittered.

"Well, if she didn't get the hint by now, I doubt she will. What the hell is she doing up here anyway? I thought she worked down on twelve," Jerro huffed, cursing the string of bad luck he seemed to be experiencing that morning. At least his boss wasn't in yet, which was somewhat of a blessing.

"Maybe she came looking for you." Daag wiggled his well-defined eyebrows.

If looks could kill, Jerro would have incinerated Daag on the spot, yet the venom in Jerro's eyes only managed to widen the already massive grin plastered over his coworker's face.

Jerro groaned, "I gotta get into my office. Can *you*—"

"Create a distraction?" said Daag. "Should I start waving my arms and yelling? Maybe parade around the office with my pants down?"

"Yeah, any of those will do, Daag. Just keep her off my scent."

"And what's in it for me?"

Whatever willpower Jerro had mustered to even be bothered with the day was quickly dwindling. "I'll buy you a round. Just…help me out, will ya?"

"You coming out tonight, then?"

"Can't. Gotta work late. Project's due tomorrow morning."

"Ouch." Daag tutted. "All right, Jerr-Bear, I'll help, but you'll owe me."

"Fine, whatever." Jerro huffed. "And don't call me Jerr-Bear."

"Sure thing, Jerrykins."

Daag continued to act as a human shield as Jerro dipped behind the cubicles to take a long, winding route through the office. Once the coast was clear, Daag strode up to the redhead and smiled widely. "Kayda! Haven't seen you in a while. How's life?"

Nighttime blanketed the city, and the glittering lights of skyscrapers and shopping outlets turned the ground into a sea of stars from the view up on the 165th floor of Kairos Global. The excessively large windows of Johan Lapaul's office peered out over Midgard watchfully, seeing as far back as the black mountains that lined the dark horizon.

The private office was as spacious as it was lavishly furnished. A big mahogany desk, housing a generously sized flat-screen monitor, sat near the far back of the room so that one had to walk a considerable distance from the door to the desk and that high-backed chair that was so akin to a throne. Bookshelves with full sets of encyclopedias and artsy-looking souvenirs stretched across the flanking walls of the executive office space. There was a minibar off to the side with an impressive selection of hard liquor and a glamorous crystal glassware set just waiting to be filled with a good whiskey.

It was quiet in the room save for the soft, methodical ticking of the metronome placed among the other artifacts that lined the shelves. Most, if not all, of the building's employees had gone home hours before, leaving Johan's luxurious office space devoid of its occupant. It was in that quiet when a door appeared.

It was not an ordinary door by any means. This door was a dark forest green; it was tall and old looking with a leafy face carved into the center of its ornate surface, staring out with hollow eyes and an unreadable expression. The door, nestled in a dark corner beside the entrance of the lush room, yawned open.

A figure slipped out, lithe and soundless. With a careful survey of the surroundings, the figure sauntered into the middle of the empty office space. Moonlight washed over the intruder's face and revealed Etcher's sly grin.

Her long, keen ears twitched, listening to every creak and whisper, but there were no living souls close by, and she was well aware of it. Her deviltail swished and flicked with feline grace as she casually strode over to the rich mahogany desk. She let her fingertips glide over the lacquered surface as she strode past it and headed straight to the minibar. She uncorked the carafe and took a whiff of the dark liquid, savoring the aroma with a slight purr. In one fluid motion, Etcher helped herself to a stout glass and poured out a generous helping of the rich bourbon.

She stood there, bathed in silver moonlight, and looked out at the world below. *Strange little mundane planet,* she thought. There were no great beasts roaming the skies or wandering the fertile earth; here was only brick and metal. Airplanes sailed quietly up above with little blinking lights. Fancy electric cars zipped by on the ground below. It was all so *ordinary*. Even with her keen perception, she could barely hear a whisper from the planet's core. Theirs was a gaea fast asleep, beaten down into recession by its mundanes disbelief of the extraordinary.

But it was still beautiful in its own way. A wonder what the mundanes were able to create and build, being so far removed from the greater powers of the universe as they were. She had to admit, she admired their capabilities. Maybe in time, their gaea would awaken when they were ready to see beyond the veil. Etcher wondered what their sleepy little planet would be like then. The view was losing her interest, however, and she backtracked, flopping down into the large padded chair and placing her colorfully clad feet atop the desk.

Tonight she had opted for sapphire-blue canvas shoes, tight dark-brown trousers, and a billowy-sleeved blouse that laced up the front and revealed a tasteful amount of cleavage. The femininely cut waistcoat was velvet and shone midnight blue when the light hit it just right. She looked exceptionally elegant as she sat there and sipped her drink, and far more suited to the executive's pseudo-throne than the usual occupant surely was.

Boredom began to threaten her once more, and she placed her glass down and started rummaging through the drawers, nosing about to get a sense of who *Johan Lapaul* really was. All she had was his name on the gold plaque across the desk, and she wanted to know more. It wasn't entirely necessary, but it was certainly fun. Everything she pulled out to inspect was placed back carefully in its original spot. Etcher, after all, wasn't some bumbling common thief who tipped rooms, looking for gold and jewels. Her efforts to sate her curiosity seemed in vain however, and she was woefully disappointed by the banality of the drawers' contents. There was nothing all that riveting about Johan, it seemed.

Although...

In a hidden part of a lower drawer, was a curious telling of the man whose space she had invaded. She found a classic-looking revolver in a velvet case that piqued her interest for a moment. She took the gun in hand, flipped open the cylinder and saw that it was loaded. Her own thoughts and mental notes amused her temporarily, but then she found a journal, which grabbed her attention most of all. Leverage—as was Etcher's belief—was much more valuable than jewels any day, and far more lethal than a bullet. She thumbed through the pages and found it sufficiently juicy to merit keeping. Etcher made the book vanish with a flick of her wrist.

Her curiosity satisfied for the time being, Etcher decided it was time to go to work. She scanned the area with her calculating eyes, pouring over all the objects positioned along the shelves. There was something particular she was looking for—something she knew didn't belong to a mundane world.

Her ears flicked up, and her senses prickled as her keen perception caught the scent of something distinctly *Ecliptian*. A roguish grin spread across her face, and she gracefully rose to her feet. She glided over to a section of the bookshelf, hips and tail swaying in a seductive dance as she approached her prey. There she stood, staring down the bookcase and caressing it with her senses as she searched for its secrets.

The latch—hidden behind the twelfth edition of the *Encyclopedia Nordica*— practically begged Etcher to find it, it pinged on her internal radar and her fingers snaked their way to it. With the latch opened, she pulled away the hinged section of shelving. There, behind the bookcase, was a large safe door installed into the very wall.

Etcher loved safes. They promised all kinds of delectable goodies and secrets, and Etcher very much enjoyed knowing things that people didn't want known. The lock looked formidable, but Etcher only had to place her hand against the cool metal surface and tell it to open. The door sprung ajar without a second's hesitation.

It was dark and late, and all the lights had turned off save for the dim glow of the security fixtures that lined the walkways.

The stillness was eerie.

In the middle of the open floor, with all the cubicles and secretary desks, was a quiet emptiness. Cheerful decorations that people hung about their cubbies and tacked to cork walls seemed dull and lifeless in the gloom. No imprint of life could retain itself in the office once the people left. No amount of family photos or quirky toy sculptures with bobbing heads or silly little catchphrases written across coffee mugs could preserve a sense of being. It was simply hollow.

Further back, past the employee lounge and the big industrial-looking copy machines, were a string of private offices—all closed off and locked, save for one. Shining through its privacy glass was the cold glare of a computer monitor, making fractal patterns along the faceted surface of the window.

Jerro sat, bathed in a desaturating light that made him look pale and ghoulish. It would have been a big office if it weren't so cramped with *stuff*— computer casings and motherboards along with thousands of different kinds of cables and odd bits of other electronics were strewn about shelves and piled on carts and desks. There were video game posters and cat funnies stuck haphazardly to the walls and a few tattered schedules that had been manually updated several times in a childish scrawl.

The packed metal-frame shelves sectioned off the two other work stations in the room that had the only other functioning computers, neither of which were on—their users had left hours earlier, leaving Jerro to work alone in the quiet gloom. He had been typing away, analyzing, fixing, and packaging up a *vital* software plug-in that would make it possible for the higher-ups to do even less computer work than they already did. It was aggravating and tedious.

It was not quite as aggravating as watching one of the higher-ups chicken peck at their keyboard, but it was close enough all the same. He scanned through his code and ran a debug program for the umpteenth time before deciding it was good enough to be called done.

He sent out the app with painfully simple and straightforward steps on how to run it, but he knew, come tomorrow, he'd have a slew of e-mails begging for him to come install it himself. Jerro sighed. Was this really what his life had become? He was just barely in his twenties, and already his existence had become dull and flavorless. The paycheck he received biweekly only numbed his frustrations. Life had been so much more exciting when he scammed credit card companies and skittered along the ragged edge of fraud. There was nothing glorious about being a software engineer no matter how awed people became when he told them he worked at Kairos Global.

Breaking into databases and creating false identities—those were fun. They needed creativity and skill; *that* was exciting for him, not these mundane tasks they had him doing. But there was serious jail time if he got caught doing what was fun. It was also much harder to justify his income when he worked a dead-end job as a cover, like when he was an assistant worker at a record store in Northfall.

He had liked that job though and liked the people too for the most part—not to mention all the free music. But he couldn't bear making up any more flimsy excuses about how he managed to pay rent or go through the "talk" one more time with his parents on how he was wasting his talents. Plus, he almost did get caught once, and that pretty much shut down his operation indefinitely.

It was sad, really. There was Jerro with all that capability, and he was stuck making apps so CEOs could generate pie charts in a few less clicks. The temptation to hack into their personal accounts was stifling—especially when they made it so painfully easy. They had a near mythical level of ignorance to technology that Jerro hadn't believed possible for a company that not only handled the bulk of internet services but also developed sophisticated software and data analytics.

When he had to help service a few of the higher-ups machines—which was not strictly part of his job description, but what he often got roped into doing regardless—Jerro had found folders labelled *Passwords* right on their desktops. They practically never cleared their browsers, and every single one of them had some vital piece of their personal information stored in their computers' key chains. He would play out fantasies in his head about how he could siphon their accounts, a little at a time, and route the expenses through nonthreatening names that they'd easily ignore. Within a month, he could probably triple his income.

But he already knew what lay down that road, and it was an all-or-nothing kind of life that he wasn't certain he wanted to commit to. Plus, having proud parents instead of the enduring disappointment he suffered from them when he worked at the record store did make life slightly easier. The only problem was they couldn't possibly understand how painfully unfulfilling having a respectable career had made his life. It was a scale he had to balance in his mind on a daily basis.

After making certain he had accomplished all he needed to, Jerro readied himself to leave. He was just about to close out his browsers when his company e-mail flagged with a new message. *Odd*, he thought. It seemed rather late for anyone to be sending out e-mails, besides himself of course. Stranger still was the sender, and Jerro had to read it over several times to make sure he wasn't seeing things: *JLapaul@kairosglobal.nova.*

Someone had to be having a laugh. No way was the head of Midgard's largest company still at work at this hour. He chuffed at the thought and was about to close down the computer all the same.

Although…what if the president of the company was still there? What if Johan really was working late and Jerro ignored him? He ran a quick scan through his inbox, but nothing seemed suspicious about the e-mail—other than the sender. Indecision and distrust kept him rooted for the moment. He chewed his lower lip, his mouse cursor hovering over the unread message with uncertainty. Jerro was just being weirdly paranoid, surely? He clicked open the e-mail and prayed his computer didn't bluescreen.

Jerro,

> *Got your app. Need to speak to you about the install.*
> *Pass code's 0956. Head on up if you have a moment.*

—J. Lapaul

It seemed viable enough, though what the hell was Johan Lapaul still doing at work? Hadn't Daag said something about a meeting with the heads? Maybe Johan was still there because he was wrapping something up—something that couldn't wait? It still didn't jive well with Jerro, and every fiber in his being itched with a bad feeling.

He considered just leaving—pretend he hadn't got the e-mail. The message did say "*if you have a moment.*" But then he remembered the accursed read receipts. Johan would know Jerro got the e-mail all right, and opened it, if Johan really was still there. On top of that, Jerro *had* just sent out his own company-wide e-mail containing the app, and unless he got up and bolted from the office right after sending it, it was a fair bet that Jerro would still be a work.

He didn't like it, but he seemed to have little choice in the matter.

He read through the message one more time before shutting down his computer and heading out of the private office space, locking the door behind him. He nearly jumped from his skin when the motion sensors kicked on and made the overhead lights illuminate the whole office floor. Jerro braced himself against a wall, having to suddenly adjust to the brightness. He wasn't sure what was more eerie: heading through a dark empty office space or a bright one where he was so very exposed.

The walk toward the elevator was the most tense experience he had ever had. The back of his neck prickled, and he kept psyching himself up, convinced someone or *something* was watching him. It made his skin crawl, and he couldn't wait to get the hell out of there. When the elevator finally came, he considered leaving once more. The ground floor button was so inviting with its little star emblem; he could have just pressed it, headed out through the lobby, said good night to the security guard, caught the late-night express, and put the whole uncomfortable experience behind him.

But the nagging at the back of his mind wouldn't let him. You didn't just *ignore* someone like Johan Lapaul, and if it meant that Johan would possibly owe Jerro, it was worth the unease, wasn't it?

Jerro looked over at the screen beside the rows of buttons and sighed. *Up or down?* The simple choice seemed disturbingly paramount. He steeled himself as he punched in the number of the top floor on the touch pad. The display then prompted him for his ID and pass code. Jerro frowned; the uncomfortable knot in his gut was getting tighter. He unclipped his ID, turning it over anxiously in his hands, then finally scanned it over the touch pad. The screen accepted it as a valid employee pass and then continued to prompt him for the code.

0-9-5-6, right? Simple enough. He typed in the numbers from the e-mail and silently wondered what would happen if it was rejected. He wasn't sure if he was anxious or relieved when the elevator started going up. If this was some weird prank, it was certainly convincing.

He tried not to think about how fast the elevator was traveling or what would happen if it didn't stop once it reached the top floor. *Stop panicking. It's going to be fine. Just install the bloody app for Johan and get the hell out of here.*

The doors slid open with a polite *ping* once he reached the very top of the building, jarring him out of his mental discord.

It was just as eerie on the top floor as it was on the lower levels—perhaps more so. He had thought his floor down on thirty was pretty lavish with its expensive watercoolers and its ultramodern furnishings, but this was like stepping into another world. It wasn't so much an office floor as it was a penthouse suite. Did anyone else work up here besides Johan? Maybe he never really *left* Kairos Global and actually lived up there; that was feasible, wasn't it?

Jerro stepped out from the lift cautiously and looked around. It seemed like there might have been a few other private offices behind the various doors, and there was a big central desk that kind of looked like a secretary's station. So maybe Johan didn't live here, but someone certainly could. There was a huge lounge area in the middle of the open room with big, comfortable seating and flat-screen televisions. There was even a stocked bar near the back—not to mention the full-on kitchen. Jerro wouldn't have been surprised if there was also a personal sauna and showers behind one of the doors too.

What the hell did these people do all day to merit an office like *this*? Were these really the same bigwigs who chicken-pecked their keyboards and couldn't boot up anything more complicated than spreadsheets and slideshows? Then again, it wouldn't have been the first time Jerro found out his bosses were totally inept.

Maybe they got paid so much because normal people couldn't maintain such opulent lifestyles and continue to be sane, maybe there was a special finesse to being rich. But even as Jerro considered the idea he knew it wasn't true. Half of Midgard already tried to live like this even though they barely had the funds. It was only Jerro who would go crazy.

He needed sleep. The night had become far too weird for him to deal with on the little amount of fuel he had left. He hadn't realized just how tired he was until the magnitude of where he was standing finally struck him. He was on the very top floor of Kairos Global, where the richest and most powerful heads of Midgard's biggest company resided. He felt like a mortal man stepping into a realm of corporate gods.

He gingerly made his way through the lavish space, spying several game systems set up in the entertainment cabinet that housed the large flat screens. Were he feeling braver and less sleep-deprived, he would have been tempted to thumb through the generous selection of games—maybe even ask Johan if he could borrow a copy. But no, Jerro was lucky that his legs were even moving at that point. Forget taking a casual detour to inspect the place—he still hadn't managed to shake the awful feeling that something was horribly amiss.

Johan's office was, of course, all the way at the back. Its double doors were closed, and he couldn't detect any sound coming from within, filling him with even greater unease. His hand was trembling as he reached out to knock on the door, but before his knuckles could even graze the shiny chrome surface, he heard the computerized lock disengage.

Etcher was closing up the safe. She had taken a good snoop through the contents after claiming her initial prize. It seemed Johan Lapaul *did* have some juicy secrets after all. She had taken a few choice photos—the likes of which she doubted Johan would ever want people to see—and then put everything else back as neatly as before. Her prize, along with the photos, she made vanish with a wave of her hand, just like she had done with the journal. As she snapped the bookshelf back into place, her sensitive ears heard the thrum of the elevator. She took a look around, making sure nothing was amiss, and then headed toward the old green door still hidden in the shadows. She could have easily slipped out and left no one the wiser, but a tiny inner whisper made her stop. Her keen perception picked up something curious—something *else* that wasn't exactly mundane. It was a person who stepped out from the lift, she could sense them through the walls, and she could hear them—*feel* them inching closer. They had a distinctly *Ecliptian* resonance to them.

Now there is curious, Etcher thought. Her tail swayed back and forth as she carefully considered the green door. There was plenty of time for her to leave. She didn't have to stick around and find out who or what was coming, but an inkling told her to wait—the same inkling that told her the jaws of a trap were starting to close.

The person was just outside of Johan Lapaul's office. She could smell them now—a young man, she figured—and he was nervous and confused. Not a trap for her, it seemed. Etcher sighed quietly and relented. She perched herself atop the desk and conjured up her violin. She might have decided to stay, but that didn't mean she would be unprepared.

The lock disengaged and the door swung open. Silhouetted in the threshold was the young man. He was tall and attractive and very much perplexed. "You're not Johan," he said. A tinge of fear soured his scent; it seemed he too sensed the trap closing in on him.

He might have bolted, but Etcher started to play her violin soft and sweetly. The enchanting melody wrapped itself around the young man and kept him rooted.

"No," she said, "I'm not." She continued playing her bewitching tune; its influence made the young man's eyes become vacant and hollow. "Come here," she said, and he complied.

He stopped within a few inches of her. They were level with one another only because Etcher was sitting atop the tall desk. Had she remained standing, she would have been a whole foot shorter than him, and that would hardly do for a first encounter. "Tell me your name," she said while layering her melody with heavy *majik.*

"Jerro Ahliss," the young man replied flatly.

Etcher tacked the little detail onto her growing mental file of the youth. "Now tell me, Jerro Ahliss, what brought you up here?"

"I got an e-mail from Johan asking me to come," continued Jerro in a dreary monotone, all the while Etcher's melody continued on, unbroken, as she artfully laced her bow up and down the neck of the violin.

"*Interesting*." She would have liked to have chewed on that tidbit a while longer, but her inner voice had started squeaking with urgency. "We are both going to be leaving, you and I, and you're going to wake up in your own bed and not remember any of this. But what you will do, and this is vital, is go to Eastown in the afternoon and find the Greenman door. Will you do that for me, Jerro Ahliss?"

"Yes," he replied dully.

"*Good*," Etcher cooed. "Time we got going, then, Mr. Ahliss."

Tuesday...

The alarm was going off.

Jerro shot up in a fit of panic, surprised to find himself in his own room. He frowned and silenced the obnoxious contraption with a forceful smack. In the sudden quiet he sat there, his hazy thoughts slow to tumble into place. Tattered images played behind his eyes—his dreams had been so strange, stirring up curious feelings—and there had been music. But as he tried to recall the details of his nightly visions it all became shapes and colors and nothing quite discernable.

He looked around his room, feeling uncertain, but there was nothing unusual about the space. His work clothes were in a pile beside his bed—which was typical—and his essentials were all scattered atop the dresser. His wallet, his phone, his keys—everything was there. *So what the hell?* Why did he feel so out of place?

His mind drifted back to the previous night. He had worked late and was exhausted by the time he was done—he knew that much. He also recalled sending out the app, but he didn't remember how he got home. A twinge of fear struck him and he snatched his wallet off the dresser. No, everything was there—his ID, his credit cards, and even the little bit of cash he carried around. He must have wandered home on autopilot, not like it would have been the first time.

Jerro sighed heavily; he really needed to stop pulling such late shifts. One of these days he was going to wake up on a park bench or fall asleep on the train and end up in God-knows-where. He rubbed his eyes and then slowly stretched out toward his toes. His joints gave out a few satisfying pops, relieving a bit of his tension. *Well,* he thought, *guess it's just another day.* He looked at the clock and stared vacantly for a while.

"Shit!" He remembered it was still the first week of *Fall.*

There seemed to be a curious number of vehicles parked by the curb outside the lobby when Jerro got to work, and more than one of them he recognized as an undercover police car. A knot started to form in the pit of his stomach; something was definitely wrong, and he couldn't help feeling as though he should know what it was.

The security guard was stone-faced, but his eyes seemed turbulent and when Jerro gave his usual morning greeting, the guard looked at Jerro sharply as though he had disrupted an important internal dialogue. He waved Jerro through hurriedly and gave no room for conversation. Jerro's feeling of unease continued to pervade him and he briskly made his way through the lobby—it seemed vital that he get to his office and check his computer.

"Uh, Jerro! *Jerro!*" It was the blonde from behind the secretary desk.

Jerro stopped on his heels and looked at her curiously. She was beckoning him over and seemed pretty adamant about it. *Damn, what was her name?* Jerro slowly made his way to her desk, biding his time as he tried to decide what to call her. *Mah-something. Mah—* "Mahra, right?" He hoped he wasn't way off.

She smiled wide and nodded. "That's right."

Thank God. "Yeah, *yeah*…you were at the, um, employee dinner, weren't you?" He only vaguely recalled that evening, having got horrendously drunk that night.

Mahra suppressed a quiet laugh. "I'm surprised you remembered. I've never seen anyone get quite so plastered before."

Wonderful. The heat was quickly rising in his cheeks. "Ah, yeah, well." He coughed, feeling his throat go dry. "So you needed something?"

"Oh yeah." She had been staring at him intently and seemed to become aware of herself all of a sudden and began to fluster.

There was a smile slowly creeping across Jerro's face as he looked her over. She was pretty cute, why hadn't he taken much notice of her before now?

"Um, I thought you should know…Johan Lapaul's office was broken into last night. Someone messed with his computer and ransacked the place. There's a detective and a bunch of officers questioning everyone who was working late, but, I mean, it's a big building. They'll likely be here all day." She smiled sheepishly. "You tend to work late, and I just thought you'd want to be prepared. No one likes a surprise interview."

The phone rang, startling them both. She looked down at the caller ID and then fixed Jerro with apologetic eyes. "Sorry! I gotta take this. *Mahra Lapaul speaking.*"

Lapaul? Lapaul? Great, he thought. He doubted the surname was just a coincidence. It would only figure that a Lapaul of all people would be at the employee dinner when he made a colossal tit of himself. At least everyone else had the good decency to be drunk enough not to recall much from that night. Weird, though—why was a Lapaul working as a secretary in the lobby?

Mahra covered the mouthpiece of the phone. "They're still working their way up from twelve, just so you know. *Ah yes, I'm still here.*"

Jerro guessed he should take that as his cue. Maybe if his day didn't go belly-up, he'd spend a little time getting to know Mahra better. She did have an attractive smile, now that he took the time to look. Perhaps she wasn't the typical self-absorbed Midgardian he was used to running into either. He'd ponder over her later though, at that moment the sense of urgency was still pressing down on him.

It was uncomfortably quiet up on the thirtieth floor. Those who were talking were doing so with hushed voices and glancing around at their colleagues with obvious suspicion. They all looked like they had something to hide. Police investigations had the uncanny knack of making even the most unassuming person paranoid. Suddenly, every little misdeed that anyone had ever committed came flooding back to the forefronts of their minds and plastered guilt all over their faces. It didn't matter whether they had broken into Johan's office or not; each and every one of them dreaded being under the scrutiny of the law.

Daag was thankfully absent from his usual post by the coolers. Any other day, Jerro would have relished the opportunity to waste time, but not today—not when it seemed so vital that he get to his office. He slipped quietly into the desk chair in front of his computer—the other two tech guys he shared the space with didn't even look up as he entered. They were likely scouring through their own computers for anything that might be incriminating.

Jerro booted up his machine and launched his browser, going straight to his company e-mail. There was a message sent out to the whole of Kairos Global that gave vague details about what transpired last night and about the ensuing police investigation. There was a lot of legal-sounding vocabulary in it, and Jerro couldn't help but sense that it carried an underlying threat meant for any employee who didn't want to cooperate with the investigation fully.

That was it, though. He didn't understand why he had been expecting something else—something more. As he thought about the break-in, he could feel the uncomfortable knot inside his stomach tighten. Why did he have such a prickling sense of unease? *He* hadn't done anything, had he?

He scanned through his inbox thoroughly just to be certain there really wasn't anything else. Then he went to his sent mail and found his own message containing the app that he had sent out to the upper management. The time stamp made him cringe. *Yikes!* Had he really worked that late? Mahra told him the police were questioning everyone who had been working after hours yesterday night; no doubt Jerro's name would be on that list.

He was getting the distinct sense that he should take a *very* early lunch—maybe even take a few vacation days while he was at it. Never mind if it looked suspicious—every inch of him was screaming for him to get out and get out now.

He logged out of his computer and shut it down, trying not to look hurried as he slipped back out of the room. Not that it would have mattered—he'd seen that glazed look in his colleagues' eyes before and knew they were in hyper-focus-mode and wouldn't have noticed him even if he came in wearing a pink bunny suit. He shut the door quietly anyway and turned to leave only to plow face-first into a wall.

It wasn't a wall, really—more like seventeen stone of pure muscle in the form of a sharply dressed, bald-headed black man named Jaiko Reedman. He was about a decade older than Jerro and looked like he crushed walnuts with his bare hands and punched solid cement in his free time. Reedman straightened the front of his blazer with a forceful tug, and Jerro hated himself for flinching.

"Heading out, Mr. Ahliss?" said Reedman in his deep baritone as he bared his pearly whites at Jerro—though it seemed more like a threat than a smile.

"There a problem, Detective?" Jerro slipped on his mask of indifference despite the detective's imposing stature.

Reedman was only an inch or so taller than Jerro, but boy was he wider and thicker. Jerro might have had the advantage of being quick and agile, but it hardly did him any favors now that he was wedged between the office door and Reedman's immovable form.

The predatory grin widened across Reedman's face. "That depends. See, I was just having a chat with your friend down on twelve, *Kayda*." He whistled. "She's quite the looker. Had a fair few things to say about you as well."

Jerro felt himself crumble internally. Maybe he should have called Kayda back after all.

"Imagine my surprise when your name came up. I figured, well, heck, I'd best say hi to my ol' pal Jerro. What they have you doing here anyhow?"

Jerro grit his teeth and met Reedman's scrutinizing gaze with his own glower. He knew what Reedman was after, but there was no way around it. "I do software development," he replied curtly.

"'Software development'—sounds fancy. But, I mean, you and I both know how capable you are with a computer."

A foreboding undertone had laced the conversation. Jerro could feel the tension crackle in the air between them. He kept tight-lipped and waited, knowing Reedman was baiting him.

When Jerro didn't react, the detective decided to change his tactic. He glanced around the office space, nodding to himself. "So you got yourself a respectable job now, I see. Place like this must pay well."

"It covers the bills." Jerro kept his responses clipped, trying to give as little as possible for Reedman to work with.

The detective continued to survey the big, swooping curves of the architecture and the modern chrome-and-glass furnishings. "I bet," he said, his eyes still roaming. "And how about extracurricular? Does it cover that too?" His gaze finally locked back on to Jerro, boring into him and searching for any whiff of guilt. Reedman was like a bloodhound in that way; once he caught a scent, he never forgot it.

"*Excuse me?*" Jerro was finding it difficult to keep his composure. He knew Reedman was pushing his buttons, but it didn't stop his temper from flaring.

"You know, *fun*." Reedman shrugged with his threatening, pearly grin. "You have fun still, don't you, Jerro? You took Kayda out, right? Paid for her meal, bought her drinks."

"Well I guess you have your answer then."

"Huh." Reedman tongued the tip of his canine tooth, looking Jerro over with his dagger eyes. "Guess so."

The detective breathed in through his nose, and Jerro couldn't help feeling as though Reedman was trying to smell him out.

"You work late last night, Jerro?"

And with that, Jerro could almost feel the noose slipping around his neck. "Yeah."

"Hmm…and did you happen to notice anything strange while you worked? Hear anything?"

"I work on the thirtieth floor. You suggesting I have super hearing? Maybe x-ray vision too?" It was hard for Jerro to keep the snark out of his tone, and it did little to dissuade the detective.

"So you didn't hear anyone come through here. It was just you, then—all alone. Is that right?"

Jerro's temper was beginning to reach critical mass. *I didn't do anything, damn it!* "Look, I worked late, then I went home. There something you're trying to get at, or are we done here?"

The detective considered Jerro carefully. There was the strangest look on his face that Jerro didn't quite know how to read.

"You know, Jerro, I really hope that's how it happened—for your parents' sake. Not sure they could handle another loss."

They stared each other down for several tense moments.

"Well, you let me know if you think of anything," said Reedman.

Yeah, I'll be sure to let you know, thought Jerro bitterly.

"Oh, you're leaving already?" Mahra blurted aloud and instantly regretted it—reading Jerro's mood a bit too late as he stalked out of the elevator. Yet to her surprise, he came over to her desk and even managed a smile, albeit a halfhearted one.

"Yeah. Not really feeling today."

She was shocked; this was the second time today they had actually spoken. Suddenly, she was scrambling for a way to keep the conversation going, but as she looked at him, she felt heavy. He seemed tired and drained. She hoped he hadn't been fired—or worse. "Is everything okay?" she said, and then she winced at how ridiculous it must have sounded. Of course everything wasn't okay! The whole building was crawling with cops, and no doubt the computer guys were getting the worst of it, what with the nature of the break-in. She braced herself for him to snap at her or shut down and walk away. Oddly enough, he did neither.

"Well, it's not great, to tell you the truth," he replied, and that playful smirk Mahra was oh-so-fond-of crept across his face.

She found herself staring at him yet again. His eyes were so captivating, so lupinesque—they had a somber kind of intelligence that Mahra couldn't help but find alluring. Then she realized they had been looking at each other silently for several moments and her face grew hot. "Uh, well…if you hurry, there's a little bistro down the block that does a special on breakfasts. And they do a brilliant chai latte. That usually cheers me up." *Stupid, stupid!*

He broke into an actual grin. "That sounds nice. Don't suppose you're due for a break, are you?"

"Oh, well, ah…" *Is he asking me out?* "Um, yeah, I can take a break for a little while. It's not like I'm chained to the desk." She tittered uncontrollably and was beaming like a loon. She could feel it, but she couldn't stop it.

"You lead the way, then?"

"Sure!" Mahra cringed internally at how eccentric she must have seemed, though for whatever reason, he hadn't run off yet. She gathered up her bag and held down a button on the phone. "Hey, I'm heading out for an early lunch. Been a bit too hectic this morning. Need to refuel."

"Sure thing, Mahra. I'll send Claire down to cover for you," replied a voice from the other end of the speaker.

"Thanks!"

She let go of the button and then slipped around the side of the oval desk. She was about eye level with Jerro's neck, what with her flat-soled shoes giving her height no advantages. She felt oddly exposed without the desk between them and became uncomfortably aware of herself. *Do I look okay? Is my hair sticking up? I don't have toilet paper stuck to my shoe, do I?* "So, ah…off we go." She swore she would die of panic before they reached the bistro.

She didn't die, thankfully, and they had fallen into a comfortable pace as they headed out of the lobby and down the street. She was glad Jerro let her set the speed; no doubt his usual pace would have had her skittering to keep up with his long legs. "So," Mahra began, and then realized she had nothing to follow up with. This was the most they had ever spoken before, and she wasn't sure what to do now that she had his attention.

He seemed to read her discomfort and chimed in to save her. "So how come you're working down in the lobby? I couldn't help overhearing the last name." He smiled at her with a guilty grin.

Gosh, he's cute. "Oh! That, well, my uncle gave me the job. I'm not really the corporate type. It's just a way of having some spending money while I finish school." *Hey, not bad, Mahra. You managed a whole sentence without fumbling!*

"'School'? You mean, like, *university* school or…?"

She burst out loud with manic laughter, then slowly died down into a nervous titter. "Yes, of course! Sorry. I realize that came out wrong. Yes, I mean uni. I'm just finishing my Bachelor's."

"Really? I finished mine about two years back. Computer science—if you didn't already guess. What are you studying?"

Mahra started to perk up; things might actually go well for once. "Graphic design. I guess you could say I'm the artsy one in the family. I think my parents would prefer if I did something a little more *secure?* But they try to be supportive all the same."

Jerro grunted. "Eh, I am doing something more secure, and my parents are thrilled with it."

"You don't sound so thrilled though."

He turned his pale, lupine eyes on her, and she felt her heart begin to flutter.

"I don't mean to pry," she said. "You just…well, you never seem happy you're coming in to work."

He let out a sharp laugh that made Mahra jump. "Is it that obvious? Damn, I probably seem like a miserable bastard. I'm not a morning person, by the way."

"I didn't think you were," she said. "Most of the IT guys aren't either. I guess there's something about being technical that also makes you nocturnal."

"Yeah, maybe you're right. How do you know the IT guys anyway? I can't imagine you still being in the lobby by the time us techies get off work." He grinned at her in that mischievous way that made the flutter in Mahra's chest pick up speed.

She gave a practiced shrug, playing at being cool and collected as she scooted along a fallen acorn with the tip of her shoe. "I sometimes have trouble with the phones. They come down and help, and I guess I'm one of the few people who actually still treat them as human. I also score points with them on account of being able to successfully turn on a computer." She smiled. "I might not be totally computer savvy, but I do have to use them enough to know the basics. For instance, I know the difference between RAM and a hard drive *and* that the monitor is not the computer, unless it's an all-in-one. Anyhow, point being, we get to chatting here and there, and sometimes they stop by during their breaks."

"Huh, I've been missing out then. You can turn on a computer *and* hold a conversation? I think that puts you higher on the intellectual echelon than over half the company," said Jerro, locking eyes with her and giving her another warm, flirtatious smile.

Her face was surely scarlet by then. Much to her relief, they had reached the bistro, and she was able to quickly duck inside with him trailing behind, giving her a moment to calm her giddiness. She headed straight to the counter—ordering the chai latte with the number two breakfast special and an extra side of avocado—and regained a modicum of her composure. She was just about to pay when Jerro stopped her.

"I'll get this—my way of saying thanks for the company," he told her with a wink.

She thought she might swoon.

A tiny blue flame flickered in the middle of the air, casting a dome of pale light over the glittering sands beneath it. In the dark sky above, the sea of stars gave out just enough radiance to give form to the enigmatic landscape. There were rows of dunes along the horizon; from their peaks, the gentle breeze scattered handfuls of grains in undulating currents.

The soft ground had kept the heat from the day, making for a warm and comfortable walk. There was no chill in the air—only the kiss of a breeze and the hush from dancing palm fronds. The tiny flame moved forward, and miles melted away in an instant. The flame slowed as it came upon a garden in the middle of the sands, fertile and vibrant like an oasis. A low stone wall with an iron gate separated the fertile grounds from the barren desert; the gate swung open, and the flame glided on through.

There was a stone path that wove its way through the sleeping garden; wild-looking plants and desert flora were abundant in the flower beds. The low palms gently swayed as the flame moved passed them, and at the garden's center was a beautiful fountain. A statue of a naked woman held up a giant dish that had streams of crystalline water cascading over its edge and into a pool at the stone woman's feet. The shadows cast from the blue flame made the eyes of the statue seem to follow the roaming guide light.

There was a wide set of alabaster stairs just further along the garden path that led up to a large oaken door bound in black iron. The handle of the heavy old door was a big iron ring.

The door wanted to be opened. It called for someone to grab hold of the ring and simply pull. But then came the soft beating of large feathered wings and a powerful, petrifying dread.

The screech of metal against metal pulled Jerro back into the waking realm. He jolted upright and startled the other passengers sitting beside him. They eyed him curiously and shuffled toward seats farther away from him. Jerro avoided their scrutiny as he acclimated to his surroundings. He was on the train headed to the High Street station in Eastown and was only a few stops away from his destination.

There was a buzz from his pocket, and he rummaged awkwardly through his trousers to pull out his phone.

Missed Call from Dad
1 New Voicemail

The unpleasant-looking *x* over his signal icon meant the call had probably gone straight to voicemail. He hesitated and considered putting away his phone without listening to the message. For a moment, he was twelve again, waiting in quiet dread for the lecture his parents would inevitably give him for skipping school early. But he wasn't twelve, and it wasn't school he was skipping out on. Yet he couldn't help feeling as though they must have already *known* he was bunking off—not that it was any of their business what he did; he was an adult after all, wasn't he?

He sighed inwardly. *Come on, Jerro. Man up. It's just a voicemail.* He tapped on the notification, and a gravelly voice sounded in his ear.

"Hello, Jerro. It's your dad. I just wanted to call, see how you were. It's your mom's birthday this Sunday. Don't forget. I guess I'll see you there. Call me back. Love you." There was the sound of buttons being pressed, followed by *"How the bloody hell do you turn—"* And then the message ended.

Shit. He had forgotten about this weekend—along with getting a present for his mom. Fortunately, Eastown was full of weird little stores that sold all kinds of quirky novelties, the likes of which his mom was rather fond of. So he had an objective, it seemed; at least he'd be able to justify his aimless meandering on the grounds that he was scoping out for a gift.

High Street read large across the walls of the platform. Jerro got to his feet and waited for the doors to slide open. There was a small influx of people heading through the station, although it was relatively light due to the hour and the day. It was a refreshing change to what Jerro was used to finding during the weekends when it was much too crowded and you were either in someone's way or behind the slowest-moving person in the world no matter which side of the walkway you were on.

He made his way out of the station toward High Street, where a few outdoor vendors had set up tents to sell specialty items and seasonal wares. There was a scattering of diligent street performers playing music or dancing around. Some were juggling flaming torches, although it was a lot less impressive during the day.

A vast majority of the shops had hanging signs outside their doors—more than one of which advertised psychics or palm readers—and the street itself was cobbled and car-free. Winding alleys branched off from the main path and reconnected with roads further out, but up on the long, wide stretch of the main walkway was all just foot traffic and carefree wandering. Jerro loved it.

There were huge statues on pedestals lining either side of High Street that depicted ancient gods sitting atop thrones or on the backs of massive, rearing stallions; Jerro could recall one deliriously drunken evening after a pub crawl where he had actually climbed up on the back of one of the stallions and pretended to ride alongside the gods—but the evening had come to an abrupt end and he had to book it down an alleyway after the police showed up on a drunk and disorderly call. Two of his classmates had spent the night in jail but had thankfully declined to mention that anyone else had been with them.

Now, sober and in daylight, Jerro could appreciate the statues without giving in to temptation, although it was still there. It was always there—that eager little flame that wanted him to show off what he could do—and in the back of his mind, he was scaling walls and running along rooftops. He forced his attention back to the bronze statues; they were tarnished save for the bases where decades of tactile hands could still reach. Odin's toes had been polished to a shine, and Hela's chariot horses had brilliantly gleaming hooves. As Jerro passed beside the godly effigies, his own hand reached up and ran along the cold metal, wearing away a little more of the oxidized surface and revealing the rich bronze luster beneath.

He felt calmer as he strode along the cobbled street; he often did whenever he found himself in Eastown. The air seemed a little sweeter, the world a little older, and all around him was the essence of something *more*. Tourists and trendy-looking people still walked about—talking on their cell phones—and airplanes still flew overhead, but the eastern borough retained a historical soul that was painfully absent from Midgard's inner hub. Jerro would have much rather lived on High Street in one of the old studio lofts than in his recently renovated block of flats in the bland residential zone of Northfall. It was a consensus shared by a vast majority, which meant such vacancies on High Street didn't last long, and those who were fortunate enough to live there weren't moving anytime soon.

He took his time as he continued along the cobbled road, eyeing various witchy-looking shops that had big chunks of crystals in their window displays or mannequins dressed in handmade leather apparel and princess-like robes. He realized there was a fatal flaw in his quest to find the perfect gift: with so many shops to choose from, they all started to feel the same.

He wanted to get something unique, something that wasn't such an obvious novelty—or rip-off, for that matter. Besides, his mom already had dozens of scented candles and incense and crystals and pretty much anything the shops happened to stock. Sure, his mom would have been happy with any of those things, but that wasn't the point! He wanted to show some effort and forethought—at least enough to make up for the fact that he hadn't called or visited for more than a few months.

There was a small alley—lined with more quirky little shops and a tantalizing-smelling chippie—that took a winding, downward path away from the main road. The exotic melody of a sitar echoed up from the narrow passageway—a rarity among the more common instruments of the other street performers. The tall brick buildings offered pleasant acoustics to the music and tempted Jerro to follow. Enticed by the curious nature of the sound, he headed along the path, adjusting into a lean with the steep slope of the narrow alley.

About midway, he found the sitar player, who was nestled in a doorway. The musician looked about Jerro's age but was filthy and ragged, yet he had the most content expression Jerro had ever seen. There was a lazy dog curled beside the youth that opened an eye to look at Jerro and then promptly closed it. For a while, Jerro just stood there, listening to the foreign melody and being enchanted by its otherworldliness. They were alone, the main foot traffic kept to the wide cobbled road of High Street and left Jerro and the musician to themselves, making the moment seem all that more precious.

The sitar player continued his melody, unperturbed by his sole listener, and the ethereal sound continued its passage into Jerro's soul. He rummaged through his wallet and pulled out a large bill, placing it in the open sitar case in front of the player and weighting it with coins so it wouldn't be blown away.

The musician smiled at Jerro with a shockingly white set of teeth. His heterochromatic eyes twinkled with gratitude and he acknowledged Jerro with a nod. Then the musician focused back on his sitar as if nothing else in the world existed.

It was then that Jerro understood why the musician had chosen to hide away in that small, winding alley, where the acoustics were better—rather than stay up on the main road, where the charity was more favorable. Jerro nodded back to the young man even though he had ceased to exist in the musician's world.

Jerro continued down the path, hoping to find a store to match the musician's uniqueness. He was nearing the bottom and could hear the bustle of another main road fast approaching, but sadly, he found no shops that struck him as singularly different from all the rest. As he turned to head back up the steep alleyway, he noticed a door that was heavily recessed into the flank of a building and partially hidden in the shadows.

It was a large and weathered-looking door. The dark forest green of its coloring was nearly black in the shade, and the ornamental, leafy face that stared out from its middle looked foreboding and watchful. There was no sign next to the door or any other kind of distinguishing mark that indicated what it lead to.

Nonetheless, Jerro stepped up to its threshold and considered it carefully. He felt oddly drawn to it. He reached out and turned the brass handle and opened the door. A sweet puff of air seeped out to greet him as he stepped inside.

At first, he was sure he was dreaming. The ceiling was impossibly high, and on it was an uncannily realistic blue sky with clouds that appeared to move. There were delicate, silvery lines—akin to a star chart—overlaying the sky-ceiling and running down the smooth alabaster walls of the interior, along the hard wood floor and joining at the shop's center in a beautiful concentric emblem—embedded right into the wood as metal inlay. The central design was inscribed with all kinds of unfamiliar symbols and it tugged at the recesses of Jerro's mind as though trying to summon thoughts that had been lost behind the ephemeral wisps of a dream.

There was a wide balcony lining the whole upper level with a shapely banister guarding it. A spiraling cast-iron staircase was at the very back of the chamber, stationed behind the large U-shaped display counter. Tall rows of shelves—thick with books and otherworldly artifacts—were spaced evenly along either side of the central walkway. Plush lounge areas were nestled into the four corners of the expansive square chamber, and a few doors—marked with what Jerro could only assume to be 'Employees Only' signs—dotted the walls of the lower level. As far as he could tell from his lower vantage point, the upper floor also had doors, but they were more numerous there than on the ground floor and were all closed and unmarked.

He moved slowly along the central aisle. His eyes roamed around, trying to make sense of the place. There were jars filled with indiscernible objects, some with animal-like appendages; others were filled with bouncing, tadpole-like things that pulsed with colored light. Eerie-looking plants seemed to follow him as he walked by, and he was fairly certain he caught a glimpse of eyes staring out from the shadows on the shelves. He spied a few recognizable objects: magnifying glasses, rolls of parchment, feather pens, gemstones, and wooden chests, but even those had a strangeness about them. And the books, on top of everything else, were written in one unintelligible language or another; others were simply marked with alien-looking symbols. The place resonated with a deep mystical quality, and unsurprisingly, as he approached the back display counter, he found a shopkeeper dressed to match.

She was an odd creature with long ears and a fantastical wardrobe—as if she had stepped out of a fairy tale. She looked like an elf, the kind that warned halflings of their doom—albeit a rather halfling-sized and swashbuckling-looking one at that with a very strange taste in footwear. Maybe the theatrics were part of the whole shop image? At least, Jerro assumed he was standing in a shop.

The shopkeeper's ears looked real enough though—they even twitched—and he spied a long, slender tail that moved much like a cat's. It was a very convincing costume, to say the least. The shopkeeper sat there with her colorful, canvas-clad feet up on her display counter and with a book in hand—which her golden eyes scanned through.

He *ahemed* to catch her attention.

The shopkeeper scanned a little further down the page and then bookmarked her place and set down the tome. She interlocked her fingers over her stomach before addressing Jerro with a pleasant smile. "How may I help you?" She studied him carefully, measuring him up and down with her unnaturally colored eyes.

Jerro was caught inside that gaze. She stared at him in a way that traveled through him, and made him uncomfortably aware of how surreal the whole experience was becoming. "What is this place?" he uttered softly as though talking to himself. "I know I've been down this street before, and I've never seen this store here until now."

The shopkeeper grinned roguishly, and her golden eyes twinkled with hidden knowledge. "That's because it wasn't here until now. Well, technically, it's *here*. It's just not a part of out *there*."

This made Jerro frown, and his eyes managed to tear away from hers and roam about the place once more. The space was vast—*too* vast—and he was becoming uncomfortably certain that the shopkeeper was not wearing a costume. He felt himself backing away; something was definitely wrong, he needed to get out.

"Leaving already, Mr. Ahliss?" said the shopkeeper.

"Sorry. Wrong store." He was tempted to turn and bolt out of the bizarre place until he realized the shopkeeper had said something very peculiar. He became rooted to the spot, halting any chance of retreat. "*What did you say?*"

The shopkeeper slipped her feet off the counter and rose from her chair in one fluid motion. She walked all the way around the display counter until she stood directly across from him.

She was a lithe, attractive specimen, and in any other setting Jerro might have found her alluring—even with her strange elfin qualities—but as it stood, his internal alarm bells were keeping any spark of chemistry at bay.

"That is your name, isn't it? Ahliss? Jerro Ahliss?"

"How could you possibly know that?" He searched himself quickly, making sure he hadn't left his ID card clipped to his belt.

"Well, I could give you some vague and mystical-sounding answer, but the truth is,"—she paused, continuing to smile with impish mischief—"you told me last night whilst I was breaking into your boss's safe."

Jerro felt as though a ton of bricks had landed on him. "You? It was you?" He couldn't believe it. *She's having a laugh, right?* he thought to himself. *Read something in the paper about the break-in and then…what? She wouldn't know my name or that I work at KG unless I'm already a suspect. Oh god, I'll have to check the headlines…* The more he studied her, though, and the more he thought about it, the less likely it seemed to be an elaborate joke.

"You don't look pleased."

"*'Pleased'?* Are you nuts?" Something inside him snapped just then, and all the built-up stress from the day came tumbling out. "My whole building was crawling with cops when I got there this morning. They think *I* did it!" *Or, at least, Reedman does.* "And I can't remember a damn thing from last night! I have no alibi, and what's worse, I was *there* when it happened!" He was fuming. He could see it in her eyes, she really *had* done it—she broke in and left a huge mess and stuck him right in the middle of. Suddenly, he no longer cared about whatever weirdness had conjured up the bizarre shop or the fact that he was likely speaking to someone who wasn't—in the strictest sense—human. He was livid that he might go to jail because some greedy little imp creature had the audacity to break into his work while he was still there. "You've doomed me!" Just like that, Jerro saw the life he had built unravel in an instant.

The shopkeeper, however, remained unfazed by his accusations. She folded her arms and inspected her nails, her strange tail coiling back and forth. "You know what I find interesting?"

Jerro didn't answer her; there was a murderous look in his eyes, and he didn't trust his mouth to speak without shouting.

"What's interesting is why you even came up to Johan Lapaul's office to begin with. Don't you find that a bit curious?"

"Excuse me?" An image flashed through his head that made his brain hurt. "What the hell are you talking about?" Another snippet of tangled memory played out as a hazy, disjointed recollection of the previous night started to fall into place.

"You came up to the top floor just as I was on my way out. You came right up to Johan's office, and let me tell you, *I* didn't open that door, and I don't think you did either."

Pieces were starting to snap together. It felt like lightning running across his brain. Then he remembered the e-mail, the code, the office, the violin—everything was starting to come back to him. "You did something to me." The sudden revelation sparked behind his eyes. "You brainwashed me with that music, and then you…" He turned around and looked at the old green door; it was the first time he had properly turned back to it. There was an antique-looking dial above the doorframe with a type of color wheel under a semicircular plate. The dial was currently set to a bland tannish yellow. His eyes drifted down to the leafy face that stared back at him from the middle of the door. *It's definitely the same one. It has to be.* "You took me home through *that*." He whipped back around became flush. "You watched me get undressed!"

She snorted with laughter and rolled her eyes. "Don't flatter yourself. I instructed you to go to bed. It's not my fault you stripped down to your skivvies."

He felt himself turn a deep red although he was uncertain if it was embarrassment or anger that colored his cheeks. "You set me up."

"I think you're missing the point here." She seemed irritatingly amused by his turmoil.

"And that is?" he snapped.

"I didn't send you that e-mail."

Jerro's mouth flapped open, but he was hard-pressed to find a good retort. He remembered enough of the uncomfortable evening now to know she was telling the truth, or at least part of it. She hadn't been expecting him when he showed up at Johan's door, and it didn't make sense that she would have written the e-mail, let alone send it from Johan's office while she was in the midst of a break-in. "Then why'd you trick me, huh?" There was still venom in his tone.

"Oh, yes. I'm sorry. It would have gone much better if I introduced myself first," she said. " '*Hi, I'm Etcher, and I'll be robbing your boss this evening. By the way, don't run and call security or anything.*' Yeah, I'm sure that would have been a much better plan, despite the fact that someone is *obviously* trying to set you up."

Her calm logic only infuriated Jerro further, and it didn't help that she seemed so damn smug about it. "Well, it still doesn't do me any good now, does it? I still look like the prime suspect. You've got to turn yourself in and clear me!"

Etcher threw her head back and laughed—it was a sound both musical and mocking all at once. "Not on your life. Forgive me, maybe you haven't realized, but my occupation tends to run south of the law. I'm not about to turn myself in. After all, I'm not the one who incriminated you, and I'll not take the fall for whoever is. Whatever is going on, I don't think I'm the one you should be concerned about."

Jerro glared at her. "Well then, what good are you? Why *voodoo* me to come here and tell me all of this in the first place?"

"Voodoo?" She chittered. "Firstly, it's *majik*, not voodoo, and secondly, you and I need to have a talk."

"About what?" he huffed.

"About a job I need your help with."

"My help? You planning on breaking into somewhere else?"

"Yes," she said bluntly. "Ordinarily, I don't recruit help, but for this kind of job, I need someone with special skills—someone like you."

"What, you need me to *hack* into something? I'm not helping you! Why should I?" He balked at the idea. *Who does she think she is anyway?*

Etcher nestled against the counter, resting heavily on her elbows and continuing to smile knowingly at Jerro. It was maddening.

"You really have no clue what you are, do you?" she said.

"What I *am* is about ready to call the police."

"Yeah? You think so, eh? Run that conversation by me. I'd love to hear it out loud."

He grit his teeth and felt his muscles tense. This snarky little shopkeeper was working his last nerve. "I'm leaving."

"Well, I can't make you stay. Actually, I *could*, now that I think about it."

A flicker of fear ran through him, but he masked it with a large dollop of resentment. "You threatening me?"

"*No,* and that's the point. See, I could just strike up a tune and make you do pretty much whatever I wanted, but I won't. I'm not that kind of person—well, not always anyhow. I'll let you walk out of here, and I'll not bother you again. However, if you do choose to help me, then I'll help you find whoever it is that's trying to set you up. I'm a fan of even exchanges."

"I'll figure it out on my own, thanks."

"Suit yourself." She shrugged.

And he turned from her, ready to storm out with all his indignant vigor.

"But, ah, Jerro," she said, and with that she tossed him a small, ornate ball with a golden latch—which he reflexively caught. "Should you change your mind, all you have to do is open it. Try to be near a wall though. It's a real pain having to improvise."

Jerro had half a mind to chuck it back at her, but he could already feel his hands curling into fists and wasn't sure they'd unfurl anytime soon. "Whatever!" he snapped and marched out of there, yanking the green door open and then slamming it shut loudly behind him. He was thankful for the fresh air that rushed over him as he stepped out onto the winding alley; it eased his mind a little and brought him back to a reality he understood.

The sitar music continued to echo down the street, but instead of filling him with a sense of awe as it had before, it only amplified the growing strangeness he could feel bubbling in his gut. Things were getting weird—too weird. He thought he heard the distant rumble of thunder and looked up to see clouds starting to roll in; they were dark near the horizon and promised to bring rain fairly soon.

Strangely, he found himself entertaining the bizarre little imp's story, and stranger still was his willingness to believe what had happened *had* actually just happened; memory or not, this wasn't the type of thing that *normal* people just accepted.

He dared to glance behind him, but the door was no longer there. *Of course it's not! Why would it be? Unbelievable things never leave behind any proof.*

Except...

He still had the pendant-sized ball in his hand. It was a beautiful little sphere—all painted and embossed and gold trimmed. He *could* open it, but that would mean he was daring to believe the story—that would mean he wasn't just writing off the whole thing as a lucid fantasy. And it was just a fantasy, right? He was just having a momentary lapse—a waking dream even—and was simply inventing some obscure reality so as to assuage his feelings of guilt and doom. There was no mystical shopkeeper. There was no disappearing store. There was only Jerro who had the sense that he was in very, very deep shit. He thrust the little ball into his pocket and thought of it no further.

"*Fuck*," he cursed under his breath. As he came back to reality, he remembered Reedman was hot on his trail, and Jerro more than fit the bill of the case's prime suspect. He had to admit, were he in Reedman's shoes, he would have suspected Jerro as well. But there wasn't anything concrete that tied him to the crime, was there?

But what if Jerro *had* gone to Lapaul's office that night? And if he had gone to Lapaul's office, there'd be camera footage and an elevator log.

Jerro needed to get home and pack. Something told him he'd better get out of town and quickly.

The dark sky was filled with twinkling stars streaked across the heavens like jewels set in black velvet. Clouds encircled the horizon and left a wide clearing above a coastline. In the mantle of the sky were five ancient lunar discs that were set in a row, descending from largest to smallest. The largest and closest of the five was full, and so was the second, while the other three were gibbous and swiftly approaching completion. Their lunar bodies illuminated the dark world below in silvery light and weakened the veil between the worlds.

In the sprawling beachside town, the frenzy of festival activity was ramping up. The winding, narrow streets were alive with jubilation. Music blared out of every bar and musicians played on every street corner. Merchants were eagerly welcoming patrons, goading their pliable customers with lunar novelties and magical wares. Street performers executed the most impressive acrobatics and carnival antics that were laced with more than a little supernatural help. Restaurants and small food stands were dishing out all sorts of exotic-smelling treats that perfumed the town with tantalizing aromas.

And bizarre people danced around, drunk off the high of celebration and more than a few draughts of ale.

The line between human and beast was greatly blurred when it came to the people of Eclipse. They laughed and danced and did as people do, but they also had horns and fangs, claws, tails, fur, and sometimes feathers or scaled flesh. They were a mix of mundane and magical, mythical folk and the odd deity or two. Some were less conspicuous than others, but all had more than just one version of themselves.

From further down the coastline came a band of dragons headed toward the bustling beachside town. They had black scales, ruby eyes, and glided silently on massive wings. When the lunar light caught them, their brilliant scales shone in a pearlescent range of deep blues and indigos. Their jewel-like eyes glistened with a heated excitement as the sound of celebration drew near. The dragons were so focused on the commotion that nearby gulls could safely glide along the air currents without fear of being snapped up as appetizers, although they never drifted too close lest temptation get the better of them.

The leader of the troupe guided the band down to a wide stretch of sand along the beach where they could all safely alight. One by one they touched down, and as they did, their bodies quivered and changed, shrinking down to more humanlike configurations—newly clad in black leather clothing. Once the last of them had fully shifted, the leader grinned devilishly and beckoned his fellow dragons with a loud ceremonial roar. The troupe hooted and hollered, rushing in as one to join the mass of wild bodies that flooded the town.

Of course, not everyone was enjoying the celebration. Some poor souls still had to work no matter the day—as was the case for the toadish Mr. Gribs. Unlike all the tall, beautiful, and half-naked bodies that filled the walkways and crowded the bars, Gribs was short and round and barely resembled anything close to human. His skin was soft and flabby, and while the pearlescent sheen of dragon scales could be seen as attractive, Mr. Gribs's pasty, pearlescent coloring only made him appear more grotesque. He had chubby hands, bulging eyes, and a wide, flat mouth.

Despite his evident shortcomings, Mr. Gribs dressed himself elegantly; he had on a good pair of trousers and a fine waistcoat with wingtip shoes to match—although they did little to help his standing being draped, as he was, with his many leather satchels.

For such a small and portly creature, he was surprisingly spry on his feet. He darted quickly between the many dancing legs that clogged the sidewalks or poured out from the clubs that had far exceeded their maximum capacities, and ducked into the darkest alleyway he could find, moving far away from the noise of the festival. He continued to weave through the lesser known parts of the town and slipped into a narrow passage between two brick buildings where he was certain no other living soul would happen upon him.

Mr. Gribs rummaged through his many satchels and pulled out a white piece of chalk that twinkled like starlight in the total darkness of the alley. With a quick and precise hand, he inscribed one of the walls with the shape of a door complete with elegantly placed *majik* symbols. A thin light crept along the seam of the drawn threshold, and Mr. Gribs pushed open the newly created portal and slipped inside.

There was a cone of light descending from an unseen source above. Mr. Gribs found himself standing in the middle of a bare open floor facing an enormous creature that was half-bathed in shadow. The mountainous beast was pale and grave; the lower half of its serpent body was coiled on the ground behind a low and equally gigantic writing desk. The upper half of the beast stood erect like a cobra, and from the sides of its upper torso came a multitude of long, spindly arms. In between the creature's shoulders was its head— cylindrical and tall like a pillar stuck right into its neck. The features of its stony face were flat and minimal, and spread across the curve of a pillar-shaped dome. There were no eyes where there should have been eyes—only one large, roving eyeball in the middle of its forehead. The creature had a crown of protruding bone along the ridge of its cylindrical cranium and wore only a silken robe with multiple sleeves that accommodated its many spidery arms.

The frenzied movements of its limbs seemed to indicate that they acted independently from the rest of the body—which stood unnaturally still. Some of the gangly hands thumbed through documents laid out on the desk while others inscribed the large, hefty tome placed right in the middle of the lacquered tabletop. All the while the creature's singular roving eye darted about in every direction, searching, collecting, and contemplating.

"What is it, Mr. Gribs?" The Ledgerman's deep resonate voice was as mountainous as his very being, and it sent a quiver into Mr. Gribs's very soul. All the while the Ledgerman continued to mark the pages of the hefty tome with his pristine penmanship, unhindered by the quick and scurried movements of his multiple appendages and wildly roaming eye.

Mr. Gribs wrung the straps of his satchels nervously before letting out a squeaky, wet-sounding croak. "There came a jin'hazua for you, sire. It refuses to exchange with anyone other than you. Might I add, it's a rather *strange*-looking hazua."

Something twitched on the Ledgerman's solemn face. "Show me," he commanded in his sonorous boom, and the toadish Mr. Gribs quickly opened one of the pockets of his many satchels and let out a bright-gold messenger.

The little ball of light flapped its elegant wings and meandered over to the Ledgerman, setting down in one of His Majesty's open palms. The messenger was like a speck of dust compared to the colossal master. It hovered there, gently bobbing up and down, as a small strip of parchment unraveled from its luminescent, round body, and then the messenger vanished with a muted *pop*. The Ledgerman spread the miniscule note flat against his open palm. The roving eye took a moment to scan it, and then suddenly, terrifyingly, all movement stopped. His many arms froze where they were, and his roving eye kept staring down at the parchment, transfixed.

Mr. Gribs was silently petrified by the abrupt and immediate stillness of his master, and when the Ledgerman's singular eye slowly rolled up and locked on to his toadish little form, Mr. Gribs felt certain he would crumble into ash and be blown away. He watched in terror as the Ledgerman dipped a hand into his silken robe to withdraw what looked like a glimmering grain, but when Mr. Gribs realized he had not been eviscerated, he managed to let out his breath and unclench his chubby little hands.

The Ledgerman held out a green dragon scale between his gangly fingers and offered it to Mr. Gribs. "Bring me Etcher Everdoor."

Jerro had taken a long, winding route back to his neighborhood and scoped out his building from across the street. There didn't look to be any police cars yet, but that didn't mean they wouldn't be coming. He didn't feel comfortable with the idea of crossing the open road to get into his building, and what's more, he knew Kristoff would be home. When the police did come—as he was certain they would—Jerro didn't want his uptight flatmate to be the last to have seen him. He circled back through the neighborhood and cut a path through the gardens behind his building before scaling the wall to the second story, where his bedroom window was still thankfully open.

Jerro pulled himself up from the ledge and had to tumble into his room, wincing at the soft thud of his entry. He remained rigid as he listened out; he could hear the TV in the living room and Kristoff shuffling about in the kitchen. When no footsteps came down the hall, he got back to his feet, feeling safe for the meanwhile. He quietly crept about his room, delicately opening the closet to look for his old rucksack. There were notes and handouts still in the pockets, along with an array of broken pens, a useless thumb drive, a pack of ancient chewing gum, and a few specks of what might have passed for oregano. He emptied out the contents and shoved them into a shoebox near the back of the closet. He wanted to make sure it didn't look like he had suddenly packed and left in a hurry.

After gathering up the barest of essentials—his laptop, some clothes, and passport—he made ready to leave. He looked over his cluttered little room and felt a touch of remorse. He had a feeling he wasn't going to be seeing it again for a long while. There were small mementos he was tempted to take but he knew he needed to travel light, and besides, what use were mementos when he was on the run? Yet at a second glance, he couldn't help but grab a book from his small collection of novels, and a model spider he had built from a DIY metal kit.

He headed over to the window and was just about to climb out when he saw a uniformed officer wander into the garden. *Shit!* He ducked down quickly and fought the urge to start panicking. Before he could wonder how and why there was a policeman in the garden, he heard the doorbell ring. He listened to Kristoff's footsteps as they headed for the front door, and then Jerro's heart sank when he heard the distinctive though muffled voice of Detective Jaiko Reedman. The bastard had planned ahead.

"Hello? Can I help you?"

Reedman stared down the haughty-looking youth that answered the door. *Must be one of the flatmates,* he thought. "We're looking for Jerro Ahliss. Is he in?"

"No, he isn't," the flatmate replied with pursed lips. "He's probably still at work."

Reedman sighed and looked over his shoulder to the band of officers standing behind him in the cramped corridor. He gave them a subtle indication with his eyes to get ready. "No, I'm afraid Mr. Ahliss left work earlier this morning," he said as he turned his attention back to the sour-faced youth. "I'm going to need to take a look around." Reedman broke into a wide, predatory smile as he held up a warrant.

I'm doomed was the only thought that played through Jerro's head. He had risked peeking over the edge of his window to see if the officer was still there, which he was—only now with backup. Jerro desperately looked around his room for some place to hide. He knew he had mere moments to either find a way out or be caught—except that there was no way out, and he really didn't want to be caught.

Think, Jerro, think! He could hear the detective stepping inside the flat with a dozen or so other officers. This was it. It was all over for him. He couldn't talk his way out of this one or make the evidence disappear—not this time. His number was finally up, and he was actually innocent for a change. He felt his mind start to wallow in defeat. He could see it now: Reedman's smug face as he slapped the cuffs on him, the disappointment in his parent's eyes, and the total and utter collapse of the life he had worked hard to build.

It made him angry—*no*, it made him livid! Beyond furious, beyond the white-hot rage that refused to be beaten down. He couldn't give that self-righteous bastard the satisfaction! He mustn't!

His hands were nervously running up and down his legs as if trying to spark some kind of epiphany. Then he felt a small round lump on his thigh and he dipped a hand into his trouser pocket. He withdrew the ornate little ball and dared to wonder. The lacy-gold filigree, the colored enamel inlays, so beautiful and beckoning in curious ways—it was like an angel caller pendant missing the loop for a chain. He shook it gently and felt something knock about softly inside, letting out the most delicate tinkling sound that seemed to ring more in his mind than in reality.

He thumbed the button on the gold latch and popped open the lid.

So much for being normal.

"You and you with me. Harrison, you take Bortnum and Hill. You three, check the other bedrooms"

"*Wait a second!* Why are you checking *my* room? That's Jerro room down there. You can't—"

"I can, and I will. Jones, take care of this, please."

"Step aside, sir," said Officer Jones, who was just as big and impassive as Reedman. He wedged himself in front of the horrified-looking flatmate and forced the young man back with his sheer mass.

Kristoff seemed to crumple before the severe expression on the officer's face and went to a far corner in the kitchen while muttering under his breath, looking rather petulant. He pulled out his phone and occupied himself as best he could, starting by dialing the number of one particular flatmate.

"Hey! Who're you calling?" demanded the officer.

Kristoff broke down into a mess of incoherent babbling as he put away his phone.

Reedman snorted. *Spoiled little runt*, he thought. "Come on." He headed down the hallway, opening the first door he found. It was a cramped bathroom with a dingy-looking shower curtain pulled around a bathtub in the back corner. He indicated for one of the officers at his side to inspect it while he and a thin, freckle-faced cop continued down the hall. There were two more doors to inspect, but one had slats running down the front and was obviously a closet. The detective sent the freckle-faced cop off toward the closet, saving the bedroom door for himself.

He knew Jerro was close; he could feel it just as surely as he knew the boy hadn't been telling him the whole truth when they were back at Kairos Global. *Crafty little bugger,* Reedman thought. It had grated at him to let Jerro walk away, he should have taken him in right then and there regardless of the trouble it might have caused. He *knew* Jerro was guilty, but he had needed proof. Too bad it came after the boy had already slipped out. No matter, Reedman had him now. Today, the detective would get redemption and never again would Jerro Ahliss walk out of a courtroom smelling like roses.

He swore he heard movement coming from inside the bedroom. *Gotcha this time!* A small thrill ran through him. Maybe it was better this way. The hunt was so much sweeter than the catch after all, and secretly, he knew that he wanted to make the little bastard feel fear and desperation so he could atone for his prior offense. There'd be no technicality this time; the evidence would be ironclad—indisputable. Reedman tightened one hand on the doorknob and had his pistol drawn in the other. He shoved open the bedroom door and brought his pistol swiftly in front of him. This was it! He had finally caught the little bastard! He could feel the words forming on his tongue, ready to lash out. "*Fre—*"

But the room was empty; nothing stirred except the curtains, billowing slightly by the open window. Reedman rushed over to it and looked out at the officers who were milling about in the garden below. "Did you see him?" the detective demanded fiercely.

The two shook their heads.

Reedman pulled open the closet and yanked aside the clothes. Nothing. Empty. He looked about the room.

"You got something, Detective?" The freckle-faced officer poked his head inside the doorway, drawn by the sudden commotion.

Reedman felt the pit of his soul roar in anguish. "No. Nothing. There's no one here."

Jerro stood paralyzed, feeling his heart jackhammer in his chest as he stared into the empty eyes of the leafy Greenman in the middle of the door. He feared the detective would come through any second, yet he couldn't will himself to move.

"No one else is coming in," said the little shopkeeper. "I disconnected the door. Go ahead. Take a look."

Jerro peered at her through the corner of his eye. There was a mental showdown happening inside his head on whether he had gone crazy and whether or not it mattered if he had. "Disconnected how?"

"Take a look and see." She urged him again.

He looked back at the ominous door. He felt as though the green face was leering at him, daring him to open it. How had he ended up in this mess? It was only yesterday that life had been blissfully normal, if not painfully dull. Now he was standing in the same bizarre shop he had found off of High Street, next to a mystical thief, and on the run from his biggest nemesis. *This isn't really happening, is it?* The Greenman gave him no answers but continued to challenge Jerro's mettle with its empty eyes. He could have stood there, transfixed forever, or he could at least accept that if all of this was a vivid invention of his poor, sleep-deprived brain, the only way to get through it was to just get through it. He straightened himself, fidgety hands toying with his pockets, as he approached the Greenman and opened the door.

He wished he hadn't.

There was nothing but eternal blackness beyond the door—a sickening, endless emptiness that was very quickly searing itself into his mind. His stomach heaved, and he slammed the door shut, backing away from it. "Where are we?" He didn't bother to disguise his fear as his voice took on a hollow edge. The image of the void was still boring into him, filling him up and pushing aside everything else.

"I call it *Blank-Space*. Think of it as the back door to reality." Etcher cheerily strode up beside Jerro and looked at him.

He stared at the door, petrified. *This is a horrible nightmare—a fever dream. It has to be.* But as much as he wanted to be normal—as much as he wanted to deny the unbelievable the way any sane, normal person would have done—he couldn't quell the quiet voice inside him that said this was very much real. It took a tremendous amount of will to tear himself away from the door and look down at the shopkeeper. *Her eyes are so strange,* he thought, *I've never seen golden eyes before…Or have I?* "What are you?"

Etcher grinned and winked but declined to answer. "You need a drink. Come on." The little shopkeeper clapped him on the shoulder and looped her arm around his, leading him away from the door and all the way to the back of the shop towards one of the lounge areas. He was vacant as they moved past the aisles of oddities and otherworldly looking wares. She helped remove the backpack from his shoulder and ease him into one of the cushy armchairs before seating herself atop the coffee table directly across from him. In the middle of her palm appeared a stout glass filled with a rich amber liquid, which she offered to Jerro. "Take it," she insisted.

Numb though he was, he did as he was told and took the glass and sipped at it. The cinnamon spice tickled his tongue, and the warmth of the liquor ran down his throat and heated him from the inside, pushing out the blackness of the void. As the liquor eased his mind and restored his sense of self the magnitude of the moment finally hit him. It was real; it was all painfully real. The shop really did exist in a dimension of its own. He really was sitting there facing a creature that wasn't human, and he was definitely going to go to jail if he didn't catch whoever set him up. He took another sip from the glass and let the liquor slowly work its magic.

Okay, he thought, *fine. This is real. I can deal with that, I think.* He drained the rest of the glass and handed it back to the shopkeeper, who graciously refilled it with whatever sorcery had conjured it in the first place.

She watched him quietly and gave Jerro the mental breathing room to redefine his prior reality. Clearly there was more to the universe than he originally thought, and somehow he knew it was only going to get stranger.

The little shopkeeper was looking highly amused but in a patient, almost sympathetic kind of way. "You know, it would have been a lot easier just to *voodoo* you, as you say, and just get on with it." She had conjured her own glass and sipped at it, licking the sweet spice from her lips and setting the crystal ware on the table.

"And ruin all this stress?" he said sardonically.

Etcher laughed. "Humor—that's good. You might just get through this." She smiled at him in her roguish manner and fixed him with another wink.

He found himself smiling despite himself. He had to admit, she had a certain amount of charm. He took another swig of his glass and steeled his nerves.

"Okay," he said with a nod, coming to terms with his growing new reality. "So—"

"So." Etcher leaned back and folded her arms. "Questions?"

"Many." He looked around the store once again, seeing it in a whole new light. The sky-ceiling was currently portraying a soft twilight with hot-pink clouds that were gilded along the edges by an unseen, setting sun. He traced along the silvery lines of the star chart that overlay the ceiling and ran down the smooth alabaster walls and along the hardwood floor, joining at the ornate concentric design in the middle of the floor. He noticed the dial atop the Greenman had changed from the bland tannish yellow he had seen before to a deep indigo. Then his gaze came full circle and rested back on the strange little shopkeeper with the long ears and swaying tail. "So you're like some kind of elf-*thing* that can cast magic and runs an interdimensional store?"

" '*Elf-thing*'—that's charming." She tittered, searching him with her curious eyes. She took a deep breath and another drink from her glass, tapping the crystal ware with her nail as she considered him. "I'm an Ecliptian. I come from a planet that is aptly named Eclipse, and I do indeed use magic, or rather, *majik,* but it's likely not the kind you're familiar with from fairy tales, not entirely anyhow." She paused. "As for the store, well, you're more or less right. Although we call it a *potion shop,* and it's best not to mention to anyone that it can move around, if you catch my drift."

Jerro took his own deep breath and let the information sink in. "So you go around with this—*potion shop*—and break into places with it?"

"*Yes,* although I wouldn't mention that either." A devilish smirk spread across her face. "Here's the thing: thief though I am, I'm not a crook, and I didn't set you up, if you're still wondering."

"Given this whole situation, I think I'm inclined to believe you." He had to admit, it really would have been easier for her if she just hypnotized him instead of going through all this hassle. If this was just an elaborate game, then it certainly had him fooled. But the back of his mind kept nagging at him. "There's one thing I don't get." He peered at the shelves with jarred animal bits and mystical, glowing tadpole things. "Okay, a few things I don't get. Point being, someone is either really patient or amazingly lucky to pin me during an actual break-in."

Etcher's brow knit together. "Just what exactly did the police say I took?"

He shrugged. "They didn't say. I was told Johan's office got tipped and his computer was hacked. Why do you need to break into a computer anyhow? You telling me there's a demand for corporate secrets in the magical world, or am I missing something here?"

Her ears flicked back, and the tip of her deviltail coiled in feline agitation. "I don't leave a mess, and I *don't* hack computers."

Idiot! he chided himself. The whole convoluted mess was starting to snap into place and make a strange kind of sense. He took a heavy drink from his glass as he pieced the information together. "They never knew you were there." *Shit.* He should have realized it sooner.

"Nope, but they were certainly banking on you being there. I wonder how your sudden disappearance might have changed things."

Jerro had to wonder about that too now that she mentioned it. "Huh." He ran a mental list of people through his mind as he contemplated who the real thief was—besides Etcher, of course. Whoever they were, they had done some careful planning and research to pin it all on Jerro. He was the perfect suspect after all. Somewhere along the lines, he had made a powerful enemy. Trouble was, he could think of more than one. "So you took me out of there right before whoever it was who that sent that e-mail could get to me."

"Yup."

He frowned. "But why?"

"I told you: I have a job I need your help with."

"But…I don't get it. What could you possibly need my help with? It's clearly not about computers, and unless you're looking for someone with extensive know-how in building metal-sheet models I doubt I'm your man."

"Metal-sheet models?"

"I got them a lot as a kid."

Etcher stared at him incredulously for a moment. "Tell you what," she began, "there's a spare bedroom up on the balcony, six doors to the left, with a hot shower and clean clothes. Why don't you wash up, take a little time to unwind, and relax a little? And then we'll talk more about it."

"Yeah, but—"

"Just trust me. Go take care of yourself first." She picked up Jerro's backpack and held it out for him to take.

He reluctantly got to his feet, not entirely certain he was ready to put a pin in their conversation, although he had the sneaking suspicion he would not like whatever it was she had to tell him next. Maybe a shower was a good idea after all, and now that he wasn't in the midst of a daring getaway, he realized he stunk of sweat. He took his backpack from her and slung it over his shoulder. "Okay, fine. But we're not through here. I expect to get more answers"—one of the potted plants on the shelves hissed at him—"a lot more."

"As you wish," she said.

He gave her one last scrutinizing look over before he headed up the spiral staircase and realized a little too late that he should have asked exactly which door's left he should start counting from. He was confronted by a daunting number of identical mahogany doorways as he reached the balcony, and none had any discernible marks. "Erm…"

"The door left of the middle would be 'one'," Etcher called up to him.

"Uh, yeah, okay," he replied. And as he looked back he realized he could see the entire shop from his vantage. The intricate design on the center of the floor, how the lines from the star chart interlaced over every surface. It was a beautiful chamber, now that he took the time to appreciate it, and it was calm and peaceful there. He looked down and saw that Etcher was watching him. "Right, yeah." He counted his way along until he reached what he hoped was the spare room and not another *Blank-Space*.

Thankfully, it was just as Etcher said. The room was a big open space with a large four-poster bed and a view of a regal-looking courtyard. The walls were decorated in a pastel blue with pale wood panel trimmings. Big white rafters were spaced evenly along the slant of the high ceiling, and though the decor was minimal, it was homey and inviting.

There was also a ginger cat nestled in the middle of the bed—a sizable and rather-feral-looking ginger cat.

Jerro put down his bag and eyed the feline cautiously. It appeared to be snoozing, although he was fairly certain cats didn't really ever sleep. He edged along the wall, keeping his eyes on the snoozing feline as he headed to the window. Outside was a luscious green courtyard with little winding pathways and a neatly trimmed hedge maze. It seemed to Jerro as though the bedchamber were a few stories up from the ground level.

He scanned the landscape, looking for any clues as to where the chamber might exist in the universe. There was a thick forest cresting the horizon with pale-blue mountain peaks barely visible in the backdrop of the sky. He thought he heard the cawing of seabirds, and he saw a tiny glimmer of water just beyond the edge of the tree line. There were some oddly shaped silhouettes flying in the sky, but he wasn't able to identify them before a rustling from behind snapped up his attention. He spun round only to find himself at eye level with a tall and shapely woman.

She wasn't a normal woman though. She had a fine coat of orange fur covering the majority of her supple body, pointed cat ears, and big, sultry eyes. There was a layer of downy white fluff running over her chest all the way to her navel, and she was most definitely naked.

"Uh…" Jerro was trying very hard not to gawk at her.

"Well then," the woman purred with a velvety voice. She made no attempt to conceal how her eyes undressed him, making him feel like the naked one of the two. Her tail swished and flicked, and Jerro couldn't help noticing how uncannily she resembled the ginger cat—which was presently missing. "So *you* are the one we have been sitting around waiting for on this dull rock." She had an exotic accent that gave her intonation a musical edge—as though she hailed from somewhere densely tropical.

"Uh…" Jerro tried a second time to formulate something more intelligible. "'Scuse me?"

"*You*"—she purred again—"we have had to wait around here for *you*. We should be on the Hellean Islands turning a profit, but instead, Everdoor insisted we wait. It is the Lunar Week, you know. I hope you realize what a costly venture you have been. I hope it is worth it." She turned her back to Jerro, casting her sultry gaze over her shoulder as her tail coiled around his thigh. She sauntered out of the room without another word.

Jerro stared after the voluptuous cat-woman. Maybe a *cold* shower was in order. *Relax. Unwind.* Etcher had told him. He was beginning to see why. If he had any hope of making it through the rest of the day with his sanity intact, he needed to take his breathers when they were offered.

The bathroom, thankfully, pulled him out of his stunned stupor and replaced it with a sense of awe. It was nothing at all like the cramped little wash closet at his flat. This, like the bedchamber before it, was all wonderfully fitted to accommodate his usually hindersome tallness. The full-body mirrors didn't cut off half his face. The shower stall not only had a large faucet head hanging down from the high ceiling but the stall itself also had plenty of elbow room for him to move about, and although Jerro wasn't much for baths, he noticed the tub was deep and long and would have surely housed him without cramping up his legs. He stripped down and stepped inside the shower, taking a long and much-needed soak.

"You are insane, Everdoor."

"Well, that's much tamer than what you usually call me." Etcher, who was unfazed by the cat-woman's chiding, continued reading through a small book that was missing its dust cover.

The cat-woman huffed and crossed her arms under her bosom, puffing out her chest. She stared down the little shopkeeper who ungraciously ignored her. "So how long is *this* new addition staying?"

Etcher flicked a glance from over the top of her book at the feline. "Long enough to complete the deal, as always," she said as she returned to her reading.

The cat-woman grew tired of standing and being ignored and decided to take up a seated position so at least she could be ignored comfortably. She sauntered over to a vacant armchair and nestled down in it, crossing one shapely leg elegantly over the other as she inspected her nails. "What makes you so certain he *can* complete the deal? Or even make one, for that matter?"

"He's here, isn't he? And he's desperate." Etcher turned a page, conjuring a stiff drink in hand that she sipped at as she read.

The cat-woman watched the shopkeeper intently, hoping to ascertain something a bit more substantial from her impassive employer. "A bit too coincidental, him showing up, do you not think?"

"Yep."

The cat-woman waited for a more elaborate answer, but when none came, she blew out her breath and shifted irritably in her seat. "So what, then? Was it a setup?"

"There was a setup. Wasn't for me though."

The feline was just about at her threshold for Etcher's inscrutable demeanor. "How do you know there is not still a setup waiting for you? A few weeks ago, you got a message from—" She stopped when Etcher's eyes peered at her warningly. "What I mean is, Jayus sent you here for one job, and you have ended up finding a means to another."

"And I agreed with you that it's too coincidental. What's your point?"

"Well, what are you going to do about it?" The cat-woman struggled to keep her tone even and calm. Somehow, Etcher always managed to ruffle her fur.

"At this particular juncture, Tahli, nothing at all."

Feeling revitalized, Jerro stood before the open closet in the bedchamber. Despite grabbing a change of clothes, nothing he had brought with him was actually clean. Thankfully, there was a multitude of jeans, trousers, shirts, formal wear, and even shoes and socks stocking the shelves. Fashion not being his strongest suit meant that Jerro picked out the simplest-looking shirt he could find—among the more flamboyant apparel—and paired it with dark-gray jeans, plain socks, and his somewhat out-of-place sneakers.

Once dressed, he began to feel like himself again. He tossed his old clothes into a nearby hamper, after transferring out the essentials from his pockets. He had checked his phone in the futile hope that it had signal, but instead, there was an unpleasant-looking *x* over the signal icon and several missed messages from Mahra, along with a missed call from Kristoff and a text from Andri—who he genuinely felt bad for inconveniencing with the whole search and seizure. He turned off the screen. There wasn't room enough in his reality to deal with either Mahra or his pissed-off flatmates at the moment. He unpacked the rest of his backpack and realized to his silent horror that there weren't any plug outlets, which confounded him since there were light switches and working lamps. He'd inquire about the power source later though—right now there were more pressing matters that needed his attention.

The cat woman was standing beside his door, leaning against the wall with her arms crossed under her ample bosom. He tried to clear his throat discretely and keep eye contact as much as he dared, although her suggestive gaze made him uncomfortable and squirmy. "Where's Etcher?" he managed to say without a hitch.

"Everdoor is in the music room," the cat-woman replied in her exotic lilt as she stretched out against the wall.

"And that would be where?" He was trying very hard to keep his composure.

The woman pointed to the wall parallel to them. "Nine doors to your left—or thirteen, if you prefer the long way round."

Jerro was halfway tempted to take the long way since it meant he wouldn't have to cross in front of the woman. He suspected she had placed herself there to inconvenience him. *Man up, Jerro, or she'll keep toying with you.* He crossed in front of her, keeping his eyes locked with hers as he passed. She pursed her lips and looked him up and down, making him hurry a little quicker than he intended.

When he had passed by the appropriate number of doors, there was a moment of doubt as he considered the new threshold before him. *It was nine, she said, wasn't it?* How either the cat-woman or Etcher managed to keep track of all the rooms without any kind of distinctive marking was beyond him. He resisted the temptation to look back at the cat-woman, certain her eyes were still boring into him. The door would have to do even if he risked looking like a fool or facing another void—the thought of which made him cringe. He wondered if he should knock first, but with his keen desire to be out of the cat-woman's crosshairs, he simply opened the varnished door and slipped inside.

The chamber within was a well-furnished music room equipped with a multitude of string instruments and a few percussion pieces propped up on stands. Rich mahogany made up the interior and embedded shelves took up large portions of the walls, housing what Jerro could only assume were books of a musical variety. The ceiling was domed and painted with a brilliant mural of mythical looking creatures, posed in a way that made Jerro recall the grand works of renaissance masters. Little spotlights surrounded the rim of the dome, and their only function was to light the extravagant painting. The rest of the chamber was softly lit by the amber lamps set high along the interior.

Etcher was playing her violin in front of a music podium with her back turned to the door. She was wholly engaged in her practice, masterfully gliding the bow along the strings while her fingers danced across the neck of the instrument. The violin's song wove into a soulful melody, caressing the air with its solemn call. It filled the room with the tale of a long and arduous odyssey in which any listener could quietly impose their own personal voyages.

Jerro wondered for a moment if she was casting another spell, but this was different than the last time. He didn't feel dull and lifeless like he had the night they met, and he was still in charge of his faculties, but he couldn't deny that he was moved by the rich melody.

He found an empty chair and quietly seated himself. Soon Jerro let himself be lost inside the music, feeling his thoughts expand and wander along the winding currents of the violin's song. He remembered his grandmother then— and her great distaste for the instrument. She had so crassly stated that the violin sounded like cats yowling, but as Jerro sat and listened to the elegant flow of every note and the vivid and winding melody that invigorated him in unusual ways, he couldn't think of anything being further from the truth.

And as he listened time lost all focus.

After what may have been hours, or perhaps only moments, the tune wound down, and Etcher concluded the violin's song. She vanished the instrument and bow with a flick of her wrist and peered at Jerro sidelong. "Answer time?" she asked with an amused smirk.

Jerro nodded slowly, reluctant to come out of his musings. "You play beautifully."

"Far more enjoyable, I imagine, when you're not being *voodooed*."

He snorted. So much for compliments. "Yeah."

"Maybe I only convinced you to believe it was good. You never know." She smiled at him and neatly consolidated the music sheet in front of her, walking the stack over to the ledgers in the bookcase and shelving the papers. "So, then, what do you want to know first?"

Good question. "Well, let's start with this job." He folded his arms and leaned back in his chair, trying to look more confident than he felt.

"Ah." Etcher took up the chair opposite Jerro, crossing one leg over the other and looking much more convincingly at ease as she adjusted the lacy cuffs of her blouse. "Well, it's a fairly simple job, really. All I need you to do is remove a seal from a door."

"Oh, is that all? And you can't do this because…?"

She clucked her tongue and checked him up and down. "*I* can't because it's a ghost seal. As the name suggests, only the dead can touch it."

"But I'm not dead." His face twitched with panic. "Not planning on killing me, are you?" he said with a teeth-clenching smile.

"No need," she replied. There was a devilish glint in her honey-colored eyes as she regarded him. "You're a reborn. You confuse the natural order. Things like ghost seals register you as dead."

"A *reborn*? And that's what, like, reincarnation?"

"Yes, but slightly different. Honestly, perhaps not the most aptly fitting name—more of a slang term. Every soul is technically reborn, reused—re-whatever from a previous life force. But with reborns, there are traces of the old life still left. Everyone else gets a clean slate, but reborns are left with a type of marker that gives them access to things like ghost seals. You could even cross through the gateway of Death and back without much of a hitch if you wanted to."

Though Jerro was not dim-witted, he felt absolutely dumbfounded by what his ears had just heard. Okay, so maybe he hadn't fully adjusted to this new reality with *majik* and ghost seals and reborns and God-only-knew-what-else. He mulled over the information for the moment. In light of all the weirdness that had compounded itself on him in a single day, he decided to try and keep his mind as open as possible and just accept whatever new weirdness came his way—that didn't mean, however, that he wasn't plagued by the notion he might have gone stark-raving mad and was currently occupying a padded cell.

Bugger it. If it was a choice of reality between this or a loony bin, he'd rather be sitting there, talking to an alien who ran a magical shop that could travel through dimensions. *I'm definitely going mad.* "Okay, so…what makes you so sure I'm a reborn? I don't remember any past life."

"Well, that's the beauty of it! You don't necessarily have to remember the past life. The trace of it exists in your soul—gives it a different signal. I have read that occasionally a reborn will 'awaken' with knowledge from their previous selves, although don't bank on that. Typically, it's much more subtle. You'll have heightened senses, varying degrees of precognition, strange dreams—the type of signs that can go unnoticed at first. I, however, have a very strong aptitude for sensing the resonance of a person's soul, which is a fancy way of saying I can *feel* what people are. In your case, I could feel the Ecliptian marker that clings to you."

"Ecliptian? That's what you are, right?"

"I'm delighted you remembered."

"And is that typical—to find an, um, Ecliptian reborn out here? I mean, on my world?" It was a strange thing to have to distinguish *his* world from another's. Only a few hours ago, there was *one* world drifting in the vast unknown of the universe. No aliens, no *majik,* and no potion shops, cat-women or otherwise.

"Well, finding a reborn at all isn't typical. It's a very rare state, but a different world does fit the bill—something about the soul not returning directly to the source it came from. As far as I know, this only happens with Ecliptian souls, but who can say? Not a whole lot is known about how and why it happens. Are you all right? You look nervous."

Jerro was chewing at his lip again. "You said reborns have strange dreams?"

"That is one potential indicator, yes."

"Strange like how?"

"Well, I'm not a reborn, but if you're asking, then I'd say it's a fair assumption whatever dreams you're thinking of are probably it."

"I had a dream before I found your store. It wasn't the first time I had the dream, but it's been a long time since I've had it. Used to be I'd have the same dream all the time when I was a kid, but eventually it stopped."

"You got older."

"I guess so."

"Not surprising. The child's mind is much more open to these things. Plus, growing up on a mundane world makes you quickly lose touch with the ethereal."

"What do you mean by '*mundane*'?"

"You know—no *majik,* no greater awareness. The gaea of your planet is in a deep slumber. No one hears it besides maybe the paona."

"Paona?"

Etcher laughed. "Sorry—*animals.* It's a distinction we use on Eclipse to define the animals from the people since that line is rather blurred for us. Although don't think that makes *animals* any less intelligent or capable. I've met a fair number of paona with a far greater aptitude than a great many people."

"Can't fault you on that one." He could have traded in half of the workforce at Kairos Global and not have lost an iota off its intellectual totem pole. It'd probably have been a much more enjoyable place to work in if said people were replaced by monkeys or guide dogs. Hell, he'd have taken parakeets even. "Okay. So, just to be clear, I'm a reborn, and you need me to remove a ghost seal so you can break into somewhere. Is that right? And then you'll help me find out whoever it is that's setting me up?"

"That's right, but we have to shake on it."

"Yeah, okay." Jerro started to laugh at the juvenile nature of the request, but when Etcher extended her softly glowing palm, his expression quickly fell. "What are you doing?"

"I told you, we have to shake. Think of it like a magical pact. It'll bind us to our promises. It's how I ensure I don't get double-crossed by my clients. My job runs south of the law, remember? Which means the people I work for aren't always the squeaky-clean and trustworthy type."

He eyed the palm suspiciously. "How do I know you're not trying to double cross *me*?"

"Look, I know you're new to the whole *majik* thing, but the pact runs both ways, I assure you." When Jerro failed to appear alleviated, she sighed long and heavily. "See? This is why I don't work with mundanes. You're unfamiliar and suspicious of the supernatural."

Jerro felt his features scrunching; *mundane* was starting to sound awfully similar to an insult. "I'm not mundane."

"Oho! Well then, prove it." She kept holding out her glowing palm. "You don't shake, we don't have a deal, and I'm afraid I'll have to return you to your world."

"You would really dump me off just like that?"

"Sorry, Jerro, but I don't run a charity. You want my help. I want yours. This makes sure we both get what we want."

"Well, I don't like it."

"You don't have to, but I'm not asking you again."

There wasn't a threat in her tone, but she was undoubtedly sincere. If he didn't make the deal, he was on his own. "Can I think about it?" he said.

She shook her head. "I've lost enough time as is, and I don't like dawdling. Besides, I miss my home. Your world just isn't my cup of tea."

Jerro could feel the gravity of the moment weighing on him. Returning to the disaster that surely awaited him back in Midgard didn't seem like much of an option, but the knot of apprehension wouldn't leave him. This moment was important, he knew that, he could feel it down to his core—he was choosing between two fates which would redefine the course of his life forever. For a moment it was as though he could see all that lay down either path, and it horrified him to realize just how delicate the tapestry of Fate truly was.

The rain had left the air smelling sweet and the dark sky clear. It was a beautiful night out, despite the chill. Yet Mahra was perfectly warm in her thick woolen coat. She had nestled herself atop a squat brick wall under a big open archway, flanking the courtyard of her upscale community. She had come to find peace for her busy mind but couldn't help drifting back to the events that had so recently turned everything inside out.

It was strange that her day could start out so well and end so badly. For a short time, she had been on top of the world—eating lunch her dream guy and not caring about anything else. The first time they had actually spoken was likely to be the last time she'd ever see him again.

She pulled out her phone and checked it for the umpteenth time, but there was still no word. Mahra slumped against the cool brick archway and peered up at the stars.

"How long have you and Mr. Ahliss known each other?"

"I—well, not long. Today…today was the first time we really spoke."

"And yet you left with him earlier this morning."

"He asked me to lunch. I didn't know anything was wrong. Please, Jerro's not a bad person. I don't believe he would have done this—"

"Miss Lapaul, are you aware that Jerro was a suspect in a prior case a few years back?"

"What?"

"I'm sorry, Miss Lapaul, but you don't know Jerro Ahliss nearly as well as you think. Now tell me, where was he going after you parted at the bistro?"

"I—I don't know. He just said he wanted to get on a train and go somewhere, and he…"

"He what, Miss Lapaul?"

"He asked me to go with him."

"And why didn't you?"

"I—they were expecting me back at work, and I thought maybe we could go another time."

She should have gone with him. Mahra closed her eyes and let the cool breeze redden her cheeks. She could still feel the little flutter in her heart whenever she thought about Jerro and the way he looked at her with his flirtatious smile. She had grinned uncontrollably when he pulled his chair around so they could sit beside one another, and they sipped their drinks and picked at their food, talking and smiling. After all the gut-wrenching nerves had died down, she found he was surprisingly easy to talk to. They had gone through the usual *getting-to-know-you* questions, but afterwards it was *'Oh, I love that film! Did you see that awful remake?' 'The one with the bad CGI? Cor, that was rubbish!' 'They should have stuck with puppets!' 'Hey, you know Nelson's voice-acting in the new Odin Sword game?' 'Really? No way!'* chatting away like they were longtime friends.

And when it came time to say good-bye, Jerro had put an arm around her and bent down to kiss her cheek. She could have melted; it could have all ended right then and there and she would have been perfectly content.

But then the detective came, and everything fell apart. She hadn't been back at work long when they detained her for questioning, and soon after that, she learned about Jerro's past. The detective shouldn't have said those things. He'd done it to provoke her—she was certain of it.

She'd left the station in tears. And yet, despite everything, she wasn't sure it mattered if Jerro was a crook. That's when she knew the love bug had bitten her right on her arse. *Stupid Mahra!* She just wanted to talk to him one last time; she needed to know. Why her? Why had he asked her to go with him? Why did he make her feel so…

The rain was starting up again, and Mahra sighed. She slipped down from the wall and pulled up her collar as she quickly navigated through the gardens and the open walkways toward her roomy flat in the south building of the Glade Apartment Homes. She fumbled with her keys to get inside the stairwell; the little iron gate stood impassively shut as she jiggled the key in the lock. It took a bout of abusive words and some forceful jarring to get it open, but before she could make it up the stairs, the wind suddenly picked up and made her skin crawl.

She looked over her shoulder and thought she saw the shadows move, and then a crack of thunder damn near made her jump from her skin. The rain came down in a heavy sheet and drenched her as she hurried inside.

The squelch from her shoes echoed off the stony walls as she marched up the steps to the second floor. Behind her, she could hear the wind rattling the iron gate and whooshing through the trees. It was getting nasty out, and much like her day, it had been so nice only moments before. She felt tired and heavy when she finally reached the door to her flat. The golden numbers on her door glinted as she approached—and then something dark appeared in the reflection, but before Mahra had time to scream, a dull force smacked her in the back of her head, and everything went black.

Wednesday...

"We need at least a full day in the market to make up for our losses." Tahli, the ginger cat-woman, cast a glance at Jerro. "And I suggest we start in Hellay and then move on to the capital."

"No can do. We're starting in Gahza'Dune, and I can only give you a few hours of market time before we need to be on the move again."

Tahli let out a long, frustrated breath and crossed her arms. "Honestly, Everdoor, sometimes I think you are determined to run this shop into the ground."

The little shopkeeper replied with a snort of amusement, paying little mind to Tahli's growing agitation. "At any rate, it'll be early morning right now. Jerro, you're clear on everything?"

Hardly, he thought to himself, but knowing that any further attempts to explain things would only confuse him more, he decided it was best just to nod and go along with it. So far, he understood that *Ecliptians* were metamorphic; they could shift between an animalistic form and a humanoid one—which explained Tahli—and that most of them could do *majik.* When he asked Etcher what *her* other form was, the shopkeeper's long elven ears flicked back and she told him it was taboo to ask, but then proceeded to explain that Tahli was from a race of jungle cat known as Kyoki that lived out in the Bloodlands—wherever that was.

He also understood that he and Etcher were going to break into the treasure room of somewhere called the Ivory Palace, which made him realize he should have asked for more details *before* making the deal, and that right now, the whole northern hemisphere of Eclipse was bathed in total darkness for something they called the *Lunar Week.*

And then of course, there was the Babble Seal. Etcher had enchanted him with the spell when they shook hands, and it instantaneously dissolved the very notion of a language barrier—a fact which Jerro witnessed firsthand when he was suddenly able to read all the book titles in the shop. Other than that, he was clear as mud.

Tahli and Etcher were still talking, and Jerro had begun tuning them out; his brain had accumulated its quota of otherworldliness—any more would start spilling out of his ears.

He kept flexing his right hand. When they shook on the deal, there had been a cool, tingling sensation that ran through his palm and wove through his very muscle fibers, and for a moment afterward, there were fine, shimmering lines—similar to the concentric pattern on the middle of the shop floor—inscribed right onto his open palm. But then the lines vanished, and even though Etcher assured him he was only imagining it, he couldn't help but fidget as though the sensation were still there prickling his skin.

Etcher had done her best to give Jerro a basic rundown of Eclipse, the universe—or rather *universes*—and all the in-betweens, but eventually, Jerro had to sleep on it and hope he'd wake up with a bit more understanding than the day before.

So now here he was, sitting in a grand breakfast hall, staring out a massive window toward a sunlit savanna, and watching some *very* exotic-looking wildlife graze on the open plains. He wondered if Etcher also stole whole sections of other buildings, since the various adjoining rooms all seemed to have their own unique views—not to mention the fact that the architecture was vastly different behind each door. His room had a pleasant beachside kind of decor whereas this place looked like it was better suited to an extravagant palace hall—what with the masterfully painted murals and resplendent furnishings. He was fairly certain the cutlery was solid silver and the big overhead chandelier was actual crystal. Despite the fact that he felt extremely out of place, Etcher was enviably comfortable in her own skin regardless of the setting, it seemed.

He became aware that he was the subject of discussion and turned his attention discretely back to Tahli and Etcher while he ate his eggs and toast. Tahli—who Jerro wasn't sure actually liked him but was fairly certain viewed him as an unnecessary and costly expense—was giving off some strong oppositions to whatever Etcher was proposing. He poured himself another helping of freshly squeezed juice and watched them over the rim of his glass.

"You will be wasting your time."

"Oh, come off it, Tahli. Have a little more faith that I might actually know what I'm doing."

Tahli huffed and crossed her legs, her tail coiling with irritation. "We shall see."

An eye roll and a chitter from Etcher only served to further vex the feline. "Well, only one way to find out if I'm right or wrong," said the impish shopkeeper.

"And meanwhile, we could already be in Hellay, making our monthly revenue. Your thievery alone will not run a potion shop, Everdoor," replied Tahli.

Etcher snickered. "My thievery is why we're still in business, m'dear."

Tahli pursed her lips and muttered something under her breath, to which Etcher only smirked.

"At any rate, let's get on with it, shall we?"

Tahli stayed quiet but gave Jerro a rather disapproving appraisal as she looked him up and down, although despite the evident venom, Jerro couldn't help feeling like he was being undressed all the same.

"Right, then." Etcher got up from her seat and circled around the long stretch of dining table toward Jerro.

"Okay, Jerro, I need you to put this on." She held up a dark opal pendant—the size of a pearl—on a thick, braided chain.

It was a tad on the feminine side, but Jerro suspected he'd be forced to wear it despite whatever oppositions he might have. "What is it?" he asked as he gingerly took the necklace and unhooked the clasp.

"It's an obelisk stone. Now I need you to focus on the pendant. What does it make you think of?"

Jerro frowned, wondering what kind of bizarre experiment this was going to be. Clearly Tahli didn't believe it was going to work—whatever *it* was. "I dunno—wait, I see a closet," he said, surprised at himself.

"Good. Now go inside the closet."

Was this some weird kind of hypnosis? Whatever it was, Jerro could vividly see a closet space in his mind's eye as he thought about the black stone hanging around his neck. He did as she instructed and imagined himself stepping inside. It was a decent-sized space—not a proper walk-in but there was enough room for him to stand inside it and turn around. There were shelves all around him that were lightly stocked with a variety of things.

"What do you see, Jerro?"

"I…I see clothes and some tinned food. There're some folded blankets, and a field guide, I think? Oh, there's a hunting knife—what is this, a survival kit?"

"Basic starter kit for the everyday traveler. What about the baskets? Do you see them? They should be filled with coins."

He did see them; there were several neatly labeled wicker baskets lining a section of cubbies, each marked with a different value. The coins looked as though they were made of glass, and each had a glob of pure color at the center matching the tint of the glass itself. Each basket was filled with its own color code of coin, which appeared to correlate to the values marked on the labels. "Okay, I see them."

"Good. Now I want you to pick up one of the coins and step out of the closet."

Jerro was becoming highly skeptical about the nature of Etcher's experiment, but did as she instructed. He picked up one of the green-tinted coins and stepped out of the closet.

"All right, now look in your hand."

"Wha—*how?*" Held between his fingers was the glassy coin.

Etcher grinned and plucked the coin from him, holding it up and turning it in the light, causing little prismatic rainbows to shine across the table. "This is a ginse coin—international currency of Eclipse and the allied worlds, more or less." She shot a devilish smirk back at Tahli—who managed to remain unimpressed. "Do you remember what the label on the basket said for the green coins?"

"Yeah. It said twenty, and it had a money symbol before it."

"That's right. So that means this coin is worth twenty ginse. Easy enough, right? These coins are mined from huge ginse crystals. Think of them like batteries that produce reusable energy. They'll be depleted after their maximum *ginwattage* is used up but will slowly recharge themselves over time. Ginse are used to power all kinds of things—even some spell work. Now I've given you a small fortune there, so don't get stupid and don't flash your wealth, but it's important you have money on you, so you've no excuse not to cover your own end, all right?

"Okay, now go back into the closet and return the coin. Make sure you put it back in the right basket. I carefully organized everything in there, so don't make my efforts vain. Things will stay *exactly* where you place them, so if you leave your space a mess, it's going to be a real pain trying to sort through it in a pinch, got it? One other thing, the space inside the stone is suspended in time, so whatever you put in there won't age or decay, and before you ask, no, you can't store paona or people in there. You're not powerful enough, and it's ill-advised either way. Plants should be alright, though." She handed him back the coin and triumphantly placed her fists on her hips, beaming at the prickly feline.

Jerro was in awe. No wonder Etcher made things appear and disappear at a whim; she must have had her own obelisk stone hidden on her somewhere. He stepped back into the closet space within his mind's eye and put the coin back in the basket with the other green ginse. He took another look around, noting the careful placement and organization of everything, although he intended to do a little rearranging when he had time.

"There's room for you to add whatever else you'd like, but for now, it's just the basics. I imagine I don't need to stress how important it is to keep your own stone safe and away from prying eyes? On that note, I'll need your thumb—since I was clearly right and you *can* use the obelisk." She shot another victorious smirk back at Tahli—who responded by inspecting her nails. "You'll need to make a blood pact with it so no one else can use it," added Etcher.

"Blood? As in my blood?" *Wonderful.* Of course there is a catch.

"Just a drop, or would you rather anyone be able to dip their paws into your stash?"

Jerro did not like the sound of that at all. He instinctively clutched the pendant; it had become rather precious to him all of a sudden. Right there in his hands was the means to never have to worry about packing ever again. He could have whatever he needed right at his fingertips. And he truly despised packing and moving and pretty much anything that involved carrying more than what fit in his pockets. Hell, he wouldn't even *need* pockets now! Okay, so he had to give a little blood; that was a fair trade-off, wasn't it? He held out his hand to Etcher and flinched at the sight of the knife.

"Just a small cut. Don't worry."

He was worried, but he let her prick his thumb anyway, and he sucked in a sharp breath at the sudden flare of pain. He watched in fascination as she placed his thumb over the crystal and then cupped her hands over his. A light started to glow out from under her palm, and Jerro felt a familiar tingling sensation spread through his own hand and forearm.

"There! It's all yours now. No one else can claim it."

"So I can keep it? Even after—"

"My gift to you. Use it wisely." She winked at him, smiled, and then clapped her hands together. "Okay, I think we're about good to go."

"Finally," said Tahli, rising smoothly to her feet.

"Ah! One last thing."

Tahli groaned and sat back down.

"You'll need to be able to contact me or Tahli in case of an emergency. As you might have noticed, your phone doesn't do much good here. You still have that capture ball I gave you?"

"Huh? Oh, you mean that angel-caller thing? Yeah. Why?" He rummaged through his pocket for the ornate little ball Etcher had given him. "What was in it anyhow? When I opened it, I saw a flash, and then your door appeared."

"I put a messenger in there." Etcher snapped her fingers, and a little ball of greenish-teal light with feathered wings appeared beside her and bobbed lazily in the air. "This is a jin'hazua. They're messengers. Pretty basic spell, but since testing your aptitude for casting *majik* will cost more time than Tahli would be willing to permit, it's easier that I just give you your own. Just feed your messages directly into it and tell it where to go, and it'll be off in a flash. As long as you have the capture ball on you, you'll be able to call the hazua to you purely through intention. You should keep the capture ball in the obelisk. You'll still have the connection to the hazua all the same." She ushered the hazua over to Jerro, and it lethargically sailed through the air and alighted on his shoulder.

Jerro peered at it dubiously through the corner of his eye. *That* had been inside the ball the whole time? Seemed like a strange way to communicate, but whatever worked, he supposed. "So…what do I do with it in the meantime?"

"Dismiss it. It'll go away until you need it or until a message comes for you."

Jerro sort of shooed at it, and the little winged ball of light disappeared with a soft *pop*. "Where does it go while it's, ya know, waiting to be called on?"

Etcher shrugged. "Haven't a clue. One of the many mysteries of Eclipse. Likely with Omeh-He—the messenger god—but some say there's a giant aviary that all the jin'hazua go to while they're not delivering post."

"So what's the range on them? Can they go anywhere? We're still in, ah, *Blank-Space*, right?" Jerro hadn't dared to check the front door again after the sickening, eternal blackness confronted him the first time.

"Anywhere at all. They're the only thing in existence that can."

"But so can you, right?"

Etcher let out a dreamy sigh. "If only. I can go *almost* anywhere. God realms and a few of the other sacred ones are inaccessible to me. As far as the Dream and Waking realms are concerned, I can go anywhere, and of course I can step outside reality, but otherwise, no, I'm not quite as versatile as our little winged friends."

Jerro began to see the merit of the strange little creatures. His phone was only as good as its signal allowed, which currently meant it was useless. He had yet to check his unread messages and wasn't keen on doing so anytime soon. Right now, he wanted to be distracted. He'd help Etcher with this job, and *then* they could undergo the tedious task of clearing his name, beginning with finding the bastard who had set him up in the first place. "Well, ah, guess we should be off, right?"

"Yup." Etcher strode toward the mahogany threshold that connected them to the upper balcony of the shop. "Come on. You'll want to see this." She grinned impishly and headed out the door.

Jerro was just about to follow suit when Tahli brushed by him, her tail coiling about his waist this time as she passed. She turned her sultry gaze to him though managed to retain a small amount of disdain in her pursed lips.

"Maybe you will not be *entirely* useless after all," she said as she sauntered ahead of him.

He'd take that as a compliment.

"All right! Now remember, Jerro, what you see here doesn't get shared with anybody outside this room, understood?" She grinned at him roguishly. Excitement was crackling in the air around the shopkeeper. She had stationed herself in the middle of the concentric design on the shop floor and faced the main threshold. Her eyes were locked on to the dial above the entryway, and she squared her shoulders, taking on a regal posture as she poised herself.

Jerro watched intently. The air became charged as Etcher focused, and things began to happen all at once. The star chart that overlay the entire shop changed drastically, whirling to reveal unseen parts of the map, and the enchanted sky-ceiling spun through a variety of weather and day-night cycles, making the lighting in the shop flicker wildly. Then finally, the chart lines thrummed and lit up, the color-wheel beneath the antique dial started turning, and Etcher herself became aglow.

Jerro felt his stomach lurch upward—much like it did when he was inside the elevator at Kairos Global. Wooziness pervaded him, and he felt lightheaded as the Greenman door bridged the gap between *Blank-Space* and reality once more. Then a polite *ding* marked their arrival at somewhere new, and his stomach sank back into place. The sky-ceiling and star chart had stopped spinning wildly, the lines stopped thrumming, and Etcher returned to her normal unlit self. The dial above the door, however, had changed to an oceanblue color, and the ceiling portrayed a clear night sky with the occasional silhouettes of gulls flying overhead. There were five moons directly above them in the dome, three of which were full while the other two gibbous discs trailed close behind.

Etcher turned and smiled at Jerro. "We're here. Ready to head out into the world?"

Jerro was hesitant to see what lay beyond the door, but his eagerness to get out of the store and out of *Blank-Space* outweighed his apprehension. As spacious as it was within Etcher's hodgepodge shop, he still felt a touch of claustrophobia and needed to plant his feet on solid ground. Knowing that an eternal nothingness lay just beyond the walls had kept him ill at ease, and he yearned to be back *in* reality once more—even if that reality comprised itself of *majik*-wielding, metamorphic humanoids on a strange alien planet. And to think, just a few days ago, his life had been relatively normal.

"Okay, Tahli, shop's all yours. Jerro and I are going to take a look around."

Tahli, who had positioned herself behind the U-shaped counter, her tail swaying back and forth behind her with her elbows propped on the countertop—squeezing together her bosom—rested her chin in her cupped hands and looked entirely indifferent. "Take a *long* look around."

Etcher snickered. "No promises." She winked and ushered Jerro toward the door.

Together they stepped up to the threshold, and for a brief moment, Jerro felt a pang of cold dread run through him as Etcher turned the handle.

When Jerro was just a boy, his older brother had taken him to the Fenris Bay pier. His parents were away, and his older brother was left to watch him. They had made it very clear that Jerro was not to leave the house as punishment for sneaking into their neighbor's yard and stealing the apricots off their tree.

His brother took him out anyway.

He remembered the sheer thrill of it all—it was like a genuine adventure and he and his brother were daring explorers out on a quest for fun and excitement. Jerro had never seen such a magical place in all his little life. There were carnival rides and jugglers and wild-looking kites dancing through the air tied to a fancy-looking shop that had a whole mess of wonderful toys.

He ate his first deep-fried chocolate bar at the pier. It was so amazingly scrumptious that little Jerro had drooled through a mouthful of rich chocolate and nougat and sweet, crispy batter; it was sheer bliss.

Then he and his brother took to some of the carnival games and shot BB guns at cans and played hoop toss in hopes of winning one of the pretty little goldfish. They didn't manage to win a thing, but Jerro didn't care; he was having the time of his life.

And the rides—oh, the rides! Jerro was spun upside down and flipped sideways and back and couldn't get enough of it. And when the sugar rush had finally faded and they had both run themselves ragged up and down the pier, he and his brother sat and watched the sunset. They said nothing for a great long while and were perfectly content with one another.

"Thanks for not ratting me out."

Jerro gave a big boyish grin in reply. It had been worth the scolding to have a day like that where he could put aside all his cares and worries and enjoy only the thrill of the moment.

Jerro hadn't felt that way in a very long time, but as he stood there on a bustling street corner of Gahza'Dune, it was as though he had stepped right back into boyhood. The sheer volume of people was astounding, and they were the wildest assortment of faces—from the totally ordinary to where the line between beast and man became hard to define. They were all dancing around and draped in colorful beads and flamboyant clothing. He could see now why Etcher dressed herself as though she had stepped out from some romance novel—except, of course, for the canvas slip-ons.

He found himself on the corner of a main road that led directly down to a beach. Crowds were gathered there too by fire pits and portable food stands, and all around him the influx of foot traffic was spilling off the sidewalks and directly into the road itself.

There were vendor stalls set up along the street and displays propped up outside the brick-and-mortar shops, tantalizing people to go inside. He could hear music playing and spied a few percussionists and brass players blaring away on their instruments. It was a catchy tune they were belting out—even Andri might have enjoyed it.

He couldn't stand around for long, however, as the constant flow of people were jostling him about. He suddenly realized that he was eye level with most of the crowd, if not shorter than a fair few of them. It was the little shopkeeper at his side that was out of place among the land of giants, although it didn't seem to disturb her any.

"Come on," she said as she looped an arm around Jerro's and guided him across the street and through the throng of Ecliptians. "You *must* have a moon bun—classic festival fare and an absolute tradition during the Lunar Week." They wove between a group of monkey-faced wanderers and around a couple who were so interlocked Jerro wasn't certain which appendage belonged to whom; it didn't help matters when there were extra extremities to account for.

There was an avid crowd of people in front of one particular food stand, eagerly holding out their coins in exchange for small round buns. Jerro and Etcher diligently made their way to the front of the group where he got a mouthwatering whiff of the fluffy white pastries up close. The buns were lined up in rows inside the display, and a sign had been posted that read '*Limit 3 per purchase.*' Each little bun had five colored dots marking their tops and smelled like freshly baked sweet bread with a citrusy note.

"*A pit for a bun!*" the woman inside the food hut called out. She had a mane of feathers instead of hair and thick bands of gold rings around her long, slender neck. She was also covered in tattoos.

"What's a pit?" Jerro whispered to Etcher, who—despite being a solid foot or so shorter than most of the crowd—seemed to exude enough presence to be noticed even at her lower altitude.

"It means a ginse. Get your coins ready." Etcher already had a ruby-red ginse in hand, which she made tumble between her fingers.

Jerro ducked into his mind closet and sought out the baskets of money. The ruby coins were labeled "*5*," and the blue ones next to them were labeled "*1*." Etcher was likely getting herself the full '*Limit 3*,' so Jerro decided to do the same.

The small buns were passed over to him in a paper bag, along with his change. Once he and Etcher escaped from the crowd and found a sheltered doorway they could retreat to—safe and shielded from the constant flow of traffic—they sat on the steps and opened their bags.

Jerro pulled out one of the buns; it was squishy to the touch and fit easily in the palm of his hand. He eyed it dubiously, hoping he wasn't making a regrettable choice—this was alien food after all. He looked to Etcher, who had already inhaled one of the buns, unlike her usual polite manner, and was starting on her second. If she was willing to tuck into them like a ravenous beast, then they had to at least be good—even if it did end up being his last meal.

Jerro brought the little white bun up to his mouth and breathed in the sweet aroma once more. The bun was warm and steamed in the cool air. He took a bite and swallowed.

Deep-fried chocolate bars had nothing on moon buns.

It was like biting into a cloud, and when he got to its center, a warm filling played a symphony over his tongue. The dough had been airy and light, balancing out the delicate citrus and rich, creamy, fruity filling that overwhelmed him with pure joy. He was glad there were another two left after he decimated the first.

He sat there in the sheltered doorway, eating the last of the delicious pastries, and stared up at the night sky with its five beautiful moons illuminating the world below in soft, silvery light. For a time, he was just a boy again, sitting in quiet contemplation and utterly at peace with the world.

When had he lost that feeling? When had childhood ended and life become so dull? How could he have let something so precious slip away without him noticing until now? He looked around at all the wild faces that surrounded him, listened to the live music playing and the distant waves of the ocean, and wondered how things could have changed so drastically.

He wasn't always like this; he hadn't always felt so numb. There was a time when even his mundane little planet had felt just as magical as this one. But it all stopped being magical that day when he was sixteen—

A loud crash brought him out of his musings. There was a troupe of festival performers making their way along the center of the main road, parting the crowd with flashes of colorful *majik*. Great tiger-like beasts flanked the troupe, decorated in a similar motley to the jumping acrobats and *majik*-wielding fire dancers. Musicians headed the gang, beating wildly on their sonorous drums and helped to part the throng.

Etcher sprang to her feet. "Come on! Let's get a front-row view before we're stuck on this stairwell." Sure enough, the crowd that was being pushed back from the road was nestling up against the sidewalks and clogging the already-flooded walkways.

"So what's this whole celebration about again?" Jerro had to call out over the clamor of the circus troupe as they made their way through the throng.

"The moons, of course. They'll all be full by Friday. Happens every five years."

"Yeah, but what does it mean?"

"It means we're having a party, Jerro. Just enjoy it." She clapped him on the back and pulled him along to the front of the sidewalk so they could watch the troupe go by.

Just enjoy it. Now there was something else he hadn't done in a great long while.

The tiger-like creatures were mere inches away from Jerro as they strode past and were taller than him, even on all fours. The muscles rippled in their powerful legs with every graceful stride, and their huge jaws lay agape, revealing big carnivorous teeth. Their fur was startlingly white and thinly streaked with silver; as the light played off them, they seemed to shimmer like a mirage.

Pale-blue eyes locked on to Jerro's. As one of the beasts passed him by, it turned its head ever so slightly and looked straight at him. He felt a shiver run down to the pit of his stomach and was transfixed by the magnificent beast. It was as if it knew him, the way it stared him down, and in that instant, he felt a distant memory start to untangle itself from the dark recesses of his mind.

A nudge in his side shattered the moment and put the memory back into the void before he could fully recall it. Etcher was indicating for him to follow, and she cut a path through the thick of the crowd and headed down to the beach.

"This place is wild."

"Yeah. It's not half bad, is it?" Etcher had taken off her shoes and was walking along the beach with Jerro, who had done the same. They had left the main hub of the festival for quieter grounds and were traversing the long strip of sandy coastline. "How do you like it so far?" She cast him a sidelong glance.

Jerro looked over his shoulder toward the fire pits and food stands where the Ecliptians were dancing around and throwing back their heads and letting out wild calls. "I think maybe I was born on the wrong planet."

Etcher snickered. "So it would seem." The waves were lapping softly, and gulls cawed overhead. Behind them, the laughter and clamor of music were reduced to a low rumble. She picked through the sand and gathered a handful of broken shells; she tossed them back into the ocean here and there as they walked. "So what would Mr. Ahliss like to do next? Still a few hours before your big debut into a life of crime."

He smirked and stuck his hands in his pockets. "Yeah, well, there's a thing about that."

"Oh?"

"My occupation used to run south of the law too."

"You don't say."

He laughed gently. "Nothing so adventurous as breaking into palaces or corporate-bigwig offices. What did you take anyhow?"

Etcher winked and tapped the end of her nose. "Client-confidentiality privileges, I'm afraid. So tell me about this criminal background of yours. Computers, I'm guessing?"

He nodded. "Yeah, it involved them."

"Care to elaborate?"

"Well, I would but, ah,"—he tapped the end of his nose, mimicking her— *"Client-confidentiality privileges."*

"Ha! Guess I deserved that. So what happened?"

He kept quiet for a time, kicking stones aside as he peered off into the distance and shrugged. "Got caught. Managed to get out of it, but it was way too close for comfort." He sighed. "Plus, fun as it was, I started to feel like there was a dark cloud hanging over me—like I was marching slowly towards my doom. I think maybe I wanted to get caught. Otherwise, I wouldn't have been so sloppy."

"Hmm." She pelted another shell fragment into the ocean, watching it sail through the air over a great distance before losing sight of it.

"You ever get caught?" he asked her.

"Never caught, exactly, but I've had my share of close calls."

"It doesn't bother you?"

"'Course not. Part of the thrill is the chase."

"Yeah, but that's only fun if you're the one chasing."

Etcher stopped and looked at him incredulously.

"What? Why are you smiling?" he said.

She shook her head and smiled. "Well, you can't seriously believe that, can you?" She let the question hang there a moment before they slowly continued their stroll. "Let me tell you something: I used to walk by this yard, and every day, this dog—tiny little thing—used to chase squirrels up a tree. This little dog would bark its head off. It was livid. And you know what the squirrels did? They chittered back at the dog. They were laughing at it. D'you see? Tell me those squirrels didn't enjoy the chase."

"Yeah, okay." Jerro chuckled. "But they only laughed because they didn't get caught."

"That's true." She threw the last of her shell pieces and dusted off her hands. "Of course one day the dog got lucky. It caught one of them and broke the squirrel's back."

They looked at each other and burst into laughter.

"That's a horrible story." He smirked.

"Yeah, well, there's a moral too."

"And what would that be?"

"Don't get complacent." She winked. "Come on, I'll buy you a round."

Ria had been working in the yard, digging out the flower beds to plant the new seeds of the season. She hadn't heard the phone ring inside the house as she gathered up the old dead and dying foxgloves to put in the compost heap, and when she came in, she had been too busy doing the washing up to notice the blinking light on the answering machine. Ria was old-fashioned like that, she didn't much care for cell phones even though she had one—which was buried somewhere in her purse. So when she got a knock at the door later that morning, it had been very unexpected.

"Just a minute," she called out, wiping the flour from her hands, adjusting the heat on the crock pot, and straightening herself out before heading for the door. Had Ria heard the phone or listened to her messages, she would have been better prepared for who was waiting outside. But as it stood, Ria Ahliss was given a nasty shock when she answered the door. "You!" she said less than pleasantly and had to grip the door hard to stop from slamming it.

"Mrs. Ahliss," said Detective Reedman in his smooth baritone. "May I come in?"

"No you may not!" Ria said sourly.

"Mrs. Ahliss," repeated Reedman, "I came here as a courtesy to tell you in person before you read the papers."

In that instant, her eyes went wide, her bronze skin paled, and she clutched the doorframe desperately. "What's happened to my boy?"

"That's what I'd like to find out, Mrs. Ahliss."

"He's alive though? Tell me he's alive!"

"As far as I know, yes, but he's in a lot of trouble."

Ria took a deep breath to steady herself, and the color slowly came back to her cheeks. She straightened out and narrowed her eyes on the detective. "Trouble you've put him in."

"No, he put himself in trouble, Mrs. Ahliss. Look, he's wanted for questioning. There's an ongoing investigation regarding a break-in at your son's work, and unfortunately, Mrs. Ahliss, your son was the only one present at the time."

"Jerro wouldn't do that. He's a good boy despite what you think!"

The detective stared at Ria with naked disappointment. "Does your son own a laptop, Mrs. Ahliss?"

She glowered at him.

"Well, there wasn't a laptop in his apartment," he continued on. "And he hasn't been home since he was last seen leaving work yesterday morning. I have to ask you, is he here?"

"No," she said curtly.

"Would you tell me if he was?"

They stared each other down. "I'd like you to leave now, Mr. Reedman."

He took a card out from inside his blazer and brushed it over his knuckles as he considered the middle-aged woman before him. She was so prim and proper, like a real 1950's housewife—prideful of her home, well dressed, and hardworking. Such a strange contradiction to her son. "The longer he stays missing, the worse it's going to look for him." He held the card out for Ria to take. "You let me know if you hear anything."

The door was finally slammed in his face.

Reedman let out a deep breath, shaking his head as he stepped down from the porch and crossed the road. He got back into his sleek black car and sat there for a moment, peering over at the side of the house and spying Mrs. Ahliss between the bushes—heading out to her garden in a huff.

Attractive lady, he thought—even if she was nearly twenty years his senior. *Spanish women always do age well though*, he thought as he continued to take mental stock of Ria Ahliss; bronze skin, long dark hair, great legs—it wasn't right that a woman like that was all alone in her house, not that she'd ever let Reedman do anything about it. *Pity*, he thought, *could have loosened her up a bit*. He laughed at himself and pressed the ignition button, starting up the car.

It was a long drive back up the coast to Midgard, but he needed the time to think. He dipped a hand into the center console and fished out a protein bar, tearing it open with his teeth. He took a monstrous bite out of the bar and chewed it thoughtfully. It had been over twenty-four hours since the break-in; Reedman had been busy contemplating the case, and there were a couple things that didn't stick.

For one, after they had finally managed to unscramble the security tapes, he had found footage of Jerro going up to Johan Lapaul's office that night, but the rest of the film had been wiped, and there was no footage from inside Lapaul's office either.

Reedman had watched what little video he had carefully and had come to the conclusion that Jerro Ahliss looked very nervous that night. There was a theory formulating in the detective's head, and he didn't like it. He suspected the boy had been coerced into the break-in, which meant there was another party involved. He also suspected that Jerro had been double-crossed by whomever the second party was. This thought brought him to another theory: Had the second party taken Jerro out of the picture? He hoped, come the end of the week, they wouldn't be pulling Jerro's body out of a river.

He took the on-ramp for the northbound freeway and let himself be carried by the steady flow of cars. The second thing that bothered Reedman about the whole sordid affair was the sloppiness of the job. Why was any of the footage left at all? And why leave an elevator log to top it all off? As much as he hated to admit it, Jerro wasn't stupid; the boy wouldn't have left so much evidence lying about. It was *too* convenient, which backed up his theory about the double cross. Jerro was no less innocent for it, but it meant there was more to the case than what was being revealed.

Reedman drummed on the wheel, finishing off the rest of the protein bar, crumpling up the wrapper, and stuffing it back into the center console. It still irked him that Jerro had managed to get away. No one had reported him going back to the flat, but Reedman was certain the boy had been there. The missing laptop said as much.

The glimmer from the ocean was lighting up the right side of his face as he drove, dancing along his profile through the glimpses between the trees. Little beachside communities were nestled around solemn-looking lighthouses, breaking up the otherwise long stretches of forest. A few motorcyclists wove through the traffic on their big cruisers, all wearing matching jackets. The bikers were flanking Reedman's slick car, and he looked over at one big burly fellow with a petite brunette—who had her arms wrapped around the burly man's waist. The big biker looked back at Reedman, then opened the throttle and took off with the rest of his gang. Reedman would have to take his own bike out for one last cruise before the snow started.

His phone rang. Reedman peered over at the caller ID that lit up on his dashboard and decided to answer it. "Yeah?"

"Got news for you, Jay, and you're not gonna like it." Jones's grizzly voice came through the car speakers.

"Let me guess, the lawyer?"

"Yup. Won't let us near Lapaul's computer. He's got so much red tape wrapped around it I doubt we could get a warrant signed."

"Wonderful. They do know I'm running an investigation here, right? Hard to get a motive down without knowing what's on that computer."

"Yeah, well, you try talking to the bloodsucker. See if you get anywhere."

"I intend to. D'you get anywhere questioning Jerro's coworkers?"

There was an audible sigh. *"Oh we got something all right. Listen, Jay, you coming in soon? You're gonna need to see this."*

"You got another suspect for me?"

"Sort of, 'cept there's two of 'em, and we're not sure who we've got."

"The hell are you talking about?"

It was dark in the bowels of Undercity, but then again, it had been dark down there for a very long time. The corridors and grand pavilions were desolate, as were the wide, sweeping balconies and open stairwells. A creeping sickness had spread throughout the dark world and turned feral all that had once been lavish and pristine. The royal gardens had turned into an

unruly jungle where a ghostly quiet had instilled itself, and in the grand hall where the Pale Throne sat, beautiful and delicate with its silver roses, was the presence of an ominous chill.

In the beginning, there had been five master architects—one for each of the primordial gods; ten thousand slaves, stolen from the Dahl'Kir mines; and an old king, prolonged by his royal blood, to bring the dream of Undercity to life. It had been a noble dream at first, and for a time it was good.

When the pavilions had been full and bustling, the old king threw the most extravagant galas. Lavishly dressed people twirled harmoniously to the music of a live orchestra that was renowned for its enchanting melodies, and the dining halls overflowed with the most succulent of foods from across the five kingdoms.

Night and day were governed by the crystal lights that bathed the alabaster walls with dancing rainbows, and in their soft glow, Undercity became a world of everlasting twilight. Above the galas and the extravagance flew the winged angelous in the open air of the cavernous halls. They nestled in their handcrafted perches by the statues of the godly and looked down on the underground world with sympathetic eyes.

Along the mountainous marble walls were strings of windows belonging to tidy little apartments. The living quarters had been beautiful and homely, decorated with gold-leaf trim and furnished with rich silks and elder oak. There was a place for every slave, their debts finally paid in full, and for every noble and peasant alike who came to call Undercity home.

But the dream had been too grand and provoked the ire of Nightmare. The old king turned mad, and Undercity became a tomb.

—Pages from The Traveler's notebook, from the chapter of "Sin and Sacrifice."

Drip-drop-drip.

A dank stillness pervaded the forgotten world; it crept into every corner, dulled the luster of the marble, and tarnished the gold-leaf trims. Through the hallways came a hollow breeze whispering with the echoes of the long since dead. The tattered banners that hung limp from the walls waved soundlessly as the ghostly air picked at their ragged edges and played tricks on Jerro's eyes.

He was beginning to reconsider their deal. He had half a mind to go back to the shop and convince Etcher they should return to the fun and excitement of Gahza'Dune and be anywhere but in this lonesome and dismal place. He surveyed the shadows suspiciously; there was something in them—something calling to him from out of the dark. The place made his skin crawl.

He moved carefully within the soft dome of teal-colored light emanating from the little winged hazua floating silently beside him. Every step he took, no matter how delicate, clapped off the solid floor and echoed through the black expanse; he felt horribly exposed. *"Tell me we're close to this door,"* he whispered, but the ghostly acoustics of the marble world made every syllable bounce off the stony walls and echo back at him mockingly. *"Etcher? Etcher!"*

"I'm here, I'm here. Calm down." She materialized beside Jerro from out of the shadows, looking ghoulish and unwell in the teal light.

He had to stifle a yelp as she appeared. *"Do you mind not wandering off?"* he said curtly; his nerves were on a razor's edge, and it did him no favors whenever the little shopkeeper kept soundlessly vanishing into the gloom.

She looked at him curiously. "You're not afraid of the dark, are you?"

"No." He cringed at her volume, soft though it was. *"I just can't see a damn thing!"*

"Huh." She clucked her tongue and looked at him sidelong.

"What are you sneering about?"

"Nothing," she said, inspecting her nails as she groomed them. "Just a curious thing to see someone of your *stature* quivering like a willow branch."

"I am not quivering!"

"Oh? Must be the chill, then." She smacked him on the back with her tail and chortled as he yipped with surprise.

"That isn't funny!"

Etcher howled with laughter and jostled him some more.

"Piss off!" he barked and pushed her back into the shadows, flinching as his words came echoing back at him sharply. Her chittering laughter died down as it drifted away, turning soon into silence. *"Etcher? Etcher! Damn it! This isn't funny."* He stared into the hollow stillness of the dark. Tiny whispers in his mind began to scratch at his mettle and weaken his composure. *"Etcher?"* he said again, a tad more desperate than before. This was not how he had planned their break-in going.

A low, gritty rumble of stone against stone echoed through the darkness and made Jerro's blood run cold. Icy dread gripped his heart, and the tiny whispers broke through his veil of calm, filling his brain with infinite horrors.

Without warning, Undercity became lit by the soft iridescent glow of crystal lights. There stood Etcher, leaned up against a colossal black granite pillar and looking triumphant, if not a tad smug. Beside her was a huge amber dial, cast entirely of the crystallized sap, that was set deep into the wall behind the ebony columns. Silver filigree flanked the dial, and behind it, ornate cog work churned away beneath the wall's transparent glass shielding. The prodigious mechanism revolved steadily while a decorative sun and moon chased each other in a slow procession around the amber centerpiece.

Jerro stood in quiet awe of the forgotten place. Though tarnished and tattered, it was no less grand than it must have been when it housed bustling life; of course, it was no less spooky either. "So this is the Ivory Palace?" he said as he moved into an open pavilion. His little hazua sailed quietly through the air beside him, bobbing and down until he dismissed it.

High on the walls before him, the banners of nobles fluttered soundlessly in the ghostly air. The sparkling light from the domed crystal ceiling undulated across the marble floor and made the forgotten world seem as though it had sunk beneath the tides.

"No, this is Undercity. The Ivory Palace will be above us shortly—though right now, we're directly under the city limits," said Etcher as she sauntered into the pavilion beside him.

"So what are we doing down here? I thought we were breaking into the Ivory Palace?"

Etcher tutted. "You weren't listening very well, were you?"

He averted his gaze.

The shopkeeper sighed and strode into the middle of the open floor. "There's a treasure room hidden under the Ivory Palace, and the only way to get to it is through Undercity."

"And the door with the ghost seal?"

"It's what's kept the treasure room locked away all this time."

"Okay, so where is it?"

Etcher pointed to the expansive set of stairs at the end of the pavilion that led up to an unlit hall. "Through there to the royal gardens, past the throne room, and then up the hidden stairwell."

Jerro felt something dark and menacing creep into the back of his mind as he stared into the black gape of the hall. It seemed the crystal lights hadn't managed to vanquish all the shadows. "If you know where it is, why not bring us closer?" He was definitely rethinking their deal.

"Because the seal won't let me. This is as close as I dare to bring the shop without being caught within the seal's influence. But even at this distance, I can still feel it pushing at me, and the closer we get, the harder it'll be for me to move."

"I don't feel anything." *Besides a keen desire to get the hell out of here.*

"Good. If you did, this would be a bust now, wouldn't it? Come on, we've a treasure room to raid." She smiled at him devilishly and urged him forward. There was excitement in her step, and she practically skipped like a dancer toward the dark hall.

Jerro envied her. He envied the carefree attitude she retained even as she ran headlong into the dark unknown. He wondered what it took for a person to get like that.

"*Come on! I didn't bring you here just to sightsee,*" she called back from the stairway.

Jerro hurried after her, passing the row of thick ebony columns and the colossal flank of a marble building that housed a multitude of little apartment windows. For a split second, he thought he spied a pale face staring out at him from one of the dark portals. He stopped dead in his tracks, but the face was gone, and only the vacant window remained. Jerro felt his soul shudder, and he hastened to catch up to Etcher.

"So what's the deal with Daag Landvik?" Reedman, who had arrived only moments before, was standing on the dark side of a two-way mirror, sipping a barely tolerable cup of reheated coffee. The young man sitting inside the interview room with the expensive designer suit and meticulously groomed features was doing his best not to look as scared shitless as he actually was, but Reedman knew. Reedman always knew fear when he saw it.

Jones let out a labored breath and was looking deflated for such a hefty man. "We were combing through the videos, like you said, and found footage of Daag Landvik and Jerro Ahliss talking by a watercooler on the day the break-in happened. Landvik swears he's never spoken to a Jerro Ahliss before in his life."

"Yeah, so?"

Jones had his own cup of barely tolerable coffee and sipped at it before answering. "Landvik works on the twenty-second floor, in the accounting department, and was *at* his desk during the time Jerro and another Daag Landvik were having a conversation."

"You wanna run that by me again?"

Jones didn't answer right away. The poor man looked as though he had already far exceeded his quota of weird for the month, and the day was only just getting started. He stared vacantly past the two-way mirror for a while as though trying to perceive something more from the fidgety young man sitting at the table within the interview room.

"Jones?"

"Yeah, Boss?"

"You gonna give me a little more to work with here?"

"Yeah," Jones sighed. "I'll show you the tapes."

"So, Mr. Landvik," said Reedman as he forcefully slapped the case file down on the table. Daag Landvik twitched; it was slight, but it was enough for Reedman to make sure he had Daag's full attention. He circled the room, prowling as he watched the boy.

Daag started to talk with an overly wide smile, showing off all his pearly teeth. "Listen, *Detective*—"

"No, you listen." The young man's expression fell as Detective Reedman's sheer mass came up to the table and loomed over it. "You're in deep shit, son," Reedman said plainly. He pulled out a metal chair, letting it grate against the floor as he sat himself down. Reedman placed his coffee on the table and leaned back, linking his fingers together over his firm stomach. "You wanna tell me what the hell is going on here?"

Daag began to look nervous. "L-look, I told the other officer. I don't know Jerro Ahliss. I've never *met* Jerro Ahliss—"

"And yet you do realize there's video of you two talking?"

The color drained from Daag Landvik's face. "*Please,*" he implored; his pearly smile had become sheepish. "You have to believe I don't know who he is. C-check the other videos! You'll see!"

"Oh, I did." Reedman flipped open the manila folder and pulled out several images of Daag and Jerro, along with pictures of another Daag sitting blissfully unaware at his desk; all with matching time stamps. "Looks to me like you've got one hell of a look-alike, so which one are you? Daag the accountant or Daag who better start saving for bail?"

"I'm the accountant!" Daag looked over the pictures splayed out before him. His knee had started to tremble, and he clasped his hand down to still it, "I'm the accountant," he repeated weakly. "I swear to you, I've never met this man. Please, you have to believe me!

"I balance checkbooks, for God's sake! I have never met that man, and I don't know why there's another me running around, but I'm not him! Ask anybody! The dates—*look!* The dates! Give me one, and I can tell you exactly where *I* was."

His composure was crumbling fast. "You have to believe me. Whoever this impostor is, I have nothing to do with them. Please! I…I have a good life here. I…I'm just the accountant." And then Daag Landvik started to cry.

"So what'd you think?"

It was Reedman who sighed now. "I think Landvik might be telling the truth."

"Seriously?" They both stared vacantly into the interview room as Daag Landvik rambled on frantically to his lawyer. Jones sipped his coffee and cringed; the bitter-tasting sediments had all settled at the bottom of the cup. "Listen, Jay, this case is a mess. Ahliss is missing. We've got two Daag Landviks, and as far as what I managed to find out behind the lawyer's back, there's nothing missing from Lapaul's computer."

"What?"

"Yeah, and that's not the half of it." Jones hushed his tone as much as his gravelly voice would allow. "I heard Lapaul has a safe in his office and that several things are unaccounted for—things that Lapaul failed to mention to the investigators."

"You think Lapaul called in his own people?"

"I think that if we don't find Jerro Ahliss first, he's gonna end up a statistic."

The gardens were much less inviting than the dark hall before them. Strange bioluminescent plants filled the flower beds and spilled over the canopy frames. The place had grown wild without a tender; hedges and fountains became shapeless in the tumble of glowing ivies and creeping vines. Neon-colored lily pads and illuminant cattails were clustered in thick bunches by mossy ponds and man-made canals, and great twisted trees swept the ground with their boughs.

But it wasn't the strange glowing plants or the feral undergrowth that made Jerro so uncomfortable. It was the silence. There was not a chirp from a cricket or a croak from a toad; there was nothing except the intermittent sound of water trickling down from the ivy-covered fountains.

"Well, this place is charming," Jerro said sourly. His mood had become marred ever since they had left the pavilion, and he had found himself more irritable and unsettled the deeper they ventured. They were making their way across the barely visible path. Leaves and vines crunched beneath his feet, bringing uneasy interruptions to the unnatural quiet.

"I imagine it was in its heyday, but I get what you mean. Not exactly the picture of paradise anymore, is it?" Etcher managed to move silently along the dying foliage and with a lot more grace than Jerro—who was having difficulty navigating through the thick overgrowth.

"What happened here? I mean, why is everything so empty? This place is massive. There must have been thousands of people here, and now nothing?"

"Well, the story goes that the old king went mad and trapped everyone down here—that or some kind of cataclysmic cave-in, maybe both. Whatever happened, suddenly all the passages from Undercity to the surface got closed off, and no one came in or out ever again—until now, of course." She winked at him.

"That's reassuring."

Etcher chuckled.

"I'm glad you find it so amusing."

"It's not *it* I find amusing. It's *you*."

"Oh?"

The lithe little shopkeeper hopped over the thick root of an illuminant weeping willow and plucked one of its softly glowing leaves, rolling it between her thumb and forefinger. "You know, you remind me a little of myself—my younger self anyhow. Before I became the cunning thief you see before you, I was always so uncertain. I was so terrified, in fact, of losing everything and everyone that I'd always imagine the worst possible outcome."

"And that amuses you?"

"Well of course." She stopped to look at him. "Fear is such a funny thing to hold on to when all it does is hold you back." Her eyes went up to the dark glass ceiling, where white jewels had been set to mimic stars; they appeared to twinkle in the eerie light from the florescent flora. "The fear of losing everything kept me stagnant for so long, and it wasn't until I embraced the possibility of total loss that I became free. Every morning that I wake up is a day I could lose it all, but it's also the possibility that I might just see something new."

"Yeah, well, forgive me if I don't exactly seem thrilled to be traipsing around some underground tomb whose only exit is through a magical doorway attached to the back of reality. Call me crazy, but I like a little more assurance of my own survival."

"I'm not so certain I buy that."

Jerro peered at her curiously. "You know I'm only here because I need your help, right?"

"And I yours, but that's not the only reason you said yes."

"Oh yeah? You think you know me so well, don't you?" He chuffed at her. "So tell me, then, why am I here?"

"Why, my stunning good looks, of course." She grinned.

Jerro smirked as they continued through the thicket.

"Honestly though? I don't think it's your survival you're worried about. There's something you're running from."

"Yeah—the law."

"No, that's not it. There's something else. I don't know what exactly, but I'd be willing to wager something happened to you when you were younger and you've been running from it ever since."

Jerro went very quiet as Etcher watched him.

"So how close are we to this treasure room?" he said after a great long while.

"We're almost there. Just wait till you see the throne room."

"Yeah. Can't wait," Jerro said a tad bitterly, and then he stopped dead in his tracks when he caught a glimpse of two dark eyes peering out at him from within the thicket. He thought it was another mirage at first, but when the illusion failed to dissipate, he realized what it was. "Is that...?"

"Looks like we found the gardener." Etcher pulled back a thick bunch of cattails to reveal a sad-looking skeleton. The skull was oblong with a big crack running down from one of the huge eye sockets, and the rib cage was wide, the shoulders hunched—as though the creature was used to standing while bowed over. Its limbs were long and lanky, and there seemed to be more leg than torso.

The tattered remains of a shirt and trousers were the only things keeping the lonely skeleton together—them and the creeping vines that had woven around the bones. "A Dahl'Kir slave by the looks of it. They were liberated from the mines during the Second Alliance War. A lot of them were brought here. They've a sensitivity to sunlight. They worked in the mines for so long they couldn't tolerate the sun after a while."

Jerro felt sorry for the lonesome skeleton. To die in such a solemn place after a life of servitude—it seemed unfair. "He shouldn't be left like this."

"Hmm..." Etcher looked around the wild garden. "How about we move him over there?"

Jerro looked to where she pointed and smiled ever so slightly. "Yeah. All right."

"Help me bind the joints first. Don't want him to fall to pieces." She handed Jerro a spool of silky ribbon.

"There we are, much better," said Etcher. They both stood back and admired their handiwork. The lonesome gardener was now resting in an old, rusted swing chair under one of the illuminant willows beside a trickling, ivy-covered fountain. "He's still missing something though."

"How 'bout a hat?" said Jerro.

"That's perfect, Jerro. Good thinking."

"Thanks. My mom loves gardening. She's always wearing one of those big sun hats." For a moment, he saw his mother's smiling face looking up at him from the flower beds with a little smudge of dirt across her cheek. 'Look, Jerro! The poppies are flowering...'

"Of course. No gardener is complete without their trusty hat." Etcher's words snapped him back to reality. She produced a straw sun hat with a soft fabric lining and placed it delicately on the gardener's head, tilting it down to shield his big sad eyes. She crossed his hands over his rib cage and propped up one of his silk-wrapped knees. "Now he can finally take a good, long rest."

"Yeah." Jerro felt a pang of guilt run through him. He wondered how his mom was doing and if she knew what was going on. His mind quickly skittered away from the idea though; best not to think of those sorts of things.

"Hey, gloomy guts, we're out of here." Etcher pointed to an archway that led into another hall.

They left the gardener to his eternal nap on the swing chair beneath the willow tree and didn't look back—which was fortunate because if Jerro had, he might have decided to leave Undercity then and there and have stopped an extraordinary chain of events from happening.

But as they left, a lonely phantom stood beside his lonesome corpse and watched the two lively souls leave the wild gardens. The lonely phantom decided to follow them; after all, he wanted to thank them for the new hat.

"Holy hell," Jerro said. The throne room hadn't failed to impress despite the weightiness that was still looming over him. He stood on the now-crunchy velvet carpet that ran down the length of the grand hall. It was akin to the inside of a stately cathedral with stained-glass windows and masterful carvings hewn from the very marble that comprised the interior. Bright crystal lights lit the windows from behind and gave the stately chamber the illusion of being above ground. Angelic statues flanked the walkway in prayer, their sad, sympathetic eyes cast down and watchful as Jerro moved toward the pale throne. Unlike the prodigious pavilion, with its colossal ebony pillars and lavish gold-leaf trims, the throne room was delicate and graceful. The white marble and silver filigree made it feel holy and sacred.

Along the walls hung long, draping banners and decorative sconces topped with the effigies of lesser gods. High above them were alcoves where more divine idols watched in silent judgment, and above all else was the most intricate piece of artwork Jerro had ever seen. Faces had been carved out across the ceiling with pale jewels set into their eye sockets to make them twinkle. The faces were painted over with a soft pigment and a skillful hand to create a holy depiction of angels and godly beasts rising up to a single bright star made of pure silvery ginse that sat right in the middle of the remote ceiling and glimmered with its pulsating energy.

"Not bad, eh?"

"Not bad," Jerro replied distantly as his upturned eyes drank in the incredible architecture. He had to admit, this alone made the trip worthwhile, although he only admitted solely it to himself.

"So, then, Jerro," Etcher said as she slipped onto the pale throne—which dwarfed her greatly by comparison—and traced her fingers hungrily over the silver roses that were set along the arms of the chair. "We've reached the throne room. There's only one more place to go before we get to our intended destination."

"The hidden stairs?"

"That's correct. Fancy a guess at where it might be hiding?"

"I dunno."

"Give it try, Jerro. If you were a mad king and wanted to hide away your wealth, where would you put it?"

Jerro looked at her bluntly. "Are you serious?"

Etcher crossed one leg over the other, her tail swishing gently as she sipped at a conjured whiskey glass. "Why not? If you figure it out, I might just tell you what I stole from Johan Lapaul."

"Huh." Jerro clucked his tongue. "Maybe you don't even know where this staircase is."

"Nope. Try again. I'll tell you if you get close."

Jerro searched her over dubiously. "Do I get a clue?"

"Sure, if you like."

"Okay then, what is it?"

Etcher smiled, and her eyes twinkled, then she began in a singsong cadence:

> *"Mine eyes do weigh upon thee,*
> *They're frightful to behold,*
> *They betray the might of avarice,*
> *Where the Mad King hid his code."*

"Wonderful, Etcher, and what's that supposed to mean?"

The shopkeeper shrugged and sipped her bourbon.

Jerro breathed out through his nose. *All right, then. Fine.* He began searching the walls and the statues although soon found there were a lot of weighty eyes upon him, but none were all too frightful. The godly effigies in the alcoves had rather-severe expressions on their faces but he couldn't pick one that stood out among the rest, so he turned to the praying angels, who were all sad and somber, and headed back toward the entrance.

Etcher tutted. "Getting colder."

Jerro sucked at his teeth as he peered at Etcher. "Mine eyes do weigh upon thee." He turned back to the foot of the steps leading up to the throne and looked up at the little shopkeeper, who was casually draped in the resplendent chair. *Not all that frightful either...although,* as he thought about it, a mad king looking down from his high perch would certainly be unpleasant to behold. Jerro scaled the steps and stood beside the throne.

"Getting warmer."

He smirked. "Having fun?"

"Quite."

"I need to borrow your throne, *Your Highness*," he said.

"Can't."

"Oh?"

"Remember how I told you the seal would start to push at me the closer I got? Well, I'm afraid I'd rather not like to stand around while you figure out the riddle."

"Then why not tell me so we can get on with it?"

"And ruin the fun?"

Jerro rolled his eyes. "Have it your way." He leaned in awkwardly so he could look out at the grand hall from the king's perspective and then let out a soft gasp. "That's incredible."

"Clever, isn't it?"

"The Mad King's code?"

"Hidden in plain sight—at least for those on the throne."

"I'll say." He was staring down the aisle of praying angels; in their parallax was a series of symbols hidden within the folds of their clothes as inlays of silver. From the velvet carpet, they had looked like nothing more than decorative striping. "Okay, so I see four symbols. What do they mean?"

"Well, that's where I'll have to give you another clue. Those symbols belong to the primordial gods—the Nakus. That's Din of fire, Sin of wood, Hoya of water, and Terra of earth. But there's a fifth: Aorisaku, the primordial god of wind. Aorisaku is often depicted as a winged horse."

"I see where this is going."

"Do you?"

Jerro sneered. "Hey, you're the one who wanted me to figure it out, so let me figure it out." He looked around the hall once more, but there was no winged horse. His eyes scanned over the sconces topped by divine effigies, and still there was no semblance to the animal he sought. When finally he had stepped down from the throne, the cocky smirk left his face. There in the alcove high above where Etcher sat was a pegasus-like creature rearing on its hind legs. "Shit."

Etcher got to her feet and lazily made her way down the stairs. "Bit of a climb, wouldn't you say? Shall I—"

"No. No, I got this."

"*Really?* Well, now I am curious."

Jerro plastered a boyish grin on his face. "Just watch." His eyes went up to the perilous alcove where Aorisaku was rearing proudly. *All right, Jerro, let's hope you're not that out of practice.* He shook out his limbs and rolled his shoulders. Poised, he ran headlong for the wall.

It was just like old times again, and before Jerro knew it, he was overcome by a familiar thrill. He kicked off the wall and grabbed the lip of a lower sconce, hoisting himself up and sidling around an effigy toward the next ledge. It was surprising how quick it all came back, and in that moment, nothing else mattered but the path of ascent. He didn't have to think; it was all muscle memory guiding his every move. He threw his faith into his footing and sprang off from ledge to ledge, never worrying about the way back down or the danger of falling. It was all just stepping stones from one point to another. He grabbed the legs of another godly figure and swung himself round, he propelled himself along the walls with the hanging banners, and pendulum-swing up to the higher sconces.

It was all one smooth, continuous motion until he grabbed hold of a banister that gave way. For the rest of his days, he would remember that quintessential moment which marked an end to his old life. He just didn't recognize it then.

One minute, he was just about to lift himself up into an alcove adjacent to Aorisaku's, and the next, he was falling, about to be skewered by the horns of a ram-headed god. In slow motion, he started to turn to right himself and saw Etcher crouch down, readying to spring into action, but there was no need. For a bare second, he remembered something that seemed rudimentary, and as the deathly ram head came up to meet him, he twisted round to face it and felt utterly free. The ram god passed through but never touched him, and when the danger was behind him, he felt himself go solid once again just in time to land atop a vacant lower sconce.

Etcher skid to a halt across the marble floor and stared up at Jerro. There was a world of thought running behind those mysterious honey-colored eyes, and when Jerro looked down to meet her gaze, he knew something between them had changed.

"I...uh..." Jerro started, but his thoughts kept cycling over the impossible incident and wouldn't let him speak.

The shopkeeper, however, straightened herself slowly. She said very calmly, "Quite the trick you've got there, Jerro. Care to finish the way, or do you need a hand?"

Jerro paused. It was all so strange and so improbable that what had happened could have happened to him. "I...I can keep going," he said.

She winked at him, and he felt renewed.

He jumped over to a hanging banner and made up for the lost ground, jumping and climbing until he reached the other side of the perilous balcony. He was tentative when he grabbed hold this time, but the banister stayed rooted, and Jerro was able to hoist himself up onto the alcove. Aorisaku's recess was only one leap away from atop the banister railing. He sprang across the gap and tucked into a roll as he landed before the mighty, rearing pegasus.

As he straightened, he felt incredibly small before the primordial god— statue or no. It emanated a quiet strength that made Jerro develop a healthy amount of reverie and fear of the divine effigy.

"*So how's the view?*" called out Etcher.

"It's incredible!" Jerro called back, looking down at the tiny shopkeeper and the rest of the grand hall. It was funny how he could feel so on top of the world while being so far underground. He had dreamed of seeing places like this, although he was fairly certain there was nowhere like this on *his* world. All the mischievous escapades and outings with his brother—they had been leading up to this moment when it stopped being make-believe and became true—a real, bona fide adventure.

"So, then, where's our hidden stairwell, Jerro?"

"Hang on. Let me take a look around." In all the excitement, Jerro had almost forgotten the whole reason for his daring climb. He turned around and looked at the fierce deity again; it was alabaster white, much like the rest of the hall, but within the marble were striations of gold and silver, and the eyes had been made of pure, glowing ginse, much like the immense silver star that hung at the center of the high ceiling. Beautiful though it was, it didn't give him any more clues.

But behind the statue? Now there was something. Jerro carefully sidled around the deity to the back wall, which had been hidden in the recess by the shadows. It was strange to have such an intricate engraving on a wall that no one would see, but there it was—a decorative archway carved into the stone with four identical notches that looked like they had once housed small globes. They were numbered with archaic-looking numerals.

"Hey, Etcher!" he called out, and as he did, he heard a swoosh cut through the air. A grappling hook came over the edge of the banister and wrapped around it before it was pulled taut. Then up came Etcher over the balcony. She landed elegantly on her feet and straightened herself, looking as regal as ever. "Well done," said Etcher.

"Thanks." Jerro regarded her curiously. "I thought you were feeling, you know—"

"Oh, I am, and speaking of which, this is all getting very draining."

Jerro smirked. "Sorry, Your Majesty," he replied with a mock bow. "I didn't realize we were on a timer."

"There's a time and a place for dawdling. Besides, I take it you saw the keyholes?"

"Keyholes?" Jerro followed Etcher's eyes over to the decorated wall. "Oh, *those* holes." He was looking over the numerals when it dawned on him. "The code."

"*Very good,*" said Etcher with genuine appraisal. "You remember the order?"

"Yeah. Uh…Din, Sin, Hoya, and…Terra?"

Etcher grinned impishly and conjured four gemstone spheres and juggled them high in the air. They were green, blue, red, and yellow with gold inlays resembling the symbols embedded into the angels. "Can't get much further without these. I did us both the favor of gathering these up on my previous visit." Etcher caught the gemstones and handed them over to Jerro. "Do the honors?"

"Yeah, sure," he said as he took them from her. "When you say 'previous visit,' you mean you've been here before?" he asked as he started slotting the gemstones.

Etcher scoffed. "Of course I have. I wouldn't waste your time if I hadn't scoped out the place beforehand. Granted, I haven't gone past the ghost-sealed door, but I know it's there. Did you think perhaps I was just very lucky in guiding you this far?"

"Well, no. I just thought maybe"—he felt a tad embarrassed by his naivety—"you know, you researched this place."

"Oh I did. But the research only gets you so far. That little ditty I recited to you earlier? That was one of the more comprehensive snippets I found when I read up on this place."

"Oh...so how long were you down here before?" *Dare I even ask?*

"Long enough to reach my goal. The repression from the seal was at least an indicator of the right direction, but these tunnels are endless. *Undercity* is quite literal once you've spent enough time poking around. It must have been days before I found the right path. Quite a trifle, and as you can imagine, Tahli was none too pleased with me for spending the time." She snickered.

"What's the deal with you two anyhow? It's kind of like watching an old married couple—the way you two talk to each other. You're not *married*, are you?" Jerro slotted the last stone. A familiar gravelly sound resonated from behind the wall, and then the entire section slid down into the ground and revealed the hidden stairwell. "Whoa!"

Etcher strolled up beside Jerro and leaned against the entrance. "No, we're not married. What's your interest in our relationship anyhow?" She smiled at him slyly.

"Ah, well, you know...just curious, I guess."

"Would you find it hard to believe that my relationship with Tahli is platonic? Or were you hoping for a little girl-on-girl?"

Jerro felt the heat rising in his cheeks. He wasn't used to being confronted with someone so forward—he was supposed to be the cheeky one, the one that made girls swoon and blush. "W-what? No! Please. I'm just asking! Jeez, where's your head at?" He swallowed, his throat had gone dry all of a sudden. "So up the stairs, yeah? The, ah, ghost seal?"

Etcher eyed him with amusement for a few unbearable seconds. "Just up the stairs and down the little hallway, you'll see the double doors. There's a big disc hanging over it. Remove it and you remove the seal's influence. I'll be up once it's done."

"Right, you're staying here." For someone who was apparently afflicted by the seal's repressive force, she sure didn't look it. But that was fine with Jerro; he needed a breather after that uncomfortable exchange. "I'll just be a moment," he said, and then he hurried up the stairs.

The light was dim along the hall; only a few small crystal lights lit the way, and they were just enough for Jerro to make out his footing—not that he needed their help. The moment he had reached the top of the stairs and saw the ghost seal—glowing with a soft blue light—he felt it call out to him. It made his stomach lurch, and the irritable feeling that had been pecking at him since the garden came then at full force. As much as the seal beckoned him, there was a greater part that wanted to turn tail and run. He didn't like the door and didn't like how the seal seemed to peer inside him and poke around at his soul. The closer he came, the more dread filled him, and he was certain that the sound of his own blood pulsing in his ears was getting louder, becoming almost deafening. It was wretched.

He desperately wanted to leave, but every time he considered bailing, he felt a little tingle in his right palm and remembered it was either this or going back to Midgard on his own to face whatever horrible fate Detective Reedman could cook up. He had to admit, no matter how strange or untrustworthy Etcher Everdoor seemed, he'd much rather have her on his team than against him. Oddly enough, he found himself daring to believe they might just clean up this whole sordid affair and he could go back to living a normal life.

A normal, dull, and uninteresting life. For a small moment, there was a quiet truth whispering in his head, but he dared not give it any stock. For now, he still needed to believe that there *was* a way back—no matter how much he hated his old life, because the other option, well, that just had far too many unknowns for him to even think about.

The ghost seal—which took the form of a large stone disc—was merely feet away from him, thrumming with that pale blue glow. It was hung over the crack of the double door by two metal clasps. It seemed surprisingly simple to remove. Jerro inched toward it and held out his hands on either side of the disc, not quite ready to touch it. At the center of the ghost seal was the carving of a dog's head with big sad eyes, and around the rim was a multitude of symbols and scriptures that would have been cryptic to Jerro had it not been for the Babble Seal spell.

"*Ow'l ah...ha na, loo eh, ee deh...*" Jerro tried out the words for himself. *May Death wash us both of sin?* He shuddered at the phrase and regretted saying it aloud because it then stuck in his head.

Remove the seal, and it stops, right? Jerro was feeling the growing turmoil bubble away in his gut and he very much needed to be done with the awfulness. He grit his teeth and grabbed hold of the seal. Instantly the urge to vomit hit him hard and nearly brought him to his knees before he yanked the disc out of the holder, bringing a strange and sudden end to the chaos.

He breathed out deeply and laid the disc on the ground beside the door. It had no resonance now, no glow; all the agitation and sickness had left him the moment the seal was removed.

"Splendidly done," said Etcher as she came up beside Jerro. She actually did look a little livelier than before.

"Thanks." Jerro felt displaced all of a sudden; his whole purpose had been to remove the seal, and now that it was done, he felt disappointed. "So that's it then."

Etcher was taken aback. "That's it? You're not coming with me to raid the Mad King's treasure?" she said.

"Both of us?"

"Jerro, I'm surprised at you. You really think I'd bring you all this way and have you open the door and then leave you here while I go and have a merry ol' time without you?" Her expression was strangely dejected. "Behind that door is said to be mountains of treasure. Of course, there is always the possibility there could be nothing at all. I'm not banking on the latter, but besides that, we came this far together, I figured we'd find out what's on the other side together too."

Jerro grinned. "Yeah, okay. I like that idea. Mountains of treasure, right?"

"I certainly hope so."

They were just about to throw open the doors and see what lay inside when Jerro remembered something crucial. "Hey, wait. Didn't you say if I found the stairwell, you'd tell me what you stole from the office?" Well, maybe not crucial, but he was dying to know what could possibly bring a cosmic thief all the way to his mundane little world.

Etcher crossed her arms. "Well, no. I said I *might* tell you."

Jerro huffed. "Come on, you know I almost *died* getting up here."

"Yes. That was curious, wasn't it?" She eyed him over and clucked her tongue. "All right, I suppose you've earned it."

He grinned eagerly. "Okay, so what was it?"

"It was a Dahl'Kir artifact."

"A what?"

"Strange, right? Or it would be if this kind of thing hadn't been happening all over the cosmos. A long while back, there was a Nautiloid cruiser that crashed into a warp gate and—"

"Hang on, a *what* crashed into *what?*"

Etcher sighed. "A big spaceship crashed into a teleporter, and all its cargo has been scattered across the galaxy ever since, turning up randomly here and there. Honestly, Jerro, I told you about warp gates and Nautiloids and Peace Keepers—"

Jerro held up his hands before he could get a headache. "Yeah, you told me a lot of things. But remember, a few days ago, there was just me, on one planet, working as a software engineer in the IT sector. Forgive me if I'm slow on the uptake."

"Oh come now, you're not slow—just naive."

"Cheers."

Etcher tittered with amusement. "Well, at any rate…shall we?"

"Please do."

The little shopkeeper pushed against the heavy doors, and the lock gave way.

There weren't any mountains. There was an entire *other* Undercity of treasure behind the door.

"Holy hell," Jerro found himself saying once more. From the moment they had walked in, another dial like the one Jerro had seen in the pavilion began to rotate and light up the cavernous treasure hoard, except this one was not made from amber; it had been cut from the biggest fire opal Jerro had ever seen. The doors had led them out to a large patio where tables spilled over with riches and mysterious-looking relics cast from precious metals and encrusted with jewels. The interior of the treasure hoard was lavish, if not ostentatious, with the amount of gold and gemstone that coated the walls, ceiling, and floors.

Giant solid-gold dragons that acted as pillars held up the vast ceiling, and onyx griffins stood regally at the entrances of stairwells and in the alcoves of balconies. There were even sphinx statues of pure alabaster, laced with gold jewelry and precious stones, watching like sentinels from their perches along the walls. And there were other beast carvings too, but they were like no other fairy-tale creatures Jerro had ever seen.

"All the paragon beasts," said Etcher with a degree of reverie.

"All the what?" asked Jerro as he trailed behind her.

"Wyrms, kerberoses, sentinels…these are all the great treasure-hoarding creatures of Eclipse. These beasts are the embodiment of greed. I'm starting to get a bigger picture as to why the Mad King went mad."

"So he was a paragon—whatever you called it?"

"Not as far as I read. He was a rylin. They're like a desert leporidae. They're supposed to be rather humble."

"*Leporidae*…hey, that's Latin, isn't it? You mean a rabbit? The Mad King was a rabbit?"

"I'm surprised you know your genera, or was that courtesy of the Babble Seal?"

"Hey, uni wasn't all for naught."

"Guess not," said Etcher. She made her way down the steps and was winding along the only pathway that wasn't littered with mounds of treasure. "Though not any rabbit you're familiar with, I'd wager. The old rylins were about two hundred feet long from nose to tail and could run like lightning."

Jerro thought up a comical image of a massive bunny rabbit zipping around like a bullet train, though he assumed his imagined creature was far from the mark. "So, now that we're here, is there something particular you're looking for?" he said.

Etcher fixed him with a sly smile. "My, you are a perceptive one, aren't you? There is one thing in particular I need. Anything else I happen to pick up will be a bonus. Here," she said as she walked up to a sizeable wooden chest and vanished away its glimmering contents with a flick of her wrist. She picked it up and handed it to Jerro. "As much as you can, try not to get too greedy. Don't want to end up like His Majesty." She winked.

"You're serious?"

"Why not? You helped me break in here. As far as I'm concerned, part of this treasure is yours. But like I said, best not to get too greedy. Stick to what fits in the chest and you'll keep the treasure lust at bay."

"'Treasure lust'? I'm not materialistic, if that's what you mean."

"Well then, you won't have a problem, will you?" She smiled at him and then headed deeper into the trove.

Jerro stared down at the empty chest. He had never really *wanted* material wealth. Money was about the only thing he really cared about having, along with a good computer and a roof over his head. Outside of that, though, was unknown grounds for him. The thrill he had got from scamming credit cards was never really about the money; in truth, it had been about the act—the fact that he *could* do it—that excited him.

Of course, that wasn't always the case. There had been a time when it was all about the money and keeping the debt collectors off his older brother's back.

If he were to truly be honest with himself, though, he couldn't deny that he was just as much of a thief as Etcher was. He looked around the immense treasure hoard and thought: *I can have anything I want.* Back on Midgard, where gadgets and high fashion were all the rage, Jerro could hardly ever see the appeal of material things, but here, where the relics and holy artifacts held real intrinsic value, he found that they sparked a different kind of itch.

Jerro took to another end of the cavernous room and started picking through treasures for whatever caught his eye. After all, he still needed a present for his mom.

Etcher moved slowly through the grand expanse, drinking in the majesty of their find. But for Etcher Everdoor, it wasn't the gold and jewels that enticed her; it was the architecture and the choices that the architects, or rather, the Mad King, had made. They revealed something of His Majesty's affliction, and that interested her a great deal more than the rare assortment of fae diamonds or crystal moonlight or even the ebergold swords and the white arhk bead jewelry. She relished the opportunity to walk among such riches all the same, but for Miss Everdoor, true rarity was hard to find, and Etcher only ever collected those things that were truly valuable.

Any good potion shopkeeper worth their salt knows the value of things. It's a skill—a magical eye, one could even say. They can look at something and know its worth with as little as a glance. But a great potion shopkeeper, such as Etcher Everdoor, saw the value in things that had yet to be—the things that gather their worth over time.

The lantern key, for example, which she found on a dresser shelf next to the spiritus orb and the quartz apple from the crystal gardens, held exceptional value—which any shopkeeper could tell you. What they couldn't say was how much more valuable it became when she vanished away the key—with its little feathered wings and tiny blue flame flickering in the ring—and made sure never to tell anyone she had it. In that instant, she had given the object a far more significant worth than it already had.

But the lantern key was not what she had come for; it was simply a bonus for finding the hoard. The sacred object that Etcher searched for tugged at her awareness from deeper within the trove. She would have to venture further to find it. She was just about to step away when she remembered she had company.

She peered over at her new companion. He was busy comparing chalices; one was ivory and the other was gold. He was diligently deciding between the two and seemed to be at a stalemate until he finally settled on the ivory—much to Etcher's surprise—and stashed it in the chest she had given him. Maybe he had an eye for antiquity after all.

It was nothing personal, but Etcher would have much preferred to be venturing on her own. She had an intimate approach to her work, and that was difficult to achieve with company. Etcher liked to take her time; she liked the silence and the moment. Usually, there was no one to distract her—no one asking questions or needing answers; she could simply be. People, quite frankly, were exhausting to her.

But she had to admit, Jerro's predicament had certainly piqued her interest, and try as she might to be unattached, she found herself growing just the slightest bit fond of him. It was that niggling thing that she felt when they first

116

met—a knowing that their paths had been crossed for a reason and could no longer be uncrossed once they happened upon each other. Somehow Fate had decided that Jerro Ahliss needed to be a part of Etcher's journey—at least for the time being.

She let out a deep breath and relented. There'd be no leaving him by himself, of course, as she was certain he would find trouble; so Etcher turned back to collect her tall companion so they might venture deeper into the hoard.

"Hey, Etcher, which of these is better?" Jerro asked as she approached him. He had a silver bangle inlayed with pearly white stones and a ruby pendant with an elegant braided chain.

She smiled inwardly to herself; both were quite the find. "Who's it for?" she asked him knowingly and tittered at his surprise.

"Funny you should ask, but it's my mom's birthday this weekend, and I thought maybe I'd grab her something...unique."

"Well, in that regard, either would do, but I imagine you wouldn't want your mom wearing the necklace of Bale's favorite harlot."

Jerro looked at the pendant with shock and gingerly put it down. "Bracelet it is."

"A fine choice and aptly fitting. Those stones are callokahn moonstones. They're often thought of as *mother* stones."

"Yeah? Why's that?"

"They promote restful sleep and were often given to new mothers as gifts of goodwill."

"Restful sleep?"

"Indeed—the one thing every new mother needs and seldom gets. That particular bangle must have been given to a mother who was dearly loved. Those engravings that I imagine caught your eye are imbued with a protection spell. Whoever made this thought highly of their dear old mom."

"Huh." Jerro inspected the bangle with renewed interest before storing it away. He looked Etcher up and down. "Are we moving on?"

"Indeed. You gathered enough souvenirs?"

Jerro smiled and held up the chest, shaking it a little; it wasn't packed to the brim as Etcher expected. "I think I got a few good ones," he said.

"I'm sure you have. Well then, let us venture deeper into the Mad King's treasure, shall we?"

Jerro grinned at her boyishly.

So maybe he is just a little endearing, she thought.

It was dark—too dark.

At first, she thought it was nighttime—maybe she was waking from a bad dream. What time had it been when she got home? It had been late, hadn't it?

But then she remembered something, and with the memory she recalled the pain and the panic that came with it. Someone had clubbed her over the head.

Oh god, have I been kidnapped? She tried to make a sound, but she couldn't. There was a cloth wrapped across her mouth. The panic began to rise steadily, and in that panic, she could feel herself become lightheaded. *Calm down, Mahra!* she thought to herself. *No use in blacking out—again.*

For the moment, she was alive, and she intended on keeping it that way. She wiggled around but found little give.

She had been hog-tied.

Okay, Mahra…just stay calm. You can do this. As she settled down, she realized why she couldn't see; another cloth had been wrapped around her eyes. *Okay…okay, you didn't see their face. They've tied you up and blindfolded you. Maybe this is for a ransom?* Lapauls were rich after all.

But then another thought came to mind and made her heart sink: *Did Jerro do this?* He was a crook; she accepted that, but this? *No. No, it can't be.* She banished the thought immediately; it just didn't sit right.

So, then, if not Jerro, then who? And why? It had to be because of the break-in. The two were connected somehow; she could feel it even if she didn't understand it. The next question was, where the hell had she been taken to? The floor was hardwood, and as far as she could tell, the space was small since the top of her head and the bottoms of her feet were grazing the walls.

And she could smell something—a familiar combination of sandalwood and perfume. It was her perfume! This place had to be her closet.

So she was at home. *Okay, home. Why though? Kidnappers don't usually keep you locked up in your own house, do they? Unless…this isn't a kidnapping.* Mahra had a bad feeling about what might happen next.

Kyddr'Ith listened from behind the door to all of Mahra's thoughts. Mundanes were an amusing bunch of simpletons after all, and Kyddr'Ith would know.

How long had it been? A year perhaps, maybe two, of living and breathing like a normal *human*—just thinking about it made Kyddr'Ith feel dirty, and now, again, Kyddr'Ith was stuck wearing mundane flesh.

But it was all for the cause. The Lord had asked for the most dedicated of the following for this holy mission, and Kyddr'Ith had risen to the challenge.

Of course, it hadn't gone exactly as planned. The anger seethed behind Kyddr'Ith's stolen eyes. It should have been done. Kyddr'Ith should have returned to the chapel with the reborn and fulfilled their duty.

The Lord had not been pleased with the failure, but the Lord was also merciful and gave Kyddr'Ith another chance to see things through. It had been Kyddr'Ith's own idea to wear the girl as bait, and the Lord had liked that plan. There was still hope that Kyddr'Ith could redeem themselves in the Lord's eyes. Kyddr'Ith prayed things would go well this time.

The girl, Mahra, was becoming tiresome with her clumsy, sluggish thoughts, and Kyddr'Ith rose soundlessly from the bed and left the room. In the kitchen, Kyddr'Ith had been preparing a special brew, one which would put the girl in a deep stupor where all but her ears would function. Kyddr'Ith wanted the girl to be able to hear.

Over the burner Kyddr'Ith had been simmering paratin seed—the sleeping plant—with crushed flutterby wings and juru-berry nectar. It was almost done; all it needed was a dash of serpentbell, and the brew would then be ready for the final incantation. Of course, serpentbell was hard to come by, and Kyddr'Ith was forced to use lesser known channels to procure it so as not to alert the Peace Keepers of a hazua delivery.

At least Kyddr'Ith was patient. The lesser of Kyddr'Ith's kin would not have survived this holy mission. *They* would have faltered. *They* would have fed. And then the planet would have been crawling with *Ecliptian* scum. There were too many Peace Keepers on the world already. *Self-righteous pigs.*

Who were they to lay claim to this dull planet? How dare they mark it a protected world? No matter, there would be no more Peace Keepers when the Lord was done; there would be no more Eclipse and no more alliance.

Just beautiful, everlasting oblivion.

Kyddr'Ith breathed out a long sigh. The mission was everything and worth suffering the skin of another mundane. Kyddr'Ith found peace at their center and became focused once again. Kyddr'Ith glanced at the clock; it was half-past the hour. It was coming soon.

A few minutes later, Kyddr'Ith could feel another mind enter their sphere of perception. The mundane was fumbling with the iron gate; they were using the wrong postman's key.

Simpletons. When finally the mundane had righted their error, they entered the stairwell and ascended. A knock came at the door a moment later.

Kyddr'Ith checked their reflection in the mirror and smoothed out the blonde hair before answering the door.

"Uh, hey, delivery for Mahra Lapaul?" said the dull-eyed delivery boy.

"That's me!" said Kyddr'Ith with the girl's usual singsong cheeriness. Kyddr'Ith smiled as Mahra would have smiled and signed for the package, being as shy and bashful as Mahra would have been when the delivery boy smiled back. "Thanks," said Kyddr'Ith with a blush, and then shut the door.

Such ungainly creatures they are.

Kyddr'Ith tore open the package and revealed the small vial filled with fresh serpentbell flowers. Kyddr'Ith grabbed a pair of tweezers and very delicately fished out one of the tiny blue bells, dropping it into the bubbling brew.

The concoction turned silver and let out a sweet aroma like honey and lavender. The brew was nearly done. Kyddr'Ith lowered the heat, letting the spell settle down into a simmer, and made ready for the final incantation.

With hands splayed out atop the simmering pot, Kyddr'Ith's eyes became solid white, and their voice took on a dark timbre.

"Ibenus tez'Drios, ow'l aha, ow'l aha. Ushra insta koosa, labat ushra, labat ushra."

The silvery liquid swirled on its own, and little flecks glimmered within the whirlpool. When Kyddr'Ith's eyes regained their normal sight, they looked down into the pot and examined their work.

The brew was finished. Kyddr'Ith smiled with Mahra's smile and filled a baster with the liquid. It was time to deal with the girl. Kyddr'Ith quietly entered the bedroom and headed over to the closet.

The girl tensed when she heard the door open.

"Good afternoon, Mahra. It's time for your medicine." Kyddr'Ith smiled as they listened to the girl's racing mind.

The gag had to be removed, of course, and after a moment's consideration, Kyddr'Ith removed the blindfold as well.

The girl's eyes went wide. "W-who...how?"

Kyddr'Ith grinned wickedly. "Oh hush now. All will be well."

"Y-You...you can't be...your face..."

"Yes, I know." Kyddr'Ith grabbed hold of the girl's jaw and puckered her lips. The girl squirmed, but Kyddr'Ith simply squeezed tighter and shoved the baster down her throat, letting the brew flow right down into her gullet.

The girl choked and coughed and seized. And then there was nothing. Her eyes became glassy and lifeless, her body limp, but Kyddr'Ith could still hear the thoughts running wildly behind her unseeing eyes. "You're going to die like this, and no one will ever know you're gone." Kyddr'Ith licked the girl's cheek and snarled. It was all too tempting to crack open her head and eat the precious matter within. But the Lord had given a holy command, and Kyddr'Ith dared not break it. *"Eat not the mundane flesh,"* the Lord had said, and Kyddr'Ith would abide.

Of course, the Lord was unspecific when it came to torture. Kyddr'Ith leaned in close to the girl's ear. "Your lover boy is going to come for you, and instead, he'll find me. And together we'll go to this very bedroom and do all those naughty things you dreamed of doing. And you'll be here, with your perfect ears, listening. He'll tell me he loves me, and we'll leave together. And he'll never know and never care that you lay here dying."

A single tear rolled down the girl's cheek as Kyddr'Ith shut the closet door.

They had been walking quietly for a while now, but Jerro didn't mind. He was feeling rather pleased with himself. He had a real treasure chest full of treasure! He was on an actual adventure, albeit with a strange little alien shopkeeper; and—dare he even say it?—had potentially dabbled in some real magic, despite having no idea how the hell he'd managed to avoid becoming a shish kebab.

Things were looking up in a curious sort of way. So what if he was a fugitive on his own world? They could sort that all out, right? If he and Etcher could travel to a lost underground city and discover an untouched treasure hoard, they could fix one little case of mistaken identity. If worse came to worse, all Jerro really needed to do was get rid of the evidence, and with Etcher's help, that wouldn't be too hard. At least it would buy them time to figure out who had set him up to begin with.

But those were thoughts for another time; he didn't want to spoil the enjoyment he was feeling. Life was good right now, and after the mountains of crap he had dealt with, he deserved a little good.

He found himself looking over at Etcher; she was a weird one, for sure, though he couldn't help admiring the way she conducted herself. He wanted that kind of confidence. Jerro was a fine-tuned bullshitter when it came to appearing indifferent and uncaring, but there was a big difference between pretending to be self-assured and actually being it. As far as he could tell, Etcher was the real deal.

"So what exactly are we looking for?" he couldn't help but ask.

She looked at him with her calculating eyes. They didn't leer at him the way Tahli's did, but he couldn't help but feel naked within them all the same.

"Hmm," she replied with deep contemplation. There was a sea of answers swimming behind her eyes, but Jerro was certain he'd have to be incredibly lucky to get a drop of that knowledge, if anything at all. She seemed to have considered him at great length when she finally decided to answer. "All right, quid pro quo. I'll tell you what I'm looking for if you'll answer a few questions of mine."

"All right, but you answer my question first."

Etcher smiled at him; apparently, he had amused her yet again. "Tricky, aren't we? Well then, you asked what we're after? Firstly, it's I, not we, doing the searching. I'm looking for a Death Token. There's said to be one here."

"A *Death* Token? What does—"

"Uh-uh. Quid pro quo. My question now."

Jerro snorted with a laugh. *Figures.*

"Do you like living in Midgard, Jerro?"

"What? Seriously?"

"That's my question. I answered yours. Now answer mine."

"Well," he began, but the usual spiel he gave when asked similar questions seemed to snag in his throat. Etcher was watching him closely, and he felt all too much like a bug under a pin. "Yeah, it's fine, I guess."

"Liar."

Jerro huffed. "Well, if you already know the answer, why even bother asking?" he snapped defensively, although he wasn't entirely certain why.

"Because"—her slender tail coiled back and forth—"I want *you* to hear it for yourself—the truth, that is."

"What's it matter to you anyhow?" Brilliant. He *was* having a good time up until then. *Why'd she have to spoil it?*

"You're very expectant, aren't you?"

"What happened to quid pro quo?" he said with a snarky lilt.

"Oh, well, please, if you have another question to ask of me, then do it. I just thought perhaps we could give an even exchange of questions and answers for a change."

"'*Even'?*" He was getting ornery. "So far, you've given me evasive answers at best. I hardly know anything about you. This whole situation is way over my head, but I put my trust in you to sort it all out. There is nothing *even* about our exchange."

"Hence why I thought we might."

"What?"

"You thought perhaps I was making a jab at you?"

"Well…" He was backtracking through their conversation; had he really just overreacted? "Well, what was that whole thing about me being *expectant*, huh?" *Great, I sound like I am twelve.*

Etcher, of course, remained infuriatingly calm. "There was a point that I was about to make, except that you interrupted me." She continued to smile at him with amusement, although it wasn't mocking or sardonic. "You *expect* a lot of truth from me and yet seem rather reluctant to give it. You asked me what I'm looking for, and I told you. But when I asked whether you liked living in Midgard, you lied.

"You *expect* me to tell you things when you're already in way over your head, and you never stopped to consider that maybe there's so much more I would *like* to tell you but have to bite my tongue."

"Yeah, but why? Just because I'm in over my head doesn't mean I can't *know* things. It always seems like there's more to the story than you tell me. It's like you're treating me like a child." He huffed and felt extremely childish.

The little shopkeeper merely grinned.

"What's so funny?"

"Well, it's just…you're not the first to have this frustration with me."

"Yeah, well, trust me, it's not amusing from my end."

"True, I'm sure it isn't. But do you think that I'm any more open with anyone else?"

Jerro looked down at his shoes as they walked along the coin-littered path. He didn't usually have so much trouble with people, but somehow Etcher seemed to know exactly how to push his buttons.

"Quid pro quo? I believe it was your turn." She smiled at him with a wink.

He looked at her sidelong. "You'll answer whatever I ask?" and then added hurriedly, "That's not part of my question, mind you."

"I'll answer as truthfully as I dare, but I would like a little honesty in return."

"Okay. Fine." He chewed at the inside of his cheek as he contemplated the offer. "So this Death Token, what's it for?"

"I need to break into Death, and I need the token in order to do that."

"Why?" He saw the look in her eyes and sighed. "Yeah, all right, fine. *Quid pro quo.*"

Etcher smiled back at him. "So in relation to my previous question, why is someone as skilled as you are working as a small wheel in a big machine? You don't strike me as a little cog, Jerro. I can't imagine you wear the role comfortably."

There it was again—that nosy way she cut right to the core of him. He huffed. "You know what? I think I'm done with quid pro quo."

"All right, my fault." Etcher held up her hands. "You asked me easy questions, and I didn't do the same. My apologies."

"Forget it." Jerro shrugged. *Damn it, I just wanted to have a good time.*

Etcher let out a deep breath and put her hands behind her head as she casually strolled along the path. They walked quietly for a while, and then she started talking. "My father is sending me there—to Death. I don't know why or what'll be waiting for me. I just know I have to go."

Jerro remained silent. He wasn't sure how it had happened, but he was pretty certain he just became privy to some very private information about Etcher Everdoor, and he didn't want to ruin it.

"From time to time, my father will send me messages telling me to do this or that. A few weeks prior to meeting you, I got a message telling me to go to Leona Mesa. It's a place in Death. Actually, the message didn't say to *go.* It was just that: *'Leona Mesa.'* It seemed urgent. His messages usually aren't quite so...*clipped?*

"So here we are, venturing into the unknown so I might find the answer to a cryptic request. If you find me infuriating, Jerro, just imagine what my father must be like." She chuckled to herself. "The truth is I'm not short of acquaintances. Despite my otherwise aggravating, enigmatic behavior, I'm actually quite likeable, and I have a decent amount of good friends scattered here and there.

"But each of them only gets a piece of me. Tahli has a piece, and my friends up north have their own little pieces. Out on the edge of the Angelous, there're a few more, and maybe somewhere in between all of that is the whole of me, which no one else knows in its entirety. And I understand that mine is a nature that doesn't allow the whole of itself to be known. I am guarded, and I am secretive, but if you like, maybe I'll give you your own little piece. It won't be the whole, but it'll be different from all the rest, and that, my tall companion, is about as much truth as those closest to me get."

Jerro let the words sink in for a while. He wasn't sure what to do now that he had been granted his request, but it was nice, and he appreciated the sincerity. Deep down, he started to get it—at least as much as he could. He realized they shared a lot more in common than he previously thought. They were both secretive in their own ways, and only a handful of people knew a piece here or there about either of them, but at least Etcher was comfortable with the fact and admitted it openly.

"I hate living in Midgard, actually…but I didn't like living at home either. I don't really know where I'm supposed to go. I just know I don't want to end up in prison…so I'm just doing what I'm good at and hoping it all works out."

Etcher took her time to consider what she had been told and then smiled and nodded at Jerro. "I'll take that as my own little piece." She winked.

The moment had gotten a bit too heavy, and Jerro blew out his breath. "So where's this Death Token?"

"Haven't the foggiest idea, but I'm thinking it's near the center of this hoard."

"You don't know?"

"I have an *inkling* and I'm hoping that my inkling is inclining to what I seek and not just something that only resembles it."

Jerro narrowed his eyes on her. "You do that on purpose, don't you? Talk like a riddle?"

She grinned at him. "See? You're getting to know me already."

They had been walking for a great long while, and still the treasure hoard stretched on with no end in sight. They had roamed through passageways and open chambers, navigated their way across pavilions and bridges, and hiked stairways to the upper levels. The trove was not merely one flat plain that stretched on for eternity; it was sectioned and divided. Hallways and bedchambers and great dining rooms littered the expanse, all spilling over with mounds of wealth. The great paragon beasts continued to loom over them as they walked, watching with jewel-encrusted eyes and blank, stony faces. They could have easily gotten lost in the hoard, but Etcher's *inkling* seemed to be getting stronger, so they continued to push on.

"Did you hear that?"

"Yes." Etcher's ears began to twitch and she stopped.

"What is it?"

"We're not alone." There were rows of pillars flanking a wide set of stair that let up to big open arches above a low wall—like windows lining an opulent balcony. Etcher ascended the steps and peered out across the vast treasure hoard, muttering quietly under her breath.

Jerro scaled the stairs after her but was unprepared for what he saw. "What the hell is *that?*"

"I don't know, but I believe it's where we're headed."

The archways were not overlooking just another part of the trove; they were flanking a giant canyon whose bottom could not be seen. The massive fissure appeared to cut right through the treasure hoard, splitting the trove in two. There was another row of archways across from them, lining the other side of the great gorge where the glint of riches could be still be spied. Along the interior of the canyon were colossal dragon statues that appeared to brace the rocky walls on their backs. But that was not where Etcher and Jerro were looking; they were craning their necks around the side of the archway to peer down the length of the canyon.

There was a dome of light atop a floating isle that stood in the middle of the gorge a far ways down. Little winged creatures circled the dome in constant procession, occasionally diving at the isle only to be knocked back by a flash from the forcefield.

"It's like the dome's protecting that island," said Jerro, hoping for some kind of reply, but when the little shopkeeper remained quiet, a bad feeling took root. "Etcher?"

"I think it might be best if I take you back to the store, Jerro."

"What! Why? No—"

"You see those little winged things flapping about the isle?" she said, cutting him off.

"Yeah, so?"

"They're Oolkas. *Reapers.* There are different kinds of reaper, Jerro, and those are the kind that come for the spirits that refuse to return to the land of the dead. I don't just think that dome is keeping the reapers out. I think it's keeping the spirits in."

"What spirits? You mean, like, *the* spirits? The people that lived here before?"

"Besides that corpse in the garden, how many bodies have we found since we've ventured through Undercity and now this place?"

"Just the one." Jerro didn't like where this was going.

"And do you know, when I spent all those days in Undercity by myself searching, how many bodies I found?"

"How many?" he asked, but he had a feeling he already knew the answer.

"None."

"So you're saying you think they're trapped in there? All of them?"

"It's possible, although that little floating isle seems relatively small to house the hundreds of thousands of people that used to live here. Whatever the case, I'd be willing to bet there are still souls clinging to this world, and I think they're stuck on that isle."

"Yeah, okay, but that doesn't explain why I need to go back. You needed me to open the door to even get into this place. For all you know, there could be more stuff down there that you'll need my help with."

"That's possible, but you seem to be forgetting something."

"And what's that?"

"Your soul never went to the land of the dead either. The Oolkas will be just as likely to take a swipe at you. Are you really willing to take that chance?"

Jerro began to see their predicament now. "What happens if they take me?"

"You'll be in Death, and unless I can get that token, I won't be able to come find you."

"All right"—he breathed in deeply—"but we made a deal. I have to help you get that token before you can help me."

"Jerro, the deal was only for the door. Your part of the debt is done."

"That's nice of you to say, Etcher, but the fact is you might still need me, and you know it. Just promise me you'll find a way to get me out of Death if it comes to that. I mean, you were planning on breaking into there anyhow, right?"

"You don't have to do this."

"Yeah, I know." He stared off at the floating isle. "But I'm kind of tired of sitting back and letting someone else run the show."

Etcher smiled. "Yes, of course. I would never make you be a little cog." She straightened out and adjusted her lacy cuffs before searching herself up and down. "You know what? I fancy a change of dress."

"What? *Now?*"

"Just a moment," she said, and then she conjured up a neatly patterned folding wall between her and Jerro.

He stood there awkwardly as he heard Etcher unbutton and unzip her clothes. "Is this really necessary?"

"It is," she replied matter-of-factly.

A few moments later, the folding wall disappeared, and there stood Etcher, looking proud and regal. She had on tight, waist-high pants with big brass buttons and a form-fitting jacket with decorative white-and-gold stitching along the trim—like an admiral's coat. It was femininely cut, so her bosom was mounted high, and a small amount of cleavage was exposed. The shoes were still canvas slip-ons, but they had the decency of having big decorative buckles to at least fit with the rest of the nautical attire. It was all a deep indigo with white-and-gold accents, which Etcher looked utterly refined in.

Jerro was feeling considerably underdressed with his casual jeans and T-shirt ensemble, although he wasn't certain he could pull off an outfit like that, especially when it all seemed *very* snug. He was uncomfortably aware that he was looking where he shouldn't be. "Are we good now? Can we go?"

The little shopkeeper's tail coiled back and forth. "What you wear becomes you, and if I'm about to do something incredibly daring and stupid, I might as well look as though I *meant* to do it. Confidence, after all, can make all the difference in the world."

"I'll stick to being comfortable, thanks. Shall we?" he asked impatiently.

Etcher smiled. "That's why I wear these shoes. Come along, then."

From the darkest shadow under the belly of a great big lion statue crept out a rather-small and portly creature. He huffed and puffed and took a moment to right himself.

His satchels were all crisscrossed and tangled, and his chubby little hands had their work cut out for them. Once situated, Mr. Gribs surveyed his surroundings. "Oh dear," he croaked, and his big eyes bulged frightfully wide. He tiptoed around the piles of golden ginse and sidled by the tables and dressers overwhelmed with jewels. Stout though he was, Mr. Gribs was not ungainly when he moved.

He soundlessly crept through the room and spied Miss Everdoor talking with a tall, handsome fellow over by the balcony arches some distance away. "Oh dear," Mr. Gribs croaked again. He barely felt comfortable with confronting Miss Everdoor, let alone *another* person.

But Mr. Gribs, cowardly and pitiful though he was, was also incredibly loyal. And besides, His Majesty might flay his flesh if he failed. Mr. Gribs gulped, he certainly didn't want that. His chubby hands wrung his satchel straps desperately as he bided his time. He wanted to make a good impression and timing was everything, but when Miss Everdoor decided on a change of dress, Mr. Gribs's pale, pearlescent skin turned bright red, and he quickly looked away.

This was going awfully. Now bashful atop of nervous? How was he ever to confront Miss Everdoor now? Oh, but he couldn't just stand around feeling sorry for himself. *Right,* thought Mr. Gribs, *Time for ac...tion.*

But Miss Everdoor and the tall young man had already left. "Oh dear," said Mr. Gribs once more, and he hurried out to catch them.

"Miss Everdoor! Please! Miss Everdooooor!"

"Do you hear something?"

"Yeah. What is that?"

Etcher turned and looked over her shoulder and saw a strange round *thing* bounding after them. "*That* is a nightmare."

"Are you...being figurative?"

"No. Literal. That *is* a nightmare—although, figuratively speaking, he's quite the fright to look at too now, isn't he?"

"No kidding. Should we, ya know, run?"

"Somehow I doubt he'll pose us any threat."

"Yeah, but you said 'nightmare'—"

"Just give it a moment, will you?"

"Fine, but if this goes south, remember, *I* told you so."

"Yes, Jerro, I'll be sure to remember it."

"Miss Everdoor! Thank goodness you've stopped." The strange, portly creature doubled over to catch its breath.

Jerro looked at the nightmare with distaste. Of all the beautiful and wondrous things he had seen on Eclipse, this was by far the opposite. The flabby skin, the toad-like face, and the bulging eyes were unappealing at best. The thing was frightful, for sure, and Jerro wasn't certain if the fine dress suit and shoes really did the toadish creature any favors. If anything, it made the little nightmare look more bizarre, especially with all the satchels.

He hadn't realized when it happened, but Etcher was suddenly holding a thin blade, like a rapier, with a beautiful lily molded into the intricate metalwork of the handguard. "*I thought you said he wouldn't be a threat,*" Jerro whispered out of the corner of his mouth.

"*He* won't be." Etcher's eyes glinted wickedly, and a sly smile crept onto her face. She pointed the tip of her sword right at the creature's double chin. "Tell me, Sir Toad, why do you call my name?"

The portly nightmare quivered before the blade. "I...I...was sent here," it croaked. "Please forgive the intrusion, but I've been instructed to ask you to attend an audience with His Majesty." The pasty toad bowed low and with surprising grace.

"*His* Majesty? You mean *your* Majesty, the King of Nightmare?"

"Yes, yes…the very same. Please, it is imperative that he speak with you." The toad squeaked as Etcher began to circle him.

"Why, pray tell?"

"His Highness said it was urgent, concerning your father. Ahk! Please don't flay me!" The toad cowered as Etcher pressed her blade against its flabby neck.

The little shopkeeper leaned in close. "*And what would* you *know of my father?*" said Etcher in a deadly whisper.

"N-nothing, madam, I swear it! Oh please, oh please, I'm only an envoy! His Majesty said you must come. I'm to offer you this invite. Here!" The toadish nightmare rummaged through his bags and produced a white envelope with a black wax seal. "If you will come, no harm will befall you. It is promised."

"And if I *don't?*" Etcher looked down at the envelope and plucked it from the toad's quivering hands, vanishing it away without a second glance.

The toad quivered. "Then I'm not to leave you. His Majesty has said that I've a persuasive persistence."

Jerro snorted. "So you're annoying?" The toad glanced at Jerro then and shied away when their eyes met, pretending as though Jerro wasn't there. It irritated him.

"Please, I must insist."

"And so you have—more than once. I don't like being nagged, little toad, but *if* you manage to survive through our current quest, then I might just take you up on your invite."

"And what,"—the toadish creature began, still trembling before Miss Everdoor—"is your quest?"

"We're going to break into that floating isle down the way—the one with all the Oolkas."

Mr. Gribs turned even paler, and his eyes bulged in fear. "N-no, not there! You mustn't break in there! It's forbidden!"

Etcher pressed her blade a little harder against the toad's flabby neck. "Forbidden by *whom?*"

"P-please…it's not for me to say."

Then Etcher smiled and winked at Jerro. She pulled away from the toad and held out her arms. "Well, I'd hate for you to break your word." She glanced at Jerro and then toward a dark stairwell running adjacent to their path.

Jerro was quick to gather her meaning.

"All right, then, I imagine you've a way to lead me into Nightmare?" she said, smiling devilishly all the while.

"Yes, of course! It's just through the shadows a little ways back."

"Well then, lead the way."

The toad's eyes lit up, and he spun on his heels and started heading back from whence he came. "I can't tell you what a relief it is that you decided to come. His Highness will be very pleased to see you," he prattled on.

Meanwhile, Jerro and Etcher had other plans. They crept away slowly as soon as the toad's back was turned and slipped down the dark stairwell and out of sight.

"I'm told there will even be a dinner for you, if you like, and—Miss Everdoor?" The toad glanced over his shoulder to find himself alone. "Oh dear."

"What was that about?" Jerro said between breaths.

"I honestly don't know."

"You don't think maybe we should have gone with him—it—whatever it was?"

Etcher did not let up her sprint as they darted along the dark passage; she seemed very focused and distant. They were rounding a corner when the path suddenly branched out into three separate dark halls. "Wonderful," Etcher sighed.

"All right, so what now? Got any *inklings* telling us which way to go?"

"Not as such, and we've another problem too."

Jerro had an inkling of his own, and he didn't like it. "Is it…what I think it is?"

"I thought you said you couldn't feel anything before?"

"Yeah, well, that was before. After I took the seal down from the doors to this place, I sort of realized I'd been feeling it all along. It's like a buzzing in your ear that you get used to. You only notice it when it's gone."

"But you notice the buzzing this time?"

"Yeah, I do. There's something else though. It's a bit different from before. I feel a little…light-headed."

"Jerro."

"Yeah?"

"Try not to panic, but we've got company."

"It's not that toad—" Jerro's words fell away from him as he saw a set of burning eyes appear in either of the flanking hallways.

Etcher had conjured back her sword and stood poised. "Jerro?"

"Yeah?" he replied nervously.

"I'm going to need you to find that second seal and remove it."

"Okay. Quick question though—what are they?"

"Poltergeists."

"Great."

The seething spirits were creeping in on them. Their eyes burned, and their teeth gnashed, and all the while their bodies flickered like white flames.

"Oh dear, oh dear…His Majesty will not be pleased," Mr. Gribs confessed to himself. He wrung his hands together desperately. *Which way has she gone?* Miss Everdoor was such a difficult one to find; it had taken Gribs such a long time just to track her this far.

But she was still in the trove somewhere—his senses told him that much at least. *Well, Gribsy ol' toad, you'd best hop to it!* he thought. He looked about the vast sea of wealth nervously; such grandeur, such magnitude—it was no place for a little nightmare such as he. The quicker he found Miss Everdoor, the quicker he would leave this place and return to his night job. Mr. Gribs chose a direction, based on his strongest inclination, and heading that way.

He wandered for a great long while. It seemed Miss Everdoor and that young man could really put some distance behind them when they meant to. But he was also certain he was getting closer. Gribs rummaged through his satchels and pulled out a bright-green dragon scale and rubbed it between his pudgy fingers. It belonged to the dragon Miss Everdoor owned and, therefore, belonged to Miss Everdoor; it was the only clue he could use to be able to find his elusive recipient. Of course, Miss Everdoor had a nasty habit of popping up all over the place, and at times, she was nowhere at all. It confounded Mr. Gribs.

There were very few creatures in existence that could move as Miss Everdoor did, and he should know; as a being who could warp through shadows, he shared a certain kinship with those that also traveled by curious means. But Miss Everdoor was unlike any creature Gribs knew; well, perhaps that wasn't entirely true. Mr. Gribs had met one such creature a very long time ago, but it was ridiculous to think that Miss Everdoor—mysterious though she was—could belong to *that* unfathomable race.

He hoped she could be persuaded to come with him in any regard. How he would manage to convince someone as headstrong as Miss Everdoor was beyond him, but he had to give it a try. Gribs wandered along the dark halls until he was certain he heard a kind of commotion up ahead. It wasn't just any old commotion either; there were shrieks and cries and the whooshes of a blade.

Mr. Gribs, being as cowardly as he was, crept through the shadows very carefully. The good thing about his unassuming demeanor was that he had a special talent for going completely unnoticed, and not even the cunning Miss

Everdoor with her keen ears and heightened senses could know Gribs was there if he really put his mind to it.

And he certainly put his mind to it this time. What he saw as he peered out from the shadows was a frightful scene indeed. Miss Everdoor was battling two vengeful spirits, and she was grinning wide and wickedly.

The spirits lunged at her, but she dodged this way and that as though they were all part of a careful ballet. Miss Everdoor moved with incredible grace and speed, spinning and weaving around the phantoms and dodging every vicious swipe and lunge they took at her. Gribs would not have been able to keep track of Miss Everdoor's precise and quick movements were he of mortal stock. But being as otherworldly as he was, Mr. Gribs was able to watch as Miss Everdoor danced around the two ghastly phantoms and slashed back at them effortlessly with her blade.

Mr. Gribs found it was no ordinary blade either, now that he had time to inspect it from a healthy distance. *It can't be,* he thought to himself, for the blade he believed to be in Miss Everdoor's hands was none other than a Reaper Blade, and such a weapon could only be summoned by those well versed in demon *majik.*

But a Reaper Blade, Mr. Gribs thought to himself. *Oh no. No-no. She couldn't be.* Oh, but she could.

Mr. Gribs watched in silent horror as Miss Everdoor grew bored of her quarry and rounded them up. "Do you know what I like about poltergeists?" she asked the two spirits, who were trading dubious glances. Their flickering white bodies seemed to quiver with uncertainty as they started to realize the roles of hunter and prey had been reversed. "What I like about you,"—she continued—"is that I can *eat* you and your god won't get mad." And then her mouth grew impossibly wide, and her teeth became deadly sharp. She lunged at the phantoms and gobbled them whole. Miss Everdoor was a Soul Eater.

Mr. Gribs let out a small squeak, and in that moment, he had forgotten to be unnoticeable, and Miss Everdoor took heed of him.

"Come out, come out, little toad," she said, peering through the corners of her golden eyes to the shadows.

Mr. Gribs gulped; his knees were trembling, and he had the utmost desire to turn and run. But if he knew anything about Soul Eaters, it was that running would be a very bad plan indeed. Mr. Gribs stepped out of the shadows with shaky steps and trembled before Miss Everdoor.

She smiled at him slyly; her mouth had returned to its normal proportions although Mr. Gribs could not erase the frightful scene from his mind.

"Well then, we are at a crossroads, it seems."

"I...I..." Mr. Gribs began, but he was too terrified to speak.

"I take it you know me?"

"I-if by '*know*' you…you mean '*your kind*,' then yes, madam, I…I know you," his scared little voice croaked.

"Hmm," she said, and she watched him curiously with calculating eyes.

"W-where is your friend?" Mr. Gribs made an attempt at polite conversation, although he had the terrible notion that she might have eaten the young man too.

"He's on an errand. What's it to you?"

So much for that. "Oh, well, I…" Mr. Gribs wrung his hands nervously and tried to look anywhere but at those piercing golden eyes that bore into him. He smiled weakly and did his best to retain what little composure he had left. "I, um"—he *ahemed*—"I must say, I thought your kind were extinct."

"Evidently not," she said to him coolly.

"Right, right, of course." He was swiftly losing ground. "And so your father, would he—" But Mr. Gribs stopped talking as Miss Everdoor pointed the tip of her rapier at his throat.

"Let me make this very clear to you, little toad: The words *your* and *father* are not permitted to leave your lips in conjunction when speaking to me. Understood?"

Mr. Gribs shrank as far as he could possibly shrink. "P-perfectly," he squeaked.

Miss Everdoor then smiled a much more genuine and warm smile and vanished away her blade. "Now then, I can't be calling you '*little toad*' anymore, seeing as you're determined to follow me around. So what's your name?"

"Pardon?" Mr. Gribs was very confused as to what was happening.

"Your name. I'm assuming it's not *Pardon* as that would make for a very unfortunate moniker."

"Oh, right, yes—my name is Mr. Gribs, but occasionally it's just Gribs for short."

"And you are the envoy of the Ledgerman?"

He was shocked by Miss Everdoor's rudeness. "His Majesty is not fond of that name."

"Well, it's a good thing *His Majesty* isn't here, then, isn't it?"

"Y-yes, I suppose it is." He cast wary glances to the shadows. Mr. Gribs could not help but worry his master's eternal eye was watching.

Miss Everdoor began circling him, and Mr. Gribs was again ill at ease. "So, then, Gribs, you've been sent to extend me an invitation and are not permitted to leave me unless I comply. Is that it?"

"Precisely, Miss Everdoor."

She laughed, and there was actual mirth in it. "Well, my little envoy, I'm afraid you will be stuck with me for a while as I've no intention of taking up your lord's proposal."

Mr. Gribs fell into despair. "Oh, but please, Miss Everdoor, whatever reservations you have, let me assuage them. His Majesty harbors you no ill will despite your—how to put it?—prior run-in with him."

"Ha! Now that I do find hard to believe. As his envoy, I trust you've an idea of your lord's temperament?"

"Well, I suppose, yes."

"And have you ever known him to let go of a grudge?"

"N-no, not as such."

"Then I'm afraid, Mr. Gribs, that my reservations are not assuaged."

Mr. Gribs sighed woefully. "Oh dear."

"Go now, Jerro. I can handle this."

"But—"

"They're not after you. You're a reborn, remember? Technically, you're one of them. The dead don't haunt the dead."

Jerro had left, although he didn't feel good about it—not that he was entirely certain what use he'd be in a ghost fight. Still, it felt wrong to leave a friend behind, and they were friends now, weren't they?

Too late to turn back now though. As soon as he took off, his motor functions took over and hauled him into a full-on sprint. He could feel the second ghost seal call to him—now that he was aware of it—and it directed his path as he navigated through the winding treasure hoard.

The light-headedness hadn't left him though, and he had a nagging suspicion as to what it actually meant. He had slowed to a jog and then a walk once he entered another vast chamber whose ceiling was so high it had succumb to shadow and the lights came only from the glowing amber stones that marked the walls at regular intervals. The same archways and balconies flanked his left, letting him know he was still traveling alongside the canyon. This room, just like the others, was littered with an abundance of wealth that twinkled in the warm gemstone-glow.

He stooped to pick up one of the many palm-sized solid gold coins that peppered the floor—there was a precise diamond shaped opening with a band of a circle inside it at the very center of the coin. Ecliptian numerals embossed across its face let him know the coin was worth *four-hundred-and-fifty*, though of what he didn't know. He did, however, know it was a *Gilden* coin—the word popped into his head where before there had been nothing and he couldn't recall how or why he knew such a thing.

For the moment he vanished the weighty coin into the obelisk pendant and looked about the cavernous room, the glittering wealth touched by something malicious, the unfathomable hugeness of it all. *How can anyone amass so much? How can it all seem so...endless?*

He strode through the room. The call was getting stronger, but the heading was becoming harder to read. Something was blocking him, and it had to do with the light-headedness; he was sure of it.

At the opposite end of the chamber were three sets of doors placed within the gaping maws of more colossal paragon beasts—away to the right were more dark hallways leading off to unknown parts of the trove, but none of them appealed to Jerro. The center of the door-heads was that of a dragon's; at its left was a lion's, and at its right was a griffin's. All three of the doors, however, called to Jerro equally, and each door sent a quiet dread through him at the thought of passing between those monstrous teeth. He stood rooted, unsure of where to go to next.

Something about the way their stony eyes glinted made him certain that the choice mattered—direly—and so he stood there, dumbfounded. *How the bloody hell am I supposed to figure this one out?* Unlike the throne room with its hidden code and Etcher's riddle to guide him, here he was hopelessly lost. He looked over the carved faces, hoping to glean something meaningful or unique that might guide his choice, but each face stared back at him with an unreadable, lifeless stare.

He was screwed.

He let out a heavy breath as he regarded the three impassive doors. Etcher was depending on him to figure it out. He couldn't just stand around while she was busy battling *poltergeists*, and all he had to do was remove another seal. He was beginning to feel slightly inadequate in their growing dynamic.

Time felt like it was against him, and as much as he wanted to nurse his wounded pride and head back to join Etcher and fight the good fight, *however the hell I'd manage that*, he begrudgingly admitted that his mundane task was the best way he could help.

He strode up to the dragon maw and considered it. *As good a guess as any, right? I hope...* But even as he stepped inside the dragon's mouth and reached for its door, he swore he heard the statue-head creak. If he hadn't been yanked out of the way at the very last second, he would have been crushed as the dragon's mouth snapped shut so quickly a few of its marble teeth cracked.

He skittered back on his heels and then stood there, petrified, having almost ended up a shish kebab for the second time that day. He might have remained standing there, caught in a daze, if he hadn't realized that his nagging suspicions had been confirmed. Someone had followed him, and it wasn't that strange little toad either. Jerro's skin prickled, and as he turned to face his savior he felt his blood run cold.

'The dead don't haunt the dead,' huh, Etcher?

Jerro's grave hero was at least two heads taller than him—even though said hero was greatly hunched—with big, sad, oval eyes and a strangely familiar hat.

"Wait," Jerro said aloud. "Are you...the *gardener*?"

The gardener, looking much less corpse-like though still pale and ghostly and a little see-through, was wearing long baggy trousers—which were patched up in places—and a button-up shirt with the sleeves rolled up to his elbows. He was a strange, gangly creature whose lips had been stitched closed at the corners and whose features were rather flat—save for the big bulbous eyes. The gardener smiled as much as his stitched lips would allow and waved at Jerro.

"Uh...hi to you too," replied Jerro.

The gardener tipped his hat.

An impression came to mind, and it seemed to Jerro as though the gardener were thanking him. "Oh, yeah, you're welcome." Jerro regarded the spirit skeptically. "So you just wanted to say thanks, or...?"

The gardener straightened from his hunch a little and looked over to the three doors, gesturing with his hands.

"Why? Well, it's a bit complicated—what do you mean? Well, no...not exactly. I mean, you know, it's a big place. You can't take it all—that? Okay, well, yeah, I took a few souvenirs, but, I mean, can you blame me? No, we just need something from here, and we're pretty sure it's in that isle—hang on, how do you know that?" said Jerro.

The gardener had suddenly become very interested in his quest, impressing images and feelings as Jerro talked for both of them.

"So...do you know the way?" Jerro asked.

The gardener gave a solemn nod and then beckoned Jerro to follow. He walked with soundless steps right up to the center door, which was now sealed off by the dragon's closed maw, and stared at it for a moment.

Jerro came up beside the gardener and waited. "You can't seriously think it's that one. The damn thing nearly ate me!" Jerro almost huffed. *A lot of good this guy is.*

But the gardener shook his head. He walked up beside the colossal griffin and clicked a hidden latch inside its beak. A doorway opened up in the wall between the dragon and the griffin heads, and the gardener disappeared inside.

Jerro had been right; he would have been screwed.

"So you've been following me since the gardens?" asked Jerro as they traversed along a dimly lit tunnel. There were more godly sculptures—similar to the effigies that had been in the throne room—lining the passage walls, although these had flickering little flames in their eyes that lent the barest of light to guide the way.

Yes, the gardener replied, imprinting the word in Jerro's mind.

"Why didn't you show up earlier?"

The gardener didn't give a clear reply then. It was more a mixture of thoughts and impressions—as though the answer wasn't simple enough to be encapsulated by words—but Jerro more or less got his point. The gardener had been curious about Jerro and Etcher but wanted to see what kind of people they were first in case they were the unscrupulous sort.

"How come you kept after me?"

Again the answer wasn't simple. Jerro gathered that the gardener became afraid when the poltergeists turned up and that he wasn't all too sure about Etcher, which planted a small seed of doubt in Jerro's mind. *Why not Etcher? What about her makes even a ghost wary?* But the gardener had moved on from the topic and was communicating something solid.

Death Token.

"Yeah! That's what we're after—well, what Etcher's after. You know where it is?"

The gardener nodded solemnly, and another mix of impressions and thoughts flooded Jerro's mind, but there was one solid word that stood out: *Purgatory.*

"The token's in Purgatory? Like, biblical Purgatory?"

But the gardener didn't seem to understand Jerro and tilted his head in confusion.

"Never mind. So this *Purgatory*, is that what the isle is? The souls are really trapped there?"

Yes.

"Okay. So why aren't you there?"

Unnoticed.

"What do you mean? You were unnoticed?"

Yes.

"What, they just forgot to lock you up in Purgatory? Speaking of which, who put the souls there? Someone must have, right?"

Yes.

Jerro frowned. "Yeah. Okay, but who?"

The gardener didn't answer. They were coming up to the end of the tunnel, where a flood of light obscured the threshold.

"What's wrong?"

Follow the bridge.

"You're not coming?"

Follow the bridge.

"I'll take that as a no." Jerro sighed. "Well, listen…thanks for getting me this far." Jerro reflexively stuck out his hand to shake and then wondered if the gesture would even be understood.

The gardener looked at the offered hand curiously and then slipped his own cold ghostly hand into Jerro's. They shook, and once the gardener got the gesture, he shook Jerro's hand more vigorously.

"Whoa, whoa! You'll take my arm off!" Jerro smirked, although he was a little unnerved by the surprising strength. "Easy, see?"

He let go of the handshake and patted the ghost on the shoulder. "Be seeing you, I guess." He felt a strange pang of guilt for leaving his solemn new friend behind, but it seemed the gardener had no desire to join Jerro any further. With a deep breath, Jerro stepped through the light.

Etcher was leaning up against a wall as she waited for the ghost seal's influence to fade. The little toad hadn't moved from his spot and kept peering over at her despite his obvious attempts to look distracted by something else. She smiled; was the little nightmare becoming infatuated with her? *Now that would be curious.* "I don't suppose I have to mention that if you tell my tall friend—or anyone else, for that matter—about what I am, I'll devour you whole?"

The little toad quivered, and Etcher smiled again. "O-of course, I wouldn't *dream* of it." He chuckled nervously.

Etcher laughed too, startling the portly nightmare. *Funny little thing, isn't he?* "So, then, Mr. Gribs, are you ready to venture into the great unknown? Although, it would seem to me that our destination is not so unknown to *you.*"

The toad gulped. "I wouldn't know all that much about it, Miss Everdoor."

"Hmm." Etcher pushed off from the wall and sauntered over to the toad; her tail coiled back and forth hypnotically, and the toad's eyes followed it. "I thought perhaps you were a nightmare in the know. Was I wrong?"

A strange pallor tinted the toad's pearlescent skin. "I…I…well, it's not my place, really—"

"But are you or are you not in the know?"

"Well, I know certain things…b-but it's nothing all that important. I just deliver the messages."

"Pity about that. I thought perhaps you knew that the King of Nightmare was responsible for that little isle over there." When the toad looked as though his eyes might pop from his round head, she knew she had been right.

But Mr. Gribs started to backpedal and stumble over his words. "W-why ever would you think that?" He grinned sheepishly.

"Why ever wouldn't *you?* As someone—who I must now assume is *not* in the know—who at least knows such an isle is forbidden, should also know that the forbidding must have come from upper management—in which case, for you, Mr. Gribs, would be from the Ledgerman." She could see the confusion behind Mr. Gribs's eyes as he tried to untangle her words. "And so, if such forbidding were to come from His Majesty, then it's only natural to suggest His Majesty had something to do with the isle. Wouldn't you agree?"

"Well, I...I suppose—"

"So His Majesty *did* forbid you?"

"No! No! Well...well, yes, but—"

"And therefore His Majesty is responsible?"

"Well, he..." Mr. Gribs wrung his hands desperately. His green tongue poked out as he moistened his wide, thin-lipped mouth.

"Mr. Gribs?" Etcher pressed on.

The poor toad had been so spun about that he wasn't sure what to deny and what to answer. He finally seemed to break down and said weakly, "It...could be suggested that way."

"Huh." Etcher smiled. "Curious thing that His Majesty should want those souls locked away. Seems to me like they might be in penance, or perhaps it's just punishment."

Mr. Gribs was about ready to faint. "Please, Miss Everdoor, I don't wish to say any more on the topic."

"Relax," she said with a wink. "You hardly said a thing."

The toad breathed a little easier and unclenched his hands from the satchel straps. "R-right. Good." He coughed and cleared his throat. "So...should we, perhaps, be going anywhere soon?"

"As soon as the seal is removed. It doesn't affect you, does it?"

"Oh, well...it does—although differently, I suppose." He was visibly relieved for the change of topic. "I am not repressed by it, though nor could I remove it. But your friend...he can?"

Etcher studied the toad carefully. "You know, Mr. Gribs, it would be dangerous for my tall companion if others were to know about his *condition*. Can I trust you'll keep from mentioning it to anyone?"

"Oh, yes. Of course, Miss Everdoor! I would not wish your company any harm."

She continued to eye him. "You enjoy having people's trust, don't you?"

And at that, the toad started to blush. "Well, it's just an honor to have the confidence of powerful individuals."

"Why, Mr. Gribs, are you trying to flatter me?"

"Well, I-I mean, I wouldn't try to flatter you—not that you're *not* remarkable—" He turned a deep scarlet and started wringing his hands again. "W-what I mean to say is y-you are a very talented swordsman—*swordswoman*,

I mean…And, well, your *condition* is quite incredible. Is it true that you can…travel to the Blank?"

Etcher's eyes twinkled. "Would you care to see it?"

"Oh, well, that would be…I…it would be an honor."

"Well, Mr. Gribs, stick around long enough, and I'm sure—" Etcher paused. Her ears flicked up, her poise became rigid. The seal was gone, but so was Jerro.

"What—"

"Come. We must go." And she took off at a run.

"Oh dear," said Mr. Gribs, running after her as quickly as his stubby legs would allow.

The phone was ringing. Reedman put down his paperwork and frowned at the extension that popped up on the display. He hesitated for a moment, clearing his throat before he answered the call. "Reedman here," he said. "Yessir, I'll be right over." He put the phone back on the receiver and drummed his fingers on his desk. Something was up.

He glanced over at his growing report and wondered if he should bring it with him but then decided it was better to travel light. He left his office and shut the door, then navigated his way through the station to the chief's office and rapped his knuckles on the privacy glass.

"Come in," came a voice from the other side of the door.

Reedman entered.

"Shut the door behind you, Jay."

"Something up, Inspector?" he asked, although he already suspected something was.

"Take a seat."

Reedman pulled out the only available chair and sat down. He felt squished by its arms—there was barely any padding stretched over its austere metal frame, but the chair wasn't meant to be inviting.

Chief Inspector Vahlin was watching Reedman closely. He was a tall, gaunt creature with shallow cheeks and thinning blond hair. He had severe blue eyes, and on more than one occasion it had been suggested that he'd make a very convincing Grim Reaper for Halloween—or any day of the week, for that matter. Of course, it was always suggested quietly and out of the earshot of the Chief Inspector.

The Chief sat with his back impossibly straight, as though a pole had been shoved up his arse—which had also been suggested quietly and out of earshot. His long, bony fingers were laced together, and his cold eyes weighed upon

Reedman as the detective shifted uncomfortably in the chair. "Good news, Detective, we're wrapping up this case."

"Ahliss has been caught?"

"*No,* but the real criminal has."

"Excuse me, sir, but I don't—"

"The cleaning man confessed to the crime earlier today. He's been detained and is ready to sign off on his statement. You and Jones will be finishing up the report. I expect to have it on my desk tomorrow morning. Are we clear?"

"No, sir, I don't think we are."

"Then let me make it clear." The Chief Inspector glowered at Reedman, and his voice took on a frightful timbre. "*You* should have been pulled off this case the moment Mr. Ahliss became a suspect."

"But—"

"*You* should have been promoted two years ago. But with that prior case being as big of an embarrassment to this entire station as it was, you were lucky to remain in property crimes and fraud. Detective Reedman, I am promoting you to homicides. You've paid your dues, and you're good at what you do, so I am allowing you to move on from this whole sordid affair, providing you put Jerro Ahliss out of your mind. And just so that we are perfectly clear, let me rephrase it: You *cannot* have anything to do with that young man. If the media got wind of another cock-up involving Jerro Ahliss, you would be lucky to remain as a beat cop. Do you understand *now,* Detective Reedman?"

"Yessir," Reedman said through clenched teeth. A bitter taste in his mouth had made his words clipped, and he figured it was better to keep the rest of what he wanted to say to himself.

"*Good.* Now, finish up the report."

Reedman nodded curtly and rose from the chair.

"Oh, and one last thing," said Chief Inspector Vahlin as Reedman headed for the door, "Mrs. Ahliss called earlier today. If you ever make another house call like that again, you will be fired. Understood?"

"Boss—"

"Don't, Jones." Reedman's jaw had been clenched from the time he left the Chief Inspector's office, and it didn't seem like it would be unclenching anytime soon.

Jones sighed. "So what now?"

Reedman didn't answer right away. Everything about the case stank; it was even worse than the first time. Begrudgingly he had to admit that it was better he got as far away from anything involving Jerro Ahliss as he could. The bastard had almost ruined Reedman's career once already. For years he had wanted to be transferred to homicides, but now that he had it felt like an empty victory.

"Should we go and have a word with Edik Bosko?" said Jones, trying to gently prod at the matter at hand without invoking Reedman's ire.

"Who?"

"The cleaning man. You know, the one who confessed?"

"Tell me you don't buy into that shit, Jones."

"What do you want me to say, Boss? Ahliss is in the wind, and besides the elevator log, we don't actually have anything to pin him to it."

"You saw the videos."

"*Yeah*...why do you think Chief wants this case done with? You want to explain any of that in a report? Besides which, we don't *actually* have footage of Ahliss going into Lapaul's office. The video cuts out before. There're no prints, no motive, and now, no Jerro Ahliss. I'm with you that there's something wrong here, but Johan Lapaul isn't pressing charges. Officially, nothing was taken from his office."

"Officially?"

"Jay, you cannot touch this case with a ten-foot pole. The media will hang you. Whatever Ahliss has done, however he's managed to swing it, you can't be involved. The station can't be involved. You weren't the only one who got his arse handed to him."

"Chief talked to you too?"

"Yeah, right before he took it out of your hide."

Reedman sighed. "Look, go and question this Bosmo—"

"Bosko."

"Whatever. Just go and talk to him."

"What're you gonna do?"

"Guess I'm transferring over to homicides." Although he intended to do a little digging first.

Jerro felt weightless. He was surrounded by a black void; it was almost like floating in *Blank-Space* but without any of the petrifying fear. He drifted along the black and felt nothing—only release. Ages might have passed, or it might have all stood still. He felt no internal clock ticking nor any measure of time; it was simply *endless*.

As he drifted, there was only a vague semblance of his consciousness clinging to his weightless form. But then the space around him shifted, and he felt himself going down with the same curious upheaval he experienced when he was back at the shop and Etcher bridged the way between the *Blank* and reality. As the rush passed over him, his feet finally met the ground, and once more he had form.

The black continued to surround him, but he himself was lit. He held out his hands in front of him and thought for a small moment there had been a symbol branded on both his wrists, but in an instant, they were gone.

His thoughts were slow to return after the eternal abyss, but one tangible word crept into his mind: *Where?*

Upon that thought, a distant shaft of light illuminated the way, and suddenly, the blank had depth. He walked toward the light; with every step, small rings rippled out from under his feet. He thought he heard chimes echoing in the distance; they got louder the closer he got to the light, and they called to him from memories long since passed.

As he continued toward the shaft of light, things started to change. The blackness began to chip away, revealing the colors of dawn beneath. With every step he made, more of the darkness flaked off until suddenly, all that remained of the black crumbled like a veil collapsing onto the ground, leaving Jerro standing in a vibrant world.

Above him, he saw beautiful songbirds flying overhead; their intricate tails left streaks of color in the air as they sailed on by. Floating islands dotted the skies, and magnificent beasts like the paragons flew between the levitating landmasses. Some ferried small children; others, the young at heart.

There was a magnificent ocean stretched out to meet the horizon on either side of the bone-white bridge that Jerro found himself upon; it too seemed to stretch on forever. As he walked along its toothy surface, he felt oddly satisfied, and still a little weightless despite his feet touching down.

It was as though he were suspended in a moment where no hunger or tiredness touched him no matter how far he walked. He travelled for a great long while, watching the ever-shifting expanse, and still the bridge continued on. The day did not slowly slip into darkness and then back into day like on a pinwheel; instead, there were pockets of starlight; bright, sunny skies; and all the in-betweens.

He was contented to walk forever in that strange and beautiful place; it was oddly effervescent. He felt a spark within him ignite, like a calling from his boyhood when he felt joyful and free. Children's laughter trickled down from the skies as they rode on their magnificent chimeras, and soft music drifted along the tops of the undulating ocean; he was at peace.

Then he saw her. She refracted in the light, sometimes she was a tall and beautiful woman draped in white and at others time she was a magnificent fox with a pelt like fresh snow. She beckoned him to her, reaching out with a delicate hand, or maybe a paw.

Who? The word came to him, though he never made a sound.

She smiled at him sadly. *I am Sovereignce. I guard the Terriss Walk.*

Where? He recalled the first word that had come to him.
We are in Dream, and you are dying very slowly.

Etcher felt the tiny voice inside her bristle with urgency. Something had gone wrong. It was possible the Oolkas had nabbed Jerro, but even as she thought it, her highly tuned intuition wouldn't let it stick. She was oddly concerned over her new companion, and it did strange things to her temperament. She was running in to save him, which was not the usual calm and collected Everdoor way; it was slightly vexing.

It had happened once before—when she watched him fall from the balcony and nearly meet his end on the horns of Armanis, the ram-headed god. She could have reasoned that she was simply protecting her investment, but she knew it was more than that. Etcher was not in the business of lying to herself after all; it was only everyone else who got half-truths.

She would have to sort through her emotions later though. One thing was for certain: Jerro was in trouble, and she was likely the only one who could save him. She knew the portly toad was trailing slowly behind her, but she couldn't worry about him just then. She was single-minded in her pursuit to save Jerro, which was another curious notion indeed.

The urgency had lent a heightened reflex to her perceptions at least, and she was able to track what remained of Jerro's essence trail all the way to the pavilion where three paragon beasts held doors in their gaping maws. A trickle of dread ran through her as she looked at the collapsed jaws of the dragon, but she knew if Jerro had met his end there, the stony beast would have smelled of blood; it was a morbid comfort.

She slowed only for a moment as she regarded the secret passage between the paragon heads. There was a trace of another's essence touching the threshold; someone had been there with Jerro. Had they showed him the way? Or led him to his doom? Her intuition said the answer lay somewhere in between. She raced down the hall, stopping only before the shaft of light that bathed the exit.

She could feel them out there: the Oolkas, the isle, and somewhere distantly within that floating island, the Death Token and the smallest hint of Jerro's soul. She stepped out through the light and into the canyon gorge.

There was a small lip of rock that she stepped out onto as she exited the secret hall. She saw a wide flat bridge in front of her that connected the canyon wall to the domed isle up ahead. Upon closer inspection, Etcher could see the finer details of it all.

She felt a touch of anger slither through her.

There were hundreds of thousands of bones making up the bridge and the isle itself. Atop the man-made landmass was a stone wall that encircled the perimeter of the floating isle, and atop the wall was the crackling dome of light that buffeted away the Oolkas.

The winged reapers were owlish; they were also of dragonesque proportions. Etcher would have fit neatly within the grasp of their sharply-clawed talons. Fortunately enough, they had no interest in claiming her living soul. But unfortunately, there was a certain history between the reapers and Etcher's kin that caused tension to weigh heavily in the air. It was safe to say they weren't all that fond of Soul Eaters.

One of the Oolkas glided down from the circling procession and landed thunderously on the bone bridge, blocking Etcher's path. The Oolka reared its head slowly and peered down its vicious beak all the while at the little shopkeeper with big, owlish eyes. The immense fowl was a dapple of black and white with tiny flecks of gold trimming its feathers. It was as beautiful as it was formidable.

"*These souls are not for you, Oullakkan.*" The sonorous words tumbled through the air like boulders raining down, though its beak never moved to create the sound.

"Hello, Shee'Den," Etcher said calmly as she poised herself before the great fowl. "I have not come for their souls—only to claim one that is bound to me."

"*There is no such soul.*"

"Oh, but there is." Etcher held out her right hand, and her palm illuminated with Jerro's contract.

The great owl tilted its head ever so slightly to look down at the concentric pattern within Etcher's palm. "*You should not be permitted to make such a deal.*"

"Well, thankfully, my dear friend, souls are permitted to make such deals of their own volition."

"*Not every soul.*"

Etcher tutted. "But this one did. Curious thing, isn't it? That isle."

"*Do not change the subject.*"

"But it's part of it. The soul I seek came here to this very isle, and now he's gone. If you have taken him, I've a right to know."

"*We do not take souls that do not belong to us,*" said the Oolka, doing little to hide its contempt.

But Etcher was immune to the slight, and she let it fall away, unacknowledged. "And a good thing that is, but this one you might have mistaken as belonging to the dead."

"*The reborn.*"

"So he did come through here."

The Oolka's feathers ruffled. *"Reborns should not be permitted to walk with the living."*

"Did you take him?"

"We tried, but he was quick, and when he removed the seal, he was drawn into the isle. Now he will be lost forever with the others."

Etcher flicked her eyes to the isle and then to the Oolkas circling above. "If I were to make a deal with you, dear Shee'Den, to break open the field that hinders you and free the souls from the isle, would you let me pass?"

"If you were to take none for yourself, then I might let you pass."

"Oh, but I would take only those indebted to me, and I'm afraid even you cannot unravel that deal."

"The reborn should not be permitted to stay."

"And yet his soul is housed in a living, breathing vessel. He is not yours to take."

The Oolka rumbled with a sound like thunder, but it seemed it could not deny Etcher's words. *"Take only he who is indebted, and free the rest. That is our deal. Now go."*

Etcher bowed elegantly, and the great Oolka took off, returning to his procession with the others. She heard a labored breath behind her and smiled. "Mr. Gribs, you're just in time."

The little nightmare doubled over and panted. "I don't suppose I can dissuade you from this course?" he asked through heavy breaths.

"You suppose correctly." She grinned and continued down the bridge. The crackle of bone crunched beneath her feet as she strode up to the wall encasing the isle. There was a silver line along the stone barrier in the shape of an archway, and at its center was a round indentation where a ghost seal had once been housed. Etcher reached out and touched the wall, but it rippled and allowed her fingers to pass through. *I hope you'll still be in that living flesh when I find you, Jerro Ahliss.* She stepped forward and passed through to the other side.

Etcher found herself stepping out into an entirely different world. There were blue skies overhead and seabirds cawing as they sailed along air currents. She was standing on the edge of a cliff overlooking a calm ocean. The waves lapped up against the rocks gently, their crests glittering as the sunlight hit them. There was a tropical heat to the air that was subdued by the salty breeze, which tousled Etcher's chestnut locks. She surveyed the horizon but only saw the endless blue; no other isles dotted the vast expanse. She flexed her fingers, feeling out the place and trying to discern where in the universes this world might be. It was strangely familiar, as though she knew this realm, but for the life of her, she couldn't figure out its place in the void of time and space.

She looked down at her feet and noticed a wide road that went right up to the very edge of the cliff, as though the isle had once extended out much farther and the road along with it. Behind her, the road continued on through a throng of exotic palms and wilderness to where she could sense a bustling of souls. There was something odd about the ground she stood on though, and she knelt down to get a closer inspection of it. Little motes of dust appeared to move in reverse, gathering back into the rock and soil along the rim of the isle.

"Oh dear!" said an exasperated Mr. Gribs. "Why, Miss Everdoor, have you got shorter?"

She stood slowly and peered at what was no longer a *little* nightmare. "Quite the opposite, Mr. Gribs. It appears you've become tall and rather dashing." But it wasn't said as a compliment; there was deep contemplation in her tone.

"W-what? Me?" Mr. Gribs blushed, and he blushed with a very handsome face. He was tall and lean and dressed like royalty. He had a strong jaw, long blond hair, and beautiful green-blue eyes. He was positively dreamy.

Etcher flicked her wrist in an attempt to conjure a mirror, but nothing came. "Now that might be problematic."

"My satchels—where are my satchels? Ahk! What happened to my hands?" Mr. Gribs was staring down at long, slender fingers and unblemished skin. "'Dashing,' you said?" He smiled at Etcher sheepishly, but with his new face, it seemed coy and attractive.

"Positively," Etcher replied, continuing to scrutinize his new form.

"How is this possible? I can only transform in Nightmare, but I never—I mean, I've not the ability to be *dashing*."

But Etcher was no longer listening; she was staring down the path into the jungle. There were souls deeper within the isle, and they were old.

"Miss Everdoor?"

But she had already started down the road.

Etcher was vaguely aware of Mr. Gribs trailing behind her; he apparently took the hint that she was no longer in a talking mood. The road was taking her deeper toward the heart of the isle, and she could hear the cheerful chatter of people up ahead.

The road abruptly led out into a bustling town square where hundreds of people were milling about. It was as if a chunk of Undercity had been raised above ground. The buildings were hewn from marble, gold-leaf moldings crowned pillars and trimmed the walls, opulent fountains poured out crystalline waters in delicate falls—the place was beautifully extravagant.

Just as in Gahza'Dune, the faces ranged from the ordinary to the exotic, except that here there was also an angelic, if not godly, accent to their features. They seemed to radiate with a celestial aura, and their faces were perfect—as though they had been chiseled.

Their dress also reflected their ethereal stature. They were draped in rich silks and light cotton cloths of the type that tastefully fall from the shoulder in a cascade of rippling folds and cinches along the waist. Etcher's stately attire with its admiral theme and Mr. Gribs's princely outfit made the two instantly stand out among the others, and the others took notice. Angelous alighted atop of roofs and peered down at the two visitors, whispering to each other, and the street-traffic paused their amicable conversations and stared at Etcher and Mr. Gribs with wonder in their eyes.

Etcher pulled herself up straight as she stood before the waiting crowd. She could feel the tension from Mr. Gribs, and she flicked him a glance that indicated that he should remain silent. Her tail wove back and forth, and her calculating gaze scanned over the expectant throng. Something was very wrong here. Despite the friendly faces looking back at her, she couldn't help but feel ill at ease. They were too orderly in their quiet expectance and looked to her and Mr. Gribs so unwaveringly that they could have been mistaken for statues.

She took a step forward, clasping her hands behind her back. "I am Etcher," she said smoothly. "Who of you is in charge?"

Life animated the crowd again, and soon they were trading whispers and glances among themselves until one of them broke away and smiled widely. She had the face of a young woman with golden hair artfully styled and twisted into a neat braid that came over a shoulder. She bowed low before Etcher and Mr. Gribs. "Please allow me to escort you." She beamed hopefully.

"And where would you take me?"

"To our king. He will be delighted to meet you both." The young woman shot a shy smile at Mr. Gribs as a touch of heat colored her cheeks.

Etcher had to hold back her laughter at the girl's quick infatuation. *If only you knew*, she thought privately. She glanced at Mr. Gribs sidelong, watching as a grin started to curl along his handsome lips. She felt herself groan inwardly; he'd be of no use to her now. "Well then, lead the way," said Etcher.

The golden-haired girl was delighted to comply. She straightened, being nearly a half foot taller than Etcher, and beckoned them to follow. The sea of people parted, murmuring and whispering to one another with apparent awe. Man, woman, and the indiscernible alike kept smiling at Etcher and at Mr. Gribs—who was relishing the attention.

"It has been so long since we've had any visitors," the golden-haired girl said. She was leading Etcher and Mr. Gribs along the main road, which cut through the town square and went straight toward a towering cathedral. Its delicate architecture and silver filigree were all too reminiscent of the throne room in Undercity.

"When was the last time someone came through here?" Etcher was careful with her words, and she glanced at Mr. Gribs again, hoping he'd retained enough of his faculties to follow her lead, although it did not matter; he was too busy smiling and waving at the crowd that seemed to *ooh* and *aah* at his appearance.

Useless, she thought to herself.

"Oh, it was maybe ten years ago now."

"How curious." Etcher peered at the sea of faces that smiled at her. She slipped into her friendly and welcoming demeanor, appearing to be indifferent to the world with an easy smile of her own. It was only the honey eyes that gazed a little too deeply and shone with too much thought that would have begged to differ. "And who was your last visitor?"

"Why, the Grand Vizier! He was sent by the gods to aid us in this time of war." The golden-haired guide seemed solemn at the mention. "Things became so awful, our paradise would have fallen apart, but the Grand Vizier brought new life to our world and made it better again."

"War?" piped up Mr. Gribs. The conversation had finally hooked his attention enough to draw him back into the present.

Etcher glanced at the princely nightmare, making sure to catch his eye. A flicker of menace crossed over her face as she smiled viciously at him, revealing her sharp canine teeth. *Remember that I can eat you, little toad.*

He seemed to gather her meaning and went slightly pale.

"Yes, the Third Alliance War...it still rages on." The golden-haired girl shot them both a questioning look, her brow furrowing in confusion. "You are Ecliptian, are you not?"

"Er—"

"Yes, we are." Etcher interjected before Mr. Gribs could stumble over his words. "What we find curious is how much you know of the war, being so far removed from it," replied Etcher without a hitch. Her eyes flicked back to Mr. Gribs for only a moment, and he shrank under her weighty gaze.

The young woman did not seem fully convinced, however, and kept looking at Etcher and Mr. Gribs questioningly.

Etcher sighed and then her features softened into something warm and sympathetic. "Forgive us, there is much we would like to say, but neither of us is certain about the details you already know. It's why we need to speak to your king first and foremost. We've important business, and I would hate for either of us to be compromised by a slip of the tongue. You understand?"

At that the young woman's eyes suddenly lit up. "Have you been sent by the gods as well?"

Etcher inclined her head. "We have both been sent by the powers that be. Please excuse us if our attitude seems strange." The words rolled off her tongue with confidence. It was hard to call Etcher a liar as such; she merely allowed people to interpret their own meanings.

"Oh, not at all! Forgive me, I shouldn't have pried."

"It is forgiven." Etcher brushed it aside. "But perhaps you could bring us up to speed? It would be helpful to know your current state of knowledge so that we might save ourselves from redundancy with His Majesty. The gods, after all, are fickle with the information they impart."

"Yes, they are." The young woman started to relax, confident that she was ferrying visitors sent by the gods over to her king. "Well, we know the war is very fierce. The Grand Vizier is able to show us what goes on beyond this realm. It is so awful what the Syndains did to the Dahl'Kir."

"Well, the Syndains are a warring race after all. It was only a matter of time," Etcher retorted, which was a true-enough statement. She was grateful that Mr. Gribs came to enough sense to realize he needed to guard his words; she only wished he would guard his expression as well. He kept looking at Etcher with unease stamped across his face. *Yes,* she thought, *I know. Something is very off with their version of reality. Now stop gawking, you fool.* It wasn't the first time Etcher wished she was telepathic.

"Too true." The young woman replied. "But we are safe here in Arcadia. The Grand Vizier was able to shield us from the evils of the war."

"How very lucky you are."

The young woman beamed back at them. "So very lucky, and now with you here, maybe we will learn how to stop the fighting altogether."

"That is the goal, is it not?"

"We will find a way to bring Arcadia to everyone, and then finally there can be peace."

Etcher felt a lump of cold dread sink in her chest, though outwardly, her mask of nonchalance remained firmly in place. The young woman seemed to believe wholeheartedly in things that had never come to pass. There was no Third Alliance War, no remaining strife between the Syndains and the Dahl'Kir, and Etcher was willing to bet that this Grand Vizier, much like herself, had not been sent by the gods.

But the most disturbing fact of all was that the young woman didn't seem to realize that she and everyone else on the isle—save for Etcher and Mr. Gribs—were most certainly dead. The little shopkeeper looked around at the denizens of Arcadia; there was a complacent attitude about them that made Etcher unnerved. The place was too idyllic—too calm. The people roamed about with such a blithe indifference that it seemed unnatural.

But under their buoyant disposition, Etcher *smelled* something wrong. It was a hint of that stagnant, dusty air and moldy earth the likes of which only ancient tombs and catacombs had; it was the smell of spirits rotting. She seemed to get a whiff of it every now and then when the occasional city goer passed them by, but it came in droves when she spied a haggard old man standing on a street corner who was simply *staring*. His face twitched with silent rage, and then suddenly, as if the moment hadn't happened at all, the man blinked and carried on with the same casual cheeriness as everyone else.

She regarded Mr. Gribs out of the corner of her eye. *This is all an illusion. They are rotting, and yet all they see is a beautiful nightmare.* Etcher thought back to the poltergeists she had devoured earlier—they had tasted *old*. Had they come from Arcadia? And if so, what were they doing beyond the isle?

"Would you like me to announce you?" said their golden-haired guide as they approached the stately steps of the cathedral.

"By all means." Etcher let the young woman hasten up the steps, and allowed herself to fall behind so that she and Mr. Gribs were walking side by side. She spied the worried look he gave her at a glance, but kept her focus in front of her. *"As best you can,"*—she began, under her breath—*"try not to say anything that might land us in a prison cell. Are we clear?"*

"Yes, of course, Miss Everdoor, perfectly." He gulped.

Etcher picked up her pace once more and was right behind their guide as they entered the cathedral. It was an exact replica of the throne room in Undercity; a procession of praying angel statues lined the center path, godly effigies were perched along the walls and in the alcoves above, and yet unlike Undercity, the throne was currently occupied by none other than the Mad King.

A Rylin, in its human skin, often had a wild mohawk lining all the way down their back and along the crest of their slender tail. They had ears that were each the length of a forearm, which were often littered with hoops and studs, and a reddish-brown complexion with strong, handsome features and a proud nose. Their dress was often minimal, being that of a loincloth or tabard. Their legs were long, and their frame was usually tall and sinewy, as to be expected of a species that prided themselves on their speed and athletics.

This rylin was no different, only that his hair had gone pure white with age, and he was sporting a beard cut to just above his navel. It was wound into one long braid and bound with silver rings. His Majesty stared down his long, proud nose at the visitors who had entered his chamber. He held a staff beside him and tapped it against the marble ground, making an authoritative clap echo through the cathedral hall.

The golden-haired girl bowed low. "Your Majesty, I bring you visitors sent by the gods." She kept her eyes on the ground and waited patiently for recognition.

The old king got to his feet and descended the steps with exceeding grace. He strode up to the golden-haired girl, towering over her, and held out his hand. "You've no need to kneel, Elwa. Please rise." He smiled kindly.

The young woman got to her feet but kept her eyes on the ground. "Thank you, Your Majesty." She stood aside so that the king could inspect the new arrivals.

"Quite the dutiful king to be at his people's beck and call," said Etcher. "And no guards at the door—you've such a trusting kingdom."

The king regarded Etcher and the warmth that had softened his features froze over. "I've no need to fear my people any more than they should have need to fear me. My duty is to serve them and keep our kingdom alive."

"*Alive,*" Etcher repeated, meeting the king's gaze with a steely look of her own.

"Elwa, would you excuse us, please?"

"Yes, of course, m'lord." She curtsied before the king and swiftly left the cathedral, casting back a curious glance at the two visitors as she headed out. Her eyes lingered on Mr. Gribs, and she smiled when his gaze met hers.

The king watched as Elwa left, making sure she was gone before focusing back on Etcher.

"She doesn't know." The little shopkeeper stated as a fact rather than a question.

The Rylin king turned his back to Etcher, let out a sigh and seemed to drift in his thoughts. He retraced his steps toward the throne and then stopped midway to gaze out a magnificent stained-glass window. Colorful lights dappled the ground and undulated softly. As the moment began to stretch on he looked over his shoulder and regarded his two visitors once more, his expression a little more calculating than before. "My people are happy here. That's all that matters. Why should I take that happiness away from them?"

The tip of Etcher's tail twitched, there was a coil of irritation growing inside her and to quell it for the meantime she began to circle the king, her hands still clasped behind her back, her stride altogether casual and unhurried—but in her golden gaze their flickered menace. "Forgive us, Mr. Gribs. I'm sure you're wondering what is going on," she said, noting the evident confusion and worry that had plagued the nightmare's handsome face since the start of their exchange with the king.

He opened his mouth as if to speak but then closed it again, uncertain if it was safe for him to say anything at all.

Etcher smiled, though there was tightness behind it. Her growing impatience to find Jerro tugged at her. There was only the slightest wisp of his essence clinging to the air, and it gave her no heading as to where he was—or what state he was in, for that matter. "You see, Mr. Gribs, our dutiful king has neglected to inform his people that they are dead—His Majesty included."

The king looked down as if ashamed, and Mr. Gribs's features twisted with horror. "D-dead?" he stammered out.

"Yes, Mr. Gribs. I suppose it was hard to notice while you were busy doting on your adoring fans."

The nightmare flushed with embarrassment and went to fiddling with the brass buttons of his coat since there were no satchel straps to wring out this time. "But they seem so lively. I thought perhaps..." He trailed off as realization sobered his expression.

Etcher watched him closely. *I know, little toad. You thought perhaps we were simply misinformed and this wasn't just a prison for the damned.*

"Have you been sent by the gods to judge me? Or is there something else you seek?"

Her ears prickled; was there a hidden meaning to his words? "Your fate is yet to be seen,"—*though I am considering eating you,*—"but there is something that might sway my judgment." She watched the king studiously as he straightened and as she continued to circle she felt a ripple of hunger. The *Mad King* was close enough to a poltergeist, surely? "A young man came through here. Would you happen to know anything about it?"

"There has been no one else but you and your"—the king considered Mr. Gribs for a moment—"*escort* in nearly ten years."

"So I've heard. But you see, I have it on good authority that he came through here, and I would hate to find out I've been deliberately misinformed."

"What are you suggesting?" The king's tone became cold.

Such a sharp transition, thought Etcher. There was no blending of his prior diminutive demeanor into the new callous one, and that set Etcher's mind wondering.

She smiled—and there was little pretense of compassion left as she dropped her own guise, her smile was a baring of teeth. "Forgive me. I've offended your honor. It's just that my good authority came from another envoy of the gods, so now I am put in the unenviable position of wondering who—if any—has lied to me."

"You are welcome to search the isle, but I assure you, no man has come through here."

Etcher bowed. "Thank you. I will be searching, and I will be determining my judgment as I go."

"Then take all the time you need." The king spread his hands wide as if to illustrate he had nothing to hide.

"You are too kind." Etcher turned to leave. "By the way, where might I meet this Grand Vizier of yours? I should like to question him as well. Perhaps he might have seen something that you did not."

The king did not reply immediately. He was watching them both carefully, weighing them in his mind. "The Grand Vizier is a busy man."

"Busier than the king?"

Tension flexed the king's jaw, but in an instant, it was gone. "The Grand Vizier works to understand the shield that binds us here."

"To bring Arcadia to all?"

And again the Mad King changed, becoming uncomfortably sober. A weightiness beyond pretense of reality bared down on him. He spoke with the disappointment of one who knew his struggles could not be comprehended by such outsiders. "The Grand Vizier studies the shield so that we might be free."

It was not the answer Etcher was expecting.

"Why am I here?" asked Jerro. It had taken a while for words to come back to him. He had felt stripped of everything when he was drifting through the void, as if being cleansed, and the pieces had only come back with effort.

Because I wished to speak with you, replied Sovereignce; her words flittered into Jerro's mind musically, but they felt as though they had been summoned from a long ways away. Even though she walked beside him, it was hard to feel as though she was truly *there.* At odd angles she was a beautiful, fair-haired woman, and at others she was a giant white fox with many undulating tails; it was as though he were looking at her through a kaleidoscope. They had continued along the bone-white bridge through the ever-shifting expanse, watching as personal dreams shaped the floating isles that dotted the skies.

Jerro waited for Sovereignce to continue speaking; he was so much calmer now—less impetuous. He watched Sovereignce and watched the world around her. Wherever she walked, she left a trail of peace and restitution behind her. It felt as though the world rippled, like a shiver of pleasure, at her very presence.

I was vain in my youth. I made a terrible mistake that has haunted me for the rest of my days. She paused, and the shapely railing of the bridge quivered and reformed into an opening. Then wide, flat stones appeared in procession along the Ocean of Dream and led out toward the horizon. *Come, I must show you something.* She jumped from the bridge to the stone plateau as though in slow motion, appearing to glide as delicately as a feather caught on a breeze as she alighted atop the platform.

Jerro jumped to follow her, venturing into the vast blue. As they proceeded from stepping stone to stepping stone, the plateaus behind them vanished, sinking beneath the rippling sapphire-blue tides of the Dream Ocean. Jerro felt a rush and a breeze roll over him as he walked above the tides. The endless abyss called to him with its magnitude. He felt as though the waves were washing over him, filling in all the gaps and holes and making him feel a oneness he had seldom ever felt. He was complete, and he was pure.

They were coming up to the shoreline of a rocky and jagged isle. Thick clouds started to roll in overhead, rumbling with the threat of a storm. The isle, a mass of vicious crags jutting out of the ocean, loomed before them. There was a wide black gape near the top of the landmass, and Jerro could hear as much as feel the menace—like creeping whispers—seeping out from it as dark mist might tumble out from the open mouth of a wakened volcano.

He was thankful that they remained on their stony pedestal, watching from nearly a mile away. Just looking at the isle filled him with dread. The rumble of thunder was getting stronger, and the jagged cracks of silent lightning zigzagged through the encumbered clouds.

I had thought once that Nightmare had no place in Dream—that it could not serve a function other than to incite terror and conflict. I had even ventured to prove my point and denied its passage to the place you know as Undercity. It was Arcadia in my day—a place of peace and virtue.

Jerro stared into the dark, jagged isle, and it as much stared back into him. He felt the anger and the rage boil deeper within its bowels. The Isle of Nightmare looked more like a wound inflicted upon the realm, oozing with its menace like a pustule sore. His heart quickened, and with each pulse, it felt as though the isle drew that much closer.

I should never have tried to balance the scales in my favor. She waved away the isle, and they were once more on the Terriss Walk, safe and serene.

But Jerro could still feel the last lingering tendrils of dread slither through him, slow to fade away. He peered out into the ocean, but the Isle of Nightmare was nowhere to be seen. Yet it had marred the Dream realm for him, knowing that it existed somewhere out there.

He sought to educate me. And in doing so, he took the place that I had helped mold in an ambitious king's mind and cut me off from it as I had done to him. But it must stop now. It has to stop. I wish to ask for forgiveness, but he will not see me. Please, you must give him this. She cupped together her hands, and within them appeared a delicate yellow rose with twinkling dewdrops gathered along the petals.

Jerro took the rose from her; he looked up as both the face of the woman and the fox stared back into his own. "But I am dying." There again was the strange symbol branded into his wrists, but they weren't fading away anymore. They were there, and they were real. He felt a cold emptiness spread out from the branding; it slowly snaked up his arms and to the tips of his fingers.

You haven't long. Sovereignce touched the marks, and the emptiness slowed. She pulled the symbol from his flesh and held it in the air between them; she regarded it carefully and then whisked it away. *She will find you soon enough.*

"Who will?"

The Keeper. She will be among you soon.

The king had watched the visitors go. He retraced his steps to the throne and glanced at the shadows beside him once he was alone. "How many more will come?"

"No more, sire. Once the soul is pulled from the boy, the isle will be strong again," someone with a calm, attractive voice said from the shadows. Beautiful eyes looked out from the dark and watched the king steadily.

"And what of them?"

"Do you seek to use them too?"

"Only the woman. The other has a strange resonance to him—similar to your own."

The voice hissed. "He is *nothing* like me, sire."

"Forgive me, old friend, I did not wish to offend you." The king sat down on his throne and tapped the end of his staff against the floor in contemplation. "But we must have that woman's soul. It is *old*."

"Older than yours, sire?"

"Much older." The king turned to look at the darkness from where the voice came. "Can you do it?"

"Of course." The beautiful eyes blinked slowly. "She has only to come to me, and I'm confident that she will."

The king nodded. "It will be done, then. She will be the last."

"Sire?"

The king slumped back heavily into his throne. "All those souls that have had to be sacrificed to keep Arcadia safe, to revert the aging—no more. With a soul like hers, we could restore all the spirits to their youth and keep Arcadia strong. We will survive through the war and past oblivion until we are the last bastion of hope once the great destroyer cleans the slate."

"We are being lied to." Etcher had not spoken until they had left the cathedral and were well away from everyone else on the outskirts of the city. The sprawl of Arcadia covered a majority of the isle and even nestled up against the coastline and cliff edges in certain places. She needed a moment away from prying ears to gather her thoughts. Jerro was here; she knew he was, but where? She had tried to call a hazua in the hopes of delivering a message to him but nothing came, vexing her further. The isle was blocking the ability.

She had found the ruins of an outdoor amphitheater where the city dwellers seemed to steer clear of. She didn't blame them—it was a part of the isle that actually felt dead, another little bit of the city that had been slowly crumbling away. And yet, here too, she saw the dust motes reforming. She had a theory, and she didn't like it.

Mr. Gribs fidgeted with his clothes and toyed with his hands as though he wasn't sure how to stand comfortably in his new skin. "How do you know?" he dared to ask.

Etcher shot him a bemused look. "Were you listening at all back there in the cathedral? Or was our guide's infatuation with you too distracting?"

"W-well, I mean…um…" He rubbed the back of his head bashfully, tousling his blond hair and looking boyish and coy.

Etcher rolled her eyes and sat down on the top row of the deserted amphitheater. She stared out into the ocean, her thoughts drifting. "Jerro's essence is here—I can feel it. The only problem is I don't know *where* exactly. And that king, so noble and dutiful, is *lying* to not just his people but to us as well."

The princely nightmare found himself feeling awkwardly exposed, being the only one standing, and chose the row just below Etcher to seat himself. He looked back at her with a mix unease and contemplation. "I had no idea they were all dead, and I-I mean, I should have known, but I had hoped perhaps…" He paused and stared off somberly.

"It's all right, Mr. Gribs. I'm just swiftly losing my patience with this whole affair." She leaned forward, and she dropped her tone so that Mr. Gribs would listen close. "The king has all these people believing they are alive and well on some paradise isle, but that isn't the worst of it."

"What could be worse?" Dread had drained the color from his handsome cheeks.

"They are stuck in a loop. That Elwa said their *Grand Vizier* came here nearly ten years ago, but no one has been down to Undercity for millennia, let alone found their way into *Arcadia*. I think their memories are being recycled to make them think they've only been here for a short time—that this supposed Third Alliance War is still going. And another thing—where are all the slaves? Ten thousand Dahl'Kir slaves were said to have been brought into Undercity after their liberation in the Second War, so where are they now? This population is exceedingly too small for as many people as were in Undercity before it closed itself off from the rest of the world."

"I don't know." Mr. Gribs had that worried look on his face. "But why would their memories be *recycled,* as you say?"

"To slow the rotting. These spirits should have all turned into poltergeists or worse by now. Souls cannot linger outside of Death without turning. They decay. They lose their sense of self. This whole island stinks of rot, but somehow the king is managing to keep them from degrading too quickly. And for all the rot that's here, the king is remarkably vibrant. He isn't decaying at all, but the rest of his people are. So, then, you ask me why I think he's lying? I ask you, how can you think he's not?"

Mr. Gribs looked down at his shoes. "I didn't know."

She waved her hand dismissively. "Forget it. At any rate, it's not my main concern. All right, enough dawdling. I aim to find my friend, and I've an inkling of where to start."

"W-where might that be, exactly?"

"If we find the Grand Vizier, I assume I may find some more answers."

"How? The king didn't tell us where the Grand Vizier was."

"No, but I imagine our informative guide might bring us to him." She grinned at Mr. Gribs wickedly. "She took quite the fancy to you after all."

Mr. Gribs turned a ghastly pallor and looked as if he might faint.

"Messengers from the gods?"

"What did they say?"

"Oh, what was that handsome one's name?"

"Handsome? What about the woman?"

"I liked her."

"I liked them both!"

The chatter was rippling through the small gaggle of young men and women that had gathered around Elwa once she had returned to the town square. They had followed her back to a courtyard where trees offered a pleasant shade and they could lazily watch the fish swim inside the courtyard ponds.

Elwa was draped across a lounge seat and was picking grapes idly from a thick bundle that was spilling over the cornucopia beside her. "I don't know his name," she said with a dreamy sigh. "But he looked at me with those beautiful eyes and smiled."

The *oohs* and *aahs* spread throughout the crowd and tapered off into little private conversations. Some of the young men and women lay on the floor, draped in each other's laps, while others fanned themselves delicately beside a fountain. They were all luxuriously sprawled out across the courtyard as if they were a part of a scene in a classical painting.

"Look!" said one of the young men, who was perched on his elbows and dressed more effeminately than his female companions, his makeup glorious and unchallenged. He whispered something to the youth beside him, and she whispered to the next. And the whisper continued to be spread to the others until it came all the way back to Elwa.

The golden-haired girl let out a soft gasp as the murmurs reached her and she looked over to the patio by an ivy-covered awning. The handsome messenger was standing there, looking boyish and bashful. He made a few steps toward Elwa, and her breath caught in her throat. He had come to *woo* her, surely. A princely envoy of the gods coming to profess his undying love? Ah! She could already see the wedding bells as he whisked her off her feet! *And the doves, they will fly—*

"Is he *admiring* himself?" said one of the women.

Elwa cocked her head in bewilderment as the messenger suddenly became infatuated with his own reflection.

Mr. Gribs hadn't realized just how much of a transformation he had undergone until he spied his own reflection in one of the ponds. At first, he nearly jumped, thinking someone was behind him, but he quickly realized the incredibly stunning face staring back at him was his own. *That's me?* he thought with utter amazement. A wide and magnificently white smile spread across his face. *I'm gorgeous!* He straightened his shoulders and turned his head this way and that as he examined every inch of his profile. *Well, Gribsy ol' toad, you're looking good now!* he professed to himself.

"*Ahem.*" A small cough sounded beside him. He nearly had a heart attack and then remembered how dashing he was and straightened himself out.

"Oh, hello, Elwon—*Elwa!* Sorry." He smiled sheepishly.

The golden-haired girl smiled back politely and rolled back and forth on the balls of her feet. "So?"

"So…" said Mr. Gribs. He tried one of those looks he believed to be known as a *smolder*, but since he had never smoldered at anyone before, he wasn't quite sure how to wear it, and the result was an awkward scrunching of his features that made him look slightly constipated.

"Are you unwell?" asked Elwa.

"What? N-no, I"—he cleared his throat—"I thought you might accompa-" he began, but his voice cracked and hit a cringe-worthy high note that brought on a bout of coughing. "I thought…thought you…" He held up a finger as he doubled over and coughed and sputtered until he hacked up something vile and spit it into the pond, which one of the fish then swallowed.

The girl looked as though she might faint.

"*Thought-you-might-accompany-me-to-the-Grand-Vizier!*" he forced out in one long breath.

Elwa smiled weakly and nodded as though in a daze. "S-sure."

In the bushes to the far back of the courtyard was Etcher, watching quietly from her hiding spot. She rubbed the side of her head and cringed as her keen ears heard every stumbling word that fell out of from Mr. Gribs's mouth. *Gods help me.*

Jerro had stood peering off the side of the Terriss Walk into the Ocean of Dream.

You are troubled, said Sovereignce as her refractive form came up beside him.

"I'm dying. Of course I'm troubled." He had felt heavy ever since they came back from the Isle of Nightmare. Slowly, like sand in an hour glass, he was returning to his old self again, and the calm serenity that had filled him before was swiftly pouring out.

Do not concern yourself with what happens among the flesh. Your journey is not quite finished here.

"What?"

Come. Though you must let another save your mortal vessel, that does not mean you must stand here and do nothing.

Jerro took the woman's outstretched hand, and the world melted away from him. A whirlwind of colors and shapes spun around him and slowly regathered into something tangible; it was like watching the world form in reverse. He had been transported to an oasis nestled in the middle of a vast, glittering desert. The clear sky was blanketed in a deep velvety blue, and the lunar bodies, which were set high in the mantle of night, shone down and bathed the world in their silver radiance.

He knew this place. He had seen it so many times when he was a boy. He stepped forward into the garden and followed the path. He walked by the stone woman who held up the dish with the crystalline water cascading over its circumference. He traced his way up the stairs and to the old oaken door with the big iron ring.

The soft, hushed sound of feathered wings came from behind him. He knew them too now, and he pulled open the door before the talons of a reaper could claim him.

He was standing again in the blackness of *Blank-Space.* He looked down and saw his reflection in the dark, mirrored ground. The reflection smiled back up at him and winked.

"Hello, Jerro," said the reflection.

Jerro tried to take a step back, but the image followed him, almost in perfect harmony save for its face that kept staring back at him so knowingly. "Who are you?"

"'*When* are you?' would make better sense," replied the reflection.

"All right, then…when are you?"

But the reflection merely smiled and started walking forward.

Jerro felt himself be dragged along with it. His body moved in time with his mirrored self, yet his head was allowed to move independently. "Where are you taking me?"

"Through time—toward the edge of the abyss."

"Why?"

The black void changed suddenly, and soon there was fire all around him. He was inside a jagged cave with spires and crags of black obsidian. His image littered the multifaceted faces of the stones, lit by the tongues of flame that danced all around though never seemed to touch. Some of his reflections looked directly at him; others were staring off and pointing.

He moved deeper within the cave and saw another him, but it wasn't a reflection this time; it was a second-self standing in the flesh across the way.

"That's you," said one of his reflections.

"Why are you showing me this?" Jerro asked.

"Keep watching."

The other-him had his back to Jerro. There was something sinister about his poise, though he wore Jerro's form the man was an imposter—he rolled his shoulders as though feeling his body out and looked over this shoulder.

Then came Etcher, walking up to the other Jerro with slow, calculated steps. She was speaking to the imposter, her expression was pained and a bitter smile spread across her mouth.

There was no sound, yet Jerro continued to watch in horrid fascination as his other-self turned and met Etcher's gaze with cold crimson eyes. The imposter grinned wickedly and beckoned Etcher closer.

He saw the imposter slip an arm around Etcher's waist and pull her in. Then the imposter plunged his hand into her chest and pulled out her heart. The little shopkeeper went limp and fell to the ground.

"No!" Jerro cried out.

"This is you. This is what you'll become," the reflections whispered.

The imposter met Jerro's mortified gaze and brought the heart up to his lips before sinking fanged teeth into the pulsing organ.

"This is what you'll become," the reflections continued on, snickering wickedly from all around Jerro.

"No..." said Jerro, his voice losing all its vigor.

"This is what you'll become."

"This is what you'll do."

"This is what you'll be."

But as the whispers continued to plague him, Jerro felt a hand gently touch his shoulder, and he whipped around.

"Don't listen to them, Jerro. You can choose. You don't have to be anything you don't want."

"*Liar!*"

"*Can't escape it!*"

The third-him smiled softly. It was Jerro's face, but it was slightly older and more refined.

Jerro asked, "Are you—"

"Come on. You don't need to stay here." His third-self beckoned Jerro to follow, and together they left the cave.

"What business do you have with the Grand Vizier?" Elwa had regained some of the color in her cheeks as they left the courtyard.

"Oh, you know…this and that." Mr. Gribs laughed weakly.

"This and that?"

Etcher sighed quietly to herself. She had swooped in to save Mr. Gribs from his own awful display and convinced Elwa to let her tag along. It was mortifying to watch the nightmare fumble over his words, and she had a feeling their guide was relieved to not be left alone with such a loon, handsome though he was. She felt Elwa's gaze drifting over to her—as if pleading for something more intelligible. "We'd like to check in with a fellow messenger."

"Oh. Of course." Elwa forced an overly wide smile as Mr. Gribs—her once princely dream of a man—stumbled over a rock and nearly fell face-first onto the ground.

Etcher winced internally. "So where is this vizier anyhow?" She grabbed back the attention of their slightly bewildered guide.

"He has a tower at the center of the isle. It's just behind the cathedral." She cast a withering glance at Mr. Gribs, who was trying to *smolder* once more. "We're nearly there," she said all too eagerly.

"Wonderful," said the little shopkeeper.

It was unsurprising why Etcher had neglected to see the "*tower*" before. The little brick column, about the width of an elevator shaft, wasn't even tall enough to break past the tree line. It was curiously bland compared to the rest of Arcadia's grandeur and almost completely hidden behind the cathedral.

There was an open archway at the front of the tower that led inside to a spiral set of stairs that led down as opposed to up. "The Grand Vizier lives underground?" Etcher inquired as if to herself as she stared into the depths. She felt a flicker of something prickle at her senses and *knew* Jerro was down there. "Well, come along, then."

"W-wait! We don't go down uninvited—"

"Then don't," Etcher replied as she ducked inside the tower.

Mr. Gribs ran a hand through his hair and checked his breath a little too loudly. "Now that we're alone—"

"Wait for me!" And Elwa bolted inside the tower.

The three of them progressed down the spiraling steps in relative silence. Mr. Gribs, who was at the rear, was looking rather put out and muttered to himself as he stared into the back of Elwa's golden head. Etcher was striding at the lead, feeling her *inkling* becoming stronger.

There was a sudden change of darkness to light as the steps let out into a vast circular room. Dazzling blue currents rippled across the ceiling, originating from a single spire of pure blue energy that shot upward from the middle of the room.

Etcher tensed as she saw the body lying directly beneath the current. Suspended above Jerro's limp form was a small chunk of turquoise from which the energy seemed to originate. His own essence was slowly being sucked up into the levitating chunk of turquoise and drawn into the blue spire of energy as though the chunk were acting like a spiritual convex lens.

Before she could control herself, Etcher had dashed into the room only to become suddenly rooted to the spot. A symbol on the ground lit up the moment Etcher had set foot in the chamber; it looked uncannily similar to the pattern on the ghost seal. *Damn it all!* Etcher chided herself; she had been too impetuous.

"Miss Everdoor!" called out Mr. Gribs as he cowered in the doorframe.

"What's going on?" Elwa had stumbled into the room after Etcher, and then she saw the young man lying on the middle of the floor. *Now there's someone dreamy*—her eyes seemed to say, uncaring of the fact that the young man was unconscious and that some very strange happenings were going on.

"Well, well, I see you've managed to cause quite the disturbance in my quiet little kingdom," said the Mad King as he slunk out from the shadows.

"Majesty?" Elwa inquired with bewilderment.

The Mad King put up his hand to silence her. His hair was looking a little wilder, and his eyes a little more feral. "Pity you came here, Elwa. I did not want to have to show you these awful things."

"Gah! Un-unhand me...won't you?" Mr. Gribs had been carried out of the doorway by another tall and handsome man who had incredibly beautiful eyes.

Elwa backed away as Mr. Gribs was dragged in by his collar. "Grand Vizier?" she said.

The unnaturally attractive Grand Vizier flicked his sultry eyes over to Elwa—who nearly swooned—and then he said. "Elwa, dear?"

"Yes, Grand Vizier?" She said, showing a blithe disregard to the fact that there was a body on the ground, Etcher was stuck on the spot, and her *no-longer-quite-so-charming* prince was being held by the scruff of his neck. Her attention had been solely focused on the beauteous man.

"Do you fancy him now?" The Grand Vizier shook Mr. Gribs, and Elwa gave out a frightful shriek.

"W-what's wrong?" croaked Mr. Gribs as he watched Elwa turn tail and run back up the spiral steps. He noticed his feet were no longer touching the ground, and when he looked down at himself, he realized he wasn't quite so dashing anymore. "Oh dear." He sighed heavily.

"Lor, what *is* that?" said the Mad King at the sight of Mr. Gribs's portly, toadish form.

"Nothing but a false prophet, sire!" The Grand Vizier glared down at Mr. Gribs. "*What in all of night are you doing here?*" he hissed in a whisper.

"Fillabir? Is that you? I thought you got transferred to grounds keeping?"

"*This* is *grounds keeping, you idiot! Now shuddup!*"

"What's going on, Lor? Put that thing down already. It's time!"

"Yes, sire!"

"And what are *you* sneering about?" the Mad King said as he approached Etcher.

"Oh, nothing—just that your *Grand Vizier* is actually a nightmare in disguise." Her eyes flicked over to Lor. "What I can't quite place is *why* the King of Nightmare is so adamant about keeping all these souls trapped here. Quite the costly venture too, wasn't it?" She returned her attention to the Mad King. "What was it exactly? About ten-thousand slaves and about two-thirds the populace to get this place up and running?"

"You know nothing of these matters!" the Mad King growled.

"And I'll dare to speculate on something else," she continued on, unabashed by the king's vehement glare, "when they first told you about this whole Third War you thought to yourself, *'perfect opportunity to start hoarding some treasure'*, am I right?"

"We were preserving Eclipse's history!" The king's voice became shrill and his eyes darted over to the masked nightmare currently known as Lor.

"I imagine your people found that a far more convincing lie than I do, when you had them start piling up the gold and jewels." Etcher sneered as much as her paralyzed state would allow.

"Don't listen to her, sire, she's just another false prophet." Lor sniffed.

"Then reveal her so we can extract her soul!"

Etcher's ears twitched and a ghost of a smile touched her lips. "That is a spectacularly *bad* idea."

"We shall see. Lor?" The Mad King stepped aside and let the masked nightmare take up the spot in front of Etcher.

The nightmare held out his hands and began to chant, murmuring low as his eyes rolled back and became white.

"I really wouldn't advise this," Etcher warned them both. She could feel the *majik* start to seep into her. "This is your last chance," her body started to quiver and her joints began to pop.

"There will be an endless paradise," the Mad King mused to himself, unhearing and uncaring of Etcher's cautioning. "We shall sail past oblivion into a bright new future and be restored once and for all..."

The masked nightmare was having trouble *revealing* the little shopkeeper, however, and the Mad King took note of it. "What are you doing? Don't stop. We *must* have her soul. I will not sacrifice any more of my people. We need her living essence."

"She is heavily guarded, sire, as though her true form is locked away." There was the slightest hint of exhaustion in his tone.

"Then break down her guards!"

Lor started chanting once again, physically struggling as he fought to break down the guards that kept Etcher's true self hidden away. The masked nightmare focused hard, and when he looked as though he might pass out there was a crackling *snap*—like the sound of a *majik* seal breaking.

Etcher started laughing, but it was a sound far more grave and menacing than her usual impish chitter. Her teeth were bared in a snarl, and her mouth had contorted into something hideously wide.

Mr. Gribs whimpered in a corner. He had a terrible feeling of what was about to happen next.

Etcher's chest was heaving, and her gaze were cast down. "Don't say I didn't warn you." She stared up at them then; her golden eyes twinkled with a dreadful glee. Then her body began to change.

Up and up she lengthened. Her body darkened, turning black as horns coiled out from her head and her face elongated into something equine and skeletal. Her rib cage protruded, cracking and popping as it inflated. Her waist and hips became thin and bony, and the rest of her turned sinewy and long.

The symbol that had rooted the little shopkeeper could not contain all of Etcher's new form, and the ground cracked, breaking the *majik* that had been inscribed onto the floor, setting her free.

"By the gods...what have I done?" The Mad King's voice was barely a whisper as he cowered before Etcher's rapidly growing form.

The masked nightmare currently known as Lor finally cracked from his beauteous image and turned into a small, gangly-looking lizard with a few too many legs and eyes. "I'm out of here!" his thin voice squeaked, and he got down on his belly and scurried away, knocking back Mr. Gribs as he hurried up the stairwell.

"W-wait for me, Fillabir!" The portly little nightmare was not about to stand around for the horror show, and he took off as well.

"Lor! *Lor!* Don't leave me, Lor!" The Mad King shrank to his knees as his neck craned up to look at the horrifying new entity before him.

Still Etcher grew, and the vast chamber was no longer big enough. It burst open, quaking the ground. The cathedral above was blown apart, scattering monstrous chunks throughout the isle as the people outside finally snapped out of their indifferent stupor and started running for their undead lives.

Etcher straightened and shook out her wild, tousled mane, grinning devilishly with her long, skeletal face and yet still managing to look just a touch regal. She levitated. Her long deviltail coiled about her demonic legs, and she folded her arms imposingly.

The creature that had taken place of the little shopkeeper was great and terrible, demonic with its skeletal features and coiling horns yet grand with the noble tilt of its chin and proud stature. Its ebony skin was so dark it seemed to choke out the light that touched it, and the raw power that emanated from its very being put a deep and dire dread into all that beheld it.

The demon looked down at the tiny speck of a king. It unfurled its great sinewy arms and reached down as the tiny lord cowered and blathered. But it didn't reach for him; it plucked the little stone that had hovered above Jerro, ripping it out from the spire of energy that suspended it in the air.

The energy flashed, and the isle trembled. "I'll be taking this." The demon's words were a sonorous boom. It scooped up the limp body of Jerro and cradled him close to its chest. Then the terrifying mouth of the demon opened wide, and it breathed in, pulling in air like a furious gale.

The souls of Arcadia were sucked up in a wild torrent, settling within the demon's lungs. The unbridled power of the beast amplified, and the marble buildings shook and crumbled until the isle itself began to tear apart.

Shee'Den had felt the tremor ripple through the dome; it even shook the walls of the chasm and sent the other Oolkas flailing as the air currents violently changed. Then the dome of light that had protected the isle of Arcadia for millennia shattered into a hundred thousand glimmering shards, and a great beast floated at the center of the destruction.

The bones of the bridge and the isle itself crumbled and fell into the void of the gorge until there was nothing left of Arcadia—only the immense demonic entity, which stood suspended in the air.

The Oolkas scrambled to get their bearings, buffeted by the waves of terrifying force that rolled off the Soul Eater's *other* self.

"Where are the souls-!? You promised you would free them!" called Shee'Den over the rumbling of earth.

The Soul Eater opened its terrifying maw and blew out its breath, scattering thousands of souls into the air. They whipped about like a whirlwind of fireflies, and the Oolkas dove in to gather them up. But when the very last spirit left the Soul Eater's mouth, the demon snatched it between two fingers, holding it back from the rest.

"We had a deal! You cannot take even one!"

"I can take those who are indebted to me. *That* was our deal, and *this* soul owes me gravely." The Soul Eater's voice reverberated along the canyon walls and made the Oolkas skitter away. The demon opened its mouth and held its fingers above its gaping maw before dropping in the soul of the Mad King and gulping him down.

"You tricked me Oullakkan! You will pay!" called back Shee'Den as it hurried away with the other Oolkas.

When the walls had finally stopped quaking, the demon peered over to the lip on the inside of the canyon wall that had once connected to the bone bridge. A tiny, toadish form stood quivering in the archway of the darkened hall. The demon smiled, although with its equine skeletal face, it was hard to know when it *wasn't* smiling. "How forgiving do you think the Ledgerman will be now?" The demon flicked its wrist, and Mr. Gribs was sent somewhere far away.

The Oolkas had fled, taking with them the souls of Arcadia and returning them to the land of the Dead. The Soul Eater remained in the gorge for a moment and turned one of its golden eyes back to the tiny opening along the inside of the canyon wall.

One last spirit remained, poking its head out from the shadows of the hall. "I won't eat *you*, if you were wondering." The demon's powerful voice resonated throughout the canyon.

The last spirit stepped onto the ledge and pointed up at the hand that the demon held close to its chest.

"Oh, I see. No, I won't be eating him either."

The demon lowered its free hand, and the last spirit climbed onto its palm. The demon then brought the soul up and let it climb over to where a limp and lifeless Jerro was laying.

The spirit knelt down and touched Jerro's shoulder before looking up into the mighty face of the demon.

"I'll let him know."

The spirit then tipped its hat and faded away.

CHAUNCY FELISZ

Thursday...

Jerro felt himself being drawn upward as the weight of reality settled over him once more. His eyes cracked open slowly, and he blinked to adjust to the light. He saw a hazy blue sky above him that was streaked with white clouds. He lifted an arm sluggishly, feeling as though it had been turned to pure lead. With great effort, he managed to scrub his face, then remained there blinking, thoughts unfocused.

It wasn't a sky he was looking up at but the pale-blue ceiling and white rafters of his room in Etcher's shop. He pushed himself up by his elbows and looked about the room. Fragmented memories trickled back to him, but there were holes in his recollection, and all the pieces seemed to bleed together, making it difficult to know what was dream and what was reality.

He rubbed his wrists absently and saw the ghost of a mark on them both; they were slowly healing in the flesh. He stared at them for a while and tried to recall what had happened. There had been a woman—or a fox, maybe. And he remembered seeing himself though he didn't like what he saw.

His attention was drawn to the bedside dresser after what felt like an age. There was a newspaper along with his phone and a little sticky note, written in a tall elegant script that read:

The gardener says he owes you one.

(The gardener says he owes you one)

He slid the phone off the paper and stuck the sticky note to the table, then gathered up the tabloid, peering vacantly for a few moments at the article that had been circled.

Etcher was sitting in one of the lounge areas that was nestled in the northwestern corner of the shop. She was thumbing through a haggard-looking paperback, sipping from a steaming cup of tea as she read. Tahli was also with her, perched in the adjacent armchair. The ginger feline was busing herself with an emery board that she used to shape her long fingernails.

It was from the balcony that Jerro spied them, and he held up the paper. "What's this?" he called down to them, slowly making his way over to the spiral staircase so he could descend into the shop.

Etcher looked over the top of her book and smiled at Jerro as he headed down the cast iron steps. "I thought it might be easier to find our culprit if you weren't also on the run as the prime suspect." Etcher placed her cup in its saucer and rose to her feet.

"*How* did you manage it?" Jerro asked. He was still holding up the *Midgardian Times* with the circled news article that stated that the case of the Kairos Global break-in had been closed and that a certain Edik Bosko had confessed to the crime.

Etcher's smile grew sly. "Well, I merely suggested to Johan Lapaul that it was in his best interest to clear up the case and that he had the wrong man pinned anyhow."

"Yeah, but *how*? *When*?" Jerro was gaping at her with a mix of bewilderment and glee.

She winked at him. "With the right leverage, Jerro, anything is possible. As for when, well…it was that first night after you made the deal. I decided to make a pit stop while you were sleeping. Took Johan long enough to find a way to wrap it up, though, if you ask me."

"So I'm good? No more police coming after me? I'm not a fugitive anymore?"

"Well, I can't promise that no one will come after you. There is still the matter of whoever set you up running free. It wasn't the cleaning man, if you were wondering. But for right now, you are currently *not* wanted for questioning or incarceration."

Jerro felt a sigh of relief well up inside him, and he let it out, feeling good—really good—for the first time in a long time.

"I'm afraid you've been let go from your job, however, though I am assured the severance package is quite agreeable."

"I hated that job anyhow." He waved his hand dismissively. He didn't care about that, not when he was a free man once more and had narrowly missed going to jail yet again. Reedman must have been livid, which gave him just a touch more satisfaction to think about. "You didn't have to, ya know. That wasn't the deal, remember?"

Etcher shrugged. "Ah well, I recall saying something similar, and yet you tagged along anyway. At any rate, I thought perhaps since you are not a wanted man, we could make a stop back in your hometown. I believe there was mention of a birthday coming up this weekend?"

"*My* hometown? You mean…?"

"Take a look." Etcher motioned to the Greenman door.

Jerro strode toward it and pulled it open without a second thought. He was greeted by a rolling hillside, looking down into the small, nestled community of Fenris County and the murky glimmer of the North Sea. Jerro walked out onto the grassy hillside and grinned wildly.

"Pretty little place. That's your mom's house, isn't it? Along that narrow coiling road?" said Etcher as she came up behind him. A breeze had rolled up the hill and made the daisies dance with the sway of the grass.

He looked back and saw the Greenman door nestled into the side of an old wooden shack. The door was wide open, revealing the impossibly large space within. It was such a fine thread that separated reality from *Blank-Space*. He grinned at the shopkeeper and looked back toward the small sprawl of houses. Sure enough, he saw his mom's yellow bungalow with its neatly manicured garden just down the way. "How did you—"

"You've been passed out since yesterday evening. I had enough time to snoop around."

"What happened anyway?" His memory was all too hazy to really know what had gone down. He remembered the ghost seal on the isle and running from the Oolkas and tangled pieces of something *else*, but he was missing large chunks of recollection and had the distinct notion that he had missed out on something *big*.

"Well, from what I gathered, you got sucked into Arcadia—that's what that strange floating isle was called—and were kidnapped by the Mad King. He wanted to use your soul to stop the isle from crumbling."

Jerro's brow knit together as he realized there was a *lot* he had missed out on.

"Everdoor saved you and brought you back to the shop. What else do you need to know?" Tahli said in her musical lilt as she slunk up to the door and leaned against its frame.

Jerro studied the feline carefully but was too overjoyed to be alive and *free* to let her mocking tone rile him. "That simple, huh?" He laughed and held up his hands. "Okay, fine. Although I expect to hear the whole story eventually." Turning his attention back to the little shopkeeper, he asked, "More importantly, though, did you get it?"

Etcher grinned and produced a small turquoise stone that had been cut into a rectangular slab and engraved with the effigy of a little winged dog. "Yes, I most certainly did." She turned the Death Token in the light to admire it and then vanished it away. "Tricky thing, really. The Mad King was using it to keep the Oolkas out. Much like a key's ability to open a door, it can also lock one as well."

"Huh." Jerro felt something untangle in his memory, but it was quickly whisked away by a buzzing coming from his pocket. He pulled out his phone as a bombardment of missed messages and calls finally caught up to his device now that it was back within signal range. "Jeez." He grimaced as he saw the screen become littered with notifications. "Hey, how'd you charge it anyway? There're no plugs anywhere."

"I had it modified. I figured since it's akin to our jin'hazuas, it was fairly important to you, but it's hardly as efficient. That thing barely holds enough energy to run for a full day."

"Modified it how?" He stared between the phone and Etcher dubiously.

"Had an engineer friend of mine fix it up. It uses ginse coins now. It won't run out of energy anymore."

Jerro was just about to express his thanks when the phone started ringing. Mahra's name flooded the screen. He felt himself wince internally; of all the people who had to deal with the backlash of Jerro's few days of being a fugitive, Mahra was one of the least deserving of them all. "Hey, I better take this."

Etcher nodded and beckoned Tahli back inside, practically dragging the curious feline away so Jerro could have some privacy.

He steeled himself as he stared at the phone. He would need to pick up the pieces and restore order to his life; this was as good a place as any to start. The tumultuous mixture of his thoughts and anxieties, however, were threatening to coalesce the longer he remained standing there in contemplative indecision.

And Mahra's name continued to blink on screen, waiting for him to answer the call.

The Owl's Court

For Grandma Judy, who taught me that you're never too old...

Preface

𐎅𐎁𐎜𐎂𐎀𐎅𐎁

He steeled himself as he stared at the phone.

Mahra's name filled the screen, big and urgent, summoning an uncomfortable pang of guilt to strum through him. And suddenly all his mettle abandoned him. A noxious cocktail of emotions bubbled away in his gut as he looked down at the angrily buzzing device that was threatening to spring loose from his sweaty palm. It was time to start putting the pieces of his life back together, or at least try and instill some semblance of it into place. He thumbed the answer button with nervous gusto lest the device acquire a mind of its own and lunge out of his hand.

And there his thoughts became nullified, leaving only a petrifying blank as the soft hiss of white noise slithered down his ear canal, searching for a voice to fill the void. What the hell was he supposed to say? *Sorry I vanished for three days, I met an intergalactic thief with a dimension-hopping potion shop and got caught up robbing an ancient underground city.* And what about the police investigation? *Yeah…I didn't actually steal from work but I am a bit of a crook.*

He settled on croaking out a shaky "…Hello?"

"…*Jerro?*" croaked back Mahra from the other end of the line.

She's been crying, he thought, and his guilt strummed out a solo on his weighty heart. It had been some time since he'd got the call from a heartbroken fling, though it didn't take long for guilt to tune the cords and revive old melodies. Calling Mahra a fling was generous though; their fleeting moment of intimacy had been a simple kiss—which Jerro tacked like a note to Mahra's cheek— marking her for later review. He had hoped to continue his appraisal at her place, since his flatmate Kristoff made any addendum to Jerro's note damn near impossible.

Jealous prick, Jerro thought, and realized that as his mind wandered, and as he shamelessly fantasized about the inside of Mahra's bedroom—or otherwise—the white noise serpent had returned, awaiting his response.

"Mahra? What's wrong?"

A quiet sob came as reply. He could hear Mahra take a few audible breaths.

"*Jerro...I'm so sorry to call like this...*" There was something ominous in her tone.

Guilt, sensing that something greater had spurred the call, departed and let in panic on the way out. Panic didn't play a soulful melody on Jerro's vital organs, rather, it came in bashing his ribcage and pulling the switches on fire alarms, yelling, "*Something's very wrong!*" To which his outward façade remained indifferent to.

Then he heard her take in a sharp breath. "*I-I think I'm in trouble.*" And with that her tears rolled out freely in heavy, ragged sobs.

There was a winter chill in the air, and a cold grayness to the world. The mountains in the backdrop of the sky were pale and distant, barely visible over the lip of the high colosseum walls.

And there was blood, staining the rough stone ground.

Black feathers dappled with white and gold drifted through the frigid air like falling snow. Along the seats of the gray colosseum, the Oolkas had gathered, quietly stationed as they spectated the scene. Their immense owlish forms were nestled together, and together they stared down their vicious hooked beaks into the carnage that the demon thief had wrought.

"*Etcher Everdoor,*" spoke the enthroned Oolka with a voice like boulders crashing. He was not like the other reaper owls that were nestled in the tiered seats; his body—lacking solidity—was encased in stark white armor, almost as if he were a man. But the body that possessed the suit was nothing more than wispy black smoke, and within the hollow helm, where tendrils of the ethereal body drifted out, were two glinting lights like stars set in a dark void. The armored Oolka held a gavel in one gauntleted hand, and a lance in the other, and on his back was a folded set of black wings, dappled in white and gold.

Etcher Everdoor knelt in the middle of the colosseum, amidst the blood and wreckage and falling feathers. Her wrists had been shackled together with heavy manacles. Crimson stains were smeared along her face, her hair, her clothes, her hands. She bared her teeth in an angry snarl and her chest moved steadily with seething breaths.

Beside her stood more armored Oolkas, though their suits were plainer than the grand white judge who sat in the high throne. The guards looked more like they had been hewn from stone, laced with little glowing lines of *majik*, and they held crude spears in their armored hands. Black smoke swirled within their helms too, and little winking starlight eyes stared out with rigid focus.

The demon thief was also changed. No longer the petite little shopkeeper, she was gangly and tall. Her flamboyant clothes had been replaced by a strange inky substance that hugged her boney contours as though she had been dipped in tar. Her hair had turned so black it seemed to consume the light, and it hung limp and matted with Oolka blood to one side like a horse's mane, and from either side of her head where the hair had left her bald, were coiling demon horns. She stared up at the white judge, her honey-gold eyes ablaze and full of wild malice.

"*You have been charged with violating the Goodfellow Treaty,*" continued the white judge, his deep resonant voice echoing throughout the colosseum. "*You have been charged with the unlawful attack against the Oolkas, entering Death without valid consent, and harboring a fugitive reborn. The punishment for which is eternal imprisonment in the Under Realms, where not even you can escape, Oullakkan. How do you plead?*"

CHAUNCY FELISZ

Crown of Caster

(Calda) Toronto

Sinaku

Yahre

Kingdom of Gep

Bellay

Belloan

Leburah

Darewood

Gahza'Dune

Undereily

Kingdom of
Inblan

Produo

Kingdom of Enllis

Canya Cemele

Thursday...

Mahra put down the phone on the kitchen counter, letting the last few sobs rattle out of her as the tension melted away from her face. She glanced at her reflection in the hallway mirror and smiled at herself.

Her eyes were tearstained and gleamed like polished glass. Her long blonde hair had the appropriate amount of tussle for a poor frightened damsel who had been holed up in their apartment. She wore only a touch of makeup, a little eyebrow liner and mascara.

The outfit had been meticulously chosen. She wore thick woolen socks that came up to her knees and a long baggy jumper that went midway to her naked thighs. A comfort jumper, aptly appropriate for a sad and vulnerable Mahra.

And then, of course, there was the star of the show: the pink cotton undies. They could be seen only vaguely through the open weave of the jumper, but on occasion, when the baggy garment hitched up, the flash of pink was unmistakable.

No leggings, of course—the thigh-length jumper and long socks were a replacement for that—and since the aim of the outfit was to look comfortable yet unintentionally provocative, it was a winning combination. With a big sad-eyed Mahra face looking helpless, if not innocent, the outfit was believably without ulterior motive. Even the pink cotton undies were girlish enough to seem modest.

To fully pull off the act, however, staging was key. There were things that Mahra would have done—the real Mahra that is—that would help solidify the image of a benign damsel awaiting her rescue. The real Mahra would have put the kettle on, had tissues stuffed in the sleeve of her baggy jumper, and had cheesy horror movies playing on the flat screen in the living room. So, it was precisely what the doppelgänger did.

The doppelgänger filled the kettle and set it on the stove, clicked on the tele, flipped through the channels, and found an old black-and-white vampire film. Then the imposter decided to take a trip to the bedroom closet where the real Mahra lay catatonic.

The doppelgänger opened the door slowly and knelt down beside Mahra, smiling wickedly at her expressionless face and vacant eyes. The creature moistened its stolen lips with its stolen tongue and whispered into the real Mahra's ear, *"Your boyfriend's coming to save me from the big bad monster."*

The wild and panicked thoughts of the real Mahra stumbled within the darkness, tripping on the gnarled roots of disembodied sounds that trickled in from the outside world. Mahra's inner self shuddered as she heard her own stolen voice speaking to her. With no touch or taste or vision to ground her, Mahra was trapped inside her own lightless mind. No matter how much Mahra screamed, or kicked, or raged inside her catatonic vessel, she could not plug back into her body and make it move. She was a prisoner, and Kyddr'Ith adored it.

Electrified by the succulent misery, Kyddr'Ith ran a finger over Mahra's cheek. The nail became a talon, and Kyddr'Ith made a hairline cut across Mahra's soft skin. The cherry-red line welled with little crimson beads as a grinning Kyddr'Ith pushed down on it.

"You know, I've had the most fun being you. And I have to say, you've got a great wardrobe to work with. The last person I was had a more sophisticated sense of fashion, of course, but they were such high maintenance. Brilliant teeth, perfect hair, tailored suits—admittedly, unremarkable. Not like you, though. You've got that natural prettiness that doesn't need much work. You underplay it, but it's there. It's just that shyness that keeps the boys from noticing you. But I suppose *this* one finally did," Kyddr'Ith said with a musical laugh. *"Too bad, Mahra, should have noticed you sooner. Ah well, I'll be sure to have fun in your place."*

Kyddr'Ith grinned viciously at the deep crippling depression that rolled in heavily over Mahra's mind and suffocated the poor girl's soul.

"You think this is pain? Just wait until he gets here…" said Kyddr'Ith, then the doppelgänger shut the closet door on Mahra for the last time.

Jerro was standing on the sidewalk of the bustling street, running his fingers absently through his tousle of black hair. Across the busy main road was the private entrance into the luxurious Glade Apartment community. The high walls spilled over with ivy growth and the overhanging boughs of reddening birch—which had been manicured to create an autumn colored canopy over the sidewalk. Behind Jerro, hidden in the shadows of an alley, was a large antique green door with a leafy face carved into its middle.

Jerro stood, quite literally, between worlds.

The Greenman door of Etcher's mystical shop stared out with its empty, wooden eyes. Behind the antique threshold was a place that existed in the back door of reality, in *Blank-Space*. Etcher's shop was a grand square chamber, its high ceiling enchanted to show the steel gray sky of the outside world. Neat rows of magical oddities lined the central gangway toward a large U-shaped display counter at the back, and behind it was the spiraling cast-iron stairwell, leading up to the generous encircling balcony of the upper level that was lined with identical mahogany doors. From the sky-ceiling, down the alabaster walls, and along the rich wooden floorboards, intricate silver lines of a magical star chart connected to an ornate nautical emblem embedded in the center of the shop floor. It was a place that had become like home.

Jerro chewed on his bottom lip as his pale lupine eyes stared vacantly, rooted in that place between the magical and mundane. He looked past the sleek electric cars that flooded the roads, beyond the sounds of horns blaring and the scent of dying foliage and apple blossoms tinged with motor oil and city dirt.

A clean city they called Midgard, and here, in the southern borough where the ritzy lived in fashionable homes with posh landscapes and hired help, where they had private gardens for the residents to walk their pretty little dogs, where there were quaint little corner shops and expensive eateries, here was supposed to be the cleanest of all.

But it stank.

It looked dull after all Jerro had seen, and even the air that he breathed, air that was so much cleaner than it had been thirty years ago, tasted sour on his tongue. He felt the city filth cling to him, gathering like dust over his skin and clothes, over his soul.

"Are you certain you don't want us coming with you?" said Etcher, who was leaning gracefully against the brick façade of the alley. She was inspecting her nails as she spoke, her slender spade-tipped deviltail coiling back and forth like a wisp of smoke.

The impish shopkeeper stood out sorely against the mundane foot traffic that passed them by. Morning commuters on their way to work, briefcases in hands, long bland coats to fight the early chill, downturned eyes, and sullen faces. Etcher was like an explosion of color against the dullness that surrounded them. Her femininely cut velvet waist coat was a deep emerald green with polished gold buttons and the chain of a gold pocket-watch to match, and her tight midnight blue pants were embroidered with intricate needlework stitched in shimmering gold thread. She wore a cream-colored blouse with billowy sleeves and a big lacy collar, making her appear as if she were ready for a masquerade ball, were it not for the shoes—which were a silly pair of green canvas slip-ons. To top off her extravagant outfit, she had long elven ears, calculating golden eyes flecked in green, and the elegant tumble of wavy chestnut hair—setting her all the more apart from the crowd.

"No, thanks, it's probably not a good idea. I think my friend might get angry if I showed up with two other women." He eyed them both warily.

Beside the little shopkeeper was Tahli, the ginger rat-woman, and by god did she stand out just as starkly. It wasn't just the cat ears and tail that contrasted her so vividly against the morning commuters; she was as tall as Jerro, for one, which put her at a solid six-foot-two, and she was curvaceous and busty, not to mention that she was covered in ginger fur, save for the white downy fluff that ran from her ample chest to navel, and of course, she wore no clothes. It was hard enough not to ogle at her inside Etcher's shop, but out there in the mundane, unmagical world she stood out like a bloody beacon.

It bothered Jerro greatly that he could still see them both as they were, while the crowd hardly gave them a passing glance. It made them seem like figments, like he was going mad. Jerro's discomfort must have made itself evident because the inquisitive little shopkeeper was staring at him.

"Problem?" she said. Her golden gaze captivated Jerro like a mouse before an asp.

"No, nothing," he said, and then proceeded to fidget where he stood until the rest of his thoughts came tumbling out. "It's just weird. I know you said you're wearing a glamor, or whatever, it's just strange to see you both, ya know…"

"Elegant? Regal? Refined? Come, Tahli, what other words might I use to describe ourselves?"

"Enchanting," Tahli purred in her exotic lilt with her nose turned up and her arms folded.

"You know what I mean," said Jerro, and a tiny smile started to curve itself into his lips.

"Yes, yes, I do. But, Jerro, there's no point in wasting more *majik* just to fool *you*. Take heart in knowing that what everyone else sees right now is a pair of trendy university students standing beside you, making you the envy of these mirthless people, trudging along to jobs they hate."

"Yeah, sure. It's still weird though."

"Well, regardless, we'll leave you to it. Take all the time you need, we'll meet you back at the shop when you're done. Hazua me if you need anything."

"Might be kinda hard to do that without someone noticing."

"Then do it discreetly," she said with a wink and then pushed off from the wall and sauntered down the road with Tahli in tow.

Jerro watched after them for a while. A weight was starting to press down on him as they disappeared into the crowd. His shoulders hunched and he pulled his leather jacket more tightly around him to fight a phantom chill.

He had the sinking notion that he had made a terrible mistake, and the feeling nestled right in the pit of his stomach. He should have never come back to Midgard—an internal voice whispered to him. But Jerro brushed it aside, writing it off as nothing more than guilt. It wasn't fair how he had left Mahra, and even though they didn't know each other well, he felt he owed her an apology and an explanation.

Yet the feeling wouldn't shake. The moment they had stepped through the door into the mundane city streets, Jerro felt himself divided. He was no brave adventurer here, he wasn't special, there was no *majik*, he was just plain old programmer Jerro. There wasn't room for anything else under the oppressive atmosphere of disbelief.

He looked back at the Greenman door longingly, the shadows turning its rich color into a cold bluish-black. He wanted to be inside the shop, breathing the sweet air, smelling the parchment and wood. He wanted to let his fingers glide along the lacquered shelves where the plants turned to follow him, where eyes seemed to stare out from the shadows between books, he wanted to sit in the comfortable lounge seats and stare up at the enchanted ceiling and watch the clouds glide on by. He was almost tempted to pull open the door, but he knew if he did, he would leave the mundane world behind and not look back.

Was this how Etcher had felt? She had been so eager to leave Midgard before they had sealed their fateful deal. He thought she had been hurrying him for her own ends, but perhaps it had been this feeling of being fractured. It was as though most of him had been left behind a veil, behind the door, and what came through were only the barest parts, the pieces that didn't challenge anyone else's reality. He didn't belong here anymore, but had he ever really?

Jerro sighed aloud. He couldn't just stand there, staring off at the luxury flats. No doubt someone would eventually take note and think him up to no good. He navigated his way across the road and headed for the entrance of the Glade Apartments, then stopped. He wasn't ready yet, not to face Mahra. He needed a little more time and a little more air.

The T-junction down the road seemed promising; there were shops and cafes where he might afford himself the breathing room he needed. He took one last look at the apartments and promised to be back soon.

A little brass bell tinkled as the door opened.

"Welcome, welcome," beckoned a kindly old lady. Her eyes crinkled and she stood up from her tidying, straightening in her long, silken dress. The embroidered dragons and cranes of her outfit were posed like an old Japanese painting, betraying her eastern origin as much as her neat salt-and-pepper bun and her kindly round face.

"Hi," replied Jerro, his gaze wandering through the shop.

It seemed fresher in there, a little cleaner than the city world outside as though the liberating perfume of flowers had created an atmosphere all of their own. The sound of the morning traffic was dampened as the door fell closed behind him, transporting him into a bubble of elsewhere. Soft gray light from the cold autumn day filtered in through the big windows, but the bushels of bouquets and stocked shelves dampened the light and created a gentle shade inside that cramped little store, and made the space feel cozy.

"Can I help you find something?" There was a stiltedness to the old woman's speech as though each word didn't quite flow into the next. The local language evidently hadn't been her first.

"Uh, yeah…I wanted to buy a bouquet."

"Is it for your girlfriend?" The old woman beamed at him, her eyes crinkling heavily with amusement.

"No, not exactly…not yet, anyhow," he said with a cough, and felt himself turning a shade red.

"Oh, I see. Well I think I have something here. Come look." Without hesitation, the old woman took his hand in hers and patted his arm gently, leading him along the narrow walkway of the little flower shop with a familial friendliness.

She brought him to the backside of a large display of roses where colorful bouquets had been placed in tidy rows. "These are quite nice, yes?" she said as she pointed out a neat assortment of white asiatic lilies, cream spray roses, blue statice, and miniature carnations.

He considered it for a moment—pretty as it was and being as unaccustomed as he was to buying flowers. He liked the blues and the whites, but the tones overall seemed too calm and muted for what Jerro wanted, they weren't vibrant enough to lighten the mood which he knew would be in dire need of it once he had actually stored up the courage to face Mahra.

"Maybe something with a bit more color?"

"Hmm, yes." She shuffled around him and muttered to herself as she searched through the store.

She picked up one bouquet, then shook her head and put it down, and tapped a finger against her shallow lips until she found something that made her eyes light up with revelation.

"These are good. Peonies are romantic and bashful, a bit like you." She winked at him. "Good for beginning love. And the Peruvian lilies show friendship and devotion, you like it?"

It was a mixture of pinks and pastel blues and soft whites, with a cheery warmth to it that reminded him of Mahra, and its delicate aroma was soothing and sweet.

"Yeah, I'll take those," he said. "Thank you."

"Do you need it boxed?"

"Oh, no, I'm not going far."

The old woman smiled and nodded and went to ring up his purchase. She bowed to him as he was leaving. "Come back again soon!" she said.

Jerro waved at the old woman and stepped back into the dusty gray of the southern borough of Midgard. Without the fragrance of the shop and its warm homely bubble, he was reminded of his fractured state. And as he stood outside on the sidewalk, with his colorful bouquet in hand, he began to feel rather foolish. He should have accepted the box, or even a bag. How exactly was this conversation going to go? *Hi, Mahra, sorry I left. Here's some flowers, I hope you're not mad at me.* He cringed inwardly.

Soon he became aware of the strange passing glances from the meandering foot traffic. Was it such an odd hour to be buying flowers? Was there a mandate for such a thing? Or maybe a dreary Thursday morning in the autumn chill was an odd time to be doing anything other than going to work or holing up inside.

Man up, Jerro, he chided himself. There was no way to make it any less arduous, he had to start reassembling his life somehow, and considering all the other confrontations he'd yet to face, Mahra was comparably the easiest of the lot. He sure as hell wasn't going to deal with his flatmate Kristoff right off the bat, nor Andri—who he genuinely felt bad for with the whole search and seizure. Those were certain to be *very* unpleasant conversations indeed, and lest he forget the scolding his dad was sure to give him, and the gut-wrenching guilt from his mother. Nope, Mahra was the least stressful of his list, even if the ill feeling was still hanging over him.

The walk back to the apartment community was a strange one. Inside his head, the little voice that told him he should leave Midgard and never return kept chirping at him. Maybe this was a mistake, maybe he should message Etcher and ask to leave, go back to the hillside in Fenris County and see his mom. His parents deserved an explanation most of all even if he had to deal with the scolding and the guilt, and really, who was Mahra to him anyhow? Did he genuinely care?

In truth, his motives weren't entirely altruistic. Mahra was pretty after all, and the thought of meeting her alone at her flat had sparked some rather provocative ideas. But to say he didn't care was too cruel to swallow. He did want to settle things with her, he wanted there to be more—more time, more talk, and more of anything else she allowed him to have.

All too soon he found himself at the bottom of a stairwell where a little iron gate barred his path. There was a dial pad and a speaker beside him where he sought out Mahra's flat number and punched in the code. The speaker made a crackling sound as it rang.

"*Hello?*"

"Uh, hey, it's Jerro."

The crackling hiss of the speaker met him as reply. A key was pressed on the other end of the line, and then the gate buzzed with a loud agitated sound.

An electronic bell rang with a soft *bing-bong* as Etcher pushed past the main door of the large book retailers. She was greeted by the heady scent of coffee beans suffused with the abundance of paper and ink. *Not bad for a mundane planet,* she thought to herself. The two-story building was packed with not only books but temptations for the bookish: table displays were laden with novelty knickknacks of a spiritual variety, chocolates, handcrafted beauty products—the social media deemed self-care essentials. One wall was lined with rows of leather-bound journals and fashionable notebooks, writing implements of the impractical and the stylish; a whole other section of the shop was dedicated to board and card games for all ages.

A sparse number of people were milling about the aisles, a handful of middle-aged patrons, mixed with university students biding time before class. They took little heed of Etcher and Tahli as the pair walked in to examine the place.

"It looks dull," announced Tahli.

"Oh come now, it's charming in its own way. Besides, I know you love shopping even on a mundane little world such as this, so you can save your mock disappointment. Jerro isn't here."

Tahli rolled her emerald eyes and cocked her hips to one side. "What could I possibly buy here that would be of use? It is all cheap rubbish, what could mundanes make that could stand up to the quality of Ecliptian wares?"

"Well, why don't you go and find out? I'm sure the chocolates are nice."

Tahli sniffed with disdain and left the little shopkeeper by herself.

With a quiet snicker, Etcher headed off for the escalator. The coffee scent was getting stronger, and Etcher discovered a small cafe on the upper level equipped with its own tiled seating area where a few of the bookstore's patrons had nestled in with their books and coffee cups and pastry treats.

Etcher quite liked the look of the place, the coffee counter, and the wrought iron tables and chairs, the glass display and the chalkboard menu. She found herself entertaining the notion of installing something similar inside her own shop, a little coffee bar in place of one of the lounge areas perhaps? She wondered if Tahli could even be persuaded to man such a thing—it was an amusing idea, one that she knew Tahli would be vehemently against, which made it all the more enticing.

"Can I help you find anything, miss?" said one of the bookstore employees. He was a twenty-something-year-old with light hair and pale eyes, and seemed overly smiley. He had a few silvery studs in one ear and the tail end of a tattoo poking out from under his short-sleeved shirt.

A university student, no doubt, surmised Etcher, checking him up and down with her weighty gaze. The young man seemed to both shrink beneath her scrutiny and be captivated by it.

"I suppose you, might." she said, smiling impishly as the young man started to fluster. "Your fiction section, could you point me to it?"

"Oh, uh, yeah. It's over there, by the fiction sign." He grinned sheepishly.

"Ah, silly me, how obvious. Thank you."

"Um, was there a particular book you were looking for?" he added, and the eagerness was making itself apparent in his voice and in the glint of his eyes. His smile was a touch more flirty, a little more expectant. The look of a young man who was used to getting what he wanted.

"Just whichever book happens to catch my eye. Good day." And with that she sauntered away from the young man, leaving him dumbfounded.

Etcher let her fingers run over the spines of the books that she passed. She filtered through their titles and the names of unfamiliar authors. She eyed the type of font that was used, the color of it. Pulling a few novels out from the shelves, Etcher examined them, reading a couple lines from the meat of them before returning them to their cramped homes.

It was as her search seemed to be in vain when she happened upon a little yellow novel that featured a world carried on the back of a cosmic turtle, and found it suitably amusing. *That's the one,* she thought, and she took the book in hand and went back down the escalator to find Tahli.

It seemed the flirty employee had moved on from Etcher, and had set his crosshairs on the tall shapely woman, and while the ginger cat-woman did not appear naked to the mundane world, the young man was certainly undressing her with his eyes.

You poor sap, Tahli would eat you alive, thought Etcher amusedly. She sashayed up to Tahli and *ahemed.* "Find anything of particular interest yet?"

The ginger cat-woman turned an emerald eye to the shopkeeper. "The chocolates do not look so bad, I suppose. And the honey lavender soap smells nice, but they use so much artificial fragrance."

"Oh, ah, we have organic soaps I could show you," said the eager young man.

"Organic? Why do you use this word?" remarked Tahli.

"I believe it's a marketing thing, Tahli," replied the little shopkeeper.

The young man looked between Etcher and Tahli with increasing confusion. "Are you exchange students then, or something?"

"That would be one way to put it," said Etcher.

"You are getting that?" asked Tahli, pointing a slender finger at the book in Etcher's hand.

"Yes. Shall we get your chocolates then? And the soap? Perhaps we can replicate the aroma with something more agreeable."

The young man was beginning to look a little dejected as he was pushed to the sidelines of their conversation, and his flirtatious smile was slowly turning into a grimace.

Tahli sighed wistfully. "Why not? But you are paying, I did not bring the appropriate currency."

"Ah yes, of course, I'm sure you merely *forgot* your coin purse."

"I want that little box too," she added.

"The puzzle box? What for? You hardly ever play games."

Tahli huffed. "It looks amusing."

"Anything else?" asked Etcher, rolling her eyes.

Tahli turned to the young man who had been fading into irrelevancy. "Show me these organic soaps you talked about."

The orange sun turned the sky into a crimson fire as it sank beneath the horizon. Under its dying light the opalescent sea shimmered, thrashing waves lapping over one another as the crested peaks snatched up the last moments of sunset.

Atop the chalky cliffs that crested the turbulent waters, was an ivory tower attached to the sprawl of a monastery. A halo of open arches left the topmost room exposed to the chill of the evening air and the encircling balcony granted a panoramic view of the exotic world. One side was framed by the alien sea and the other was flanked by rolling hills and grasslands—the speckle of wildflowers danced in the breeze, losing their seeds and pollen in undulating currents.

The long warbling calls of draconfowl could be heard as they slithered through the naked skies on delicate feathered wings toward the yolk of the setting sun. The humps of whale-ish creatures poked out between the frothing waves as they headed for deeper waters, and standing in one of the tower archways, was a man, peering out into the darkening world.

The cool air drifted past him and mixed the salty-sweetness of the shimmering ocean with the rich fragrance of spices and incense that diligently snaked up from the lower chambers of the monastery. He stood tall with his habit pulled tight around him. He was hairless and sinewy, and covered in intricate little scales of every variety of blue imaginable. He had a strong jaw and a proud nose, and had he flesh instead of scales it would have been easy to call him handsome.

The scaled man stood in a simple monk's robe, plain and cotton-white, and had with him a long wooden staff full of knots and twists that had been smoothed down to reveal the beautiful weave of the wood grain. The man held the staff close to him as if for comfort and watched the sun sink beneath the waves, transforming the crimson sky into a deep purple.

There was something in his hand, which he ran his thumb over subconsciously. A little scrap of toothy parchment with a note penned in precise lettering that was tall and elegant. But he dared not look at the note as he heard the sound of footsteps clap off the polished floor behind him. The man tucked the paper into the folds of his robe and turned in time to see another of his kinsmen ascend the tower steps.

"Abbot E'Kilh, Morrigah Faus is here and demands to see you." The kinsman, much like the man he addressed, was scaled and robed, but the kinsman looked younger and boyish, and his coloring was that of sea-foam green and emerald.

The Abbot let out a long exhale, and in the same moment, drew himself up and squared his broad shoulders. He headed forward with an elegant stride, moving with purpose toward the tower steps, descending into the monastery below.

As he made his way down, the smell of spice and incense became thicker and the warmth and the glow from the torch fires danced along the spiraling stairwell walls. The Abbot stepped out into the large open hall where the other scaled holy men were busying about, preparing supper and finishing their daily chores.

The decorations of the monastery were modest, relying more on the shape of the rooms, the pillars, and the vaulted ceilings to give the space character. Stained glass windows let the last of the dying light undulate across the floor in iridescent waves, and a thick carpet that lined the center gangway were about as much adornment as the monastery could expect, save for the religious relics and statues that were scattered about.

The Abbot walked down the carpeted gangway through the open hall, past his busy kinsmen, and toward an old heavy door to the meeting chamber. The sound of commotion was audible before he even reached the chamber door. An angry voice, gravelly with age, was arguing against the softer, calmer tones of the Abbot's fellow monks. Steeling himself before he passed through the threshold, the Abbot drew himself up as tall as his already fine posture would allow and pushed open the door forcibly, making his presence known.

The two young monks, one purple and the other amber-brown—who had been saddled with the grave misfortune of receiving Morrigah Faus—were visibly relieved that the Abbot had come to take the unruly old codger off their hands.

Morrigah, however, was not so pleased.

The old man who was causing such a fuss was a deep ruby color, and his intricate scales had flecks and streaks of orange and burnt umber making him look like a brightly lit fire, even in his twilight years. He didn't stoop as an old man might; instead his posture was straight, if not defiantly so, and though his scaly flesh drooped and wrinkled around his eyes and neck, he was spry and spirited and invoked no sense of pity as the elderly often can. The fire in his amber eyes burned just as brightly, rebelling at his age. "*Magh fastas!*" the old man Morrigah cursed. "You devil! You fiend! Where is it? I demand to see it! Where is the statue of Urg'Ra?"

The Abbot breathed out slowly, letting the insults roll over and away from him as if they were like water passing over a stone. "Urg'Ra rests safely within the holy chamber, but if you must see it, I will show you."

"Damn right you will," Morrigah growled. "What made you think you could keep such a secret? The sacred stone of Urg'Ra's fire! It belongs to the people, not in some pompous counting house."

"Might I remind you, Brother Faus, that the relic remained safe in a *monastery* such as this for hundreds of years. It was only lost when the people thought it wise to move it," said the Abbot flatly. He turned and beckoned Morrigah to follow, nodding at his fellow monks to dismiss them. They skittered away before the Abbot could change his mind.

"*This is impossible,*" Morrigah whispered with a mix of reverie and fear. "You...you cannot have this, you should not!"

The holy chamber that the Abbot had brought Morrigah to was the only room in the entire monastery that could be considered lavish, and lavish it was. Gold framed paintings made by master artisans, marble statues, lost treasures, and holy relics filled the chamber and topped podiums and stands. Glass displays encased rare stones and the ancient jewelry of long-forgotten kings. Sacred blades and gold-plated armor were lined up along the walls—some incomplete and others chipped and damaged, though all were polished to a shine nonetheless. And at the very back, in a great shrine to the fire god Urg'Ra, was the little ruby statue of the dragon-headed man holding a golden sun.

The Abbot looked at it gravely. "But, indeed, we do have it. Now you have seen it, it's time for you to go—"

"No!" Morrigah pulled a blade from his robes and pointed it at the Abbot. "I cannot allow you to keep it. The Dulvaras'Kahn cannot have this much power! I will not let you. Can you not see? One faction cannot grow so uncontrolled, you will doom us! You and Ruld and the rest of the Dulvarus ilk! Was the war against Pelingross not enough? Ruld will not stop until the Peace Keepers stomp down on our necks and are forced to snuff us out like a dying flame!"

"Ruld is a fool," said the Abbot plainly, unmoved and unafraid of the blade pointed at his heart.

"You would denounce your own leader? What game are you playing, Jayus E'Kilh?" Morrigah kept the blade firmly out in front of him despite the flicker of doubt that crossed his burning amber eyes.

"Not a game I play lightly, Morrigah Faus," replied the Abbot, and in one fluid instant he had shifted his stance and held his wooden staff behind his back like a weapon, his free palm out facing the blade, and his ocean blue eyes became cold and fierce.

Morrigah didn't move. Instead his bright eyes locked onto the Abbot, thinking hard and weighing cautiously. The air became charged with tension, and if Morrigah's scaled flesh could have sweat, little watery beads would have crested his forehead. The sudden force that emanated from the Abbot was so commanding that the outcome seemed plain before their conflict could begin. Better judgment won out and the old man Morrigah put the blade away.

"This will not end well, for you or for any of us," said Morrigah.

"Have faith Brother Faus, not all tales end in tragedy." The Abbot straightened himself, his staff no longer a weapon and his posture tall and stately.

Morrigah looked back at the ruby statue, drawn by its quiet power. "I won't let you keep it."

"You're welcome to try and take it."

"Yes, I am. But another time, and it will be bloody."

"Yes, it will be."

The Abbot stepped aside as Morrigah stalked out of the holy room. Once the Abbot was alone he sank to his knees. He rubbed his bald scaled head, massaging away the tension and said a quiet prayer to himself. Seizing the moment of privacy, the Abbot fished out the note he had hidden inside his robe:

(We need to talk —Etcher)

The print was neat and elegant, and cut him as deeply as any blade. The name alone was enough to send an icy shudder through his bones. He could feel the ominous pulse behind the simple statement, the demand which would not take no for an answer. He made a fist and crumpled the note. The price he had paid for the statue had been high, and he wasn't sure if it had been worth it.

Jerro knocked on the door.

He could hear footsteps moving from within, and then the turn of a latch. The door opened slowly, and Mahra's face peered at him through the gap and smiled at him weakly.

"Hey," she said, biting her lip as she pulled open the door to let Jerro in.

"I hope this doesn't seem too cheesy, but I brought you these." He held out his small bouquet of Peruvian lilies and pastel pink peonies.

Mahra brightened a little, though her eyes were still tear-stained and downturned as though the weight of her thoughts made it hard for her to look up at him.

"They're lovely," she said, holding the bouquet under her nose and breathing in its soft aroma.

She flashed him a somber smile and went to place the flowers delicately in the sink, running the tap over their stems.

"Mahra?" he said as he came up beside her.

She held herself so timidly in her big baggy jumper with her long blonde hair falling over her face.

A warmth bloomed inside Jerro and rose the heat to his cheeks as he looked her over. Even though Mahra's eyes were bloodshot, and even though she wore that silly outfit and knee-high socks, there was something oddly provocative about her. Jerro's thoughts started to tiptoe toward the gutter.

"Sorry," she said meekly. "I'm glad you came—thank you—I was beginning to feel a bit silly, like I shouldn't have asked, I just—"

"Mahra, it's okay. I mean, I was kind of a jerk to just leave like I did."

"Is it really over? I haven't gone back to work the past few days. After the police interrogated me, I just couldn't stomach it. And then I thought they were watching my place." Her shoulders hunched, and her hands groped at the material of the knit jumper.

"It's over," said Jerro. He felt awful to see her like that, all the pain and turmoil he had caused her. Before he knew it, he was slipping his arms around her waist and pulling her close. "They got the guy, the investigation's over," he said as he rested his chin atop her head and stroked her back.

She seemed so small in his arms, deflated from the cheery Mahra he remembered. But she was also warm, and as she nuzzled into him the warmth grew. He pulled away from her slightly, slipping and finger under her chin to lift her gaze to his.

"You think you can forgive me for leaving?"

Mahra's face turned flush, and her glossy eyes darted away. "Could we talk in my room? It's been a rough few days and I still have this horrible feeling like I'm being watched."

"Yeah, of course." He let Mahra lead him through the spacious apartment toward a cozy bedroom.

It was comfortable, much like the rest of her place. But whereas the chic living room and adjoined open-faced kitchen were friendly and inviting, the bedroom was small and intimate and held the sense of Mahra.

A generously sized bed, covered in a plush, earthen-toned duvet of chocolate brown and burnt orange, took up a large portion of the room. Its color scheme echoed throughout the chamber.

Necklaces were arranged to hang decoratively off the orange walls from repurposed silver coat hooks. In one corner was a tidy maple-colored desk and matching chair, dressed with a small stack of books, a closed laptop, artsy pottery, and ornaments of a spiritual motif. There was a gold and bruised-purple colored tapestry filling one entire wall and a closet with bamboo slats occupying another. It was a space that said, "I like to feel comfortable and safe," and that the outside world is out, and here is in.

Jerro liked it immediately.

They sat down on the bed together, and without thinking it, Jerro had put his hand over hers. "Just first, let me say I'm a real bastard. But honestly, Mahra, I didn't mean to leave you in the dark."

He waited, but when she only nodded he had no choice but to continue, lest the oppressive silence nip at them both.

His words started to tumble out in bursts. "I had to disappear for a while. I had some friends help me out. I *never* broke into Johan's office, but I knew no one would believe me so I had to get away until things got sorted. I'm just sorry that you got tangled up in everything in the meanwhile." It was a decent half-lie.

"I would have believed you," she replied in a small voice. "I wouldn't have turned you in. You didn't have to just...*go*."

The levees that held her emotions at bay were threatening to break, Jerro could hear it in her hitching speech. All the pent-up thoughts and feelings that she must have been left to stew in were bubbling dangerously between them.

"I didn't think I had a choice," he told her, and there was a modicum of truth to that.

Etcher had offered to help him, and it had been Etcher that persuaded Johan Lapaul to tidy up the investigation and find a scapegoat. If he hadn't left, Reedman would have thrown him in a jail cell, and whoever was really behind the break in might have got him then.

There was still that missing piece of the puzzle, and the small voice inside his head was beginning to squawk at him again.

"Mahra," he said, "you told me over the phone you thought you were in trouble. Has anything else happened? Did anyone come up to you, or...?"

"No." She frowned at him, mirroring the concern that was plaguing his face. "I thought you said everything was okay though?"

"Yeah, yeah, sorry, it is." But deep down he felt that it wasn't.

"Are *you* okay?" She looked at him with her big sympathetic eyes.

Jerro felt the primal parts of his brain begin to light up. Here was this pretty girl sitting beside him, looking up at him almost pleadingly, and after all the stress and turmoil, he could use a break, some form of relief. He smiled at her. "I'm a lot better now," he said with a wink.

Her cheeks turned flush again and her eyes flittered away from him. "Jerro," she said, "just answer me one thing, back at work—when you invited me to lunch—was I just an excuse to get away?"

He leaned in close and turned her face back toward him. "No, Mahra. If it had been anyone else I wouldn't have even bothered. Besides, I wouldn't be here now if that was the case."

"Really?" She had turned a deep red, and she looked so demure, so enticingly shy.

"I was on my way to my mom's when you called, and I came to see you instead," he told her, and as he glanced down he saw that her big knit jumper had rode up, revealing a sliver of pink.

His smile spread into a grin, and he leaned in for a kiss.

"These are from a local seller, they use honey from their own beehives to make the soaps," said the flirty bookstore employee, who had been showing Tahli various soaps and creams and lotions, which the cat-woman had been adding to their ever-growing pile.

Etcher had become saddled with fragrant beauty products, and was staring off through the shop's big windows into the dreary outside. The clouds were getting darker, thicker; it looked like it might rain.

The store employee, whom she had decided to think of as 'Kevin,' had become a blur in the outer ring of her focus, and his conversation with Tahli was more a constant murmur in the outskirts of her mind. She continued to stare off into the distance through the open windows and passed the bustling streets with its electric cars and solemn looking people, and felt her finely tuned intuition *ping*, and the sensation made her frown. Something was wrong, something bad was about to happen.

She closed her eyes a moment and saw the world through her senses, felt all the passing souls move around her as if by radar. She could even feel Jerro's soul, despite him being outside her usual range of perception. It was a funny thing she hadn't quite noticed before, she hadn't considered since Undercity.

Back when he had been taken, she had trailed his essence to find him, she had been so dogged in her search then. But now, without effort, she knew where he was. He was beyond her immediate scope—so that she couldn't sense any souls that might be near him—but she knew *he* was there. That wasn't the problem, that wasn't the bad.

"We need to get going," she said to Tahli, though her eyes remained glued to the windows, to the heeding where she knew Jerro was.

The ginger cat-woman might have argued, but the serious air that had overcome the little shopkeeper wasn't something to trifle with. "What about your book?" said Tahli carefully.

Etcher turned to 'Kevin' and locked her stern eyes on him. "Thank you for your help, but we must be on our way. Here, this should cover the lot, keep the change," she said as she handed him several large bank notes.

"Oh, ah, you have to be rung up actually, I can—"

"No, we don't have time," she said to him firmly, and he shrank under the fierceness of her eyes.

He took the notes from her and smiled meekly. "Yeah, I guess I can just ring that up myself for you then," he said as he took a visual stock of their haul.

"A pleasure doing business. Come along, Tahli."

"I thought you said we would give Ahliss time?" asked Tahli once they were out of the bookstore and heading swiftly down the road, back to the Glade Apartments.

Etcher cut through the crowd easily, and her fierce determination seemed to create a barrier which parted the flood of the wary foot traffic. "Ordinarily, I would. But I need to check something," was all she told the cat-woman.

They navigated through the streets and found themselves back by the alley where the Greenman door was hidden. Etcher crossed the street and went straight up to the main entrance of the apartment community, towards Jerro's heading, and she paused. She was close enough now for the neighboring souls to be within her radar. She sent the tendrils of her keen perception outward, felt the souls within the building where Jerro resided, felt the room where he was in.

He was not alone.

One soul, not too far from him, had an essence that burnt low like an ember—and then there was another, a soul that Jerro was entangled with.

Etcher's eyes widened with alarm. "To the shop, Tahli, now!"

Things had been going remarkably well. In fact, Jerro had very little else on his mind beside the beautiful young woman that was interlocked with him. The touch of their skin, the warmth of it, the electric feeling that was crackling through him. It was just what he needed to erase all the stress, the stinging silence, the endless questions: a purely enjoyable release.

He was more than a little surprised when Mahra turned out to be just as keen as he was, but then again, after days of being holed up inside her apartment, maybe a release was what she needed, too. It wasn't the first time that Jerro suspected women might actually covet sex as much as men.

He had only gone for a kiss, but he didn't mind at all when her hands started to wander, or how deeply she kissed him back. And when the clothes came off, well, he didn't mind that either. And he certainly didn't mind how she slid on top of him. And it was all going so very, *very* well.

But then a door appeared and Etcher came bursting out.

Both Jerro and Mahra hastily untangled themselves and put an abrupt end to what was about to be a very enjoyable release indeed.

"Etcher!" He found himself yelling in a mix of shock and frustration. "What the *fu-?*"

"That's not Mahra, Jerro!" Etcher shouted back.

Jerro, who had groped wildly at the bedding to cover himself, saw that Mahra—or what he thought to be Mahra—stood in full view of everyone. And while her naked body remained unchanged, the face had contorted into something hideous with a mouth that unhinged and bared long needle-like teeth. But the eyes were the worst of it; the sockets were deeply sunken in, and nestled at their centers were beady little black eyes like an insect's. It was an unsettling contradiction to have such a face on such a body.

"*Jeez!*" Jerro scrambled to get away, but the bedding had entangled him and the shock of everything made him clumsy and slow. The creature lunged at Jerro with clawed hands outstretched, and from one of the open palms he saw a crimson wormy-thing slither out from the flesh and coil around the fingers.

The creature came at Jerro, and he could feel the warmth from its needle-toothed mouth caress his face. And before Jerro blinked, Etcher was between them—blade in hand. The creature hitched in its descent toward him and mouthed something that Jerro didn't quite catch as it contorted itself to get away, but it was not fast enough to avoid the vicious swipe that Etcher landed, lacerating the creature from shoulder to navel and dousing both herself and Jerro in a putrid black ichor.

It howled with a shrill, horrifying voice that clawed through Jerro's brain, searing him with agony. The creature fell back as it screamed, but before it reached the ground, and before Etcher could stop it, the creature crushed the blood red worm in its hand and the entire retched parody of Mahra vanished in a ball of crimson fire.

Time returned to its normal pace and hit Jerro unforgivingly with the enormity of what had just happened.

"Holy shit!" he cursed, panting wildly. "What the fuck was that?"

"That,"—began Etcher—"was a *slithe*. A doppelgänger." She had conjured a silk handkerchief and wiped away the black ichor from her face.

"A wha—"

But Etcher had already walked away from him and headed for the closet. She opened the slatted bamboo door and stared inside it, contemplating quietly to herself.

"Give me a hand with this, Tahli," she said after a moment.

"What the hell is going on?" Jerro's panic started to rise as the shock subsided and released him from its numbing stupor. He grabbed messy handfuls of the sheets and scrubbed the putrid blood from himself.

"…slithe…face eater…soul stealer…" Tahli started muttering, in fact, she was trembling.

"*Tahli*—" Etcher said warningly.

"Doppelgänger…darkling…" The feline was starting to hyperventilate. "We cannot be around him…he brought this on us! Cut him loose, Everdoor! He brought the slithe, it will find us! Leave him, Everdoor! Leave him!" She was shouting and pointing at Jerro, trembling with full blown hysteria.

Etcher's expression became dark. "Tahli," she warned again, but the ginger cat-woman wouldn't stop.

The hysteria had taken hold and Tahli hissed as she spoke, pointing her accusations at Jerro and looking wild. Her fangs were growing, her body started shifting. She was becoming more catlike, more beastly.

"If you do not cut him loose,"—Tahli's voice had transformed into a low guttural rumble and she was an inch away from turning into something big and feral—"then I will…"

Just like that, Tahli was no longer the sultry cat-woman, she had become her *other* self. A mixture of jungle cat and savanna predator. The immense feline that took her place had shimmering stripes that played tricks on the eyes, protruding carnivorous fangs and a thick ruff of fur framing her large angular head. The creature-Tahli snarled, her muscles twitching, a wild hatred flashing through her brilliant eyes. The long sinewy limbs became poised, readying to strike, readying to lunge full force at Jerro and tear him asunder with tooth and claw.

Jerro could see it happening. The horrid fear anchored him in place as he watched the beast of Tahli coil back like a spring. He was transfixed by the premonition of his own hideous death and was trapped in the moment as he saw the tension in the creature's limbs release and propel the gaping jaw and splayed claws at him.

"KANRA ARAN'CHANTAS PEGWA!" Etcher thundered, shaking the walls and charging the very air with her ire.

In that very moment the beast of Tahli skittered to a halt and recoiled like a terrified kitten, shrinking as she did, changing back to her more human-like self. The power and ferocity of Etcher's command still crackled through the room and weighed down on everyone. The silence afterward was deafening and dreadful.

Jerro felt as though his heart had plummeted right down into his gut. Never had he seen Etcher angry, nor had he ever heard her yell with such a powerful and frightening finality. For the first time, he was afraid of her. When he was able to tear his eyes away from Etcher he saw Tahli standing down, meek, and a little afraid herself. Her head was bowed and her eyes kept to the floor.

"Forgive me," she said in a quiet voice, and she turned and left the room through the Greenman door.

Etcher sighed, returning slowly to her normal and not-so-terrifying self. "Get some clothes on Jerro, and help me."

Jerro—whose panic had grown into a confusing, tumbling mess between Tahli's hysteria, Etcher's thundering, and Mahra-not-so-Mahra turning into a monster—remained dumbfounded for a moment at the command given to him. But when the shopkeeper turned an ominous golden eye on him, everything snapped into place.

"Right...yes...coming," he said, as he hastily pulled on his clothes.

And then he saw what was in the closet.

"Oh shit!" Jerro fell to his knees and huddled over Mahra. She was bound and unconscious and breathing shallow breaths. "Mahra! Mahra! Why isn't she waking up?" He turned to Etcher desperately.

"I don't know. Get her in the shop, Jerro, Tahli will deal with her."

"*Tahli?* But—"

"Do it, Jerro," she said sternly and the memory of her previous and terrifying anger was all too fresh that Jerro dared not question the little shopkeeper further.

He scooped up Mahra and hurried through the Greenman door.

Finally, when Etcher was alone, she breathed out long and heavily.

She looked down at her clothes which had been splattered with the slithe's oily black blood and stripped them from herself, vanishing the ruined apparel away and donning on something fresh and clean. Pity, she had liked the green outfit too.

She knelt down to inspect the closet now that it was quiet and the tedium of people's questions and concerns had left the room. She expected more from Tahli, but then again, Etcher couldn't fully blame her, what with Tahli's history. Jerro reacted as expected, which only compounded the tension of the whole affair. *How tiresome*, she sighed again.

Etcher took a moment to gather herself. *A slithe*, she thought, *now that is interesting*. And as she considered the situation, a greater picture came into focus. No doubt a slithe was behind the break-in at Kairos Global, and no doubt that spelt something bigger in the works.

No blood, she thought. What little Etcher knew of slithes told her there should have been a body count, some bloody trail to follow. But this slithe hadn't killed Mahra, even though it was wearing her form. She had believed slithes ate their victims in order to mimic them, but Etcher quickly gathered that it was a tad more complicated than that.

A lot of trouble and care had been taken in setting up the trap, which was unusual to say the least. *This was meant to look clean*, Etcher realized as she stood there. The break in, the set up, it was meant to raise the least amount of questions and rouse few suspicions—had it worked, of course.

Had it worked. Etcher pondered on that a while. If she had not been there on such an auspicious night, Jerro would have been taken, Johan Lapaul's office would have been trashed, and Jerro—with his prior history—would have been deemed the culprit who had split town. The only good questions would come from the parents, and those would have eventually faded into irrelevancy. A little media hype for a while and nothing more. *Clean*.

And no bodies.

Etcher prowled through the room, moving gracefully like a dancer as she inspected the surroundings. The bed was a mess of oily blood, sheets, rumpled duvet, and strewn about clothes, a few of which were Jerro's. She took her time as she tidied, putting the room back together. She disposed of the soiled linens and found fresh bedding to dress the bed with. She even folded the small pile of clean clothes that had been neglected and put them in the appropriate spots. In the closet she found a bag, which suited her intent, and beside the desk was a rucksack with a compartment built for a laptop. Carefully, and with the thought of a young college girl in mind, Etcher started to pack.

She was thankful that Mahra kept a tidy home, making Etcher's job all the easier. She had meticulously combed through Mahra's drawers, hiding places, and unsent love letters—more than one of which had been about Jerro—until she had exhausted all possible resources. The slithe had left very little to work with.

She moved on to the kitchen and found a bouquet of flowers in the sink. She lifted them to inspect. They were fresh, and no doubt bought by Jerro. She frowned at that, what a wicked thing to have happen to him, to them both. How long had the girl been trapped in the closet? How long had the slithe been waiting?

She vanished the flowers away, perhaps Jerro would still want them for Mahra, perhaps not. It was too fine a bouquet to leave behind in any regard, and it would raise unwanted questions if anyone came looking.

Etcher continued to comb through the apartment, searching for some hint at the slithe's intentions. The living room gave her nothing, though for a moment she stared at the flat screen television, watching the climatic end of some horror flick. The monster of celluloid lay bleeding out, uttering with its last breath its curses and damnation of man, questioning who the real monster truly was, before it expired and the bloodied hero was reunited with his love. Etcher clicked off the tele and lay the remote down where she suspected it took up its usual residency. Their monster hunt had only just begun, she knew, the slithe was only the prelude, and it roused worrisome questions.

She continued her investigation through the apartment, leaving no room overlooked yet still finding nothing. She returned to the kitchen, almost drawn by it, and studied it once more with a scrutinizing eye. She started pulling out the cooking utensils, the pots and pans, cups, dishes, studying them until she found the clue she needed. The barest hint of spellwork marked a pot that had been scrubbed and stashed away in a cabinet, but mundane dish soap was hardly enough to fully mask the trace of *majik* within it, although admittedly, Etcher had nearly missed it. Were it not for the vial of serpentbell she found hidden far back in the cupboard she would never have given the pot another look.

Behind her golden eyes the treasure trove of knowledge was building, ideas formulating. She stood back from the grand scheme of things, analyzing the bigger picture, adding puzzle pieces where they fit best and went back to regarding the situation at hand. She came to several conclusions, none of which boded well.

Once her mental discourse had been exhausted, she gathered up the now packed bag and rucksack and headed to the store. Should anyone come looking it would seem as though Mahra Lapaul had left on a trip. In a way, it was almost true.

"Hold it down!"
　"Cut it! Cut it!"

A blood curdling shriek ran through the dark hall, echoing inside the walls and the minds of everyone within. But those that heard it, felt it, only sneered wickedly at the agony filled cry.

"You brought this on yourself Kyddr'Ith, you will suffer!"

"Failure," another hissed.

Kyddr'Ith's writhing form had been laid out across a flat stone slab, held down by chains made of a strange glittering light—like starlight. The body no longer looked like Mahra's, nor was it anything recognizable.

On the flat stone the squirming vessel revealed itself without any borrowed faces or forms. Black and inky, the body had tendril-like extrusions that might have been arms and legs, were they not continually shifting in length. It was an amebic shape that couldn't hold still, constantly quivering and undulating as though unsure of itself and what it wanted to be.

The others had form. They leaned over Kyddr'Ith with their perfectly stolen faces, grinning wickedly with someone else's teeth and tusks. Their eyes twinkled with malice, and not an ounce of remorse could be found in any one of them.

A tall, handsome creature with scaled skin the colors of deep purple and gold, wearing the humble robes of a holy man, leaned down to the blobby mass that might have been a head and whispered into what might have been an ear.

"You failed again o' favored one and *I* shall brand you for it." His voice was smooth and sinister. The scaled man rose up and beckoned one of the others, grinning all the while with his perfect teeth.

A small feathered creature, no bigger than a child, skittered over to the scaled man with a long and vicious metal rod clutched in its hooked snout. The tip of the spiked rod had been stained with a pearly substance that reflected light of its own accord.

Visibly, the black oily mass that was Kyddr'Ith trembled in fear, thrashing and tugging to break free, but the starlight chains bound the inky body to the slab and wouldn't budge. The scaled man took the rod and shooed the jittery creature away. He smiled with malice down at Kyddr'Ith, and then he began to carve.

The shrill cry of agony filled the dark hall once more, and the others smiled with wicked glee.

Drip-drop-drip.

Moisture pooled on the underside of rafters and fell in heavy droplets to the stone ground below. Quiet had returned to the dark chapel, instilling itself like an eager new tenant. The prior cacophony of screams had been swept away, leaving no trace of what had transpired. The quiet saturated the damp cellars, although that was nothing new—quiet was often the only resident of the chapel's lightless underbelly.

Kyddr'Ith lay huddled in that stale silence beside moldy provisions and long forgotten canisters of spoiled food. The parody of Mahra had been abandoned; without the body close at hand Kyddr'Ith could no longer copy her form, and since Kyddr'Ith hadn't eaten her brains the form could not be called at will. The doppelgänger was forced to take on a different guise.

The new body was that of a young hairless boy, whose brains Kyddr'Ith had eaten in a time long ago. The boy had an elfish quality to him; it was in the way the body held itself, in the point of the ears and the long delicate frame. Mostly, it was in the ocean-blue eyes that were a size too big and the androgynous elegance of his round face, a face which was used to smiling. The boy clutched his sinewy arms with his thick hands, his bare calloused feet tucked under his slender body. Despite the darkness he shone with a cherub's radiance.

It was that same captivating light that Kyddr'Ith had found beautiful once, and envied him for it.

So Kyddr'Ith ate his face, cracked open his skull, and sucked down the precious gray matter within and became him. It was the first person Kyddr'Ith had ever truly become and it brought a familiar comfort.

Over the bare shoulder, uncovered by the simple tunic in which the boy was clad, was an ugly scar—puffy and red from its newness. The scar formed the shape of a symbol that had three circles preceding one another with curving, interlocking lines that joined it altogether. A symbol that marked Kyddr'Ith's failure.

Kyddr'Ith could have moved the mark to some unexposed part of the body, but that would have been a cowardly thing to do. A failure Kyddr'Ith may be, but a coward Kyddr'Ith was not. There was no reason to hide the mark in the chapel anyway, they were all slithes there, except of course, for the Lord. There was no one worth trying to trick or fool. Even so, Kyddr'Ith had needed time alone after the ritual concluded and the others had quickly lost interest soon after, leaving Kyddr'Ith to retreat to the cellars.

The scar, slowly losing its puffiness and angry color, settled down and healed, leaving neat lines in the flesh. It was an elegant design—if only it had not been so permanent—Kyddr'Ith might have worn it fashionably. But, alas, the beautiful-horrid mark meant that Kyddr'Ith would never be a perfect copy again; no matter how flawless the impersonation, how convincing the mannerisms, or how much better Kyddr'Ith played the role, the mark would always remain. Kyddr'Ith felt unclean.

But, Kyddr'Ith *had* failed, and failed because the temptation had won out. It had been too irresistible to punish the girl, pitiful creature that she was, and deserving of torture that she was, it had cost Kyddr'Ith greatly. A deep and heavy disgrace weighed down on Kyddr'Ith. All the praise for being better than the others, more patient, more controlled—all for nothing, all undone by Kyddr'Ith's petty need to sate a dark impulse.

There was no way Kyddr'Ith could have known that the reborn had otherworldly help, no way to anticipate that an Ecliptian, of all things, would come bounding into the room and rescue Jerro. But Kyddr'Ith should have guessed something was wrong the moment Jerro had entered Mahra's flat, the very moment when Kyddr'Ith could no longer read his mind. Arrogance had betrayed the doppelgänger, so certain was Kyddr'Ith that the deed could still be done, that there was still time to see the plan through and nail the final stake in Mahra's heart, that the curious changes in Jerro would be answered once Kyddr'Ith brought him back.

How the Ecliptian had managed to disrupt them at that pivotal moment was curious enough in itself, but what bothered Kyddr'Ith the most was the feeling of kinship with the small woman. Something called to Kyddr'Ith as though a dark secret lay hiding in the woman's breast, and Kyddr'Ith wondered. But Ecliptian or not, the fact was that Kyddr'Ith had, if but for a moment, the reborn within reach and could have completed the sacred duty the very same moment he walked into Mahra's flat.

It all could have been done with.

And yet, Kyddr'Ith just couldn't resist taking the time to torment Mahra. It had been so sweet to savor the reborn while Mahra's crippling thoughts brought the catatonic girl to newfound depths of utter misery.

Pitiful creature, Kyddr'Ith thought viciously, teeth baring in an unnatural snarl on the boy's cherubic face. Why did Kyddr'Ith have to suffer in the end, though? Why did it have to fall apart? It would have been perfect, Kyddr'Ith would have taken the reborn right after he was spent and savored in his horror as reality dawned on him.

Would it really have been worth it though? Deep down, Kyddr'Ith knew they should have taken Jerro the moment he was in their clutches. So why then did Kyddr'Ith risk it all for something so petty?

The other slithes were hardly any better, truth be told; they savored torture and bloodshed as much as Kyddr'Ith. There was a primal need encoded into their very matrix that demanded such satiation. Born from blood and torment as they were, it was only fitting that violence became inherent to their survival.

But Kyddr'Ith had been denied fulfillment of those primal urges for years. In that regard, Kyddr'Ith had outlasted the best of them; too bad Kyddr'Ith couldn't best themself.

Or could they?

Surely, Kyddr'Ith, favored by the Lord, could have gone just a little longer—being as close as they were to victory. So what had happened? What had changed that weakened Kyddr'Ith's resolve? Was it truly just arrogance? A serpent coil of anger hissed in Kyddr'Ith's ear and uttered an unnerving revelation.

True, Kyddr'Ith was better than most of them, better at imitating another, better even than the real person was at being themselves. But in being so good, Kyddr'Ith had unearthed a fatal flaw: Kyddr'Ith had been human *too long*, had played the roles of Daag and Mahra too well, been forced to keep all primal desires at bay, to keep it clean.

The real truth, the one that Kyddr'Ith now harbored at their core, sent a cold shiver of shame and disgust through the boy-Kyddr'Ith's stolen form. Kyddr'Ith had acted out Mahra's fantasies because they were no longer hers alone.

So there it was, a horrid truth. Kyddr'Ith had become infatuated with Jerro. These things did, on occasion, happen. It was difficult enough to go as deeply undercover as Kyddr'Ith had and come back without being tainted by borrowed feelings. But those feelings would fade, eventually. And in the end, Kyddr'Ith's love and devotion to the Lord was far greater than any imparted sentiment. The reborn *would* be brought to the chapel and the Lord *would* be freed.

In that, Kyddr'Ith was resolute.

The quiet of the cellars had grown tiresome and empty and Kyddr'Ith was in dire need of guidance. Rising on calloused feet, Kyddr'Ith strode along the winding walkways and past the aqueducts to leave the cellars. And as they climbed the cold spiraling steps up to the outer narthex and toward the hall of worship, the boy-Kyddr'Ith left self-pity behind.

It was hardly any brighter than it had been below, but what need did slithes have for light? Only dim fires rested in the sconces high on the walls that shed the barest amount of light, accenting the dark chapel in foreboding contrast. Kyddr'Ith pushed passed the heavy doors of the inner sanctum and headed for the Lord. Rows of pews lined either side of the vast chamber of the inner church, framing the open walkway that led straight to a massive tomb of ice where the upper sanctuary should have been. Colossal, and stretching up past the vaulted ceiling and beyond the reach of sight, the wall of ice bared down on the chapel like an unforgiving master.

Within that icy tomb was a creature of eternity. Its vastness and depth were as terrifying and endless as the void of space, and within its body of darkness, stars twinkled and supernovas winked out. The creature brought on a vertigo feeling, not just because of its extremeness, but because of the heavy choking waves of its ancient aura that rolled off it in endless procession. This was a creature that had been since the dawn of time, and would be past the horizon of existence. Its demonic head was without much adornment, save for the horns, and the multitude of crimson eyes. Its dark body made up for its lack of features with a plethora of arms and a set of sturdy legs.

There the God of Destruction stood, trapped in a single moment for all of time. The dark deity was poised for a fight, bracing itself for impact. Whatever—or whomever—had locked the dark god in the frigid tomb hadn't concealed the ethereal being entirely. There were small patches here and there uncovered by the icy prison, a piece of cosmic skin, an eye, a finger.

One such eye looked down from its high perch into the great hall of worship and watched as Kyddr'Ith—dwarfed by the god's enormity—advanced along the central gangway and approached the god's cloven feet.

Kyddr'Ith knelt and gave a prayer. At once the god's mind filled Kyddr'Ith's, and in that moment there was no distinction between the two.

In that moment, there was only endlessness.

Enveloped by the dark god, Kyddr'Ith became eternal and weightless. There was no pain, no worry, only a beautiful and purifying oblivion. And nothing else in all creation mattered.

But the god receded and Kyddr'Ith felt hollow when it did. To touch eternity and then be so suddenly and unforgivingly forced back into a small and insignificant form, was frightening and lonesome. Kyddr'Ith shivered, but it was a feeling not unfamiliar. Kyddr'Ith experienced the painful separation many times before, and would many more times to come until the god was freed.

But it wasn't all for naught. The God of Destruction—Lord of the Slithes—had left Kyddr'Ith with a plan, one that would redeem the doppelgänger's failure.

"Thank you, my Lord." Kyddr'Ith bowed, ocean blue eyes swimming with hope, a spark of giddy anticipation lighting in the slender limbs and settling into the smiling face. The boy-Kyddr'Ith turned and went to make the necessary preparations. The last impressions of the dark god played over in Kyddr'Ith's mind and brought a sense of overwhelming comfort: "*We will retrieve the vessel, together.*"

"Did you find anything?" Jerro blurted at Etcher with a bit too much zealotry. He had been pacing through the store, letting his mind work himself up into an impetuous tizzy, and he unleashed some of that anxious energy on the shopkeeper as soon as she walked in.

When Jerro had arrived in the shop with an unconscious Mahra in his arms, Tahli had—with few words or eye contact—taken the girl from him and disappeared through one of the downstairs doors, locking it behind her. It had left Jerro with very little else to do other than worry himself to death.

He had been hovering over the intricate summon circle that marked the center of the rich wooden floor—the nautical symbol that Etcher used to make the shop move between the cosmos within a blink and ferry their way between the mundane world and wonders of Eclipse. The first time he had ever entered the shop, he had been awed by its improbableness; now he looked hopelessly lost in his frenzied state against the grandeur that surrounded him.

The enchanted sky-ceiling had become blanketed by darkening clouds, mirroring the changing weather of the outside world, and drizzle appeared to fall though never seemed to touch as far as the encircling balcony and shapely banister of the upper level. Amber lamps, set along the alabaster walls, had flickered on as the sky-ceiling darkened, and the vast square chamber was filled with an ominous gloom.

The shadows that gathered over the tall rows of shelves—flanking the central gangway—appeared menacing, looming over Jerro with all their magical secrets and wonders. The hissing plants seemed to leer at him, the jars of glowing tadpole things and curious oddities mocked him with their hidden knowledge, and the eyes that flickered in and out of the shadows between the books and scrolls and heavy wooden chests glared with a gleeful wickedness.

Etcher's face tightened, agitation doing little to hide itself. "I found something, although it's not much to go on."

"Well, what is it—"

"Jerro, I'm going to say this once, for both our sakes. Stop panicking, or the next person to be hog tied and locked in a closet will be *you*." There was a touch of humor in her smile as well as a touch of seriousness.

Jerro bit his lip, and nodded.

"Come along then."

He followed Etcher through the store, heading along a neat aisle of alchemic-looking wears and bottles filled with colorful liquids, and reached the very same door Tahli had disappeared through earlier. Though the door had been undoubtedly locked when Jerro had jiggled the handle, it gave no resistance to the small shopkeeper. She twisted the knob and headed on through without a hitch in her step.

Inside was a room Jerro had never been in before. It was dimly lit, aside from the narrow spotlight that illuminated only the middle of the chamber and seemed to come from nowhere. There were no windows to this room, and the atmosphere inside was hot and humid, making it uninviting at best. The ceiling had been enchanted—much like in the main body of the shop—though this ceiling revealed a sky dressed in murky clouds that drifted by in a blanket of midnight, which only added to the dreariness.

Mahra was currently occupying the space on a large flat slab in her still-unconscious state with Tahli working close beside. There was an L-shaped work bench surrounding the ginger cat-woman, with strewn about books, medical tools, labeled vials, burners, glass beacons, and magically inclined looking machinery.

The rest of the chamber was filled with shelves packed thick with jars and other curious Ecliptian wares, not unlike the main body of the shop; the difference between them was that this room was much more cramped due to the sheer density of *stuff*. There were thick bundles of dried spices and herbs hanging overhead, seeming to levitate of their own accord, and large potted plants with big leafy fronds had been arranged in such a way that it seemed as though a small slice of jungle had been uprooted and shoved into the chamber.

A soft ribbit at Jerro's feet alerted him to the toadish creature that was crawling along the wooden floor. It walked oddly, which was largely due to fact that it only had two hind legs and a wide flat head about a size too big for its small body.

"Do not let it out," said Tahli without looking up.

Jerro realized this statement was directed at him and he quickly shut the door before the toadish creature could hobble to freedom.

The amphibian croaked with disappointment and continued along its ambling way.

There were other creatures strewn about the room. Most were in manmade habitats with colored overhead lamps to keep them warm, some had running water and little ponds, but others among the bizarre reptilian assortment had no confinements at all, although they looked as if they should. Instead, the uncaged creatures rested upon thick tree branches or atop shelves and in between books. There was a rust-colored lizard, similar to what Jerro could only describe as an uncomfortably large iguana, that was sun bathing under a heat lamp on one such branch. It had a decorative frill and a horned nose with dexterous eyes that followed Jerro's every move.

"This was all I found," said Etcher, placing a small glass vial on the counter next to Mahra. Little blue flowers were inside the glass container; they were bell-shaped and delicate-looking.

Jerro gave the orange iguana a wide berth as he made his way over to counter. As he stood there beside Mahra's catatonic body, he could see the gentle rise and fall of her chest, which ignited a small spark of hope. *Thank god she's alive*. The fact that she was still comatose, however, weighed on him heavily, and he tried not to think about what he had been doing with the creature that wasn't her when Etcher had burst into the room.

"What are they?" He reached out for the vial but his hand was smacked away none too gently by Tahli, leaving a stinging hairline scratch across his knuckles.

"Do not touch that unless you want to end up like the girl," she said sternly. Her prior timid demeanor had evaporated, returning Tahli to her usual feisty self.

Jerro withdrew his hand carefully, as if any sudden movement might make the vial explode.

"This is serpentbell, Jerro. A dangerous little flower native to Eclipse that spits out a pollen which affects the lungs. Ingesting the flower causes asphyxiation."

"But Mahra's still breathing," Jerro noted.

"True, but serpentbell is often used in spellwork. There were traces of it in the kitchen, but not enough to derive the type of spell." The latter was addressed to Tahli who nodded solemnly.

"Witchcraft," said Tahli.

"Witchcraft," agreed Etcher.

"Sorry, what's significant of that?" Jerro asked the question cautiously for fear of incurring any wrath, or being hog-tied and locked in a closet.

Before Tahli could answer with what was sure to be vague and insulting, Etcher chimed in.

"There are many types of *majik*, Jerro. What I use, what most Ecliptians use, is not witchcraft. It's elemental, it draws from the foundation of reality, but witchcraft is raw and primal, often unpredictable and most definitely dangerous. Few witches exist on Eclipse. It's not a *majik* that gets practiced lightly, and unfortunately for us, it'll take a witch to undo this spell."

"So we find a witch, right? I mean, we're not just going to leave her like this?" He could feel a sharp pang of guilt and urgency rise in his throat, though he fought to keep his voice from showing it.

Etcher sighed. "We'll find a witch, but it won't be easy. Of the witches that do exist, I trust even less. In the meanwhile, we'll have to get her to a doctor."

"What'll that do? You said we need a witch."

"Jerro, she's dying."

"Wh—"

"She will be fine, so long as we take her to a doctor. But she *is* in a coma, possibly for days. She hasn't eaten, she hasn't had anything to drink. Her body will shut down if we don't get her proper care now."

"I tried every potion I know, but I could not get anything down her throat," said Tahli. "She looks pale and underfed, but I do not think she is fully dehydrated, yet."

"Well that's a real comfort, Tahli," Jerro said sharply.

"We'll take her to Druvon," said Etcher, ignoring Jerro for his own sake.

"In Produo?" asked Tahli. She too had decided to ignore Jerro, although it wasn't for his benefit.

"He's in Yahre now, by the river. We'll have to leave immediately."

Etcher turned on her heels and left the room, conjuring in her hand a small ball of red light attached to delicate feathered wings—her signature colored jin'hazua. She spoke quietly to the little floating messenger as she left the room and closed the door before Jerro could follow.

216

"I would leave her be," said Tahli flatly.

Jerro looked back over his shoulder at the ginger cat-woman who was busy cleaning Mahra's face and tending to the small cut on her cheek, then to the abrasions around her ankles and wrists where they had been tied. He felt awkward being alone with Tahli and the memory of her earlier transformation. The way she had very nearly attacked him was playing over in his mind.

He had never seen her so terrified or uncontrolled. Granted, he had only known Tahli and Etcher for a handful of days, but so much had happened in that time that he felt as though he knew them. Evidently, there was still a lot to learn.

Slowly, cautiously, he made his was over to Tahli and stood on the other side of where Mahra lay. He had a numbness inside him as he looked at the unconscious girl. What he had thought had been her—what he had done—left him unsure of what to feel. Right then and there he just wanted to make Mahra—the *real* Mahra—better, and pretend everything else hadn't happened.

"Can I do anything?" he found himself asking.

Tahli glanced up at him. "And what exactly is it that you think you can do?" It wasn't curt, but it certainly wasn't said with any warmth either.

Jerro shrugged. "I dunno know, I just want to help."

Tahli studied him closely for a while, and then rolled her eyes and relented.

"Sit down, you can clean her wounds with this." She slid over a medicine bottle filled with a watery-orange colored liquid. It had a fruity-floral smell when he uncorked it, like mangoes and lavender.

"What is this?"

"Paramin nectar, it is a cure-all, although you would have to combine it with other ingredients for more severe ailments. Dab a cotton ball with it and gently work it into her wounds."

Jerro did as he was told and quietly went to work. The action was soothing, as though he were at least trying to put things back to how they were, if of course, they could ever really be put back. Mahra continued to breathe softly; she was almost peaceful if her eyes hadn't looked so sad. He brushed away invisible strands from her face as he looked at her.

What a mess, he thought. He had been stupid enough to believe it was finally over. Just that morning things seemed to be getting better, he wasn't on the run anymore—even if he was avoiding his obligations. He had been ready to put his life back on track, he had even been hopeful, and now that was all gone.

"Tahli?"

"Mm," she grunted back.

"Back at Mahra's, after the slithe vanished—or whatever the hell it did— why did Etcher call you her slave?"

He recalled Etcher's thundering words which had stopped Tahli in her tracks. *Know your place, slave!* At least, that was what the Babble Seal had translated for him inside his head. Of all the new languages that he had heard, this was the first time he had ever heard Etcher speak in such a tongue, and he prayed he never heard it again. There was something powerful to the language, something dark and sinister.

The air became chilly between him and the cat-woman, and Tahli's coat bristled. "Because the word for apprentice and slave are one in the same where Etcher comes from, and because I would never have been allowed to leave the Bloodlands without a Master."

A whole whirlwind of questions came barreling through Jerro's mind, but judging by Tahli's mood he figured he'd better ask his questions carefully.

"What kind of place does Etcher come from where *slave* and *apprentice* are the same thing?"

"The kind of place that does not look too kindly on people snooping about her business," Tahli remarked coolly and made it quite clear that a change of topic was in order.

But Jerro wasn't quite done. "Why were you going to attack me?" The question had been plaguing him along with the hundred other niggling inquiries.

Tahli might have answered, at least she had opened her mouth to say something, but the door swung open and Etcher beckoned them both.

"Come on, Druvon is expecting us, we need to get her inside the clinic."

"Yes...this is not good. Lucky you brought her when you did, organ failure would have been inevitable," said Druvon in a slow and drawling monotone.

He was a peculiar creature to say the least, a tall bluish *thing* with shimmering skin and a long serpentine neck that connected to a bulbous head, akin to a giant caterpillar that had been affixed to a squat body. His shoulders were hunched, and the torso was thick and sturdy, but the arms were unnaturally long, looking gangly and thin compared to the rest of his boxy frame. He wore a long purple and gold robe that brushed the ground and he seemed to glide rather than walk.

"Hmm, yes, we'll start her on a drip, that'll replace the lack of fluids, and I'll give her a shot of vitamins too and start a feeding tube. I can keep the body from declining, but little else," said Druvon as he adjusted the frameless half-moon glasses that were clipped to the bridge of his flat nose. Archaic symbols, carved into the lenses, caught the light at odd angles.

"That's fine, Druvon, it'll have to do for now," said Etcher, who was leaned up against the doorframe to the operating room.

Druvon's clinic was small and humble. Not like the hospitals Jerro was used to, all sterile and white. This felt more like a palm reader's den, with tapestries and golden effigies, brass alchemy-esque machinery, crystal balls and the scent of incense. But the decor was spaced out and let the floor breathe. The high ceiling and tall windows also aided in giving the room enough space, although Jerro imagined that were it not dark outside, the room would have felt even more open with actual sunlight to brighten it. With the Lunar Week still in full force, perpetual night prevailed, and so, bright overhead lights and gas lamps had to give the chamber its form.

"There's something else you should know. The girl's mind is very active. She can hear us, although she doesn't understand our dialect. She's from an Earth planet, correct?"

"Terra Norse," answered Etcher.

"Whoa, wait...what do you mean she can hear us? How long has she been hearing us?" *Oh shit,* Jerro thought, *oh shit.* "And what the hell is *Terra Norse?* Earth, I'm from *Earth,* we're both from Earth. What the hell is going on?"

Jerro was becoming infuriated by his own ignorance, but moreover, he felt a deep and ugly shame fill him. Mahra could actually hear them? Had she heard everything? *Oh god, what have I done?*

"You're from *your* version of Earth, known to some as Terra Norse. The original Earth is down the spectrum from us," replied Druvon as though the knowledge were commonplace.

"Perhaps we should step outside," said Etcher, placing a gentle hand on Jerro's back to lead him away.

"No, you know what? Enough!" He pulled away from her. "Stop treating me like I'm some bloody child! I want to know things too, don't just leave me in the dark or tell me to stop asking questions because they're inconvenient. I'm too goddamn tired for this right now. Apparently someone has it out for me because all this shit keeps happening and I'm the common bloody denominator. I want answers!"

"You're upsetting the girl," said Druvon plainly.

"And how the hell would you know?" Jerro snapped.

"Because I've been reading her mental activity, I'm reading it right now. I can tell she recognizes your voice, but she doesn't understand what you're saying, or any of us for that matter. Pity, I thought Dragon's Tongue was common speech in the Angelous. My Earth dialects are rather rusty. Tell me, is your native tongue English, Latin, or Norwegian? Perhaps French?"

Jerro was about ready to pull his hair out. "Forget it!" He turned and stormed out of the clinic.

"That went well," said Etcher.

Tahli sniffed disdainfully. "Define '*well.*'"

The little shopkeeper pushed off from the wall and straightened her vest. "Keep an eye on him. I'll be back when I can. Get rooms for both of you. I should still have an account at the Vouladun down on Penrose and Agith." Etcher headed for the Greenman door that had been tucked away at the back of Druvon's clinic.

"Where are you going?" asked Tahli.

"To get answers."

Friday...

The week had felt long, which was truer for some than most.

But in reality it had only lasted as long as a few moves on a chessboard. The Lunar Week was coming to its end and the final moon would be full, thinning the veil between worlds and giving way to endless possibilities.

For Jerro, Friday began with a head-splitting hangover.

Tahli had retrieved him from a bar the previous night and dragged his wobbly drunken hide to a hotel room where he passed out as soon as his body hit the soft plush bedding. There he remained—long passed the hour he had actually awoke—unwilling to move, and afraid that if he did his bizarre and twisted reality would dawn on him and leave him empty and alone.

But he was alone, and he was afraid. Try as he might to stay in the unfocused haze of his hangover, laying still on the plush bed to deny his wakefulness, the thoughts kept bleeding through and with them came all his wretched feelings of guilt and shame and bitterness.

He thought back to the start of the week, how he very nearly hadn't gone into work that day, how things had very nearly been undefinably—perhaps *fatally*—different. Why did it all have to fall on him? What had he done to merit so much attention? And where the hell had Etcher and Eclipse and *majik* been when he was younger? When he still believed he might be special? How dare they come for him then, how dare it all happen when he was so much older and calloused, when he had obligations and a life, when he had lived for years so desperately alone.

If he was so important, then where was it all when *he* needed *them*?

And now he was here, and there was *majik* and lost cities and wonders beyond his imagination, and still, he was miserable. When Mahra got better, *if* Mahra got better, what then? Because, no doubt, she had heard every nasty little sin he had committed with that foul monster. The things he had done, the things he had felt, and all of it tainted by a fake wearing Mahra's face. It was all just an ugly trick.

And then there was Etcher, who had up and left and hadn't been back since the clinic. What the hell was that about? Weren't they friends? Weren't friends supposed to wait for you to calm down? To still be there when you came back to apologize for blowing up? Not to leave you dumbfounded with a thousand questions and only a prickly cat-woman who barely tolerated your existence as company. Meanwhile the girl you actually liked was dying on a slab because you couldn't tell the difference between a fake and the real thing.

And if he hadn't answered the phone he might have been back in Fenris County with his mom, having a home cooked meal, listening to her tell Etcher and Tahli embarrassing stories.

And Mahra would be dying in a closet.

Fuck.

Right then and there he hated all the *majik* and trickery. What the hell use was it anyway when all it did was cause this much trouble? Slithes and multiple Earths and god-only-knew what else. Fat lot of good it did him, any of it. So he had some shiny trinkets from an ancient city, so what? And, oh yeah, he could occasionally pass through solid objects and mess around with ghost seals and sense the dead. Wonderful, a great party trick if he ever got back to his normal un-magical life.

He grabbed one of the plush pillows and buried his face into it. He needed a little normality, just a touch. Everything was happening so fast that he barely had time to breathe or stop and think about what the hell he was doing. He just needed everything to slow down before it broke him.

Truthfully, he wanted to cry. But that never made him feel any better, crying was like a punch in the gut that left him wretched and used up after. None of this cathartic release that girls seemed to get.

Reluctantly he got up and the whole world spun.

He clutched his head and peered around the hotel room cautiously for fear that any sudden movement might flip the world on him again. His pale, bleary eyes rested on a bottle near his bed with a note that read:

†ɔfȝ† Iℶ⪽f⪽ʰ -
⪽ǐ⪽ʰ Ǝↄʰ ⊥⪽ʰ†⪽ʰǐ⪽†⪽ʰ
—(ⱦⱶ†)

(Drink this. You are welcome. —Tahli)

He could hear the cat-woman's sour tone in his mind as he read the note. He looked at the pale-gold liquid inside the bottle dubiously, but in the end, decided he should probably drink it as instructed. Despite the cat-woman's evident disdain toward him, he doubted she would poison him. If Tahli really wished him harm she could have left him at the bar last night and let Fate decide the outcome.

Although, from his scattered memories he recalled befriending an Ecliptian with a mighty resemblance to a bulldog who had offered Jerro a sofa to crash on—had Tahli not come to get him of course. There was also a vague recollection of dancing a little too closely with a few too many pretty girls— one or two of which whose genders traipsed along ambiguous. The fragmented imagery stamped more guilt and awkwardness on his already encumbered mind, and he quickly skittered away from the tattered memory. He further recalled drinking something called wulfbru ale, and peppermint shots, and another nasty something called *Rebyum* or *Rebbium*. It was by far the strangest thing he had ever drank. Once poured, a vapor wafted off from the top of the green-black liquid, like mist on a lake, and formed into a little laughing skull that slowly dissipated into the open air. It was that which had undoubtedly caused the ungodly hangover, as shortly after downing the vile drink he blacked out.

At any rate, he was in dire need of something to alleviate his splitting headache. He popped open the rubber stopper on the bottle and downed the fragrant liquid inside. It had a slight medicine-sweetness, and a hint of something like bergamot. A moment passed and Jerro felt no change, and just when he believed he had been duped, Jerro flopped back down on the bed and realized the world had stopped spinning. Daringly he swung his legs back around and actually stood up. The tonic had worked! No longer did his brain feel as though it were sloshing around in an acrid soup of pain and regret. He actually started to feel clear, fresh, like he had slept restfully instead of the deadweight coma that he had fallen into upon being plopped on the bed.

He walked in a slow circle around the room. No spinning world, no hangover. He was good—well, *good-ish* besides the horrid feeling of guilt in the pit of his stomach, but it was a start. As he looked about the room he noticed something strange. It was daylight, bright and warm and— *Shit, how long was I out for?*

He went to the window but was unprepared for the strange contradiction that confronted him. Outside was dark, he could see the five moons in the sky, and the late night party-goers finally tapering off as they stumbled through the streets to find a warm bed. And yet, light was clearly streaming in through the window. He decided to close the lace curtains and contemplate the odd duality later. Although the tonic had cleared his mind, his body still stunk of booze, what with the sickly aftermath of the peppermint shooters oozing out his pores.

He needed a shower.

The hotel room that Jerro had been dumped in was by far the nicest place he had ever stayed. After bathing and dressing—he had found a small pile of clothes in the closet, although he wasn't sure if Tahli had left those along with the tonic—he took a moment to appreciate his surroundings.

The room was comfortable and spacious, which could be said about his room in Etcher's shop, but the defining difference between the two was the grandeur. At Etcher's his room had pale blue walls, a high slanted ceiling with white rafters, and a king-sized four-poster bed. It was a homey beach-style accommodation that Jerro had taken to with ease. But *this* room was the very definition of ritzy. The richly stained wood furniture and trimmings, the marble floors, big classical paintings in gold leaf frames, plush bedding with dozens of pillows, the *free* mini bar, exotic-smelling soaps and lotions, and the black granite bathroom—it was lavish to say the least. Typically, lavish was not Jerro's scene, but he could get used to this.

He had taken his time washing up; in fact, after his initial rinse-off in the shower, Jerro had opted to take the large bath for a spin and loaded it up with bubbles and any other intriguing smelling bath oils that he found stocked in the cupboards. The end result—after an hour-long soak—had left him pruny and smelling like the inside of a perfume house, but his body had been heated to an enjoyable loose-muscled wobbliness and his mind was still riding on the lucid effects of the tonic. He had dressed subconsciously and practically floated out of the room once he was finished getting himself ready.

The rest of the hotel was like a palace. Crown molding and vibrant murals laced the ceilings, alabaster statues lined the walls; there were crystal chandeliers, plush carpets, and swanky looking attendants ready at every beck and call. Jerro got the distinct impression that if he were to ask, someone would tie his shoes and spoon feed him—if he were into that sort of thing. There was also music playing throughout the hotel, that of a symphony orchestra, which kept their composition light and airy, although Jerro had yet to find any speakers or said orchestra.

He did, however, find his way to the lobby, which was crowned with a big domed ceiling—enchanted like in Etcher's shop—portraying a sky of cotton-white clouds silently drifting by in a sea of perfect blue. But whereas the shop's ceiling showed what the sky was actually like beyond the Greenman door when connected to reality, this was set to a fine summer's morning and definitely not reflective of the perpetual night outside, nor the autumn chill.

"We find that the Lunar Week can be disorienting for some, so the hotel was enchanted to appear lit by daylight during the hours in which it normally should be," one of the attendants—a snooty looking man with a hook-nosed and a slicked-back mane of raven feathers for hair—said matter-of-factly to Jerro. The attendant had apparently caught Jerro staring up at the ceiling and decided to chime in, although he had done so without making so much as a sound as he approached.

"Oh, right," Jerro said warily, managing to stifle the yelp of surprise. Typically, Jerro had found the average Ecliptian to be pleasant and easygoing, but this man gave him the distinct impression that they would not get along on a personal level.

"You look like you're in need of some assistance, *sir*." The attendant spoke in a dry and humorless tone, and the way he said *sir* made it clear that he did not actually think Jerro was deserving of the addressor.

"Yeah, I suppose." *Well aren't you a bundle of laughs?* thought Jerro bitterly. "Can you tell me which room my friend's in?"

"Name?" the snooty bird-man inquired.

"Uh, Tahli—um, you know I actually don't know if she has a last name."

"Hmmm." The attendant narrowed his gaze disapprovingly on Jerro. "Are you both under the same account?"

"Probably." Jerro shrugged, meriting more disdain. "Try Etcher Everdoor?"

The attendant's eyes went wide for a moment, but the shock was quickly hidden away behind a mask of indifference.

"Are you certain you're under that account?" The vinegar had left the attendant's tone somewhat, replaced by a subtle hint of fear.

Jerro grinned inwardly. *Pompous prick.* "Yeah, actually, I am. I work directly with Etcher, see?" He held out his right palm where the invisible contract had been sealed between him and the little shopkeeper.

He wasn't sure what had possessed him to do it, or how he did it for that matter, but the emblem that had been branded into his hand revealed itself with a soft, iridescent glow.

The attendant paled. "If you would just come over here, I'll find your friend's room in the directory." He gave a sheepish smile that his face was unused to wearing.

The feather-haired man led Jerro to a big, black granite counter where other, more smiley, attendants were checking in guests. He slipped behind the desk and picked up what looked like a pen with a crystal nib and started tapping on a small tablet of clear glass.

"There we are, Jerro Ahliss and Tahli Bruunblud Al'Florun. You are, I presume, Mr. Ahliss? Room nine-fourteen?"

"Yeah, that's me." *Bruunblud Al'Florun, what kind of name is that?*

"She's in room nine-fifty-six. Was there anything else I could help you with, sir?" asked the attendant with a forced and somewhat weaselly smile.

"No. Thank you," said Jerro, turning on his heels to leave and casting a wary eye back at the attendant who continued to smile at him. *I think I liked him better being pompous.*

"Who is it?" called out Tahli from behind the door.

"It's Jerro." *Your favorite person in the world,* he thought to himself in wry amusement. "Can I come in?"

There came a huff as a reply followed by hard footsteps.

"What do you want?" Tahli said as she opened the door, although she said it looking down her nose at him.

"I just wanna talk." He held his hands up, hoping to invoke a temporary truce.

The ginger cat-woman clucked her tongue and moved aside, letting Jerro pass.

He stepped inside the room and was shocked by what he found. "Whoa…" The word escaped him with a quiet breath as his eyes sailed upward until his neck was craning. Slowly his gaze traveled around the voluminous chamber and back down to rest on Tahli. The ginger cat-woman had evidently gone for a deluxe suite, to put it lightly, which made his own grandiose room seem like a chantey by comparison. The luxurious abode was furnished like a palace hall, and she even had her own kitchenette and separate sleeping quarters. *How much did this cost?* he wondered privately.

Tahli sashayed over to one of the lavish sofas and draped herself in it as if accustomed to luxury.

Still dumbfounded by the opulence, Jerro couldn't help but stand and stare at Tahli. He was suddenly reminded of an article about the absurdly rich he had read on one website or another, the likes of which had pictures of tigers with diamond studded collars lounging indoors in some billionaire's summer home. The thought of Tahli being akin to someone's pet, however, was a thought he dared not mention aloud.

"I see you drank the tea I left you." The tip of her tail was coiling with feline curiosity, and she watched him through the corner of her emerald eye.

"Uh—yeah, I did. Thanks," he said somewhat awkwardly, returning his wandering thoughts back to reality.

He sat himself in an extravagant armchair across from Tahli, although was nowhere near as accustomed to its lavishness as she was—despite the fact that it was extremely comfortable. His jeans-and-t-shirt ensemble made him feel like an intruder in some outlandish new world, though his discomfort may in part have been due to the ever-present disapproval radiating off of the cat-woman.

"Worked well, did it not?" she said, sounding mightily pleased with herself.

"Like a charm." Jerro tried desperately to keep the snark from his tone, without Etcher for backup he was having difficulty keeping a cool head. "Look, Tahli, about the other day…"

"Forget it." Tahli waved her hand dismissively. "If you came to apologize, I do not really care. It would not make me like you any better. Do not waste either of our time and just get to what you truly wish to talk about."

Jerro blew out his breath slowly. She certainly had a knack for being difficult. "Okay. Any word from Etcher? I mean, we're just sitting here until she gets back from wherever the hell she went. I kinda feel a bit useless here and I'd like to do something more than just sit around and wait."

Tahli snickered quietly, and he had an idea of internal dialogue. "Message her yourself if you are so concerned. She gave you a hazua, unless you have forgotten how to use it." Tahli, of course, made no attempt to hide the barb from her words.

"Fine. I will." He glared at her.

And the smugness grew on cat-woman's face.

"You know, Tahli, I'm really trying to be nice here."

"Do not bother," she said flippantly.

There was a throb of aggravation pulsing in Jerro's temple. He got to his feet and sucked in the air through his teeth. "You know what? Forget it." He was about to leave but his tongue hadn't quite finished wagging and he found himself turning back on his heels. "You can treat me like I'm some deadweight lay-about, but at the end of the day *I* was the one that got dragged into this. I'm really *not* trying to be the pain-in-the-arse that you make me out to be, so you can be pissed off at me all you want but don't forget it wasn't just your life that got messed up by all this."

His better sensibility came to and he silenced his tongue before the next bought of words could leave his lips. He marched out the door and let it fall heavily behind him.

The walk back to his room was thankfully a quiet one. If by accident or not, Tahli's and Jerro's room were on the same floor, albeit at opposite ends. It afforded him time to think as he navigated his way through the adjoining hallways back to his own private suite.

He began to prioritize what he felt needed to be accomplished. Firstly, he'd send a hazua to Etcher and find out where the hell she had gone to, secondly— and though this merited an internal cringe—he needed to get Mahra up to speed on what was happening. Comatose or not, the fact remained that she could still hear, which meant she was probably very confused and very afraid. Jerro owed her an explanation at the very least, although he wondered how much she'd really want to hear from him of all people. Given the option though, it was probably best he be the one to explain things rather than, say, Tahli, who would be less than tactful.

Thirdly, he'd have to find a way to sort things out back on Earth—mainly to stop his parents from worrying themselves to death as they most likely were. Of course, that also meant he'd have to check his voicemails and somehow smooth things over with his angry flatmates. Hopefully Kristoff hadn't put his stuff to the curb and rented his room out already, which he might have...*prick*.

The third thing, and all it entailed, would have to wait, preferably for as long as Jerro could put it off. Despite how much he dreaded visiting Mahra, he had little to no desire to put forth the mental capacity needed to address the last part of his checklist. So far he had actually managed to keep most thoughts of home—and how everyone else might be doing—at bay. Now was hardly the time to start untangling that massive knot.

He reached his room, unlocked the door, and slipped inside. Then felt his brain draw a resounding blank as he realized he had no idea what to say to Etcher, as per part one of his list. An overwhelming desire to leave his room again and check out the pool area of the hotel, or perhaps the spa or dining room, crept up on him and wished to delay all pressing obligations indefinitely.

But Jerro mustered whatever willingness still remained and forced himself to summon the little teal-colored hazua that Etcher had given him.

With a soft *pop* the dainty ball of blue-green light, bobbing on delicate feathered wings, appeared right before Jerro's nose and lazily hovered in the air as it awaited instruction. Jerro batted the little messenger aside to stop himself from going cross-eyed.

"Sorry, just...can you not be right in front of my face, please?" The hazua's wings seem to hang miserably as it bobbed in the air.

Jerro groaned and rubbed his forehead. "Okay...look, I'm sorry, really, I am. It's been a rough morning, okay? Just, ya know next time, not quite so close. Look, come on, cheer up, all right? I've got an important message for you to deliver, I need your help...*okay?*"

The request seemed to perk up the sullen messenger. Of course Jerro then spent the next twenty minutes trying to decide what to write.

The teal hazua lethargically followed behind him at a reasonable distance as Jerro marched back and forth through the room, stopping occasionally at the dresser by the bed as if he might actually write something, then abandoning the thought to resume his marching. Eventually he gave up on trying to hash out some long-winded letter and settled for something simple, scribbling it down on the hotel's complimentary notepad:

Where are you?
—Jerro

It seemed to encapsulate the heart of what Jerro needed to know. He fed the note into the hazua which rolled back lazily, pulling the scrap of paper into its illuminant body, and disappearing with another muted *pop*.

Jerro was surprised to see the hazua return only moments later, just as he was headed for the door to confront part two of his list.

"Was there a problem?" he asked.

As reply the hazua lurched forward and a small strip of parchment unraveled from its body. Jerro took the note, seeing that it wasn't the one he had sent, and read the tall elegant lettering:

Jerro, Went to find answers. Got held up, be back soon. Be nice to Tahli. —Etcher)

"That's it?" Jerro snapped.

The little hazua shied away and vanished with its signature pop.

He groaned aloud. "*Be nice to Tahli.*' What am I, a toddler?" He thought about trashing the note but his better judgment told him he should keep it, so in his mind he focused on the onyx pendant that hung about his neck under his clothes, and saw the closet space of the Obelisk stone. Inside his mind's eye he was standing within that space, with all its shelves, with its baskets of glassy Ecliptian coins that Etcher had given him, and the barest essentials any traveler would need. Blankets, spare clothes, guide books, a hunting knife, some other bits and pieces he had yet to fully rummage through, and of course, his treasure chest filled with his haul from Undercity.

He opened the decorative chest and looked at the ivory goblet and gold trinkets inside, and at the silver bangle intended for his mom. He stared down at the sparse note in his hands, feeling a coil of irritation start to build, and he shoved the scrap of paper into the chest and slammed the lid shut. Then he was focused back on reality, grabbed his leather jacket and he left the hotel room, heading for the lobby.

The snooty bird-man wasn't there as he headed for the front doors, and Jerro said a silent thank you to whatever god might be listening. He strode with purpose all the way past the grand main entrance and out onto the hotel's entrance patio, only to be struck by the unnerving transition from daylight to night.

The dark streets of Yahre were softly bathed in pale moonlight and the warm amber glow of cast iron street lamps. Their delicate radiance gave a wholesome feel to the elegant city, which Jerro had paid little mind to during his prior drunken excursion. Nocturnal critters gave their songs to the faux night, infusing the world with a mysterious sense of life, and the odd morning bird called to distant mates—unperturbed by the preternatural darkness. At the backdrop of it all was the rumble of water that flowed in abundance throughout the city in cultivated pathways. Right then and there, sober and clearheaded, he realized what a beautiful place he was fortunate enough to be standing in.

The wide roads were cobbled and tree-lined, with handfuls of horse-drawn carts clapping along the stony streets on their metal-shoed hooves. Most of Yahre's architecture was dominated by tall white buildings made elegant by their fine, lacy filigree cast into the molding. Gargoyles crested building tops and jutted out from corners, while stone angels lined bridges and cathedral roofs. Yahre, by far, was the most breathtaking place Jerro had ever been to.

The throne room in Undercity had been magnificent, but Yahre inspired a different kind of awe. Not only did the architecture lend the city grace, but the landscaping elevated it to new levels of beauty—quite literally. The city was tiered; some parts were stacked above the lower levels on magnificent pillars or by the very structure of the land. Some seemed to float all by their own accord and had waterfalls pouring over their lips into manicured pools. And the flow of the wild river, which cut straight through the heart of Yahre and tapered off in manmade canals, wove the sound of its gurgle and the smell of its moisture into the canvas of the city's elegance.

If elves existed on Eclipse then they must have lived in Yahre, decided Jerro. It was at once a civilization and woodland paradise, a community that had built itself in harmony with the world around it, and it was stunning even in the dark. It wasn't just the amber lamps and lunar light that helped illuminate the world either; there were firefly-like things bobbing all around, glowing butterflies, trees adorned with radiant spheres, and shimmering plants that made the night seem friendly and inviting.

Of all the disaster and guilt and stress that Jerro felt, stepping out into that beautiful place—into the no doubt cultivated view from the grand hotel—helped alleviate a little of his turmoil. Few Ecliptians were still wandering about the streets, many of which were clad in elegant flowing gowns dyed with rich colors—a staple of the city's high fashion, so it seemed.

The predominate face among the variety of races were what Jerro thought of as the '*pearl people.*' They had pale skin and soft features to their smooth faces, with shimmering white hair that draped all the way to the ground, pointed ears as long as Jerro's forearm, which were littered with jewelry, and big pearly, pupil-less, eyes. They were bewitching.

The parades and parties had died down for the meanwhile, being that it was technically late morning, although there was still a smattering of performers and shopkeepers dressing up their stores and stages for the final night of the Lunar Week. It was sure to be a remarkable event, and Jerro caught himself wondering how the grand finale in Yahre would compare to the parades down in Gahza'Dune.

He realized as he stood there in awe of the woodland city, his breath misting in the air, that he had absolutely no idea where to go. He had intended on going back to Druvon's clinic to check in on Mahra, but being that yesterday was predominantly a hazy drunken blur he wasn't entirely sure *where* Druvon's clinic was in relation to the hotel. He thrust his hands into his jacket pockets, eyes sailing about but found no revelation.

"Shit," he cursed aloud.

"D'you need help?"

Jerro spun on his heels to find himself face to face with another finely dressed attendant. This one, however, had green skin and features reminiscent of a floral origin. She, or maybe he, had the general shape of a human body, but everything else was petals and vines. The strangest thing about the attendant, however, was the face—which was more a porcelain guise than a real human countenance. The eyes of the mask were an infinite void of black, and the pert nose and petite lips made the porcelain face reminiscent of the type worn for an exquisite masquerade, all jewel encrusted and sparkly, bewitching and a little scary.

The question took a moment to register before Jerro realized he should answer. "Erm, yes. Actually, I do. Can you tell me where Druvon's clinic is?"

"Druvon?" replied the attendant. The ambiguous mellow voice lent itself to either sex and further kept their gender debatable. "Do you mean Dr. Ashadon?"

"If Dr. Ashadon is about eight feet tall and blue, then maybe."

"Yes that's him." She—or he—replied with a smile to which the porcelain mask strangely conformed. "Dr. Ashadon is a *rovel*, they're rare, not many still around. His clinic is just down this street, right on the corner of Penrose and D'Kaht. This is Penrose and Agith, see?"

The flowery steward pointed to the black iron post where a neatly written sign was swaying gently on the corner of the intersection. "It's about a kilometer down the road, you shouldn't miss it." The genderless attendant smiled as widely as the decorative living-mask would allow.

"Um, thanks," said Jerro, feeling as though he were obligated to do something more.

He quickly ducked into the mind-closet of his pendant and grabbed the first ginse coin he could find, bringing it into reality and pretending to draw the coin from his pocket as he handed it to his floral host. The attendant smiled even wider, graciously accepting the purple-hued ginse.

Jerro had tipped them a fifty.

"D'Kaht…D'Kaht—*Ah!*" Jerro found the front of Druvon's big-windowed clinic after a half-hour meander down the road.

He praised his stars for the open sign hanging inside the window and let himself in. The front door rang with a pleasant little bell. He was struck first by the heady incense and the low sitar music playing on some unseen speaker, then by the sight of the receptionist.

"Can I help you?" It was a pearl person that greeted him.

Unlike the androgynous hotel steward, this Ecliptian was definitely female, and the nurse's uniform was well fitted. She wore all white with red trim and her long pale blonde hair had been twisted into an intricate bun. Little ringlets hung down beside her ears, framing her hypnotic face. The abundance of delicate gold chains and hoop piercings in her elven lobes jingled lightly every time she moved her head, playing a delicate *tinkling* sound like fairy chatter, adding to her spellbinding façade.

"I'm here to see Malira," Jerro said a little dully, as if in a dream.

"Your name?" her soft melodious voice inquired, big pearly eyes staring like open pools.

"Jerro Ahliss, I came here yesterday with Etcher Everdoor." His mind felt sluggish and slow and he fought to retain the lucidity the tonic had granted him earlier.

"*Oh,* you brought the Earth girl, didn't you?" There was sadness tinging her reply.

"Yeah…Is she okay?"

"Well, as okay as she can be, I suppose. She hasn't woken up yet. Dr. Ashadon has done all he can but *majik* like that won't be broken easily."

Jerro felt remorse weigh on him heavily and break through the hypnotic web the pearl nurse emanated. Instead of going out yesterday and getting blind drunk, he should have stayed with Mahra and answered some very important questions. "Can I see her?" he asked.

"Sure, I'll take you to her room."

The shapely pearl woman got up from the desk and was a good half foot taller than Jerro. She waved him through the side door and led him down the hall, past an abundance of big amethyst chunks and hanging tapestries, and into an antique-looking elevator that brought them to the top floor of the narrow building.

Mahra had been moved from the operating room to a little private chamber with a window view looking out over the encircling forest toward the mountains. She was hooked up to an IV drip and had a tube down her throat that connected to a big brass machine with slowly winding clock parts.

The sight of her in that hospital room brought sorrow and shame crashing down on Jerro's heart.

"I'll leave you be." The pearl nurse smiled somberly and shut the door behind him.

Someone had put out fresh flowers beside Mahra's bed and brushed her hair, doing their best to make her look comfortable despite the graveness of her condition. Jerro pulled up a vacant chair and sat down, gently placing his hand over hers.

"Okay, Mahra," Jerro began, the Babble Seal effortlessly guiding his speech back to his native tongue. "Um, it's me, Jerro." He stopped and had to clear his throat, shoving down his nerves with a deep steady breath. "So this is all probably terrifying and confusing, but I'll do my best to explain it.

"The truth is I'm different. I didn't actually know that until Tuesday and not until after I left the bistro." He scrunched his eyes at how ridiculous he sounded but forced himself to keep talking.

"I'm what they call a *reborn*. Basically there's something special about my soul and I can do things—*sometimes*—and all the weird languages you've been hearing, the only reason I can speak them too is because my friend, Etcher, put a spell on me. She can probably do the same for you too, once we get you better…" The latter made Jerro pause. *If* an evil little thought squeaked at him from the recesses of his mind.

"I'm so sorry, Mahra. This whole thing is a mess. I barely understand what's happening myself, but—but here's what I know…" Then, he let the whole strange tale of his bizarre week tumble out.

"I *want* cream cakes! I want them *now*." A little girl with golden pigtails and a white lacy dress was stamping her feet as she demanded the sweet treats from a tired and apologetic-looking woman clad in governess apparel.

"Lulu, sweetie, you can't have any cakes until supper. Your mama said so," replied the woman. Her accent was posh but her dress made it clear that she was hired help and not of any real blood relation to her charge.

The girl blew a raspberry in reply. "Mama's not here. I. Want. *Cream cakes!*"

"Little girl," purred Tahli. The ginger feline had been watching from across the buffet room and decided to intervene.

The woman gave Tahli a wary look but politeness kept her from speaking.

"Who are you?" the little girl said rudely, uninhibited by any sense of manners.

A wicked smile curled Tahli's lips. She knelt down to the girl's level, whispering quietly in her ear. *"If you do not shut up, I am going to roast you over a spit and eat you for my breakfast."* Tahli's eyes twinkled dangerously and she licked her fanged teeth.

The color drained from the little girl's face, eyes ready to pop from her skull. She squealed in fear and ran off.

"Lulu!" the tired woman cried, and ran after her troublesome charge, shooting back a-venomous look at the cat-woman.

"*Peh,* foreigners," Tahli said to herself and continued to the buffet table for a quiet meal.

"Terrorizing little girls now?"

The ginger cat-woman looked over her shoulder and chuffed. "*I* was hardly the terror." She peered at Jerro disapprovingly through the corner of her emerald eyes. "I suppose you have come for something else?"

"No, actually, I was just hungry and saw the buffet was complimentary. Besides, I just got back from the clinic…" His words tapered off and he quickly busied himself by grabbing a plate.

Tahli watched him, idly picking through the fresh cut fruits as she did. "Any news?"

"No, not really. Mahra's the same, although her color looks a little better. I decided to sit down and tell her what was happening—since she can hear."

The cat-woman gave out a long, heavy sigh. "I would not keep beating yourself up. What? Do not look so surprised. Just because I do not like you does not mean I am heartless. You had no way of knowing it was a slithe. No one ever does."

"Do you—I mean, have you run into them before?"

Tahli nodded.

"I'm sorry."

"There is nothing quite so cruel as finding that a slithe has stolen the face of someone you love." Tahli became distant then, and her gaze looked to something far, far away.

Jerro, feeling that the topic had taken a dark turn, decided to switch gears. "Oh, so, I heard back from Etcher."

"Of course *you* did." Tahli huffed.

"Erm—what's that supposed to mean?"

"Nothing. What did she say?"

"Well, it wasn't all that enlightening, only that she was held up and would be back soon." He decided to leave out the part about being nice to the ginger cat-woman.

"Typical. *'Held up'* could mean any number of things. We might end up stuck here for days."

"Seriously?"

"Would not be the first time. Best to get comfortable."

Jerro groaned and took his slightly over-stacked plate to an empty table. He was surprised when Tahli joined him. He started eating, but his mind was nagging at him. "Has Etcher—" He paused, trying to find the right words, then shook his head and went back to his plate.

"*Just* spit it out."

"...All right," he said with a sigh. "Does she do this often? Disappear and not leave any word."

"You have *no* idea. If you have not noticed, Everdoor does what she wants, when she wants, and does not stop to fill in the details. I have learned to know when to drop a question when it is clear I am not getting any answers. *Ugh!* The amount of times I wanted to scream at her."

"Oh thank god, I was worried it was just me."

"Hardly." She returned her attention to her plate and let the conversation hang there.

They sat quietly for some time, eating their food and idly watching the other hotel guests mill about. It was as the awkward silence grew thick and uncomfortable that Jerro put down his fork and finished chewing his bit of toast and what he decided to think of as bacon. "So what exactly do we do now?"

Tahli drummed her nails. "Sit. Wait. Nothing else to do. No shop, no sales, we are simply stuck until Everdoor gets back from whatever it is she is doing."

"Wonderful," Jerro said a tad bitterly. Nothing seemed to be going smoothly. Even his brief reprieve the other morning had been shattered by the events that followed soon after. And the sickening guilt that hung heavy in his gut had been plaguing him ever since Mahra's apartment. It had been a whole week of madness and impossible events, and while he resented being thrown into the thick of it, he was strangely unprepared to take his rest now that it was forced on him. He *had* wanted a break from everything, he just didn't expect to feel so restless when it came. But what was there to do? Mahra was at least stable, the police weren't after him back on his world, and though he knew eventually things would pick up again—and no doubt quickly—he just couldn't wrap his head around actually taking a break.

He felt numb.

Surely he should have welcomed the reprieve, but without all the excitement and adventure to keep him occupied he found himself confronted by the dusky parts of his mind, the parts he seldom trod and had diligently kept locked away. The fact of the matter was that without Etcher there with him he was hopelessly lost and ill-equipped to deal with the demons that started creeping out from the far reaches of his subconscious. He had very quickly become dependent on the little shopkeeper to lead the way and it made him feel hollow and small now that he had time to think about it.

Tahli had been watching him as he drifted away with his thoughts.

"What?" he said as he noticed her eyes on him.

Her tail flicked. "You look love sick," she said flippantly, poking her food with the end of her fork as if it were a small rodent in her clutches.

"*Excuse me?*"

"Love sick."

"Yeah I heard you the first time."

"*Humph*, then I guess you are slow as well."

"Cheers Tahli, I really missed your berating. Here I thought we might actually enjoy a meal together without insults."

"We are not friends," she stated as plainly as if she had told him *'the square root of nine is three.'* "If it were not for you, I would not be stuck in Yahre."

"You're saying this is *my* fault? I didn't make Etcher leave—"

"Oh yes you did. You asked for answers, she went to get them. Now she is held up, we are here with nothing to do. Simply put, your fault."

Jerro narrowed his eyes on the ginger cat-woman. "What the hell is your problem with me? I didn't ask for any of this, I got thrown into it. Etcher asked *me* to come along, not the other way around."

The other guests were beginning to peek over at them as the conversation started to elevate.

"True, she did. And here you are looking pathetic and sorry for yourself like a love-sick pup, and about as useful as one."

"I am not *love sick* over Etcher if that's what you mean."

Tahli smiled sourly. "Of course. It must be the girl then."

"She has a name." Jerro's teeth were clenching.

Tahli brushed the conversation aside with a flick of her wrist. "Go eat elsewhere. I would rather not make a scene."

"I lost my appetite anyway," Jerro replied bitterly as he got up from the table and stormed away, trying not to make eye contact with the other hotel guests that were staring at him.

Be nice to Tahli, he thought venomously. *Peh, fat chance of that happening. I was being nice—she started it—she...*He continued to grumble away in his mind as he stalked down Penrose Street toward *elsewhere.*

Despite his dramatic exit he actually was still hungry and his stomach growled at him. As his feet moved automatically he had the flittering notion of going back to visit Mahra, but all he would end up doing is moaning on about how unbearable Tahli was. He decided that was probably *not* something Mahra would want to be subjected to.

Jerro continued on past the clinic in hopes of finding somewhere else to eat. Breakfast cafes and coffee shops were open despite the strange contrast of faux-night, but they failed to catch his interest. He continued on, putting as much distance between himself and the hotel as he dared before his hunger won out. He found himself standing outside a corner shop embedded in the side of a stately alabaster building, where watchful gargoyles stared down from the rooftop. The shop advertised '*hot sandwiches and deli treats!*' painted neatly in black and gold along the bottom of the storefront window. It was as inviting as any and would have to do since hunger had taken the reins.

On the inside was a tidy little restaurant all too reminiscent of the bistro he and Mahra had eaten at back in Central Midgard. There were a sparse number of patrons, most of which had their faces buried inside newspapers or were absently looking over the tops of their steaming mugs into the quiet dark streets of the outside world. The granite floors, blackboard menu, and cozy little booths lining the windowed wall lent the restaurant a friendly demeanor.

If he weren't so painfully reminded of the last time he had seen Mahra—the real Mahra—smiling and happy when they had sat together, trading their stories and finding common ground, the place might have even seemed charming. As it stood, Jerro was tempted to leave, but his stomach gurgled out an angry 'no' and forced him to wander up to the counter and order.

Another pearl person greeted him, but they were nothing like the hypnotic nurse at the clinic. This massive specimen was distinctly male, with his white mane styled up in a tall pompadour making him two heads taller than Jerro. His long ears were pierced with matching rows of evenly spaced gold studs, his finely manicured sideburns went down to his impressive jawline—graced with a cleft chin—and his handsome face was square and pleasantly symmetrical. He looked like a macho-man rockabilly and was distinctly out of place wearing a plain t-shirt and heavy black apron.

Jerro placed his order without much thought, picking the first combo brunch that struck him, paid, and sat down in the most secluded corner he could find. He rattled his brain for a while as he wondered what to do, sitting there anxiously until the same pompadour pearl man came out from behind a set of swing doors and laid out Jerro's brunch.

"Kavet?" said the man. He, like the lady nurse Jerro had encountered at the clinic, had a melodious quality to his way of speaking, although his voice was a deep baritone.

"'Scuse me?" Jerro frowned. The Babble Seal was having trouble deciphering the man's thick accent.

"*Kavet*...cov-ee?"

Cov-ee? What the hell is cov—*oh!* "You mean coffee?"

The man smiled and nodded. "*Cov-ee,* yes. You'd like some?" He held up a big steaming container with a deliciously familiar aroma.

"Yes. Thank you."

The man poured the dark, steaming liquid evenly into Jerro's mug and smiled again before returning to his station behind the counter.

Jerro pulled the mug close and warmed his hands on it, savoring the rich aroma and the nostalgic comfort it brought him. *Ah dearest caffeine, how would I ever live without you?* Jerro reached for the tray of white ceramic containers and tested their contents, finding what was most likely cream and sugar, and added a liberal amount of both into his mug. The liquid turned from its deep dark color to a milky chocolate—which Jerro sipped at carefully.

He burnt his tongue and the back of his throat, despite his efforts, but the soothing taste of coffee was worth it. For a moment, Jerro was at peace. He could relax and take his time.

The brunch—which he tucked into like a ravenous beast—had been absolutely wonderful. The bread was warm to the touch and the thick crust crackled as he pulled it apart; it must have been freshly made—the dough inside was airy and soft and buttery on his tongue—such a thing was hard to replicate in anything less. And the root vegetables were flavorful and wholesome, retaining some of that earthy quality. The thick links of sausages had been beautifully chard, the skin breaking with a satisfying snap. It reminded him of his boyhood, of the scrumptious meals his mother would cook with vegetables pulled straight from their garden and meats which had been left to sauté in rich stock.

Jerro mopped up the remaining savory juices on his plate with the fresh bread and devoured every last bite of his meal. Then he sat back, content with his full stomach and still-hot coffee, and actually managed to relax. Amazing how a good meal could brighten his mood, especially without any prickly company to dampen it.

Be nice to Tahli...he thought again and breathed out a laugh. *As if it were possible.* He stared out of the big windows and watched the dark world outside pass him by. How beautiful and strange it was with its weeklong festival of night, its hidden cities and dark secrets, its weird metamorphic inhabitants, its *majik,* its power, its sense of purpose. He had taken to Eclipse so quickly, almost flippantly, as if all its wonders were something strangely familiar. He thought he should feel more overwhelmed by his awe, but after his initial debut into the curious world, it had all become natural. He felt at home.

Home.

...Shit!

Part three of his mental agenda nagged at him. After having messaged Etcher, and checked in on Mahra, the last chunk of his list was still awaiting his attention, and it was by far the worst segment of the lot. Without the buffer of parts one and two, he was left exposed to a line of thinking he had doggedly avoided since the start of his adventure:

Did his parents know about the break in at his work and the investigation against him? Granted, he had been cleared of any charges, but as he counted in his mind the number of days since anyone had seen him last back on *his* Earth, he had a sinking feeling.

With a deep sense of dread, Jerro brought out his phone. He hadn't checked any of the other messages since he got the call from fake Mahra, choosing instead to deny knowledge of any missed calls and voicemails that had piled up on his phone once it had reconnected with Earth's network.

Which was another thing: he had been *right there* on the hillside by his mom's house and was so close to making the trip back home, but then the call came and he was whisked off again on another wild ride.

Things did not look promising as he scrolled through his voicemails. There were four new messages from his dad and seven from his mom.

"Shit," he cursed aloud.

He brought the phone to his ear to listen to the most recent message his mom had left him, and for a moment he had the fleeting hope she might simply be calling about her birthday party. But as her shaky voice crackled through the phone's speakers, that hope was crushed immediately.

"*Jerro, sweetie,*" began the recording, tears threatening on the very cusp of every word. "*Please, sweetheart, I—I just need to know you're okay...I just—*" He ended the voicemail before the sobs could start.

He felt wretched, and although he knew this was a possibility, the reality of it was still difficult to bare. He had no desire to worry his parents, their lives were tumultuous enough after what happened—

An image of his older brother flittered through his mind, and Jerro quickly avoided it, wandering instead into the mind-closet of the Obelisk stone where he sought out the bracelet intended for his mom's birthday. He brought the bangle into reality and turned it over in his hands, admiring the beautiful filigree, the pearly moonstones, the fine engraving...

"*Those stones are callokahn moonstones,*"—Etcher's voice echoed through his memories—"*they're often thought of as mother's stone...They promote restful sleep and were often given to new mothers as a gift of goodwill...That particular bangle must have been*

241

given to a mother who was dearly loved. Those engravings…are imbued with a protection spell. Whoever made this thought highly of dear old mom."

Restful sleep. Now that was something his mother surely needed and was surely not getting in his absence. He hadn't thought much of it at first, but it dawned on him that his mom probably hadn't had a restful night's sleep in a great long while, what with how much of a terror both he and his brother used to be. And how everything turned out after.

He had to get the bracelet to her, and a note, at least enough to say he was alive and that he was sorry. His eyes drifted over to the display counter where the pompadour pearl-man was busy wiping down the glass. Their eyes met and the pearl-man perked up.

"More kavet?" he asked in his heavy guttural accent.

"Uh, no, thanks."

A thought nagged at Jerro and he got to his feet and headed to the counter where rows of beautiful little cakes, housed in fancy boxes, lined the inside of the display. He stared at the bangle in his hand and measured it against the circumference of the cakes. It could fit around one of them, and if he wrapped the bangle in butcher-paper it wouldn't damage the cake either.

"Do those come with the boxes?"

"Yes." The pompadour man nodded affirmatively. "I can give you little tag too and ribbon. You want as gift, no?" The man's deep baritone voice poured out melodiously.

"How di—"

"These cakes a little too feminine for you." The man smirked. "Plus I see you looking down at jewelry." He lowered his voice and leaned in. "Did you get in trouble with the missus?"

A tiny smile cracked across Jerro's face and he laughed. "No, it's for my mom. It's her birthday this weekend."

"Ah, say no more. Might I suggest this one? Is made with fresh strawberry and cream I get from local farm." The cake he pointed out was wrapped in a flawless white fondant with decorative pink icing and tiny edible flowers.

"You have strawberries here?"

"*I* have strawberry." The pompadour man winked. "I grow myself. I have little garden on roof where I grow all my produce."

"That explains why brunch was so good."

"Of course it was, I cooked it."

Jerro felt his smile widening. He liked this strange pompadour man. "Forgive me for saying this but you don't seem like the other, um, actually I don't know what to call them, ah—*you*."

"The *Lanka?* Course not. I'm not so stuck up. Here they walk as if strung up by their noses. Besides, I was not born in Yahre, I was born further south in Leburah." The man's chest puffed out and he seemed mightily proud of his heritage.

Jerro simply nodded so as not to offend.

"My father is *Rockus*, but my mother is *Lanka*. I get her good looks," he said as he swiped his hand over his tall pompadour, "and my father's strength."

The man struck a heroic pose and flexed his impressive plethora of muscles. He had been imposing before, but as his body bulged and seams of his clothing stretched to their limits, Jerro became certain that—should the man wish it—he could have popped off Jerro's limbs as effortlessly as plucking the legs off a bug. It was a display that would have made Reedman wary, and Reedman was about as big and menacing as they came.

"How come you moved to Yahre then?" Jerro asked cautiously. The man seemed friendly enough and Jerro aimed to keep it that way.

"Well, unless you're jeweler or smith, there's no work in Leburah. Besides, I like making little cakes and good food for hungry people. My mother taught me to cook." He shrugged. "I find it more interesting than mining. My father, well, he's not so pleased with my talent but he always has me cook when I come visit. Besides," —the man looked around and whispered to Jerro— "even he likes little cakes. I caught him eating once."

There was a grin now fully affixed to Jerro's face. "In that case I'll take two, one for my mom, and one for me."

The man seemed pleased by this. "Do you like wildeberry? Is very tart but how I make, you swear wildeberry could never taste so good."

The man's jovial aura was swiftly elevating Jerro from his pit of self-loathing. "That sounds good, I'll have that. How much do I owe you?"

The pearl man thought about it for a moment. "Five ginse, you take both."

"Really? Are you sure?"

"Of course. When you taste it, you'll come back for more and I charge you full price next time."

"Okay, deal." Jerro handed over a glassy red coin that had a little glob of solid ruby color at its center.

The man fished out the cakes nimbly and set them on the counter. "You want me to wrap or you want put jewelry in box?"

"Oh, yes—I mean, yes I wanna pack the bracelet too. Do you have butcher paper? Also, would you happen to have a notepad and pen I can borrow? I'd like to leave a note inside."

The man looked at Jerro for a while, indiscernible thoughts swirling behind his pearly eyes. "Tell you what. You write note and give it to me with jewelry, and I package all so cake doesn't get damaged, fair?"

"Yeah, that'd be great, thank you."

The man shrugged. "No problem. Your mom will love cake and you will have to buy every year from now on." He went and grabbed a pen and notepad. "Is fountain pen, you write with before?"

"Yeah, back in school. I think I can manage." Jerro graciously took the pen and paper and sat back down, staring blankly at the notepad.

He sighed, and for a moment the blank page was daunting. There were a hundred-thousand things he could say, might say, *should* say, none of which seemed adequate for the enormity and urgency he felt he needed to impart.

Finally, deciding that he didn't want to waste any of the man's paper or time, Jerro kept the note simple and to the point. He looked it over carefully; it was hardly everything, but he hoped it would be enough. He folded it in half and headed back over to the counter.

"You're done?"

Jerro nodded.

"Hmm. Must be important note for you to look so glum, if you don't mind my saying."

"It's okay. It is. I've kinda not been the best son lately—er—for a while, actually."

The pompadour man nodded. "It can be hard, carving own path in the world. Some people get left behind when searching for who you are. I'm not always good son either, but I try, all we can do is try. Our mothers will always love us. Is our blessing and their curse." He smiled softly.

Jerro felt a hard knot rise in his throat and kept quiet.

"Well, anyway, I wrap this for you and your mom will feel better when she eats cake. And so will you." He winked and gathered up the pieces, leaving the wildeberry cake on the counter for Jerro.

Jerro peered at the little orange-and-white cake and felt his mouth water. It was like a miniature piece of art and he was reluctant to bite into it. Should it prove to be anything like his brunch then it was best kept for another time when he really needed cheering up. He closed the lid of the decorative box and vanished the wildeberry cake away inside the Obelisk.

The man returned to the counter shortly after, holding open a new box for Jerro to inspect. It was a bigger then the one the cake originally came in and was partitioned in half with his note and bracelet in one side and the cake securely wrapped in the other.

"Wow, that's perfect. Thank you!"

"No problem."

The man smiled and closed the lid, fastening the box with a bright red ribbon, which he took a blade to and ran the loose ends over so that they coiled into delicate ringlets.

"I have good penmanship, if you want, but I would have to know what language you want written," said the man, motioning to the decorative blank tag that was hanging down the side of the box.

"Oh, no, it's okay, really. This is perfect."

The man huffed and took up the fountain pen, a smooth line of text flowing out of the nib as he inscribed the notepad. Though the lettering was in a foreign script, it was written so beautifully—with elegant loops and swirls—that Jerro could tell the man had more than just *good* penmanship.

"Is up to you, but if you write here, I copy in my best writing on tag, if you want." He shrugged, but Jerro noted his expression.

"All right, it's a beautiful box, wouldn't want to spoil it with my sloppy writing."

"Well, I wasn't going to say anything, but I study calligraphy; most people's writing is sloppy compared to mine." He grinned.

Jerro smiled at that, feeling uplifted once again. He took back the pen and wrote '*To Mom, from Jerro*' in his neatest print on the notepad and handed it to the man.

"Hmm, this alphabet, is Earth writing, no?"

"Yeah, that's where I'm from."

"Ah! I thought so, your ehta looked too natural."

"Huh?"

"*Ehta.* This my ehta," he pointed to himself, "my native self is much bigger. You know, in town most people stay in their ehta, is easier to get around, outside town we're all big beasts." He laughed.

"*Oh.* Right. I didn't know it was called that. I guess you could say I'm all ehta then." He laughed quietly at his own poor joke.

"Must be strange having only one body; I can't imagine."

"I can't imagine having more than one."

"Fair point."

The man looked over the note again, studying it carefully, then, with the same beautiful calligraphy he had used before, the man wrote Jerro's simple note on the tag.

He stood tall and awaited Jerro's appraisal.

"She's gonna love it," Jerro announced. The whole packaging was more impressive than any of Jerro's previous floundering attempts at gift-wrapping, and he hoped the contents would give his mom some peace of mind.

The man nodded. "Good. Birthdays are special. That bracelet is as beautiful as my cakes, she will be happy."

"Yeah, I'm sure she will."

"By the way, what did I write? I don't read Earth script, only recognize it."

"Just '*To Mom, from Jerro*,' simple."

"Jerro? This is your name?" And the way the man spoke made Jerro's name sound heroic and regal.

"Yeah that's me."

"Jerro, I'm Yohza, good to meet you." The man named Yohza stuck out his massive hand for Jerro to shake.

"Yohza," repeated Jerro as they shook. He imagined the name probably didn't sound as epic coming off his own mundane tongue. "Say, Yohza…how come this place is so empty? Last day of the festival, I figured it would be more packed."

"That's because everyone is sleeping off hangover, come three o'clock this place will be packed. Thankfully, I have workers coming in to take care my shift. This year, I will enjoy the Fifth Day *with* the crowd. My husband too, he's been nagging I take time off." Yohza laughed to himself at that. "What about you?"

The information had taken a moment to register, the word *husband* had taken Jerro off guard but he recovered quickly before his expression could accidentally insult the man. "You mean why aren't I sleeping off a hangover? Well, I certainly tried to, but ah—a colleague of mine left me some special tonic, cleared me right up."

"You came prepared then, smart man. Don't suppose you have any extra?"

"Not on me, but I might be able to get you some." *Might* being dependent on Tahli's unpredictable mood. "I'll send you a hazua if I do."

"That would be very kind. Ask hazua to drop off at my flat on top of shop, otherwise I might lose it during the festival."

"Sure thing." Determination snuck into the backdrop of Jerro's words and he realized that 'might' wasn't an option. He was intent on getting Yohza the special tonic even if it meant sucking up to Tahli. It was the least he could do as way of thanks. "Well, uh, I should probably be sending this out." He smiled, yet felt a little empty at the thought of leaving. He hoped he wasn't over thinking it, but it was possible Jerro had just made a new friend.

"Of course. And if you find yourself near Hanova Street tonight be sure to stop by the Black Dog. I will likely be there."

"I like the sound of that." Jerro beamed and shook hands with Yohza one last time. "I'll see ya around, thanks again!"

"My pleasure. Next time bring friends so they will buy more of my cakes."

Jerro had wandered into the more heavily wooded area of Yahre and nestled down on the bank of a calm lake. In the moonlight the water looked just like black glass laced with gentle ripples and lazy undulations.

Weeping willows were leaned over the dark water, dipping their blossom heavy fronds into the lake. Small rings radiated out from where they touched as a soft breeze swayed the spindly branches. Near the heart of the lake water birds sailed quietly along, leaving V trails behind them and causing the fallen blossoms to delicately twirling across the water.

A soft melody of night critters danced on the edge of Jerro's consciousness as the illuminant bodies of fireflies and glowing butterflies tumbled about in thick bundles, dotted around the banks of the dark lake. Their reflections caught on the water's surface like twinkling jewels, mimicking the stars that streaked the clear sky above.

It was beautiful there, calm and quiet. The cool air played through Jerro's hair and kissed his skin, soothing away his tension. Jerro held the magnificently wrapped box in his lap and considered it thoughtfully for a while. He knew its arrival would only provoke more questions, but it would at least let his parents know he was alive.

He called his teal-colored hazua to him. The little ball of blue-green light popped into existence and gently bobbed in the air beside him. Its soft glow cast a dome of eerie color around Jerro and the lunar-tinted world.

He let out his breath and stared at the hazua. "Okay. I need you to do something for me. I need you to deliver this to my mom's house. Put it right on top of the side table in the main hallway by the front door. There's a dish of coins on it, put this box beside it and make sure no one sees you do it. Do you understand?"

Having neither facial features nor a head, the little hazua did a loop-de-loop in the air.

Jerro took that as a yes. "All right, well, here you go." He held up the decorative box—which was considerably larger than the hazua—and wondered how exactly the winged messenger would manage.

He didn't have to wonder long. The teal colored hazua expanded and sucked the whole package up into its round body before resizing itself to its original proportions. The hazua then rolled back lazily in the air and disappeared with a muted pop.

Jerro breathed out a sigh of relief. His mental checklist was almost complete. He'd deal with his flatmates some other time.

Blue and white lights flashed steadily, warning the crowd to stay back. Silent police cars surrounded the scene, vacant save for the occasional officer radioing their muffled conversations to dispatch. A ribbon of yellow caution tape gave the investigators a wide berth from the civilian crowd that nestled up as closely as they could against the barricade.

Part of the road had been blocked, much to the displeasure of the morning commuters and the nosey foot traffic that eagerly wanted a peek at the source of the commotion. A row of uniformed officers stood impassively around the perimeter and stared down the crowd. All too soon the news reporters came pouring in like an ugly flood, shoving their microphones under noses and jabbering away with their speculations.

By the alley, which was safely hidden behind the ring of police cruisers and impassive officers, was Detective Reedman.

There was another man beside him, though the weedy specimen was much smaller by comparison to Reedman's massive bulk. At nearly six-and-a-half foot tall, Detective Jaiko Reedman was a beast of a man. He was finely groomed, dark-skinned, and mean looking—with sharp angles to his chiseled face, a large square jaw and thick angular eyebrows. Yet far from unattractive. A point which Reedman put careful consideration into when styling his closely cropped facial hair and sculpting his physique.

His new partner, however, was very lacking, and made more so by Reedman's impressive stature. His partner *looked* like a homicide detective: slightly sloppy, unkempt mousy-brown hair, tired apathetic eyes, a long brown trench coat, rumpled shirt, and permanently clasped cigarette between his thin lips. He slouched as he stood, pushing out the little doughy paunch that clung to an otherwise weedy frame.

He had a face whose features looked as though they had been squished toward the middle and his pert nose was perpetually upturned as if he had just smelled something awful.

"Whadda mess," spewed out the detective between his partly closed lips. He plucked the cigarette from his mouth and brushed out the ember on the bottom of his shoe, then stuck the crumpled butt in the hand of the closest officer. "Take care of that, will ya?"

The officer grunted disdainfully in reply.

"Bet you're glad you transferred from property crimes, ey Reedman?" the man said with a sneer.

"I dunno, seen claymores leave a nastier mess," Reedman replied evenly, although his deep, resonate tone held the slightest growl. It was safe to say he wasn't fond of his new partner.

"Oh, yeah, right. Forgot you're a vet. Don't get many of you, don't usually pass the psych."

Reedman grunted.

"So, can't confirm anything yet, what with the face *missing* and all, but we're fairly certain that's Daag Landvick."

"Yeah, I'd be willing to wager that was him. I recognize the suit." Reedman breathed out heavily through his nose as he looked at the human remains in the alley. A pervasive metallic stench accompanied the scene, corrupting every breath Reedman tried to expel.

In a crumpled bloodied heap was a body. It had been bent in ways that would make a contortionist cringe, but that wasn't the worst of it—the worst was the head, or rather, what was left of it. It had been cleaved in half, exposing the inner cavity of the skull. The face was entirely missing, as was the brain. And the torso was soaked in blood from the neck down.

It had not been a clean cut either; it was ragged and cracked around the edges as if it had been *crunched* off. What was left of the severed tongue lulled to one side, the hollow head was upside down, and the torso had been twisted back into a loop with the legs and arms folded over the body, turning it into a tight ball, like someone had wadded Daag Landvick up and had tossed him in the bin.

The once-designer suit, polished wingtip shoes, and silk tie were largely untouched, aside from the blood, as was Daag's white-gold wristwatch and the contents of his fully stocked wallet.

As Reedman stood there and let the ungodly scene poor into his ever churning mind, he noted two things: The kill had been recent, and this was most definitely a murder.

"Wouldn't'a found him if it weren't for those damn gypsies rummaging through the bins. Apparently the gypsy-boy that found the body screamed so loudly they thought a girl was getting buggered in the alley and one of those rent-a-cops came running out the shopping center. Guess he was hoping to be a hero. Probably pissed his pants when he saw this mess," Reedman's partner said crassly.

"Has the boy said anything?"

"Nah. You know how it is, bloody gypsies. Been prattling on in Romanian or some such. We got half the world under one common tongue and they go on like they're too good to speak it. Not like they don't understand, mind you, but they don't wanna talk to cops, not even to help with a bloody murder."

Reedman glanced at his partner. "So we are calling this a murder then?"

"Fuck." He lit up another cigarette. "I'd love to call this a wild animal attack or freak machining accident. But mister designer suit here isn't exactly a factory worker and an animal would have gnawed on more than just the head. Fucking psycho did this. What I dunno is how they balled up the body like that." He gave Reedman a quick glance up and down. "Whadda ya think, Reedman? Think you could turn someone into origami?" He snickered.

"You volunteering?"

"Ha!" The man spat out a laugh.

"Let me talk to the boy."

"Suit yourself. We had to cuff him in the back of the police van so he wouldn't bolt."

"He might press charges."

"Yeah? How's he gonna do that in Romanian?" said the detective, and started to lead the way.

"Thorneback, why don't you let me head over there. You already tried talking to him once, right?"

"*Peh*, yeah I get you. I'll be over here then. Tell me if he says anything interesting."

Reedman strode briskly over to the police van that Thornback had singled out. When he opened the back he saw a scraggly looking youth that was more dirt then boy, with ragged clothes and dark, greasy hair that was difficult to discern the natural color from. What was clear, however, were his icy-blue eyes, and they stared hard and accusingly at Reedman. The boy said something in his native tongue and spat on the floor of the van as Reedman entered.

"Romanian, huh?" Reedman said with a quiet laugh, rummaging through his trouser pocket to pull out a small key. *"A ty govorite po-russki?"* asked Reedman as he gathered up the boy's wrists and undid the cuffs.

The boy was so shocked that he didn't move when Reedman approached him. "Da," he replied.

Reedman let loose another string of Russian and waited for the boy to answer.

The tension was slowly leaving the boy's shoulders as he rubbed his freed wrists. He nodded in answer to Reedman's question.

The conversation went on like that for a while. With Reedman asking a question and the boy either nodding or shaking his head as reply, occasionally giving a few words of his own. And when it was all said and done, Reedman backed out of the van and held the door open.

Gingerly, the boy climbed out behind him, watching Reedman all the while. He flinched when Reedman grabbed his shoulder and handed him a folded bill from his wallet.

"Yest," Reedman instructed. *Eat.*

The boy hesitantly took the bill and hid it away inside his filthy shirt. His eyes were darting about, looking between the police barrier and the detective.

"Go on then."

The boy dropped his gaze to the ground, looking sullen for the moment, and then started to take off, but before he could disappear, he turned back and spoke a few words to the detective, then finally disappeared down a small alley.

"What the hell was that about?" Thorneback had slunk up beside Reedman and was watching the big man carefully with his own beady eyes.

"He said a monster did it."

"Ha! You learn to speak gypsy overseas, did ya?"

"School, actually." He glanced at Thorneback.

The unkempt detective clucked his tongue. "You think it wise to let 'im go? Only lead we got so far."

"He's hardly a lead." Reedman unfolded a piece of paper from his blazer pocket and handed it to Thorneback.

"Well look-y here, signed statement and everything." The detective whistled. "Aren't you all prim and proper on the job."

Reedman huffed. "He didn't see anything; the alley was deserted when he decided to go dumpster diving. Then he found that." He jutted his chin out toward the disfigured bloody heap of Daag that lay besides a scattering of garbage. "The dumpster tipped over with him when he tried to jump out, wasn't very full to begin with, but someone had gone through the trouble of piling a few bags on top of the body as if to hide it."

"These businesses go through a ton of rubbish, they'd have been full by the end of the day and the trucks come tomorrow."

"We wouldn't have found the body for months, if at all."

Thorneback nodded grimly. "So you think your boy Jerro did it?"

Astonishment stamped itself all over Reedman's face as he peered at the scraggly detective.

"Yeah, don't act so surprised. I could give a toss what you lot do in blue collar crimes but it's been hard not to hear someone yacking on about the little bugger. Gave the station quite the run around, what was it, three years ago?"

"Two."

"Yeah well, '*Infamous Ahliss*' I keep hearing. He some techie kid, right? Didn't really think much of it, but this poor sod was involved in the latest debauchery with Ahliss, wasn't he?"

"Not exactly."

"What's that supposed to mean?"

"Don't ask."

"It's my job."

"You wanna look through the case? Go right ahead. You tell me if he was involved or not."

"*Touchy*. What crawled up your nickers and died?"

"Nothing. Tell me what forensics finds." Reedman strode over to his car and pulled away from the scene.

Jerro laid back in the grass along the bank of the lake and felt the gentle tug of sleep start to close in on him. His eyes were being lulled by the dancing glowing insects and the low buzz of their nightly calls. He could feel the ground supporting his body and each breath, alleviating the weightiness of his mind. He could so easily fall asleep…

Distant memories called to him…

He saw a being who was a kaleidoscope of woman and fox. She spoke without words and showed him through the Land of Dream…

She had given him a flower and asked him to do something very important…

He had promised…

He was supposed to go—

Jerro.

The dream started to lose its validity—

Jerro!

The memories started to slip away, back into the recesses of his mind—

Jerro!

He shot up with a start.

"Etcher?" he called out, but he was alone.

The sudden jolt had set his heart racing as adrenaline pumped wildly through his veins. But he was alone, and everything was calm. He pushed himself up to his feet unsteadily and looked out into the dark waters of the lake. He felt strange, like something was tugging at him, pulling at the pit of his stomach as though he were hooked to a tether. The feeling became eerie and his skin turned to gooseflesh.

The insects danced in their gentle undulations, the weeping willows swayed, and blossoms tumbled weightlessly through the air, and he felt ill at ease.

He had a sudden desire to step back. And in the very next instant the air right before Jerro turned red and hot. Tongues of flame lapped out as a tiny fissure scarred the air and bent the lunar light inward.

Then a ball of fire burst into life in front of him. A wave of energy knocked him to the ground as the fire leapt out.

But it dissipated as quickly as it came, and where the fire had once been now stood a familiar and somewhat singed little shopkeeper.

"Etcher!" he exclaimed.

But the shopkeeper was busy hopping around as she patted out the tiny clinging tendrils of fire which were burning holes in her elegant clothing.

"Damn, this was my favorite shirt," said Etcher, poking a finger through a hole in her midnight-blue silk blouse. She then produced a handkerchief and wiped the soot from her face.

"Etcher, how the hell?"

Ah, Jerro," she said, looking him up and down. "You're here. When are we?"

"We're in Yahre...don't you remember?"

"Not *where,* I said *when.*"

"I...er, Friday?"

Etcher looked up at the dark sky with its four full moons, with the fifth both the furthest and smallest in the row, edging closer to completion. "Friday morning?"

"Yeah..."

"Oh good. I've only been gone a day here," she said more to herself then to Jerro.

"What?"

"Nothing to worry about. Well, come along then."

"Hey, now wait a second!" said Jerro as he scrambled to his feet after Etcher. He reached for her arm to stop her but the evasive little shopkeeper turned with him and they found themselves standing uncomfortably close.

"I know you have questions, but to save me the trouble of repeating myself I'd rather divulge said answers in front of both you *and* Tahli. Is it safe to presume she's still at the hotel?"

"Yeah, I guess, but Etcher..."

She held up a hand to silence him. "Jerro, please. I *will* answer your questions, but I have a great distaste for tedium, and it would be incredibly tedious to have to retell my tale more than once."

Jerro chewed on the inside of his cheek to keep quiet, avoiding eye contact as much as he could with their close proximity.

"Right then," Etcher breathed out and continued to head up the grassy hill. "How's Mahra?" she asked once Jerro had caught up to her.

"Okay I guess. The same mostly." His mood dampen and he was suddenly less interested in how and why Etcher had appeared before him.

"Well, I have good news and bad news. Frankly, it's more bad news than I care to impart but things don't always go the way we like."

"What's the good news?" he dared to ask.

"I found a witch that can cure Mahra."

"That's brilliant news! Wait...What's the bad news?"

"The bad news is that it's *the* witch, and she's just as likely to turn on us as she would be to help us. Actually *more* likely to turn on us than help us, given the reputation, but I'm trying to be optimistic."

Jerro didn't like the sound of that at all. "So, can't we try someone else then? Someone *more* likely to help then less likely?"

"I'd love to, but this particular witch is one we have to go see regardless of Mahra, so we might as well try and enlist her help."

"And why do we have to go to her, exactly?"

"Well that would be part of the tale which I've yet to tell, so for the meanwhile, you'll just have to wait."

Jerro looked around as they walked and noticed that something was missing. "Etcher?"

"Mm?"

"Where's the shop?"

"*Ah.*"

And the way she said 'ah' did not put Jerro's mind at ease. "Etcher?"

"It's part of the bad news, I'm afraid, and will also have to wait to be told."

"How did you get here?"

She shot him a rather blunt stare and Jerro decided he should probably stop asking questions before he ended up in a closet.

They continued through the thick of trees and back into the hubbub of Yahre. The cobbled street which they followed ran beside the river and up over a bridge to one of the higher tiers. Manmade canals ran off from the tumultuous waters, and laced the upper levels of the city, trickling down from the ledges in delicate waterfalls that filtered into an intricate network of fish ponds below—where mermaid creatures were lounging about, some perched atop of rocks while others rested their arms over the lip of their pools and idly chatted with other city-goers.

The foot traffic was still light, though Jerro noticed a few of the pearl people turning their heads in wonder at the singed little shopkeeper beside him—who strode forward with such determination as if she *meant* for her clothes to be burned.

He was glad there weren't more people about; though Etcher might have walked with unchallenged confidence, he himself was feeling very uncertain. His thoughts started to wander as an uncomfortable quiet settled between them, and he remembered what Yohza had said would happen come three o'clock. Would Yahre truly awaken then? Now that Etcher was back, would they even stick around long enough to see the fanfare?

Jerro felt a strange sense of loss. He had privately hoped that whatever happened next, they'd be back in time to see the grand finale of the festival, and so that Jerro could meet up with Yohza at the Black Dog on Hanova. He missed having a carefree night, drinking with his mates—last night hardly counted. He considered mentioning it to Etcher, but he wasn't sure there was a way to bring it up without also inquiring about where the hell she had been.

"Is there anything else you *can* tell me?" he found himself asking.

"Not really." Etcher looked at him sidelong.

"Great."

"What about you? Nothing to tell during your stay so far?"

Heat flooded his cheeks and kept his tongue silent. There was plenty to say all right, but nothing he was entirely certain he wished to share. For one, he was rather embarrassed to have gotten so plastered the night before that *Tahli*, of all people, had to come to his rescue, and his whole dealings with Yohza and his mom's gift felt strangely personal. He shrugged. "Just been passing the time till you got back," he said airily.

"For what it's worth, I hadn't intended on being gone so long."

Jerro refrained from speaking, hoping *something* more vital might be shared, but the little shopkeeper kept mum, which meant the rest of their trek continued in awkward silence.

Soon enough though, the grand white façade of the Vouladun hotel broke through the tree line as they headed down Penrose Street. Only this time there was a frenzy of commotion before the main entrance.

Massive black steeds, with finely groomed manes and golden bridals, clapped their hooves impatiently on the cobbled road outside the hotel. The carriages they drew were large and ornate with richly stained wood and polished metal inlays. The drivers who sat quietly upfront where dressed in heavy black clothing and their faces were obscured by their tall, stiff collars and top-hats, casting deep shadows over their indiscernible countenances.

Valets from the hotel hurried to open the carriage doors for their regal looking passengers. An entire entourage poured out, looking stately in their bright and colorful outfits. They formed a guided path from the middle carriage to the hotel and stood at attention for the small group that exited. There were seven of them in total, heading down the guided path the entourage had formed. The group stood out starkly from their vibrant associates in that they were clad from head to toe in long black gowns that had only narrow slits in the fabric across the eyes.

"What's going on?" asked Jerro, watching curiously from the sidelines.

"The grand finale of the Lunar Week calls for the most prestigious of performances. Those esteemed guests will be fulfilling that requirement."

"Do you know them?"

"I might take a guess, but typically the last performance is a surprise. They could be debutants, or perhaps world-famous vocalists, instrumentalists. But if I were to wager, I'd say that they were the Al'Florun singers from the Bloodlands." Etcher's tail coiled with curiosity and her honey eyes studied the group closely as they disappeared inside the hotel. "We should be on our way."

Jerro felt the air around Etcher change, becoming cold and serious. He didn't like it.

They had to use a side entrance to get into the hotel as the main doors were being blocked, if not intentionally, by the entourage. Once inside, Etcher let Jerro take the lead, and they navigated their way through the bustle toward the elevators. The attendants seemed to be in a flurry, darting about like a mad rush of bees, and gossip was spreading quickly amongst the hotel guests about the mysterious new arrivals. Jerro caught wisps of the chatter here and there, although no one else seemed to think they were the Al'Florun, and there was certainly no mention of the Bloodlands.

The name niggled at him, but he couldn't place his finger on why. He would have asked Etcher, but her icy mood stilled his tongue and put an uneasy feeling deep in his heart. They rode the elevator up in silence to the ninth floor, and stepped out into the lavish furnishings of the hallway as they headed to Tahli's room.

*Tahli…*A thought dawned on him, but his attention was drawn away as Etcher rapped her knuckles on the door.

The ginger cat-woman's hard footsteps came swiftly. No doubt she expected another run in with Jerro.

"Everdoor!" Tahli spoke with a mix of shock and irritation.

"Pleasure to see you again too, d'you mind?"

The testy feline moved aside and let Etcher pass, staring into the back of the little shopkeeper's head as she did.

"Really, Tahli? The Diva suite?" said Etcher as she looked around.

Tahli crossed her arms. "You did not specify which room I should book," she replied in her sultry lilt, although there was the slightest hint of petulance in her tone.

Etcher snorted. "I'll keep that in mind."

"So?" Tahli said expectantly. She had walked away from the door and let it fall toward Jerro, who luckily caught it before it could smack him in the face. "Why are your clothes burnt?" It was more of an accusation than a question.

"Because she appeared in a ball of fire," said Jerro as he brushed past Tahli and made his way to one of the comfortable armchairs.

Tahli sniffed with agitation, glaring at Jerro as he passed. "So I am last to know what goes on now?"

"If you're quite done, Tahli, I might explain myself. *Yes,* I did appear in a ball of fire, as Jerro says, but so far I've asked him to wait patiently for my recount of what transpired since yesterday. And now, it's your turn for patience. I need a bath and a change of clothes, and I would appreciate if you had room service bring up their finest lunch platter with two bottles of Sanka Blush and three glasses."

Tahli set her jaw firmly and went over to a rather posh-looking rotary phone to call room service, muttering under her breath as she dialed.

One of the many good things about the Diva suite was that it came with a magnificent bathroom—more of a bath-*house* than a room—equipped with its own sauna, a large hot tub and even a miniature pool. The bad thing was the cost, and that it was coming out of Etcher's pocket.

The little shopkeeper sighed as she took a mental tally of the week's expenses. She stripped down and looked at the singed and slightly ragged clothes. There would be no fixing them, velvet and silk didn't patch well, burned and frayed as they were. She tossed them in the laundry bin—yet another outfit of hers that had been ruined. She would need to take a trip to the tailor's very soon.

Etcher, now naked in the florescent light of the expansive bathroom, surveyed her petite body in a full-length mirror. It was a form she had grown rather accustomed too, she even rather liked it. Short though she was, it was a good body, lithe and agile. It was curvy enough without being cumbersome, and proportionate in a way that made her flamboyant clothes sit nicely. Of course, it was only a shadow of her true self—the reminder of which lay on her back in the form of an intricate gold seal which was branded into her flesh.

Etcher stood with her back to her reflection, looking over her shoulder to examine the branding. There was a hairline fissure cracking the outer rings of the concentric design over her left shoulder, just barely chipping into the inner part of the symbol, though looked as if it were threatening to break deeper. She tentatively touched the crack in the design and remembered her time in Arcadia.

The Mad King and the false prophet had tried to trap her, and had forced out her other self.

It didn't end well for them.

A mirthless smile coiled into the corner of her mouth. The feeling of being whole, though short lived, had ignited a longing which she so often had to repress. Its weight was a bittersweet burden.

Etcher let out a lengthy exhale. Though she hadn't shown it to the others, she was very tired, and the events that had transpired since the day before had left her mind heavy. A great deal of troubling questions had arose, and Etcher pondered them carefully. She owed Jerro and Tahli a story, at least enough to fill in some of the gaps.

But they didn't need to know everything, nor would she tell them all the sordid details: how her long and arduous journey had taken her to unknown parts of the cosmos, how she had jumped not just between worlds but also between realities, how it had been more than just a day for Etcher Everdoor…

She lowered herself into the steaming bath, housed in the back of a great porcelain tortoise. The heat from the aromatic waters seeped into her aching body and purged her weary soul. Yes, she'd have to tell them a story, and like all great tales it would be grounded in truth, at least in part.

"Your *wine* is here," said Tahli with a curt knock on the bathroom door. She didn't bother to hide the saltiness in her voice.

The door cracked open and the humid aromatic air from the bathroom rolled out in a light mist and perfumed the living quarters. Etcher emerged, groomed and refined in her new clothes. It was a much more somber theme than she usually donned: deep black with crimson trim, a high stiff collar, blood-red scarf, and the polished silver chain of a pocket watch with silver buttons to match.

It made her look grave and menacing.

Whatever pointed quips Tahli might have said died on her tongue at the sight of the austere looking shopkeeper.

"Thank you, Tahli," said Etcher. She sauntered past the cat-woman to the kitchenette counter where the wine and a fine-looking cheese platter had been placed. Etcher gathered up the food and drink and brought them over to where Jerro was seated, setting the coffee table and pouring them each a glass of the pale rosy-colored wine in one flawless motion.

"Thanks," Jerro said cautiously as he picked up his glass, eyeing Etcher with wonder.

The little shopkeeper took up an armchair and motioned for Tahli to come join them. Once they were all seated, Etcher sipped at her wine, crossed one slender leg over the other, and let the silence hang there as she nibbled on a piece of cheese.

Neither Tahli nor Jerro dared to speak. They traded weary glances; the stern countenance of the shopkeeper had instilled a sense of dread in both of them.

Etcher drained half her glass and dusted her fingers as she settled back into the chair. "There are some things that need explaining," she said evenly, but there was coldness to her voice that kept the tension around the group, "before I can tell you both what happened."

Her eyes rested on Jerro and made him quiver. The cheery, carefree shopkeeper had been eviscerated by the grim host that sat before them. They were reminded that Etcher Everdoor—who lived without a rudder, who smiled easily and jumped into the fray without hesitation—was most definitely in charge.

It was like sitting in front of an asp, coiled up and ready to strike. No sudden moves, no sound to break the thin barrier that kept the serpent at bay. Their attention was wholly captivated, which was precisely what Etcher had wanted.

"*I* make the shop move," she said plainly, and kept her eyes on Jerro. "The shop, in turn, hones this ability of mine so that I can pinpoint where I want to go. Without it, it's like trying to aim at a spinning target in the dark. Do you accept this fact, Jerro?"

He nodded slowly and kept very quiet.

"Good, then we can begin."

Evenings by the shoreline were no less colorful than the day. Illuminant sea creatures swam through the opalescent waters and made the undulating body a glittering mass of eerie lights. The clear night sky let the large red moon bathe the world below, and the ivory chapel was painted in a cacophony of borrowed colors.

The chill in the air had deepened and the tower's open arches made the upper chamber frigid. Jayus E'Kilh had returned to the tower after his dealings with Morrigah Faus, though he didn't stay there long. The blue-scaled man retired down the winding stairs to his private quarters where a hearth was burning steadily. His fellow kinsmen had finished their evening chores and made ready for a well-deserved rest.

But the Abbot couldn't sleep. Instead, Jayus E'Kilh sat before the hearth and watched the tongues of fire dance as the logs crackled and murmured under their bite. He was numb for a while, no thoughts of Morrigah Faus, or of the statue of Urg'Ra, of the certainty of war, or the doom that followed him steadily. For a moment, there was peace.

But it wasn't meant to last.

"Such a funny thing to find you sitting here, unoccupied and unhurried. I had entertained the notion that you *must* be busy to ignore my messages. I find I am mistaken."

Cold, icy, dread slithered down Jayus's back. He peered through the corner of his eyes and saw a familiar little figure sitting beside him. *Soundless*, how could she be so soundless?

"Etcher Everdoor, you find me in a rare moment."

"Oh, I'm sure it must be. You, of all people, know I don't take kindly to being ignored."

Jayus fought the desire to gulp. He studied Etcher closely; she sat so casually, so calm, draped on the couch, legs crossed, and tail coiling lazily. But he had no illusions, he knew that should she wish to, she'd slice his throat before he had time to blink.

Her honey-gold eyes turned on him and made his soul quiver; the little flecks of green caught the firelight and made her petrifying gaze seem to burn like embers. He was frozen in those eyes, knowing that they peered into him, and through, slicing apart his words and tearing out the truth behind them.

Etcher was a devil that had its claws around Jayus's heart the very moment they made their first deal. His palm itched as he thought about it. A deal with Etcher was binding, everlasting and never forgotten.

She waited patiently as she stared at him. The magnitude of Etcher's patience was a terrifying thing, she could wait for the stars to burn out. And when you thought you were safe, when the years had put enough distance between you and the past to lull you into false security, she would come to collect on those deals and you'd be helpless to stop it.

"There's been a lot of commotion since the statue was returned to us. Morrigah Faus threatened a clan war."

"Nothing unusual then," she replied silkily.

Jayus took pause. He had no excuse that would be convincing, no lie that would make it past those piercing eyes. He didn't want to talk to Etcher, he had no intention of replying to her messages. He knew she would come, sooner or later—he had merely hoped for more time. "What do you want?"

Etcher smiled, and it made Jayus's heart fall to new found depths of horror. "I came to ask a question, Jayus, one which I hope you'll answer plainly."

The Abbot said nothing and waited in quiet dread.

"*Who* sent you the tip about Urg'Ra's fire?"

She might as well have asked him for his soul. "I don't give out my contacts." He tried to sound firm and confident, though there was little to draw from.

Etcher drummed her nails on the arm of the couch. The smile played about her lips and she continued to watch him with those calculating eyes.

Jayus felt his fear building. The silence that hung between them was palpable and heavy, choking out the air from his lungs. The seconds seemed to press into him, and the longer the silence built between them, the more his dread grew. He knew he had to say something, lest she ask again. He wouldn't like how the question was posed a second time.

"Why do you want to know?" He stalled, hoping that if he could prolong giving the answer, Fate would smile on him and grant him refuge.

"That little venture," she purred with menace, "caused me quite a lot of trouble. Trouble, I might add, that has posed some interesting questions." Her nails drummed steadily on the arm of the couch, *brrum-bum-bum-brrum-bum-bum*. "It seemed to me that there was greater purpose in sending me off to that little Earth planet."

"It was a trusted contact, verified. I wouldn't have sent you on the venture otherwise."

"That wasn't what I asked."

"I—" but his words fell flat. "I can't tell you."

Etcher sucked in her breath and rose from the chair.

Jayus felt small.

"*Can't* tell me, or *won't*?"

"I would be putting myself at risk..."

"You're at risk now." Her eyes twinkled devilishly. "Who is the greater threat to you?"

Jayus swallowed and closed his eyes. There was the immediate threat of the devil-woman, and the one that loomed down the road. The only thing that separated them was time.

Time, he thought. Time had become a giant clock that played at the back of his mind, always. Pressuring him, hurrying him, weighing him down and slicing away at his days, bringing him ever closer to an inevitable and terrifying end. It seemed he was always scrambling to prolong his time, just a little more, just enough to get him through to the next day. Etcher offered him time; appeasing her meant he would survive the next few moments, days perhaps. It meant he wouldn't have to go behind the green door with the hollow leafy face, wouldn't have to go inside the room at the very back of the shop, wouldn't have to remember what it meant to cross the devil.

"I didn't ask for the contact, they approached me, I had no choice—"

"*Jayus,*" Etcher said calmly, almost melodiously.

He looked down at the hard floor and his eyes traveled along the peaks and valleys in the stone toward the warmth of the fire where they sought refuge in the mesmerizing flames. He let himself go numb, enough to loosen up his tongue so he could speak. "The Raven Witch sent me the message and instructed me to contact you." He felt the weight of the world collapsing. How had he entangled himself so thoroughly? How had he got caught up surrounded by these demons? If Etcher didn't kill him, the Raven Witch surely would. He felt his gaze be drawn upward to the golden eyes of the demon thief.

"The Raven Witch," she repeated, a snicker dancing in her lips. "You've doomed me."

Jayus felt empty and with it came a strange sense of calm. "I had no choice."

Etcher laughed, tittering with jittery giggles that developed and became robust. Soon she was laughing deep from the pit of her stomach. A hearty and sincere-sounding laughter that brought tears to the corners of her eyes. "Of course you didn't! Oh! Poor Jayus…what god did you spite to end up in such a spider's web?"

He felt confused. "You're…you're not mad?"

"Mad? I'm furious!" she said as she continued to laugh. "But what good's being mad at you? Ah, Jayus, I hope the next life brings you happiness, this one's been nothing but strife."

He went cold and his heart thumped hard against his chest.

And Etcher kept laughing. "Aw well, I suppose I wouldn't have believed you if it were anyone else. Well then," —she sighed and took a deep breath to compose herself— "well, I guess I'm buggered." She looked at him and winked. "Next time, Jayus, forewarn me when someone's putting a noose around my neck. Here, you could use a drink." She had conjured up a stout glass and handed it to him. "A toast: may it not be our last." She clinked her glass with his and downed the amber liquid.

Jayus sipped from his glass, his thoughts turned blank. The sudden and drastic change unnerved him, but he had seen her like this before. At one moment she was cold and cruel, ready to peel the meat from his bones, but in an instant the ruthless killer was replaced by the happy-go-lucky little shopkeeper. He never fully believed that the killer was gone in those moments, simply lurking beneath the skin, ready to strike whenever needed. A darkness that held firm at the core.

"Cheer up," she said.

He breathed out slowly and took another sip. His heart was still racing and was slow to settle down. He had never trusted any of the perceived camaraderie, but he didn't dare insult her either, so he had no choice but to play along. "This hardly seems amusing to me. She'll come for me, and when she does—"

"She won't come for you, Jayus, she won't go near you."

"Why not? I know the darkness in her wake; she's more powerful than you." It was a daring thing to say, but given the change in her mood, sincerity was expected and Jayus sincerely believed the Raven Witch would eviscerate him—like she had so many others in the war of Pelingross—and not even the cunning Etcher Everdoor could do a thing to stop it.

Etcher tilted her head back and forth as if weighing his words. "I don't think you know me well enough to make that call." She winked. "Besides, I protect my investments. Unless of course you *are* right and she offs me. Then I guess you're buggered too."

"That's not a comfort."

"It wasn't meant to be."

Etcher sipped her blush-colored wine and leaned forward, picking up a little silver knife to spread a soft herb-speckled cheese over a slice of toasted baguette. She nestled back in the chair and chewed thoughtfully, looking between Jerro and Tahli in silence. A little of the iciness had broken away and the cheerful Etcher they knew was starting to show through once again. Of course, the version they had got of Etcher and Jayus's exchange left out the subtle threats, the fear in the scaled man's eyes and the knowing of what Etcher would do, should he have denied her.

Jerro was first to speak, albeit tentatively. "So the *Raven Witch* is behind all this?"

"I wouldn't go as far as saying that," replied Etcher, finishing the baguette slice and dabbing her mouth with a handkerchief. She leaned in toward the platter again and plucked a large, juicy grape from a laden vine that was nestled around the display of exotic cheeses, and popped the fruit in her mouth.

Jerro had been following suit, picking cheeses and pairing them blindly with different breads and crackers and fruits until he found a combination that he liked.

Meanwhile, Tahli had been resolute in sitting stiffly in her chair, one leg over the over, sipping the wine occasionally—though more from obligation than enjoyment.

"You don't know who the Raven Witch is, so I understand your assumption. But believe me when I tell you that *if* the Raven Witch wanted you, she would take you, plain as that. No, I believe she sent me to intercept you before the real threat could snap you up."

"The slithe, you mean?"

"Precisely."

"Then why did the slithe want me?"

Etcher shrugged. "It's hard to say, but I'd be willing to wager the Raven Witch has answers."

"I have a question," pipped up Tahli, looking none too pleased. "*Where* is the shop?"

Etcher sighed. "*Ah.* About that..."

Music was playing loudly through the speakers of Reedman's car. It was a nice crisp sound produced by the high-end audio system, which suited the high-end car. The sleek, electric vehicle had sporty contours and aggressive angles—a real gem against the older, shabbier cars of Reedman's fellow officers. It was as spotless as the day he drove it off the lot.

The luxury model was prized for its performance, its speed and energy efficiency. Reedman prized it for all those things too, but had found that the clear audio system and sound proofing had been the real treasures.

It was moments like these, when he tried to push aside the gory scene of Daag Landvick's mutilated body, that the car's undersold features afforded him much needed peace. He sat in his pearlescent-black car with its limo-tints and genuine leather seats, and stared vacantly at the cement wall of the underground parking lot that confronted him.

The soulful bellows of a throaty singer continued to pour out of his car speakers, harping on the bittersweet taste of an unforgiving world. A retro sounding tune from mid-century—music he had been subjected to as a boy, which brought a strange nostalgic comfort in adulthood.

Reedman was not a superstitious man, but he couldn't help feeling cursed. He wished he had never met Jerro Ahliss, and though he had resolved to keep his distance from the troublesome youth it seemed as though all roads kept leading back to the boy. The deep notes of the singer were doing their best to keep darker thoughts from intruding on the detective's peace, but the thoughts kept niggling their way through the lapses in his focus and played havoc on the forefront of his mind.

He was absolutely certain Jerro had not killed Daag; he was not certain, however, that Jerro wasn't connected to the gruesome murder.

Again an old theory played in his mind. There had been someone else, they had coerced Jerro into going to Lapaul's office and double crossed him, trying to pin the whole break-in on the boy. Something had gone wrong, Jerro had got away, somehow, and even showed up to work the next morning as if nothing had happened.

Maybe nothing did. Begrudgingly, Reedman had to accept that Jerro may have gone to Lapaul's office and done *nothing,* and that the break-in had taken place *after* Jerro had already left. Why Jerro would go to Lapaul's office, if not to break-in, was still a mystery. Maybe it really had been just an innocent trip up? Maybe he was leaving something for the boss, a note or report? Whatever had brought Jerro Ahliss to the top floor of Kairos Global Monday night hadn't left the boy with any feelings of guilt, because if he *had* done something nefarious, he sure as hell wouldn't have come into work the next day.

But it didn't feel that squeaky clean. There was something up with Ahliss the day Reedman had confronted him; deep down the boy must have known he was in trouble. But if Ahliss really was innocent, if not ignorant of what had happened, then it meant someone was after him, and now that Daag had been turned into a human pretzel it was a fair assumption that the same person was still gunning for Jerro's balls.

He refused to believe that Edik Bosko—the man who had confessed to the break-in—actually had anything to do with it, nor did he believe Bosko was the elusive other party that was pulling the strings. He did believe, however, that Lapaul had fixed it so that the whole thing would be swept under the rug. No telling what corporate bigwig types might be hiding. Johan Lapaul had not been happy to help the police snoop about his office, and whatever was unofficially stolen was something Lapaul wanted to handle outside of police help.

Thoughts of corporate secrets and sabotage were giving Reedman a migraine, and his hand instinctively sought out the center console to fish out a small bottle of liquid-gel caps that boasted *'Fast Acting Relief!'* He popped two capsules in his mouth and swallowed them dry, grimacing.

Almost instantly his stomach lurched and reminded him that its lining was dangerously thin and that the half-eaten bagel he had ripped into earlier had hardly counted as a meal. He stuck his hand back into the center console and snatched out a protein bar, tearing open the wrapping with his teeth and chewing the gummy bar angrily.

What a shit day.

He reluctantly turned off the stereo and got out of the car, stretching his long legs and letting his aching joints pop. He had been roused out of bed at the ass-crack of dawn to witness the gory mess and had not been allotted his morning run. It compounded his aggravation.

He wasn't unused to long hours and little sleep, but property crimes seldom ended up so bloody and they seldom needed Reedman to drag himself out of bed at four in the morning. Murder scenes, however, tended to scorch themselves into the spongy matter of the brain and give little room for reprieve.

Welcome to Homicides.

The office was unusually active, swarming with cops busying about as though the police precinct were an anthill that had been kicked over. Murder was not unheard of in big cities like Midgard, but the flavor of Daag's evisceration tended to raise certain alarms. You understand when someone gets knifed in a mugging, or a domestic gets out of hand, it makes a morbid kind of sense, there's still order in the world. *People* murdered one another all the time, but only monsters and madmen left you mutilated and crumpled you into a ball.

Reedman was wedging his way between two portly officers as he tried to reach the back of the precinct were his own little private space resided. He wanted to get away from the buzz to organize his thoughts. No doubt he'd be pulled off from the case since it was too closely tied to Ahliss; no doubt he'd be asked to put it out of his mind while they scrambled for a tidy answer. It would be left gnawing at him, like the break-in, and though he wouldn't be allowed any direct involvement it didn't mean he'd stop digging.

"Where the hell have you been?" came Thorneback's craggily smoker's voice. "Hope you had fun lazin' about, we've got work to do."

"What's going on?"

"One of *Infamous Ahliss*'s flatmates called. There's been another murder. An' no, it's not Ahliss, fuck knows where he is."

Reedman stood dumbfounded as the information processed, and with it came another metric ton of questions. He felt his brow knotting together and held up his hands to halt Thorneback's tirade. "Listen, I dunno what you've heard but I can't be on any case involving the kid. Chief made it pretty clear…"

"Yeah I talked to him an' all. Gave me the same spiel, but we came to an understanding. Strictly speaking you won't be on the case, more of a consultant. You know more than anyone about the Jerro kid and I could use your insight. Aw, don't give me those doe eyes, s'not like I'm asking you to marry me."

"I just—"

"What? Heard I'm a cantankerous old bastard who's hard to work with? Yeah, well you heard right. It's why I'm getting the credit and your name stays off the paperwork as much as possible."

Reedman chuffed. "So that's how it's gonna be?"

"You can bugger off and work on a nice tidy murder if you prefer. Take all the credit you want for those."

Reedman peered down at the weedy little man with wonder. "I guess I'm coming with you then. I'm driving though."

A small band of police cruisers had already sectioned off the entrance to the bland rectangular building of Jerro's residence. Nosey neighbors were piled up along the sparse lawns and sidewalks, many of which were bleary-eyed and pajama-wearing. The stay-at-homes and the forever-on-welfare made up the majority of the crowd. There was a constant murmur running between them, which only intensified as Reedman pulled up in his shiny black car.

Thorneback got out first, eager to light up a smoke—which he had been expressly denied within the confines of Reedman's luxury ride.

As Reedman got out, he took a moment to survey the surrounding residential community. A lot of windows and gossip-hungry neighbors; hopefully someone saw something this time. Which brought another curious question to mind: how had Jerro escaped without anyone seeing him?

"You're gonna need to see this." It was a female officer that addressed them. Her features were hardened and she looked a little pale—the other officers looked worse.

"Whose puke is this?" snapped Thorneback.

"Mine, Sir," said another officer weakly. He was doubled over and leaning heavily against one of the cruisers.

"Make sure forensics don't mix it up with any actual evidence."

The officer nodded as best he could, keeping a fist against his mouth in case he lost what little was left of his breakfast.

Thorneback trailed behind Reedman, looking around with his scrutinizing beetle eyes. At the top of the stairs there were three other officers guarding the door to Jerro's shared flat; none of them looked like they'd be accompanying the detectives inside.

"We didn' touch nothin', go right ahead," The braver of the three said to Thorneback and Reedman.

It wasn't hard to miss what had caused all the upset. The front door led straight into a big rectangular space, which was both living room and kitchen, separated only by the kitchen island. Wedged in between the island and cabinets was a body, drenched in its own blood. Like Daag, the face had been cleaved off, or maybe bitten, and the brain cavity was disturbingly empty and exposed.

The remains hadn't been balled up like Daag's though, instead the gangly youth was slumped on the floor, legs splayed out and lopsided head resting to one side as if the body had been plopped down like a rag-doll.

There was a trail of dried blood leading from the body and down the hall, disappearing into what Reedman knew to be Jerro's bedroom. He followed the gruesome path and pushed open Jerro's door with a latex-covered hand.

The room was a mess. More so than it had been when Reedman had first been there. The mattress was flipped up against a wall and the closet doors had literally been ripped open, one of the sliding panels hung precariously, held in place by a piece of fabric that had snagged it.

Drawers had been turned out. Papers, clothing, knickknacks and otherwise were all littered about the floor, some smashed or shredded. It looked like a pissed off bull had been plopped inside the room and had a fight with a matador. But it wasn't the wreckage that caught Reedman's attention, it was the note that had been painted across the bedroom wall in blood.

WHERE ARE YOU ☺

The message was punctuated by a drippy smiley face that had a crooked grin. The wobbly eyes glared at Reedman, its hollow grin leering. His migraine had returned, and with it came a feeling that the worst was yet to come.

It was slowly inching closer to noon. Sunlight peered out weakly through the breaks in the steel-gray sky, streaking the hilly landscape below. The air was crisp and the sea breeze carried with it the hint of colder weather still to come. Days like these were some of Jerro's favorite, Ria recalled fondly. For a small moment in time she had pushed aside the days of endless worry, the fear and uncertainty, and tried to appreciate today as Jerro would.

He loved this weather because it was times like this when you could *feel* the turning of the seasons, the end of a sparse and humid summer, the end of niggling bugs that got in your hair and buzzed in your ears. It was as though the cold cleaned the slate, preparing the year to be tidied away so that by the end of winter, things could start anew.

The moment did not last long enough, and Ria felt her throat tighten and her eyes water. She sniffed, trying to hold back the tears. But Ria Ahliss wasn't some old biddy who spent her time crying by herself, bemoaning the cruelty of having such a careless son! No word, not even a silly text message. She hated using her mobile phone but even that would have been something. She took a deep breath and tried to calm herself. When the sadness subsided she was left open to the twisting spark of anger that wanted to rage at Jerro and give him a piece of her mind. But even the anger couldn't hold, and soon it lay way to fear and the cycle started over in her mind.

She prayed that Jerro would call any day now as if nothing had happened, and then she could breathe again, they could go back to being a family.

To try and alleviate her worries, Freddy had been coming around more often, bringing flowers and treats. Since that awful detective had shown up on her doorstep and they got the news about Jerro's work, Freddy had insisted on sharing a meal with Ria daily.

She wasn't sure how to feel about it.

After Noah had died, they fell into such a strange routine. Whenever things needed fixing, Freddy came round, and whenever Ria knew he was neglecting himself she would make his favorite dish and bring it to him. Their houses, after all, were only down the road from each other. But they still lived separate lives, and the times they did share were always met with apprehension, like a tinderbox that could go up in flames with a single spark.

The past few days had been so very different, and she could almost see Freddy for the man he was before the tragedy marred her image of him.

She realized she missed Freddy, and in that moment she dared to admit how much she missed having a full house with her children and her husband. Times were sweeter then, the boys younger and innocent. But they grew up too fast and reckless. Noah was like a torrent pulling his younger brother in, leading him down dark paths.

She wondered if things could have ended up any other way. Noah had so much fire in him, so much anger. He had got the worst of both Ria and Freddy, though she loved him still. And Jerro was such a sweet boy before it happened, caring and loving.

Deep down that sweet kid was still there, and she knew that her youngest son, with all his flaws and absent-mindedness, would not have left her so hopelessly out of the loop unless something terrible had happened.

Tears threatened to break free and Ria fought them back with her waning strength. She had been sitting out on the patio for long enough, she needed to get moving, keep busy and keep her mind away from crippling thoughts. With effort she got up from the stony steps; the days had started to make her feel her age.

She headed back inside and passed through the kitchen, fussing with this and that, attempting to tidy an already immaculate space.

She'd go for a walk, she decided, head down to the beach and collect shells, look for bits of sea glass or a nice bit of driftwood Freddy could carve into something interesting. It was a good plan, she liked it, but she didn't get much further than the hallway.

There was a box waiting for her on the side table near the front door. It was most definitely for her because the beautiful calligraphy read:

To Mom, From Jerro

She lunged at it as if possessed and then stopped herself before she tore through the bright red ribbon with her fingernails. Delicately, cautiously, she carried the beautiful box into the living room and sat down on the couch, setting the box on the marble coffee table before her.

Her hands were trembling as she undid the pretty ribbon with all its ringlets. Her heart pounded as she lifted the lid.

When she peered inside, she found a magnificent little cake, wrapped in clear tissue paper, its sweet-succulent aroma drifted up her nose and tantalized her taste buds. She licked her lips without meaning to and had to tear her eyes away from it and the intricate decorations of tiny edible flowers which adorned it. As her eyes moved through the box, she spied the silver bangle and more importantly, the note.

Ria pulled out the folded piece of paper, her hands still shaking and her heart skipping beats. She opened the note and scanned the message several times. Her brow furrowing, mind working. In the end, she felt blank.

Mom
I'm so sorry. There's so much I want to tell you but can't right now.
I'm okay, safe—But I have to stay away until things are settled.
I love you.
Please wear the bracelet, it'll protect you.
Happy Birthday Mom.
Please enjoy it.
Love, Jerro

(P.S. Tell Dad I'm sorry too)

Ria stared at the message, unsure of what to think or feel. She had been hoping and praying for any kind of sign that her son was alive and well out there, somewhere. But now that she had it, she found more questions than comfort.

How had the package arrived? Where was Jerro? Why couldn't he come home? A tumultuous concoction of anxiousness, fear, wonder, and confusion started to bubble in her brain. She fought it back, scrunched her eyes shut, and took a deep breath. When she opened them again she stared down at the bangle. It was an elegant piece of jewelry, filigreed and old with a comforting weight as she picked it up to examine it.

It was the most beautiful present Jerro had ever given her; she only wished he had given it to her in person. She rubbed her thumb over the fine engravings and turned the bangle in the light so that the pearly stones shone in a variety of hues. It must have been expensive.

Uncertainty plagued her as she wrestled with her mind for an appropriate response, but keeping the noxious cocktail of emotions at bay had left her with nothingness.

She slipped the bracelet on her wrist and looked at it.

Slowly she felt something tangled and heavy unravel inside her heart. A weight she hadn't realized she'd been carrying until it was gone. She breathed, and it felt like the first breath of a lifetime. Calmness flowed through her, and as it did, her shoulders relaxed, she hadn't even realized she'd been tensing.

Ria sat back in the couch and continued to breathe steadily. Jerro was alive. He was *alive!*

She found herself smiling, her eyes trailing back to the box and to the little cake left inside it. Carefully she undid the tissue paper and brought the pastry to her mouth, its aroma strong and succulent. She took a bite and closed her eyes. A symphony of flavors played over her tongue. The creamy fondant gave way to a light spongy center, delicately sweet and laced with the most tantalizing mixture of fresh strawberries and cream. It reminded her of sunny days and springtime, picking berries in the garden, watching her boys run through the sprinklers, laughing with glee.

In that moment, she was whole.

Etcher sat quietly as she looked into her wine glass. She poured herself another helping and refilled Jerro's glass as well; Tahli's was still mostly full. She sipped, stared out of the large windows and sighed.

"I could give you the simple answer as to where the shop is, however, it would raise more questions."

When she said nothing more, an oppressive quiet started to creep in and weigh on Tahli and Jerro.

"So why don't you start where you left off..." offered Jerro, looking between Tahli and Etcher. The cat-woman appeared pricklier than ever, as though the iciness had shifted from the shopkeeper to the feline.

Etcher remained silent, seemingly lost in her thoughts. Her face might have been serene if there wasn't so much turbulence behind her golden eyes. Finally she put down her glass and laced her fingers over her stomach. "Yes, I suppose that is the best place to start."

The news should have blindsided Etcher, but of course, Etcher had already formulated her suspicions. She knew of the Raven Witch, as was Etcher's business to know of such things, and she knew of the reputation that followed, which was none too pleasant. And though anyone else might have packed up their bags and called it quits right then and there, Etcher found the circumstances strangely advantageous. It made sense that the Raven Witch would be behind Etcher's fortuitous timing in intercepting Jerro. Witches were known to have visions and premonitions of the grander scheme of things; this witch was no exception.

It resonated with Etcher's feeling of destiny; she had thought that Fate itself had crossed her path with Jerro's. As it turned out it was a dark prophet instead, which was close enough all the same. It struck her though, how vital Jerro was beginning to seem in the grand scheme of things, what with a slithe being after him, and that the Raven Witch should see to it that Etcher come to the rescue. *Funny,* she thought, *I feel as though I've been through this before.* It was not the first time that Etcher had pondered over her tall companion, and how quickly they formed a friendship. And though Etcher would be careful in admitting it, she had taken to the boy almost as quickly as he had taken to her as if they were already old friends.

But Etcher was carefully selective of her friends, and seldom made ones so quick. Something itched along her back as she thought about it, and a small dull pain deep in her mind pinged, warning her that only a headache lay down that line of thinking. She let the sensation go just then and focused her attention on the present.

Poor Jayus, she thought, returning to the matter at hand. The man had truly entangled himself in the worst possible way, putting Etcher into a precarious situation as well. Jayus was useful, and she intended to keep him within her grasp, which was much better achieved with him alive rather than dead. It was true that the Raven Witch might very well eviscerate him for having such a loose tongue, but it seemed unlikely, contrary to Jayus's belief.

To Etcher, it was rather obvious that Jayus had been chosen *because* he would divulge the information. Any other contact could have sent Etcher to Jerro's planet, but not all of them would have revealed their source, not without making it exceptionally tedious.

And if the Raven Witch had chosen Jayus for that purpose, it stood to reason that said witch would be expecting Etcher to come pay a visit, and how curiously fortunate it was that Etcher so happened to need a witch to cure Jerro's friend. Why, it seemed to Etcher like an open invitation into the Raven Witch's lair.

Wonderful.

Of course, it also seemed like a trap. A clever trap, to be sure, because Etcher did need a witch and her curiosity would not allow her to walk away. It was a much more persuasive invitation than the King of Nightmare's—whose approach was entirely wrong. The King *demanded* that Etcher come see him for an audience, and no one demanded anything of Etcher if they truly wanted to get it. Where was the persuasion? Where was the enticement? The bait? His kingliness was lacking greatly in finesse if he thought a simple invitation and an urgent demand was enough to get Etcher to come to his beck and call. No, this was much more seductive in its approach.

Clever, very clever, Etcher thought. She appreciated the method; it took imagination and planning, it was cunning and indirect—it was how Etcher would have done it. A small bubble of excitement rose inside the impish shopkeeper, a feeling that she was getting closer to obtaining another puzzle piece to the mystery of Jerro's predicament, and to the grander works at play. *Very well,* she thought, *I have my heading, I best gather the others.*

"What will you do?" said the scaled monk, his voice mirthless and flat.

Poor Jayus, Etcher thought again. She looked him up and down, weighing his mood and thoughts, moving the mental chess pieces in her internal game. "I'm not so sure you'd like to know."

He grimaced. "You're going to see her, you're going to confront her."

"Oh come now, *'confront'* makes it sound so hostile, I'm merely going to drop by and have a little chat." She said with an impish smile. "Well, Jayus ol' friend, I'll be leaving you now. Don't work yourself in a tizzy, pick some of those fine fruits you enjoy so much that you keep hidden in your locker."

If the blue man could blush he would have turned crimson.

Etcher grinned and bowed her head, sauntering over to the shop door. Had she spared Jayus that little jibe she might have made it to the Greenman, she might have turned the handle and disappeared inside. But those few precious seconds in which she lingered had cost her greatly.

"My, what have we here?" It was a voice that slithered up Etcher's spine and wrapped its claws around her neck. A voice that nestled deep into her brain and brought heart-skipping dread, and Etcher hardly ever felt dread.

She spun on her heels, blade in hand, ready to slash at the thing that had appeared behind her. "Jayus, *run!*" she ordered.

But Jayus E'Kilh did not move, he remained where he sat, his eyes rolled back and his body sat motionless like a doll.

"Jayus!" she called again, more urgently. Of course, that was the only thing she could do. Her body froze where it stood as if time had abandoned it and only her eyes could roll, and her tongue waggle.

"How curious…" The voice hissed with reptilian pleasure—it belonged to a man, whose scaly flesh showed a kinship to the petrified Abbot. He was tall and proud, purple hued and gold trimmed, and wore a holy man's habit. He was known as Ruld, leader of the Dulvarus'Kahn in his current form, but Etcher ventured to suspect there was something else beneath the borrowed face.

The little shopkeeper's heart was beating fast and her mind was being swept away in a frenzy. She yanked the reins away from her panic and forced a calculating anger into the saddle.

This man had snuck up on her.

No one ever snuck up on Etcher Everdoor, and yet this man had. It shouldn't have been possible, because every living thing burned brightly with an essence, every living thing that could sneak had a soul. But this man was missing that vital spark, he was dark and hollow as if he weren't really there.

And although she sensed no vital spark, what she could sense was the reptilian mind, his cold alien intelligence that was pressing into hers, scratching and wriggling its fingers, trying to bore its way into her treasure hoard of thoughts, and it was winning.

"You're thinking very hard," The man smiled wickedly. His handsome face was angular, tilted upward with defiance as he looked down his proud nose with vicious violet eyes. His perfect teeth gleamed in the firelight, bared like a predator ready to take a bite.

Etcher forced anger into her limbs, forced anger to deny the petrifying hold on her muscles, and finished the strike she had intended to lacerate him with. The blade slashed through the scaled man without leaving so much as a mark.

And the man laughed darkly. "Ah, such a pity. You wasted precious energy on something so futile. *Tsk tsk*…a demon blade, isn't it?" He let his fingers creep along the blade's length, letting his hand slither up the hilt, over Etcher's hand and along her arm where it danced its way across to her collarbone and toyed with the lacing of her blouse. "One of those deadly five. Are you a bladesmith? Hmm? Come on now, lower your wall, I'll have your thoughts one way or another." He licked his scaly lips.

"And how will you take them?" Etcher said with effort, a moment of biding time to calculate, to find which glass to break in the quickly rising emergency. "Will you turn me dull and lifeless like the Abbot?"

"Him? Oh no, not like that, I need him for my little game, and this game requires two. I can only be one. He's a useful pawn, he thinks he's a double agent, how precious, don't you think? He thinks he's pulling a fast one on Ruld, but I beat him to that years ago. No, you I'll *eat*. I've no use for a pawn that won't yield, and you're not going to yield, are you? My, those secrets that dance behind your eyes, they look delicious…"

The scaled man leaned in, his teeth parting as they came up to Etcher's eye, his hot, moist breath caressing her skin with an intrusive touch.

But his teeth never made contact.

He drew his face back slowly, though his hands continued to wander, gliding across her neck and around to her back. "What have we here?" He smiled. And as he smiled he slid another wandering hand across Etcher's torso, undoing the buttons of her waist coat on the way up to the lacing of her blouse, loosening the garment so that he could slide it down her shoulders.

He kept uncomfortably close, letting his fingers glide across her naked flesh in a sickening caress as he circled her. "Now that is some powerful *majik*," he said, tracing the intricate lines of the golden *majik* circle branded into Etcher's back. "And what's this? Someone has been naughty." He toyed with the hairline fracture in the outer ring of the circular design. "What *are* you, I wonder? Care to share? No? Hmm, what a pity."

He drew a clawed finger along the fissure gently, creating little flecks of *majik* to spark along the lines. "You're something else. I feel like I *know* you…there's just something about you, something under that spell." He slipped an arm around Etcher's waist from behind while the other hand snaked up her hips and slid across her chest and up to her heart. And then he hissed in serpentine pleasure, his body pressing flat against the curve of her back. He brought his teeth to her ear, a quickness in his breath.

"I. Know. You." The violet eyes became wilder, the fangs longer, and his hand pressed painfully against her sternum, feeling the two hearts beneath. *"You're the Keeper."*

Something in the man's words sunk deep into Etcher's mind and ignited a feeling that had been hidden beneath the bindings of *majik*, beneath the bindings that kept her trapped inside her little form. Urgency pumped through her veins, reigniting anger and pushing it into her bones, into her fists. Her *majik* started flowing as the man's teeth got nearer, and as the seconds sluggishly passed, the rapier in her hand transformed and became crimson, the lily moldings in the hilt turned to thorny roses, and Etcher pooled up her might and drove the blade through her stomach and into the man's gut, causing him to howl and scream, and to finally release Etcher from his grip.

Black putrid ichor gushed from the man's wound as Etcher pulled out the sword, and crimson blood flowed heavily from her own, but the hold which rooted her loosened just as she had hoped.

The man was not dead, however, instead he seethed with rage, clutching at the ugly gash and steeling himself for retaliation. The black ichor continued to pour out and soak the ground, bringing the man to his knees, but only for a moment.

Anger, much as it had empowered Etcher, was driving the man upward, bringing him back to his feet, lunging him forward. It was only an instant that Etcher had bought herself, and in that instant she looked at the Greenman door and said a silent goodbye, then she pulled herself into the *Blank* and disappeared.

"Whoa—wait a second, you left the shop at—at, um, well you left it anyhow," Jerro stammered. Though Etcher had left out large chunks of the details, she had at least boiled down her retelling to include the fact that a slithe had her in its clutches and she avoided being eaten by disappearing into *Blank-Space*. Any business about the stabbing, or mention of the Keeper, what she felt, were blatantly omitted.

"Yes, I left the shop, but it isn't on Dahl'Kir."

"Dahl'Kir…isn't that—"

"Yes, where the slaves from Undercity came from."

There was a pained expression on Jerro's face as he tried to piece things together.

"Jerro, Dahl'Kir is halfway across the galaxy from us, but like I said, I didn't leave the shop there. The shop returned to its place of origin right as I pulled myself into *Blank-Space*, it's trained to do so in cases of great peril."

"What do you mean *trained?*"

"Well, there's a certain amount of sentience to the shop, like a residual consciousness after years of accumulated energy. To put it plainly, the shop is sort of alive. I was in danger, so, the shop reacted by going home, so to speak."

Jerro frowned and his eyes squinted with the headache that was surely building in his frontal lobe. "And where is home?" he asked with trepidation.

"That would be Death."

"…What?"

"I told you, it went back to its place of origin. Jerro, I built the shop with my father when I lived in Death."

Confusion and anguish swirled into Jerro's face as he tried to process what his ears had heard. "Huh? What do you mean you *lived* in Death? If you lived there why do you need a Death Token to get back? Why didn't you just have the shop take you back? What the hell-!?"

"Jerro, breathe, you're turning blue."

He pushed out the air from his lungs and slumped back in the chair, breathing in deep and staring in bewilderment at Etcher. His gaze sloshed over to Tahli as if for reassurance, but the cat-woman was staying curiously quiet, and if Jerro didn't know any better, he would have sworn that this was all news to the prickly feline as well.

"Look,"—Etcher set down her glass—"I lived in Death, a long time ago, and I was exiled—*No*, I will not answer any questions on that matter—and the shop will not take me back for the very reason which I won't discuss, but it will return by itself in times of danger. When I pulled myself into the *Blank*, it was a clear signal to the door that I had no other choice. That man—that *slithe*—was like nothing I've ever experienced before. It was not the same one from back on Earth, either. I would never have made it back to the door, and I couldn't risk him getting a hold of me and gaining access to the shop.

"He said it himself, he was going to eat me. Now, as far as I understood that's how slithes are able to turn into other people. Obviously, Mahra's case is thankfully different. So, I hopped into the *Blank* and have been aimlessly skipping through the cosmos trying to get back here. I'm sorry if the answer isn't as neat as you would like but it's been a long and arduous journey and that's about as much as I'm inclined to say on the matter." There was a forcefulness to her voice that made the statement resolute and final, and both Jerro and Tahli recoiled.

Etcher let out her breath, long and heavily, and settled back into the chair. "I'll permit you a few more questions Jerro, let's just leave certain topics aside, shall we?"

"Yeah…okay…" he said, and swallowed to moisten his dry throat. "So, ah, I guess we're headed to Death, then, right? You needed to go there anyhow."

Etcher raised an inquisitive eyebrow at him. "Though your enthusiasm is admirable, aren't you forgetting something?"

"…Uh…"

"*Mahra*, Jerro. She's still in need of a cure, and since the Raven Witch has crossed our paths it seems we owe her a visit, don't you think?"

"Right. Yeah, of course. Sorry, I just…it's a lot to take in."

"I know. Well, I suppose we should be off."

"What, *now?*" said Jerro.

"Yes, of course now. There's no better time."

"How though? We don't have the shop—"

"He has a point," interjected Tahli, who was looking no less icy than before.

"Yes, he does. But there's more than one way to travel, there's always Hoya."

Tahli shivered with revulsion. "I will *not* subject myself to that again."

"Tahli…"

276

"No, Everdoor, no! I will not, I have no desire to set foot on that *beast.* I-I have able feet, I will walk or run or climb but I do not fly!"

"Tahli, the Al'Florun are here."

The ginger cat-woman paled as much as her fur coat would allow. "They cannot be here."

"Ah, but they can. We saw them entering the hotel, they were brought by hollowmen carriages."

"I'm missing something, aren't I?" Jerro chimed in.

"We need to leave," said Tahli, blatantly ignoring Jerro.

"True, however, I actually don't know where the Raven Witch lives."

"Everdoor!"

"Don't start with me, Tahli. Look, we can leave almost immediately, we'll just need to stop over in Faerie first. There'll be someone there who can tell us where the Raven Witch is."

"...Um, should I even bother asking?"

"This might be one of those times where it's better if you don't, Jerro," said Etcher. "Just, follow along. Tahli, how long did you rent the rooms for?"

"Two weeks," Tahli replied sharply.

"Two weeks? Gods help me, Tahli. You rented the *Diva* suite for two whole weeks? And you accuse me of frivolous spending."

"It was not frivolous! You left me for a month in Bargos last year!"

"All right, all right, calm down." Etcher pinched the bridge of her nose and squeezed her eyes shut. "It's fine, two weeks gives us more than enough time. I dare say, this may not take more than a day or so to resolve."

"Excuse me?"

"Not right now, Jerro."

"*Are* we going yet?"

"Yes, Tahli, for the life of me! Come on then, there's a full-length mirror in the bathroom."

"Why are we—?"

"Jerro, please, just watch."

"*Humph.*"

"Don't start, Tahli."

Jerro had been standing patiently, and quietly, after they had shuffled into the bathroom with Etcher. He watched the little shopkeeper inspect the full-length mirror before them while Tahli—who had kept hold of her wineglass and was now sipping it more enthusiastically—tapped her nails impatiently on the marble countertop by the dual sinks.

Etcher was looking the mirror up and down and pulled it away from the wall; it was the kind that was housed in an ornate heavy wooden frame with wheels for feet, the mirror itself was attached to joints so it could be easily tilted within the frame. Etcher circled the mirror once, twice, tapping her lips with a thoughtful finger. She stopped in front of her reflection, her black-and-red-suit-wearing twin staring back at her, returning the careful scrutiny in Etcher's golden gaze. "This'll do. Lucky for us it's the Lunar Week."

"What does that have to do with anything?" Jerro had directed his question to Tahli since Etcher seemed too captivated in what she was doing to answer.

"The Lunar Week makes the veil between worlds thin, otherwise we would need a base spell to prime the mirror and endow it with *majik* before drawing the portal door—*Hic.*" Tahli covered her mouth and stifled a burp. She swigged down the last of the wine and left the bathroom, returning only moments later with the unfinished bottle of Sanka Blush and pouring herself another helping.

Jerro merely stared in bewilderment. Partly, he was surprised that Tahli had even bothered to explain, though the explanation was hardly all that illuminating; and partly he was stunned by the sudden reckless behavior from the ginger cat-woman who had gone from stone-cold sober to hiccupping and tipsy in about three glasses flat.

He craned his head away from Tahli and back to Etcher, who was inscribing very precise circles and archaic symbols onto the mirror with a piece of white, glittering chalk. The intricate pattern became a beautiful filigree covering the glassy surface of the mirror. It was done so perfectly, so cleanly, that he would have never guessed it had been done with a naked hand had he not witnessed it himself. *Is this why she's called 'etcher'?* he thought. Were all the patterns and star charts that laced the wooden floors and alabaster walls of the shop also made the same way? Had Etcher drawn them with some *majik* pen?

The finished summon circle Etcher had inscribed onto the mirror was different from the large nautically themed symbol of her shop floor. This sigil had moon phases interwoven into the design, complex knots and braided patterns. There was more whimsy and swirls and something tantalizing and familiar. Jerro felt himself be drawn to the magical diagram, it was pulling at him, urging him. His heart was beating faster and his memories started to dance with notes of recollection. The white-and-silver tigers of Gahza'Dune, the desert oasis in his dreams, the cave of fire, a yellow rose...

"Tahli, I need a tear."

"Do you not have fairy tears? Oh! That is right, they are in the shop," the ginger cat-woman replied sourly.

"Yes, Tahli, we're all very annoyed that the shop isn't here. You can berate me as much as you like later, unless, of course, you'd rather stick around for the Al'Florun to sniff you out? Hollowmen carriages, remember? They came with an entourage, you know what that means?"

Tahli flexed her jaw and her lips curled as if she had tasted something sour. "Khlarii trackers."

"That's right. So, a tear if you'd be so kind."

Tahli straightened defiantly, although Jerro noted that she was clutching the marble countertop as if to steady herself, and that the wine bottle was now empty. She sauntered over to Etcher with a heavier step than usual and looked down her nose at the little shopkeeper.

"And if this does not work?"

"It'll work Tahli, felines are close enough to fae, at least as much as we need on a day like today."

"*Humph,* how lucky we are." Tahli plucked a hair from her brow and winced as her eyes watered.

Etcher caught the tear on her pinky and dabbed it into the center of the inscribed mirror.

The surface rippled like a pool and kept rippling, bouncing back from the edges of the mirror within the wooden frame. The pull that had called to Jerro moments before ignited again, though the tangled memories that had begun to take shape lay dormant this time around.

"What did you do?" he asked in awe.

"I made a door between the Waking Realm and Faerie. Faerie is, after all, our reality's mirror realm." Etcher stood aside and held out her arm, presenting the rippling portal to Jerro and Tahli. The ginger cat-woman harrumphed and stormed through first, disappearing into the silvery vortex and causing the ripples to undulate wildly.

"You're next, Jerro."

He gulped down a breath and approached the mirror. "I just walk on through then, yeah?"

"Just walk through," Etcher said reassuringly.

But the nervousness continued to grip Jerro and he fidgeted on the spot "Yeah…" he said.

"Together, perhaps?" She slipped her dainty hand into his and led him forward, stepping into the mirror and casting back a smile before she disappeared into the vortex almost completely. Only her arm remained beyond it, hand in hand with Jerro's.

"Yeah, okay…just walk through." He closed his eyes and held his breath, stepping headlong into the undulating mirror before nightmarish images of *Blank-Space* could hinder him.

Jerro nearly toppled over Etcher on the other side and started to mutter an apology before the strange new world of eerie twilight captivated his senses.

Bruised colors filled the sky as a sun of eternal setting hung about the world's lip but failed to sink under the horizon. The air was alive with dancing firefly lights, sparks of *majik*, windswept glittering leaves. Impish laughter echoed from the distance and time felt slow and fragmented.

Things moved as they should in the soundless breeze—Etcher's hair undulating, Tahli's tail flicking back and forth, butterfly wings batting—but time itself had a thickness to it like it was tangible and heavy, and Jerro had the strangest notion that he was seeing past and present act as one, that somehow this place existed in a different spectrum of Time, adhering to an entirely different kind of law.

"We should keep moving." Etcher touched Jerro's side gently and urged him forward.

"Yeah…" he uttered back, his eyes drinking in the surreal world and getting intoxicated by it. The thick tree line that flanked the herringbone brick path before them portrayed every variety of color in every variety of season. Their fronds were heavy with glistening fruit and peppered with morning dew. The mixture perfumed the air with something heady and wild, something fresher than the cool winter morning on a mountainside or the taste of first light on a springtime lake. It confused Jerro's senses, made his insides churn with unnatural feelings. Curious elation and solemn loneliness were so interwoven as to be nearly indiscernible, a confounding mixture that put Jerro into a daze.

Every now and then Etcher would pat his arm, reminding him that he was tangible, grounding him back into a semblance of reality. He would tear his eyes away from the intoxicating world and look down into the piercing honey orbs of Etcher's eyes, finding a moment of clarity, only to have the seductive twilight colors in his peripherals hook his attention away and set his gaze adrift once again.

Absently, he followed along as Tahli headed their trek, though her footsteps were losing their feline grace and becoming ambling and heavy. She was catching her toes in the grooves between the intricate brickwork of their path and bumping into trees.

"Tahli," said Etcher softly. In her hand was a small vial filled with a familiar orange liquid.

"No." Tahli pushed Etcher's hand away, vial included.

"Tahli, they won't find us here. They can't, they're not allowed. Faerie has its own law."

"I do not want to be sober." She straightened out defiantly but then careened into Etcher.

"Tahli, enough now. They're not going to get you, *I* won't let them. Tahli, please." Etcher held out the vial again, grabbing Tahli's arm with her open hand, and halting the feline's progress.

Tahli tried to pull away but Etcher held like a vice and didn't budge. It was about then that Jerro was able to pull himself out of the enchanting dizziness of Faerie and realize something strange was transpiring between the shopkeeper and the feline.

"Tahli, I'm sorry. I left you in Bargos, and I left you again in Yahre, and now I've lost the shop. And you can be mad about those things, Tahli, but I need you clear-headed. They won't ever take you again, I made you that promise, and I don't break my word. Have I ever?"

"No," Tahli said quietly, she was holding back a sob, though whether it was induced from the booze or a genuine emotion was hard to tell.

"So, then, drink this please, Tahli, you'll feel better, you'll remember that you're safe." Etcher held out the vial, keeping her other hand gripped around Tahli's arm.

The ginger cat-woman took the vial shakily and pushed off the stopper with her clawed thumb, downing the fragrant liquid inside with one big gulp.

A moment passed in tense silence, and the sobering effect of the tonic seemed to vicariously affect Jerro as well. He remembered that they had a purpose, and that there was a sense of urgency nipping at their heels, that Mahra was counting on him. And though the bewitching world of Faerie still pulled at him, he managed to resist it better now, and as Tahli regained herself and stood again with sturdy feet, balance returned to their trio in more ways than one.

He quickened his step and kept up beside Etcher—Tahli still determined to take the lead. Neither shopkeeper nor feline spoke more on the matter that had transpired, and Jerro felt it wise to keep the mention of it from his tongue. "So, where in Faerie are we headed?"

"To Tahli's favorite place of course, the Market."

"The market?"

"No, no, *the* Market. A one of a kind. The originator of commerce, birthplace of merchants and shopkeepers alike."

"…Shopkeepers like you?"

"Not quite, I'm not from Faerie, if that's what you're wondering."

"Where are you—?"

"Hurry up, Everdoor! The Market is bristling!" yelled back Tahli, who was now a great distance ahead of them.

"Just wait until you see this place," said Etcher with a wink. She grinned at Jerro and quickened her step, leaving his inquiry to fall short and forgotten. He had no choice but to hurry along with them lest the bewitching world take hold of him again. Yet for all his quickness he was surprised at how quickly Etcher closed the gap on Tahli and left him trailing behind.

The path was getting narrower and the trees were nestling in until he was pushing past branches and bramble, seeing only the fleeting glances of the little shopkeeper as she disappeared into the thicket.

Panic rose inside his chest as he fought past the dense foliage; he didn't want to get left behind, not in this place. His panic made him rush and made his footing clumsy and the heady air of Faerie was closing in.

He was still headed straight, wasn't he? Or had he got turned around? Behind him the path had vanished, no herringbone brick, no path at all, only trees and thicket. His feet still ambled forward but Jerro was feeling himself become entangled—snared in an enchanted web—and the more he moved the more his judgement clouded.

Was it just over that hill? Was that the flutter of Etcher's hair? Was that Tahli's orange fur he saw zipping through his peripheral?

Something was encircling him, chittering with laughter. He caught snippets of unfamiliar movement between the trees: sometimes snow white skin and golden hair, or copper flesh and midnight tresses, a shapely leg, a slender arm. The world was spinning, or maybe he was, and he couldn't find his way. He felt dazed and heavy. Maybe he should lay down, maybe take a nap, he was so tired all of a sudden.

He staggered forward and forgot why he came.

It was such a nice evening, the twilight still giving shape to the world, the crooning of invisible birds, the warm air, the touch of *majik*. And there he was, in a clearing, soft leaves and luscious grass. He wanted to lay down, he couldn't think of a reason not to. It was so very nice out after all. Why had he come here?

He knelt down and his head swayed, feeling too big before his neck. The grass was thick and springy, the leaves were soft, the ground was warm. He should take a nap, just a small one. It was so nice, so very nice there in the clearing.

And the things were still circling, giggling, and smiling. Were they women? Yes they were, they were pretty women, he liked pretty women. His face was smiling back, his eyelids halfway open, and the women were getting closer and he thought he should lay down.

"Jerro."

His eyes snapped open, the heady feeling was gone and there stood Etcher, a beacon in the fog, clearing away the bewitching haze on his mind. Jerro struggled to his feet and looked around, suddenly he found himself standing on the herringbone path once again. The women were gone, as was the strange cloudiness that had confounded him so. "What happened?"

"Nymphs. Sorry, that was careless of me. They don't usually take interest in me or Tahli, it slipped my mind they were even here."

"Nymphs? Like the sexy kind of nymphs or—?"

"Is there another kind?"

"Uh…"

Etcher smirked. "Hmm, suppose I should have let you be a while longer. They were taking a fancy to you after all."

Jerro's face turn hot. "So are we, ah,"—he coughed—"are we at the market yet?"

"It's just up ahead. You sure you want to come? I could just leave you here a while, I think you'd have plenty to keep you occupied." She grinned devilishly.

Jerro thought about it. He genuinely considered it, in fact. *Nymphs,* he thought, *Sexy Nymphs*…was that giggling he heard in the distance? He thought maybe he saw a curvy figure slip behind the trees. But as his thoughts slunk down into the gutters of his mind he was assaulted by an image of Mahra lying on the hospital bed, with the feeding tube sticking out of her mouth.

Damn it, he thought. What a way to add insult to injury. As enticing as an orgy with a bunch of frisky nymphs sounded—and it was enticing—he figured Mahra probably wouldn't find it all that forgivable. Jerro felt bad enough about sleeping with not-Mahra, but that was a mistake anyone could have made. Sleeping with nymphs, however, well, there really wasn't a good excuse for that. "No, I better come along." He nodded affirmatively and urged Etcher forward lest he be tempted again.

"Fair enough," she said.

Jerro traipsed behind her, unable to help himself as his eyes darted glances at his surroundings, but all sign of the nymphs had gone. Etcher's presence had made them vanish. "So…" he began as his thoughts started to spill from his head without meaning to, but when he realized the nature of the question he was about to ask, he stopped himself.

Etcher raised a curious eyebrow at him. "So what?"

"Nothing," he lied.

Etcher rolled her eyes and smirked at him. "Were you wondering *why* the nymphs leave me and Tahli be, perhaps?"

Damn it. "Yeah, alright, I was. You don't have to answer though, it's a stupid question."

"But you're still curious about my relationship with Tahli? It's all right, perhaps it's better I be direct. The nymphs leave us be because Tahli is interested in men and I am what you would call asexual. In other words, we're not much fun for the nymphs."

"Oh."

"Was there anything else you wanted to know, since we're on the topic?"

Jerro's face said it all, even if his mouth wouldn't.

Etcher took note, her amused smile ever present. "Just ask me, I promise I won't bite," she said with a wink.

Jerro fidgeted as he walked, his eyes focused on the herringbone path. "So, being *asexual,* does that mean to you don't like, you know—"

"Sex?" Etcher was chuckling now. "You know, for someone who seems so sexually charged, you can be quite the prude."

Jerro's face scrunched. "I'm not a prude, I'm just, you know, trying to be polite."

"Sure you are. Well to answer your question it's not that I *don't* like sex, I've enjoyed it from time to time, but I've never had a desire for it, does that make sense?"

"Not really."

"Perhaps it's difficult for someone like yourself to understand."

"What's that supposed to mean?"

Etcher raised hands to quell the argument. "I'm not taking a jab at you, merely pointing out that you are a young man with an active libido, correct?"

"Well, yeah," he said, feeling strangely bashful.

"Well I don't really have that kind of drive. It's like saying I *like* cake, but I don't love it, I don't find myself going out of my way to get it. It's nice when it's there, but I don't miss it when it's not. I just don't *need* it."

"Oh."

"Were you perhaps offering?"

Jerro's face went flush. "What? No! I-I wasn't asking—"

Etcher burst out laughing. "Apologies, I couldn't help it. Look, I understand that you're curious, you want to know about me. But if you have something to ask, just ask me outright. I know I'm not always receptive to questions, so take this opportunity while it's here."

"Okay…well,"—he began—"does that mean you don't have any preferences then?"

"You're asking if I prefer men or women? The answer is neither. But if you were to ask who I've slept with, the answer is both. Gender to me seem *arbitrary*."

"Oh."

"Is this making you uncomfortable?"

"No, no I'm good. I mean I have friends with different preferences or whatever. I've just never met anyone like you, I guess, but it kind of makes sense."

"Good. I'm glad we've sorted that out. Now, let us make haste, the Market is waiting!" She grinned at him, looped her arm around his and led the way along the path.

The Market of Faerie is a collision of markets. A labyrinth of identical herringbone brick roads lace the expansive emporium, running through each cultural borough with similarly meandering pathways, making it very, very, easy to get lost, and many have.

There are people in the Market that have lost themselves so entirely that any memory of an existence beyond the Market walls has abandoned them altogether, and they themselves have turned either merchant or beggar. It is as if the Market of Faerie is alive, and as such, claims the livelihood of the unwitting so that it might perpetuate itself everlasting.

Though the Market is treacherous, though it will claim you should you linger too long or forget why you came, it is marvelous to behold. All corners of the world bend so they might meet here, at the heart of Faerie. From the golden sands to the tropics, from the meadows to the springs, to the highlands and the arctic; all manner of merchant, shopkeeper, trader, and traveler come to the Market to buy, barter, and sell.

But unlike the markets of the Waking Realm, things can be traded in Faerie that you would never think to give away. A favored memory, an ounce of your time, the color of your eyes, the name of your kin. In Faerie, anything and everything can be bought and sold. A person would be wise to keep themselves guarded, for swindlers and golden tongued liars, thieves, and muggers will take anything which can be took. There is much to lose in Faerie; the seasoned traveler knows this best of all.

Of course, there is also much to gain. Whatever you might seek, no matter how obscure, strange, or rare, you can almost guarantee it can be found in the Market. Whether or not you can afford it, however, is a whole other matter.

—Pages from The Traveler's notebook, from the chapter of "Festival and Faerie."

"Now listen carefully, Jerro, we're about to step into the Market and I need you to be cautious. First of all, put some coin in your pocket, enough to look reasonable but not more than you're willing to lose."

"Why?"

"Because you're likely going to be pickpocketed, and if said pickpocket finds nothing to pinch they might start looking elsewhere, and that necklace of yours is infinitely valuable."

Jerro clutched the black Obelisk pendant through his shirt and cast a wary glance into the bustle of the marketplace. He could see the whirl of commotion just beyond a massive entryway flanked by two giant golden dragon statues—interlaced with impish pixies and dancing bears.

"What's the second thing?"

"The second thing is this: *if* you get into trouble, you should reveal your contract but *only* if there's no other way out of your predicament. While an association with me may grant you certain liberties, it may also garner unwanted attention. Now, I can show you how to display the markings—"

"Oh, you mean like this, right?" He raised his right hand, and for the second time he revealed the elaborate sigil that Etcher had branded into his palm. The soft glow illuminated the hidden contract and made his flesh tingle with *majik*.

"Yes, like that. When did you learn to do that?"

"Back at the hotel, some mouthy attendant wouldn't tell me where Tahli's room was so I just sort of…*did it*."

"How curious."

"Is that weird? You look surprised—does it mean anything?"

"How so?"

"Well, I dunno…I mean, back before we left the shop—before Undercity—you were talking about *'testing my aptitude for majik'* or something. And then after what happened in the king's chamber…"

"You mean when you passed through the statue unscathed?"

"Yeah…"

"Jerro, are you asking if you can learn *majik*?"

"Well…I—it would be cool, and I…well yeah, I am. I wanna learn *majik*."

Etcher grinned. "I think that could be arranged. You show potential."

"I do?"

"You do." She looked at him thoughtfully. "All right, look. I'll give you something, another gift if you will. An old notebook of mine, it has the basics of conjuring," she said, and in her hand appeared a small journal. It was bound in leather and had braided patterns molded into the cover with a fanciful metal clasp to keep it shut. She offered it to him with a smile. "Though I'm not the right person to teach you *majik*. I actually know very little, truth be told."

"Are you serious? What about your violin? Or jumping through dimensions?"

"*True*, that is *majik*, of a sort. But, you see, I'm a specialist. I mastered only a few avenues of *majik*. The music, sure, although my ability to *jump* is more an inherent thing. Otherwise I'm only skilled with locks, swordplay, and scripture. All in all, it's a rather limited repertoire. Tahli, on the other hand, is exceptionally gifted with potions and her bindings are expertly done. She also excels at hexes and channeling, not to mention her scripture may someday rival mine, although I do pride myself on my written works."

"What are you getting at? Are you saying *Tahli* should teach me *majik*?" He was thankful the prickly feline had already headed off into the Market before them and spare him from whatever jibes she'd surely make with the topic at hand.

"Well, comparatively she knows more *majik*, but no, I don't think that arrangement would suit either of you. You'll need a proper teacher if you truly wish to learn, but that doesn't mean you can't practice some basics on your own. That book should help you out. But I wouldn't recommend practicing here. Keep it out of sight, for now, agreed?"

"Yeah, sure. Thanks, Etcher."

"You're welcome. Shall we?"

He nodded, though he was reluctant to stow away the leather journal. His fingers played with the clasp, wishing to unlock the pages and drink in the knowledge that lay inside. *Majik*, real *majik*, there in his hands, but it would have to wait. If the Market was anything like his own experience with crowded shopping plazas and big cities, he couldn't risk having his nose stuck in a book and end up taking a wrong turn down a bad alley. The sheer bustle and vastness of the Market was intimidating enough, but this was Faerie after all, and he was willing to bet it was a whole lot more dangerous and unpredictable than anything he knew.

"Beggin' your pardon, madam, but you are planning on paying for those, aren't you?"

Tahli huffed. "I am not a thief. I am waiting for my master, they will pay you."

"That's all well and good, but I can't let you leave until then." It was a dopey-eyed creature that spoke, sitting on a high perch of pillows beside a big antique-looking brass cash register. The portly little merchant had spindly arms and legs—that hardly looked accustomed to carrying around the flabby body. Whiskery hairs stuck out of all four of its long ears in bushels, and its wrinkly face was dotted with warts and moles. It was a frightful thing to be sure.

"*Tsk*, do I look like I am leaving? I am still inspecting, there is more I intend to buy."

The ugly creature groaned. It picked up a long, thin pipe and stoked it with tobacco, keeping one big dopey eye on Tahli while the other swiveled around to watch the dried leaves take flame.

The shop which Tahli perused was cramped and dusky, housed inside a patched-up tent and nestled between two brick buildings. The front of the shop was exposed to the herringbone path granting a clear view of the other shabby vendor installations that lined every available inch alongside the road. Colorful globes of faerie lights hung in the air above their entryways, others hovered above the passing foot traffic, lending the world additional luminance in the bluish twilight.

A multitude of people were in constant procession going up and down the herringbone path, buying and bartering from various merchants, perusing the wares, chatting amongst friends. There was an electric energy to the Market, a brimming of life that crackled in the air and set the heart thumping...

So much to see, so much to buy! Endless shops, endless hopes and dreams on sale at every street corner. And the smells, oh the smells! Spices and incense, food of all varieties. Gold, raw metals, bundles of herbs. Some smells savory, other repulsive, but all of it tangled into a cacophony of enticement. A smell that is unanimously attractive and ugly and manages to linger with you, summoning the most vivid sensations whenever the olfactory catches a whiff of it.

It is truly a one of a kind experience to walk the streets of the Market and breathe in all that it has to offer, to see all that there is to see. The extraordinary is in such multitude that the eyes become drunk. Every part of Eclipse exists in its own little slice, in its own little borough. Turn the corner and suddenly you're in the tropics, with palm frond roofs and beach-themed goods, bongos playing off in the distance, the smell of a nighttime luau, and lots of tanned bodies and smiling faces. Turn again, you've found winter: mountain men and yeti creatures offering thick coats, cuttings tools, gemstones. Another corner and you're in the desert, hookah lounges a plenty, exotic spices, dancing girls, and lots of rugs and antique lamps.

Go further still and you've reached the borough of Faerie's Faerie, a place where the natives staked their own claim in the Market, a hodgepodge of everything the fairfolk dared to shove together. A mixture that in its final product was a calamity of crammed tents, brick buildings, vast toadstools, carved-out oaks, disembodied pools and Stonehenge look-a-likes, and a very odd assortment of faerie merchandise. Strange toad people, fair ladies, water cretins, boogeymen and bogarts, all thrown together trying to tantalize patrons with their magical and improbable wares. In a way, it had a kinship to Etcher's shop, albeit far less organized. And it was exactly where Tahli had come to spend some coin.

"Ah, there you are." Etcher had spied the orange feline from down the road, Tahli's arms brimming with goodies.

"Buy these," the cat-woman said, without so much as a hello.

"You have your own money, Tahli."

But the ginger cat-woman responded with a look that could slice through bread.

Etcher sighed. "Fine, I'll take it as my punishment for leaving you."

Tahli held her nose high in the air and handed over the assortment to Etcher. "I have more things to see, hold onto these for me after you pay."

"Oh, but of course, Tahli, it would be my pleasure," Etcher said dryly to Tahli's back as the feline bounded away. "Well, how much do I owe for these?"

"Twelve arhk beads and a crystal flower."

"I'll give you fifteen beads and a dragon tooth."

The ugly creature squinted at Etcher and puffed out a large smelly plume of smoke. "Which tooth?"

"An incisor."

"Peh, no deal. It's a crystal flower or nothing."

"I have a forest *sprit*."

"Don't need `em, I got plenty."

"And what about fire?"

"Those I don't have so much, but I'm not looking for any either."

"Wind?"

"Hmmm." The faerie merchant smacked his lips, contemplating hard. "What else you got?"

"I'll give you the beads, the wind sprit, and a kilo of Cyndir tobacco."

"Is it honeysuckle?"

"Better, it's ambros."

"Deal."

Etcher conjured the agreed upon exchange. The wind sprit was a strange looking embodiment of tangible air currents, like a small tornado. It had a serpentine body, a big ball head, and little windy wings. It was housed in a big cylinder jar and the windy creature was bobbing its ball head back and forth, its serpent wind-body wiggling, as though in a dance. The arhk beads varied in size, though all were beautifully polished, pristinely spherical, and colored in a springtime green with delicate striations akin to jade. Beside them was a large brick-shaped package wrapped in brown wax paper and stuck with an oval gold-and-black label that read:

(Abien Cynnados Smoking Herb Handpicked Ambros 1-kg)

It had an exotic aroma similar to patchouli and raw vanilla, and something else unfamiliar yet enticing. The faerie merchant wrapped its spindly arms around the goods and scooped them into a drawer beneath the register. Etcher, in kind, vanished away the goods Tahli had laden her with. "Come on, Jerro, if we avoid Tahli long enough she'll have to pay for her own bloody shopping spree."

"I take it that was expensive?" asked Jerro once they were far enough along the herringbone path to be out of earshot of the bizarre faerie merchant.

"Not really, it would have been if I had handed over a crystal flower. Truth be told, it would have been a fair price for the lot. Tahli has expensive tastes, though she knows quality when she sees it. No, I got away rather light on that one. When you know someone's weakness, it's easy to set your own price."

"The tobacco?"

Etcher winked. "Precisely. Good tobacco, to be sure. I didn't swindle him on that, but all in all I made out better in the deal. Vices can cost you dearly, remember that Jerro."

"I'll try and keep that in mind."

"A wise decision." She looped her arm around Jerro's and ushered him down one of the branching paths. "I know time is of the essence and all, but there's something you really must see, since we're here."

"Oh?" He had become strangely accustomed to Etcher taking his arm and leading the way, as she often did. It was an odd sort of comfort.

She tapped the end of her nose and winked at him. "Just you wait." She grinned.

Together they wove their way through the hustle and bustle, moving along with the flow of traffic and into yet another exotic part of the Market. And as monkey-faced travelers, faerie folk vendors, toadstool shopfronts, and the hodgepodge of Ecliptians wearing their native bodies or human-like ehtas passed them by, neither one of them noticed that they were being followed.

The dog had been tracking Jerro since he entered Faerie. It had watched him in the forest as the nymphs attempted to seduce him, keeping low and distant so as not to alert the Soul Eater of its presence. It had followed Jerro's scent as he meandered through the Market—the Soul Eater close at hand. Now, it waited from across the road, eyes following Jerro and the Soul Eater as they made their way through Faerie's Faerie toward the Flower District, where scent merchants and Araelia fanatics gathered in droves.

When they were far enough away the dog continued to track them, sticking to the thicker crowds to keep its essence off the Soul Eater's radar. It watched and waited on the outskirts of the borough, eyes locked onto Jerro as he and the Soul Eater continued their casual meander down the herringbone path.

"So, Jerro, there's been something on my mind, but I'm unsure of how to tell you," she said casually, the tip of her deviltail flicked back and forth and her eyes peered sidelong at him.

"Well, what's on your mind?" An internal bell had started ringing inside Jerro's head, summoning a conflicting mixture of curiosity and caution.

The little shopkeeper, clad as she was in her black suit and blood-red trim, had kept an austere air about her. It made Jerro nervous, and as Etcher seldom revealed her inner thoughts, he worried over what might have prompted her to speak. He waited with bated breath for whatever might tumble out from behind her guarded tongue.

"A thank you, of sorts."

"...For what?"

Etcher remained silent a while as her gaze traveled along the vendor stalls and traced over the curves of fine wares and glimmering artifacts.

Experience had taught Jerro that it was best not to prod when Etcher fell into these quiet lulls, although he very much wanted, *needed,* to know exactly what it was she intended to tell him.

She stopped walking and slipped her arm from his, turning to look up at him with her golden gaze.

Jerro froze under her scrutiny.

"I have to thank you for getting me back home."

"How d'you mean?"

Etcher dropped her weighty gaze, removing the pressure that had kept Jerro rooted, and linked her fingers behind her head as she picked up her casual meander once more. "Well, as I was skipped through the dark, finding my way back without the shop to help guide me, there was one thing that gave me a heading. An inkling that I was at least traveling in the right direction."

"...Okay..."

She flicked him a glance and smile. "It would appear that we've become tethered, somehow, ever since Undercity, at least."

"Um, what does that mean, exactly?"

Etcher shrugged. "Well, it would appear that even halfway across the galaxy I could sense you out there. Even from the *Blank*, you're like an ember in the darkness. Perhaps it's your curious soul, or maybe our deal that binds us, although that usually doesn't happen. I don't imbed tracker spells, since they have a nasty habit of going both ways and I prefer to be secretive, as you know."

The words digested slowly, and quietly, for Jerro. He remembered the weird sensation he had felt tugging, as if from the core of him, right before Etcher showed up in a ball of fire. A fact she had failed to explain when they were back in Tahli's grand suite. "So that's why you showed up in front of me, specifically?"

Etcher nodded. "That would be why."

"And ah, why were you on fire?"

"*Ah,* that. I had inadvertently made a pit stop on the Zotah."

"What's that?"

"That would be our sun."

"Oh—*oh* shit. How did you—"

"It was a very quick stop. As soon as I jumped in, I jumped out, and nearly landed on you. My apologies about that."

"Uh, yeah…no worries." *The sun?* he thought. Who the hell could make even a *quick* stop on a blazing ball of fire and not be turned to ash? Although, granted, Etcher was unlike anyone else he knew. "So, you just popped in, saw everything was on fire, and popped back out?"

"Something like that. Although I recognized it was the Zotah and knew I was getting close. That, coupled with the fact that the tether which binds us had become much stronger."

"Oh." Jerro fought back the raging tide of questions and curiosities before it could tear down the floodgates and erase the one pivotal answer that he needed. "When you showed up, you asked *'when'* was it, not where."

"I did indeed."

"How long did you think it had been?"

"Well it obviously felt like much longer."

"*Felt* or *was?*"

Etcher studied him curiously. "Hmm. I fear you're spending too much time with me, you're beginning to get too quick."

"Etcher…"

She sighed. "There are worlds within worlds, as you have seen. And worlds which abide by their own versions of time. In some, a blink in this world could be years in another; in others, years in ours only a blink in theirs. By the fact I was only gone a day, we can rule out the latter."

A weighty gravity was starting to push down on Jerro as the implications dawned on him. "Years? Etcher, are you telling me…you were gone for *years?*"

"It was a long and arduous journey, like I said."

"Yeah, but Etcher—"

"Jerro, please." She stopped walking and turned to face him. "What's done is done. I'm here now, and I've you to thank. So thank you."

"You might not have come back at all."

"I'm well aware. But I couldn't let the slithe have the shop, nor me, Jerro. I couldn't give him that much power. What choice did I have?"

"Weren't you scared though?"

She shrugged. "Years pour into a lifetime as long as mine are negligible. Arduous, but negligible."

"You never did say how long—er, well, how old you are."

"Let's just say, I'm older than I look."

"Yeah I gathered that."

"Look, never you mind about all that," she said. "I'm glad I made it back, let's just be thankful for that, shall we? Besides, there are more interesting things to occupy your mind with." Etcher stood aside and held out her arm, presenting yet another decorative entryway to Jerro, housed inside a very long wall.

The wall stood at least twenty feet tall and appeared to separate Faerie's Faerie from another borough. A thin veil hung down over the opening of the archway, diffusing and muting the place beyond the threshold.

"That thing I wanted to show you, go have a look," she said, and pointed her chin toward the opening.

Jerro approached the entrance slowly. Though the back of his mind buzzed with the flurry of his unanswered questions, the threshold called to him. It was beautifully adorned with a multitude of gem-cut flowers woven together into a gigantic wreath that comprised the archway. The gem-flowers twinkled in the soft glow from the hovering faerie lights, gold leafs gleaming, the emerald vines and glowing ginse rosebuds resplendent even in the twilight. Quartz wildflowers, diamond blossoms, topaz lilies, and marigolds made of amber— all luscious and seductive in the purples and blues of the twilight sky that accented their precious petals.

From the moment Jerro brushed passed the hanging veil and stepped into the Flower District he was struck by the voluminous *scent* of the borough. Bafflement was wrought across his face at the stunning and unexpected change. He turned on his heels to face Etcher, the question rising in his eyes before he could even speak.

"The Flower District has a very potent smell and not all the other denizens are fond of it. Therefore, *majikal* barriers have been put in place to keep the scent within the borough's confines. It also adheres to its own moment in time. As you can see, it's early morning here," said Etcher, reading Jerro's face.

"It's incredible," he uttered softly, quickly being swept away by the cacophony that infiltrated his senses.

The scent that struck him was an amazing and overwhelming mixture of fresh flowers and heady pollens. The succulent sweets of fruit blossoms, the deep and potent allure of roses grounded in the underlying musk of marigolds, the delicate honey-like aroma of lilies and the soothing aromatics of jasmine and lavender—all of it threaded into a formidable floral mixture as though Jerro's nose had been buried inside a bouquet.

It was wonderful.

He breathed it in and felt it seep into his lungs, his skin, his clothes, cloaking him in a blanket of earthen goodness, invigorating the olfactory of his brain and trigging nostalgic memories of childhood, of springtimes in open fields, of the backyard in full bloom.

The second thing that struck him was the color, which was enhanced by the warm gold-pink glow of early morning light. There were such beautiful and bountiful assortments of vibrant flowers stacked up high in thick rows across vendor stalls. Amazing multitudes of blossoms were bundled together, strung up from the ceilings of open shops, spun into decorative wreaths, piled into large vats. There was color everywhere.

Loose petals danced through the Market and were swept along in the undercurrents of the passing foot traffic, peppering the ground and rooftops. It was an overwhelming and invigorating experience to simply stand there and drink in the sheer fullness his eyes and nose perceived.

And once his first two senses had been struck, the rest of the Flower District came at him with its utter abundance. People were there in the thousands, much as they had been in Gahza'Dune—where the foot traffic was so thick it was spilling off the sidewalks and into the main road. But here, there were no sidewalks. The multitude of people were already well packed into the heart of the street, churning and moving against the flow of comings and goings.

People were bartering with vendors, stuffing large bags with flowers in exchange for coinage or other goods. Some vendors, with decorative wreaths draped over their shoulders or loaded in baskets set upon their heads and backs, sought their customers out; others sat in the middle of the road with huge burlap bags all around them—piled high with their floral wares. There were people threading blossoms with expertly quick fingers, crafting their wreaths and decorative floral arrangements right then and there, others were shredding down their flowers to make confetti; some were stewing them to make dyes, perfumes, and potions; and some vendors were simply chewing on their petals with dopey eyes as they casually exchanged their goods with their patrons.

A peppering of food vendors kept the crowd fed and happy as they walked and shopped, and the scent of the vendors' mouthwatering goods sailed atop the floral headiness to tantalize taste buds, further saturating the sheer fullness of the borough. It was a beautiful orchestra of sensory stimulation that ignited a bubbling excitement and cheerful giddiness that was hard to contain.

Jerro was ready to throw himself into the thick of it, ready to buy something, anything that would engage him with the crowd. He was being drawn in by the hustle and bustle and needed to obtain a souvenir of this wondrous place so he might keep a piece of it alive with him always.

Etcher grinned at the boyish glee that was spreading throughout Jerro's face. "Well go on then, lead the way," she urged him.

He didn't need any more encouraging than that; he strode forward, moving headlong into the crowd and let himself be caught and guided by the currents of the other shoppers. He was carried along the winding streets and under canopies that kept the more delicate flowers safe from the light. Eventually he was drawn to a particular stall selling a plethora of fresh flower crowns, but it was the stark image of the merchant that initially drew him in.

Sitting atop a makeshift stage on a large plush pillow was the vendor, who had a strong resemblance to a giant langur. The creature had brilliant white fur covering its lanky body and a dark chocolate face. It was draped in rich silks and an abundance of gem-encrusted jewelry, conducting itself with an air of authority and ease. Seldom did the vendor maintain eye contact, as though the hands, feet, and tail independently bartered and traded with customers while the head surveyed the borough.

Jerro tore his eyes away from the monkey-merchant and began perusing the assortment of beautiful floral crowns. Then an image of Mahra spilled into his mind, and the thought popped the effervescent bubble that had carried him thus far. Was it right to be off having fun while she was lying in a hospital bed? While she was dying? And the dreadfulness of his thoughts plagued him until his guilt bled through his face.

"Something wrong?" asked Etcher, peering up at him with a mix of curiosity and concern.

He tried to smile, but it felt too heavy and instead he frowned. "It just…feels kind of wrong being here while, ya know—"

"*Ah*. I see. Perhaps I didn't make it clear when I mentioned that this borough adheres to its own moment. Time is different here. Akin to what I had told you earlier, only a blink might have passed in the rest of the world despite the lengthiness of our stay in this district. We could spend all day here, Jerro, and barely any time would have gone by out there. There is an exact conversion for time spent here as to out there. I believe about an hour in Flower District time is roughly point-two of a second in the rest of the Market? Something like that."

"Seriously?"

Etcher nodded. "On top of that, flower markets work best in the early morning, and so this place is centered around that period of the day. Time will appear to pass here, though it will never truly become night. It loops from dawn to noon and back again, but even within that cycle we are moving at a different rate of Time."

Jerro looked around with renewed interest at all the busy people bartering with shopkeepers and traveling merchants, but the heaviness stuck with him.

"Do you feel guilty for being here?"

"Yeah, I suppose."

"Hmm, I'm afraid there's not much can be done about that. Perhaps it would seem careless to be off having fun while there are still perils and uncertainties looming over us, but you know, your misery does Mahra no good."

Jerro groaned. "Yeah, I know. Doesn't stop it though."

"Well, maybe we can use this time to find something for Mahra?" She paused, weighing her thoughts behind her eyes. "I did see there was a bouquet back at Mahra's flat. I took it with me into the shop, although unfortunately left it there. I wasn't certain if you would want it or not."

Jerro wasn't certain either.

"At any rate, there are much finer flowers here," she said with a wink. "What about this? Mahra looks like a girl who would like snapdragons, don't you think?" Etcher had plucked a floral crown from the assorted rows and handed it to Jerro for inspection.

It was a beautiful arrangement of blues and soft whites. The predominate feature being that of the blue-and-purple snapdragons, intermittently laced with tiny white rosebuds, miniature bluebells, and sparkling glass beads, threaded along a rich green vine that had been woven into an elegant crown.

Jerro had to admit, it seemed like something that would suit Mahra, what with her whimsical bedroom decorations and spiritual motifs. And though, at a guess, Jerro assumed Mahra's favorite color might be orange or yellow, some kind of warm, earthy tone, he liked the blue crown for being different, something that would stand out in her collection—providing she ever got back home, of course.

He was smiling despite himself as he looked at the crown. "You know, I used to like snapdragons a lot when I was a kid. My dad showed me how to make them 'talk,' although my mom hated when we'd pull them off the stems to do it."

"They are a fun little flower, aren't they?" Etcher said, smiling back at the warm nostalgia softening Jerro's features. "Admittedly, I'm rather fond of them myself. On occasion, when Tahli is in more of a cattish mood and we'd get a shipment of them in, I would nip her paws with them."

Now that was a strange thought to digest, but in that moment, Jerro was reminded of the big cat he had seen on his first day at the shop. "I kinda forgot Tahli could change into a cat—well, a more normal looking cat." So long as normal meant something akin to a large feral tabby.

"I'd wager that with you around she's felt the need to assert her dominance and make you as uncomfortable as possible. We won't be seeing much of a cattish Tahli for a while."

"Why though? Why does she hate me so much?"

"Jerro, she's a cat. Cats are jealous creatures, not prone to sharing. Forgive this analogy, but you're a bit like the big lumbering puppy I just brought home who now runs rampant in what she believed would always be *her* space."

"*That's* how you see me? Like a big lumbering puppy?"

"Well you are very adorable, aren't you?" said Etcher mockingly, and went to pinch his cheek.

"Piss off." Jerro pushed her away, though he was smiling.

"At any rate, Tahli isn't used to sharing my attention."

"So she *is* your cat? Like litterbox and cat-toys kind of cat?"

"No, not like that. She's my apprentice, and will someday inherit the shop from me, so long as we get it back, of course. But Kyoki are...how to put it?

They need companionship, they're very loyal and, well, without delving into Tahli's past too deeply, she lost her companion and it wounded her in ways that are hard to truly grasp. I am a substitute of sorts, and hence why she doesn't like sharing me."

"Oh…I didn't know."

"You wouldn't, and it's wise if you pretend as if you don't."

"Tahli mentioned something before—while you were gone—that she'd lost someone to a slithe. Or at least it seemed that way."

The air around them both became weighty, and Etcher's face became grave. "It's a very unhappy story, and not mine to share."

"Sorry. I wasn't trying to pry."

"It's all right. We all have varying degrees of darkness coloring our pasts, Jerro, it's why I find it so important to seize the happy moments when they come." She smiled and let the heaviness of the moment lighten. "Anyhow, why don't you get that crown for Mahra? We can leave afterwards, if you like."

Jerro looked at the crown in his hands and imagined Mahra's smiling face as she wore it. It was one of the nicer images that had graced his mind during the tumultuous day. "Yeah, all right, thanks, Etcher…but ah, well, maybe we could stay for a little bit longer."

The little shopkeeper grinned and her deviltail coiled with impish glee. "Well, you know, with all these flowers this happens to be an excellent spot for beekeeping, and bees, of course, make honey, and honey…makes *mead*." She winked.

Jerro found this to be a tantalizing offer, and quickly found that guilt was swept away by the boisterous and adventure-seeking urges he all too often had to keep in check under the joyless supervision of better sensibility. "Well, I guess we could hang about for a drink or two."

"A wise decision indeed. Very fine mead here, I assure you."

"Yeah, I bet." He laughed.

Etcher ushered Jerro toward the langur-esque merchant to purchase the flower crown—who greeted them with a beckoning hand and eyes that sought out something far off in the distance.

"Twenty eagle feathers, any color. No downy." The langur merchant chittered at them.

"Um—" Jerro looked to Etcher for help.

"That's a curious exchange," said Etcher.

Upon speaking, the langur merchant shot its gaze down toward the little shopkeeper and let out a series of clipped monkey calls. "You!" The langur merchant pointed at Etcher with a long dexterous finger. "You, Potion Keeper. You buying crown?"

"Actually, my friend intended on purchasing it."

"Bah." The langur merchant waved its hand dismissively at Jerro. "Mundies only bring ginse. You can trade. You have phoenix charms, yes?"

"Perhaps. But that's a high price for a flower crown."

"No. I give you crown, you trade for this." The langur merchant pulled out a necklace from under its silken robes.

The amber pendent—hanging from the elaborate braided chain—was in the shape of a teardrop and carved with the emblem of an eye.

"It's real Dyna token. You trade for it, you trade!"

Etcher held out her hand expectantly. "I'll have a look first, if you don't mind."

The langur chittered. "You see, it's real!" it said, and slipped the necklace over its fluffy white head and plopped it in Etcher's hand. "We have deal?"

"Just a moment," said Etcher. She turned the emblem over and studied it carefully, holding it up and examining it in the light. "Why would you trade *this* for a phoenix charm?"

The langur's eyes darted about and it lowered its voice. "I'm tired of flower business, want to do feather business. Feather crowns make more than flower, I can get out of here."

"I'm afraid I don't see what use I would have for this."

"No! You have use, I *seen* it. You have dark journey ahead, you need it! You do. You want crown for your friend, too, don't you? Take both! Just give me phoenix charm."

Etcher sighed as she looked to the crown in Jerro's hand, to the look on his face, and then to the strange desperate plea of the flower merchant. "Fine. Here." She donned the Dyna necklace and hid the pendent under her clothes, then conjured a glowing red stone dressed with beautiful peacock-esque feathers. It looked like a little fat bird, the way the feathers were arranged, and it had a long ribbon of parchment stuck into its tail with a scrawl of ancient runes inscribed along it.

The langur's eyes went wide with excitement, and it chirped and chittered frantically, snatching the charm from Etcher's hand. "You make good choice! Go on now, go on."

The langur merchant waved them away.

"What was that about?" asked Jerro after they had made their way from the flower booths and headed toward a row of tall brick buildings that flanked the open road.

"Apparently, the merchant wants out of the flower district."

"I got that bit—sort of—I meant the necklace? What's a Dyna-thingy anyhow?"

"Dyna token? It's like a charm, of sorts. It clears your mind and helps you see the truth of things. Dynasta, where the charm gets its namesake, is the Goddess of Truth."

"Well it sounds useful."

"Sure, but I typically have little trouble reading people. I can smell a lie a mile away, so to speak, so it's not all that illuminating for me."

"Then why are you wearing it?"

Etcher smiled devilishly at Jerro. "Because I'm superstitious. The merchant seemed insistent enough, maybe it'll prove its usefulness in another way."

"*You're* superstitious?"

"Of course I am. Look where we are. On your Earth superstition might seem foolhardy, but it has genuine validity here."

"I guess you make a good point."

"That isn't to say you should buy into every little thing you hear. Some people are actually just full of it, even on Eclipse."

"Good to know some things are universal."

"Indeed. Now, about that mead." Etcher skipped her way toward one of the brick buildings and stood aside from a dark wooden door. A small hanging sign over the threshold read '*The Olde Azalea*,' with painted flowers along the trim. There were floral patterns set into the stained glass of the door and the along the windows of the building.

"I'm guessing the flower motif goes a long way around here."

"Welcome to the Flower District." Etcher smirked. "After you."

Jerro pushed past the creaky door and stepped inside the cool dark interior of the floral pub. He took a big whiff of the place and noted that under the penetrating scent of the district's flowery perfume there was the nostalgic and oddly comforting aroma of stale beer, whisky, wood varnish, and tobacco. It was strangely homey.

"You can get this round, they're more than happy to accept ginse here," said Etcher.

"Thank god for that," Jerro replied, sighing with genuine relief as he led the way towards the bar.

It was quiet inside the pub, a smattering of other metamorphic patrons enjoyed a quiet pint to themselves, a few others enjoyed their pint with a pub lunch. There was that carefree resonance to the place that pubs often have during late mornings on a weekday, when most everyone else is slaving away at their nine-to-five while a lucky few have managed—somehow—to idly spend their time inside a cozy watering hole.

Oh, how Jerro envied that. The amount of times he'd walked by—usually late—on his way to work and spied some happy bastard sitting in the window seat of the local pub as if to advertise their good fortune. A big content smile on their silly faces as they sat back with their pint, a nice juicy fry-up in front of them and not a care in the world.

Come to think of it, Jerro could be that happy bastard today. Feeling a little more renewed, and even less guilty, he strode up to the counter and smiled at the big, dragon-faced bartender.

The imposing barkeep with said dragon face was about as tall as if Etcher were sitting on Jerro's shoulders for a game of chicken fight. He was richly adorned in shiny black scales that turned indigo when the light accented them, and his plain clothes were stretched to their limits across his thick, imposing mass. Jerro was reminded of a far less friendly version of Yohza.

Upon seeing Jerro, the barkeep narrowed his ruby eyes and merely grunted, letting out two small tongues of flame from its scaly nostrils.

The smile fell from Jerro's face.

"Two meads please," Etcher chimed in. "Lupigwen, if you have it."

The bartender looked Etcher over carefully, then shot a curious glance at Jerro. "He's with you?" he said in a deep rumbling voice.

"He's paying." She smiled.

As if the little shopkeeper had passed some kind of secret test, the dragon-faced bartender grinned with a fierce set of stark-white dragon teeth, and the ferocious demeanor lightened up, although there was still a touch of mischief and malice lingering about. "Aye, we got Lupigwen. Ya opening a tab?"

"Oh, I dunno about that. We're only staying for a drink or two, isn't that right, Jerro?"

"Ah…" *Crap,* he thought. The allure of a luxuriously lazy day of sitting and sipping had already embedded itself in his mind and wasn't keen on making way for better sensibility. "I mean, we could still do a tab, even if it's just for a few?"

Etcher smiled. "You make a fine point. We'll open a tab." She winked at the bartender, and the bartender in turn, grinned.

A pleasant little bell rang as the door to the clinic opened.

"Hello," began the pearl nurse with musical cheeriness before her eyes locked onto the person standing in the doorway. Shock kept her rooted, and a sudden heart flutter made her dimwitted and slow.

A tall, ebony-skinned man walked in, although it seemed as if he glided. His green eyes were hypnotic and his smile was worn easily, if not a little mischievously. Tribal feathers and beads adorned his finely braided mane, framing a handsome face. He moved smoothly, as if in slow motion, and the world around him became a soft haze and he became the center. There was a heady radiance that poured off him, a mix of some tropical musk and a dark mysterious allure.

The pearl nurse was smitten.

"Wat a fine morn'n I find me'self `ere in da *great* city of Yahre." His exotic lilt was like honey pouring into the pearl nurse's eardrum, rhythmic and deep and unabashedly sensual.

"H-how may I help you?" The pearl nurse said with effort, summoning the words as if from a dream.

The man smiled with his million-ginse smile and set the pearl nurse's heart a-fluttering. "I com' `ere t'check me'self in, want t'be looked at before da party starts tonight, ya know? Been `ave'n dis strange sensation run up me arm every time I move it." He rolled up his light cotton sleeve and presented the well-defined appendage for the nurse to inspect.

Obediently, the pearl nurse leaned in and *inspected* his arm, turning just the slightest shade of soft pink as she ran her fingers over the thick cords of muscle.

"I-I don't feel any swelling, or—"

"Well it also com's across me torso, maybe ya could take a look at dat too," he said smoothly.

The poor nurse looked as if she might swoon. "Well I could...uh, check you out in the back, there's a room..." Her words were breathy and floating, and her pearly eyes were in a daze.

"Why don't we do dat?" The man winked and let himself past the swing doors into the back.

The nurse followed after him, though she hardly recalled summoning the will to make her legs move. She opened the door to a small examination room and stood aside to let the man in. He brushed by her ever so close and let her get a great whiff of his bewitching scent.

"Should I take dis off?" he asked, though never bothered to wait for a reply as he pulled his shirt over his head and stood before the pearl nurse like a wolf before a lamb.

"That would be lovely—I mean fine—that's fine..." She beamed at him, and then something caught her attention and a little of the cloudiness left her pearly gaze as she turned away from the man. "W-was that the bell?"

"*No*, ya just imagine'n tings," he said as he stepped up to her, catching her chin with his finger and turning her face back toward his own. "Now, `ow `bout dat check up?"

"Took ya long enough." A kinsman of the suave man spoke through the drags of a slender cigar. He was propped against a wall in a back alley, hidden in the deep shadows of the faux night.

"I `ad t'make sure ya `ad enough time," said the suave man. He had left the clinic only moments before and sought out his comrade around back.

"Sure, sure, dats wat it was," said the kinsman in a slow calm. He was thinner than his handsome counterpart, and more agile looking, and though he wasn't quite as intoxicatingly good-looking as the other man, he was better dressed. His trilby hat was cocked to one side, his silk shirt with its big collar was left unbuttoned near the top, exposing the shapely collarbone beneath. He wore a suede jacket and matching trousers that were well fitted, and his wingtip shoes were polished and gleaming.

"Wat ya find out?" said the man.

The hat-wearing kinsman took another long savoring drag off his fragrant cigar. "Ya not gon' like wat I found."

"An' why is dat?"

"`Cause dat mundie girl belong t'da devil," said the kinsman. He pulled out a slip of paper from inside his jacket and handed it over.

"Dey didn't pay us enough for dis," said the man as he looked the paper over.

"Wat we gon' do?" asked the well-dressed kinsman.

"Don't ya worry ya pretty `ead over it. I'll deal wid it. Don't tell em no'tink."

The kinsman breathed out a heavy cloud of fragrant smoke through his nostrils and eyed the paper in the other man's hand. "Me tink dey bad for business. Why we deal'n wid dem anyhow?"

"`Cause better we deal wid dem den if dey deal wid someone else." The man folded the paper and tucked it into his shirt.

"Do ya tink dey know?"

"About da devil? Not sure. Why don't ya find out?"

The kinsman put out his cigar and pushed off from the wall. "Why me a'ways do'n ya dirty work?"

"`Cause I'm better look'n den you." The man winked.

The kinsman grunted in what might have been a laugh and then disappeared into the darkness without as much as a sound.

The pleasant buzz of tipsy was stumbling dangerously close to the line of blind drunk, at which point better sensibility had salvaged enough of itself to smack Jerro upside the head. "D'they have any coffee?" asked Jerro with only the slightest of slurs.

"Calling it in already?"

"Ah, come on Etcher, I don't wanna be munted. I do actually feel a little bad still."

"Oh, all right," said Etcher. She waved the dragon-faced barkeep over and ordered a coffee for Jerro and an exotic sounding herbal tea for herself. "I suppose you have a point. Besides, if we don't find a lead, Tahli will all but bankrupt me if left to her shopping spree."

Jerro let out a giggle-snort of a laugh. "Did you really leave her for a month in Baros...Barga, uh...?"

"*Bargos.* Yes, I did. And I paid for that too, dearly."

"S'not really nice, Etcher."

"I know, but Tahli seldom goes on adventures with me and I was in the midst of an exciting endeavor into the heart of the Kali'Goh. An ancient city on the far side of the Angelous run by a cult of some *very* peculiar folk, let me tell you."

She sighed whimsically. "It was a marvelous time. There I was, standing at the lip of the gorge into Kali'Goh, thinking of how I'd infiltrate their precious hidden temple. I ended up using one of their ceremonial tapestries to hang-glide down into the main chasm, pickpocketed the guard, snuck into the holy chamber and took the jewel of Ahkmar right from the head of the statue. I was out before they noticed the tapestry on the ground. Of course, once they caught on, I had to stow away on an airship, which they followed after vigorously, then I circled back and raided the holy room again whilst they were gone. I imagine they were none too happy when they got back."

Jerro had a lazy smile on his face as he listened to the tale and envisioned the daring adventure, although imagined himself in place of Etcher, minus the flamboyant clothing.

"Yer coffee," said the dragon-faced barkeep as he set the ceramic cups and teapot down on the table.

"Thank you, we'll close out that tab, too, I think, right Jerro?" said Etcher.

"Huh? Oh yeah." He nodded absently then scrubbed a hand over his face and through his dark mane, squeezing his eyes shut for a moment and then forced them back open and into focus. "I wish I could go on adventures like you," he said dreamily, then proceeded to stir in a liberal helping of cream and sugar into his coffee.

"Undercity wasn't adventurous enough?"

"Well, yeah...but I mean, I was knocked out for most of it, which by the way,"—he said as he licked the stirring spoon clean—"you have yet to fill me in on all the details."

"Yes, I suppose I do owe you an explanation for that." Etcher added a large dollop of honey to her tea and sipped it carefully, setting the cup down gracefully in its saucer. "It was quite bizarre. That little nightmare, Gribs was his name, followed me the whole way through," she began, and went on to tell him about how Mr. Gribs had been turned into a handsome prince on the isle, how the people of Arcadia were all dead but unaware of it, how the Mad King had tried to steal Jerro's soul and how the whole place eventually fell apart.

It was a mostly true retelling, only that the version he got left out how Etcher had been transformed into her dark demi-god soul-eating self. Instead, Jerro was told of a normal-ish Etcher who had snatched the Death Token from the pillar of light that was attempting to steal Jerro's soul, and that the whole isle fell apart because of it—which was more or less how it happened.

"Whoa—I really did miss a lot."

"Indeed you did."

"So you got me out of there before it all fell apart?"

"Well, I carried you out, actually. Have you been gaining weight by the way?"

"Har har, very funny." Jerro was both amused and slightly embarrassed at the thought of the tiny shopkeeper hauling him out from Arcadia and back to the shop. "What happened to the toad then?"

"Well he ran for the hills once things turned south, not a very courageous nightmare that one."

"No kidding, you think he'll show up again?"

Etcher shrugged. "You know, he might, truth be told, I never did take up the invitation to see his king."

"Yeah I dunno if I'd be in a hurry to meet the *King of Nightmare* either."

"Especially not since I stole from him."

Jerro choked on his coffee, though managed to avoid spraying himself and Etcher with the hot liquid at the expense of the back of his throat. "You what?" he croaked.

"Technically, I was stealing back something that did not belong in his possession, but either way, I'm still the thief in the mix. He wasn't happy last we met."

"What'd you take?"

Etcher sipped at her tea once more, stirring in another helping of honey and pouring a little more liquid from the teapot into her cup.

"There are these small gemstones called dexus orbs, they catalogue all the literature in the great temple libraries from which they originate. Although their true significance is that they can recreate any of the text within said library. Access to that kind of knowledge yields with it incredible potential."

"No kidding. How'd he even get one in the first place?"

"You remember when I told you about the nautiloid cruiser?"

"Er, vaguely."

"You know, '*the big spaceship crashed into a portal*' that whole thing?"

"Oh yeah!"

"Well, long ago—*very* long ago—there was a move to set up a colony on another world outside of the Angelous, which is a big deal, mind you, since we've mainly kept to our own galaxy. But anyhow, the idea was that Eclipse, along with several of the other allied planets, were going to set up this new colony together, like a utopia, if you will. So they loaded up all kinds of treasures and literature, tools, technology, you name it.

"But for whatever reason something went horribly awry and the nautiloid lost control and crashed right into a warp gate. There was a huge explosion, the gate was destroyed, and the entire nautiloid vanished. Ever since then, however, pieces of the cargo have been popping up all over the galaxy. Funny enough, it's only ever the cargo though, nothing of the crew or of the ship itself."

"That is weird."

"It really is. Another mystery for the books, I suppose. Profitable for me, however, as whenever someone catches wind of an artifact turning up from the nautiloid, I usually get called in to collect. For a price," she said with a wink.

"Was that the same deal with the jewel of Akbar-or-whatever?"

"No, that was purely for fun."

"You have quite the life."

"It's seldom dull."

"I wish I could say the same," he said as he absently stirred his coffee.

"Well, all things considered, it's been rather adventurous these past few days, has it not? And even if you *were* unconscious for the better half of our excursion into Undercity, you've still managed to have a little fun."

"Yeah, it has been fun," he remarked, though there was little effort given to the statement.

Etcher cleared her throat and shifted in her seat so that she could slide one leg over the other. "So at what point were you planning on asking?"

"'Scuse me?"

"Oh come now, don't be coy."

"I don't—?"

She looked at him bluntly. "Jerro, really, I know it's been on your mind."

"Etcher I'm not sure—"

"About staying *here*. Or am I mistaken?"

Jerro's eyes lit up, though his vocal cords were snoozing on the job, still healing from the burn, and instead of words he produced a soft grunt.

"Is that a no then?"

"W-what? No! I mean yes! I mean, yeah I'd like to stay—can I?"

"Well I dunno, you haven't asked me properly," she replied airily.

Before Jerro could overthink the situation and be inhibited by an endless torrent of *what ifs* and *should I really?* his vocal cords piped up. "Etcher, can I please stay?"

She looked at him through the corner of her eye and sipped her tea, an impish smile curling into her lips. "With me, you mean? In my shop? Providing we ever get it back, of course."

"Yes."

"You'd be embarking into a life of crime, you know? Can't have you just lounging about, you'd have to help me on my escapades."

"Etcher, I'm already a criminal. Yes!"

"It'd be dangerous."

"It's been dangerous."

"You'd be leaving your old world behind. I suppose you could still visit it, though."

"I know, but I,"—he frowned—"I haven't felt like I've been at home in a long time, not until I came here."

"Hmmm," said Etcher. "I will consider your proposal to accompany me as my—what shall we call you? Underling, perhaps? On one condition."

"What's that?"

"You'll need your parents' blessing."

"Are you joking? Etcher, I'm not a kid."

"*Ah*, but you do have family ties, and I am no kidnapper, pardon the phrase. Jerro, at some point or another, you do need to see your parents and explain a few things, otherwise they'll keep probing for answers, and that is dangerous. Mundane your world might be, it is not entirely without magic, and there are magically inclined people walking side by side the local inhabitants. Your parents could get themselves in tremendous trouble if they started poking about in matters which are beyond them."

"Yeah, but what am I gonna say? Hey, sorry I disappeared, I'm traveling with a cosmic thief across the galaxy because some shapeshifting monsters are after me. By the way, I'm a reborn."

"*No*, you tell them a convincing lie with enough half-truths to be believable and allow them to fill in that which you neglect to mention. People already have an idea of the story they want to be told, you simply need to guide them to it. A person will readily believe their own lies over yours any day."

Jerro narrowed his gaze on her. "Boy, Etcher, sounds like you've had a lot of practice with this sort of thing."

She winked.

"So…is that a yes then?" he asked as he peered down into his caramel colored coffee.

Etcher rolled her eyes and smirked. "Of course it's a yes, you fool. Loathe though I am to admit it, I've grown rather fond of you, and I suppose I could use a good partner for my adventures."

Jerro was beaming and blushing simultaneously. "Do we shake on it?"

"*After* you've had a word with your parents then we can hash out the details of your stay. Tahli will be none too thrilled mind you, you'll have to make peace with her eventually."

"I'll deal with my parents first, thanks."

Etcher laughed. "Can't say I blame you. Well, suppose we best push on then. As nice of a reprieve as this has been, we better get back to the matters at hand. I've an idea of where to look for some answers about the Raven Witch."

"Ah, right." He winced internally. There he went again, forgetting about Mahra and all that she entailed.

He didn't feel as bad about it this time, though, which made him think maybe he should have. Strangely enough he was filled with a sense of renewed vigor. They'd find the Raven Witch, cure Mahra, get the shop back, and, well, take it from there, but at least he now had a future he was actually looking forward to. Goodbye mundane Programmer Jerro, hello Jerro the Adventurer! He'd be ready for whatever life had to throw at him now! He could take it!

It was a nice thought to have, even if it was naive.

The inside of Reedman's car had settled into a weighty silence and neither detective dared to break the grueling tension. To add to the oppressive mood, the rain had started to drizzle and made a constant patter on the windshield.

Thorneback, deprived of his nicotine fix, had resorted to angrily sloshing a lollipop back and forth inside his mouth while Reedman sat unmoving—arms crossed and eyes boring a hole into the bland façade of the council flats in front of them.

Through the hazy rainfall, Thorneback's beady eyes followed after the coroners—who had donned police-issued rain jackets. The grim hooded figures made their way carefully down the stairs with a gurney stretched between them. The lumpy body bag atop their stretcher was no doubt holding the faceless remains of Kristoff Abilgaard.

Reedman had taken notice of the slow ambling movement. The dour scene snatched him away from his solemn reverie and reminded him that he was still on duty. "What now?" he grunted at his partner.

Thorneback caught the lollipop between his molars and cracked the hard candy, squeezing it until the candy sphere shattered. He proceeded to crunch the sugary fragments until they stuck like mortar to his teeth. "Hell if I know," he said as he sucked at the glassy paste with his tongue. "What would you do?"

"Go back to the precinct, inform the chief, start putting together all the evidence."

"Sure, and what would you really do?"

Reedman eyed the wiry detective in his peripheral. "I'd go down to Fenris County right now and warn his mom."

"Oh yeah? And why's that?"

"'Cause whoever wants Ahliss didn't get their answers. They're carving their way through everyone that knows him. Daag, Kristoff—the other flatmate's in protective custody so he's out of reach. But they'll keep looking for anyone affiliated with Ahliss. If the mom isn't next on the list she will be soon enough—*shit*."

"What?"

"There was a girl, Mahra Lapaul. Seems like she had a thing with Ahliss, better check in on her as well."

"So, which one first?"

"The mom. The girl didn't know Ahliss well enough, she might not even pop up on the radar, for now, anyway."

"Right then." Thorneback nodded. "Let's get on with it."

"You serious? Maybe you don't know but chief doesn't want me going near the mom."

"What'cha do?" Thorneback winked with a sneer.

"Nah, nothing like that. She just doesn't like me, I made one too many house calls about her son."

"Well, guess you're making one more. You drive, I'll call in. Have 'em put someone else on the girl."

"Chief's not gonna like this."

"You let me handle him. You're just a consultant on this anyway. No press, no signature."

"Yeah, and you get all the glory."

"Peh, real fucking glorious up in that flat. Just drive, will ya?" Thorneback got out his phone and began to dial.

Reedman started up the engine and the car came to life with a rumbling purr. He was eager to be on the move and get far away from the blood and gore. They pulled away from the curb and headed for the freeway, leaving the quiet police lights and solemn officers behind them.

"So where are we headed?" asked Jerro.

"We're going to Dune Hut. There's a merchant there—*Delluige*—he trades in information and rumor mostly, he'll be a good place to start," said Etcher, stretching her legs as she got up from the booth and headed for the door. "Don't forget to pay the tab."

"Oh, right." Jerro nodded and made his way for the bar. He smiled at the dragon-faced barkeep—who sneered back—and readied a glassy ginse coin in his hand.

"Cashing out?" the barkeep said in a deep rumble.

"Yeah, please."

The barkeep slipped a receipt Jerro's way and waited quietly.

Jerro looked down at the paper and frowned. "Um, are you missing a decimal?"

"Nope." The dragon-faced barkeep grinned.

There was a sudden and grinding halt to Jerro's thoughts as he looked down at the extortionate amount. "H-how much was the mead?"

The dragon-faced barkeep tapped a clawed finger on one of the many repeating lines on the list.

Jerro continued to stare at the receipt, hoping that it might rearrange itself into something less horrifying. "We drank *that* much?"

"Including the rounds ya bought for me, aye, ya did."

"I...wait, what? When did I?" He turned and looked over his shoulder at Etcher, who smiled and winked back at him from the door.

"So, ya gonna be needing any change?" said the dragon-faced barkeep, and he folded his big scaly arms over his big barrel chest.

"You could have warned me they were ninety a pop!" said Jerro after he had caught up with Etcher.

"Well, good mead is worth every pit. Besides, had you worried over the price you would have tarnished your enjoyment, and mine at that."

He was tempted to keep on grumbling but considering how every ginse he currently owned had been given to him by Etcher, he really wasn't in a position to complain. It was just in his nature to dislike the spending of currency, especially since everything up until that point had seemed so cheap. At least there was still plenty lining the baskets in the Obelisk mind-closet.

"It was pretty good mead," he relented.

"Indeed it was. Very smooth, and perfectly sweetened. Some meads can get rather sickly when they're not done right."

"I wouldn't know, I've never had mead before today."

"Well, you have now, and I dare say you're in for disappointment."

Jerro rolled his eyes and smiled as he kept in time with Etcher. They headed through the throng of flower merchants and back toward the jewel-encrusted archway that separated the boroughs, passing through the light, silky veil that hung limply inside the barrier. As they walked through, Jerro was assaulted with the same disorientation he had experienced back in Yahre when he transitioned from day to sudden night. The bruised colors of the twilight sky tinged everything in blue, and the soft pastels of the colorful floating faerie lights added a different kind of vibrancy to the world.

Jerro noted that things were almost *exactly* the way he had left them. The same people that had been perusing, the same gestures and conversations he had overheard—all as he remembered it the moment before they left Faerie's Faerie. Etcher had been right; barely a second had passed since they had gone into the Flower District. He looked back at the archway in wonder. The moments he could now feel ticking past made him realize that within the space of those seconds, people were living out whole lifetimes beyond the veil.

He looked back at Etcher then. 'Years' she had said. She had spent *years* trying to get back from Dahl'Kir after she left the shop, and all it had been for Jerro was one blurry drunken night out. The thought made the universe seem infinitely vaster, stranger, and very much *alive*. At any given moment, no matter how boring, dull, or slow, there were markets bustling with flower merchants, drinks being drunk, afternoons being spent, and cosmic thieves trying to find their way home.

"Hey, Etcher?" he found himself saying.

"Hmm?"

"Has it always been like this?"

"How d'you mean?"

He looked around at the bizarre faerie merchants, the giant toadstools, bogarts, glittering lights, the wild looking patrons. An Ecliptian with ram horns and cloven feet was bartering with a mermaid, who was suspended inside a large ball of floating water, for what looked like a clutch of tiny golden chickens.

"It just seems so weird. Back on Earth, *my* Earth, the universe seemed so small. I mean, I hardly ever *thought* about the rest of space, not seriously anyhow. Fantasized about it, I suppose, but it never seemed real. You know there are planets out there, and the likeliness was there had to be life, but so what? It's not relevant when you have bills to pay and a job to go to, it's not really *real*.

"I just find it crazy to think that I could be living my mundane life back on Midgard while all this was going on, and I never had a clue."

Etcher took pause and considered this for a moment as they meandered along the herringbone path. "That's a truth shared by many, though. Think about all the billions of people that have no idea that *you* exist. Just because you don't see a thing, doesn't mean it isn't there."

"I know that."

"Yes, I'm certain you do. You know it, but you never really understood what it meant until now."

Jerro felt a strange tingling sensation in his brain as dendrites created new pathways and connections, broadening the scope of his reality. "After seeing all this, I don't think I could ever go back to living a normal life."

"No, I imagine not, and we shall certainly endeavor to keep things interesting for you." She smiled. "At any rate, Dune Hut's just up ahead."

Jerro breathed in deeply of the arid twilight, feeling the strange crackle of *majik* that permeated Dune Hut. Fewer of the floating faerie lights dotted the place, and instead wrought iron lampposts—gently assaulted by tumbling bundles of moths—lined the roads and bathed the world in amber. Unlike Faerie's Faerie with its storybook whimsy, here was a sensation of something ancient and timeless, a feeling of grandeur that saturated the very ground.

There was warmth radiating up through the golden sands that obscured the herringbone path, and a potent aroma, though not of flowers, but of incense and curried meats snaking its way through the bustling crowds.

Jerro, of course, hardly took notice of Dune Hut's finer details; instead his eyes kept drifting off to the smiley half-naked belly dancers who moved their hips in fluid undulation and glided through the parting throng, clapping their cymbals and jiggling their jingly clothing. To be fair, it was hard not to watch, what with the drummers and musicians that kept after them and directed any wavering attention back to the dancers with the beat of their loud, sonorous drums.

"You should stay outside," said Etcher once they had reached a low domed hut with a leather flap for a door.

"What? Why?" replied Jerro, a little bewildered to be so suddenly pulled away from the hypnotic movement of the dancers' hips.

"Because the merchant inside this hut is not going to like you. It's not personal, he doesn't like anybody."

"So, why can't I come in? If he doesn't like anyone he's not going to like you either," he said, and found himself looking over Etcher's head to watch in disappointment as the belly dancer troupe moved down the path and out of sight behind a flock of spindly glass people that were dancing and pirouetting their way across the sands on singular appendages like music box ballerinas.

"Quite true, he hates me in fact, all the more reason to keep his loathing to a minimum."

Jerro groaned. "So I have to stand around outside doing nothing, staying out of the loop *again*."

"Jerro please, you're sounding like Tahli. You're free to shop around, there's plenty to do here."

"Etcher, I don't wanna get lost! This place is massive."

"Oh come now, even if you got lost, I'll always find you. Have we not proven that point? Besides, you could always *not* get lost too, you know."

"I don't even know how we got here. I couldn't even tell you how to get to the front gate and we walked through it."

"And I said I'll come find you."

Jerro huffed. "So long as you don't appear in a ball of fire again," he mumbled quietly.

"I'll try not to. Anyhow, the fact of the matter is you'll still have to wait outside. Why not shop around to occupy the time?"

"Yeah, but Etcher, I don't even know what a *sprit* is or how much a crystal flower is worth, how am I supposed to buy anything without getting swindled?"

"Well, if the price sounds too cheap or too expensive, you're being swindled."

"Etcher—"

"Do you want to find the Raven Witch?"

Jerro paused and looked to the ground. "Well, obviously."

"Then I need to speak with the merchant in this tent. I need to find out what he knows and I can't do that with you there. If Tahli were here I'd tell her the same thing, now, please, Jerro, let me do this."

"Etcher…"

"Jerro," she said firmly.

"Yeah, all right, whatever. Go on then. But you better come get me when I get lost!"

"Always, Jerro. Even through time and space, I'll find you." She winked and ducked inside the hut.

The heat rose in his cheeks. It was an oddly intimate thing to say, it was oddly intimate how she said it, and he was ill equipped to process the feelings that assaulted him thereafter.

He stood numbly for a moment until his feet began to carry him away from the hut and toward the closest open stall he could find.

The dog watched.

As the Soul Eater vanished inside the hut and left Jerro by himself, the dog found the moment it had waited patiently for. The dog crept along the outskirts, keeping to the shadows and the crowds and slinking ever closer towards Jerro. It found a narrow gap inside a crooked alley and there it waited once more, waited for Jerro to see it.

Jerro found himself before a curiously aquatic-looking vendor, who was stationed under a tall lamppost and was sitting cross-legged on a pillow, calmly smoking from a large hookah pipe. The aquatic vendor was nearly as tall as Jerro even at that vantage.

The strange Ecliptian had a face like a cuttlefish, though the eyes were keen and forward-facing. Its head was crested in a mohawk of long, flat fins that ran down the back of its neck to its shoulders—a substitute for hair—and its humanoid body was sinewy and elegant like a swimmer's physique, with the addition of blue rubbery skin, webbed fingers and flipper-like feet, and a very long tail topped with a butterfly-shaped fin.

There was a dog curled up beside it, if you could call it that, and if you included gills, webbed paws, and fins in that description, and if said dog was also colored similarly to a lionfish. The canine creature opened one big watery eye to look at Jerro, sniffed the air in his direction, and growled softly before resuming its pseudo-nap.

"Can I help you?" said the vendor, although it never paused from its smoking, nor did the tentacle mouth move in a manner to suggest speech.

"Uh…" replied Jerro, looking around at the vendor's set up.

Behind the aquatic merchant was a big tent where the glimmer of hidden treasures occasionally winked and beckoned the curious onlooker with an air of mystery and a touch of danger. Jerro slowly brought his attention back to the dog, beside which was a low table where an assortment of antique lamps and mystical objects had been placed.

"I'm just looking to be honest." he smiled meekly.

"Fancy a smoke?" asked the vendor, and again the only move its tentacle mouth made was to suction at the hookah pipe and blow out the most intricate smoke-rings Jerro had ever seen. The vendor held up an unoccupied hose from the hookah and presented it to Jerro. The fragrant aroma of the shisha was spicy and sweet and laced with a touch of citrus and coconut.

Jerro's mouth watered. He cast a weary glance back at the domed hut where Etcher had left him. She hadn't said anything about *not* sitting and taking a casual smoke with a vendor, nor did she mention anything about the proper etiquette of how to handle said situation. But then again, there were a lot of important things that Etcher often neglected to mention.

"I, ah,"—the tobacco was tantalizing and the calm demeanor of the aquatic merchant was equally endearing—"um, sure, why not?"

The merchant seemed happy at this, although it was hard to tell as the face changed little, but its color seemed to brighten at the very least. Jerro took the offered hookah hose and seated himself on an empty pillow, casting a cautionary glance at the amphibious dog beside him. The merchant placed a thumb over the end of its own pipe and nodded at Jerro.

Jerro brought the pipe to his lips, noting the cobra-headed topper of the hose, and sucked in the smoke. It tasted even better than it smelled, fruity yet savory, with none of the sickly aftermath that exceptionally fragrant shisha often had. The smoke danced along the tip of his tongue, rolled down his throat in a cool wave, and filled out his lungs. With it came a pleasant lightheadedness that made the world seem a little easier and less chaotic.

The vendor tapped him with its pipe and indicated for Jerro to cover the nozzle.

"Oh, sorry." Jerro covered his pipe with his thumb and let the vendor have a turn.

"You're new here," said the vendor, and on the third instance of 'speaking' Jerro realized that it was a version of his own voice that was speaking to him— something a little deeper than his usual tone and laced with euphoric calm that was not inherent to Jerro—and that it was coming from inside his head.

"Yeah, I am," he said warily, plagued by the slightly horrifying notion that the vendor might be reading his mind as well as speaking directly into it.

"Have a gift then," said the vendor, calmly turning to the low table beside the amphibious-dog, puffing out elaborate smoke-rings all the while. It sorted through a wooden tray of ornate little trinkets with a long, pointed finger until it found what it was looking for. It held up a golden hoop earring; it was simple and unadorned, though thicker than the average piercing, like a small chain-link.

"Oh, uh, I'm okay, thank—"

"You should take it," the vendor cut in with its mind-speak. "It's the fashion." And indeed, the vendor itself was sporting a fair few golden hoops, albeit even bigger and thicker, along its plethora of fins.

"Um, my ears aren't pierced…it's okay."

The vendor stared at him calmly, the look of parental patience across its serene face. "It's the fashion," —it said again— "you're staying, aren't you?"

"How did you—*ow!*"

Before Jerro had time to react, the vendor had leaned over and pinched his earlobe. He felt a sharp hot prick, an uncomfortable stretching, and then an unfamiliar weight in the afflicted lobe, which throbbed dully.

With a careful hand, Jerro reached up and touched the gold ring which now adorned his left ear. "…Thanks," he said with trepidation, worried the vendor might *gift* him with anything else.

"Now you look more Ecliptian," it said.

"Yeah?"

The vendor nodded, and held up its pipe, showing Jerro that it was his turn.

Jerro took a deep long drag and felt the soothing lightheadedness roll over him once again. As he idly watched the crowd he noted that a lot of the

Ecliptians did indeed have an assortment of gold hoops in their ears, a few even had them on their faces. There were other studs and gems and tattoos and what have you, making them look like the motley collection of the wild things that they were, varying from neutral to extreme. So in the end, Jerro decided he rather liked his new fashion statement, even if it had been forced upon him.

"Do they mean anything? The rings?"

"Different things to different people, mostly to mark a special occasion."

"So what's special about this occasion?"

The vendor looked at him with a surprisingly dexterous eye that turned a full 180-degrees. "You're present."

"Um…"

"And the moons will be complete tonight, maybe you'll be complete too."

"Excuse me?" There was a strange and somewhat troubling undertone to the vendor's cerebral speech, and Jerro decided it was time he pushed on.

"We'll see," said the vendor as if to itself.

"Hey, ah, well thanks again for the *gift*. I should…"

The vendor nodded and took back the hose from Jerro and stared off into the crowd.

"Right." Jerro got to his feet and left quietly, making sure to put a good amount of distance between himself and the peculiar amphibian.

Food became the driving force of Jerro's meanderings as he wandered through the exotic borough of Dune Hut. He needed something to occupy himself, other than window shopping lest anyone *else* decide they wanted to force another present on him, and food allotted him the opportunity to meander without being bothered. Eating meant that you were busy, which in turn meant most people left you alone, and that was precisely what Jerro wanted. Without Etcher to be his chaperone, he was very much convinced that he would not only find himself in trouble—to which his throbbing earlobe attested—but he'd also get lost in it as well, so he decided on food.

As if to answer his prayers, a row of food merchants were lined up along the side of the sand-covered herringbone path as he rounded the corner, and he said a silent thank you to whatever gods might be listening. Being carried as he was by the current of the foot traffic, Jerro allowed himself to be ushered toward the nearest stall, where the aromas were not wholly unfamiliar.

Crispy deep-fried morsels, marinated meat chunks with grilled veggies, skewered fruit cocktails, frozen treats. Battered, fried, broiled, grilled, marinated and sautéed—the vendor had it all, and all came on a stick.

Jerro's mouth watered as the tantalizing aromas beckoned him to come hither. A black chalkboard had been scrawled with a list of menu items, and that was where the familiarity stopped.

"Nectaroons drizzled in teyo sauce with porcelain cocoa...deep fried red bellies with tangrium seasoning...huh..." Jerro quickly discovered that the exotic menu was outside his realm of knowledge and that all too quickly he was next in line.

"What'cha order?" A grisly looking creature with a sweat-stained apron, furry belly, and quill-covered back addressed Jerro with one beady eye; the other was scarred and closed. The vendor looked like a mutant bear-porcupine and was nearly twice Jerro's size, looking all the more cramped inside the food stall.

"I, uh—"

"Come on, come on, there's a line forming."

"I dunno, sorry, I-I dunno this food."

The bear-porcupine leaned in and inhaled a great whiff of Jerro then grumbled to himself. "Mundie, is? Don't feel like a mundie but you smell like one. Here, order number seven, mundies like number seven."

"Yeah, sure, I'll take it."

"Two pips or a hollow seed."

"Excuse me?"

"The price!" The creature snarled.

"I don't have pips or . . . seeds . . . I have money."

"Peh, six ginse then."

Jerro pretended to fish in his pocket for the money while he quickly dipped into the mind closet and retrieved the glassy coinage, giving it to the grisly vendor and then stepping aside from the line.

The vendor grunted the order to a monkey-faced cook who used both arms, a foot and its tail to dice veggies, handle frying pans and season kebabs. The cook gave a clipped sounding "Oo-oo ee!" in return.

A few minutes later a greasy brown bag was slid across the counter in Jerro's general direction. Without daring to bother the ill-tempered vendor, Jerro took the bag, hoping that it was his number seven and that it was edible.

At a distance, Jerro opened the bag and pulled out the foreign concoction. It was some kind of meat with fruits and grilled vegetables separating the chunks, doused in some tangy smelling sauce, making it an ordeal to eat without looking like a mannerless heathen.

Jerro slurped, bit, gnawed, and chewed at the skewered kebab, finding the flavors to be reminiscent of something familiar and delectable. Was that beef? Or perhaps pork? And the vegetables were like bell peppers, the fruit like pineapple, it tasted and smelled like a meal he understood.

He greedily devoured the dripping chunks of meat and vegetable alike until a horrifying revelation hit him. As there was less food and more skewer, Jerro noted that the shish of his kebab was none other than a quill from the back of the porcubear vendor. With a fist held firm against his mouth, Jerro forced down the last bite and tried very hard not to let any of it come back up. Half of the kebab still remained on the quill but Jerro's appetite had taken a jaunty stroll elsewhere.

There were no bins in sight, much to Jerro's aggravation, and nowhere that wasn't packed with vendors and shop stalls and colorful twirling glass people, where he could safely dispose of his leftovers out of sight. He was also unsure about what the rules of littering might be in Faerie and wasn't too keen on finding out. As he begrudgingly considered stowing the half-eaten kebab away in the Obelisk stone, he noticed a large black dog watching him intently from further down the way.

He looked around to see if anyone else had taken notice, but the crowd simply continued on its endless comings and goings and was unperturbed by the large animal.

Jerro, seeing an opportunity to rid himself of the questionable kebab, waved it out in front of him in the dog's direction. It licked its lips and wagged its tail, sniffing the air with eager anticipation. Jerro proceeded with his plan, though he proceeded cautiously. The dog looked friendly enough, even if it was as big as Great Dane, but a younger Jerro had learned the hard way that even a friendly dog can bite.

He worked his way through the crowd until he was only a few feet from the dog. "Here boy." He whistled, reaching out with the kebab but keeping his body at a distance.

The dog thumped its tail against the ground in enthusiasm, sniffing the air and inching forward with the same amount of hesitance as Jerro, its big floppy tongue almost within reach of the aromatic food.

There were millimeters separating the tip of the dog's mouth from the quill-stuck-kebab, but still the dog was reluctant to fully close the gap.

Jerro was getting impatient and leaned in closer to lengthen his reach. When he did, his necklace slipped out of his shirt and dangled in plain view about his neck. In that very same moment the dog's expression turned into something sly and mischievous, and it shot passed the kebab, snatched the necklace in its maw and yanked the chain from Jerro's very neck. It leapt back before Jerro could grab hold of it, resting low on its front paws, rump high in the air and tail wagging with impish glee.

"HEY!" Jerro yelled.

The dog chomped its maw playfully, the loose ends of the chain that hung down from either side of its massive jaw danced in the air.

Without a second thought Jerro had thrown aside the half-eaten kebab and lunged at the dog, but it darted out of the way with a spring in its step. Jerro rushed at the animal again, and again the dog darted away, heading down a dark crooked alley.

And so their chase ensued.

Blindly, Jerro ran after the beast, skittering corners and hopping over obstacles as the dog headed deeper into the winding back alleys of the Market. The dog was quick and nimble, but so was Jerro, the only difference was the speed. A scattering of Market patrons yipped and yelled as both the massive black dog, and Jerro, came barreling toward them. One of the glass people spun like an iridescent top as Jerro shot passed and clipped its glassy shoulder.

"Sorry!" Jerro called back.

The dog darted between legs as Jerro jumped up on shop canopies and even stepped-stoned on a few heads, giving out his apologies hurriedly as he ran. But the stone was too precious, and Jerro wouldn't stop his mad dash even if it meant pissing off a few locals. He wouldn't lose the Obelisk, especially not to some devilish mutt.

Deeper and deeper the two wove through the back roads, skittering, hopping, darting and jumping until they were inside the heart of the Market where vendors and shop stalls were no more and wandering patrons were replaced with thick limbed trees, the herringbone road traded in for dirt paths and woodlands.

The dog stopped on its paws and turned back on Jerro, snarling with menace. Jerro, in turn, dug in his heels and came to a grinding halt.

He held up his hands in surrender, his eyes kept on the necklace but self-preservation had taken the lead. Suddenly he took heed of the massive jaws, the sharp teeth, the sheer enormity of the beast, and was reminded that while good dogs can bite, *big* dogs bite harder.

"Easy now," he cooed, side stepping slowly, hoping to lull the dog into security long enough to snatch his necklace back and book it out of there before the dog could retaliate.

The dog growled and Jerro stopped.

And then it snickered and spat out the necklace, turned away from Jerro and darted into the woods and out of sight.

"Wha—?" He would have stood dumbfounded had it not been for an urgent tapping in his brain that told him he should grab the necklace quick before something else could nab it. And so he did, with a grimace.

Both chain and pendant were coated in a viscous saliva. He held the pendant in his hand and was thankful that he could still slip into the mind-closet without having to don the chain. There were blankets and hand towels inside the Obelisk, as per courtesy of one Etcher Everdoor who had stocked up the stone ahead of time.

He cleaned off the necklace and pendant—though it still stunk of dog breath—and placed it around his neck, stowing the soiled hand towel inside the mind closet and tucking the pendant under his clothes once more.

As he took note of his surroundings, and as he recalled the unusual manner in how the chase had ended, Jerro realized with sinking dread that he had been set up. "Shit."

He looked all around but saw only woodland, and not even the hustle and bustle of the Market was audible through the sound barrier of trees. It had finally happened—he was lost.

A fleeting guilty hope made him wonder if the nymphs had led him out, but there was no haziness this time nor dreamy feelings and no glimpses of curvy women with long flowing hair, no musical laughter. He chewed at his lip.

"Shit," he said again. If he turned around and headed straight back, surely he'd return to the familiar herringbone path…right? Then again, the chase had twisted and turned and wound all about, which he now perceived as being intentional.

His senses were prickling and his tension was high. Someone wanted to draw him out and away from the crowd. Was he going to be mugged? Or worse? He wanted very desperately to leave but couldn't will his feet to move.

The teal hazua might save him. If he called it and sent a message to Etcher, surely she would come and help him out. His eyes shifted around, unsure if he was being watched. The trees seemed sinister then in the dim light, the quiet insect calls and the beginning *whoops* and *hoots* of night creatures ignited his sense of dread and worry. He started to call for the little teal hazua in his mind but was stopped by a quiet tendril of music that slipped into his ears and sparked a comforting familiarity.

A sitar was playing in the distance. It was a tune he recognized, though he didn't recall why. His body started to move and he headed for the sound, his mind grasping desperately at the music, trying to untangle the hazy recollection. He had heard this song before, he was sure of it.

The tune seemed to change direction, and as he would come to one clearing the sound would shift to his left, or to his right. He followed the zigzagging path, driving deeper into the woods and further from civilization. Eventually, he found himself confronted by a wall of overgrowth, the sitar music playing diligently from behind it.

He pushed through the thicket and nearly toppled out the other side. The twilight world had turned to sunlight beyond the barrier. Birds were chirping, a thin stream gurgled, and on a large flat rock in the middle of the grotto was a booklet.

Jerro eyed the surrounding cautiously. The music had become faint once again, although now it seemed to echo from all around him, drifting further away as time ticked on. He stepped up to the large, flat rock and looked down at the little booklet. It was painted with a mural of witches and goblins and black cats and boogeymen in the style that children's books often are—playful and loose-lined—and had big blocky letters along the top of the cover that spelled out:

'Horrible Tales'

He looked at the book dubiously, unsure whether this was a trap. But despite his apprehension, he couldn't deny his curiosity and his urge to pick it up. Daringly, he did so, and when nothing else happened he found himself unclenching. He flipped open the book to its chapter page and saw a heading that immediately caught his eye:

'The Raven Witch of Darcwood'

"No way," he uttered aloud.

He flipped to the chapter and scanned through the text. It all started in singsong fairy tale rhyme but it very clearly mentioned the Raven Witch and her place of residence inside the heart of Darcwood.

I went to buy a pop'ee-seed,
And mother said to me,
Take half the loaf and spare the roast

Stir clear of Darcwood, see
For the Raven Witch has a cooking house
Two-dozen acres wide,
She'll snatch you up
Like a plump ol' duck
And bake you in a pie

And if you tread those marshy banks
Don't venture too far inside
For at the heart of Darcwood
Sit the Raven Witch in disguise

Oh! I went to buy my pop'ee-seed...

The tale went on, and eventually the child in the story was indeed caught and baked into a pie, and of course, eaten with a dollop of fresh cream. The image played out in horrid clarity inside Jerro's mind.

He stashed the book inside his Obelisk stone and looked around. The clearing was still bright and cheery, and birds were chirping happily, the sun beaming warmly, and he had the very strong urge to leave as quietly and quickly as possible.

Jerro backed away from the stone, and over the gurgling stream and back toward the thicket through which he came. Though he was tempted to send off a hazua to Etcher instructing her to *'Come get me'* and *'now!'* he decided he'd rather take his chances out in the twilight forest first rather than stay in the middle of the clearing, so exposed and vulnerable.

It seemed, however, that his worries were ill-placed, for as soon as he stepped through the thicket he found himself back on the sandy herringbone paths of Dune Hut.

The violin was playing a lofty tune. Its delicate melody brushed against the damp catacomb walls, bounced with the *drip-drop-drip* of water droplets, and skipped like a dancer into the Ledgerman's dark and spacious writing chamber.

At first the king—too consumed with his work—his singular roving eye gathering, collecting, contemplating, his ears listening only to the internal chatter of a busy mind and the constant scratch of the pen nib against the parchment, did not notice that the background melody was no native to the ambience of Nightmare.

But then the roving eye stopped, and when it did, his multitude of long, spidery arms stopped as well, poised in a moment. The hefty ledger lay open in front of him, the quill in one of his many hands paused in the middle of its precise and careful scrawl, the ink pooling on the end of the nib and threatening to drip. The King of Nightmare took notice of the lofty music then.

The sound continued on its dainty serenade, moving through the vast chamber. It was a barren room, save for the massive desk, and the only light came from above, creating an illuminate cone that cut through the blackness and kept the grim monarch half in shadow, half in horrifying detail. And though the melody was light and distant, it was most definitely calling to the grisly king.

His Majesty's colossal serpent body uncoiled slowly as he slithered out from behind the low writing desk, his torso, clad in only a silken robe with enough sleeves to accommodate his plethora of limbs, stood erect like a cobra, his many arms poised outward, ready to strike, clawed hands open and waiting, twitching only with the anticipation of the hunt.

He slipped out of his chamber and glided through the catacombs, the scaly flesh of his serpentine belly moved like silk over the slick stone floor, soundless and sinister. The singular eye remained unblinking, unmoving, focused and terrifying as it stared dead ahead. The flat expressionless face of his cylindrical cranium, with its bone-crown-growth cresting his kingly head, was gruesome in its plainness.

The sound of the violin strengthened, its elegant music a foreigner to the dour underbelly of the hellish realm, and yet the melody continued on with confidence, unperturbed by the fear-soaked tunnels, the faded and distant echoes of screams, and the palpable dread.

The Ledgerman approached a large round door in the lightless tunnels where the foreign sound emanated. His Majesty ducked down low, tucking in his many arms, and crouched like a spider as he confronted the door, because though the threshold was vast, the king was vaster still.

Without so much as a touch, the door creaked open and dim amber light flooded out of the warm chamber within. Shadows clung to the Ledgerman and the firelight served only to accent the terrifying features of the gruesome monarch. With a gliding, slow and deadly slither, the King of Nightmare slid into the chamber, filling the room with his abundance, stretching up to where the light dared not touch. Only the large singular eye, illuminant with its own internal glow, pierced the shadows of his high perch and looked down into the fire lit chamber below.

"Hello, Saragan." The Ledgerman's voice was resonate and grave, deep and chilling, and as ancient as the earth.

The violinist, a thin lengthy man with a wild tumble of crimson curls and high-cheekbones in pale skin, dressed in a fine emerald suit that was trimmed in gold thread—posh with his fitted waistcoat and brass buttons, his narrow upturned nose and dancing fingers that caressed the neck of the violin—did not answer right away. He remained where he stood and carried out his elegant tune, though dwarfed by the mighty king, though strange and foreign to the Realm of Nightmare, he played on and the music skipped and spun and pirouetted through the chamber as though to mock the ghoulish figure that towered over the violinist from a dark corner.

And when he had finished, he opened his strange gleaming eyes. They were black and shiny like polished onyx, save for bright green ring of the iris. The man held his violin and bow down at his side, his long elegant neck stretching up to look into the shadowed face of the king. "Hello, Gunar." His voice was soft and delicate like his music.

The Ledgerman remained still and poised, half bathed in shadow, glowing eye unblinking, arms unmoving, watching the lithe violinist with deep contemplation. When the moments passed silently in heavy droves, the Ledgerman spoke once more. "Why have you come?"

Saragan, the violinist, smiled sad and sweetly. "You paid a visit to my realm not that long ago and made no stop to see me, I was curious as to why?"

"I had an urgent matter to attend to," the Ledgerman said in careful calculation.

"There is nothing urgent in Death," said Saragan with a gentle laugh. "What was your business?"

The king made a move then, his long talon-like fingers clicked and clacked together deliberately like a metronome. A measure of his thoughts. "A business which beholds me not to speak."

"Oh," said Saragan. "Hmm." He too made a move and gently tapped the bow against his violin, competing with the metronome clack of the Ledgerman's claws. "Why Leona Mesa? No one goes there anymore, not even the tenant, not for a long time."

"It was on behalf of that tenant that I went. I will say no more."

Saragan nodded, strange glossy eyes turned down, tracing lines in the floor. "Ah." Then he smiled again, returning his gaze to the dizzying heights of the Ledgerman's shadowed face. "I'm sorry to have bothered you then." He picked up his feet and headed for the door, but before disappearing into the dark catacombs, he stopped and turned back to the king. "Your business, was it resolved?"

Something like a growl emanated deep in the Ledgerman's throat. "It is in the process of being resolved, much to my frustration."

"Oh, forgive my asking then. Good luck with it, Gunar."

The Ledgerman said nothing.

"One last thing—there was a strange delivery not that long ago. I find my realm flooded with an abundance of old souls which were thought to be lost. My Oolkas said they came from Arcadia. Would you know anything about that?"

A gooseflesh chill permeated the air and the darkness that hung in deep pockets around the Ledgerman oozed with fear and dread, but still the king said nothing.

Saragan's brow farrowed and for a moment something dark and menacing crossed his brilliant eyes, but the menace never entered his voice and the moment passed quickly. "I fear we, too, have unresolved business." He nodded to himself. "Another time perhaps. Goodbye, Gunar, though I feel we will be seeing each other again *soon*."

The Ledgerman watched as the God of Death walked out into the dark. When all trace of the violinist's dancing airy presence had gone with him, the Ledgerman bellowed. His Majesty's frightening call trembled the walls, slithered down through the catacombs, and made the denizens of Nightmare scurry into the deeper shadows.

And when the bellowing stopped, the Ledgerman breathed in deep and exhaled another mighty call; this time he spoke two words punctuated with deep rolling R's and a commanding finality. "MISTER GRIBS!"

It is noteworthy to mention that during the late spring, on the western side of the Lonely Mountains facing the untamed wilderness of the Bloodlands—a land dubbed by the ancients as Lebhinen Thy Geho—that the raw beauty of this forbidden continent inspires the deepest wonders of the heart. A call that grabs the wild within us and beckons it forward, dares us to be bold, to run free, to live wholly and purely in an unencumbered nowness. A call that dares us to be authentic, like the moment we are from birth, but by the burden of society's expectations is replaced by a mask until we are but parodies of ourselves—conformed to another's vision of what they think we should be.

But the land I now face, a place of raw and wild purity, has no such guise. It is ruthless in its authenticity, callous with the hand of death, which can claim any at a whim. It abides not to society's civilized laws, but to ancient tradition, to old gods who do not dine in the council of the Elders, for they are not welcome in the realm of civilized gods.

In many ways it is Eclipse's true heart: beautiful, bold, fierce, and terrifying. Qualities which brought forth the demon's war.

But that was another time; now the land is both cherished and feared by the outside world. Protected in the sense that it is both a prison and reserve for the native dwellers of this land. The heart though it may be, and vital though it is, the civilized world has seen fit to tolerate the Bloodlands' necessity but not to dine with it. Forever will the Bloodlands be cornered to its own table, viewed from afar as exotic and dangerous, appealing for the softer-hearted Ecliptian to look at, to flirt with, but never to marry. To accept the Bloodlands as kin would be to call attention to the masks we have donned, and to the purity we have lost. There are but few willing to make such social pariahs of themselves...

The Traveler put down his pen and closed his thick leather-bound journal. He remained where he sat and watched as the high sun illuminated the feral continent before him. The wind tussled his cropped wintered beard and made his long, pointed ears twitch. It caressed the thousand laugh-lines that gathered around his bright eyes, it played with the rim of his worn leather hat and jostled his clothes as it snaked through the grass and tossed dandelion seeds into the air.

He smiled as he watched the world before him with his ageless piercing blue eyes. He was an old man only by the color of his hair, but he did not stoop, he was not riddled with aches and pains, he did not tremble, nor stammer. His soul burned with an eternal youth that radiated from him even as he sat quietly in the grass on the mountainside.

A dampened thump took his attention away from the exotic wilderness of the Bloodlands and turned it toward the dragon that had landed at his side. The beast was vast, his scales a cold blue like a winter morning sky, and his neck and spine were crested with soft white fur like fresh snow. The dragon folded his mighty wings, covered in a fine layer of downy fluff, and nestled down in the grass beside the Traveler.

"Hello, Holixben," said the Traveler.

"Hullo," the dragon replied with a deep guttural rumble that echoed out from his colossal windpipe. "You've come back I see."

"No, Holixben, I never left."

"Hmm," the dragon rumbled.

The Traveler sighed gently. "I've written this passage many times. I've watched the sun pass overhead, the dandelions glide through the air, gently dancing their way down into the meadows and fields of yonder. And yet, every time feels like the first, as though it were brand new."

"Is this a dream?" Holixben asked, his voice carrying over the mountains and seeming to emanate from them.

"No, not a dream, a memory."

"Are they not the same?"

The Traveler smiled and patted Holixben's smooth scaly side. The massive lungs beneath expanding and contracting with slow gentle breaths. "In many cases you are right, dear friend. But this memory is on a loop. I believe I'm caught in a trap."

"Hmmm. What trap could hold you?"

"A trap that I made myself, to avoid another trap I imagine."

"Too many traps," said Holixben. His nose pointed north, his ears flicked up and alert.

"This is where you leave me, Holixben. I shan't keep you from your prey."

"A wise decision," the great dragon replied, and unfurled his mighty wings and stood on his mighty legs, then took off at a glide down the mountainside and let the wind currents catch him.

The Traveler watched Holixben fly away, flipping open his journal and sketching the mighty beast before Holixben became a blip on the horizon.

"Too many traps indeed, dear friend," the Traveler said quietly to himself.

"The old man won't budge."

"Well, he can stay in his happy place until oblivion, it won't make a difference."

"Why bother holding him then? What use is he?"

"He knows things, and if he won't tell us, it's better he not be telling anyone."

"Peh, what a waste. How did we get saddled with guard duty?"

The two chatting sentinels tossed dice between them atop of a wooden barrel, playing their cards in respect to the rules of the game, idly chatting to pass the time. Beside them was a large metal door, bolted, and engraved with angular runes and the vicious, angry pattern of a strange *majik*.

In the door was a tiny glass porthole where the sentinels would, from time to time, check in on their prisoner. Beyond the miniscule window was a cylindrical room bathed in white—no adornments, no bed—just an old, bearded man, sitting on the bare ground. His legs crossed, his back straight, and his eyes closed. And in the corner of his mouth was the slightest touch of a smile, his mind very far away, stuck in a loop.

The sleek black car cruised down the highway toward Fenris County. The detectives had barely said a word to each other the whole ride down as though a dark ominous cloud were trailing close behind them and they were trying to outrun it.

Reedman felt a subtle urgency rise in his chest. Despite his ill feelings toward Jerro Ahliss, he didn't wish anything bad for the parents, not after all they had been through. Reedman knew too well what it was like to lose loved ones, and no one should ever have to bury their kid.

The exit was coming up and Reedman quietly merged onto the off-ramp and out into the commercial roads, navigating his way to the quieter residential hub of the county. The road to Ria Ahliss's house was disturbingly calm. Reedman felt the itch of anxiousness prick him, he hoped and prayed that they weren't too late.

He pulled the car into the open driveway of Mrs. Ahliss's home, and drummed his fingers on the wheel, peering at the lace curtains and trying to spy inside the yellow house. He unclipped his seatbelt and went for the car door.

"Hold ya horses," said Thorneback. "I think it's best I go in alone, don't you? If I need back up, I'll call ya."

Reedman rested back heavily in his padded leather car seat. "Yeah, all right." He didn't like it, but chances were Ria Ahliss wouldn't be happy to see him and they needed her cooperation, especially if it meant putting her in protective custody. The wiry detective gave Reedman a nod, then got out of the car. Instinctively, Thorneback's hands ruffled through his pockets for his nicotine fix but after a moment's consideration, he decided against it, despite the obvious cravings. Thorneback pushed his fingers through his thinning hair, tugged at his shirt and adjusted his trousers—which had clung awkwardly to him during the two-hour-long drive down. With a quick check in the side mirror of the car, a grunt, and another nod to Reedman, Thorneback headed up the porch.

He rapped his knuckles against the door and waited, casting a glance back at Reedman, though the other detective was concealed by the tint of the windshield.

"Just a minute!" a voice called out, and the sound of footsteps followed.

A handful of seconds later the door opened and Ria Ahliss's elegant bronze face appeared in the threshold, looking curiously at Thorneback.

Reedman watched from the car, feeling a small moment of relief that the mother was alive and unharmed. He saw her peering over at him, though he knew she couldn't see him through the tinting. He continued to watch as the two of them talked, until finally, she let Thorneback inside and shut the door. Reedman sat back and waited, but the ill feeling had yet to subside. The dark clouds were rolling in.

"So, Mrs. Ahliss, I'm sure you're wondering why I'm down here," said Thorneback, hands in his pockets, beady eyes scanning over the interior of the tidy home.

Ria contemplated the man slowly, unsure of what to make of the shabby detective, though she was certain his appearance had to do with Jerro. "Any news about my son?"

"Well that's the thing—mind if I take a seat?"

She pointed with her chin to the sitting room and let the detective seat himself; Ria took to one of the lounge chairs across from the detective—who was now occupying the sofa.

"I have some bad news—not about your son, but his flatmates. One of 'em's been murdered, and a coworker, too."

"Oh my god."

"No, no it wasn't god that done it." The detective started tapping his foot. "See, thing is, Mrs. Ahliss, I've got a bit of a problem."

Ria did not like the sudden change in the man's tone and the hungriness that crept into his eyes. Most of all, she didn't like the fact that she was suddenly rooted to her chair.

Thorneback nestled into the sofa and with one hand pulled out a slightly crumpled pack of cigarettes. He shook the pack with a practiced flick, pulled a stick free with his lips, then fished out a lighter and lit it, taking a deep savoring drag. "Mind if I smoke? Judging by the look of the place, you probably do. Nothing you can do about it though, ey?" He winked at her.

Ria felt alarm build inside her, but it manifested itself differently than she was used to. She was honed and focused. There was no panic, though she knew she was in trouble. She knew the situation had become deadly serious, that something was very wrong, and that one way or another she was going to have to figure her way out of it.

Thorneback breathed out a noxious cloud through his nose and looked Ria Ahliss over with his intrusive eyes. "You know, Reedman's had some naughty thoughts about you, I can see why. You're not half bad for a woman your age."

He leaned forward, taking another long drag, then he put the cigarette out in the little vase that decorated the coffee table before him, slowly poisoning the daisies and wildflowers that adorned the pot.

"Honestly, I don't really see the appeal of smoking, but I mean, I have to keep up appearances and all." He wet his lips, linked his fingers together, letting them hang limp between his knees as he leaned in toward Ria, staring with his cold beetle eyes.

"So, about my problem—ya see, I didn't expect to find a mundie with a protective '*coating*' so to speak. Felt it as soon as you opened the door...*tsk tsk tsk*...someone's been making my life miserable, haven't they?

"The other two were easy to crack. Most mundies, their thoughts are spilling out their ears, there's no barrier, nothing holding it in. I can just lap it up. But not you. Now why is that, Mrs. Ahliss?" Thorneback bared his teeth in a predatory smile and rose to his feet, taking a few steps toward the armchair where Ria sat.

"You wanna know where your son is? So do I. I really, *really* do, Mrs. Ahliss. More and more, I think he might actually be the one. I have a few lingering doubts, of course. They're all so bloody certain that 'Jerro Ahliss' is the holy fucking grail, focused *everything* on Kyd's word. But how things have gone? Makes me think they might be right."

The man moved right up to the chair where Ria sat and placed his hands on the armrests, lowering his face down slowly to level his gaze with hers. His beady eyes stared deep and the vicious smile about his ugly mouth grew steadily. "Guess I'm just gonna have to take whatever's in your head the hard way. 'Course, I also think of it as the fun way."

The mouth stretched horrifyingly wide and the teeth lengthened into needle points, but as soon as he went to chomp down on Ria's skull, a flash of light knocked him back and sent him tumbling over the coffee table, smashing the potted flowers against the floor.

Ria felt movement slip back into her body and she sprang up from the chair. Her heart was racing, pumping adrenaline through her veins like a rampant bull on the loose, but her head stayed focused and clear. "What are you?" she demanded.

The slithe wearing Thorneback's face hissed as he got up. No longer was he smiling, there was real anger now in the borrowed face, and he lunged at Ria.

She brought her arms up to brace herself and the flash of light happened again, rebounding the creature and sending him howling across the floor. This time she saw the source of it. The light slowly faded into the bracelet around her wrist.

It'll protect you.

Jerro really had gone all out for her birthday this time round.

The creature was quick to draw itself back to its feet, hissing and seething with rage. It was careful now, circling Ria, trying to back her into a corner. Working its way through her house in a steady dance, its beady eyes searching her up and down. But then its attention snapped to the front door moments before Reedman came bursting in with his gun drawn.

"Freeze! Thorneback what the—" But the words died on Reedman's tongue as the slithe's influence petrified him on the spot.

The creature carefully made its way around Reedman and shut the front door as best as it could shut with its newly broken latch. "You are all starting to wear out my patience."

Reedman's eyes followed the monster that only halfway resembled Thorneback anymore. The teeth were hideously long, the ugly mouth wide, and the eyes were tiny and insect-like.

The creature took the gun from Reedman's hands and shot at Ria, but again, the light flashed and the bullet ricocheted off the protective barrier and lodged itself into a wall. In that moment, the creature found the source as well.

"Give me that bracelet!" it screeched, darting at Ria and making her flinch, though the creature stayed out of range of the barrier.

"Get away from me!" shouted back Ria.

"Have it your way then." It snarled and shot Reedman in the gut instead.

"No!" Ria cried.

Reedman winced as the bullet hit him. The searing hot pain bloomed from the entry wound and the petrifying force released him and let him crumple to the floor.

But Ria had already taken action, and in the very same instant she had cried out, she had also come at the creature, her bracelet-clad wrist held high as she smacked it down onto the beast. Light burst from bangle as she struck. The creature screamed and was shot to the floor so heavily that it bounced, and Ria struck it again.

The creature thrashed against the light, only to be sent flying across the floor and tossed into a wall, smashing the china cabinet. The glass doors burst open, the wood buckled, and the plates and vases came spilling out, shattering across the ground where they hit.

Skittering to its feet, the creature dove into the kitchen. Ria chased after it with her bracelet held high. No bloody monster was going to come into her home and smash her fine china and get away with it!

But as she ran into the kitchen, she found the monster grinning, holding the beautiful box Jerro had sent her in its clawed hands. It winked at her with its ugly beetle eyes, made a fist in which something went *crunch*, and then vanished in a flash of crimson fire, taking the box with it. At least she'd already eaten the cake.

"Oh my god," said Ria in the aftermath of all the strangeness.

Then she heard a groan from the hallway and remembered that Detective Reedman was bleeding out on her carpet. She rushed out to the detective, finding that he had dragged himself up to a wall and slumped against it, clutching the bleeding wound on his abdomen.

"Oh god! Mr. Reedman! What the hell are you doing here?"

"Is it gone?" he managed through labored breaths.

"Yes, it vanished."

"…Good."

"Mr. Reedman…how did you get here?"

"Thought I'd come pay you a visit," he mustered in a wispy voice. "Do me a favor and call an ambulance."

"Yes of course!" Ria was about to step away when Reedman grabbed her wrist.

"A mad gunman forced his way into your house and started shooting…" he said in a rasp. "You don't tell 'em about the other stuff. Okay?"

Ria nodded. She headed to the kitchen and grabbed the phone.

A portly little toad in a fine dress suit with polished wingtip shoes and an abundance of leather satchels, crisscrossing over his round torso, was busy humming a happy little tune to himself as he penned his memoirs in an old journal.

Mr. Gribs was taking some much-needed time off. After the atrocious incident—which he dared not think about—and of course, the vehement scolding he got from His Majesty—which he also dared not think about—Mr. Gribs had decided to cash in on his holiday time. Besides, after *that-which-he-dare-not-think about*, he had been relieved from his duties as the king's envoy, though was permitted to resume his usual work.

Funny, he thought, *why didn't His Majesty eviscerate me?* Though he was very glad *not* to be eviscerated, he did wonder why the king hadn't punished him further. In fact, as colossal of a failure as Mr. Gribs's ill-fated venture had been, he had gotten off exceedingly light, as though His Majesty had a lot more on his mind.

The king did look rather worried about the whole affair—which worried Mr. Gribs immensely—but in the end he had been politely told to bugger off elsewhere, in fewer words than that. So he did, he buggered off good and far, and went back to plaguing accountants, bankers, misers, and worrywarts with his rather tame, yet haunting, nightmares. He was very nearly back into the swing of things when he decided he very much needed a holiday.

Truth be told, he'd only been back at work the one night, but the whole unthinkable situation had caught up to him and he just couldn't muster the *oomph* he needed for his work. A good nightmare should always come from a place of passion, and well, Mr. Gribs just wasn't feeling all that passionate about his night job at the moment. He was letting people down.

It had been a great long while since his last holiday, sometime around the second eon he recalled. He was usually very content with his meager stature in life, and his role as His Majesty's personal messenger afforded him a boost to his feelings of usefulness, although that job was now out the window. Mr. Gribs sighed, being just a lowly nightmare simply wasn't enough anymore.

Since Fillabir had come back to Mr. Gribs's department of tame-yet-haunting-nightmares without a job, the ol' lizard was more than happy to cover for Gribs and keep as much under the radar as possible. Gribs did feel partly responsible for ruining Fillabir's previous employment, so it was only fair that he gave the ol' lizard something to occupy himself with until he found another suitable position.

Mr. Gribs let out another long and labored breath. He potted his feather quill and stared out of the round window of his quiet little lodgings. The boggy, tree-speckled landscape of Darcwood stared back at him, almost quite literally. Darcwood had its own personality—a dreary and menacing one that weighed down on you as much as the thick, boggy air. It leeched away any feelings of hope and wonderment and replaced them with a strong desire to go elsewhere, lest the dreariness bury you in the muck.

It was a good place for a meager nightmare such as he. Most people stayed away, and the things that did live there were as much akin to Mr. Gribs as he was to them, so neither bothered each other much. His small log cabin occupied a plot of ground midway toward the heart of Darcwood—just enough to be within the veil of dissuasion but not close enough to annoy the central tenant.

He shivered at the thought. Though he had never seen the tenant during those few and fleeting instances that he occupied his little cabin in the woods on previous occasions, he was well aware of the stories and had no desire to tread any further toward the heart of Darcwood than need be. No, midway in was just enough for his time off. There was a good amount of open space free from people and obligations for him to relax a little, to take a much-needed look back at his collection of thoughts, to organize the mental cabinets, and do some tidying up.

Mr. Gribs slipped down from his chair and moved through the den toward the living room where a small fire was burning. It was a strange blue fire, and instead of heat, it was giving off a rather refreshing chill to combat the horrid humidity. The portly toad stared at the hypnotic cobalt flames for a moment, wondering absently what he should have for lunch. In that same moment he felt the most awful chill run down his spine, and thought someone had called his name, and angrily at that. But as soon as he turned his attention to the instant, both the spine-chilling sensation and the thought became nothing more than an echo in his memories.

"Huh." Mr. Gribs shrugged, and thought nothing more of it.

This was Darcwood after all, and all manner of spine-chilling oddities tended to live amongst the trees, and what with the bogarts and banshees, there was bound to be someone wailing something or other that might have sounded like Mr. Gribs's moniker. That was the nature of such baleful spirits, always whining and wailing in their long warbling calls that could sound like just about anything. Mr. Gribs often wondered if said spirits were truly going on about anything at all.

He left the fireplace and headed for the hat rack by the front door, picking out a simple fedora to place upon his large, round head. He looped the handle of a wicker basket over his chubby arm, then left his log cabin and ventured out into Darcwood.

It was a good day for mushrooming, dark as it was due to the Lunar Week, although the very nature of Darcwood was to be, in fact, dark. The thick tree growth made sure of it, blotting out the sky with their tangle of fronds and dampening the light even when it was present. But with the enhancement of the faux night, there was sure to be all sorts of curious flora in bloom. If Mr. Gribs were very lucky he might even find himself the rare and coveted *noctrahellun* fungus on a day like today. The very notion put a spring in his surprisingly spry step.

There was a network of boggy rivers and lakes, lacing their way through Darcwood like a nervous system. Crocodilian eyes poked up through the surface of the algae-infested waters, the glint of lunar light giving them form in the midnight-colored world. They watched with mild interest as Mr. Gribs hummed to himself, adding his tune to the cacophony of chirping, chittering night life, while rooting around in the mud with his little trowel, occasionally finding something of interest to put into his wicker basket—which was already quite full.

He followed along the marshy banks of one little winding river, finding it to be a haven of curious mushrooms and plant life. Even in the dark, Mr. Gribs could see very clearly. Given that he was a nightmare, the darkness was an old friend, and it brought him comfort and safety. Truth be told, his night vision was probably better than his day vision, and that, too, made the darkness all the more appealing.

He paused to take stock of his growing assortment of mushrooms; some of his collection was edible, while others were not so much, although that made little difference to his indomitable digestive system. He was very pleased with what he had gathered, but he wasn't quite ready to call it quits; he was simply enjoying the pleasure of the carefree meanderings of his holiday, making his way along the curve of the bank in slow progression.

This was just what I needed! he thought and breathed in the thick and cloying scent of Darcwood with a very satisfied *ahhh!*

Toadish, as he was, he found the invasive smells of decaying flora, mixed with the boggy amphibian scent of the local wildlife and the damp algae, to be, against all odds, rather pleasant. This was going to be a wonderful trip, he assured himself. Besides, he *had* put in centuries of loyal service, a matter which may have made His Majesty so lenient with the punishment; he deserved a good holiday. He even toyed with the notion of using all of his accumulated vacation time to do a soul-searching endeavor—where he might travel the world, try exotic foods, meet new people, do wild things. But then he caught his reflection in the glistening black swamp waters and came hurtling back to reality.

All right, so he was *not* the most pleasant thing to look at, and granted, taking a world trip would probably raise some serious, if not dangerous, questions as to why a nightmare was on holiday. He thought about the *thing-which-he dare-not-think-about* without meaning to and recalled his stunning transformation back on the isle of Arcadia, though he managed to not think any further lest he recall *Miss Everdoor's* transformation.

If only he had stayed so dashing! Then he could go anywhere in the world, the multiverse even! But alas, Mr. Gribs's big toadish face with its bulging eyes, flabby pearlescent skin, and wide, flat mouth all stared back at him in utter defiance and said firmly through his thoughts '*fat chance of that ever happening again,*' to which he added, '*Well damn.*'

He was ruining his time off with such lamentations. It would have been nice though, as improbable as it was. Hadn't he read somewhere about a frog turning into a prince? How did it go again? A kiss from a princess? Not like that was likely to happen either. He let out a long croaking-sigh. "Well, Gribsy ol' toad, there's no point crying over that which can't be helped!" he said aloud, and a set of crocodilian eyes popped under the boggy waters as if it wanted to stay out of the conversation as much as possible.

To hell with it, thought Mr. Gribs. He was going to have a good time, by gum, whether or not it killed him—although he surely hoped it wouldn't come to that. And strangely enough, it appeared that Fate was smiling upon him during his hour of self-loathing, for Mr. Gribs's big, bulging eyes caught sight of something of great interest over at the base of a rotting tree stump.

There was a little patch of black velvety mushrooms, all about a few inches high, with small white spots cresting the pinnacle of their domed heads. This interested him greatly because the dainty little fungi were a telltale indicator of a possible *noctrabellun* nearby. For where *beliforn dames* could grow, so, too, could the rare and illustrious fungus. Now that would truly be a find! And worth more than just a pretty penny, not that money was ever much of a concern for Mr. Gribs.

The true value of finding a *noctrabellun* mushroom was cause for a variable amount of reverie amongst those whom declared themselves experts in the field of mushrooming. And no matter how objectionable Mr. Gribs was to look at, he'd be allotted a certain degree of praise from his peers. Who needed princesses anyhow?

Prickled with excitement, Mr. Gribs followed along the river bend, finding more patches of the tidy little *beliforn dames*, which heightened his feelings of exhilaration. With his nose and eyes glued to the ground, he followed the thickening trail of black-capped mushrooms and headed straight to an overgrowth of tangled hedge weeds.

The thick and thorny bush was a nightmare to get through, in a manner of speaking, which fortunately for Mr. Gribs, being that he was in fact an *actual* nightmare, meant that he was able to reason with the prickly plant, somewhat. "Now see here, be a good fellow and let me through, won't you?" The bush quivered a bit but didn't so much as budge.

"Really, now? Must we split hairs? I know you're not a fellow, but *we're* fellows enough aren't we? Now, unless you want me creeping through your shadows, which could be unpleasant for both of us, I ask that you clear the way."

The bush moved this time, much to Mr. Gribs's delight, and not only was he rewarded with a clear path, but there, in a very damp marshy patch, was the beautiful, awe-inspiring, rare and coveted mushroom: the *noctrabellun*.

Mr. Gribs rushed forward with boyish glee, stopping only inches before the impressive fungus lest he topple over it. He *oo'ed* and *ahh'ed* at it, rubbing his chubby hands together with wide-eyed enthusiasm across his big, toadish face.

The *noctrabellun* was indeed a beautiful mushroom. A solitary stalk, pale and glimmering in the darkness, was nearly half a foot in length and was topped with a wide umbrella cap as velvety as the night sky and dotted with twinkling speckles like starlight. It had an elegant netting hanging down from the rim of its cap like a lady's veil, where crystalline dew drops gathered. It was a marvelous specimen, and fragrant, too! It let out a wonderful earthy scent, wholesome and satisfying.

It wouldn't do to simply pluck the mushroom, oh my, no! Mr. Gribs went about digging around the fungus with his trowel so that he might take the living specimen home, and who knew? Even cultivate and grow his own? Oh! The notion was extravagant and filled his head with fantasies. Those fantasies, however, were quickly popped like a balloon on a pin.

"*That* is my mushroom," said a slow and deadly voice.

As it turned out Fate had indeed been smiling down on Mr. Gribs, smiling with a wicked, crooked-tooth grin. Mr. Gribs looked up and let out a little whimper. "Oh dear," he croaked.

Jerro stood rooted as his eyes scanned the bustling streets of Dune Hut. He craned his neck to peer over his shoulder, but there was only an alleyway there to greet him. The forest was gone, there was no sign of the clearing or what had happened, save for the children's book which Jerro took mental inventory of. *Well, that was…odd…* he thought and tried very hard not to be as disturbed by the unexpected transition as he really was.

He decided that he had enough solo adventuring for the time being, and at the risk of incurring the wrath of Etcher, he headed straight for the domed hut where she had left him, mustering a belligerent confidence as he reached for the leather flap covering the threshold, squared his shoulders and—

Decided against it. He let out his breath as if the air were escaping from his inflated ego and slumped up against the wall of the hut, letting himself slowly slip down until his rump had reached the ground. He folded his arms and crossed his legs, and waited.

As unnerved as he was, and as eager as he was to be back within familiar company, he didn't want to mess up Etcher's plans. And though there had been something alluring about storming in and making demands—which would have included the words '*I want to get the hell out of here*'—and feeling high and mighty, he was fairly certain the moment would have been short lived, although the repercussions wouldn't have been. And so he waited, but not for very long.

Soon after he resided to his fate, Etcher's head popped out from behind the leather flap, inquisitive ears flicked upward in curiosity as she regarded him.

"Something wrong?" she said.

Jerro, who was not expecting the little shopkeeper to be done so soon, was still lost in the jumble of this thoughts and stared at her a little dumbfounded. "Uh…yeah, um, sort of? I'm okay though, I think."

This only deepened the little shopkeeper's inquisitiveness. She slipped out from behind the flap and looked down at Jerro. "Should we take a walk?"

"Uh…well, what about the merchant? Did you get what you needed? I can wait here, you can go back in, I'll just—"

"No need, I was about finished anyhow."

"Oh, right." Jerro cleared his throat nervously and got to his feet, dusting off the sand and grit that had conformed to him. "So you got something useful then?"

"A tidbit of enlightenment. Though I'm more curious as to what put you in such a state."

"Yeah…" Jerro fiddled with a stray thread hanging from the hem of his sleeve. "You mind if we get Tahli and head out? I'll tell you on the way."

"We can take the High Roads to Darcwood," said Etcher as she led the trek out from the Market and back into the twilight autumn forests of Faerie.

"I still find it curious how Ahliss even came upon that book," remarked Tahli. She had been none too pleased that Etcher had slipped away during her shopping spree, and that said spree was being cut short.

"Well it *is* curious, but regardless of who led Jerro to it and why is out of our hands. We still have to find the Raven Witch, and with what I learned from Delluige I can corroborate the nursery rhyme's validity. We don't have much choice in the matter, and we can't afford a detour in finding out who is helping us from behind the scenes."

"Or leading us into a trap."

Etcher rolled her eyes. "Yes, Tahli, it could be a trap. It could be that the Raven Witch herself even led Jerro to the book. But again, what choice do we have?"

Tahli muttered under her breath.

"At any rate," said Etcher, shooting a cautionary glance at the cat-woman. "The High Roads aren't too far up ahead."

"What exactly are the High Roads?" chimed in Jerro. He had been keeping close beside Etcher in case the bewitching quality of Faerie ensnared him again, although it was getting easier to resist. Like adjusting to a sudden change in the weather, he found the longer he stayed in it, the more comfortable he got and the less that the wiles of the realm could trick him.

"The High Roads are a bit like a back way in, a pseudo *Blank-Space* if you will. They aren't outside of reality as such, but they're like back doors. Since Faerie mirrors the Waking Realm there's usually a hidden path somewhere or other that can lead you in and out from Waking to Faerie, and vice versa, you just have to know where to look. Or know how to create your own path."

"Like that mirror we used back at the hotel?"

"A bit like that, yes, and funny you should mention it, the High Roads all connect to mirrors back in the Waking Realm."

"What, like, *any* mirror?"

"Well, yes, any mirror is potentially a gateway in or out of Faerie. Though not every mirror is open, shall way say? Just because a mirror is a door, doesn't mean just anyone can use it, and some mirrors need a lot of convincing to be opened, as was the case with the bathroom mirror."

"So what's gonna happen to that mirror, anyhow?"

"Oh, don't worry about that. Being that I was its creator, so to speak, I am also its gatekeeper. No one else will be able to use it without my granting it first."

"So if someone were to come into Tahli's room and see the mirror in the bathroom—?"

"They would see a mirror with a lot of graffiti on it, and not much more than that unless they're versed in gateway *majiks*."

They continued their trek in silence, a strange feeling of gloom settled over Jerro as they did. In the back of his mind he felt the pressure of time start to gather and swell into an uncomfortable lump behind his very thoughts. He looked over his shoulder cautiously, feeling as though something was watching, that something was coming. The endless autumn forest stared back at him, fragmented in hitching moments of time as if looking at the world through a kaleidoscope. Leaves fell in a loop, others moved in slow motion, and the world whispered to him.

There was something sinister in the breeze, in the way the trees moved. The feeling of gloom was closing in on him, uttering his name in a soft hiss. A dark thing was coming, and it was coming for him.

"Jerro, don't dawdle," said Etcher, and the little shopkeeper's voice cut through the ominous chill and banished the moment as if it had never been.

Jerro stared back at the forest, but there was nothing sinister about it anymore, though time was still fragmented, and the world was tinged in twilight; it was only the ill feeling that lingered with him. "Yeah, coming. Sorry." He picked up his pace and caught up with the others.

The tree line thinned suddenly, and the herringbone path gave way to rocky ground that in turn gave way to the edge of a cliff. An endless chasm confronted them, competing with the horizon as it stretched beyond sight in all directions before them—as if a great big chunk of the world had simply vanished, and in its place was the chasm and the thin network of perilous pathways stretching out over top of the colossal gorge like a deranged spider's web.

The pathways were floating over the bottomless abyss, and when Jerro dared to peer over the edge he saw a thick darkness dotted in starlight and nebulas, as if he were staring into the void of space. It was worse than the *Blank* by far. He skittered back, bumping into Tahli who hissed.

"Mind your step," the cat-woman said coolly.

"Tell me that's *not* the High Roads!" he said, not minding the cat-woman at all. There was panic in Jerro's voice. Heights were not a problem for him, and ordinarily he wasn't prone to vertigo, but the thought of walking along those thin rocky roads—that seemed to be held up purely by their own volition atop the monumental endlessness of that cosmic void—filled him with a sickening dread.

"Easy, Jerro. Don't give in to it. The High Roads play on your fears. Come now, I've seen you scale walls and leap into the fray, don't let your wits abandon you now," said Etcher.

She had brushed her hand lightly across his arm, urging him back to a place of stillness and serenity.

Jerro gulped in the air, squeezed his eyes shut, and tried to push out the fear. He shouldn't be afraid, he knew that, he'd done plenty of perilous things before, Undercity was a testament to that and he had no reservations when he blindly chased after the massive hound in the Market.

So was the chasm playing on a different fear? What was even left to be so terrified of after everything?

Then a thought crept up to the forefront of his mind and made him squirm internally. He started thinking about his brother.

No, he wasn't afraid of that, he just didn't want to think about that, he reasoned with himself, and felt very much like a bug under a pin. But the thought pushed on, and pressed down on his mind, memories manifesting in the image of the deep cosmic void that had seared itself behind his eyes.

He didn't want to think about how his brother was gone and how everything changed, and how he'd been waiting ever since for something—*anything*—to happen to pull him out of the limbo he had settled into, how he had cast off his vitality like a coat and hung it in some dark closet, forgetting what it was to truly feel alive, because any day now, his brother was sure to turn up and then he could start living again. No sir, he didn't want to think about how much time he had wasted on that improbable hope, how many years he'd let slip by in a stupor. No, it wasn't that, he just didn't want to think about it, that was just something in the back of his mind—*always*—it was just a thing that was there, that's all, just a thing, just a small unimportant thing. "Yeah. Right. Sorry, I'm fine," he heard his lips lying aloud. "So, shall we...?"

Etcher cleared her throat, looking sidelong at Jerro for a moment, and in that moment her golden orbs held him, saying quite plainly, *I see right through you Jerro Ahliss.* And then the weight of the moment vanished and released them both. "Right, well, for this venture, we'll be traveling in style—" began Etcher as if nothing were amiss.

Tahli's face contorted with fear. "And what does *that* mean?"

A mischievous look carved itself into Etcher's countenance as she grinned, and with it all memory of the strange and petrifying moment had gone. "You'll see."

Her palm became aglow with a springtime green and in the air high above her, a beautiful summon circle shimmered into reality. The surface rippled, and out from the portal flew a massive sapling colored dragon, shattering the image of the magical design—the pieces fizzled out before the glowing shards could reach the ground.

Hoya alighted on the ground beside Etcher. The beast's powerful wings kicked up the loose earth into whirling eddies, and a strange springtime scent came with it. The great beast snorted out the air from its perfectly curved nostrils and butted the end of its smooth nose against Etcher, who was only about as big as the dragon's head.

"Good to see you too, Hoya, how've you been?"

The dragon replied with a rolling guttural sound that put a little tremor in the ground.

"Yes, my apologies for not calling on you sooner. We haven't had much opportunity for flight. Anyhow, Hoya, this is Jerro. Tahli you've met."

The feline folded her arms and her hair stood on end as she let out a low hiss at the dragon.

Hoya moved her giant head over to inspect Jerro, turning to greet him, and in the process, nearly knocked Tahli over with her long dragon tail. The sapling colored creature breathed in Jerro's scent and nuzzled at him with her nose.

"Uh, hi," said Jerro. There was a look of utter amazement and boyish glee infusing in his eyes as he looked into the big, watery opals of the dragon's gaze. What had he been so frightened of before? He was having trouble remembering.

Jerro was taken in by how beautiful the dragon was. There was something of a smell like fresh grass and morning dew, of flowers blooming and the world warming, and it rolled off the great beast in a comforting melody. He dared to place his hand on the dragon's snout and was rewarded by the warmth and smoothness of the dragon's skin. He let his hand glide, trembling only slightly with the sheer volume of his excitement, along Hoya's face, contouring with the ridges and the muscles of her impressive form, along the intricate network of scales that soon followed. There was raw power right beneath the skin, he could feel it in the density of her powerful jawbone and in the thick cords of the muscles and tendons. But there was also gentleness in her watery eyes. And when the dragon looked at him, he felt a happy, effervescent bubble grow steadily inside him.

"You're beautiful," he said quietly, and meant it.

The dragon was evidently pleased with the compliment, and started butting Jerro again with her head, leading him toward her side where a finely crafted saddle sat high on the mantle between her shoulders.

"Uh—" Jerro stammered, pushed as he was by the powerful head.

"It would appear that Hoya's eager to take you on your maiden voyage."

Jerro beamed at Etcher, eyes glazed with delight as his inner-child self took full rein of his faculties. "We're really gonna ride on a dragon?" Somewhere, deep down, was the ghost of a dream half remembered finally coming to life. His child-self was about ready to throw his arms up and shout with all the excitement of a five-year-old being told he could have *any* toy he wanted from the store, even the loud annoying one.

"That is the plan."

"*I* object to this plan," cut in Tahli, who was looking even more ruffled than before. "I told you, I will *not* ride on that—" Tahli stopped speaking when Hoya grunted, narrowing her opal gaze on the feline.

"Well, Tahli, fine by me if you want to stay behind, but don't complain about being left out," said Etcher as she nimbly scaled up Hoya's side and reached down to lend a hand to Jerro.

Jerro was promptly aided up to the saddle by Hoya's tail, which made it quite evident that the great beastie was *very* eager to give Jerro his maiden flight on dragon-back.

"I do not like this!" Tahli snapped, though her resolve was faltering, and her defiant cross-armed stance had dissolved into a fiddly one.

With a groan and a quiet snarl, Tahli relented and headed for the saddle, although at that same time Hoya decided she needed to give her legs a good stretch and consequently left Tahli scrambling to grab hold.

"*That* was intentional," Tahli hissed once she had climbed aboard.

Etcher hid a quiet laugh under her breath and adjusted herself in the saddle. It was a long, spacious piece of hardware, and made to accompany two well enough, which meant that Tahli had to straddle her way in right behind Jerro and hold onto his belt, which she seemed none too happy about, and which Jerro felt rather uncomfortable with as well.

"Everyone ready?" inquired Etcher, and where Jerro replied with an eager yes, Tahli merely grunted. "Right then, off we go!"

Etcher patted Hoya's side. The dragon reared down low, the muscles swelling in her limbs and back, and she stretched her wings out wide. Sheer strength radiated out from Hoya's pores, and in one powerful wingbeat the ground fell away beneath them, the air rushed over them, gravity sucked at their stomachs and at their cheeks and any other piece it could suction, though couldn't hold on long enough to keep them down, and they took flight.

In the small private room of the narrow clinic was an empty quiet. There was the bed Mahra was occupying, and the big machine that was keeping her fed and nourished, methodically *beeping* and *clicking*, and there was even a bouquet of flowers someone had left on the side table. But what made the space empty and quiet was the lack of essence.

Though the blonde-haired girl lay on the bed, she might just as well not have been there, because her thoughts were locked up in a deep darkness inside a body that could not, would not, move. She was like a doll placed upon a shelf in some forgotten room, and the absence of her presence was what made the space so lacking, and the sounds so empty.

Moments were being sucked down into a black hole, and every *beep* and *click* and *drip* that went by stole another second from Mahra that she'd never get back. It was a sink-drain of time, and even the flowers could feel it, feel their liveliness spilling in the vacuum of that emptiness.

But the empty quiet was suddenly intruded upon by a scuffling from under the bed, where the shadows were the darkest. And a *huff* and an *oh dear* came to further disrupt the vacuum, like ripples on a pond, playing havoc on the once still façade of stagnant water.

Mr. Gribs clambered out from under the bed and doubled over. Truly, the shadows under the bed had been some of the darkest in the room, but not dark enough for his liking, and that made them difficult and treacherous to cross through, though he managed all the same.

After he regained his breath his big bulbous eyes scanned through the boxy chamber, seeing Mahra, and the machine, and the door that was thankfully closed and to which he wandered over to and locked. Then he muttered to himself and rummaged through his satchels and pulled out a scrap of paper, reading it to himself in a low murmur. He nervously twiddled his thumbs, his eyes looking at the big machine, reading off a mental checklist just behind his gaze. The portly nightmare walked up to the whirling contraption with its churning gears, and brass dials, and strange gizmos, and he looked over his little scrap of paper once more, checking it thoroughly, then he pulled some knobs and flicked some switches and the machine quietly powered down.

Then came the part that Mr. Gribs was not happy about, not happy about at all. He went over to the unconscious girl, cringing, grimacing, his podgy hands squirming, and he removed the tape which fastened the drip to her arm, and he pulled the long needle out from her vein, turning a ghastly color when he did. Then he slowly pulled the tube from her mouth and throat, and at this he had to take pause, for his queasiness was taking him over. He gasped at the air hungrily, steadied himself as best he could, then he hugged his arms around Mahra's torso and dragged her off the bed and pulled her into the shadows from whence he came, and together they vanished.

Then the room became a little emptier, a little quieter, and only the flowers were left to lament the difference.

The line between dreaming and waking had become a muddy blur. Without sight, or touch or smell, or taste, it was hard to know when the mind had truly woken up. It wasn't a thing that Mahra could get used to, this strange sluggish movement from one state into the other, though never truly feeling as though she was ever actually asleep or awake.

All she could do was hear, and without a connection to her body, it was hard to know if she hadn't just gone mad. Was she awake now? There was the ticking of something, was that a clock? It didn't dissolve into erratic patterns like numbers in a dream, so she assumed she was awake. There was the dim whirring of machinery, low beeps and drips, and so continuing her assumption, she assumed she was still in some hospital room on a strange alien world.

It had been disquieting to listen to Jerro when he came earlier—listen to the bizarre story he told her, listen while she could feel nothing, taste nothing, see nothing. She was trapped by her listening and it didn't feel real because she couldn't interact with what was being told. It felt as if she was at the bottom of a deep dark well and all around her were the recordings of sounds being played back at her, recordings of things happening, people talking, chairs moving, feet stomping. For all she knew she was still back in her closet slowly losing her mind.

It was a crippling thought, but then she realized how much more crippled could she really be? She had been downgraded to a collection of ideas, with nothing tangible to anchor them to reality, besides whatever her ears overheard. She felt dead.

The worst of all was not being able to feel her own breath, as though she was paused in the moment right when you breathe in a deep one and right before you blow it out, except she couldn't blow it out because she couldn't feel it, no matter how well she imagined, or how much she panicked trying to let out that infinite breath, it never came. It hung with her, and made her nervous, uncomfortable, scared—a whole plethora of emotions that also couldn't be blown out.

Eventually she found herself receding from her ears to somewhere deeper in her mind. She started looking back through her memories, reviewing her choices. She realized with quiet horror that her mind had become more like a dusky, abandoned mansion, littered with cobwebs and leaves, broken glass, rotting floorboards, crumbling lace.

She had been neglecting her inner mind, her deeper thoughts. And when the panic started to fade and she further receded into her mind, she started cleaning. She swept up the trash and put back the tables and chairs, threw out the moldy muck, and started taking stock of her thoughts. How much time had she spent avoiding thinking about the important things? How much time in honest quiet had she given herself to reflect? The answer was always and none.

There was always a movie on or music or someone talking, or she was busy thinking about her college assignments, or what she would wear, what was for lunch, on and on and never giving herself a small moment of quiet where her mind could at least breathe.

She looked into the dusky, abandoned mansion of her mind and found a fair number of truths amongst the wreckage. Sometimes painful, sometimes happy, but she found them all the same. She started looking at herself, her choices, who she was, what it meant to her to *be* Mahra Lapaul, not a *Lapaul* like how the world saw and thought of Lapauls, no, what being *Mahra* Lapaul meant to her. She came to the bitter conclusion that for the better part of her life she had been greatly underselling who Mahra Lapaul truly was.

It was obvious, now that she took the time to look at it. Even the slithe had said how she undersold herself, how her shyness had kept people from noticing her. It made Mahra angry when she finally confronted the truth of it. How many lonely nights she had spent, how many times she'd cried, how often she let people hurt her, and she could have stopped it at any point if she had only taken the time to *look!* To really look at herself! Not through the self-loathing, or the pity party that she often liked to throw for herself, not through the depression; if she had just looked at herself honestly without any of those dark glasses she might have realized that she actually was worth a damn, and anyone else could be damned if they didn't see it!

It was too late now though, which made her really mad. She had wasted so much time hating herself, and thinking so little of herself, instead of saying bugger it all and just getting on with her day. If she had only known sooner. If she had only stopped and paid attention.

There was something bittersweet in knowing that the guy she had a crush on for the better part of a year actually liked her, *really* liked her, apparently, which she recalled with a squeamish ugly feeling at the remembered sounds of Jerro and that *thing* in her bedroom, in her bed. She'd burn those sheets, she was sure of it. If she ever woke up, of course.

Could she look at him the same? She wondered. How different would it all be? What would this weird world look like, feel like, when she woke up?

He had told her so many strange things, fairy tale things, make-believe things, but she supposed, after what she *had* seen and what had happened, maybe anything was possible. She wouldn't truly believe it until she saw it with her own two eyes though, not until then, because it was hard to believe anything in the physical world while she was so incorporeal.

She hoped they could fix her, Jerro and his friend, the one he called Etcher—*Etcher*, who he kept talking about. *Etcher,* whose name he spoke with a degree of reverie that ignited a curious spark of jealousy inside Mahra. *Etcher,* who seemed like some kind of superhero the way Jerro described her. Well she intended to size this Etcher person up when she could, see if she really was all that. Jerro certainly seemed to think so, and the sinking feeling came again.

Had the slithe ruined that? Was Jerro done with her now? Over her? Was she even sure she wanted anything more from him after everything she heard him do? Could she be near him without thinking about *that?*

It wasn't a fun thought, so Mahra set it aside for the time being and went back to her tidying, slowly fixing up her mansion. It was a pretty good one, as she cleaned it up, sure it had its secret pathways and scary shadows, and there were monsters in the basement—but Mahra had gone down there, too, and had a good chat with them and they all decided to acknowledge one another and give each other a wide berth. But all in all, it was a good place, and Mahra liked it, which meant to a degree, she had to like herself. It was because of that, because she found that she was indeed someone likable, that she felt so disappointed and angry at how she had let herself be treated, how she had treated herself. She vowed that would change, damn it all, if she ever got out of the dark.

Her ears had picked up movement, and it drew her out of her inner thoughts and back into focus. Someone was in the room, muttering in some foreign language, clicking things and doing things and fussing about things very close to her. She wasn't sure she liked the sounds, especially not the dull *thump* sound of a body being dropped, nor the way the ambient sounds of the room went silent, deathly silent.

Where the hell was she? What the hell was going on?

Then there was a woman talking, and boy, she did *not* like that sound most of all. Not the slow deliberate drifting way the woman spoke, no, not at all, as if every word was something being pulled off a shelf then put back again, as if they didn't actually string together. Mahra would have had goosebumps if her body were still connected, so instead she got mental shivers.

And more things were happening, and the person who had been muttering in the hospital room was now muttering and stammering and moving about quickly. And the woman said something else and the other person made a sound like a croak.

Then there something bubbling, and water hissing like it hit something hot. Metal things clanked and some wooden things bumped and then—

And then there was a smell. *Yes!* There was a smell, an earthy smell! Mahra smelt it, she was sure she smelt it.

There was chanting now, low and sinister sounding, and someone poured something near her head...no, not near, *in!* In her mouth, she knew it because she could *taste* it. Oh my god, she tasted it! And it was warm, no, bloody hell it was fucking hot! *Ow-!!* It burnt her throat! Shit! She could feel it.

And it was all moving faster now, yes! Mahra could feel it, feel like she was being dragged up from water, feeling gravity slowly, deliberately, a little too heavily, push down on her.

And then she gasped. She heaved, she sucked in the air, and yes, it was the first breath of a lifetime, and god it never tasted so sweet. She breathed, and breathed, and her eyes felt warm, and there were tears and she could feel them. Thank fuck, she could feel them!

And then she opened her eyes—

Her body was heavy and tingling, her chest was heaving, her nose was smelling, her tongue was tasting the hot fleshy taste of her burnt mouth and she was seeing...it was all blurry at first, all strange and weird. It was coming into focus slowly. She was in some dark cellar maybe? It smelt like damp earth, and something a little boggy, even swampy? But there was candlelight and rocky walls, and the floor was cool though the air was thick and humid and—

"Oh, h-hello there," a portly thing said with a ribbit.

And Mahra screamed.

This was not how Mr. Gribs had envisioned his holiday being spent, not in the slightest. As he stood there, wringing his pudgy hands together in silent terror as the Raven Witch ordered him around—although very few words were actually spoken and most of the ordering had come from a look in her eyes or a tilt of her chin and Mr. Gribs inferred the meanings as best he could—he wondered what would become of him after it was all said and done?

Would the Raven Witch spare his life? Would he be made into a sacrifice for the spell they were laying down around the unconscious girl? Would he be cut down ruthlessly much as the Raven Witch had done to his precious Noctrabellun mushroom? He recalled that with unmasked horror, how she had stepped up to the beautiful, rare, coveted fungi, and snapped it from the stem like she might a common toadstool right before his bulging eyes. The very thought of handling such a precious specimen with unbridled brutality sent shivers of revulsion down his spine.

But what was he to do? He knew the Raven Witch's reputation all too well; you didn't last in Darcwood long if you didn't. And, oh, how foolish he had been as he followed the path of those devious Bellaforn Dames without stopping to look at where it was leading him to. Right into the heart of Darcwood, that's where!

Well, he wasn't going to tell the Raven Witch what she should do with her mushrooms, nope, not on your life. And when she said "come" with the strange drifting quality of her voice that echoed with a cold hatred buried far back behind her dark molasses eyes, well, yes ma'am I'll be right there! Coming, right-o. There wasn't a choice in the matter, unless Mr. Gribs decided he'd rather be a smoldering pile of ash then do as she commanded.

No, Mr. Gribs was very much of the mind of living to see tomorrow, no matter how much of a coward he might look or how much he might have to grovel, *surviving* was a very prevalent notion in the forefront of Mr. Gribs's mind. That was precisely what he was doing, surviving by doing exactly as the Raven Witch instructed, and every moment that kept him breathing was a happy, and terrifying, moment indeed.

So he watched, and waited, until the Raven Witch turned her spine-chilling gaze on him again and pointed to the far wall where a row of utensils were hanging down from steel hooks. He noted that it was the big ladle she was pointing to, and so he hopped to it and snatched up the ladle in double time and handed it to her, cowering only a little when she plucked it from his clammy hands. She spooned out a big helping of the steaming liquid from her cauldron into a stone dish and handed it to him with a type of baster then pointed at the girl.

"All of it," she said. And Mr. Gribs went about doing just that, filling up the baster and pouring it into the girl's open mouth.

And then the Raven Witch was chanting and Mr. Gribs wasn't entirely certain what he should be doing, so he stood there awkwardly after he had finished searing the girl's poor throat with the hot, earthy-smelling concoction.

Then, all of a sudden the girl woke up, just like that! And then she started screaming at Mr. Gribs, and he wasn't quite sure if she was screaming for her throat or simply just screaming. Either way it scared him half to death and he stumbled backwards and landed at the Raven Witch's feet, at which point he fainted.

"Enough," said a tall woman draped in a black dress.

Mahra noted that there was a finality to the command, and something else, something darker, older, scarier behind the cold monotone word. She clammed up her mouth immediately, and simply stared at the woman in black, then to the hideous toad-*thing* that had collapsed at the woman's feet.

The woman stepped around the toad creature, never looking down as if she hardly noticed it was there. She moved silently, you could almost call it elegant—like watching smoke billow and twist and snake in the windless air. She was beautiful, were it not for the frightening emptiness of her eternal gaze, the cold darkness behind those molasses eyes. Her long, dark hair fell in wavy tresses off her smooth white shoulders and down past the small of her back. She was shapely in ways that radiated raw sexuality and was accentuated by how the silken material of her black dress hugged her hips and her chest as if the cloth itself lavished touching her.

Mahra found herself watching after the woman in awe, *envying* how confidently she moved, how beautiful she was, how unabashed and unashamed she was of her own vivacious curvature. And Mahra was also deeply intimidated by her as well, and became too aware of herself, wearing nothing more than a hospital gown, unwashed, eyes a little crusted, mouth tasting—and no doubt smelling—awful. She felt like something a cat had dragged through a hedge, and probably looked it.

But if the woman thought this, she didn't show it. She looked past Mahra toward a stairwell that led up from the stony cellar, and she walked toward it, never saying anything more.

Mahra looked to the unconscious toad, who was slowly rousing, and to the woman as she ascended the stairs, and then Mahra decided that she best get to her feet and get going, that somehow the woman was expecting Mahra to follow. She didn't know how she knew, she just did.

It didn't dawn on Mahra until she reached the stairs that the task should have been a lot more difficult than it was. She had scrambled to her feet and skittered quickly across the stone floor after the woman in black without a second's hesitation, or a stumble, or any general weakness that should have been expected to accompany a person after being in a dead-weight coma for the past few days.

Whatever had been shoved down her throat had done a hell of a number on her, that was certain, and even the blistering sensation inside her scorched mouth was starting to subside. All the strange things Jerro had told her suddenly didn't seem all that strange as she headed up the steps and into a fire lit room where the smell of a juicy pot roast was weighing down the boggy scent of the air, and a lot of jarred things on shelves stared with cloudy eyes, and bundles of herbs hung overhead, and a steaming cauldron or two were spewing out colorful smoke; no, she was beginning to think that Jerro had given her the tame version of how strange things really were.

"Uh, um…where am I?" Mahra said timidly, and was surprised at the croak in her throat. So maybe the scorch marks hadn't quite healed yet.

The woman in black didn't say anything at first. She instead went over to a crockpot and lifted up the lid, sending a plume of fragrant smoke into the air. She ladled out two helpings in two china bowls, then her eyes drifted up to reach Mahra's, seeming as if they were being dragged from somewhere very far, like the wreckage of a ship being pulled up from the bottom of the ocean.

Mahra felt petrified as that horrifying gaze set upon her.

"You're in Darcwood," the woman said. Then she placed a spoon in each bowl, took one for herself and left the other as she headed out the room, which Mahra suddenly realized was a kitchen. "Gribs will explain," the woman called back before disappearing behind a door.

On cue there came a huff and a wheeze from the top of the stairs and there stood the toadish creature. This time Mahra held in her scream, though her face didn't hide her distaste.

"Oh, right. Yes," the portly creature huffed. "Right well, um, shall I take you to your room?" It smiled, and Mahra really wished it hadn't.

"Yeah, sure," she said with a grimace.

The wind ran its silken fingers through Jerro's hair, nipping his nose and reddening his cheeks as he clung to the saddle on the dragon's back. He felt exhilarated as they soared through the twilight skies of Faerie, even with Tahli clinging to him for dear life and sinking her clawed fingers into his sides. He could have sworn the ginger feline was terrified; she was pressed so flat against his back he could feel her little tremors vibrate through his spine.

Below them, the weird twisting paths of the High Roads looked like a knotted web stretched over the top of the gorge while the cosmic void winked up at them through the breaks and gaps in the winding roads, quiet and waiting. It was mildly less threatening from up there, as if the High Roads were like a net holding back oblivion, keeping the darkness trapped beneath the labyrinth of pathways.

Every glance Jerro stole downward tied stones to his heart and made images of his brother bloom in his mind. He kept his gaze forward as much as he could, toward the slight curve of the horizon, kept his mind focused on the brilliant beast beneath him that was guiding them through the air.

He could feel Hoya's calm and methodical breaths expanding and contracting in her colossal chest, the powerful and fluid strokes of every wingbeat, the slow, deep *thump-ump* of her giant heart. He watched the sparse clouds sail by, occasionally finding himself with a face full of cold moisture whenever they passed through one. He was quietly thankful for the warmth of Tahli's fur at his back, and Etcher at his front to break the full force of the frigid wind, although he wished he had on goggles to stop his eyes from drying out.

"How much longer!" cried a desperate Tahli, still pressed firmly into Jerro's back.

"Not too much longer now, the mirror to Darcwood is coming up. We're going to fly straight through it, and when we do, plug your nose, close your eyes, and hold your breath!" replied Etcher, calling back loudly to be heard over the whooshing sound of the wind.

"What? Why?" Tahli yelled.

"You'll see. I'll warn you when we're close."

Jerro opted to stay out of the conversation. He was enjoying the feeling of freedom on Hoya's back, the way his problems seem to be falling away from him with every mile they crossed through the sky. He didn't want the journey to end, he'd gladly stay up there on Hoya for hours more, simply letting the world roll by beneath him. He dared to reach down, despite Tahli's protests, and touch Hoya's smooth, scaly skin. She had an internal warmth that radiated through her thick hide and she gave a little rumble like a purr as he stroked her.

The sudden lurch in Jerro's stomach told him that they were beginning their descent, bringing the void frighteningly closer. He snatched his hand back and gripped the saddle, squeezing his eyes shut. He didn't want to look where they were going lest he stare too deeply into the cosmic nothingness and forget to hold on.

"We're almost there, get ready!" called out Etcher.

Despite himself, Jerro dared to peek at where they were headed, then gripped the saddle tightly with one hand, plugged his nose with the other, and took a deep breath. Hoya had leveled out her flight and they were sailing parallel to the rocky paths of the High Roads. He stared dead ahead into what looked like a large rippling pool tilted on its side, as if the laws of gravity had bent, allowing the watery surface to stand perpendicular to the ground without pouring out.

It was dark and murky within the mirrored pool. Jerro could not see their reflections; instead he saw a halo of tree cover surround the rim of the rippling surface, glimpses of night sky, of dotted stars and full moons, and the occasional silhouette of a night bird shooting out between the trees.

Hoya's nose was just about to push through the portal, and Jerro realized with a mix of awe and horror what the mirror truly was. He shut his eyes quickly as the watery surface engulfed Hoya's head, enclosed around Etcher, and pressed into him.

Immediately he was struck with a cold, wet sensation, and a sickening lurch as gravity flipped and Hoya shot through the murky water that had been the mirror and arched up toward the sky, leveling out as she headed back down to the new ground.

They landed heavily, at least that's what Jerro felt, and they were accosted suddenly by the warm and humid air, the weight of the bog and oppressive dreariness of this new place.

He opened his eyes and looked back at where they had come from. He had been right—they had shot right through a large pool of swampy water and up into Darcwood with its miserably thick air of swampy stink.

Jerro was half tempted to keep his nose plugged—the cloying smell of decaying foliage and algae was immense. The humid air amplified his discomfort, making his skin feel sticky and damp, and his clothes cling intrusively like an unwelcome guest.

This miserable place is Darcwood? Of course it is, of course it had to be! Where else would a witch live? Jerro thought bitterly as the unpleasant atmosphere quickly soured his mood.

Then as Etcher nimbly climbed out of the saddle, Jerro realized he had no desire to jump down onto the spongy wet ground of the marshlands. He wanted to take off with Hoya again, go somewhere else, somewhere nicer than this. But Tahli had dismounted as soon as she was able, leaving Jerro to sit alone atop of the sapling-colored dragon. For a moment he saw himself taking to the skies, and never looking back. How fun and freeing that would be. And then it hit him how much he wished he could cut the ties that bound him and be off on his own wild adventure. It wasn't fair how quickly he had been saddled with so much obligation just when his enjoyment of life had been rekindled.

But it wasn't his dragon—it was Etcher's—and he couldn't just leave while Mahra was counting on him, on *them*, to fix the mess they were all in. With reluctance he dismounted, though he stole a moment standing there, looking into Hoya's deep watery eyes.

"Thanks," he said, smiling gently, wishing and hoping that it wouldn't be the last time they flew together.

The great sapling-colored dragon purred and butted her nose against him, then she crumbled into little shining flecks of green light that fizzled out before they touched the ground.

He turned and saw Etcher with her palm upturned, the glow slowly fading.

"We'll be sure to fly back." She winked at him.

Tahli huffed, but Jerro grinned.

"Right then, we should get going—though Jerro, you may want to call your hazua. The name of this place isn't purely figurative," said Etcher.

Jerro gave a nod and thought of his little winged messenger. Soon, the teal hazua popped into reality and created a soft dome of light around the group.

"Let's push on. The Raven Witch awaits." Etcher turned and led their party toward the heart of Darcwood, navigating her way through the swampy wetness with ease.

As soon as Jerro stepped forward, a new fear bloomed inside him. The marshy ground depressed and suctioned at his heels as he moved, and he found himself wishing for a pair of sturdy boots. At any wrong step his sneakers might be sucked off his feet and vanish into the muck. He sighed quietly as he followed after Etcher, trying hard not to breathe through his nose.

Mahra was feeling much more comfortable now that she had been allotted a good meal, a nice long shower, fresh clothes, and a brush for her bedridden hair. She was calm as she groomed herself, staring at her reflection in the big trifold mirror, as she sat in the plush chair at the vanity table.

There was a multitude of beauty products laid out before her—all pristine and new. Porcelain containers with glittering eyeshadows of every variety, rich stained wood handles of velvety soft brushes, tiers of foundation product, creams, oils, toners—all laid out on beautifully handcrafted shelves, like a prima donna's dream come true.

Of course Mahra was no prima donna, nor was she prone to painting her face with anything more than a little eyebrow liner and mascara, but the plethora of goodies was tempting, and she was considering doing something more elaborate with so much to choose from, so many sparkly, shiny new things to dress up with, so many colors and brushes and tools. She felt a little childhood spark of excitement—like getting ready for a costume party. The possibility of things she might be, a chance at trying something new.

She brushed some mascara under her lashes, dared to paint her eyelids with a little color, refined her brows and plucked a few hairs that blemished the symmetry. A little eye shadow, a little liner, some fancy facial creams and toners. She examined her handiwork with careful scrutiny, not too much to feel like a lie, not too little to feel like incomplete, just enough to make her feel more like Mahra, *the* Mahra, and hopefully the one and only Mahra now that the slithe was gone.

Although, perhaps it was a Mahra new-and-improved. Now that she was awake and in control of her body once more there were the whisperings of promises she had made in the dark void of her mind, the list of things she had vowed if she ever got out of that pit. Well, now she was out, and it was time to cash in all the checks her internal dialogue had written.

It was a tall order. Mahra had lived a lifetime of meekness and undervaluing herself. Those were deep rooted habits that would be hard to break, they were woven into her very foundation and now she'd have to tear it all down and start anew with only the good bricks that were left. She'd build the tower of who she was right this time, no matter how long it might take, no matter if she'd have to tear it down again, she wasn't going to waste herself anymore.

She squared her shoulders and stared her reflection dead in the eye. "Mahra Lapaul, you listen to me," she began aloud, "you're going to make something of yourself, damn it. You're done being a doormat, all right?" She gave herself a nod, and a little spark of fierceness brightened her eyes. It was as good a start as any.

She gave herself another look over. The outfit was treading into uncharted territory, much like her daring endeavor with the makeup. The shirt was lacy, low-cut, and a little see-through, the trousers were tight, the boots were knee high, and the undergarments…well, now there was something else to top off this new Mahra. The bra mounted her chest high and the underwear was so scandalous, Mahra felt a little devilish spark of confidence creep up on her whenever she thought about them. Not that she was planning on showing them off, but in *knowing* she was wearing them she felt just a little bit good about herself.

A polite knock came at the door just as Mahra was feeling anxious to get going and do something with all her budding confidence. She suspected it was the toad. "Come in," she said.

Mr. Gribs poked his big bald head out from behind the door. "Um, yes, hello again, Miss Lapaul, might I come in?"

Mahra nodded. She watched the portly little creature walk into the room, strangely agile despite his short stature and assortment of satchels crisscrossed over his round torso. He was like a beach ball with gangly arms and legs that moved like a ballet dancer.

The toad straightened himself out and stood at attention before Mahra. "I suspect you have some questions?" he smiled timidly.

"Yes, I do…what *are* you?"

"Oh, well, I am a *nightmare*." And he seemed exceedingly proud with himself at the statement.

"Uh, what d'you mean, 'nightmare'?"

Mr. Gribs noted the confusion on Mahra's face and muttered under his breath, looking down at his shoes in contemplation. "Hmm, you're from an Earth planet, correct?"

"Yeah…" replied Mahra, and she couldn't help but note the use of 'an' Earth instead of 'the' Earth.

"Hmm, yes, yes, I see. How to explain then? I am…well *we* are—nightmares that is—we are real, tangible creatures. We give people their nightmares. I myself am an embodiment of the types of nightmares that I specialize in. Um, you know, self-doubt, anxiousness, paranoia, uh…have you ever had those nightmares were no matter how high you climb, the walls keep stretching up further? Or ones where you're trying to run and catch up to someone but you keep falling behind?"

"Yeah," she said again.

"Well, that is some of my handiwork!" Mr. Gribs said with an excited smile. "That's the kind of thing I do."

"That's awful," said Mahra, although regretted it as she witnessed the smile fall abruptly from the toad's face.

"Oh, I see why you might think that. B-but nightmares are important, they give you a chance to face your fears! If you confront your nightmares you can learn a lot from them. Happy dreams are all well and good, but in every nightmare there is a lesson that your mind is trying to tell you. My role is more of an educator. Though, I do regret when I must visit the same person again and again, some people are slow to learn or change their ways." Mr. Gribs looked genuinely remorseful as he wrung his chubby hands together.

"I never really thought of it like that."

"That's all right, a common misconception. Most people don't look forward to a nightmare, understandably, but mark my words, they are still important! Of course, too much of anything is a bad thing, anyone plagued with nightmares is a sorry state, most of us don't enjoy having to go to the same person too often, it gets very dull. But you see, the sleeping mind calls *us*, and our nature demands we follow through. We'll trade off with each other if it gets too much, you know, shake things up a bit. Sometimes it works, and the person in question gets the point."

"Huh." Mahra thought about this. It was different to view a nightmare as a tangible person, like a handyman out on a call. "So, whenever I had those nightmares, that was you making them happen?"

"Oh, no no, not me, specifically,"—he blushed, and it was awkward looking— "your Earth has its own jurisdiction. Not as much *majik* there, harder for the nightmares to take tangible form. Not like here. But I imagine something similar to myself helps shape your nightly visions."

"I see." And Mahra realized with surprising certainty that she did see, that in her heart of hearts she knew it to be true. "Okay, so next question. That woman, who is she? And are we still on Eclipse?"

"Eclipse? Oh yes! Most definitely. H-how exactly do you know that by the way?"

"My friend Jerro told me."

"Jerro...why do I know that name?"

"Jerro? Jerro Ahliss? Tall guy, dark hair, blue eyes...athletic looking," described Mahra, and she resisted the urge to include *handsome* and *dreamy* in her definition.

"Oh my!" The toad looked frightened. "Y-you don't mean—your friend, is he...*friends* with one Etcher Everdoor?"

"Yeah, that's right!"

Mr. Gribs turned an unsightly shade of green and looked as if he might faint. "O-oh..."

"Are you all right?"

"Um, well, I-I...um..."

"Do you know them?" she added carefully.

"I-I..." Mr. Gribs looked like he might burst and wrung his hands together furiously. "Oh no, what have I got tangled up in?" he muttered helplessly to himself. He seemed to inflate with his inner turmoil. His eyes searched around desperately until finally he blurted out a tumbling explanation of his encounter with Etcher and Jerro and his mission from the King of Nightmare, managing to exclude certain words like *reborn* and *soul eater*.

And again Mahra was struck with the same serene acceptance from before. "Yeah, okay that makes sense, Jerro mentioned something about that. In

Undercity? Gosh, it all sounded so strange when he told me, I wasn't sure what to make of it. I suppose it really happened then? And that whole thing about him being reincarnated or whatever?"

Mr. Gribs sighed with palpable relief. "Oh good, you already know about that. Yes, your friend is a *reborn*, very peculiar indeed. A-and, Miss Everdoor, what do you know of her?"

"Just what Jerro told me about the shop and what she does. Why they left together." There was that pang of jealousy again.

"Oh I see. Well, seems you know more than me, I'm not sure how much help I'll be then…"

"What about the woman? The one who *did* whatever it was she did to me?"

"Ah! Yes, *her*. Well, she is known as the Raven Witch, but, she does have a more conventional name: Miss Lupine Blackfeather. I-I don't know why she wanted you here, perhaps she's friends with your friends? I can't really say, she hasn't told me much and I dare not question her."

"Why not?"

"Oh Miss Lapaul, you must understand—Miss Blackfeather is very powerful, very dangerous. She has a certain reputation. I don't mean to frighten you, but you must be careful, just do as she says."

"Wait, does that mean I'm a prisoner here?"

"I-I don't know. But, I wouldn't recommend trying to leave unless she tells you to, if you understand me?" A strange expression crossed Mr. Gribs's flat face and his attention became focused, his eyes distant. "I-I believe Miss Blackfeather wishes to see you. I'll take you to her, all right?"

"Yeah okay," said Mahra, and suddenly there was a smear on her previous calm façade.

Together, Mr. Gribs and Mahra navigated their way through the strange house, if it could even be called that. It was more an amalgamation of different rooms pieced together with no particular sense of theme to unite them. A kitchen here, a bedroom there, a dining room or two, here a drawing room, there a den. As if each piece had been added as an afterthought, though all throughout the winding corridors and adjoining chambers was the succulent aroma of food drifting through the air.

"Is she expecting guests?" asked Mahra, breathing in the delicious scent.

"Hmm? No, I don't believe so, why do you ask?" said Mr. Gribs.

"Just seemed like there was a lot cooking in the kitchen, and the place smells so good, like she's making a feast or something?"

"Oh I see. No, Miss Blackfeather is very fond of the culinary arts. You should try her crème brûlée. Marvelous, really!"

Mahra had to admit, the pot roast had been pretty damn good and not only because it had been the first real meal she had eaten in days. "Seems a bit sad though, doesn't it? To make all this food and have no guests?"

"I hadn't really thought about it, I don't really know what goes on with Miss Blackfeather. All my knowledge prior to meeting her had been merely mythical, you know, tall tales you hear, rumors and such. I never expected to actually *meet* her, but I can sense enough that she is indeed a person to be cautious of, you mark my word on that."

"I guess so. She broke whatever that *thing* did to me to put me in that coma."

Mr. Gribs nodded solemnly. "An awful fate for anyone, I'm glad Miss Blackfeather was able to break you out of it."

Mahra smiled at that and looked down at the strange, cowardly nightmare. "Thank you, by the way. I don't think I ever said so, but thank you for bringing me here."

Mr. Gribs turned scarlet. "O-oh, not a problem. My pleasure really."

"Your pleasure to take orders from some powerful witch to raid hospital rooms?"

"Oh well, you know, I'm just happy to be of service. And not to be flayed alive."

Mahra stopped on her heels and stared the toad down.

"I-is something the matter?" said Mr. Gribs.

Mahra shook her head, then stuck out her hand toward the nightmare. "No, but, I feel like I owe you. And we never were properly introduced. You can call me Mahra, by the way. Pleasure to make your acquaintance."

Mr. Gribs cautiously took the offered hand and shook, his smile growing steadily with it. "Mr. Gribs, at your service. And the pleasure it all mine, Miss Lapaul—erm, *Mahra*."

"There, that's better." She smiled back. "So, how much further?"

Mr. Gribs retracted his hand shyly, a contented smile growing over his grotesque face. "I believe our illustrious host is waiting just beyond those double doors through the drawing room up ahead."

"Right," said Mahra, blowing out a long breath. "Okay then. Are you coming with me? Or did you want to stay back?"

Mr. Gribs started wringing his hands again. "To be honest, Miss Mahra, I'm hoping to stay out of the way enough until she forgets about me, and then perhaps I might be allowed to leave."

"I understand," she said, and meant it. "Well, thank you again Mr. Gribs, wish me luck."

"Good luck!" he said and watched as Mahra headed through the drawing room towards the double doors.

The room was dimly lit by the fire in the hearth. The shadows flickered with the dance of the flames, gilding the furniture with its warm glow. And there lay the Raven Witch, draped along a narrow couch beside a threadbare lounge seat. The open chair had a solemn feel to it, as though its occupant had not been back in a great long while.

"Sit," said Lupine Blackfeather, and Mahra did so.

Mahra took up the solemn armchair quietly and waited. There was a certain deadliness in the quiet, in the strange apathy that clung to the beautiful woman. What could make those deep brown eyes so cold? Her face so indifferent and distant? What could cast such a shadow over the woman that held such a tangible weight? Mahra found herself fidgeting in her seat, fearful and vulnerable before the Raven Witch called Lupine. She waited, and the silence weighed a little more with each passing moment.

"Gribs told you enough?" The words were given with effort, as though summoned from beyond the veil of time.

"Yes, he did. Thank you," Mahra said, gulping down her nerves as her heart hammered out a terrified tattoo in her chest.

"Good," the witch said, her eyes never wavered from the hearth and her hand had slithered up from beside her, her fingers twirling in the air, and with them, the fire danced and swayed, bound by her hypnotic resonance.

By now the quiet had become unbearable, and the gaps inside their conversation were becoming like sinkholes, threatening to drown Mahra within their deafening silence.

"Miss Blackfeather, can I just ask," she began, feeling her skin prickle with gooseflesh as the Raven Witch's weighty gaze slugged through the air to fall upon her. "Can I ask why you brought me here?"

The eyes lingered for an uncomfortable amount of time, simply staring, looking through, drifting into an icy void. "Your friends will be here soon, I'm doing them a favor," said the Raven Witch finally.

Mahra let out her breath, realizing that she had been holding it. "Oh, I see. You mean Jerro...and Etcher?"

The Raven Witch nodded, and removed her petrifying gaze from Mahra, returning it to the fire. "When they come you will wait in the other room. Come out when I tell you."

"O-okay."

"One other thing—" The witch paused, gathering her will to speak as she battled the apathy that made the tedium of talking all the more tiresome. "You have *majik* in you."

"Excuse me?" Mahra recoiled as the Raven Witch glanced at her again.

Lupine Blackfeather took in a deep breath, then sighed it out. "The *majik* that put you under should have turned your mind to mush. But here you are, like it never happened. Your mind is malleable, and I can sense the *majik* in you." She looked drained by the bout of words, and behind her cold eyes was a restless stirring that her usual silence had kept at bay.

"I'm sorry, but I don't understand—"

"You will. Ask Jerro about Etcher's notebook."

"Um, okay."

The Raven Witch continued to stare at Mahra, thinking, sizing her up. Then she slipped from the couch and drifted over to where Mahra sat and placed her hand lightly on Mahra's forehead.

Mahra froze beneath the delicate touch, her own fingers dug into the threadbare arms of the chair, horrified of what might happen next. She felt a tingling in her forehead where the Raven Witch had placed her hand, and then the tingling seeped in deep, went through Mahra's brain, and sent little shivers through her eardrums and down her throat.

"Now you'll talk like us." The Raven Witch removed her hand and laid herself back down on the couch. "They'll be here soon, go wait in the other room."

Mahra turned to look at the door to which Lupine Blackfeather had singled out. "Okay," she said, feeling confused and uncertain of herself, though glad to get away. She'd wait, she was happy to wait, if it meant that the next person she might see was a friendly face and she could get out from under the Raven Witch's horrifying scrutiny.

Jerro was having some serious regrets in his choice of footwear. The marshy ground continued to threaten his shoes, suctioning them a little more with each step, and more than once the mud had bubbled up and spilled over inside his sneakers, feeling cold and mushy against his now damp socks.

And the mosquitos—now there was an insect he truly wished wasn't universal. Mosquitos on Earth were bad enough; Ecliptian mosquitos were worse, and big. He had done his best not to squeal like a schoolgirl the first time one of those bird-sized abominations lumbered over to him through the air. Tahli had been the one to swat the wretched creature out of the way, then she conjured a glass jar filled with what looked like talcum powder and brushed her fur with it. She eyed Jerro as she did and reluctantly passed it over to him so he could dust himself, too.

The monstrous blood-suckers never bothered Etcher, of course—they gave her a wide berth. And of course the little shopkeeper had no trouble navigating her way through the marshy woodlands, even in her silly canvas slip-ons. And how she was not drenched in sweat in her dour black-and-red suit was a mystery. Just looking at her made Jerro feel ten degrees warmer.

"Are we almost there?" said Jerro, trying very hard not to sound petulant and whiny, the teal light from his hazua casting a gloomy accent to his features.

"Indeed, just a half kilometer to go," replied Etcher.

Jerro groaned quietly, and with his next step his foot sunk right under the muck and came up minus a shoe. "Oh for fu—" he sighed and scrubbed a hand over his face, trying to tame his bubbling frustrations. "Great."

Etcher was smirking. "You know, you have a pair of boots in the Obelisk."

"What? Why didn't you say so!?"

"You are the one who did not bother to look. I suppose Everdoor should tell you when to blow your nose as well?" cut in Tahli, mocking him with her eyes.

Jerro held in the angry torrent that was ready to break free from his mouth, though he couldn't keep the glare from his eyes. He dipped into the mind closet of the Obelisk stone and looked around, finding the aforementioned boots on one of the bottom shelves, and there was also a clean pair of socks he was very thankful for. He brought the items into reality and leaned himself against a gnarled looking tree, changing his socks and shoes for the new ones and stowing his old, soiled socks, and one sorry-looking sneaker inside the Obelisk.

The boots came up to his knees and had a good flexible heel, and were thankfully water-tight. He rolled up his mud stained trousers to stop them from sucking up any more of the swamp muck and managed to feel just a tiny bit relieved. The remaining half kilometer didn't seem as daunting anymore.

"You know, you could have warned me that we'd be trekking through a bloody bog," said Jerro.

"True, but you read the poem, 'marshy banks' and all. Crass, though Tahli is,"—and at this Tahli huffed and rolled her eyes—"I can't always be telling you what to do. But, I admit, it was unfair of me not to mention it. Although I did find it rather humorous watching you get this far in those shoes," said Etcher.

"Hardy-har-har. Yeah, real funny. And why aren't you sinking in the mud?"

Etcher chuckled. "Because I'm more nimble than you. Come on, we're almost there."

They continued their journey in relative silence, save for the cacophony of chirping insects and night creatures giving out their nightly calls.

It was a tedious, humid, sweaty, half kilometer, and Jerro was glad to be done with it. The land became a little firmer the closer they got to the heart of

Darcwood, and the heavy unpleasant smell thinned out, too, though the sticky humidity remained in full force—layered over the air like an algae-infested duvet. They stepped out into a vast circle of trees, in the middle of which stood a sprawling estate.

It was a weird hodgepodge of incoherent pieces stuck together as if several two-story houses and a few bungalows had been glued into one—like a child's science presentation gone wrong. Soft light emanated from a majority of the assorted windows, though the glass was hazy and nothing of the inner sanctum could be seen.

Jerro waved away his tiny messenger, and its absence cloaked them in a small pocket of darkness on the outskirts of the estate. "*This* is where the Raven Witch lives?" said Jerro, cringing at the sight of the atrocious architecture. And as his eyes looked over the strange dwelling they glided upward toward the canopy, tracing the gnarled faces of knots and cracks in the gloomy trees.

Despite the vast clearing of land, the trees had stretched out their limbs, weaving and intermingling with one another so as to cloak the hodgepodge house from the sky. Only thin slats of dusky moonlight stole their way into the secretive underbelly of Darcwood, outlining the many peaked rooftops of the strange estate. A diligent billowing of cotton-white smoke snaked out from one of the many chimneys and brought with it the aroma of salted pork and sage, which helped combat the remaining boggy smell. The aromatic vapor drifted up into the canopy and dissipated among the leaves of the tall, wooden sentinels.

"Evidently so," said Etcher, looking over the amalgamate house with careful scrutiny.

"Well, are we going to knock?" said Tahli, arms folded and her hips cocked to one side.

"Might as well. Suppose we'll just pick a door, shall we? That one looks bigger than the others." Etcher singled out a large oak door that was oddly fitted into one of the many brick façades. A lone antique street lamp stood beside the threshold and appeared to mark it as the entrance, casting a solemn glow over the door.

There was a quiet feeling of dread steadily building inside Jerro as they approached the door. And he noted with uneasiness that the woodland inhabitants had become curiously mum at the heart of Darcwood. Not a chirp or a croak or even the dull drone of a mosquito's wings.

Etcher knocked, and the sound echoed through the clearing, cutting through the unnerving quiet and replacing it with a dreadful feeling of vulnerability. Here they were out in the open, *exposed*, and with a clear *tap-tap-tap* to mark their location for anyone that might take an unwanted interest in them.

The sound echoed back at them, bouncing off the surrounding halo of trees—and Jerro did feel *surrounded*. He looked into the knots and the twists of the bark in those old wooden sentinels and felt as if they were indeed watching quietly, whispering to one another in a language he couldn't hear, only feel in the jitter of his nerves.

The door creaked and groaned as it opened, sending a little tremor of shock through Jerro and Tahli.

Yet Etcher, as always, was calm. In fact, there was a sly, knowing smirk on her face, and before the door could fully open to reveal their host, she spoke. "Well, well, Mr. Gribs. We meet again."

The toadish nightmare went wide-eyed. "H-hello, Miss Everdoor."

"Who is this? This is not the Raven Witch," said Tahli, eyeing the portly nightmare with disdain.

"No, he isn't," answered Etcher. "Is the Raven Witch in? I believe she's been expecting us."

"Y-yes, she is," Mr. Gribs smiled nervously. "Forgive my asking, but I haven't been introduced to you before, miss...?"

"*Tahli.*" Scowled the ginger cat-woman.

"Miss Tahli, r-right. Well, please come this way," said Mr. Gribs with a small terrified ribbit.

Etcher strode in after the nightmare, leaving a bewildered Tahli and Jerro to trail behind her.

"You know, Mr. Gribs, I find it very curious that you should be here. Are you still following me, perhaps?"

"N-no, Miss Everdoor! Actually, I was on holiday," the portly nightmare moped, wringing his hands together as he led the trio through the house. "I went too far into Darcwood and Miss Blackfeather found me and, well, was rather insistent that I help her."

"With what, exactly?"

"I think it's best if she explain. Please, if your friends would be so kind as to wait here in the drawing room, Miss Blackfeather is expecting you through those doors. She'd like to speak with you alone." Mr. Gribs was trembling ever so slightly, casting his wary eyes between Etcher and the other two.

Etcher turned to Tahli and Jerro. "I suppose you should make yourselves comfortable."

"I do not like this," said Tahli.

"Yeah, me neither," agreed Jerro.

"We're the guests, we best do as we've been told. For now." Etcher winked at them and headed for the door before they could voice any other complaints.

Jerro huffed as he let himself down into one of the armchairs. "And now we wait, *again.*"

"What did you expect? Let us just hope she does not leave without us this time." Tahli draped herself across one of the lounge seats and busied herself with her nails.

"Care for some tea?" Mr. Gribs chimed in. Neither of them had noticed that he had left, although they certainly noticed him upon his return—now that he was laden with a large silver platter filled with tea cups, an exquisite china teapot, little cakes and sandwiches, and an assortment of ceramic containers.

He dressed the nearest coffee table—which sat between Tahli and Jerro—and poured them both a cup of steaming amber liquid. "There's midnight honey if you care for it, or sugar cubes if you prefer," he offered graciously, looking slightly less timid now that Etcher had gone.

Jerro stared the tea-set down dubiously. "How do we know it's not drugged or something?"

A look of utter shock crossed the nightmare's face. "Oh my no! I assure you nothing's been tampered with, you see?"

Mr. Gribs poured himself a cup and drank from it, smiling as much as his ghastly face would allow.

Jerro, however, remained unconvinced. But when Tahli took up her cup—held it under her keen nose and smelled it, then finally took a sip—the nostalgic aroma of the fresh brewed tea, and the tantalizing little sandwiches and treats won Jerro over, and he reached for his own cup.

"Would care for a biscuit? They were made fresh this morning," said Mr. Gribs, becoming ever more the doting host.

"Sure," said Jerro, and took one of the chocolate-covered biscuits from the plate and dipped it in his steaming cup. He ate it slowly, keeping an eye on Tahli in case she had any reaction. Both the tea and the biscuit were delicious as it turned out, although he didn't say so aloud. He did, however, help himself to one of the cream-filled tea cakes and added a large dollop of honey to his cup. And then he took a sandwich, and another biscuit.

"Anyone up for a game of rummy?" asked Mr. Gribs. He had produced a deck of playing cards and was shuffling them expertly between his pudgy hands.

Both Tahli and Jerro looked at each other and shared a mutual feeling of bewilderment at how utterly strange the day had become.

The cave was dark and damp, and the wind whistled and moaned.

By the mouth of the black gape was a shallow ledge, overlooking the twinkling lamp lights of Yahre. It was colder up there by the cave, and the shadows clung more fiercely.

The air whistled softly as it sighed out from the cave's maw, creating a constant noise like static that blurred the edges of thought and focus. The darkness, and the hollow whistling wind, were what Yama had come for. He took off his trilby hat and ran his hand smoothly over his closely cropped hair. There was reluctance in his step as he entered the cave.

Yama was enveloped by the darkness, melting away the line that separated shadow from form. In the darkness he sat, he put his hat back upon his head, tilted it slightly, straightened his jacket and the big, loose collar of his silk shirt, and prayed.

It wasn't a prayer to a god, or any other ethereal entity for that matter. It was a prayer of happening, a prayer that shook his celestial-self free from the confines of its meaty shell. His spirt-self drifted through reality, the world turned to smoke and haze around him, moving past like a rolling fog.

When the world stopped moving and took shape once again, he found himself in a cathedral—an ancient and long-forgotten place hidden deep inside the bowels of the under realms. It was dark, much like the cave where his fleshly vessel sat lifelessly, though dim flickers of firelight danced near the tops of the arched ceiling, lending nothing of their luminance to the ground.

It didn't matter, Yama could see.

His steps made no sound as he walked toward the center of the chamber he was in. The narthex of the cathedral was surrounded by ornate walls in which horrific fallen gods had been shaped into the black bricks and dark stained wood. Gargoyle creatures with demonic faces, depictions of monsters devouring each other whole—a telling of the ultimate end of everything.

Yama did not like this place.

He waited in the middle of the narthex, staring at the large doors that led into the nave, which in turn led toward the transept and up to the sanctuary where the cathedral abruptly ended and where a tower of ice stood as though it had been plunged into that tainted alter, entombing the dark god. Yama could not see into the nave, however, because the door was firmly closed, but he knew what lay behind it, and knew he had no desire to see it for himself.

Beside Yama, another door opened, one that led out to other hallways and chambers that circled around the main body of the dire chapel—to where the acolytes of the slumbering god congregated.

A boy with a shaven head entered through the side doors. His bright eyes alert and keen, his gangly limbs betraying his slow transition into manhood. His tunic was simple, his feet were bare, and his arms were laden with bottles and scrolls and wooden boxes.

The boy frowned at the spirit-self of Yama, bringing an unnatural scowl to the smiling face. "Have you news?" the boy demanded.

But Yama did not speak. He looked the boy up and down, weighing what he saw, and wondered.

The boy let out an exasperated sigh, his features softening once more. "I am busy, what have you come to tell me?"

"Me don' com' to tell ya no'tink, me com' to find out more," said Yama in his own perpetual calm.

The boy seemed frustrated at this, his bright blue eyes glanced between Yama and the main doors fervently. With reluctance, he set down his magical wares and strode up to the projection of Yama. "What do you mean? I gave you plenty, what's wrong? Didn't you find the girl? Her friends?"

"About dos friends, we can't find no'tink about dem. Who are dey?"

"*You* can't find *anything* about them?" The boy stared incredulously at Yama, and the kindly face was once again marred by a deep resentful anger that was foreign to his features. "A Khlarii can't find them?"

"Dey be hiding well. Who are dey?" Yama said, keeping his tone dull.

The boy's agitation grew, his blue eye twitched. "*I* told you already. There's a young human male and an unconscious human girl, a kyoki and some other Ecliptian. She's small, strange..." the boy added almost as an afterthought.

"No'tink else? No'tink ya forgot? We can't find dem," repeated Yama.

"None of them?" The boy's eyes went wide with a reptilian rage. He paused for a moment, wrestling with himself to subdue the anger which broke his character. Again his eyes flittered over to the main doors. He seemed too hurried, too occupied to don his friendly mask for Yama and play the role of the skin he wore.

"What use are you then?" The boy glared at the spirit projection, dropping the last of any pretense. "You're a Khlarii, aren't you? You *find* people, that's what you do! That's what you're good at! Do you have any idea how much it cost to put Bloodland performers in all the major cities? To pay for the hollowmen so you and your brother could have speedy transport? How can you come here and tell me you can't find them?"

"Me told ya dey be hiding well," said Yama calmly, blatantly ignoring the venomous rage that was quivering beneath the boy's skin.

"*Useless*," the boy hissed. "How hard is it to find a pair of humans, a kyoki and—" The boy stopped, unable to find the right word to describe the other. "The kyoki alone should be enough—they're not supposed to leave the Bloodlands. *You* know that."

"If it's so easy, why don't ya find dem ya'self?"

The boy grit his teeth. He had had his fill of Yama and went to gather his things, turning his back to the disembodied projection. "I have other things to do, things which *you* are impeding," he said. "And as a matter of fact I *will* find them myself, but I hired you and your brother to keep an eye on them in the meantime. Now do your job! Find the girl and you'll find the others. She has to be admitted somewhere, she'll die otherwise, she's in a coma."

"Maybe dey be treating her dem'selves?"

"And if they are, it's your job to find out *where* they're treating her. You're wasting my time! If I had known you were so incompetent—Send your brother next time! He at least seems capable."

"It's true, him got da brains and me got da looks."

The boy scowled. "Get out. Don't come back until you've got something to tell me!"

And Yama did as commanded. The world turned again to fog, rolling backward as his spirit-self drifted through reality toward its meaty shell.

His body perked up and Yama stared into the darkness of the cave, glad to be back, glad to be away from that terrible place. He got to his feet, pulled out a slender cigar from his jacket and lit it. Between the savoring drags Yama called a hazua to himself. The ball of white light bloomed before him, illuminating the cave.

"Dey don't know," he said to the hazua, and with that it vanished with a muted *pop*.

Etcher stood by the door and stared at the woman on the narrow couch. She allowed time to pool in the stillness between them, the tendrils of her heightened senses pouring over the room, over the woman, over the essence of another soul waiting out of sight.

"Won't you sit?" said the woman, a strange drifting quality to her voice prickling at Etcher's curiosities.

The little shopkeeper wandered over to the hearth, her footsteps slow and deliberate. She faced the fire, clasped her hands behind her back, and spoke without looking at the woman clad in the slinky black dress.

"There was a moment when I actually worried myself over who and what you might be. And now I find you're nothing more than a *magpie*. Isn't that right, Frihey? And I suppose I should find your name clever?"

The woman's heavy gaze dredged its way upward to look at the back of Etcher's head. "I didn't choose it."

Etcher chuffed.

"To angelous, all corvus are ravens," the witch added.

"So you were with the angels then?" Etcher clucked her tongue. "I suppose the rest of your siblings are up there still? You know I have a great distaste for magpies. I hate your kind with every fiber of my being. And yet, I cannot summon a hatred of you. Now why is that?"

Etcher turned to meet the weighty gaze of the woman, and the clash of their mutual heaviness might have cowed any onlookers, but there was kinship between them and neither felt the dreadful density that another surely would.

"You don't remember," said Lupine Blackfeather as point of fact.

"And what is it that I don't remember?"

The woman took in a great breath, pulling deeply from her internal reservoirs. "We were friends, you and I, in the Time before Time."

"Oh? Well, that's a curious thing, since I wasn't alive then."

"In a way you weren't, you were different before. You became something new."

Etcher watched the woman carefully, a spiral of thoughts whirling inside the little shopkeeper's head, until she made one vital decision.

Etcher conjured a crystal cut carafe filled with a dark liquid, and poured out a liberal helping into a glass, handed it to the woman, then poured another for herself and set the carafe on the table between them. She sipped her drink and sat down in the nearby armchair. "So what happened?"

The woman drank from her glass slowly, biding her time as he rekindled her will to speak. In the moments of silence the witch's apathy seemed to grow, as did the cold and quiet anger. Whatever had happened to mar her so had been pushed down into her very core until it could go no further. She oozed with a dark resentment directed at something far, far away. And every word she spoke sought to break that moment, tried to shake loose the binds that kept her darkness held so firmly at her core. "The Etcher before was different, and after the Dawn you became you," she said finally.

"My first memories were of the Dawn, I believed I had awoken then."

"That's true enough."

"But you say I came before. I was there, when all the others were created?"

The woman nodded.

"Well that's quite a thing to claim. So do you know why I hate magpies?"

The woman nodded again.

"And will you tell me?"

There was a pause, and the woman looked to the fire. "It's easier if I show you."

Etcher raised an inquisitive eyebrow as the witch slipped from the couch and stood before her, offering a pale hand.

"Please," she said, looking more worn with every syllable.

Etcher inhaled through her nose and set down her glass, tapping her fingers against the arm of the chair as she considered Lupine. "All right, show me." And when their hands connected everything was bathed in white.

For a moment Etcher could only see that blinding whiteness, and then slowly the world around her developed like an image bleeding through film.

A serene daytime landscape took form, there were lots of tall shade-giving trees and elegant weeping willows—their long wispy fronds swaying delicately in the breeze. Thick grass blanketed the ground and the gentle rolling hillsides which flanked Etcher; a picnic paradise.

And as birds twittered and the sun kissed the world with a comforting warmth, Etcher's eyes were drawn immediately to the trio nestled near the base of a fine old oak.

"Who is *that?*" said Etcher, and there was a touch of accusation in her tone.

Lupine Blackfeather stood beside her and seemed so much more elated than before. "That is us, in the Time before Time," she spoke with ease, and then she pointed to the smallest of the three. "That was you, *Etcher Prior* if you like."

Etcher's double was laying on the grass, her head resting in someone's lap, a cheeky smile across her face and a more genuine kind of aloofness than to the calculating Etcher of present, the double even wore a tartan summer dress.

"Not her, I mean *him.*" Etcher pointed at the young man that Etcher Prior was cozied up to.

"That was Sünhey, my brother," said Lupine of the youth who was Jerro's double.

"Gin!" proclaimed Mr. Gribs, laying down his cards triumphantly.

Tahli huffed through her nose and Jerro groaned.

"Can we play something else? I'm tired of losing," said Jerro.

The smile fell from Mr. Gribs face. "What would you prefer?"

"I dunno, poker? Black Jack? *Or maybe nothing,*" he muttered the latter, resting his head back in the chair to stare up at the ceiling.

Mr. Gribs started to fiddle nervously with the straps of his satchels as Jerro made both his boredom and frustration evident. "P-perhaps we could talk about something, help pass the time? You seem well since last I saw you— how've you been?" said Mr. Gribs with a meek smile.

Jerro eyed the toad. "Yeah, why don't we talk? What happened after I last saw you, *exactly?*"

The portly nightmare stammered for a moment. "W-well, I, um…" He paused and coughed, then grabbed his tea and drained his glass. "Got dismissed you see, and, um, decided on a holiday…and, well, ended up here…"

"Got *dismissed?*"

"Y-yes," said Mr. Gribs as he fiddled fervently. "His Majesty was none too pleased that I returned without Miss Everdoor…and what happened to Arcadia…"

"Yeah, I bet."

Mr. Gribs gulped and got up from his chair. "W-why don't I bring us some more refreshments?" Apparently talking hadn't been such a good idea.

"Why don't you sit down? I'm curious to hear your side of what happened in Arcadia," insisted Jerro, eyeing the toad disdainfully.

"Uh, um—" But Mr. Gribs didn't get much further than that. The doors opened and out Etcher strode, bringing both Jerro and Tahli to their feet.

There was a serious look on Etcher's face as she beckoned Jerro over. "She wants to talk to you," she said.

Jerro remained where he stood, rooted with apprehension, and all the vinegar he had mustered at the little toad had drained away from him. "Are you sure it's safe?" he found himself asking, the stern countenance of the shopkeeper had put him ill at ease.

"It's safe," she replied, and stood aside from the door to let Jerro pass, and the way she gestured him over made it clear the topic wasn't up for discussion.

Jerro hesitated forward, casting a weary glance at Etcher before he entered the dimly lit room.

Etcher closed the door after him and turned to the other two. "Mr. Gribs, if you would excuse us, I need a word with Tahli."

"Y-yes of course," said Mr. Gribs, eager to get away.

Once the toad had left and only Etcher and Tahli remained in the room, the little shopkeeper let out a heavy sigh. Her demeanor lost its rigidness as she walked over to the couch where Tahli had been seated and let herself down. "Sit with me, will you?" she asked.

The ginger cat-woman did so, looking thoughtful and curious.

Etcher slipped one leg over the other and conjured a stiff drink in her hand. "Tahli," she said.

"Yes?" replied Tahli.

Etcher sipped and stared off at the wall, tapping a finely groomed nail against the stout crystal glass in her hand. "I know that things have been less than ideal this past week—"

The ginger cat-woman *harrumphed.*

"All right, the past *few* weeks, and I regret to inform you that it's not looking like it'll be getting better any time soon."

"*What* does that mean?" asked Tahli.

"Well, things have got a lot more complicated than I particularly like. I know you're not happy with Jerro, and I've a few things to show you that probably won't change your opinion of him for the better." Etcher extended her hand to Tahli, palm softly aglow. "You remember Bagohven?"

Tahli crossed her arms and cocked her jaw. "What mess are we in now?"

"A big one, Tahli," said Etcher, her hand still extended and glowing. "It's worse than Bagohven."

Tahli squeezed her eyes shut and breathed out an irritated breath. "You owe me, Everdoor."

"Yes, to the moons and back, agreed."

"I told you he was trouble!"

"Yes, you were very right Tahli, but it turns out there was no avoiding it this time."

"Ah! So you admit the other times *were* avoidable?"

An impish smile curled into Etcher's face. "Well, I dare say I have a knack for seeking trouble out."

"And dragging *me* into it."

"I did warn you before you took the job."

Tahli huffed and slipped her hand into Etcher's. "You should have warned me better."

Jerro stood in the fire lit room, staring at the tall, elegant woman before him.

There was something about her face—something strangely familiar in the shape of her cheekbones, the ridge of her brow, the contours of her lips—that made Jerro feel as though he were staring into a more elegant version of his own countenance. And the sadness behind her cold eyes, that subtle rigidness to her expression of a relative long forgotten made Jerro feel guilty for not knowing her.

She moved forward with graceful steps, gliding almost, and Jerro's breath hitched, his muscles tense. There was a quiet and deadly power coiled within that vivacious body, and the guilt he felt was replaced with a shuddering chill.

"Don't be afraid," she said softly.

His jaw flexed. *Easier said than done,* he thought.

She reached out a dainty hand and gently touched the side of his face. "The slithes are coming for you to awaken their god. Your body is the vessel." There was a strange airiness to her speech, like memories whispering to Jerro from the recesses of his mind.

"What do you mean? Why me?"

"Reborn," she breathed out.

"Because I'm a reborn?"

She nodded.

"Okay, so how do we stop them?"

But the woman was shaking her head. "You don't."

"Well what am I supposed to do then?"

The woman stared at him for a moment. Her dark molasses eyes looking deep inside him. "Make the sacrifice."

"I don't understand...I—"

But the woman slipped her hand away from him as she turned and walked toward the shadows.

"You can come out now," was the last thing she said before she disappeared.

"Huh?" said Jerro.

There was another door in the room that creaked open and out came Mahra.

Mahra hadn't heard much from the other side of the door, but she did distinctly *feel* as much as hear Lupine Blackfeather's voice telling her to come out. And so she did. Of course, she wasn't prepared for who was waiting for her.

There Jerro stood in the middle of the fire lit room, gawking in bewilderment at her.

She realized in that instant that the love bug still had its jaws firmly clamped upon her arse, because at the very sight of him her heart began to flutter.

Damn it, Mahra! she chided herself. But he was oh so nice to look at, and a year of quiet longing was a hard thing to snuff out. Yes, in the back of her mind she could still remember those awful sounds, and yes, there was a strange squirming mixture of feelings when she considered him, but despite all that she just couldn't help herself; she was still head over heels for the gaping fool.

"Hi," she said meekly, and grimaced. *So much for New-and-Improved Mahra,* she thought.

He kept on staring at her, his mouth hanging open in blatant shock.

"Um, okay…I guess this is a little weird, but, um, it is me. The real me—not that *thing*." She looked down at her shoes and remembered what she was wearing. The high boots and tight trousers, the revealing top and all that lay beneath. She squared her shoulders and looked at him a little more fiercely.

"If you don't believe me, your friend should know, right? Etcher? You told me she could sense these things." She was having difficulty holding onto the more dominant version of herself and she prayed Jerro would say something soon lest she crumble back into her usual meekness.

"Mahra?" Jerro said finally, checking her up and down with a cautious eye. "How did you get here?"

"Mr. Gribs brought me, and Lupine cured me."

"*Lupine?*"

"The witch, that's her name." Mahra coughed, feeling her throat start to clam up as her nervousness vibrated through her.

"It's really you…"

"Yep…" She tried to smile, and felt it hang awkwardly on her face. *Oh god, please stop staring at me like I'm an alien!* "So, here I am. This is all a bit different, ay?—*Ahk!*"

Jerro accosted her with a tight embrace. "You're okay."

Once the initial shock wore off, she melted into that warm hug. It was lovely, even if he did smell a little like a bog. "I'm okay," she agreed, and was indeed feeling very okay in his arms

He kept on holding her, and she nestled into him, feeling for the first time in what felt like forever, safe and comfortable. But as much as she wished to stay cuddled up to him, there were things they needed to talk about, things that couldn't wait.

She pulled away ever so slightly and looked him in the eyes. "Jerro," she said, and she could see the cringing guilt twisting into his face. They both knew about the thing that hung in the air between them, and neither of them were eager to talk about it. "Thank you for saving me."

The tightness eased in Jerro's expression at that. "I'm sorry I wasn't there sooner, I didn't know…"

"I wish you had been there sooner, too, but I know it's not your fault." And again the heaviness started to weigh down on both of them and Mahra knew the awful thing needed to be dealt with sooner or later. "I'm not mad at you, you know."

Jerro looked away as the cringing guilt returned. "Mahra—"

"Jerro, it's okay, well, it's not *really* okay. It was a bad thing that happened…"

"I know Mahra, I'm sorry—"

"Just, let me finish, please?"

"Yeah, sorry."

Mahra breathed in deep and forced herself to face him. "I'm not okay with what happened, but I don't blame you…and, well, in a weird sort of way it's kind of flattering that you liked me so much to, well—do *that*." She felt the awkward squirminess of the topic afflict her, trying to fizzle out her words. "God that sounded less cringing in my head. Look, I don't know how you still feel about me, I'm not entirely sure how I feel about you either to be honest, but maybe we could start again? Can we try and be friends and just see how that goes?"

"Of course, Mahra. I *do* still like you—I'm…sorry about what happened. It doesn't feel good for me either, I wish I could take it back."

"Me too." She sighed, then shrugged at him. "So…friends?"

"Friends." He smiled back.

The air was slowly clearing between them. It wasn't perfect, but Mahra was feeling lighter now that they had at least broached the dreaded subject. And now that things *were* clearing she found that she was blushing as she looked up at him, and he was smiling back a little too eagerly. Still entangled in his arms, a tingling heat spread throughout Mahra's body and made her breath short and her heart quicken.

"I, ah, like your new look by the way," she said, reaching up to touch the gold hoop in Jerro's ear while simultaneously untangling herself from him. She was trying very hard not to look as flustered as she actually felt; it was getting awful hot in that room and not because of the fire in the hearth.

"This?" he replied, reaching for the earring too as if he had forgotten about it. "You know, I think you're the first person to actually notice. I'm glad you like it."

The heat was continuing to rise, and Mahra could feel the giddiness bubbling inside her threatening to spill out and make her do something impetuous and stupid. "It suits you. Um, so ah, your friends are here, aren't they? Were you going to introduce me?"

"Yeah, right—they're out in the other room," he said with his boyish smile, and his eyes lingered on her for a heart-skipping moment before he finally led her towards the door.

"This is a mess."

"It really is."

"No, Everdoor, I mean it, this is a *real* mess! What are we going to do?"

"Tahli, we do the best we can."

The cat-woman hissed. "And when that falls on its face, then what?"

"Tahli, please, you saw for yourself, there's no way around this. If I hadn't been there—if the slithe had got him—there would be no here and now for you to be mad at me."

"That is hardly a comfort."

"Well, look, we can't do much without the shop. I'm too handicapped without it and risking another jump would be dangerous. So, first things first, I'll get the shop, then…well, we'll just have to see."

"Everdoor!"

"What do you want me to say, Tahli? Most of our library is in the shop. If we've any hope of figuring this out, there may be an answer there, otherwise…"

"Otherwise, what?"

"I'll need to talk to my father."

Both of them went a little cold at the mention.

"You still do not know what is in Leona Mesa?" asked Tahli cautiously.

"I know what's there, I just don't know why he's sending me to it. I suppose I'll find out since the shop is in that general heading to begin with. Perhaps I'll find some answers."

"I pray you do. And what about Ahliss? What do we tell him?"

Etcher drained the rest of her glass and stared off. "Nothing about Sünhey—if we can avoid it—at least nothing involving the parts about Sünhey and the old me. But he'll need to know something, enough to understand why the slithes are after him and the gravity of the mess we're now in."

"Wonderful." Tahli huffed. "Why does it have to be you? Why is it always *you*, Everdoor? Could it not be someone else for a change?"

"Well, m'dear, because they'd bugger it up."

"Do not look so smug about it."

Etcher kept on smirking anyway. "Oh, come now, Tahli. You wanted a life of excitement when you joined on."

"*This* is not excitement. This is peril, grave peril!"

"Yes, but it is a little exciting too, don't you think?"

"I am not immortal!"

"I won't let anything happen to you."

"Peh."

"I haven't yet."

Tahli folded her arms and looked away, her chin held high and disdainfully.

"You know, I like you better when you're a cat, at least you don't disagree with me as much then."

Tahli turned a harsh emerald eye on Etcher. "I am not your pet."

"True, but you're a very lovely cat when you are one."

The ginger cat-woman crossed her legs and bent down to help herself to a small tea cake from the platter Mr. Gribs had brought in earlier, occupying herself with eating it and ignoring the little shopkeeper as best she could.

"Look lively, they're coming out," said Etcher.

On cue the door opened and out came Jerro and Mahra.

"Ah, Miss Lapaul, I trust you're feeling better?" said Etcher.

"Wait, you *knew* about this?"

"Lupine explained what happened, Jerro, I wasn't keeping secrets from you, it just seemed better you saw for yourself."

"Oh," he said, taking pause to quell the argument that was building on his tongue. "Okay…right, well, um, Mahra, this is Etcher and Tahli."

"Hi." Mahra gulped and realized with mounting dread that Jerro had been a bit too vague on the details when he had told her about his new friends. The tall curvy ginger cat-woman was intimidating enough—all hips and fur and nakedness—but it was the little shopkeeper that made Mahra nervous in ways that brought all the insecurities to the forefront of her mind. There was a quiet and deadly self-assurance that pulsed steadily within Etcher's stately poise, leaving Mahra to feel terrifyingly inadequate.

"Would you care for some tea, Miss Lapaul? Perhaps we might sit down for a moment and discuss our next course of action," said Etcher.

Tahli made an audible sound of discontent and rolled her eyes. "What is there to discuss? We need to get the shop."

"Oh be polite, won't you? A moment of patience would be appropriate, don't you think?" Etcher and Tahli looked at each other then, a volume of words transpired silently between them.

Tahli relented and went back to nibbling on a tea cake.

"I don't want to hold things up," started Mahra with an apologetic smile.

"Nonsense, Miss Lapaul, take a moment with us, won't you?"

Mahra's smile was quickly turning into a grimace. She felt trapped, standing there before those two imposing women—before Etcher's golden gaze that watched her so closely. She might have stayed rooted where she was had Jerro not taken her gently by the hand and led her forward. She sat with him and waited, feeling the tension build around their motley crew.

"Now then,"—said Etcher—"has Jerro got you up to speed on what's been going on?"

"More or less,"

"I imagine this is all quite a bit to take in, but please do try and keep up. There is some urgency to our predicament."

"*Some?*"

"Tahli," Etcher warned.

The cat-woman scoffed.

"At the moment, we can't get you back home, Miss Lapaul—"

"Please, call me Mahra."

"*Mahra,*" Etcher corrected. "The thing is, even if we could get you back, I wouldn't advise it, not now. The slithe might try and use you again and I'd rather not place you back in that situation. That being said, Tahli is right that we do need the shop back, do you understand the significance of the shop?"

"Jerro told me."

"I figured he would, despite that he was expressly told not to reveal those secrets to anyone."

Jerro—who had been picking through the remaining cakes and biscuits—had suddenly found the urge to gather up his teacup and hide his face inside it.

"I'll forgive it, given the circumstance. However, you, Mahra, cannot tell anyone these things you've been told. It would not only garner you unwanted attention, it would likely put you back in danger, is that understood?"

Mahra gave a quiet nod.

"Good. So, for the time being, you will be joining our little group until we can safely return you home. I had packed some things for you—clothes and the like—but unfortunately they're in the shop."

"Can I say something?" asked Jerro.

"Go on."

"How exactly are we going to deal with the slithes? The witch—*Lupine*—told me why they were after me, something about their god?"

"*Ah.*"

"'*Ah?*'"

"Jerro—"

"No, Etcher, this is serious! What was she talking about? What did *you* talk about for that matter?"

Etcher drained the liquor from her glass and conjured herself another helping, her tail twisting with agitation. She took a long hard look at Jerro until he started to squirm under her gaze.

"All right fine. Here it is: the slithes want to use you to awaken Abaddon, God of Destruction, to bring an end to everything. I have no idea how to stop it, the only thing I do know is that we need the shop first and foremost. I have a library there that may have answers, and failing that we will have to look elsewhere for some plan of action. But that's it, that's as far as I know what to do. The shop is in Death, so I will go and get it. All of you will stay here—"

"What? No!" Both Tahli and Jerro rose their oppositions in a cacophony of complaints.

"Enough, both of you! Look, the shop is in Death, you can't come with me."

"*I* could."

"No, Jerro, that's a monumentally bad idea."

"I have to agree with Ahliss on this one."

"Oh not you too, Tahli?" Etcher groaned. "And why do you think *that's* a good idea?"

"Because last time you left, you lost the shop and barely made it back."

"Tahli's right," chimed in Jerro

"You know what? I liked it better when you two were at each other's throats. This is not a topic up for discussion. You are *safe* here in Lupine's house."

"Safe? How? I thought you said the Raven Witch—"

"I know what I said, Jerro. It turns out we're old friends."

"Oh, really? How convenient. And you didn't know this because?"

"It's complicated, she changed her name. She wasn't the Raven Witch when I knew her."

"Etcher, we're not staying here!" insisted Jerro.

"Ahliss is right," purred Tahli. "I will not be left behind again."

"Really, Tahli? And how do you plan on following me into Death, exactly?"

"I can follow you to the gate. You will go through Dream, will you not? That is why that little toad is here."

"Mr. Gribs?" asked Jerro. "Did you plan this Etcher? Kinda funny how he showed up here as well as back in Undercity. You sure you're not friends, too? Or did he also have a name change?"

"Both of you BE QUIET!" Etcher snapped, and a sudden and terrifying silence descended in the room.

The little shopkeeper sipped her bourbon and drummed her fingers on the backrest of the couch. She let the silence hang in the air for a great long while as she started off at nothing and let her temper cool off.

Mahra kept her eyes down, Jerro sipped from an empty cup, and Tahli's coat bristled as she fidgeted with her nails.

"The shop is the first priority," began Etcher calmly once again. "But Jerro, coming with me into Death is dangerous, and besides which, you may not be able to handle it. Remember the poltergeists in Undercity? Imagine how you'll feel in the land of the Dead? *Billions* of souls around, how well do you think you'll cope?"

"I can manage it."

"You don't honestly know that, and neither do I."

"Etcher, you can't leave us behind again, *please!*" Jerro begged.

"You will be putting yourself in tremendous danger," retorted Etcher.

"And you wouldn't be? You said you were banished, what if you get caught? Aren't there guards or something?"

"Ahliss has a p—"

"Don't you say it, Tahli," warned Etcher, and she raised her finger to silence the feline. "I find this plan foolhardy—I can feel you rolling your eyes, Tahli, don't start."

"Why not? As if your plans are always perfect? As if you do not run into the fire?"

"Tahli, of all the times you choose to side with Jerro, you had to pick this one?"

"You *owe* me, Everdoor."

"Unbelievable," said Etcher.

"Ahliss will go with you to get the shop, and we will wait in Dream on the other side of the gate."

"'*We*?'" said Etcher.

"The girl is not staying here," said Tahli. "That would be *rude.*"

"You're impossible, the both of you. Your united front is my anguish." Etcher huffed. "Well, Mahra, since I can't talk sense to them, what do you think?"

"M-me?" Suddenly all eyes were on Mahra, and suddenly she wished the ground would open up and swallow her.

"Yes, you. You've an outside eye on this calamity, what's your take on it?"

"Well—I, um…I don't want to stay here either." She dropped her eyes quickly to her shoes.

"Then it's settled!" said Jerro with a victorious grin.

"…Although I don't think it's safe for you to go with Etcher," Mahra added in a quiet voice.

And Jerro's grin fell immediately.

"Look, don't get me wrong, I don't really understand what's happening. But, well, you're probably right, Etcher—that Jerro shouldn't go with you—but I think if you leave him behind he'll just get into trouble," she managed to blurt out, and then firmly clamped her lips shut.

Jerro stared at Mahra incredulously.

"Ha!" Etcher chortled. "Well at least that's a valid argument."

"What, really?" said a bewildered Jerro.

Etcher rubbed her temples with one hand and nursed her drink in the other. "Yes, really. Mahra raises a very good point."

"And I did not?" snapped Tahli.

Etcher shot the feline a look.

"Hey, you know, I'm not a complete idiot, I can stay out of trouble," said Jerro, though his tone was unconvincing.

"No you can't, you're as bad as I am," sighed Etcher. "Trouble flocks to you like a moth to a bonfire."

Jerro folded his arms and glared at Tahli as the feline quietly laughed to herself.

Etcher drummed her fingers against the backrest of the couch, shaking her head quietly and peering into the dark liquid in her glass as she swirled it. "For the record, I was against this plan." She looked at them both. "But all right, we'll have Mr. Gribs take us to Dream. You and Mahra, and I suppose Mr. Gribs, will stay near the gate, and Jerro and I will go into Death in search of the shop."

Victory was beginning to radiate through Jerro's face once again, although the knot of his thoughts twisted apprehension into his brow and curled down his lips. "So, wait, just so we're clear, the slithes really are after me to awaken the God of Destruction?" he asked.

"Yes," replied Etcher.

"So then, that night back at my work—that was them setting me up? They were going to take me?"

"Yes, on both accounts."

"Etcher, if you hadn't of been there—*ow!*"

"What's wrong?" said Mahra.

"My hand." Jerro flexed his right palm and saw his contract with the little shopkeeper light up and then shatter, and finally fade away.

"Our deal, it's done."

Jerro looked up at Etcher fearfully. "But, wait—"

"Don't worry about it. It's just our deal that's done, nothing else has changed."

For a moment there was relief on Jerro's face, but the fear hadn't fully dissipated. He rubbed his now naked palm and frowned with the weight of this thoughts.

Etcher finished the last of her drink and rose to her feet. "Suppose we should push on then. Mr. Gribs!" she called.

The portly nightmare poked his head through the open doors. "Y-yes?"

"Passage for four into Dream, if you will?"

Mr. Gribs smiled grimly and turned a ghastly shade of green. "Oh…right, o-of course, Miss Everdoor.

CHAUNCY FELISZ

Dream & Death...

W as it you who died, or me? The things that were can never be again, my younger days are gone, and you with them.

You feel dead, but so do I. Did I expire, is it why I feel so hollow around you? When I see you, you're like the echo of a memory that can never be. We've become so distant, so different you and I, and I wonder if we ever truly knew one another. Did we ever take the time?

Could I have understood you with all your complexities with my young mind when we were together? Could you understand me now that I am so foreign from the little girl you'll always see?

I love you father. But you are gone, gone because I left, and our changes will tear us apart if I stay. Because I am not the little girl anymore, and you were absent during my growing and cannot see the person I now am...and I cannot see you other than how I knew you. I cannot see you for the person that you are—only the guise of a father I never truly dared to question, the mask of a face I dare not stare too deeply into.

Who are we anymore? Where is my dad? Where is the girl? Did such a time before this ever exist? And if so, how do I get back to it? Tell me, father, how do I get home? I love you father, but you are gone, and I am gone too.

—Pages from Letters Unsent

Etcher stood outside of the sprawling house, leaning up against the brick façade bathed in lamp light as she looked up into the gnarled faces of the encircling trees. Though she had agreed to their plan, she wasn't happy with it. She would have rather gone it alone into Death, it would have been easier.

She had taken a quiet moment to herself to organize the whirl of her thoughts. The things she now knew painted the bigger picture with horrifying clarity, all that was missing was how to stop the impending doom. Those missing fragments gnawed at her.

In another life she had known, she had been there when it had all started, and she had played a part in stopping it. But the Etcher of here and now was a brand new person, and the Etcher that came before was foreign to her. There were no sparks of revelation, no hidden memories or déjà vu when Lupine showed her own account of what had happened in the Time before Time. But Lupine hadn't been there when the Etcher of before and Sünhey did—whatever it was they did—to stop the dark god. There was nothing to show, and the vital piece remained blank.

However it had happened, whatever was done, Etcher Prior had been severed from the Etcher of now right after the dark god had been sealed away; all that remained were the echo of feelings—the kinship to Lupine, the burning hatred of the other magpies, and, she supposed, her affinity for Jerro. Those were the only remnants of who she was, and when she thought of her prior self, she felt much as she would for a dear friend who had been lost. They were two different people, Etcher Prior and the Etcher of now, but they were bonded through time.

She felt that she cared about Etcher Prior and what had happened to her, even if she didn't fully know what that entailed. Perhaps Etcher Prior had known what would happen. Had she sacrificed herself so that the Etcher of now could go on?

The little shopkeeper sighed.

She had felt the threads of Fate pulling together the very night she met Jerro, and all that had happened thereafter seemed to resonate with a higher purpose, but it was draining all the same.

Etcher had little responsibilities, save for those few that she chose to uphold. She was free to come and go as she pleased, to do what she liked, dine where she fancied, travel and explore, spend without fear of poverty. How tiresome it was to be so relied upon, to have so many people's needs thrust upon her. For the longest time, there had been only her and Tahli, and the feline was self-sufficient enough and needed little from Etcher besides an open purse, and the occasional insight into the cryptic little shopkeeper's mind.

Sure, the ginger cat-woman would nag and pry, but they had an understanding, there was balance between them, and most of Tahli's complaints were simply hot air. In the end, Tahli seldom stood in Etcher's way.

But Jerro needed answers. Jerro needed to be watched, and taught, and shown. He needed looking after, he was unpredictable and often irrational. He hurried in without a second thought, he let his emotions roll him over and take the reins. He was like a fire that needed constant tending lest he burn the whole house down. And even as she thought this, Etcher was smirking to herself. What a pain he was, but how much fun all the same. Etcher enjoyed his company, even if his very existence might doom them all, and she felt a deep rooted need to watch out for him. She felt that she owed Etcher Prior as much.

Her senses pinged, and she knew her motley crew were approaching. The door beside her opened and out they came, headed by a very nervous Mr. Gribs.

"Ah! Miss Everdoor, I've found what I was looking for. Miss Blackfeather was kind enough to point me in the right direction. There's a cave not too far from here, it should have the deepest darkness I need in order for me to take all four of you into Dream."

"Very good, Mr. Gribs. Lead the way," said Etcher. She did not stop to speak with the others or make eye contact, there was still much on her mind and she needed whatever quiet she could salvage to steel herself. They'd have plenty of questions and complaints soon enough.

They traveled through Darcwood in relative silence, leaving the firmer ground and less offensive air of Lupine's inner sanctum for the boggy muck they had traversed earlier. It was Mr. Gribs that spoke the most, giving a few words here or there at intervals whenever he saw some noteworthy patch of flora he wished to point out to the others—as if he were their tour guide.

It wasn't long before they came upon the dark, hungry mouth of the cave. The air that sighed out of its wide gape was no less pungent than the muggy air they had already been breathing, and there was an earthen wetness and heavy algae scent that made the cave all the more uninviting.

"So, how's this gonna work exactly?" asked Jerro. He had been keeping close to Mahra during their journey with his little hazua lighting their way and had said nothing the entire trek until the sight of the grim cave mouth bared down on them.

"Well, we'll all need to link hands. Tightly, mind you! It must be tight. I suppose I'll be holding Miss Everdoor's hand," and at that Mr. Gribs turned a horrid shade of pink, "Miss Everdoor will hold Miss Tahli's hand and so on."

"Do we need to do anything else? Like say a spell, or…?" it was Mahra that spoke, and she seemed fidgety and uncertain as she did.

"Oh no, Miss Mahra, not for this kind of *majik*. Just hold on tightly and follow forward. I'll be leading you all through the shadows into Dream. Erm, Mr. Ahliss, I'll have to ask you to dismiss your hazua, it needs to totally dark for this to work."

Jerro waved away the winged messenger and instantly the oppressive darkness of faux night descended upon them. There was only enough dim lunar light stealing its way past the canopy to give the group any sense of form.

Mr. Gribs nodded. "Right, well—as I transition us from Waking to Dream I dare say the scenery will change quite dramatically. You'll feel a strange *shifting*, you'll understand when you go through it. Then things will solidify once we're safely on the other side. Just keep hold until then," said Mr. Gribs.

"Well, into the black we go. Lead on Mr. Gribs," hurried Etcher. The little shopkeeper took the toad's pudgy hand in hers—which startled Mr. Gribs—

and held out her other hand for Tahli, and down the chain they went until they were all connected.

Finally, they marched forward.

As they ventured into the cave, a complete darkness blanketed them. Of course, the dark was of little hindrance to Mr. Gribs, Etcher, and Tahli—who could all see well enough in the blackness to avoid the dips and crags and rough cave walls. It was Jerro and Mahra that were left stumbling about, nearly pulling down the entire chain were it not for Tahli's firm and forceful grip. And the deeper they went, and the more uncertain the terrain became, the more Mahra held on for dear life to Jerro, and Jerro in turn, held onto Tahli as firmly as the cat-woman held back—which was fueled by more than just a little spite.

Then the shifting happened. It was a disorienting feeling—like being caught under a wave and rolled in a riptide. There was a sense that the ground was still beneath their feet, but it was as if that same ground rolled with them as gravity lurched and everything whirled. The blackness became streaked with light, twisting and pulling until color began to branch out around them, blooming like streaks of lightning.

And finally, the blackness melted away, and the world came into a hazy focus, slow to settle after the spinning, shifting, whirling transition from Waking into Dream. It was the sudden change in brightness and color that took a while to register. They had come from the bleak and pungent dark into a sudden vibrant world, warmed by the hot pink and soft-orange glow of a dawn lit horizon. Child laughter and wind chimes echoed from the distance, the skies were stunningly blue and painted with gilded clouds. Strange songbirds left watercolor trails behind them as they flew, floating isles populated the skies above them, glittering lights faded in and out around them like hazua messengers, and the world brimmed with a sense of effervescent elation.

"Wow," uttered Mahra quietly. She was not alone in her awe, as Jerro stared just as wide-eyed at the new world surrounding them.

They had been brought to a meadow, where lush grass was sprinkled with dainty little wildflowers. A calming breeze swam through the open plain, turning the meadow into an undulating sea of green. A halo of thick evergreens and weeping willows encircled the meadow from a distance, and the sound of far off chimes infused with laughter and bird songs accented the world's ethereal nature.

Mr. Gribs cleared his throat audibly and fidgeted with his satchels. "We've arrived, as promised—erm, if there's nothing else—"

"Actually, Mr. Gribs, you'll be staying with Tahli and Mahra. Don't think you've escaped your leash so easily," said Etcher.

"O-oh. I see."

"Don't worry, Mr. Gribs. Once we have the shop, you'll be free to do as you like. You could even go back to your holiday."

"Wait, where's this gate supposed to be?" Jerro had broken free from the allure of the vibrant world and suddenly looked serious.

"It's a bit further away from here. But there are some things we need to go over before striding up to Death's gate. First things first, we'll need accommodations," replied Etcher.

"Okay, but I don't see anywhere—"

"Just watch, Jerro." Etcher broke away from the group and sized up a piece of open land. She scrutinized the grass plains before her, walking in a careful circle as though she were stalking prey. Then she stopped, her palms began to glow, and with a forceful strike she thrust her hand high into the air and the ground shuddered before her. Up sprang a cabin, filling in the empty spot she had been surveying.

The others stumbled back as the large wooden house suddenly jumped up before them. The cabin seemed to stretch out before it settled, taking up a good chunk of the open meadow as it nestled in. It was an accommodation fit for far more than just their small group, with big double-doors and wide stone steps leading up to the spacious porch. The cabin ended up being at least three generous stories high, if you included the attic.

One of the many stone chimneys was smoking gently, and the polished windows gleamed pink in the dawn of morning light, giving a dreamy edge to the log house. It was a picturesque sight—like it had been pulled from an oil painting—with the evergreens as its backdrop and the beautiful blue sky above. The richness of the wood's lacquer made the cabin's silhouette stand boldly against the soft colors of the meadow.

"How?" Jerro was at a loss for words and his mouth hung wide-open with surprise.

"This is Dream, a place of raw creation. Though before you get any ideas, it takes a considerable amount of practice to do what I just did," said Etcher.

"It's incredible!" said Mahra, full of naked awe.

Etcher was a touch amused by the girl's praise, and a small smile crept into the little shopkeeper's steely countenance. "Dream served me well as I prototyped my initial designs for the shop, before I came to its final rendition."

"You came here with your dad, you mean?" asked Jerro, his faculties returning and the bewilderment slowly fading from his slack-jawed expression.

"Yes." Etcher made a noise like a cough, which was in no small way a dismissal of the topic. "Well, go on, I didn't make the cabin just to look at."

The others were snapped out of their reverie and on command began to filter in up the wide steps and towards the main doors as Etcher stood aside and watched. She remained outside even as Mr. Gribs ascended the stairs at the tail end of the group—he looked back at her nervously.

Etcher stared at the toad sidelong. "Mr. Gribs, there is a pantry in the downstairs kitchen. If you would be so kind as to bring out a light lunch for everyone, I would appreciate it. Help yourself to whatever you like as well."

"Y-yes, Miss Everdoor," replied Mr. Gribs with a croak and he hurried inside.

The little shopkeeper stood there, in the meadow, surveying the tree line, the brilliant sky, the songbirds and the floating isles. There was weariness in her eyes in that quiet moment, and something close to lament. She thought about her father then and felt a pang of guilt inside her. How long had it been since she'd seen him? How long since she'd written? She'd lost count of the days, the years. It was a funny thing to lie about—to let the others think she suffered a classic case of the absent father—but it wasn't that at all.

She was the absent daughter. She had been the one that left.

"Ah, Holixben, I see you've arrived again."

"Again?" replied the sky-blue dragon in its deep rumbling resonance.

"Yes, again. This would be the six-hundred-and-twenty-fourth time, to be precise," said the winter-haired Traveler as he closed his leather journal and looked out toward the Bloodlands. His long elven ears were flicked up in contemplation—much like the dragon's own.

"So many times, are you not tired of it?"

"I suppose I might be, but this is one of my favorite hours. The day never looked as perfect as this again, and of course, you are my favorite dragon. You don't know it now, but you help sire a new race of dragonkind. Your blue vohrans and the mountain griffins will give birth to the *Holigiffs*, a wise and gentle race as ever there was."

"Hmm, and what will happen to the vohran?"

"Oh, you survive, but your red brothers of the north will not approve of your new offspring."

"They are rigid, it will be their downfall."

"Perhaps it might," agreed the Traveler, and he noted the glint in the great blue dragon's eye as the colossal beast looked down the mountain range. "Go get your hunt, Holixben, I hope we will meet each other again someday, out in the Waking world."

"If you wish it, we will." And with that the dragon took off, diving down the mountainside and catching itself on the upward winds.

The Traveler smiled softly to himself. "Perhaps a change is in order." He looked to the sunrise and sighed, enjoying the memory one last time. Then the world around him started to dim and fade, and as it dimmed, the shapes lost their forms, melting into shadows and then into flatness until the Traveler was alone in a dark room. He could feel his body back as he had left it in his jail cell, sitting upon the cold hard floor.

He eased his eyes open to the blinding white that surrounded him in his cylindrical prison. No adornments here, no beautiful horizon, no dragon friend—only a blank slate surrounded him, save for the door with the little porthole.

The bearded man got to his feet gracefully, and when he stood his full height he seemed almost regal with his barrel chest, his thick arms and sturdy legs. He lifted his leather hat to run a hand through his wintered mane, composing himself before he walked up to the chamber door and tapped his knuckles on the porthole. "I'd like a word with whoever's in charge."

Outside, the two guards who had been playing with their dice and gambling their coins did not register the knocking right away, and the old man's voice did not carry beyond the thick steel door. But upon chancing an upward glance, one of the guards did notice the man smiling at them through the porthole, and with a start, the guard knocked over the barrel they'd been using as a table.

"Oi!" yelled the other.

"Look you fool!"

The Traveler waved at them from behind the window, thinking quietly to himself *Yes, that's right, I'm awake…go on and get your master, any day now would be nice…glad to know they put the dimmer of you lot in charge to guard me…'*

Hurried footsteps echoed off the stone walls as the guard navigated the winding halls toward the narthex of the dark chapel. He was not pleased to find the doors to the inner sanctum locked, and he bashed his fist against the heavy wood urgently. As the sound faded into silence the guard waited with increasing unease.

There was someone coming—the soft clap of footsteps could be heard rising from behind the door—and when finally the threshold opened it was the face of a shaven-headed boy with bright blue eyes that looked out.

The boy narrowed his gaze and hissed.

The guard looked down at the boy curiously, squinting with scrutiny until he saw the scar over the boy's shoulder. The guard straightened up and sneered. "What are you doing here Kyddr'Ith? Come to beg the Lord for forgiveness?" The boy's eyes remained hard. "I've been forgiven. Why are you here? You're interrupting something *delicate*."

"Where is Dren'Ma?" the guard asked airily, craning to look over Kyddr'Ith into the sanctuary.

The boy-Kyddr'Ith smiled bitterly and stood aside from the door. "Dren'Ma left after my punishment. So busy, that one, playing the inciter on Dahl'Kir. The Lord put me in charge, did you want to see? Ask for yourself?"

The guard wet his lips, eager to be inside the sanctum, to be with the Lord. "Move aside," he said, and pushed Kyddr'Ith out of the way as he let himself in.

The reverie in the guard's eyes as he walked toward the entombed god had captivated him so thoroughly, that he didn't notice what lay around him. "My Lord," he uttered with awe and longing, taking a knee before the icy wall. "My Lord I—" but then he stopped. And with his head bowed and eyes to the ground he noticed something that he wished he had seen before entering the holy chamber.

Strewn about the floor were the disheveled robes of his kinsmen—stained black by their foul blood. The inky masses of their undisguised bodies arranged in a circle around the diagram in which the guard now stood. He looked to Kyddr'Ith with unmasked horror in his stolen eyes. "What—?"

And Kyddr'Ith smiled.

"You know we were gaea's first?" said Kyddr'Ith, walking in a slow and deliberate circle around the other slithe. "What everything was—in the beginning—before they chose what to be. But the few of us that didn't choose, that became what we are now…we still have that raw creation inside of us, the building blocks of a *temporary* vessel for our god. I'm so glad you came, as it happens, I needed just a little more blood."

"N-no!" The guard recoiled, turning back to look at their god with pleading eyes. At once the guard stopped moving, captivated by the colossal mind that filled his own, finding peace in the oblivion right before Kyddr'Ith cut his head off and bled his lifeless body onto the diagram on the floor.

"Was there anything important, my Lord?" asked Kyddr'Ith of the frozen deity. "Ah, I see…so the old man is awake…b-but the ritual…yes, I understand. I'll go," Kyddr'Ith said with a bow, though was reluctant to leave.

There was no defying their god, however, and Kyddr'Ith left the sanctum, closing the doors on the way out and taking a quiet moment to themself. There was a bubbling eagerness growing inside Kyddr'Ith's narrow frame, a jolt of exhilaration. Kyddr'Ith could taste the beginning sweetness of real hope—a feeling that the end goal was close at hand. It was going to happen, it was going to become real, their beautiful everlasting oblivion.

Their completion.

Of course the old man would choose *now* to wake up. Of course he would interrupt when Kyddr'Ith was so close. Why did he even matter anymore? Kyddr'Ith grumbled to themself and left the narthex, traveling down the halls toward the lower prisons.

As if the others could sense a change at hand, the dark chapel was buzzing with more activity than usual. It had been empty before—right after Kyddr'Ith's disgrace—but now the place seemed to crawl. There were slithes everywhere, all different forms, all different faces, each eyeing each other with uncertainty. Maybe they didn't even know why they had come back, maybe it was just a feeling that they should. Or had the Lord called them to make sure Kyddr'Ith had all the blood that was needed?

The very notion made Kyddr'Ith smile, knowing that the Lord stood beside them in what was being done, what *needed* to be done. Only Kyddr'Ith could smile so confidently as they traversed the dark halls and passageways. It made the others watch after Kyddr'Ith with deep suspicion. Although they often looked at Kyddr'Ith that way.

It was the purpose with which Kyddr'Ith walked that incited the distaste of the other slithes. But the others were often so clumsy in their resolve, as if they didn't fully grasp the meaning behind their actions. In a way, Kyddr'Ith loathed them, they were not as careful with their plans, nor as farsighted. They gave in to baser instincts on a whim, they were too self-assured of their superiority to any other. It made them sloppy.

But not Dren'Ma, Kyddr'Ith had to admit. Dren'Ma was murderous, but Dren'Ma had a mind for strategy and knew how to play the long game. It was only fitting that Kyddr'Ith's rival be the one to carve the insignia of failure.

And how fortunate for Kyddr'Ith that Dren'Ma left so quickly after the disgracing ritual; if not, it would have been Dren'Ma, and not Kyddr'Ith, making ready to become the vessel. No one else would have been worthy enough, nor as quick and eager to spill their brethren's blood.

As Kyddr'Ith headed down the stairs, smirking at the other slithes that hissed and glared back, Kyddr'Ith found a deep pleasure in knowing that come tonight—when all the moons were full in the Waking—Kyddr'Ith would finally one-up Dren'Ma for good.

"Oi, where's Fremu? Why are *you* here, Kyddr'Ith?" said the remaining guard by the heavy sealed door with the little porthole.

"The Lord had other work for Fremu and sent me to speak with the old man. Go find Moowsk, they can stand watch with you." The guard continued to eye Kyddr'Ith suspiciously.

"If you have problems with the Lord's command, I shall be sure to voice your grievance," said Kyddr'Ith with a hint of malice.

"I'll go get Moowsk," replied the guard begrudgingly, and left.

"Now then," said Kyddr'Ith, letting their stolen face settle into its natural cheeriness once they were alone with the man. Kyddr'Ith turned their bright blue eyes to the porthole where the wintered Traveler was looking out. "I know you can read my lips, and I can read yours. So, why don't you tell me what you want?"

The old man looked thoughtful for a while before he finally spoke. *I've met you before, you're Kyddr'Ith, aren't you?* his lips mouthed.

"I don't remember giving you my name, Traveler. You've been paying more attention than I thought."

I paid attention while I was awake.

"Evidently. So what is it? Do you want out, is that it? Bored of sleeping?"

You'll never let me go, it's pointless to ask.

"So what then?"

I ask to reason with you.

"Reason? So you've nothing better than to waste my time."

Your God lies. It won't be the paradise you think…It won't last, your oblivion.

"Oh, how would you know, Traveler? You're just afraid! But there is no reason to fear. Once it's over, once we are joined as one, we will have peace. We will all be whole in the endless void, together with the Lord. There will be no thought to corrupt us, no scattered consciousness. It will be still and quiet."

You cannot bring the end before its time without consequence. One day you will have your peace; don't force it. But know, even when the end does come, it won't last. The end is just the gateway for the new beginning. Over and over until this existence has served its purpose.

Kyddr'Ith hissed. "Don't bore me with your baseless theories. There is no continuum. *This* is it. There was no before, there will be no after! This *one* noisy, chaotic, mad existence is all there is and we will bring it to its rightful end! It should have been done with long ago, it wasn't meant to go on and on like this! It wasn't meant to twist and change! It should have ended at the Dawn of Time! It shouldn't have been allowed to mutate!"

You don't know what you do.

"If this is all you have to say to me then I am done with you! Go back to sleep, Traveler, enjoy your memories, your singularity, while you still have it. The end is coming, there will be no repeats."

We exist on a pendulum, repeating is what we do.

Kyddr'Ith bashed the door with an angry fist, making the angular runes and vicious looking inscriptions that barred the door flash with a violent potency. "Heretic." Kyddr'Ith spat, baring needle-like teeth through the porthole.

Then Kyddr'Ith left the prison, and left the man to stare in somber contemplation.

"So if Etcher made this house, and all this food, does it mean it's actually real?" asked Mahra, looking studiously at the thick slice of freshly baked walnut cake she held up on her plate. It smelled real enough, and it tasted real, really good in fact, but Mahra was still wrapping her head over a great many oddities and seemed to fixate on the reality of her slice of tea cake.

"You will not get full from it, it will not nourish your body, but maybe your mind," answered Tahli. The ginger feline had taken to a plush settee and draped herself across it in true feline fashion, her long striped tail coiling back and forth as she lay stretched out across the seat cushions. There were plenty of other armchairs and sofas to go around, so no one had any complaints about Tahli taking a whole piece of furniture to herself.

"Where even *is* Etcher?" Jerro asked, rising to his feet. "She's not leaving without us, is she?"

"Miss Everdoor will be with us shortly. Don't worry, Mr. Ahliss, she hasn't left," chimed in Mr. Gribs.

Jerro reluctantly lowered himself back down beside Mahra on the loveseat. "What are you, her personal assistant now?"

Mr. Gribs swallowed nervously and gave a weak smile. "Perhaps for the meanwhile, yes."

"You hoping she'll accept the King's invitation if you play manservant?" Jerro said with a mocking snort of laughter.

The toad paled at that and went to wringing out his satchel straps.

Jerro might have gibed at the portly nightmare further were it not for the *look* Mahra shot him. A look that very plainly said she disapproved of how he spoke to Mr. Gribs and that he should stop it immediately. The look was so stern and foreign to Mahra's usual cheery disposition that it caught Jerro off guard, and he found himself a little bewildered and hurt by the silent scolding. So, he took to occupying himself with his tea cup—despite the fact he was getting rather sick of tea.

"Well, um, does anyone want anything else?" asked Mr. Gribs, casting a small appreciative smile at Mahra.

"I will take a fresh coffee with some brandy—be generous with it," ordered Tahli, never bothering to look at the toad.

"Right away, Miss Tahli." And the toad was off.

"I might enjoy keeping him around, he does make himself useful," said Tahli after Mr. Gribs had left. And her eyes directed the comment at Jerro and delivered with it a quiet insult.

"So, ah, Tahli, are there other Ecliptians like you?" chimed in Mahra, feeling the horrid tension crackle through the room like a live wire.

"Like me?" Tahli purred. "What do you mean?"

"Well you're just so interesting looking, I mean besides Mr. Gribs—which, he's a nightmare so I don't think he counts anyway—the few people that I've met so far look sort of normal."

"So I am different?"

"Not in a bad way! From what Jerro told me there's a lot different around here, and I've already seen enough to make my head spin, but you're like something out of a real myth. It's just, sort of amazing."

Tahli was grinning widely while Jerro stared at Mahra with blatant disbelief.

"Oh don't gawk! Sorry, forget I mentioned it," said Mahra, as she shied away from the accusative expression on Jerro's face.

"Ha! Why are you sorry about it? You are right, I *am* different. My ehta is as close to my true self as I could make it. Most Ecliptians decide to look so human, like they are ashamed, but not me."

Jerro rolled his eyes. "She hasn't seen everything yet, Tahli."

"And neither have you. Peh, you think because you got a head start you know so much now? You think that earring makes you one of us? You do not know anything about this world."

Jerro touched the gold hoop in his lobe protectively and scrunched his face at Tahli. "I'm not saying I know everything, it's just she—you can't—there's more impressive stuff out there than just *you*." And as the words left Jerro's mouth he immediately regretted them.

Tahli looked at Jerro with dagger eyes and a sudden deadly rigidness ran through her body as if she might strike.

"Okay, please, both of you, don't do this! Can we please not fight? We're here in a meadow in *Dream* for crying out loud! In a cabin that Etcher imagined up! And this is the most beautiful place I've ever seen and—" Mahra's eyes began to well up, and her face scrunched as if to stem the flow of impending tears. "I'm sorry, I just need a moment." Then she got up and hurried away.

The void of Mahra's absence settled in like a bitter chill.

"Good going," tutted Tahli.

"*Me?* Are you serious?"

"You asked before why I do not like you, as if there is something wrong with *me*. This is why I do not like you! You act so arrogant, as if you are beyond reproach. And what is more, you cling to that girl like she is a bird with a broken wing. She is fine! She does not need your babying, but she is too love-struck with you to tell you to go away."

"Excuse me? What are you talking about? Why is this suddenly about me and Mahra? I'm not babying her! You're just mad that I'm not gawking over *you*!"

"Oh you gawk plenty," Tahli huffed. "You do not get it, you do not understand it at all. I like this girl better than you. She looks at this world with wonder, she questions it, embraces it. But you? So busy whining and feeling sorry for yourself! I cannot stand how you hover over her, you make her small by doing that, and you undermine her thoughts because she does not agree with you. So yes, this *is* your fault."

"You know what I think? I think you're bitter. I think the only reason you seem to suddenly like Mahra so much is so you can use her to get at me."

"Do not flatter yourself."

"Oh yeah? Mahra tells you how *'amazing'* you are and suddenly she's your favorite person?"

"No, I liked her from before. She has a kind face, and a good soul. I felt that when I was tending her wounds back in the shop!"

The latter took Jerro off kilter for a moment, remembering how Tahli had taken care of Mahra, and how for a small moment he and the cat-woman hadn't been at each other's throats.

"I just don't think you should be using her to stoke your ego—oh yeah, laugh! I'm sorry Tahli but you *aren't* the most impressive thing here, and Mahra's only seen us and now this place. This isn't funny, Tahli. You say underhanded things about me all the time and I make one remark against you and suddenly it blows up!"

"That is not why I am laughing. You are a hypocrite."

"I'm the hypocrite? Oh yeah, that's rich." Jerro was shaking his head, his jaw cocked to one side with his aggravation. "No matter what I do, it's never good enough for you. I'm taking a walk before I say something really nasty," he said as he started to rise from his seat.

"You are right. I do gibe at you," said Tahli, and that too caught Jerro off guard, halting his attempt to leave. "But you just cannot stand that anyone else might think highly of me—that is why you said what you did. You could not stand that your friend might actually like me. And talk about me stoking my ego? I will admit that, but you are doing just the same with her. It is true I do not like you, maybe I will never like you, but understand that I have been here far longer than you and this is *my* world you are treading into but you show me no respect.

"You disregard me. You think I do not matter and even though you say how you try to be nice, you do not think anything of me. You are not sincere and it is why I do not accept any of your false niceties. You think I am just some bossy store clerk, but you have not been through what I have been through with Everdoor. You have not been there through the blood and the broken bones. Oh! Now you see it, of course, because she does not tell you those stories. She does not tell you how I have to pick up the pieces when everything falls apart—how I have to be the confidante to things that would plague your nightmares. No, I am just Tahli to you, some pushy feline. But Everdoor trusts me with her life. I earned that. Can you say the same?" Tahli got up from the settee and strode away, leaving a rather pitiful looking Jerro alone in the spacious lounge of the cabin.

"Well now, I was expecting a crowd," Etcher announced as she strode through the main doors, seemingly unaware of the previous conflagration that had unfolded—though Jerro's face told her enough. "Ah," she said as she seated herself in the armchair beside Jerro's loveseat and crossed one leg over the other. "What happened?"

"Yeah, so—might have got into a tiff with Tahli in front of Mahra."

"*Ah*," she said again.

"Yeah." Jerro sighed, looking rather miserable. "Etcher...do I—am I useful?"

"You've been plenty useful to me. Why would you ask such a thing?"

"Yeah, okay, I know I helped you in Undercity but it's not like my part was all that...*big*."

"So you're bothered because you haven't got to play a bigger part in this theater of adventure?"

"No, yes—I just...Tahli said some things. It's fine, just the usual picking at each other."

Etcher breathed through her nose audibly as she looked at him. "Jerro, Tahli is less tactful than I am. She's also very blunt with her feelings. It can be difficult to deal with a person like her, however, you always know where you stand with Tahli—for what it's worth. She'll be upfront with her thoughts and she has little tolerance for people that aren't, which is why I drive her absolutely mad. But I have a thick skin, and I'm also her boss, so she has to put up with me." She gave Jerro a gentle smile and a laugh but it wasn't enough to brighten his mood.

"It's fine, Etcher, really, let's just...do what needs to get done."

"Well I suppose that's sort of a discussion for everyone."

"Yeah, I guess."

Etcher cleared her throat and helped herself to one of the tea cakes. "Unless of course we just left."

Jerro snapped up from his aimless misery and stared at Etcher with bewilderment stamped across his face. "You serious?"

The little shopkeeper shrugged. "Well, it's not like they can follow us any further. I made this house to occupy them, and Tahli's been to Dream many a time. I'm confident she can handle herself. Mahra, however, might not be too pleased by your sudden departure but you can always blame that on me, if you like."

"Etcher, I dunno—"

"Honestly, Jerro, I'm rather tired of having to check in with everyone. I'm tired of conveying my plans, of explaining and answering questions. Granted, there are things I still need to tell you, but if it's all the same, I'd be much happier taking a quiet exit."

It did sound good, and what with the friction Jerro had caused with the other two women he wasn't all that keen on hanging about either. "Let's get the hell out of here."

"Glad you agree!" said Etcher. She uncrossed herself from the chair and pulled out a large plump envelope from inside her waistcoat and left it on the coffee table as she got up.

"What's that?" asked Jerro.

"Instructions, a note, that sort of thing. Truth be told I was waiting until you were alone."

"Hang on, did you expect me to have it out with Tahli?"

"Well, I wasn't counting on it, but it's not entirely unexpected. Come on! You can be mad at me along the way."

Jerro was ready to run after Etcher, but before he did, a thought nagged at him. "Just a sec!" he called, and he brought out the blue flower crown from the Obelisk and left it on the table next to Etcher's envelope.

"Here, perhaps you'd like to leave your own note?" said Etcher, handing him a pen and paper.

Despite all that had happened, Jerro was beginning to enjoy himself. In the back of his mind he realized he should feel guilty about how Mahra would react once she found out he had left her again, but truth be told, he was simply too relieved to feel bad.

He was back on an adventure with Etcher, and that alone brought him insurmountable joy. There was freedom when he and the little thief were off on their own—especially when the two of them were springing into action and putting ground behind them. It was as though nothing else mattered, like all his other silly little problems really were small and insignificant. They were out *doing* something, it didn't matter what, only that they were doing it.

And it seemed he wasn't alone in his joy. Etcher had a much easier air about her the further they walked into the forest line and put the cabin out of sight. Her step became springier, her smile a little more impish. She had even changed her dress from the austere black and red suit to something far more colorful. Now the little thief looked much more like her flamboyant, swashbuckling self.

The sky blue of her billowy silken blouse with its lacy cuffs and collar, the iridescent sheen of her dark velvet waist coat, the polish and filigree of her brass buttons, the high fitted chocolate-colored pants, and the matching blue canvas slip-ons, all radiated the effervescent and mischievous nature of the Etcher Jerro knew—and much preferred to her dark and brooding self.

"Jerro," she said, breaking him out of his musings, "I imagine you'll be feeling strange soon, the gate is getting near. The forest is going to change abruptly and the world will look very different. We need to stay within the tree line so as not to be seen."

"Seen? What do you mean, seen?"

"Jerro, the gate is guarded, and there will be a huge influx of souls being ferried through. I can't just stroll up to it. Death Token or not, if the guards see me there'll be no way of getting through."

"Yeah but—"

"Don't worry, I have a plan. You'll see."

Jerro, of course, wanted to complain and press for more answers, even if he knew he wouldn't get them. It was frustrating, all the not-knowing, all the things his inexperience made him so naive to. Tahli's voice came swimming back to him, though the sting from her words had lessened. Begrudgingly, Jerro had to admit that the ginger cat-woman did have a point, even with his head start into the world, there was still so much he had to learn. He was still very much out of his depth.

At least Etcher didn't see him as useless, although he wondered if she was pandering to him at times. To his credit, she *had* said she wanted him to join in her adventures and he very much believed the request to be genuine. And when Etcher was around he did feel important, like he had a purpose, like he was the daring adventurer he so quietly wished to be. The trouble was when she was gone. Not for the first time he realized he needed her a lot more than he felt she needed him.

A familiar sensation plummeted right down to the bottom of Jerro's stomach, as if he had reached a sudden stop on an elevator, and the feeling plugged the spiraling whirlpool of Jerro's thoughts before they could feed into his self-loathing. They were getting close to the gate all right.

The air seemed to shimmer and shiver right in front of them, rippling like a gown of silk caught in a gentle breeze. It was rather reminiscent of the portal they had flown through to get to Darcwood. And as Jerro walked into it, he saw firsthand the abrupt change Etcher had mentioned, although she had understated just how drastic the change would be.

As Jerro stepped through the veil, the world on the other side of the rippling portal was suddenly painted in hues of blue and lit in a fading twilight. Jerro tested out just how thin the separation between the two worlds was; with one step back, everything was in the honey golds and hot pinks of the effervescent Dream realm, and with a step forward, the world became dark and blue, and cold.

They traveled quietly in that strange blue world for what felt like miles, though might just as well have been only a few feet. The trees became thinner, their branches became spindly and their leaves became a soft glow of silver moonlight. Chirping insects gave out their calls almost lazily in the twilight, and a feeling of sleepy calm was draped over the world. The long somber cawing of a crow gave the twilight place its final signature. This was Death, or at least a piece of it, that had come to rest in a pocket inside of Dream.

Jerro didn't feel as he expected he would. The headache and the nausea he had experienced in Undercity weren't present here, nor was the sickness when he had touched the ghost seal that had blocked Undercity's hidden treasures. He felt an uncanny sense of peace, a lightness to his body as though it were barely anchored to the ground. The anxiousness from before, the impatience of his youth, the need to hurry, were all gone—but he wasn't empty, there was merely a stillness inside his soul.

He remembered this feeling, he had felt this before, but where? When?

For a moment he stood there, looking up into the dark blue sky, the twinkling stars coming into focus in the halo of his vision. He hadn't realized how tense his body had been until he felt his breath move so easily in and out of his lungs in that new, yet familiar place. All of the worry and the tension that plagued him from before, the constant buzzing in his mind that he was never really conscious of—it had poured out of him and left him with an effortless tranquility.

"Jerro?" said Etcher, examining him with her inquisitive golden gaze.

"Yeah, I'm okay," he replied, reading the deeper question behind the word.

"Well, I suppose that's a relief."

He didn't smile, although he felt the warm bubble of humor slowly rise through him, bringing a pleasantness to his calm. He brought his eyes down to look at Etcher, seeing her in an entirely new light.

Though her little frame was human-like, and though she spoke like a person, acted like one, she was something very different. The body was only a guise—Jerro realized—it was a shell that contained the curious greater thing that she was. Shining through the honey orbs was the real Etcher, a creature totally foreign to Jerro. There was something packed and crammed into that little body that was older than time, old but not elderly. It was keen and curious and quite assuredly dangerous; it was a thing lying in wait, wearing this person-guise as one might wear a costume.

The thing that was Etcher was an observer, watching and calculating what it saw through its person-like shell. But it didn't truly belong, it was alien to the worlds around it, and because of this—because the thing behind the eyes seemed to hail from a place governed by different rules than those that structured the realm of mortals—it was slightly indifferent to what it saw, unaffected, a little callous.

All this Jerro recognized and understood in the blink of an instant, but it was a hard thing to hold onto. Even his serene calm was fading, balancing out with his usual self. He was left with a degree of tranquility and the constant nagging of undefinable familiarity, but the profoundness of his heightened state had dimmed and left him feeling a little less than before, a little numb.

"Shall we continue?" said Etcher, and Jerro could no longer see the thing behind the eyes, the being inside the shell. It had been eviscerated by the cheeky smile, the mischievous poise of the Etcher he believed he knew.

Jerro nodded, adjusting to his curious state of half-calm. And the niggling feeling kept scratching at his brain, that knowing without definition of this place, of Death. Even before they spied the gate, he knew what he would see.

The forest came to a sudden end, and beyond it was a great circular chasm whose depths stretched into an infinite darkness. At the very center of the gorge was the gate, stationed in the middle of the cross section of two massive bridges that stretched across the diameter of the colossal chasm like a giant 'x,' connecting each quadrant of the circular gorge to one another.

The gate, if it could really be called that, was comprised of a vast round podium that filled in the entire cross section of the immense intersecting bridges. There were four colossal pillars surrounding the base, each rivaling the tallest skyscraper Jerro had ever seen, that had been carved into the effigies of winged dogs, sitting with stately poise, their sad round eyes staring out at the world in somber contemplation.

The thing that truly made the immense structure a gate—in the sense that it separated one passage into another—was the column of pale blue light, housed within the confines of the pillars, that stretched up toward the dim twilight sky. The column was the doorway into the other realm, and a constant flock of winged *things* were filtering into that light from all four directions along the crossing bridges. They disappeared into the column despite the mass and volume of them all. Great cords of the winged creatures walked while others flew, following along the paths of the crisscross pathways as they filtered into Death.

As Jerro and Etcher inched closer, staying hidden in the silvery underbrush of their dwindling cover, Jerro saw what the creatures were and knew their purpose instantly.

They were reapers, in a sense. The same winged dogs which had been carved into the pillars of the gate, the same creature that had been sculpted into the Death Token and the seals in Undercity. They were the couriers of souls, ushering the departed into the land of the dead, and there were millions of them, flocking in constant streams from land and sky into the portal.

"*How* the hell are we supposed to sneak in? There's so many of those—" Jerro almost said the word, it was so close to the tip of his tongue, though he couldn't quite form it.

"Dyrash," said Etcher.

"Dyrash?" replied Jerro, feeling the prickle of familiarity once more. "I know something about them, I think—they bring the good souls to Death, don't they?"

"Well, good and bad are relative. Most souls will be ferried by a Dyrash, but some need more persuading and are brought by the Oolkas. Of course, there are also those that are brought by the Morig." Etcher went curiously quiet at the latter, and Jerro got that distinct notion it was a topic better left unquestioned.

"So, ah, how are we getting in?" he asked.

"With this," she replied, and conjured in her hand a big red rubber ball that was attached to a thin wooden pole by a string, almost like a fishing rod with an excessively large bobber.

"Uh, I'm missing something, aren't I?"

Etcher winked and bounced the ball in her hand, testing out its weight. Then she tossed the ball over the underbrush they were hiding behind and held fast to the rod. The ball bounced and rolled and then stopped, sitting on the open ground about a half kilometer away from the mouth of the nearest bridge.

"*What are we doing?*" whispered Jerro, crouched beside Etcher, peering between the bushes as he stared at the rubber ball expectedly.

"You'll see," was all she said.

Despite the modicum of calm that had remained with Jerro, his patience was beginning to wane as they stayed in painful silence, staring at the ball, which Jerro soon realized had absolutely nothing special about, contrary to what he had hoped. It was the most bizarre and oddly mundane thing he had ever seen in Etcher's hands.

"Etcher…"

"*Shh!*" Despite Jerro's obvious restlessness, the little shopkeeper was keenly focused. She twitched the rod in her hand slightly to make the ball roll in a small semicircle and waited.

It was then that Jerro realized the purpose of the whole charade. "*Etcher,*" he said again, though this time with pressing urgency, "*uh, Etcher…it's coming closer—*"

"*Just relax, will you?*" she whispered back.

But Jerro was finding that a hard request to deliver on. His calm was starting to fizzle out as one of the Dyrashes broke away from the flock, flicking up its inquisitive ears when it noticed the ball on the ground. Of course, that wasn't what bothered Jerro so much. What bothered him was realizing he had greatly miscalculated the measurements of the Dyrash, and as the bear-sized beast padded with surprising feline grace toward the ball, which Etcher was slowly reeling in and drawing the creature ever closer, Jerro felt a sinking dread at what was about to happen next.

The strange ethereal winged dog was a soft brown-gray color, save for the chest and feather tuffs around its elbows and ankles that were a pale icy blue. Its eyes were big and round and purely white, glowing slightly, and leaving wispy smoke trails in the air as the creature moved. It had the features of a Great Dane with the lankiness of its limbs and the structure of its lean body, but its head and pointed ears were distinctly that of a German Shepherd's. The more curious features of the beast, however, were the gold lantern that it held on a big ring in its maw, giving the creature a perpetual grin, and the long dexterous tail with its pale glowing tip, around which delicate icy blue butterflies fluttered.

As the Dyrash approached the ball with its head cocked in canine contemplation, the end of its monkey-esque tail started to coil back and forth, and it considered the red rubber ball at great length, following after it cautiously as the ball rolled lethargically toward the tree-line, but when the ball jolted and bounced, the ethereal creature stopped in its tracks. The Dyrash jumped down on its long front legs, bring its wagging rump high in the air, and it chomped playfully on the metal ring in its mouth that held the lantern.

"You've got to be kidding me," said Jerro under his breath, as more of Etcher's absurd plan started to piece together.

But the little shopkeeper was unperturbed by Jerro's disbelief, and she winked at him as she yanked on the rod and brought the ball bouncing toward them.

The Dyrash pursued with evident gusto, bringing the great beast of a dog hurtling toward the underbrush.

"Get ready to run!" said Etcher with a smirk.

"W-what?" Jerro scrambled to his feet after the agile little shopkeeper as she skipped away into the denser forest.

The massive Dyrash was right behind them, making bounding strides and gaining fast. And though the creature could clearly see Jerro and Etcher by now, its main interest was on the bouncing rubber ball that was still tethered to the rod in Etcher's hands.

The little shopkeeper skidded to a stop once the cover of the twilight forest had safely shielded them from the gate and any wandering eyes. The great ethereal dog dug its paws in quick, stopping only inches away from toppling over Etcher, and when it looked at her, its white eyes seemed to light up even brighter. The creature jumped all around in canine glee, yipping with a strange, distant echoing sound as if the bark were disembodied from the dog.

"What a good *kutya*," cooed Etcher, rubbing the massive dog's head.

The beast responded favorably, rolling on its back and spreading its sizable wings as it wriggled, inviting Etcher to pat its downy soft belly—the lantern still firmly clasped in its maw.

"You can't be serious. You lured one of them with a *rubber ball!* How? And why?" Jerro stood there in utter disbelief, watching the giant spirit dog wiggle with glee as Etcher rubbed its belly.

"Because, Jerro, this will be our ride into Death."

"Oh, I see. So we'll just saddle up on its back and fly through the gate? Yeah, very inconspicuous."

Etcher snorted with amusement at him, though her attention remained focused on the Dyrash. "So what's your name then, handsome thing?"

The Dyrash rolled back onto its legs and sat up straight, giving another echoing bark through its mouthful of lantern.

"*Pangwien,* is it?"

The Dyrash yipped.

"That's a good name. You fancy a game of fetch?"

And oh yes, Pangwien did indeed fancy it. The Dyrash dipped down on its front paws again, rump high and wagging in anticipation.

Etcher plucked the rubber ball from the string and tossed it far into the deeper forest, sending the gleeful Dyrash to go chasing after it.

"Etcher, *what* are we doing?"

"We're playing fetch."

"Oh, *ha ha* you know what I mean."

Etcher glanced at him and smiled. "You know, no one ever plays with them. They do have a true canine spirt. They're playful and inquisitive, and very loyal. People forget that."

"Okay, but what good does that do us?"

"Just watch, Jerro, it'll make sense soon enough."

The Dyrash was running back, though it no longer had the lantern ring in its mouth. The rubber ball—made tiny by Pangwien's colossal jaws—was clamped firmly in the end of its maw, and it dropped it expectantly at Etcher's feet. "You want the ball, do you?"

Pangwien reared down once again.

"Well, you'll have to catch me first!" And Etcher was off, and the great ethereal dog sprang into action, jumping and bounding after her, while a confused Jerro chased from behind.

"Here, Jerro, catch!"

"Huh?" said Jerro, reflexively catching the ball that came hurtling toward him, and then, of course, the giant dog came hurtling too. "Oh, shit!" He ran without thinking, the great dog bounding after him, yipping gleefully.

He darted between the trees, driven by mindless automation and adrenaline, but the spirit dog was nimble and fast and the forest proved little hindrance to it despite its largeness. Jerro's aimless heading drove him right out into a small glade, which caught him off guard and halted his progress. Of course, it didn't stop the great dog. "Oh n-no no! S-stop!"

Thud!

The Dyrash had dug in its paws, but not soon enough, and the great big beast hurtled right into Jerro and flattened him against the ground.

Pangwien whimpered softly, its ears flicked back and its shoulders hunched, making the giant beast look very apologetic. The Dyrash carefully padded up to Jerro and nudged him with its cold nose.

Jerro was in a daze for a moment, winded as he was by the crash. He propped himself up on his elbows and clutched the back of his head. He was certain he felt a tender lump beginning to form. "Damn it," he hissed under his breath, and Pangwien whimpered again, dipping its head low and trying to make itself small, while looking up at Jerro with very sad, smoky white eyes.

Jerro looked at the pitiful beast and sighed. "I'm okay," he said, and reached out to pat Pangwien's soft head.

The Dyrash thumped its long tail against the ground and nuzzled into Jerro, then gave him a great big lick across his whole face with its cold blue tongue.

"Ahk! Yeah, okay, Pangwien, that's enough. It's okay."

But Pangwien seemed unconvinced, and Jerro had to rub the spirit dog's massive head and pat its side for reassurance.

"You really are just a big dog, aren't you?" Jerro said with a smirk. He began to rise, and Pangwien insisted on helping, letting Jerro use its colossal head to help pull himself up. "Thanks," he said, smiling a little more. As Jerro stood up, he noticed a gold hoop in one of the spirit dog's ears. "Who gave you that, I wonder?"

Pangwien yipped and sat up straight—towering over Jerro—its dexterous monkey tail weaving back and forth, causing the delicate butterflies to chase after the glowing tip in tumbling waves.

Jerro considered the inquisitive canine before him. "Is it true? No one plays with you?"

Pangwien let out an echoey-grumbling-whiny-growl.

Out of the corner of his eye, Jerro noticed that the rubber ball was in the glade with them, and he went over to pick it up, which made Pangwien wriggle with anticipation.

"You still wanna play fetch?"

The Dyrash trembled with excitement.

"Yeah, all right you big silly thing. Fetch!" he yelled and threw the ball back into the forest.

Pangwien was off, bounding after it.

"Probably not what you expected a reaper to be like, ay?" said Etcher, who was leaned up against a silvery tree.

"Definitely not."

"Sorry about all that, by the by, I didn't think you'd get trampled."

Jerro shrugged. "S'alright. I used to have a collie named Pepper when I was little. Pangwien sort of reminds me of her. She'd sometimes ball me over, too." He smiled at the memory, but then felt a pang of sadness strum through him. "It seems kind of cruel, they're really just big pups that want to play and run around. I feel sorry for them."

"Me too."

Pangwien was back with the ball, looking exceptionally pleased with itself, and when Etcher went to grab the ball back, the Dyrash jumped away.

"Oh, I see, it's going to be like that is it?" she grinned and darted after the great beast again. "Come on Jerro! Pangwien thinks he can outrun us." And the chase was on once more.

They ran and played for a blur of time, and wrestled and chased and tossed the ball around. And for a little while, nothing else mattered. They were all smiling, laughing, yipping, barking, until all three of them collapsed in a heap, Etcher and Jerro resting against Pangwien's downy soft flank, while Pangwien lie stretched out across a litter of shiny leaves along the forest floor. The twilight filtered in between the silvery trees and the sleepy calm startled to settle over them.

"Pangwien?" said Etcher, breaking the quiet. "I have a favor to ask you, it's a big favor, and it's all right if you say no."

Pangwien's tail wove and coiled gently, and its ears perked up, its expression a little more serious.

Etcher leaned back to look up at the Dyrash. "Would you take us into Death? There's something very important we need to do at Leona Mesa."

The great beast stared at Etcher with its burning white eyes—the tendrils of smoke drifting upward in fading serpentine trails—and the beast became very still. A strange kind of intelligence was working away inside its head, revealing that the Dyrash was not just some ordinary dog. There was a great wealth of cleverness behind the canine façade.

Pangwien got to its feet and dipped its head down to where a large golden lantern had suddenly appeared. It scooped up the metal ring into its maw and turned to look at Jerro and Etcher. The lantern was illuminated by the same icy glow as in its tail, and more delicate butterflies fluttered inside the glass chamber of the ethereal contraption.

Pangwien let out a sound, not quite like a whine, but one of beckoning, and the latch on the hinged door of the lantern swung open. Some of the butterflies poured out, though they stayed close to the lantern.

"Thank you, Pangwien." said Etcher sincerely. The little shopkeeper stood aside and held out her arm, presenting the lantern doorway to Jerro.

"Erm, how exactly are we supposed to fit in there?"

"Step up and see." Etcher winked.

Jerro took a tentative step forward and looked up into Pangwien's burning white eyes and grinning canine face, noting the beast's calm stillness of intelligent contemplation.

The lantern light seemed to beckon Jerro, inviting him to step inside its little glass chamber. He had been moving steadily toward it, and with each step the lantern seemed to grow, and Jerro felt oddly light, as though he might be floating, and before he knew it, he was inside the light, fluttering around it with the other butterflies.

Etcher smiled at Pangwien and stroked the spirit dog's head. "See you on the other side," she said, and she stepped up to the lantern, becoming one of the delicate butterflies herself as she slipped inside. The door on the lantern closed and Pangwien turned its gaze upward, leaping up to the nearest tree bough and working its way toward the open sky. And when Pangwien was above the forest canopy, it stretched open its massive wings and took flight.

The cabin lobby was suspiciously empty when Mahra finally decided to come back and face the crowd.

"Hello?" she said aloud, her voice carrying through the vast space and echoing off the wood-and-stone walls.

No Jerro, no Tahli.

She walked tentatively back to the seating area where the tea was still steaming and the nibbled bit of walnut cake was as she had left it. Where had everyone gone? Had Jerro and Tahli decided to take their squabble elsewhere? Should she not have left?

That last thought sounded an alarm bell inside her heart as her eyes drifted toward the large envelope on the coffee table, then to the little half-folded note and the beautiful blue flower crown beside it.

The envelope was addressed to Tahli and had been penned in tall elegant lettering, but the little piece of folded paper had a much simpler print and was addressed to Mahra. She had a horrible sinking feeling as she reached for the note that was propped against the crown. Deep down she already knew what it was going to say, and as she read the first few lines, she was struck by an awful déjà vu—

Marha,
    I'm really sorry—Etcher & I are headed off for the gate, seemed better if I left. I'm pretty shite at this, aren't I? I imagine you'll be pretty mad, & I won't blame you if you hate me by the time I come back but I hope you won't.

                    —Jerro xx

P.S. I got the crown for you while you were in the clinic, thought it suited you.

D.P.S Please don't hate me too much, I really do want to work things out.

Mahra felt a hot salty wetness swell around her eyes. "God damn it, Jerro," she said in a tiny voice, picking up the flower crown from the table and heading for the main doors. She needed air, she needed to be away.

The tears were streaming freely before she reached the doors, her breath was hitching, and the wretchedness she felt had turned into a lead ball inside her heart, plunging her into a thick and heavy sorrow. She threw open the front doors and ran down the steps toward the grass of the meadow, collapsing in a heap on the soft ground where she let the rest of her sadness pour out.

And then it started to slow, the wretchedness began to lighten, and her breath became a little easier. She sat on her knees in the Dream meadow, the note in one hand, the flower crown in the other. She dried her eyes and looked up the magnificent morning sky.

She got left, again.

But really, how much farther could she have gone? This was their waypoint, she knew that, even if she didn't understand everything. But damn it all, *again?* She felt numb with shock, too dumbstruck to feel the hot prickle of anger that she might have, should have; instead there was only a sad bewilderment. But as she knelt there in the meadow, thinking back on herself and all that had led her there, as she listened to her internal dialogue recanting the story of how she ended up in Dream, something started to bubble inside her. She started smirking at how ridiculous it all sounded. And perhaps it was the last of the nerves rattling out of her, but soon she was laughing, staring up into that impossible sky with its floating isles and imagined chimeras sailing through the open air.

"Jerro, you colossal ass…I don't hate you," she said to herself. The crown in her hand caught her eye then—with its dainty snapdragons, its creamy white rosebuds, and intricate woven vine. She had to admit, it *was* a beautiful crown, although that didn't mean she'd let Jerro off the hook when he got back.

She found herself placing the crown on her head, enjoying the comfortable weight of it and the feeling of whimsy it gave her.

"I wish I had a mirror," she said airily, and though she wasn't sure why, she began to picture an old antique hand mirror, the kind that her gran used to have. She imagined so clearly the flowery filigree of the handle and the frame, the little bit of wear on the mirror itself around the edges, the tarnish of the silver, the heaviness of it in her hand.

The exact mirror appeared next to her in the grass, easing into existence until it solidified. Mahra saw the thing appear out of the corner of her eye and had to stifle a yelp, thinking at first it was some horrid scuttling creature nestling up beside her.

"Um," she said, looking around as if expecting to find its owner, but she was alone in the meadow. The breeze ran its fingers through the colorful wildflowers, the distant sound of chimes echoed through the air. There was calm and bliss.

Mahra chewed at her lip as she grabbed the mirror and inspected her reflection, admiring how magical the flower crown looked on her head—like she was an elven princess with flowing golden locks who knew her place and purpose in the world, and not just some college-girl secretary who was hopelessly out of her depth. She started to wonder, started glancing around the meadow and back at the cabin to make certain she was alone.

Then she got to her feet, holding the mirror to her heart. "If Etcher could make a cabin,"—she said aloud as a torrent of thoughts whirled through her head—"and this is Dream…" She was staring off at the tree line, a feeling growing deep inside her as her gaze drifted skyward. "Then I could make anything." And in her mind she was building, refining the details, focusing on the weight and the feel, remembering sensations from dreams past. And the feeling started to come true, become tangible, and whatever sadness remained had been vanquished.

"Maybe I really do have *majik*," said Mahra. Had Lupine Blackfeather been telling the truth? If Mahra had *majik* inside her, and this wasn't just the manifestation of Dream, then she would ask Jerro about the notebook—

whatever it was—and it would be part of his repayment in making things up to her.

She looked beside herself, hope and glee swelling inside her heart. She rolled her shoulders and felt her muscles move, felt the reality of her wish upon her back.

The white wings spread wide, trimmed in golden feathers that glittered in the warm morning light of Dream. Mahra held out the mirror and looked herself over once more, smiling at the confident young woman that stared back at her, remembering again all the promises she had made to herself.

If Jerro wanted to leave her behind without so much as a word, then that was his loss and he could prove how much he wanted to work things out when he came back, but in the meanwhile, Mahra wasn't going to sit and wait around to be saved again.

"I've always wanted to fly," she said with giddy excitement, and her eyes sailed upward to the floating isles.

Pangwien was soaring through the twilight sky with the flock of other Dyrashes toward the immense beam of light at the center of the gate. Its wings were stretched wide, catching the air current beneath the elegant array of icy blue feathers and brown-gray downy fluff, feeling the wind carry its ethereal body as though the great beast were weightless.

The pale beam drew closer and hundreds of Pangwien's brethren were encompassed by the light, slipping between the rift in worlds. There was a sensation of happiness at returning to its place of origin, at its long journey finally coming around full circle. Pangwien's spirit swelled, energized as it already was by the weightless freedom of flight. The Dyrash yipped and howled in its strange echoing call—which its brothers mimicked, brimming as they were with their own magnitude of happiness. And the beam of light that was the gate swallowed the great beasts, bringing them all home.

Pangwien passed through the barrier, and the weariness of the other worlds was washed away, only a purity was left, an authentic certainty of self. On the other side, Pangwien was no longer flying, but swimming, its wings and feet moving the great cleansing ocean behind it as Pangwien headed for the surface and broke free, only to fall once again into the sky and sail the air currents down toward the ground, leaving the band of the ocean barrier above.

The world was a soft dawn, and the ground Pangwien flew toward was luscious and vast, spilling over with plant growth, with epic mountain ranges and magnificent waterfalls, and the bright and shimmering Lifestream that coursed through the space between land and sky.

Pangwien and the others headed for the undulating Lifestream—that vast network of delicate butterflies flying over the world in one thick cord. Their fluttering congregation resonated with a gentle azure glow, and the Dyrashes circled the floating current, pouring out the contents of their lanterns, sending dozens of butterflies flittering out to join the great convoy. A few wayward spirits broke off from the Lifestream and headed toward the lush world—some changing on their way down into other beasts, other people, other plants, and stones.

Pangwien opened its lantern too, and the butterflies that had gathered inside quickly vacated, and the few that had kept to Pangwien's glowing tail also broke away to join the others. There were only two small flickers left in Pangwien's lantern when it closed. The Dyrash beat its wings and glided away from the Lifestream, heading deeper into the world of Death toward Leona Mesa.

The world changed beneath Pangwien's lithe form, moving from forest into desert, from tundra into meadows, mountain ranges into valleys. As Pangwien flew, small flocks of white birds joined alongside the great beast for a while, dipping and diving and chirping with glee. A few of the birds changed back to butterflies and followed after Pangwien's guiding light, while the others—content as they were—left Pangwien and returned to the world below.

The great Dyrash headed for the mountains and plateaus, gliding past the colossal waterfalls toward the thick jungle growth that crested the flat tops of the high grounds. There Pangwien descended, and when its big padded feet touched down, Pangwien's lantern opened once more and the last two butterflies fluttered out, transforming back into Etcher and Jerro.

Etcher was first to speak, her calculating eyes surveying the expanse. "Thank you, Pangwien. Will you be joining us any further?"

The Dyrash turned its massive head to look at the small gathering of pale butterflies around its glowing tail.

"Ah, I see," said Etcher. She reached up and stroked Pangwien's head and rubbed its big pointed ears.

The Dyrash nuzzled into Etcher's hand for a moment, then Pangwien turned to Jerro, giving him a great big lick across his face, and took to the skies once again.

"Goodbye, Pangwien," called out Etcher, waving at Pangwien's shrinking form as the beast disappeared against the horizon.

"Etcher..." came Jerro's bewildered voice from beside her. He seemed transfixed by the world around him. Far in the distance was the pale ribbon of the Lifestream coursing over the horizon, and the plateau they were on afforded them a grand view into the succulent valleys and grasslands and the great stretch of land thereafter.

"It's not what you expected, is it?"

Jerro shook his head.

"It's actually quite a lovely place, I have missed it."

"You really used to live here?" Which in Jerro's mind was a funny choice of words. How did one exactly *live* in Death?

"Yes, those were simpler days." Etcher said with a touch of somberness.

"Etcher, I almost—"

"You almost joined the others, I know."

"When the other souls were flying out, I could feel the flock of them calling to me. I wanted to go, I wanted to leave it all behind…"

"Jerro, you mustn't give in to that. You're not dead, you don't belong here, not for a great long while I should think." She smiled gently at him.

"It would have been too easy."

"Yes, it would have."

"I shouldn't have come."

Etcher sighed. "Ah well, nothing for it now. Come along, we're nearly there."

"Leona Mesa?"

Etcher nodded.

"That's where your dad wanted you to go, isn't it? What do you think we'll find there?"

"Well, besides the house, I'm not sure."

"House?"

"Yes, Jerro, my house—were I grew up with my father." Etcher winked at him and looped an arm around his. "It's just this way."

Jerro let his dumbfounded self be carried along by Etcher as they traversed a little dirt path through the jungle landscape of the plateau. There were streams carving their way through the ground, heading off into the unknown, and the gushing sound of a waterfall was fast approaching.

Jerro was in awe at the place. The enveloping serenity and calm he had first felt when they had approached the gate was so much stronger this time, only now the feeling lingered. There was nothing to worry about, there was no burden, no pressure of time; he felt free.

Songbirds were calling out to one another, frogs croaked, and insects chirped and chittered. The smell of fresh water was getting stronger, and the taste of fruit trees was on the air. Jerro had to stop; he could feel the sensation swelling inside him—of being overwhelmed by the magnitude of serenity washing over him. It seemed so effortless, so easy to just be. How could he have lived a life any other way? All the needless pain and suffering, the self-inflicted torment, it was bubbling to the surface and spilling out, draining out of him after what had felt like a thousand years. Why had he kept such ugly things inside him?

He wanted to let everything go and evaporate into the Lifestream with the others, he could almost feel himself lifting, floating, changing.

"Jerro," came Etcher's voice, tinged with gentle warning.

He forced his eyes open, he hadn't even realized he had closed them. "I'm sorry...I just—"

"It's all right, but let's keep moving, shall we? Focus on the path, on how much you want to see my little house and nose about all my childhood things."

He smiled. "Yeah, okay."

The feeling inside him started to change, sparking with a familiar excitement, the spirit of adventure that Etcher often inspired.

"You're going to have to put those athletic skills of yours to the test, mind you. Do try not to fall." She winked at him, taking back her arm and skipping off along the path, beckoning Jerro to follow.

He hurried after her, his excitement infusing with glee, and the great edge of the plateau was fast approaching, the roaring waters of the fall spilling off to the side of their dirt path. Ahead was a wide-open valley, hundreds of feet down, and in the middle of the valley was the mesa. From the lip of the plateau down toward the flat-topped hill were floating chunks of rock, like stepping stones, making for a very adventurous bridge.

There was no hesitation this time, not like in Undercity, no feeling of being rusty. Jerro was ready to go all out, and he sprang from the lip of the plateau onto the first floating platform and let the momentum and faith in his footing carry him all the way down. He jumped and tumbled, rolled and sprang his way across the segmented path. A very agile Etcher was further down, progressing with weightless feline grace.

Oh how he had missed this! He should never have given it up, he should have kept his silly promise to Noah and upheld their dream. Quietly, he vowed this wouldn't be the last time, no matter where he ended up he'd find a way to keep the momentum going.

The fantasy he and his brother shared came bursting into the forefront of his mind, of running away and becoming acrobats in the circus, traveling the world, performing incredible feats in front of a full house. Maybe in the great vast multiverse there was another him living out that dream. It made him happy to think that, but it also sharpened his determination. If there was a Jerro out there on some other Earth, being all they could be, soaring through the air and doing flips and jumps and feeling as good as he felt now, then the Jerro he was had no excuse. He would top those other Jerros, he would give them something to be proud of, to even envy.

Their descent along the broken path brought them ever closer to the edge of the mesa, until it was just one more leap away. Jerro threw himself into that final lunge and landed on the grassy earth of the flat-topped hill, tucking into a roll, and arriving beside Etcher.

The little shopkeeper smiled at him. "Well, just beyond the trees there is a clearing and you'll see my childhood home." She seemed so prim and stately, standing as she was, her breath unhurried and unrevealing of the athletic descent she had just engaged in.

Jerro's heart was beating fast, and his breath was moving in steady droves. So maybe he was a little out of practice. Even so, their week of adventure had rekindled a lot of long forgotten flames for Jerro and had put his rusty skills to the test. He was going to be better for all that had happened those past few days, he promised himself, he was going to be more.

Etcher smiled at him strangely, as though she saw the thoughts and determination that swirled inside his head. "Come along then," she said, and led the way through the dense woodland into the clearing.

Sure enough they came across a little log cabin with a friendly façade and a small deck equipped with a solitary rocking chair. Etcher stood there a moment, staring at something beyond the cabin, through the stream of time at memories long since passed.

"You really grew up here?" asked Jerro, a strange sensation ran through him. The little cabin was far more humble than he imaged, and in his mind's eye he thought of a young Etcher and a faceless father living out there on the tree-speckled mesa, in a place of infinite calm and safety. What kind of childhood would that have been like? Was it solemn and lonely? Or were they content, living together in their quiet slice of serenity?

There was something sad in the air as he looked at the little shopkeeper beside him, who continued to watch the cabin as an outsider stares into the warm hearth of someone else's home.

"Etcher?" he said. Concern crept into his voice and broke his own serenity, pushing aside the excitement and promises that had gathered within him.

"Yes, right," Etcher said as she cleared her throat, clasping her hands behind her back and drawing herself up in regal form. She strode forward, ascending the wooden steps toward the green-painted front door. She twisted the handle and let herself in, striding into the tidy living room with obvious familiarity of the space. She didn't need to look as she avoided side tables or navigate her way around the couch to the narrow hallway where she disappeared through a door into another room.

Jerro did not stride in; he took his steps carefully, his eyes wandering around the space, drinking in the scene and thinking about what it said of the people that lived there. It was so much more colorful than he thought it would be. The warm tones of the wooden interior were paired with richly stained tapestries that hung on the walls, and the decorative rugs on the hardwood floor infused the space with a decadent vibrancy. There was a quaint little sitting room with blue furniture and brightly patterned blankets and throw pillows near a brick fireplace.

The cabin's big windows flooded the space with light, making it warm and inviting. There was an open-faced kitchen with tile flooring and pastel green cabinets, and a two-seater breakfast table, just behind the sitting room. And to Jerro's left was the little hallway that Etcher had disappeared down, lined with more vibrant tapestries and worldly souvenirs. A few tall shelf cabinets were dotted about, packed thick with books and knickknacks, pretty stones, and framed pressed flowers and leaves that a young Etcher might have collected from the woodlands outside. There were bits of driftwood and seashells too, and sea glass in big jars, even a little toy sailboat propped haphazardly against a stack of wilderness books.

Who were these people? It was bizarre to think that Etcher had grown up in such a modest little place. Not the grandiose adventurer he knew, whose shop was filled with palace dining halls and personal music rooms, and dozens of bedchambers and god-only-knew what else. Not the Etcher who wore such fine tailored clothing, who held herself with regal confidence, who played the violin with masterful expertise. No, he didn't know the Etcher that lived in that little cabin at all.

He progressed further into the log house, searching for family pictures but never finding any, hoping to glean something of Etcher's mysterious father. There were, instead, black and white photographs of brooks and streams, framed in simple glass panels, lining the hallway further down. At the end of the narrow hall he saw two doors standing opposite one another, one of which was ajar. He let himself in quietly, finding Etcher standing with her back to him as she inspected a shelved cabinet.

Jerro thought this room to be the strangest of all. There was a little bed beside the window in the corner dressed in childish bedclothes that were decorated with a repeating print of playful Dyrashes. Beside him was a tidy desk with more books and little found treasures from out in the wild, an inkwell and feather quills, and a leather-bound journal lying flat on the tabletop. All along the walls were pictures of butterflies, some drawn like that out of an anatomical journal, others had been painted with more whimsy and little scenes, and there was an area on one of the walls that was entirely covered in papers that had intricate concentric diagrams on them with lots of notes scribbled into the margins.

The other strange piece of decoration was a little green dragon model made out of flat board pieces that was held together with fishing wire and hung from the ceiling, and when Jerro pulled the string dangling down from its middle, the wooden dragon flapped its wings as the body bobbed up and down.

"Enjoying yourself?" said Etcher with a tiny smirk on her face.

"This is...*different*..."

Etcher snorted. "Well, what does your childhood room look like?"

Jerro thought about that for a moment. "It was messier than this."

"Well I was a rather particular child, shall we say?" Etcher continued to thumb through the shelves, finding nothing of interest and looking as though she were readying to leave.

"So, is anything here? I mean this is it, right? Where your dad wanted you to come to?"

Etcher shrugged. "It's the place, but I don't see anything useful."

"Are we just gonna leave then? Where's the shop anyhow?" He had almost forgotten their main purpose for venturing into Death.

"It should be around, though not in the house. We'll go find it in a minute, I'm not quite done with my search."

"What's that?" asked Jerro, pointing with his chin to the journal on the desk.

"Ah, *that*. Call it a family tradition," said Etcher as she approached the desk and picked up the unused-looking leather tome. She unhooked the clasp and flipped through the pages. "I was documenting things that I observed around Death, creating a sort of guide book."

"Why'd you stop?"

"It wasn't hugely interesting to me, it's where my father and I differ. While he is happy to stand on the sidelines as an observer, I much prefer to dive in and experience it firsthand. He thinks that sort of thing is meddlesome, though."

Jerro could feel the dreaded question forming on the tip of his tongue and pressing against his better judgement. "Where is your dad?" he blurted out.

Silence met him, and Jerro cringed.

Etcher stood there, idly flipping through the pages in the journal, many of which were blank, before she closed the clasp and set it back down on the desk. "Not here, evidently. I suppose he's off doing what he does."

Jerro could feel the bite in her clipped words, but the questions kept pilling against him. "And what does he *do*, exactly?" He tried hard not to wince when she peered at him sidelong.

"He documents the history of the world," she replied matter-of-factly. "It's a more inclusive guide than mine ever was."

"What is?"

"His journal, or I suppose *the* journal. *The Traveler's Guide to Eclipse*. I doubt anyone will ever read it though."

"So, why does he do it?"

But Etcher had already headed out, and Jerro hurried to catch her.

She stood in the hall between the two doors, staring down the unopened threshold. Jerro stood quietly besides her, watching and wondering what would happen, why they had come here if there was nothing.

The little shopkeeper grasped the doorknob and turned it, the door creaked and groaned as it opened. It was the smell that came at them first, a scent of old books and parchment and varnished wood with only the slightest touch of stagnancy to the air. Inside was a large writing desk with more inkwells and feathered quills, stacks of thick parchment paper tucked into little cubbies, and a large antique-looking birdcage on the upper shelf of the desk with a half dozen golden hazuas, flying in lazy circles within it.

There was a big armchair next to a little fireplace off to the side, and all along the walls were decorative souvenirs, no doubt gathered from all over Eclipse. Tribal masks and engraved brass plates, tapestries, wood carvings, mounted horns and ceremonial swords. There were tall lacquered vases gathered in one corner, with intricate murals painted across their delicate façades and bundles of dried cattail reeds protruding from the open mouths of the vases. On the far back wall was a large window, though the shutters had been pulled and there was a curiously familiar dial beside it like the one in Etcher's shop above the Greenman door.

Jerro had a funny feeling he knew whose room this was and he dare not ask about it. Quietly he watched Etcher as she approached the writing desk as though stalking prey. She circled it from afar before coming up close and considered the ornate piece of furniture silently.

His attention started to wander, and Jerro's eyes caught sight of a small cluster of framed photographs hanging on the wall beside him. They were mostly of a young, smiley Etcher with gleeful golden eyes. Pictures of her in tartan dress staring inquisitively into tiny streams or grinning wide with a handful of mucky stones. There was one of her on a bench looking up at the clouds, and another of her twiddling a feather between her thumb and forefinger.

And in the middle of the cluster of framed photographs was a picture of young Etcher standing beside a big, barrel-chested man. His dark beard was closely cropped, and his bright blue eyes seemed to stare through the photograph right into Jerro. These were the only colored photos Jerro had seen in the house, and the only ones that weren't purely nature shots.

The man had to be Etcher's father, Jerro surmised, despite that he and Etcher looked so different save for the long, pointed ears. The man was standing pridefully, one massive hand placed on young Etcher's tiny shoulder and the other on his hip, his barrel chest puffed out. The little Etcher beside him was grinning at the camera and cradling a ragged looking stuffed animal to her tiny chest. Upon closer inspection, Jerro noticed that the toy in her arms looked suspiciously like a Dyrash and that it had been hand-sewn with mismatching button eyes and a silly lolling tongue.

Jerro turned away from the picture and stared at the Etcher he knew, the one that seemed so foreign to the little girl in the photographs, the little girl who hung pictures of butterflies on her walls and collected sea shells and rocks.

The Etcher he knew was carefully going through the draws of the big writing desk, pulling out books and papers, sifting through them, then putting them back exactly as she found them. This Etcher looked so serious with her calculating gaze, and he thought then of the creature behind the golden eyes, the slightly callous thing that surveyed the world and pretended to be part of it. She had said that her father was the observer, that she was different, but he wasn't certain that was entirely true.

"There's nothing here," stated Etcher. "Come on, let's go get the shop."

"Really? Isn't that kind of strange?" he asked, although he had no clue as to what constituted normal between Etcher and her mysterious father.

"It is, but I see nothing here for me. Perhaps I arrived too late and whatever the matter was has already been resolved."

"So, shouldn't he have told you?"

Etcher's tail flicked. "Perhaps he didn't think I would come at all."

Jerro held back his torrent of questions; the air was getting chilly between them and he didn't want to pry. "So, off to the shop then?"

The little shopkeeper nodded and promptly left the room. "Close the door after you," she said.

Jerro took one last look around, stealing another glance at the photographs. Then his eyes shifted over to the birdcage, lingering a moment as he wondered why it was there. The hazuas Etcher conjured were always so colorful, but never gold. He wondered if her father had made them.

Etcher was already back outside by the time Jerro caught up to her. She was surveying the woodlands that surrounded the cabin and had a worrisome look on her face.

"Is something wrong?" he asked her.

Etcher frowned, her long ears were flicked up and her posture was rigid. "The shop should be over there," she said as she pointed to a direction toward the woodlands.

"*Should* be?"

"Yes, but I don't sense it."

A lump of cold dread hit Jerro. "That's not good."

"No, it isn't." She continued to frown as she started toward the trees.

Jerro kept close beside the little shopkeeper, quietly observing her and keeping his questions at bay. He had been so focused on her, on the strange contrast of the young Etcher and the one of now, that the calming serenity of the realm had evaporated from him and was replaced by a deep-seated concern for his curious little friend.

Jerro was slow to open his eyes, the ringing still playing in his ears. He saw Etcher beside the now unmoving cylinder, peering into it with her hard eyes. Jerro approached slowly, and what he saw inside the cylinder was somewhere entirely different, as if he were looking through a window. It was a place of stone walls and floor stretching far out in all directions.

As Jerro moved around the cylinder, peering inside it, he realized he was looking into a massive and vacant colosseum. Encircling the main body of the arena were tiered seats; the only break up among them was the large podium and vast throne set high and far to one end.

It was a strange gray place and it made him feel cold and small.

"Etcher, where is that?"

"The Owl's Court," she hissed.

The air was cool and fresh, running its silken fingers through Mahra's hair, through the feathers of her imagined wings. She felt so unbelievably alive, exhilarated by the sensation of weightlessness as the wind carried her.

She never wanted to leave. This place was too wonderful, electrifying her very soul, bringing much needed joy to a heavy heart. She glided on the air currents, intuitively feeling the subtle changes in the wind and tilting her feathers as she needed. It was like she had done this a hundred times before, like in every dream where she was flying, there was no question about what to do, she need only to spread her wings and do it.

She had set her course for the nearest floating isle, but as she breached the treetops, she saw the vast horizon spread out in front of her, tantalizing her with grander things. She caught sight of the gleaming ribbon of an endless ocean to her left and the long, stark-white bridge lacing its way atop the glittering waters, joining island to island and disappearing off into the unknowable distance.

The bridge called to her. She tucked in her wings and dove, letting the wind pick her up and slingshot her out toward the ocean where she thrust open her wings once more and continued her glide. The ocean air had a salty-sweetness to it, and the warmth of the morning light kissed her skin even as the cool air washed over her. She had never been so happy to simply *be*.

The bone-white bridge was getting closer and the fine details of its composition were becoming visible. A gravity defying lattice work and filigree made up the railing, while the bridge itself appeared to be suspended over the glistening dream ocean on delicate legs. The bridge, in its entirety, was elegant and wispy, shaped as if the material were as malleable as blown glass.

Mahra descended, tilting her wings and spreading her feathers wide to slow her landing so that she alighted gently upon the chalk-white stone. On either side of the wide bridge, the undulating ocean seemed to stretch on forever, filling Mahra with a euphoric calm.

What a beautiful place, she kept thinking to herself, enamored as she was by the magnificent world, by the way the soft clouds moved, the way the sky was a perfect harmony of colors, by the distant melodies of songbirds who sailed up high.

For all the trouble she had been through, the entirety of it seemed small in comparison to the joy she felt on that bridge of Dream. She wanted to bottle that feeling, to keep it with her when the dark times came, knowing inevitably that they would. An *up* was always balanced with a *down*, there was no skirting around it, she realized, and she had learned the hard way what happened when you tried to avoid the bad, tried to customize your reality so that it fit into a pretty shape. The dark was a part of light, and what became so clear to her as she breathed in the salty-sweet air, was that good and bad needed each other to exist; if you took one away, than the other went, too.

So as she stood there, she savored the moment, tagging it in her memory so that the bad, when it came, didn't have to be as grueling. She would remember the feeling of the sun on her skin, the sights, the smells, the melodies, and the calm of the world. She would remember this beautiful moment, and let it live inside her heart forever.

"You," came a voice. It was gentle and airy, and sounded very far away.

But when Mahra turned she found the voice's owner standing right beside her. "Uh—" Her mouth hung open and her mind drew a blank.

"You know him, don't you?" said the voice, though the lips of the owner never moved, and the owner themselves seemed to be a combination of things. At once, there was a beautiful fair-haired woman clad in white, standing beside Mahra, as well as a giant ethereal fox with many tails. The woman-fox moved with a strange fluidness, and the world shivered with pleasure in her wake. The being circled around Mahra, then headed down the bridge, looking back to beckon Mahra to follow.

And Mahra did so. She hurried after the strange woman, the snow-white fox. She caught up beside her and stared. Looking at the woman was like looking through a kaleidoscope, and the fox and the woman showed through at different angles, yet were definitely one in the same.

"Who are you?" she asked, despite knowing deep down that the being was something integral to the realm and might well be the embodiment of Dream.

"I am Sovereignce," she said, *"I guard the Terriss Walk."*

"You mean this bridge?"

"Yes. This is the backbone of Dream, the thread which links all realms together."

"It's beautiful," Mahra said, and meant it with all her heart.

Sovereignce smiled, as both the woman and the fox, and a gentleness filled her eyes. *"You found your wings in Dream. I'm glad for you."*

"Found them? Did I always have them, then?"

The woman laughed, and the sound was like wedding bells and jubilation, the feeling when a child sees their best friend come to play. *"I like you. You learned so quickly, what else have you made?"*

"Oh, well—I imagined some bobby pins so I could keep the crown on my head," said Mahra bashfully, it was hardly as grand as wings. "Also a mirror, although I left that back at the cabin." At least that was a step up from hair accessories.

"A practical choice," said Sovereignce. *"You see them up there, those children flying on the backs of chimeras between the floating isles?"*

"I wondered what they were!"

"Yes, conjured by the dreams of the youthful. A child can build so effortlessly, but those that let their heart age seldom come here, they seldom build anything but walls. Not you though, you made wings, you can fly."

Mahra smiled to herself, feeling her cheeks go flush with the compliment. "I've always wanted to." She shrugged shyly.

"And you embraced it. Don't think so little of that." The woman-fox turned to Mahra then and placed a hand, or maybe even a paw, on her shoulder. *"My dear little dreamer, I have something I need you to do for me."*

"What is it?"

"That young man of yours, I need you to remind him of his promise to me. Remind him of the rose, will you do that? The dark is coming, and your time together is running thin."

"What does this mean? What's the Owl's Court?" Jerro's fears were mounting, and the seething rage inside Etcher was making him ill at ease.

Etcher drew herself up tall, her expression became hard and stony. "The Oolkas, it's where they pass judgement on the condemned."

"So what do we do?"

"I tell you what we do," she said firmly, raising her glowing palm to the sky, "we get our shop back."

There was a powerful explosion of green light as Etcher's majik conjured a great summon circle in the air above them, and out came Hoya, shattering the image behind the dragon's grand form. Hoya alighted beside them, the dust and earth billowing out beneath her giant wings, and the dragon nuzzled her nose gently against Jerro in recognition.

"Come on," said Etcher, wasting no time as she hopped into the saddle and reached down to give Jerro a hand.

"Gaz-Ut!" She snapped the reins, and Hoya was off, lunging into the sky with one powerful wing beat.

The ground fell away beneath them as they surged through the open air and broke through the tree line. Jerro's stomach lurched as gravity tried to suction at him and the wind whipped through his hair, his clothes, while Hoya's giant heart beat steadily inside her massive ribcage beneath the saddle.

He could still sense the anger inside his friend, but it was changing, becoming honed into a forceful determination. There was something deeply personal about whatever was going on, he could feel it, but he didn't wish to stoke those fires just yet, he wanted to bring back some of the Etcher he knew, the one that made him feel safe. "Do you think we'll be back before the last celebration?" he found himself saying. "If we could go back to Yahre that is."

Etcher's ears twitched, and she turned slightly as if to look at him. "You liked it there?" she called back to him over the sound of the wind.

"Yeah, I did. It was beautiful."

The little shopkeeper smiled softly, but there was heaviness in the air around her still, and in the quiet between them. All she left unsaid was beginning to pile up, threatening to tumble past her lips. "I think we will," she said finally, but those weren't the words she wanted to say. "Time doesn't work the same here in the deeper realms. It breaks down in Dream, and in Death especially."

"So what will happen? How long will we be gone?"

"It isn't something measurable, Jerro, but usually, little time would have passed for all that we appeared to spend here."

"Like in the Flower District?"

"No, not exactly," said Etcher, and then she went quiet, contemplating something far off in the distance.

The miles were melting away under them as Hoya flew. They seemed to be running parallel to the Lifestream, which remained a constant glittering ribbon over the horizon beside them. The Dyrash could be seen as tiny specks descending from the ocean barrier far, far overhead, diving out from the purifying currents into Death, then darting off again to seek out lost souls and bring them home once more.

The terrain was getting wilder, the trees taller, thicker, blotting out the ground with their giant evergreen fronds. And then there was the snow, and the chill in the air, the icy bite as the wind nipped at their naked skin while they rode on the back of the sapling green dragon. The thick evergreens were quickly dusted in white, and the mountains were rising in the distance like pale ghosts in the backdrop of the sky.

"In the Flower District," said Etcher once again, breaking the weighty silence, "the time spent can be measured, it has a constant conversion rate. But here, there is no such consistency. What might feel like an hour, a day, a year, might only amount to a moment, or an instant, or half the time. There is no

420

telling, and it could even run longer. An hour could be decades, or it could be that when you return, you would have come out sooner than you left."

"Whoa, wait—wouldn't that create like a time paradox or something?"

Etcher smirked. "Hard to say. The point is, most likely little time would have passed, it all depends on the exit you take. Nothing is written in Death, or in Dream, not like in the Waking where the past is always behind you, the future ahead, and the present as your constant marker moving along a linear stream of Time. But here—past, present, future—they could happen whenever, you could change the whole history of the world here, there is nothing set in stone."

"Isn't that…kind of dangerous?"

"Extremely. You saw what happened to Arcadia when the King of Nightmare tried to manipulate their reality. All of them dead, their own king driven mad, and all trapped in a pocket of nightmare left to rot until the end of days."

Jerro stared into the back of Etcher's head, weighing the implication of what he'd been told and the strangeness behind her voice as though all the unsaid words were pressing against her heart. "Etcher,"—he began—"why would the Oolkas take the door?"

She turned and looked at him then, a look of regret in her eyes, and something else, something like an apology swimming inside her golden gaze. "Jerro, I—"

"ETCHER!" he yelled, but it didn't matter. Even as Etcher was turning, seeing the thing that burst into life before them moments before it fully formed, it was already too late.

The massive owlish Oolka descended upon them, appearing as if from nowhere, and dwarfing even the sapling-colored dragon. The great bird's black and gold wings were spread wide, blotting out the light and turning its own silhouette into a menacing shadow that threatened to swallow them whole.

The Oolka's claws were outstretched, the razor tips reaching for Jerro and Etcher, missing by only a hairsbreadth. The vicious claws sunk deep into Hoya's flank, and the dragon roared with agony, twisting in the air and letting loose a torrent of green fire onto the massive owl.

The bird shrieked and kicked away, flapping its colossal wings in a flurry of singed black and gold. But even as the owl retreated, more of the Oolkas were coming, screeching with their ugly calls, wings and claws coming at them as they popped into existence.

Blood from Hoya's wound was trailing behind them through the open air as the dragon banked and dove for the ground, and the Oolkas took their swipes at the green dragon—tearing open her flesh and sending more crimson trails to streak through the sky—and nicking Jerro and Etcher as well.

Hoya spat fire back at the attackers, but there were so many, as though the three of them were in the eye of a tornado of wings and beaks and claws;

slashing, biting, screeching with wretched owlish voices. And Hoya was moaning, whimpering, wincing, as the owls slashed at her, riddling her body with blood and pain.

And the ground was rising up to meet them.

"Brace yourself!" Etcher called out.

Hoya had spread her wings to slow her descent, but not soon enough, not with the Oolkas threatening to tear open the thin membrane. They were going to crash, hard and heavy.

Etcher was twisting in her saddle, she got her feet out of the stirrups and grabbed Jerro's hand. "Jump!" she told him. And they did.

And before Hoya could plummet into the hard stone she started to fizzle out into flecks of green light, and what hit the ground was a plume of glittery dust that twinkled and shimmered before it faded out of existence.

Jerro and Etcher rolled once their feet touched down, but their own landings were still grueling, and Jerro fell out of his roll and lay splayed across the ground, feeling the impact thrum through his bones and steal the breath from his lungs.

Etcher rose slowly, and the hatred was burning in her eyes again, a wildness that shone within the gold. In her hand was a rapier, but unlike the one Jerro had seen before, the hilt of this blade was molded with black irises, the petals of which were contorted in such a way that they almost looked like faces, shrieking in agony.

"You dare-!" she spoke in a guttural rumble.

The Oolkas were landing all around them, alighting on the high stony seats around the colosseum in which Jerro and Etcher had fallen, and keeping a cautious distance from the vehement shopkeeper.

"You dare strike at me, Shee'Den!" Etcher spoke with such enunciated venom that a visible ripple of hesitation ran through the gathering owls, save for one.

The largest of the Oolkas landed inside the colosseum in front of Etcher, bathing her in its massive shadow. It reared up high, looking down its vicious hooked beak at the little shopkeeper, its chest filled with pomp and purpose.

"You are in violation of the Goodfellow Treaty, my strike is of retaliation." It spoke without moving its beak, and the sound of its resonate voice was like boulders tumbling together.

"You lie, Shee'Den. Your strike means *war*." In a flash, Etcher whipped up the rapier and from the narrow blade came a shrieking gust of wind that hit Shee'Den across its entire body.

The owl screamed and stumbled back, its wings flinging out at its sides for balance, and the surrounding Oolkas screeched with their ugly calls, taking to the air and readying for the counter attack.

"Get to the door, Jerro!" Etcher called out behind her, holding the blade firmly in her hand.

Jerro had scrambled to his feet in all the commotion, his fear and confusion threatening to boil over as Etcher made the first swipe. "What about you?" he said, hesitating to move. His eyes darted around. This was the same cold, menacing place he had seen back by the standing stones in the glade, back where the door should have been, but they were on the very outskirts of the massive colosseum, and the door was a tiny blip in the center nearly half a kilometer away.

"Hold it open for me." She looked at him then and gave him an impish smile.

The Oolkas had become a dark, churning cloud in the sky above them, blanketing the cold gray colosseum in faux night. And Etcher continued her attack, slashing through the air, weaving the blade with elegant majesty, sending waves of shrieking wind at the owls and knocking them down, knocking loose their feathers and blood, letting it fall like black snow and crimson rain.

But the owls did not stay down, nor did they all remain the same.

Shee'Den doubled over, his wings wrapped around his owlish body, and his entire writhing mass twisted and wriggled, tightening into a ball that was half his usual monstrous proportions. Then the wings flung open and the great owl was no more. What stood in place was a winged suit of polished white armor— possessed by a wispy black smoke that seemed to fill in the armored limbs and torso and seep out from the regal looking helm. And within the blackness were two twinkling lights for eyes, like stars set within a void.

The changed Oolka held a long white lance in one gauntleted hand and aimed the pointed tip toward Etcher, beating his wings in one forceful swoop and propelling himself forward like a missile.

Shee'Den was not alone in his transformation. Some of the other Oolkas had wriggled and shifted, but theirs were forms less grand, their armor more gray and stony than the white knight. They had no wings in their new bodies, though they were still filled with the same black smoke, their eyes still like shining stars. They lined up along the sidelines of the vast colosseum, the rest of the unchanged convoy continued to circle in the skies above, diving at the demon thief when they dared.

And those bipedal configurations, with their free moving fingers, started to chant, holding out their new dexterous appendages in spiritual gestures, conjuring *majik*, building it up before they sent it hurtling out.

As Etcher danced around the other great fowls, whipping her blade about her, jumping and pirouetting like an acrobat, the first of the armored owl's *majik* hit her and drove her down to the floor.

"Etcher!" Jerro yelled, watching with naked horror.

But Etcher did not stay down, and as she rose, and the viciousness in her eyes ignited, there was something changed about her too. Maybe it was the shadows, maybe it was the flurried confusion of it all, but Jerro could have sworn she was taller, that her hair was getting darker, that her face was longer, and that her eyes burned.

Shee'Den was coming at her, his lance at the ready, but Etcher struck him away with her sword, the shrieking *majik* from her blade buffeting the white knight, changing the air and making his black wings fail him. Shee'Den tumbled to the ground, bracing himself on his armored legs, springing up to lunge again.

The two of them fought, and the clash of Etcher's rapier and its strange screaming *majik* sent torrents of vile wind through the flock of Oolkas above and into the circle of those chanting suits of stony armor, breaking their chain of *majik*, turning them to rubble from which their wispy black bodies seeped out and had to regather into their old owlish selves.

But for every Oolka that Etcher struck down, the felled reaper would release themselves into wispy black clouds and pop out of existence, only to return as though from nowhere, and return whole and unscathed.

More of the Oolkas were landing, more writhed and changed and became suits of armor, chanting and building up their *majik*, readying to strike once again. The remaining unchanged Oolkas dove at her, swiping with their claws, and as the armored suits threw their *majik*—and as Shee'Den struck with his lance—the little shopkeeper seemed to grow wilder. The fury that burned inside her was putting speed into her limbs, made her a mad blur that darted through the colosseum.

In all the fighting and bloodshed, Jerro had been nearly forgotten. Etcher had been drawing the reapers attention away from him until there was a clear path to the door, and when Jerro looked to the small green blip, he envisioned the carved leafy face of the Greenman, igniting within him a feeling of such intensity that he was running toward the threshold before he even realized what he was doing.

It called to him like home. It was his harbor, his sanctuary, the place that had become his everything, it was just behind the door. It would all be all right as soon as they made it, as soon as they were back and Etcher was at the helm, the universe would be their oyster once more.

And he was running, beating his feet against the ground, driving himself toward it.

But not all the Oolkas had forgotten about him, and with a shrill cry, one of the owlish monstrosities dove for him, their razor claws splayed out.

He skid along the ground, the cold hard stone searing his naked arms and elbows, pulling up his thin shirt to graze his sides. But the adrenaline was pumping, numbing out his nerves, and silencing the pain. He could hear the sickening screech of the owl's claws scraping against the ground just above his head, the clamor as it fumbled and twisted to get at him.

He sprang up, getting back to his feet and throwing himself once more into his mad-dash-run. He wanted to reach the door so badly, he needed to return, needed to be back inside, but the yards that separated him from the threshold might as well have been miles. It seemed too far, too long for him to get there, and more Oolkas came, another landing heavily, blocking the door and blotting out his hope.

The air was rife with feathers and blood, and the shrieks of the Oolkas and Etcher's blade alike, the crackle of *majik* from the bewitched suits of armor that chanted from the sidelines, trying to shoot Etcher down and halt her onslaught, the sound of old hatred burning bright.

And every time their *majik* hit her, there was the sound of glass cracking, and every time she got up she was further changed.

And the owls were varying their tactics, popping out of existence and back in, appearing right behind Etcher, taking their cheap shots while they could before she slashed them down. Even the white knight that was Shee'Den disappeared midway through his lunge and popped up beside the demon thief, striking her hard with his lance and sending her hurtling across the colosseum floor.

The carnage halted Jerro's progression; he couldn't tear his eyes away from the hideous scene. He might have said something then, might have screamed it, but everything had become numb, he wasn't sure anymore where the shrieking ended and his own voice began.

As Etcher slid across the ground and finally came back to her feet, she stood there, seething in rage, staring down the white knight. Her once elegant clothes were ripped and frayed and doused in blood, and her face had been torn open where Shee'Den had struck her. Her jaw hung unnaturally to one side, revealing a set of teeth that had become far more vicious and elongated than before. The skin was knitting itself together right before Jerro's eyes, the jaw was resetting, and Etcher stood tall, her golden eyes a bright burning fire.

That was when the *majik* struck again, and the sound of cracking glass made a deadly snap.

The chanting Oolkas had been gathering up their power before they hurtled it at Etcher, and it struck with such force that part of the colosseum wall collapsed on top of her, and where the demon thief had once stood was now a pile of stone.

"NO!" Jerro screamed, and knew he was screaming then. He felt the sickening panic and disbelief punch him hard in his gut, bringing him to his knees.

But Shee'Den was also screaming, and there was rage in his sonorous voice. The white knight bellowed at the stony suits of armor. "Bind her, you fools! Bind her NOW! Stop attacking!" And his rage gave way to urgency and panic.

Before the chanting Oolkas could regather, a tremor ran through the ground, and the pile of stones that had toppled Etcher began to quiver.

The white knight took a step back, and the other Oolkas seemed to do the same, cowering before the trembling stones. Even the torrent of Oolkas in the sky hurried to get away from the rubble, bringing back the frigid light into the colosseum, though it brought no comfort.

The stone pile burst open, and what stood there was no longer the Etcher Jerro knew. What stood there was an amalgamation of the little shopkeeper and some other demonic *thing*, it was an awful parody, a halfway state. The changed creature was long and gangly, taller than the grand white knight, and oozing with a dreadful energy. Etcher's body had become unnaturally lanky, as though she had been stretched, and her arms and legs were spindly and thin. Her clothes had turned into an inky substance, hugging her now boney contours as if she had been dipped in a black resin up to her neck. Her hair had become a wild horse's mane, so black no light could escape it, and it hung over one side of her face, over the predator's snarl and vicious teeth that only barely resembled the shopkeeper countenance anymore.

There were coiling horns on either side of her head where the hair had left it bare, and an unsettling skeletal quality had crept into her features, giving her an almost equine semblance. She still held the sword in one hand, and it too had changed, become bigger and longer to match her new proportions. She pointed the blade at Shee'Den and spoke in a growl. "That trick won't work again." With the other hand she struck forward and it disappeared into a newly created fissure in the air, like a portal.

Behind Jerro, he could hear the white knight struggling, and when he was able to tear his eyes away from the demonic entity, he saw that Etcher's disembodied hand was clasped around Shee'Den's armored head.

Suddenly, the white knight was flung forward, and the changed Etcher flickered from existence, reappearing in front of the armored owl and driving her blade through his torso.

She turned her burning gaze on Jerro and spoke. "Go, *now!*"

And the Oolkas burst back into a flurry of movement, screeching and diving for the demon thief, taking to the land and sky. Reassembling themselves as quickly as Etcher cut them down.

It was partly terror that got Jerro moving again, but once he was running, he didn't stop. The strange creature that Etcher had become continued to fight the onslaught of owls, leaping from Oolka to Oolka like stepping stones and coming down hard with devastating blows, popping in and out of existence much as they had done with her. The Oolkas screeched, the blood was arching through the air, their feathers set loose. She kept their focus on her, keeping them off Jerro's heels.

And Jerro ran straight for the door, slamming into it with his full force. He twisted the handle and threw it open, hurrying inside into that sweet air of the shop, of safety. He had never been so glad in all his life, so happy to see the world inside the shop so peacefully untouched by the tumultuous battle that raged just outside it.

"Etcher!" he called out.

The strange demonic creature that was Etcher turned her head in recognition of Jerro while she held back the onslaught of Oolkas that had been pushing the battle ever closer to the door. With a powerful swipe of her blade she threw back her oppressors, her body twisting around to face the shop.

Jerro held the door firmly, ready to slam it behind her as soon as she was in. He didn't even care to question the monstrous form she had taken—it didn't matter—once she was back it could all be explained, it would all be put in order. Once she was in.

It all seemed to move so slowly as Jerro watched, and the yards that separated them might as well have been miles. A great convoy of owls took to the sky, the suits of armor around the outer ring of the colosseum had doubled sometime during all the commotion, and they were chanting and gathering their *majik*, and Etcher turned for the door, started to fade as she readied for the jump.

And then the *majik* held her. It grabbed hold and slammed her into the ground and the sword flew from her hand and evaporated.

"NO!" The word screamed out from Jerro, though he could barely hear himself over the deafening sluggishness of time. He stared at Etcher as she was flung down, felt grim horror as their eyes met and the burning glow started to fade from her golden gaze. He saw her lips move, forming silent words that seemed to say *'I'm sorry.'*

He could feel the sickening dread bubble up inside him as he stared at the regretful half-smile on her changed face, watching as she reached for him with her glowing palm. And then he felt the door try to pull away from him, he saw the lines of spellwork inside the shop light up, he could feel it closing the gap between reality and the *Blank*.

"No, no! *ETCHER-!!*" he screamed again, holding the door with both hands until it ripped away from him and slammed shut.

The force of the shop yanking itself out of reality knocked him down, and the Greenman pulled away from that awful place. The dial above the door spun, the enchanted sky overhead whirled.

Etcher felt the last spark of her energy flicker out as the Greenman door closed, vanishing with her young friend safely inside.

"Goodbye, Jerro," she said to herself.

And as the shadow of the Oolkas descended upon her, everything went black.

"No, no, no!" Jerro scrambled to his feet and lunged for the threshold, throwing it open like a madman once everything had stopped spinning. But there was no Etcher on the other side, there were no Oolkas, no colosseum.

He was back in the cabin in Dream, and there stood Tahli, holding open the thick envelope that Etcher had left behind. The feline stared at Jerro, at the frantic mess he must have looked.

"No—no, she's gone. They took her, they took Etcher," he breathed out in a fervent chant. "They took Etcher," he said, and he fell to his knees.

"True Heresy"

The Veranda...

The birds were chirping.

Along the shoreline, the waves lapped lazily, their frothy hands reaching up the sandy beach to rake in shells and seaweed. The salty-sweetness of the ocean perfumed the air, infusing it with calm. The trees danced in the delicate breeze, their leafy fronds mimicking the sea-sigh of the waves. And further up from the beach, where the ground became firmer and greener, there were butterflies fluttering between the manicured flower patches and topiaries that lined the neat path heading up the hill.

It was on that ever-springtime-green hillside where the veranda sat, and it was on that veranda where an elderly couple were playing a game atop their checkered coffee table. The couple were so old their features had become androgynous. The cocky blue-eyed elder was named Tav, and the pipe-smoking elder who sat across the table was named Aleph, and on the board in front of them there were a lot of chess-like pieces strewn about. There was no sense of order to the game, no clear definition of who was winning, but as the two looked down at their progress, Tav could be seen smiling, while Aleph displayed a stern countenance on a well-lined face.

"It's your go," said Tav with a cheeky wink.

Aleph puffed at the pipe, letting out a plume of fragrant smoke through their nostrils. "Roll."

"Roll? Are you sure? Well, aren't we daring?" said Tav mockingly, the cocky smile never leaving their face.

Tav rummaged a knobby-knuckled hand through a velvet pouch for a die, and Aleph did the same. And when they were ready, the two cast their polyhedrons and inspected the results.

The smile seemed to falter on Tav's face.

"You know what that means," said Aleph, a touch of smugness had brightened up the solemn countenance.

Tav narrowed their keen blue eyes on Aleph. "Humph," Tav said. "Don't look so pleased with yourself, you only get one move with it."

"I know," replied Aleph, who had gone back to rummaging through their own velvet pouch. The gruff elder pulled out another chess piece and placed it on the board, confronting the strange spread of Tav's counter pieces.

The little chess piece had been carved into a dancing bear, balancing on a big ball as if it were part of a carnival. It looked rather out of place amongst the other pieces that were so much closer in resemblance to people—the hooded thief and the cat woman, the golden-haired girl and the young man, the portly toad, the detective, the monk, the lonely mom, the faceless servant, and all the other pawns that unknowingly played their part.

"There," said Aleph triumphantly.

And Tav was no longer smiling.

~To Be Continued~

Traveler's Guide to
to
Éclipse

A Short Compendium of Things

WWW.CHAUNCYFELISZ.COM

Ecliptian Lexicon

Language of Demons in Deus Calligraphy Script

- **Wenga nital lukot:**

/wen-gah NEE-tahl loo-KOT/

Literal Translation—"We need speak."

Wenga is the form of 'we' when a superior addresses an inferior. *Lukot* is the command form of "speak."

Note: In the demon language, rank and power are most important and there are several forms of verbs and addressors used depending on one's perceived rank.

Dragon's Tongue in Rhona Script

- **Jobym spabax. Urag eoh zagqagrakah:**

/job-EE-um spa-BAKS. OO-rag EE-oh zag-kag-RAK-ah/

Literal Translation—"Drink this. You are welcome."

Note: Dragon's Tongue is the most common language throughout the Angelous Spiral due to Ecliptian colonization and intergalactic trade.

Spells & Majik

A Word on Titles

- **Opsyrican**—the highest level of majik wielder among mortals. Has mastered both the basic and universe elements.
- **Master Majikan**—has mastery in 5-7 elements; or can freely wield both through Gibith and Serplex casting and has mastered at least 2 elements.
- **Majikan**—a generic term for any majik wielder.
- **Medji**—has mastered 1-4 elements and or specializes in a specific branch of majik. *Channelers*, *Potion Makers* and *Smiths* tend to fall in this category.
- **Ketch**—an apprentice majik wielder who has yet to master any element or specialized trait.

Note: Witches fall in their own category and their internal ranks and terms are a subject to be discussed in other tomes.

A Glimpse of a Grimoire

Witchcraft

Ecliptian Witchcraft is tricky for many reasons. Unlike typical majik casting, Ecliptian witchcraft will often mix different languages of power and techniques that would otherwise destabilize a traditional majikan's spell. It has been described as a raw, elemental, and rather unpredictable branch of casting, and is not considered majik in the strictest sense.

- **Waking Nightmare Spell**

This spell requires a specialized potion and incantation in order to work. The goal of this spell is to put the target into a type of eternal sleep-paralytic state. Typically this spell would render all but the target's eye-sight useless, but it can be modified.

- Incantation: *"Ibenus tez'Drios, ow'l aha, labat koosa, ow'l aha, labat koosa.*
- Variation: *"Ibenus tez'Drios, ow'l aha, ow'l aha. Ushra insta koosa, labat ushra, labat ushra."*

This spell uses a mix of the Language of Demons and Ug'Roosh. The Ug'Roosh dialect is very old and originated from the planet Syndaious. It has long since been recognized as a language of power and thus is occasionally used in Ecliptian spells.

In the variation "Ushra insta koosa, labat ushra, labat ushra," means *"hear instead of see, only hear, only hear."*

Majik

All forms of Ecliptian majik draw first from the 3 Keystones of reality: *Dream, Stone,* and *Time.* But there are 2 fundamental paths to casting: *Gibith* (also known as *Daentimaus*) and *Serplex* (also known as *Anjiteus*). A gibith caster cycles through the Faerie spectrum of elements and a serplex caster pulls their majik linearly from the Waking spectrum of elements. It requires great skill in order for a Majikan to use both forms of casting, typically Majikans can only use either serplex or gibith. *See chart for more details.*

<u>Note</u>: *Demon spells can only be summoned through gibith casting, and Angelous spells are only accessed through serplex casting.*

- **Knot-In-Cloth Spell**

This is a fairly basic spell, and is usually the first a Ketch learns to cast. The spell produces a *Jin Hazua*—the winged messengers of Eclipse. Hazua Hazco are naturally occurring light sprites around Eclipse, though they lack consciousness and are ephemeral, dying each night as new ones are created during the day by the Zotah (Eclipse's sun). A Jin Hazua on the other hand, is a golem construct created by a Majikan and is permanent unless properly dispelled. In order to perform the spell, a knot is tied in an unstained white cloth and the caster enchants it with the essence of sunlight.

<u>Note</u>: *Pure cotton is preferred for this spell and most beginning majikans will be unable to successfully perform this spell with anything less. Advanced majikans can simply create Jin Hazuas without using a cloth at all.*

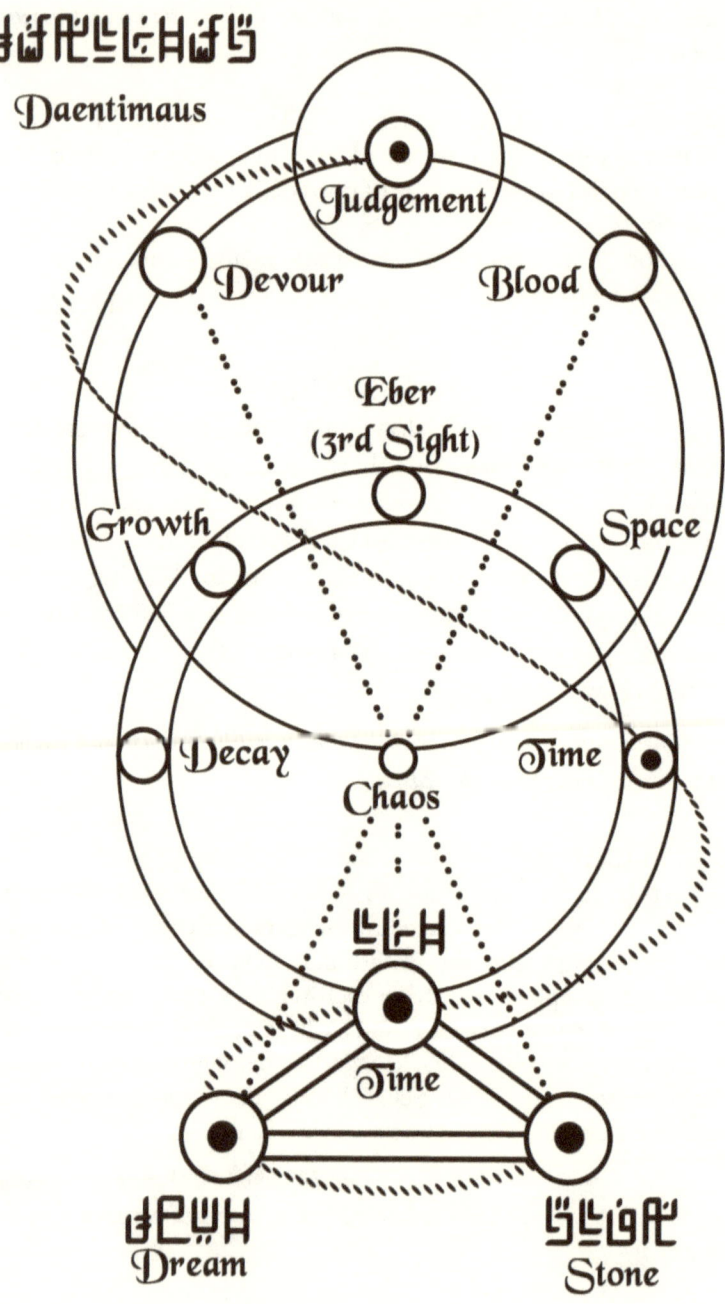

438

They walked briskly through the trees and over thin, rocky streams. The birds were calling out and skittering things rustled through the bushes. A woodpecker was drumming against a hollow tree trunk and the sound echoed through the woodlands, but the sounds failed to be as charming as they had been only a moment ago. Soon they came across a winding footpath and followed it the rest of the way, until finally, they walked into another clearing.

There were tall standing stones placed in concentric circles inside the makeshift glade, their surfaces had been carved with elaborate star charts and interconnecting spirals, and the lines thrummed with a dim light that brightened as Etcher approached.

"Etcher," said Jerro nervously, "what is that?" And he pointed to the thing at the heart of the circles, a black pulsating cylinder, crackling with little threads of lightning. There were scorch marks on the ground surrounding the angry amebic mass, and a dark feeling crept inside Jerro the longer they stood in view of the black writhing thing.

"That is where our door should be." There was a gritty sounding anger creeping into her tone and a hardness to her expression that Jerro had never seen before and wished would go away.

"What does it mean?" he asked in a small voice, cautious of turning her ire against him.

Etcher stepped forward, eyeing the black mass. "Someone has moved the door."

"W-what? How?"

"They took the space it occupied and moved it somewhere else," she almost growled.

Jerro didn't like this side of Etcher, this was more than just anger. Anger he could deal with, and Etcher's anger, though frightening, had been previously so controlled and temporary. Even when she was cold and callous, those moments paled in comparison to this new menace. This was hatred, and it was dangerous.

"So what is that thing, then? Missing space?" he asked carefully.

"No, you can't just move space, you have to switch it. It's like taking two pieces of a jigsaw and forcing them to trade places." Etcher stepped up to the black mass. It rippled angrily, as if trying to move away from her.

Jerro watched in horrid fascination as Etcher pushed her fingers into the writhing cylinder, seeing a light bloom from her palm and run through the surface of the black mass in spidery cracks. The blackness shattered, bursting with a blinding brightness. The thrum from the standing stones intensified until it became deafening, making Jerro wince and cringe.

And when finally, the cacophony of light and sound reached its sickening pinnacle, the writhing mass became like a portal into another place, and the calm and quiet returned to the glade.

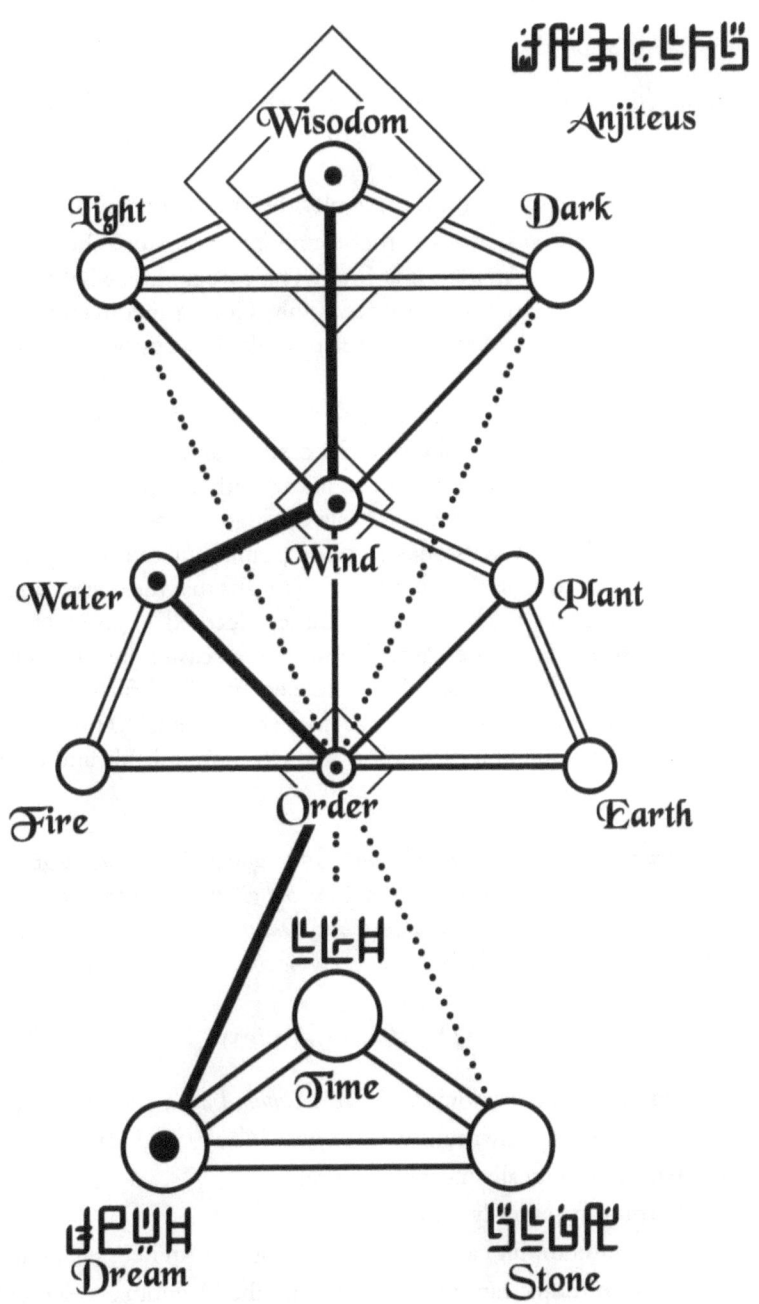

Anjiteus

Wisodom

Light

Dark

Wind

Water

Plant

Fire

Order

Earth

Time

Dream

Stone

Daentimaus & Anjiteus

(Faerie and Waking)

Firstly, it is worth noting that the *Keystones* are viewed differently to the *Elements* on the casting charts. Because of this, in Daentimaus there can be both a *Keystone of Time* and an *Element of Time*.

Both forms of casting have 2 principles they must adhere to:

- There is a *Core* node—neither element nor keystone. For Daentimaus it is *Chaos,* for Anjiteus it is *Order.* The core node is what separates the keystones from the elements. Only Gods can directly unlock the potentials of the keystones, for mortals the keystones are merely the foundation.

- 5 nodes must be unlocked in order to reach the desired element—As you can see from Anjiteus, if the caster wanted to access the Wisdom Element, they must follow a linear path in order to do so. With Daentimaus, the caster can cycle through the nodes (they don't have to use all three keystones as node points but can if they wish). The benefit of this gibith style of casting means that the caster can skip over certain nodes that they might be less learned in so as to reach the desired element, whereas with Anjiteus the caster must unlock the core node in order to reach the basic elements (and further must unlock wind in order to access the higher elements). However, due to Anjiteus' structural nature it is a much more reliable and controllable majik.

<u>Note</u>: *There was only one majikan recorded in Eclipse's history whose mastery of majik was so great they could not only use both serplex and gibith casting styles fluidly but could apply either gibith or serplex to Anjiteus and Daentimaus however they desired. This Opsyrican was known only as Bale—he lived during the First Eon of Eclipse.*

Points to Review

- **Daentimaus**—synonymous with *Gibith, Faerie,* and *Demon.*
- **Anjiteus**—synonymous with *Serplex, Waking,* and *Angelous.*
- **Gibith** specifically means a cyclical.
- **Serplex** specifically means a linear.
- **Angelous majik** can only be cast using the Anjiteus elements.
- **Demon majik** can only be cast using the Daentimaus elements.
- **Most Majikans** can only use either *Anjiteus* or *Daentimaus* elements.

Sacred Weapon Summons—Betchico Demon Blades

There are 5 different Betchico Demon Blades that can be summoned and they will take on a unique form that fits the desires and fighting style of the summoner. The Betchico Demon Blades are summoned through the Daentimaus (Faerie) elements, though they represent the 5 *Hundagas*—demon nakus. The Betchico Demon Blades are as follows:

- **Reaper Blade**—Devours soul energy upon each landed strike and funnels it to the summoner.
- **Blood Blade**—Causes massive bleeding upon each landed strike and can fuel blood majik.
- **Screech Blade**—Creates different pitches depending on how the blade is swung which cause a variety of effects on the targets within range *(such as nausea, confusion, vertigo, etc.)*
- **Time Blade**—Manipulates time depending on how the blade is swung, can create time pockets if the summoner is skilled enough.
- **Stone Blade**—Causes petrification to any area that is struck with the blade, effectively making the target immobile.

Betchico Demon Blade summoning falls under the category of weapon majik—though these Demon Blades are a high level spell and can typically only be casted by those of demon descent or by a Master Bladesmith *(a Bladesmith is someone who specializes in blade-related majiks).*

Since these Demon Blades are a summoned item, they will disappear if the summoner dispels them or if the summoner runs out of energy and or is knocked unconscious.

It is exceptionally rare for even the most skilled majikan to be able to summon more than one sacred weapon at a time. Lesser weapon spells can be summoned in conjunction, however. As Sacred Weapon Summons require a lot of energy from the summoner, it may render the summoner unable to use any other majiks while such a weapon summons is in effect.

These 5 Betchico Demon Blades are considered among the most powerful of demon weapon majik—but there is one ultimate demon weapon that takes the form of a scythe:

The Cajah Jin.

Note: The Cajah Jin is the god-tier weapon summons of demon majik. Its compliment, the Shakahn Ryu, is an angelic hammer summoned through the Anjiteus elements, and is also considered a god-tier weapon summons. The Cajah Jin and the Shakahn Ryu can be combined into a singular, immensely powerful weapon, though this has only been performed by the Goddess Shadow and the Opsyrican known as Bale.

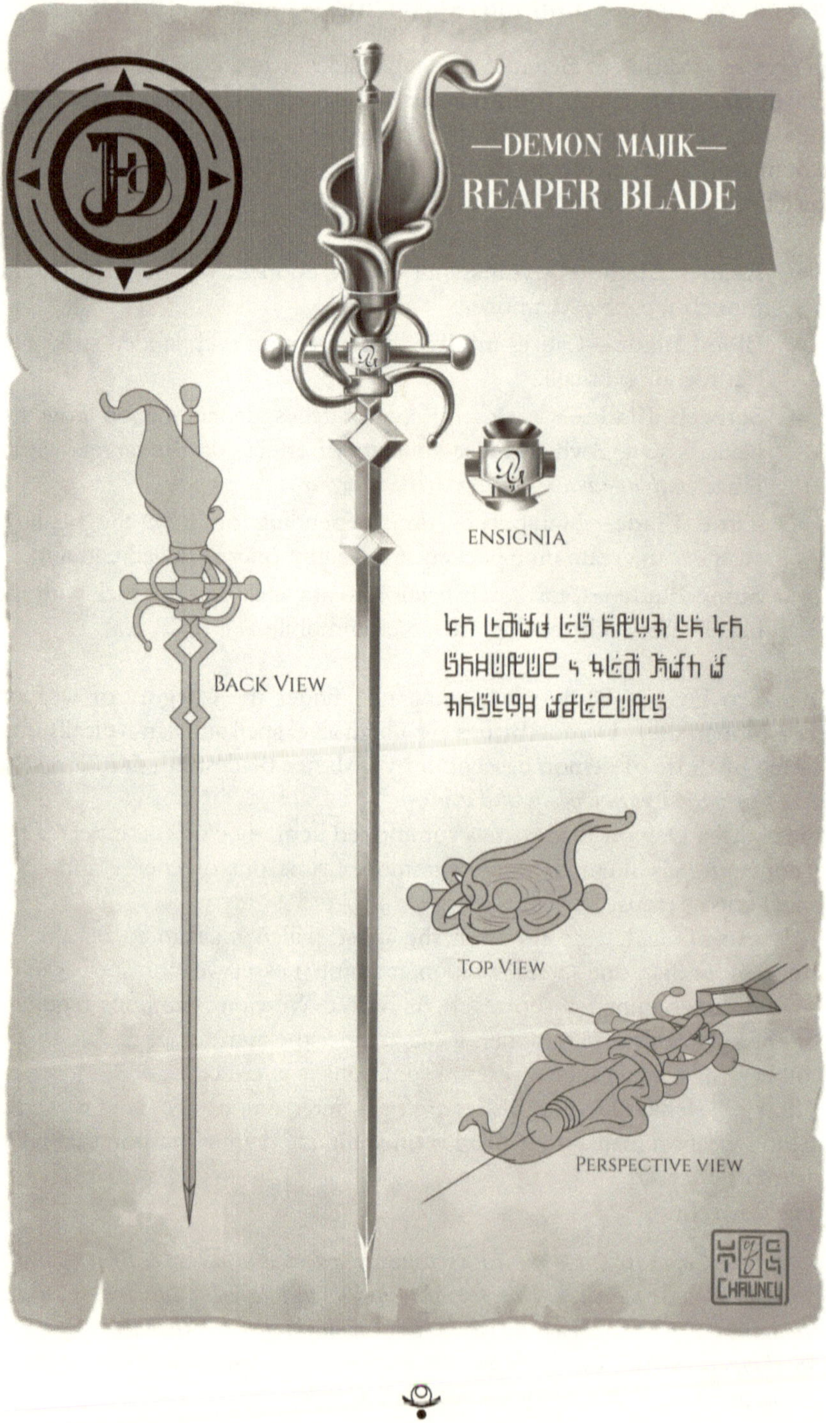

—DEMON MAJIK—
REAPER BLADE

ENSIGNIA

ᏞᏒ ᏞᎷᎯᏋᎯ ᏞᏋᏝ ᏒᎯᏞᏴᏕᏒ ᏞᏒ ᏞᏒ
ᏕᏒᏁᎳᎯᏒᏦᏋ Ꮥ ᏒᏞᏋᎯ ᏒᎯᏞᏒ Ꮻ
ᏒᏒᏒᏝᏝᏩᏒ ᏫᏫᏞᏝᏴᏞᏒᏕ

BACK VIEW

TOP VIEW

PERSPECTIVE VIEW

Artifacts

Eclipse has many majikal artifacts—some are of rare antiquity and can no longer be reproduced, some are created through summoning, some through enchanting, but when an Ecliptian thinks of an *artifact* what they really mean is a majikal item that retains its majikal ability and is not tied to the duration of a spell—once it exists, it *exists*…unless destroyed *(not dispelled)*.

Lantern Key

The Lantern Key falls under the classification of *Resurrection Artifact* and will bring back to life whomever holds the key in death—there are, however, conditions in order for this to work.

The state of the corpse is important; passed a certain point of decay the soul will not return to the body with the Lantern Key alone, so it is best to keep the recently deceased somewhere that will slow the decaying process until the proper procedure can be performed. Additionally, if the soul has already moved on to the next life, resurrection becomes near impossible—for most resurrection spells, one full lunar cycle is used as the cut off. <u>Note</u>: *Though Eclipse has 5 moons, each adheres to a relative 23/28-day cycle.* It is preferable that the deceased be buried or kept in a protective tomb while the Lantern Key is in effect, and here is why:

Once dead—*and providing that the key is on their person and the soul is still lingering in Death*—the soul will be recalled to the body under the next full moon. Since this is a frequent occurrence on Eclipse there are very few instances where the deceased would have to wait a full lunar month before the soul is recalled, however, this does mean that the deceased's corpse will be vulnerable during that interval no matter how short. It is best to have arrangements made beforehand and or a very trusted guardian who won't just steal the key for themselves.

Any bodily injury, illness, or condition, regardless if it is responsible for the death, is healed in full by the key upon successful resurrection—even some old scars have been known to heal completely. The Lantern Key can be used again and again, however, the key does need a rest period of exactly 28-days in order to restore its potency—regardless of any moon phase.

It is worth noting that the process of making Lantern Keys is said to be lost and that the current remaining few are *it*. This is not true, the process of making Lantern Keys *is* still known by a specific race of Ecliptian, however, they have asked to remain anonymous and in this regard, I will honor their request.

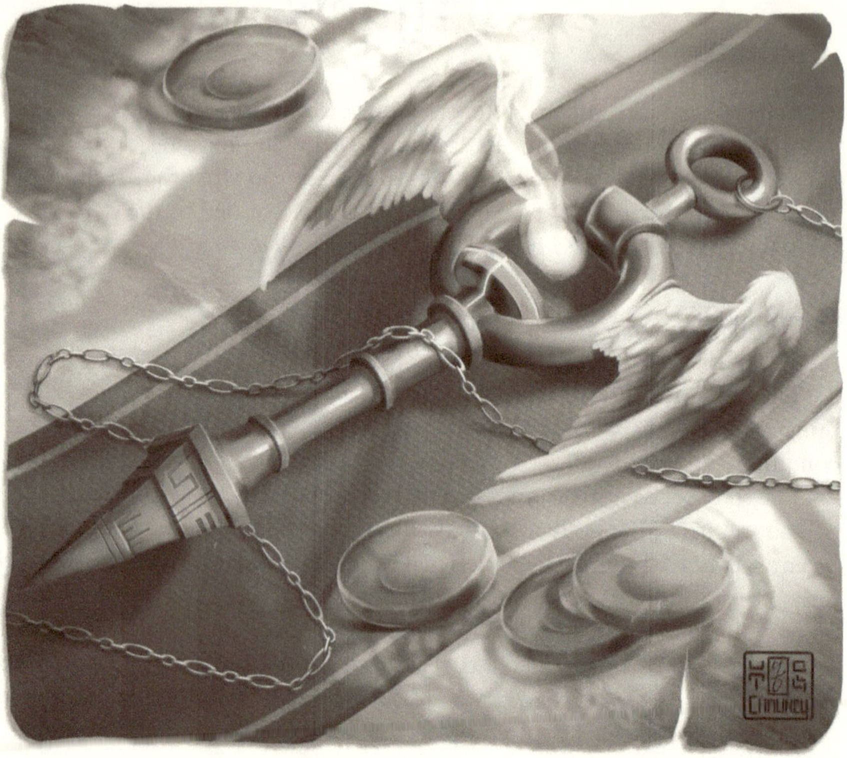

It was recorded by several historians that King Zurrundi was given a Lantern Key as a gesture of goodwill by the neighboring monarchs of the Desert Kingdom during his inauguration ceremony. Both king and key were lost in the mysterious collapse of Undercity.

Festival Fare

During the Lunar Week—which happens every 5 years in the Northern Hemisphere of Eclipse—*Moon Buns* are a classic dessert served during the festivities. Filled with a rich, creamy, fruity filling surrounded in an airy pastry, they often sell out all too quick and because of this many vendors have strict limitations on how many any one person can buy in a day.

But it's not just Moon Buns that are a festival favorite: *Blossom Cakes* find their way at nearly every celebration year round. They are a dessert jelly made from *teyö* fruit and contain a candied blossom inside them with a soft sponge base. The sponge is airy, honey-sweetened, and a delicate compliment to this special treat. However, since teyö fruit are rich in fiber and other such nutrients, eating too many blossom cakes in one sitting is ill advised—a point which vendors are quick to point out to foreign travelers, providing said vendor is in a helpful mood.

BLOSSOM CAKE

Notable Mention

In Yahre, Kingdom of Sep, there is a world renowned café owned and operated by Yohza Tennaboh—a Master Chef. While his delectable cakes are available year round, they, like the blossom cakes, are often bought for special occasions. A particularly sought out favorite are his cakes which feature the special chocolate-and-honey-crisp flowers, the making of which is known only by the Master Chef himself. Not all of Yohza's cakes have these particular edible flowers, as they are extremely time consuming to create, most will have either chocolate or fondant flowers instead, but all of his cakes are decidedly delicious.

YOHZA'S FAMOUS CAKES

The large flowers are not fondant but made of wafer thin honey crisp petals coated in chocolate. Both the craftsmanship and taste of these cakes have made them world famous

Curious Flora

Like the denizens of Eclipse, who range from the extraordinary to the seemingly mundane, so too, does the native flora. While you can still expect a potato to be a potato, there are also plants with majikal and medicinal properties, and some that have been engineered for very specific purposes that have changed the nature of intergalactic colonization.

Teyő Fruit

The pips of the Teyő fruit are numerous and are safe to consume

11CM

Teyö Fruit

The teyö fruit has a strange, glassy appearance and is filled with a hydrating nectar that is syrupy in consistency and delicately sweet—with a subtle plum-like flavor. The protective "glass" skin is tough and rubbery and is not meant for consumption—though the skins can be processed to make a variety of useful ingredients from gelatin powder to natural preservatives. Teyö trees are native to the Northern and Middle kingdoms of Eclipse, though the tree itself is highly adaptive and will tolerate most soils. This tree flowers and fruits simultaneously during the late summer and all throughout autumn.

The 'nectar' is rich in potassium, vitamin C, and dietary fiber. It also contains a potassium-protein compound that helps the body retain fluids and nutrients, proving to hydrate more efficiently than water. The fruits will keep for a long while, even after being plucked from the branch which have made them excellent for not only international but also intergalactic export—the teyö tree and its fruit are thought of as so distinctly Ecliptian that they have become the official plant of Eclipse.

Many allied and colonized worlds grow teyö trees as the plant is so hardy and because the fruit contains such useful properties. In an unofficial capacity, the teyö fruit has become a symbol of peace and or truce and in some cultures, a fresh teyö fruit is given from one person to another to signal the end of an argument and to ask for reconciliation.

This practice has also been adopted by many merchants and business-types, where they will offer one another the fruit to signal that they are entering a deal in good faith. Teyö flavored candies and treats carry similar meaning and are often exchanged for such reasons.

The teyö tree was seen as such a boon that the Syndains even feature the fruit on their currency and in many official seals. While Syndaious and Eclipse have had a sordid history it is still unanimously agreed that the Teyö tree was one of the best exports to have come from Eclipse. To this day whenever a Syndain and Ecliptian do business with each other there will always be a teyö fruit present in the exchange.

Note: As the tree and fruits are so resilient and beneficial it is also seen as a symbol of strength, endurance, success, and good health. Teyö trees are such a welcomed sight that many business owners will plant them out front to entice customers. For homeowners a Teyö tree planted in front of the house shows that they are welcoming of guests, while having them only in the back garden shows that they are more private but that guests whom are invited in will be considered as family.

Dragon Root

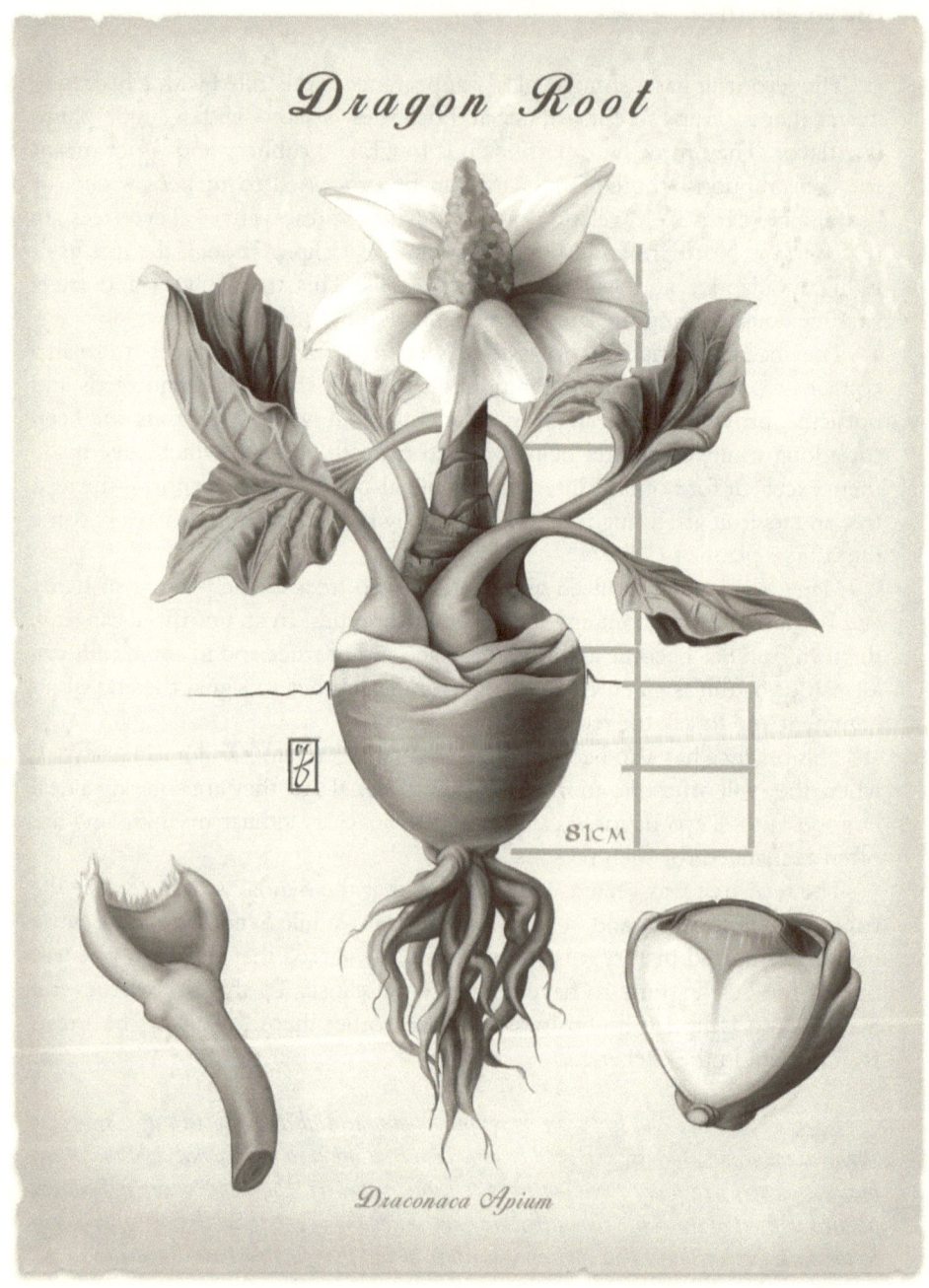

81CM

Draconaca Apium

Dragon Root

This botanical is renowned for its medicinal and majikal properties. The bulbous root is densely packed with vitamins and minerals. Most species (and races) of Eclipse cannot eat the root raw due to its overwhelming nutrients. As its namesake implies, dragons are fond of this root—and are among the few that can eat the root without any special preparation beforehand. Aside from the pygmy varieties, dragons tend to be on the larger side by Ecliptian standards, and as such, the root is ideal for providing them with a balanced diet (in conjunction with the other foods they eat), but even the pygmy and dwarf sized dragons are fond of this root.

The plant is predominantly used to cure stomach and digestion issues, and while eating the root raw is not recommended for most, small amounts of the prepared root can provide a daily amount of vitamins and minerals to the average person. For this reason, Dragon Root is popular in soups and stews, particularly for combating viral illnesses.

The entire botanical has its use, however, and both the stems and leaves are used in cooking and medicine as well. They have considerably less nutrients and can therefore be eaten with less—to sometimes no—preparation, without making the consumer sick. Both stem and leaf have a "bitter greens" taste, and make for a nice flavor and texture to soups, stews, and stir fries.

Dragon root is also a popular ingredient in holistic teas, and much like ginger, will help with nausea. Dragon root teas are known to settle stomachs and are great for motion sickness. The root is also used in combination with cattlehead plume to make *Mulley Tea*—a medicine used exclusively to cure hangovers and intoxication.

Unfortunately, Dragon Root—while considered a very hardy botanical that is naturally resistant to bacteria—just does not grow well outside of Eclipse. Though it is found all over Eclipse itself, the only successful offworld cultivation of this root is on Kerratio—Eclipse's second largest moon and home to a thriving civilization with a large population of dragon species. However, since the root keeps for an extraordinary amount of time they fair well for intergalactic export.

Note: The root has a similar taste to the common parsnip and is very hard and slightly fibrous when raw.

Pocket Garden

This strange amalgamation of a botanical is a Fae construct that will grow into a full garden, filling in a half-acre plot of soil. The garden contains flowers, berries, vegetables, and up to 5 fruiting trees, depending on soil quality.

Activating the botanical is quite simple—the cap is removed from the central "seed" and then the entire botanical is placed on top of soil soon after. The botanical *must* be placed on soil within the hour or else it will die. If the plot of soil is smaller than a half-acre it will fill in the entire space and grow as much as can comfortably fit within the space allotted.

Once the Pocket Garden has been activated it will rapidly expand and will incorporate any preexisting vegetation into its half-acre radius of growth. A central tree will sprout where the botanical was initially placed and will act as the life blood of the garden. The roots of the central tree will dig deep in search of water and can even go so far as to tap into aquifers, and through its own network of roots will supply the other plants of the garden with water.

While these gardens are capable of surviving harsh conditions, they will fail if the central tree dies or the aquifer dries up and the rest of the environment remains inhospitable.

These circular gardens will navigate their way around bridges, ponds and foot paths that have already been constructed on the land, so people tend to plan out any such additions they would want in their garden before planting this botanical. Although these gardens grow out radially, if two or more Pocket Gardens are planted close enough they will join and create new shapes—even square or triangular layouts.

The implications of this majik botanical are quite obvious and they have been used in many terraforming expeditions to great success. Varieties of the pocket garden have been developed over the years to create orchards, farmlands, even exclusive herb and flower gardens. They were initially made by the Fae to promote reforestation of other worlds and to keep Eclipse green and vibrant.

Note: the caps of the Pocket Gardens can be used in trade, and skilled botanists and potion keepers will happily take them off your hands.

End of Compendium

This has been the *Traveler's Guide to Eclipse, a Short Compendium of Things*. There are many, many other facets of Eclipse to explore, and what you have been given here is a variety bag of tidbits which have hopefully enticed as well as delighted.

Did Yohza's cakes live up to expectation when you saw the picture of those artisan constructs of sugar and chocolate? Did the teyö fruit make you crave one? (I had to get myself an aloe water, when I was painting them, though it was a sorry substitute!) Did the majik diagrams leave you with more questions than answers?

Then stay tuned, and keep an ear and an eye open for the next volume of Everdoor! Where you will no doubt be given more questions without answers but which will also contain another *Short Compendium of Things* where we might explore additional aspects of Eclipse, and perhaps a few more artifacts, diagrams, and spells to further contemplate.

Note: For the full version of this compendium pick up "Traveler's Guide to Eclipse: A Longish Compendium of Things" —containing color illustrations on premium paper— available on Amazon, or visit www.ChauncyFelisz.com

Thank You for Reading

I suppose one might put an Acknowledgment section here—Everdoor has had so many it seems with the various versions and reprints—but in this edition, there's something that feels a little off about doing so.

I am truly thankful for everyone that has helped me, encouraged me, believed in me…but I am also apprehensive to include everyone's name in a book whose future is so uncertain, and has thus far been so tumultuous.

I hope you know who you are, those of you that I cherish, and if you are holding a copy of this book and read it through, please believe me when I say I am truly grateful for you—even if I may never know you—that you hold a piece of Eclipse and Everdoor in your mind, no matter how small, means more to me than I can transcribe into words.

So, thank you—thank you for being here.

(And thank you also for putting up with my gratuitous use of em dashes.)

Who Am I?

At this point, I am to pretend that someone else has written a very lovely and concise *About the Author* section—but seeing as I am the one writing it, and you and I are well aware of it, that would seem rather disingenuous. And as you can see I have chosen a *very* tasteful painting of a self-portrait I did (which a reputable publisher might voice some concerns about but which I am very fond of so I'm including it). I can't say I actually have horns nor multiple arms, but I do sport some fun tattoos and a mohawk for what it's worth.

If you really are dying to know more about me I'll tell you this much: I was born in England, I have been traveling the world since I was 2 months old, I live in America at the time of writing this, my accent is a muddled mess (due to having lived in England, America, and Scotland throughout my life), I was raised on Nintendo, I like to paint pretty pictures, make up stories about other worlds, design geeky t-shirts, and occasionally sing a song or two.

And if *that* isn't enough for you, you can always check out my website and see some of the other things I've done:

Alright, that's it. Away with you now, the book is done! There'll be another, don't worry…but really now I must insist, shouldn't you be doing something? How long have you been sitting there, reading? You haven't forgotten about your tea that's surely stone cold by now, have you?

Well, if you won't go, then I will.

Goodbye. See you in the next one.